T0370462

The
Toll
of
Folly

J. WILLIAM WHITAKER

THE TOLL OF FOLLY

iUniverse books may be ordered through booksellers or by contacting:

*iUniverse
1663 Liberty Drive
Bloomington, IN 47403
www.iuniverse.com
1-800-Authors (1-800-288-4677)*

*ISBN: 978-1-5320-9432-3 (sc)
ISBN: 978-1-5320-9853-6 (hc)
ISBN: 978-1-5320-9433-0 (e)*

Library of Congress Control Number: 2020904761

Print information available on the last page.

iUniverse rev. date: 10/20/2020

I will destroy the wisdom of the wise,
and bring to nothing the understanding of the prudent.
Where is the wise? Where is the scribe?
Hath God not made foolish the wisdom of the world?

—1 Corinthians 1:19–20

To my father, who showed me the rules; my mother, whose intellect and unswerving loyalty shaped me forever; and my wife, whose tolerance and dedication provided blessed support and was paramount in nurturing our three sons.

Contents

Book 1
The Storm Rises

Book II
The Wind Builds

Book III
Tempest

BOOK 1

THE STORM RISES

1

War Council

August 3, 1914

WITHIN THE HOUR OF THE FORMAL DECLARATION OF war with Germany, General Joseph Joffre received a request from Defense Minister Adolphe Messimy to meet at his office. Knowing the minister as he did, Joffre was not surprised by the urgency implied by the text of the summons. He had long observed that politicians, even more competent ones such as Messimy, become impulsive in the face of uncertainty. To Joffre, however, this war had long seemed inevitable, and since becoming chief of the army general staff nearly three years previously, he had done everything he could to minimize uncertainty. Now, what remained was to implement the plans that had been the product of his efforts to deal with the German menace.

As for today's meeting, it would no doubt help Messimy better understand the army's immediate plans, but also, as Joffre expected, it would provide the defense minister a venue to remind him of the government's ultimate authority in the coming battles. That was a refrain he had become all too familiar with during these last years working with Messimy in formulating France's response to war with Germany. Planning was one thing, however, and from his own experience, Joffre knew implementation based on the often rapidly changing exigencies of the battlefield was another more difficult matter.

It was not that Messimy was incompetent. Joffre acknowledged that he was no doubt the minister best suited for his job of any presently in the government. He had been an officer in the past and would likely make a competent one now, if only he could understand priorities. Messimy had resigned his commission in protest over the army command's hostile actions directed toward the Third Republic during the later years of the 1880s. What he failed to understand, Joffre felt, was that France's survival and strength took precedence over constitutional law and party politics. Events of recent days had reinforced such concerns when incompetent politicians such as Prime Minister Viviani curtailed essential military actions in the naive hope that the Germans could be appeased.

Messimy had helped to correct the worst of Viviani's edicts, but such misadventures could be deadly under present circumstances. As Joffre set out for his meeting with Messimy, he was determined to resist future intrusions by government officials now that war with Germany was reality.

By the time Joffre arrived, the afternoon sun had brightened and warmed Messimy's office, necessitating that the blinds be closed. The dimmed light only enhanced Joffre's large figure, arrayed in a uniform fit for such an important occasion; nor could it conceal the contrast between the stolid and laconic Joffre and the volatile, expressive Messimy.

Joffre recognized the minister's animated appearance and fine line of sweat across his brow, features he had often observed in subordinates facing battle or other great challenges for the first time. Yet this was no uprising in Africa. Nor was the opponent disgruntled natives. Now, France confronted the most formidable army on the continent. Joffre sensed that Messimy would need to be carefully guided in the days ahead but acknowledged he at least had potential. Viviani was another matter, and Joffre was determined to have nothing to do with the prime minister if possible.

Messimy began haltingly as he unrolled a large topographical map on his desk.

"Well, General, it seems that the time of speculation is past, and the test of reality is now upon us. What are your plans at present?"

Joffre began speaking in a soft, near monotone voice. "Monsieur Messimy, the intelligence regarding our frontier is incomplete, especially in the northern reaches of our common boundary with Germany and along the Belgian border. Recent reports, however, have given us a better understanding of the troops that we face across our common frontier in the south. Our First Army, commanded by General Dubail, is centered here at our southern flank, running from the Swiss border toward Alsace." Joffre indicated on Messimy's map, his large hand obscuring much other detail.

"Even before the order for mobilization, its VII corps under General Bonneau was fully formed on its right flank and is now in position to attack into Alsace toward Mulhouse. Farther to the northwest, centered on Nancy in Lorraine, is the Second Army under General de Castlenaugh. These two armies will be the first to reach full mobilization and be capable of launching an attack against the Germans in Alsace and Lorraine."

"What do we know of the forces across from them?" Messimy asked.

"We know that they will be well fortified. Metz is the key to the whole of their western frontier. If it can be taken, then the road to Berlin will be open."

"Any idea of their troop strength?" Messimy continued in his questioning.

"This is where recent intelligence has been most helpful, especially from loyalists in Alsace. There are at least two armies centered near Metz. The northernmost of these is almost entirely made up of Bavarian troops under the command of Crown Prince Rupprecht. He may also exercise effective control of the southern army as well. Fortunately, there are few if any Prussian troops in the area."

"What does that imply?" asked Messimy uncertainly.

"It means this area is very unlikely to be the center of any large-scale offensive unless Prussian troops are brought into the sector in large numbers. Their general staff welcomes all German forces, but you can be assured that the most critical phase of their planned offensive will rely on Prussian forces."

"What makes you sure that they have one?" Messimy persisted in a tone that belied his uncertainty.

Joffre replied slowly, as if dealing with an inexperienced subordinate. He had discussed this matter in the past with Messimy and was surprised by his last question. "It is certain that they have not only planned an offense but have refined it for at least a decade. That is how the Prussian mind works. Nothing will be left to chance if they can avoid it. Everything about this plan has been thoroughly rehearsed, and their commitment to it will be absolute."

"What do you expect from them?" asked Messimy, with more evident concern in his voice.

"We know that it will involve a massive consolidation of troops designed to hammer any resistance in front of them. We suspect it will come from the north and likely involve Belgium, probably just above the Ardennes Forest."

"What makes you believe they won't direct their attack farther to the north?"

Joffre paused a moment to let his rising frustration subside. He and Messimy had been over this ground many times before, but now that such a threat had tangible reality, the minister seemed to conflate its risk. After a sip of water, he continued.

"There are two major problems with such an attack. An invasion to the north would soon bring the line of their attack in front of Liege and the line of Belgian fortifications. The time necessary to reduce such fortifications would likely be far longer than the Germans have allotted to neutralize us in the west before dealing with the Russians, who will be concentrating for an invasion into the Prussian homeland itself.

"Also, if they elect to extend their entire front that far north, it will virtually ensure that they will weaken other sectors due to the necessity of stretching their regular army forces over so vast an area. That should make them more vulnerable to attack in these weakened locations."

"Aside from those two armies in the south, what do you know conclusively about the remainder of their troop disposition and strength?" Messimy continued.

"As I stated, at present, that information is less clear."

Joffre drew his hand along the map from Nancy up through Lorraine and Verdun to that nearly triangular portion of France that jutted out into Germany and bordered on Luxembourg. To the north lay a small portion of Luxembourg and the dense tracts of the Ardennes Forest comprising much of the south of Belgium.

"As mentioned, our best intelligence expects their offensive to be initially directed through Belgium where border defenses are less robust. What exactly lies in front of our armies is hard to know since much of this area is shielded by Belgium and the Ardennes. We know that some of these troops are Prussian and under the command of Crown Prince Wilhelm. Farther to his south are at least the equivalent of one if not two armies under the command of the duke of Wurttemberg. We can expect that such nepotism will not be rewarded by the insanity of allowing such commanders the role of leading the primary offensive. There are at least two armies comprised primarily of Prussian troops under their most senior field commanders, von Bulow and von Kluck, who are somewhere to the north of these princes. It is the position and action of these armies that will determine the course of the German offensive."

As Messimy studied the map before them, his gaze focused on that part of Belgium to the north of the Ardennes Forest. "General, you have given good reasons why the Germans will not choose to swing farther to the north in Belgium. I know the region of the Ardennes from my time in the army, and I know it to be very poor ground for launching a major offensive. What if the Germans choose to extend their lines far to the north in the hopes of enveloping our left flank?"

"That is a possibility that needs to be excluded, as it has great bearing on the position of our Fifth Army, along with the British, who, when fully deployed, will be next to them on our northern flank. German troops invaded Belgian soil immediately upon declaration of war, prompting their government to ask assistance from us. I have ordered three cavalry divisions under General Sordet to reconnoiter German strength in the northern areas of Belgium, east of the river Meuse. If the Germans plan to attack through this area, our riders should give us advanced warning and allow us to plan accordingly."

"Well, General Joffre, how do you propose to counter this German offensive?" Messimy asked somewhat officiously.

Again, Joffre paused before replying. It seemed to him that this whole exercise was a summary of much that he and the minister had talked about many times in the past. It was as if Messimy was uncertain if all those conversations mattered now that war with Germany was a reality. His reply was direct and confident, leaving little doubt who would be in charge in the coming days.

"By an offensive of our own, Monsieur Messimy. You know my feelings on this matter as well as the feelings of the general staff. We have been rushing from the first second of mobilization to bring our five armies to full strength and in position to attack at the earliest opportune moment. The attack will use coordinated artillery fire and infantry with as many troops as can be brought to bear on the sectors deemed must vulnerable. We have spent much time and money on developing the transportation network to get these troops into place and believe we will be able to strike the Germans before they can get to us through Belgium."

"Are your plans in place now, General?"

"The events of the moment will dictate our actions, Monsieur Messimy. It is more important to have armies with the will to attack as events dictate rather than to push ahead blindly with some preconceived plan that might be endangered by the reality of conditions at that moment," Joffre replied as teacher to student.

"Nowhere in the plan is a specific timetable set out or a first set of objectives called for," continued Messimy, whose apparent concern clashed with Joffre's calm restraint.

"Exactly. That rigidity is for German planners. We must rely on our speed and adaptability, attacking where the enemy presents us with the best opportunity for success. Presently, the First Army will be in position to launch an offensive into Alsace, and the Second can soon follow on their left in Lorraine.

"Then, dependent upon what our cavalry excursion across the Meuse tells us about German movement in the north of Belgium, we will be able to align the Fifth Army in a position facing to the north to confront a German advance or act in coordination with the Third and Fourth Armies attacking the German center. I must caution, Monsieur Messimy, that such a discussion is only speculation at this time, and any final actions must await further developments."

"General, I appreciate your thoughts. You know that I fully support this offense initiative you have planned. You know also that I am ultimately responsible for your actions as the representative minister of the government. As such, it is vital that this type of close communication be continued."

This was a demand Joffre had expected and one he was unwilling to fully agree to. "I must insist, Monsieur, that in the war zone I have full authority to deal with matters."

"That is your prerogative without question, General, but ultimate oversight and responsibility for your actions will rest with the government and the president of the republic. As the member of the government most responsible for the actions of the army, I must also insist upon a frank exchange of timely information."

"Monsieur, I fully understand your responsibilities as well as the authority of your position. We can only hope that circumstances give us the time to communicate in the manner that you expect."

"I appreciate your understanding in this matter, General. For the moment, what do you want me to tell the premier and the remainder of the ministers?"

"You may tell them that the army is ready to avenge the loss of Alsace and to humble our enemy. At the appropriate moment, we will prove our intent by an offense into occupied Alsace and will follow shortly afterward with an attack through Lorraine."

"General, your hour and the hour for our country is at hand. God give you the strength and wisdom to prevail."

"Thank you, Monsieur Messimy. Now I must excuse myself, as I'm sure you understand that many things demand my time today."

"Good day then, General, and best of luck."

Joffre departed, pleased with this first meeting. Messimy had insisted on the government's prerogative yet readily conceded to him authority where it was most needed. He now planned to use it expeditiously, knowing the fate of France depended on his efforts in the days ahead. Unlike Messimy, he felt confident that he was prepared for what was to follow and that he would succeed.

2

Sanctuary

IT HAD BEEN NEARLY A WEEK SINCE THE WAR'S outbreak, and for Sara Morozovski, the reality of a war that invalidated so much of the work that had dominated her recent life had been made even more bitter by the necessity of her present circumstances. She now found herself in comfortable bourgeois surroundings in the home of Marta Frisch, a grand dame of the German socialist movement. The sunny, well-lit dining room, cozy library, and small but comfortable bedroom seemed to contrast sharply with the present turmoil in the surrounding city. At times, it seemed almost surreal to Sara, as if she were in another universe surrounded by like-minded people furtively observing the workings of a city they had formerly known, now gone mad. Yet, on reflection, Sara took comfort in the realization that she would have it no other way.

Marta's husband had been a prominent attorney and leader of the German workers' movement. Marta had proven to be a great partner in her husband's work and often used this home to host many significant gatherings though the years. In this most difficult time, it was only natural that Marta's home would continue to provide a location where the faithful could rally.

Sara had gained entry here through her contacts with Rosa Luxembourg, perhaps the most notorious and outspoken figure of the present German Socialists. Her ready transition into these welcome surroundings seemed remarkable to Sara given her French citizenship, a status that now carried a high risk of internment. Sara was truly thankful for Marta's support and that of many of her friends, but her dependency on her new host served as a painful reminder to her of how much had changed in her relatively young life.

Perhaps all of this had been preordained. The daughter of a wealthy Parisian banker, Sara had eschewed the prerogatives of her birth due to the influence of her wise and supportive governess. From Lydia Gold and her husband, Karl, she had come to know large segments of the working class of Paris, finding that—but for the luck of birth and the vagaries of fortune—many were the equal of the more fortunate classes populating the world of her parents. Their plight, however, was often influenced by forces beyond their control, and as Sara matured, she sought ways to help rectify such injustices.

Given the societal limitations she faced as a bright and committed Jewish woman, Sara seized on one of the few options available to her and studied law in Paris. There she had also been drawn into socialist politics inspired by the charismatic French leader Jean Jaurès. With a law degree in hand, she accepted a position overseeing the establishment of a new Berlin bureau of the French socialist daily, *L'Humanité*.

It was in Berlin that Sara had come of age, stimulated by the opportunities that a burgeoning industrial economy provided for the working classes. Here she had made important contacts not only among the Socialists but the well-organized pacifist community as well. Both shared a loathing for war, viewing it as an anathema to working people everywhere, who would inevitably bear a disproportionate burden in a deadly process in which the ruling elite and their capitalist cronies would realize disproportionate benefits.

She and her colleagues had much to show for their efforts in those years, expanding opportunities for workers and, through wide-scale demonstrations, increasing awareness of the destructive potential of war. Then, in a few weeks, all was undone by the assassination of an heir to the Austrian throne in a far-off corner of their empire, which had served as a catalyst to draw the entire continent, seemingly transfixed by irrational notions of ancient enmities and fear, into generalized war. For Sara, the reality of this new and abhorrent condition had been made worse by her being trapped in Berlin at the war's outbreak, unable to find a means to return to France in those final hectic days as all watched the peace of the continent implode with a sudden and irrevocable end.

Now sheltered in this quiet and refined home, hidden from the network of interior agents, Sara carried on her daily life in the best circumstances possible while she studied the newspapers and queried visitors about details of events in the city, which only weeks before had seemed to be her second home. The news, however, quickly dispelled that notion. *L'Humanité* had been one of the war's first casualties, being forced to close shortly after war had been declared with France. The existing German press gave extended coverage to the massive gatherings in Berlin in support of the troops assembling for departure to the fronts, and it paid lengthy tributes to their heroism in defense of the Reich in its hour of need. These stories were accompanied by photos of men gathered in long enlistment lines or marching resolutely to their fate while surrounded by large throngs of well-wishers.

There was no deviation from a story line universally promulgated. German excellence and resulting ascendency had threatened the other major states of Europe who were unwilling to concede any of their power and privilege. To impede German power, an alliance had been formed, and through a dastardly misadventure in the Balkans, Britain, France, and Russia had declared war against Germany. Now it was time, through the power of their army, for Germany to claim its rightful destiny.

There was scarcely any mention of dissent, as little existed. There were few if any counterdemonstrations, and strikes at the major weapon plants were never threatened. As Rosa Luxembourg had predicted, the large socialist representation in the Reichstag had voted nearly unanimous support for the kaiser's proposal for war funds, the last act of that body before being disbanded. It was as if all the large group of people she had known who opposed this day had disappeared. Now, as she scoured the news, the lack of any organized protest by the groups Sara had devoted so much of her efforts to came as a bitter disappointment, as it was to the many others who gathered during those first days of the war at Marta Fritch's home.

Sara noted that only Marta seemed unwilling to concede failure during these difficult days, a resolve that further enhanced her in Sara's opinion. Perhaps it was her experience in difficult times in the past, but Marta refused to concede the triumph of German nationalism, even as so many she knew had done so.

In her conversations with Sara and others, Marta had expressed her belief that this was a time that would require patience and discipline to maintain their network of close and trusted comrades for the future challenges she believed to be inevitable. To Marta, a person's nationality mattered far less than his or her past and continued commitment to the cause of socialism. For this reason, Sara and other foreign nationals with strong past sympathies to the workers' movement were to be welcomed and supported.

The Prenzlauer district where Sara was now sequestered had long been a stronghold of the working class. The authorities had always feared the potential of discord that might come from this district in the event of war. In the absence of any organized resistance, it soon became apparent, from what Sara could infer from her reading, that an unwritten truce had gone into effect, possibly under edict from the kaiser between the Socialists and the authorities, sparing Marta and her associates undue harassment. Sara hoped such tolerance might provide the breathing space for her repatriation but knew instinctively that Marta and her many associates were still under close surveillance and would have to move with caution.

At the end of her first week with Marta, Sara was presented with expertly forged papers showing her to be a German national. She was warned that if she were ever taken into custody, there was a real chance they might be discovered to be fraudulent, so all appropriate precautions should be followed in traveling in the city and surrounding countryside. Forewarned, Sara struck out on short excursions into the district, being careful to conceal her identity and avoid any actions that might cast undue suspicion on Marta Frisch and her circle of associates.

These brief expeditions gave Sara a firsthand glimpse of conditions now faced under this new state of war. She had long noted the efficient manner that Berlin society conformed to the norms of expected social behavior, which now seemed to make the transition to the demands of war easier. There was little grumbling and virtually no attempts to jump the queues that had become necessary due to food shortages and the limited number of trams running in the city. It was like the citizens had accepted this state of self-denial as a necessary first step in obtaining their just rewards from the struggle they were now engaged in. To Sara, it seemed a bit absurd, but, if anything, these demanding times seemed to make these spartan people more content.

Sara had also met others who, like herself, had been stranded in Berlin and were seeking a means to escape the embattled German Reich. Various discussions with Marta had touched on escaping to Switzerland or even to France itself, but they had lacked any substance. It was therefore quite significant when Sara met Hans Schwartz at Marta's one evening, who was introduced as the principal leader in arranging the means of repatriation for people in her position.

Hans Schwartz had a reserved and almost mysterious air about him, making it difficult for Sara to clearly discern his background. What was clear was his understanding of the peculiar logistics that had knitted German commerce together before the war. It was this knowledge that was proving very helpful in the strange work he now found himself dealing with.

Sara was intrigued also by his questions, which often seemed tangential and lacking some clear relationship to a means where she might reach the borders of France or Switzerland. When at last he uncovered her unusual relationship with Karl Gold, the husband of her old governess, Lydia, a subtle smile came over the face of her potential deliverer. In her younger years, Sara had spent weeks of her summers with Lydia and Karl, who was a livestock dealer who had even taken her on a trip to meet with his suppliers. Hans Schwartz seemed intrigued by the details of that trip far more than any history of Sara's subsequent involvement in socialist causes.

As he departed from Marta's that evening, Herr Schwartz broke his impersonal demeanor, giving Sara a brief smile while indicating he might have an opportunity of interest for her. She smiled warmly in response, even though it was difficult to know what that might be from the unusual conversation she had had with him that night.

The following day, Sarah was given an address in far eastern Berlin where she would meet someone who might be able to help conceal her and provide a means to escape Germany. It was breathtaking news, and Sara took care to dress inconspicuously and leave at an hour when her movement would be disguised by work traffic.

Following a series of train rides where she blended inconspicuously in the large crowds, Sara found herself in the far eastern outskirts of Berlin. Here the trappings of the city clung to the edge of large tracts of cultivated land, which disappeared toward the eastern horizon, rarely interrupted by hills or cityscape. It was a flat landscape of pine and aspens, surrounding what had once been a rural village, which included a guesthouse and restaurant.

Sara recognized the restaurant as the address given and entered cautiously at the hour specified. It was a spartan facility with little in the way of decoration, just the kind of place that farmers would feel comfortable in. She was relieved to see a pleasant middle-aged woman sitting at a well-lit table by a bay window. Sara approached cautiously and then was comforted by the plain, honest features of the woman, similar to many farm wives she had met in her younger days.

"Excuse me, are you Frau Heilman?"

"Yes, I am. You must be Sara," Frau Holman replied with a cautious smile. "Please join me for coffee."

As Sara was settling in, Frau Holman said, "You may also call me Ruth, if you would like."

Taking a seat with her back to the restaurant, Sara replied quietly, "I'm happy to have found you this morning."

"I hope you didn't have any difficulty getting here?" asked Ruth, her face softening with evident concern.

"Nothing significant, and what few inconveniences I encountered are insignificant to the excitement of finding you."

"What have your friends told you to make you excited to meet a farmer's wife?"

"They implied that the war has caused a shortage of farm help, and consequently, there might be an opportunity that would be mutually beneficial to my needs as well."

"You will excuse me for saying so, Sara, but you don't strike me as the type who would have any experience in dealing with animals."

Sara smiled as she replied, "What you must have heard about me no doubt would lead you to think that, but I can tell you that my experiences are far more than you suspect. As a girl, the husband of my governess often took me with him to collect livestock. I got to be fairly handy with the animals, and I suspect I still could manage as well as I did in those days."

"Was your friend a farmer?"

"No, he was a trader, just like I was told your husband is. He had come originally from the area around Strasbourg, but his family had moved after the German occupation. Karl still had many family members throughout the region, and they have been reliable contacts through the years as his business developed."

"You say his name is Karl? It wouldn't be Karl Gold, would it?"

"The same. Do you know him?"

"By name and reputation only, but my husband has had many connections with him in the past," said Frau Heilman, with a smile that suggested their relationships had been on good terms. "Let's finish our coffee so that I can show you our farming operation. I think it's time to meet my husband, Aaron, as well."

After walking a short distance from the guesthouse into the surrounding countryside, the women soon came to a long, well-maintained lane leading to a large collection of farm buildings, surrounded by many animal pens where two men were already moving a group of pigs into a waiting lorry. The older one, a tall man with the physique of someone used to hard work and a sun-darkened countenance acquired by long days out of doors, upon seeing their approach stopped what he was doing and came to meet them.

As he approached, Ruth called out, "Aaron, please come here. I would like for you to meet Sara Morozovski. Sara is the young woman that Marta Frisch mentioned to us."

"I am pleased to meet you, Sarah," he replied with a look of skepticism clearly apparent in his features.

"I sense, Herr Heilman, that you don't believe I could be of much help in your operations here. If I can borrow your staff for a moment, I might possibly convince you otherwise."

Taking the heavy staff from Aaron, Sara proceeded to the pen, where a large sow was resisting any further attempt to lead her to the loading ramp and had slowed the process for the remainder of the herd. Approaching the large animal with rapid assurance, she struck it on its nose and then quickly, while holding her ground, gave it a swift blow to its rump, compelling it to move rapidly up the ramp into the waiting truck. After directing several other hogs into the truck, she paused and returned to talk with the Heilmans.

Aaron smiled broadly as she returned, his craggy face transformed by surprise in seeing such an unexpected demonstration. "I thought Ruth had lost all her senses when I saw you coming down the road with her, Sara, but I guess I'm the one who made the mistake," Aaron said apologetically.

"If you would have asked, Aaron, I was going to tell you that Sara has been trained by an old friend of yours, Karl Gold," said Ruth.

Aaron laughed. "Gold. He's a crafty old Jew but a reliable one. I can see where you got your skills with animals, Sara."

"Karl always said that you had to handle the women to get what you wanted, so I learned rather early how to deal with the sows."

"That's good, because I could really use someone like you. I don't know if Ruth told you what we do, but our operations have been complicated by this war."

"I heard something about that from Hans Schwartz."

"We deal in livestock, and the war has caused the demand to skyrocket while drying up the supply of available labor. I expect I operate a lot like Karl Gold in that I have many clients and farmers that I have worked with through the years. Now the army has become our largest client, and we are organizing to bring cattle and hogs to holding areas here and all along their route, where they can then be processed."

"Will you be based here in the east?" asked Sara.

"It would be easier if that were the case, but the demands will be too much for this area alone, and much of the shipping will require that I use my network to the west so that the army can be better supplied in any advance toward France. I will be leaving in two days to begin coordinating my efforts farther to the west. How far that will be will depend in great part on the army's needs."

"I can help you with the work, but in return, I would hope to be provided with a possible means of escaping to France," Sara interjected.

"I cannot guarantee that with certainty, but if the army has success in the west, then we will move with it. If you help me, I will do the best I can to help you escape, should the opportunity arise."

"That's all that I could ask."

"Sara, you have to know that this is risky, and to be honest, you might be safer hidden here in Berlin."

"Aaron, if I might call you that, I'm willing to accept the risks if they offer a good chance to return home. With this war, there will be much unfinished business that I cannot attend to here in Germany. You should also know that if you take me with you, I will do everything that I can to guarantee your own safety and repay your confidence in me. If the time should ever come, however, that my presence endangers you, then I would want you to do whatever might be necessary to protect yourself."

"I expect that nothing of that sort will occur if we are careful. If you are serious about this, then I would suggest that you get home and pack for living out of a suitcase for the next several weeks. Be back here tomorrow or even tonight, and you can begin helping with some of the animals that we are collecting. In the next two days, I anticipate leaving for Westphalia."

———

So it was that Sara took on a new sanctuary with the Heilmans and in the next days would become familiar with a routine far different from managing a newspaper. Her life now consisted of gathering and processing hogs and cattle to send to centers for ultimate distribution to the army. This was no small task, as the increased demand caused by the war made nearly every day hectic at the receiving pens. Furthermore, Aaron's operation had several other advantages that only served to increase the demand for his services.

Aaron had acquired, through the years, considerable knowledge of the peculiarities of his business, and through his own skills, he had earned a reputation for reliability that had proven advantageous in his relationship with quality suppliers. He had also established excellent relationships with other operations across the country. These centers were usually quite similar in organization and management to his own. More importantly from Aaron's perspective, many were controlled by some of his relatives or longtime associates. When war was declared, it was only natural that the army would come to Aaron for help in procuring the supplies that would be essential for their immediate as well as future needs.

Sara would learn more about this network of dealers firsthand in the coming days, as it was Aaron's intent to visit the many collecting areas that he had under management or was familiar with, to assess their readiness to meet the demands of the army. To help in that regard, he had been issued a document that gave him free reign to travel throughout the country and ready access to petrol to facilitate his movements.

Aaron had arranged for two of his young nieces to accompany him prior to Sara's arrival. Now, the younger of the two girls would stay home and help his wife, Ruth, Ruth's sister, and her husband manage the affairs of his large operation around Berlin. On the evening of her second day with the Heilmans, Sara made one last trip to Marta Frisch's home to thank her for her kindness and to make final preparations for departing with Aaron the following morning.

Her arrival was greeted by many of her new acquaintances anxious to wish Sara well on her coming journey. It was almost a going-away party, with the large dining room table filled with an assortment of pastries. Talk naturally centered on the day's events, but few dared to mention the uncertain future that their departing friend would face in the days ahead. Instead, they all spoke of the necessity of remaining in contact so that at the end of the trials ahead, they might ultimately fulfill the dreams they shared that now seemed so imperiled.

As Sara was preparing to say goodbye, Rosa Luxembourg made a sudden and unexpected appearance, arriving in her usually frenetic way. Sara was thrilled by the appearance of her diminutive friend, as she had feared that Rosa might have been retained by the authorities.

"Rosa, I'm so relieved to see you. I had hoped to have the chance to thank you for helping me find this blessed sanctuary."

"It was something that had to be done, but now that I see that you are safe and about to return to France, it gives me hope for the future."

"Your vision for that future has always impressed me, Rosa, but I worry that your dreams may blind you to the risks for your own safety."

"That advice coming from someone who is trapped here in Germany because she ignored her own safety; that is why I like you, Sara. As different as we are, we are in some ways kindred spirits and will always be."

Rosa's declaration seemed to affect Sara, as she took a moment before replying. "I am honored that you think of me like that, Rosa, but if we are kindred spirits, I only hope we can both temper our actions until the time comes when they can once more prove effective."

"Survival may be less important than outcome, Sara. What good is living if we abandon our convictions?"

"Well then, I wish you survival with convictions."

"And triumph, Sara. Never forget triumph. My wish is that we both not only survive but live to see the day when we prevail."

"I look forward to that day, Rosa."

"I look forward to welcoming you back to Berlin when it happens, Sara."

With that, the two embraced one last time. Then Sara watched sadly as Rosa departed as quickly as she had arrived. She could only wonder at that moment what might be in store for two such kindred souls in the coming days.

3

Artist at War

MARIE BONNEAU AND HER MOTHER HAD REMAINED in Paris despite the urging of close friends to return to Lyons as war threatened. Marie had been in Paris that last night of July when word spread that Jean Jaurés had been murdered. The news had brought an immediate sense of foreboding to her, in realizing that with the death of this man, so long opposed to war, hope for a peaceful settlement of the crisis roiling Europe had virtually disappeared. From that moment, Marie sensed that life as she knew it would be changed dramatically, and the coming days would no doubt be challenging and fraught with danger.

For Marie, the realization of what she was losing was sobering. She had grown up in a privileged household in Lyon where she had been the center of her parents' universe. She had at an early age shown a proficiency in music, much like her mother, and had been tutored by a series of teachers in Lyon who encouraged Marie to apply for the music academy in Paris for further studies.

Accompanied by her mother, Marie arrived in Paris as a young woman having successfully passed the rigorous admission recitals to study in the city's Institute of Music. She settled into a new and busy life in this most cosmopolitan of cities. Paris had been a revelation to her then, and coming of age in a city that was reemerging as the capital of the world in arts and style served to accelerate her development as an artist. The city had also provided much else to enrich Marie's maturation into womanhood.

In those years, she had made many social contacts, the most important of whom had been Robert d'Avillard and his cousin Thomas. Marie had met Robert at a carefully arranged reception at her aunt's home in Paris. Her aunt knew Robert as a former prized pupil of her husband and as a rising young captain in the Army Engineering Corps recently returned from duty in Africa. She also sensed he would make an ideal match for her beautiful niece. Through Robert, Marie had also met Thomas, his cousin, a theologian, philosopher, and priest.

The two in many ways were very different. Robert was quiet and restrained and, given his intelligence and worldly experience, was often an imposing figure to Marie. Thomas, on the other hand, was expressive and had an intuitive sense for the feelings and thoughts of the people he encountered. Marie was comfortable with him almost from the moment they first met.

In Paris, Marie relished her musical studies and, through long hours of practice, developed her natural talents to become a remarkable artist for her age. Thomas, who expressed a love for the arts, began to take on the role of Marie's unofficial impresario, helping her obtain recitals in prestigious religious settings and ultimately in some of the city's chic salons. A dedicated teacher, when he was back in Paris during the summers, on leave from his many priestly duties in Strasbourg, Thomas also took on the role of tutor, introducing Marie to subjects that transcended the narrow curriculum of the music academy.

Marie also began to sense her own physical maturation during these years, more from the attention and deference of others than any specific realization of her own. No doubt, this maturation had influenced her relationship with Robert, which had progressed to the point where there had been serious talk of engagement. Robert's increasing interest in Marie also led to a closer engagement with Thomas, who tried to support the relationship by acting as a confidant and tutor to Marie.

All of this had been swept aside as the threat of war intensified through July, ultimately resulting in Robert's sudden transfer to Lorraine as a staff officer in a combat unit. This sudden departure confirmed Marie's doubts about her suitability as an officer's wife, and despite her concerns for Robert, she now fully realized the difficulties that their many differences would pose to their future together.

This insight was both unsettling and a relief to Marie, as it seemed to open her mind to other possibilities. Then in turning to Thomas for advice, she fully recognized the depth of her feelings for him. Upon learning that Thomas was being called back to Strasbourg to help address many issues that the crisis had provoked in this city divided by German and French loyalties, Marie's emotions burst into the open.

Accompanying Thomas to the train station on the morning of his departure, Marie unashamedly professed her love to him in a moment of such emotional intensity, unfettered by pretense, that it seemed to stun Thomas. Then, miraculously, he reciprocated her feelings, and for an all too brief an instant, they shared a bliss that seemed out of keeping with the fears and uncertainty surrounding them. Then he was gone, leaving Marie only a memory that she drew on in the trying days ahead.

Seeing first Robert and then Thomas depart had been a prelude to the even greater shock that now came to Marie with the reality of war with Germany. What remained was her music, and she was now thankful for the discipline of that training that had helped her deal with other anxieties in the past. Yet nothing could truly resolve the turmoil that had come with Thomas's departure. Her candor now seemed unsettling, but her discomfort could not diminish the memory of his reciprocation of her feelings. It was a revelation like nothing she had previously experienced.

Marie had been further unsettled by the transformation she was witnessing in Paris. Conflict with the historic enemy certain, the impending war had released pent-up fear and emotion, with young men from all walks of life declaring their loyalty to France by joining a growing list of contemporaries enlisting for the battles to come. The city was ablaze with the tricolor of the republic, and everywhere strains of the "Marseillaise" and the Sambre and the Meuse could be heard throughout the day. The spectacle reached a feverish pitch with the appearance of the regular army troops led by cuirassiers, with their polished silver breastplates and helmets trailing long horsehair plumes, marching along the broad boulevards en route to the front.

Marie watched this in wonder, all the while trying to cope with her emotions and uncertainties at this historic moment. She understood that her future and indeed that of all her contemporaries would be inextricably linked with the fortunes of these amassed young men and the decisions of their leaders. Yet she felt almost helpless in realizing how little her past training had prepared her to help at such a critical time.

In all the collective faces of Paris, however, Marie's sensitive eye detected others as well with different emotions from the seeming universal elation that gripped the throngs lining the streets to cheer on the marching soldiers. She thought that she could see in some of the soldiers' faces features that belied their concern for the gravity of the challenges in the days ahead. It was in the actions of the women, however, where these concerns were most evident. Many clasped their lovers or sons in one final desperate embrace, loathe to let go for fear of never seeing them again. Among the older generation, animation was often replaced by wariness and resignation as they drew on their memories of the Prussian War some forty years previous.

Perhaps it was the artist in her, but Marie was surprisingly moved by the sincerity and breadth of emotion she witnessed in those days. Yet despite her feelings, Marie was frustrated with what little control that she or virtually any of the people that she knew had over the events that would follow. Her training had ingrained in her a work ethic that rebelled against such a state of impotence. Instinctively, she resolved to rededicate herself to help the young men now bearing the awful responsibility for her safety and that of the country. As fortune would have it, she would not have long to wait for such an opportunity.

Marie's mother, through a contact with one of her friends whose husband was a doctor, became aware of the pressing need for volunteers to help in the city's hospitals to prepare and care for the anticipated war wounded. Marie's mother was soon enlisted in preparing dressings and other sterile materials for distribution throughout the city. It was work for which her mother and her friends had little experience, but the concerns they might have had were soon overcome by the demands of the numbers of wounded that began to return to the city with the opening battles of the war.

Marie watched as her mother's demeanor changed in response to her new duties. Her mother's enthusiasm at the end of a hard and demanding day contrasted sharply with Marie's increasing frustration at what seemed the frivolity of her daily routine. Marie's mother was quick to recognize her daughter's unrest and suggested that she join her and her friends working at a Red Cross center in the time that she had free after her studies.

So, Marie was drawn into the war effort. Leaving every day after her studies for the Red Cross center, she spent the rest of her day helping prepare packages of sterile dressings for the wounded entering the city. The surroundings were equally sterile, with the smell of antiseptics and brightly lit green walls unpunctuated by flowers or frivolity, reminding all of the serious nature of the work. It was a work that Marie sometimes found repetitive and dull, but she quickly reconciled herself to the drudgery by recognizing that her efforts might well be essential to the lives of many stricken soldiers.

It was this belief in the importance of her work that gave Marie the energy to do what might be assigned and to volunteer for other duties. Since she often came in later in the day when much of the preparation and packing was well under way, she soon began to volunteer for work transporting the prepared materials to various points of need throughout the city.

It was during these first visits outside of the confined and sterile surroundings of the dressing center that she first came to see in person the wounded men who were the focus of her work. This occurred in the various hospitals she visited, introducing Marie to a world far different from any she had ever experienced. These facilities generally had brightly lit corridors, leading to a multitude of rooms designed for the reception and treatment of the wounded, which in total gave the appearance of a factory dealing with the products of misfortune. These surroundings were animated by medical personnel and fleeting glimpses of wounded men being transported throughout the hospital or by ambulance. This was a sight that was sobering, but from her distant perspective, it was difficult to gain a true appreciation of the individual soldiers. This would change as the numbers of wounded increased, making it virtually impossible to escape their presence while performing her duties.

The first time she had the opportunity to observe close-up the effects of the terrible armaments of modern warfare, the sight was horrible to bear. This was a response shared by nearly all the uninitiated. Many men were so disfigured that they had a gruesome and unworldly appearance. Others were missing arms and legs that would forever consign them to a future limited by their handicap. At first, it took all Marie's self-control to not show fear or revulsion in such vivid sights. She was thankful that she had learned from the demands of her performances a means to better control such emotions. The last thing that she would have wished was to give the wounded any more distress by an inappropriate response or facial expression.

She was surprised to learn, however, how quickly she became inured to the sights and sounds of this intimidating world. As she became better conditioned to her surroundings, Marie gained more confidence and a greater sensitivity to the needs of those unfortunate soldiers. She soon was able to look past the broken bodies to glimpse the spirit of the men consigned to them. What she saw all too often was pain, uncertainty, and fear. Marie knew that for many, these mental scars would be as difficult to heal as their physical wounds and hoped for an opportunity to help alleviate them.

With each new visit, Marie familiarized herself with not only the hospitals and clinics but also the many personnel who worked there. The medical staff quickly came to recognize Marie as well, impressed by her work ethic and the effect her warm personality had on those around her. For Marie, a smile or other acknowledgment of her efforts only served to give further impetus to her work. At the end of a rewarding day, she would think of ways to improve on aspects of her work and try to implement them whenever possible. All of this was not lost on her mother, who spoke with pride of the positive effect of her daughter's efforts.

Despite the changes in her lifestyle, there was much of Marie's former life that she could not forget or abandon. Foremost in her thoughts was how this war, whose terrible effects she witnessed almost daily, was impacting her friends and loved ones. She was especially concerned with Robert, who might be thrust at any moment into some terrible combat, and Thomas, who was trapped behind German lines in Strasbourg. For Marie, the wounded were a sober reminder of the deadly nature of this war, haunting her work with fears that the men she now attended might someday be someone she loved. For the sake of those presently suffering, she did all that she could to purge such thoughts from her mind.

It seemed miraculous, but in a brief time, Marie considered herself initiated into this new realm. How different it was from her previous life of discipline and beauty, now replaced by chaos and fear. It was now clear to her that she could never go back to those past days. If some semblance of those times was to return, it would have to be paid for dearly in present misery. The hope that she might be able to lessen that misery gave her something more substantial to live for than mere acquiescence.

She had been encouraged that very afternoon, when in passing through a receiving area, she happened upon a nurse struggling to help a patient back onto a cart. She quickly lent her support, and upon helping lift the man up to the head of the cart and straightening his covers, she was rewarded with a smile that transformed his heretofore grim countenance. It was a simple gesture that seemed to give her more pleasure than any triumph on the recital stage. If only that excitement could mitigate her fears for Robert and Thomas.

She now knew that there would be many challenges for her and her mother to face in the coming days, but she had also seen enough to know that regardless of the risks, if she could provide some comfort to these soldiers, she was staying in Paris.

4

The Enemy Engaged

IN THE YEARS THAT ROBERT D'AVILLARD HAD BEEN in the army, he had spent much of his time designing and building structures and rail lines. He had done so in the hope of improving the country's military readiness to further discourage German aggression. In that time, he had surveyed or examined virtually the entire eastern frontier with Germany and the lands abutting Belgium. The declaration of war had dashed any hopes he might have had regarding the deterrent effects of his work, but he took consolation in the fact that the construction done during those years would prove valuable in the coming days. He also sensed that the knowledge that he had acquired would also prove helpful, especially in his new capacity as chief engineering officer on the staff of General Ferdinand Foch, the commander of the Twentieth Corps of the French Second Army.

Robert had joined Foch's staff in the early summer of 1914, shortly before the crisis provoked by the assassination of the Austrian archduke in Sarajevo. Subsequent events that followed in July necessitated his transfer from Paris to Nancy, where the Twentieth Corps to which he was assigned was being assembled. Now with the declaration of war, Robert had thrown himself into the logistical problems presented by the terrain in front of them in France and across the border in Germany. He and all of Foch's staff were keenly aware that time was essential if an effective attack was to be launched to seize the first initiative against the German forces opposing them.

The Second Army was deployed along the crown of hills in front of Nancy in the portion of Lorraine remaining in French hands. With full mobilization, the corps would be strengthened not only with increased manpower but also with trucks and horses needed to effectively transport artillery and other equipment to a rapidly changing battle site. All of this would require meticulous planning to effectively deploy the arriving forces to ensure a timely and coordinated attack.

It became apparent to Robert from the study of the enemy terrain in front of them that any offensive by the Second Army into occupied Lorraine would by geographic necessity be confined to rather narrow tracts. He had hoped that by close study, he might discover another route that, by using modern engineering techniques, might provide added advantage, but the more he reviewed the information available to him, the more he became convinced that the best pathway to the east still lay along the ancient route toward Morhange through Chateau Salins—a route stained by the blood of countless generations in the past.

Now, with the certainty of combat looming, he met with General Foch in his hastily remade headquarters, whose slapdash décor reflected Foch's mood as he rushed to attack the enemy before him. Upon his arrival, Foch appeared even more animated than usual to Robert, and Foch quickly focused on Robert's presentation as the two stared at a large topographical map in front of them.

"I was hoping for some secret new discovery that might allow us to surprise the Germans, but I must confess I have come to the same conclusion as you, Robert," Foch stated with evident disappointment.

"What we now need is a timetable for an offensive as soon as we have adequate resources," he continued.

"The reports of the early mobilization are quite encouraging, General. If anything, we are ahead of our projections. If this continues, we should be able to launch an attack toward Chateau Salins within the week."

"Excellent! I seriously doubt that the Germans will have the capability to attack before then. If we are lucky, we may catch them below full strength, which would give us even more of an advantage. I would favor launching the first wave of an attack even before we are at full capacity, if the remainder of the corps can be mobilized shortly afterward."

As Foch spoke, Robert began to calculate in his mind the number of arriving troops and those needed for an effective first strike. It was very much an unknown in many ways. The easiest part of the calculation would be in estimating the strength of the French forces on any given day, as he was fully aware of the schedule of mobilization and the transportation links that would be utilized. It was the number and makeup of those forces opposing them that would be more difficult to determine without further information. In that regard, the intelligence section was fortunate to have established contacts with many families of French origin in the immediate area across the border and had already gotten much valuable information regarding the number and makeup of the German forces there. As the time drew nearer to an anticipated offensive, that information would be critical in determining the final details of an offensive.

What was proving to be of even greater interest was the information coming in from aerial photographs obtained by the newest addition to the military's arsenal, scout planes that had been combing the area when weather permitted. Their photographs provided a clear view of the valley in front of Chateau Salins, giving Robert hope that such technology would be of enormous benefit in the days ahead.

Staring at the black-and-white photos of the terrain lying in front of them, he searched for any clues of enemy installations and fortifications. His trained eye could see little evidence of significant military construction and virtually no troop deployment for at least the first fifteen kilometers up to Chateau Salins. There was evidence of purposeful activity at significant intersections and in the proximity of other more strategic locations, but the extent of this did not seem at present to be enough to deter a plan of attack through the broad valley leading toward Morhange.

The information that they had already obtained from Morhange confirmed what any competent tactician would suspect, given the strategic location of the city on a high promontory overlooking the valley. The aerial photographs showed that already significant fortifications were in front of the city and along the border of the valley as it funneled toward Morhange. Here would be a major challenge for the French forces unless they could seize an unexpected advantage by an early attack that might find the German defenders unsuitably prepared.

An attack on Morhange would be dependent on the unusual calculus of a modern tactical offense. This attack was based on the supposition that the speed and flexibility of an attack, especially if carried out with the necessary ardor, could render obsolete the fixed defensive fortifications of the enemy. The formula for engagement was based on the calculations of the planners of the general staff that an infantryman at full speed could move at least twenty yards before entrenched German riflemen could get off their first and each subsequent shot.

Based on these key assumptions, Robert had witnessed numerous drills in which the infantry practiced wide-scale assaults running at full speed to gain advantage in time and space during their attack. He had also watched the even more complex and potentially deadly drills that coupled the forceful charge of the infantry with coordinated artillery fire. Such tactics were practiced in the belief that they would optimize any attack against a fortified enemy. Now, as the troops began to pour into their assigned areas, Robert could sense that the moment was near when all the theory and drill would be replaced by the reality of attack.

On the morning of the thirteenth of August, a mere ten days from the declaration of war with Germany, Robert waited in General Foch's office with the morning figures that gave him confidence that an attack could soon be launched.

Soon, General Foch arrived from his morning briefing with General Castlenau, entering the office and quickly fixing an inquiring state on Robert. He followed with a staccato burst of inquiry, reflecting his barely controlled excitement.

"Well, Robert, what can you tell me of our readiness now?"

"I have very good news, General Foch," Robert replied with more emotion than usual. "Throughout the evening and into the early hours of the morning, we have gathered nearly a full complement of transport vehicles and pack animals. We also have more than enough feed to support the animals for more than two weeks. When a decision is made, I am confident that we can support any forward movement."

"Well, that is good news—and timely as well," Foch replied with a broad smile lighting his face.

"You know that I have been pushing General Castlenau, who in turn has been arguing with general staff headquarters for an attack as early as possible. Joffre has it in his mind that the most likely success of plan 17 will be a coordinated attack toward the German center by the three armies on our left. He has been reluctant to see the front shift too far to the south, but by force of our repeated arguments and by the good fortune of our readiness, he and his staff are now inclined to approve a coordinated attack along our entire southern frontier using the forces of the First and Second Armies.

"I have learned this morning that such a plan is virtually certain to be approved as soon as the troop strength is sufficient. I have informed General Castlenau that the Twentieth Corps is prepared to launch an attack at the first opportunity, and I am pleased to report that he has given us the assignment of leading the first wave of the Second Army's offensive.

"My question to you, Robert, is how rapidly can the artillery be put into position to initiate this offensive, and when will suitable transportation be available to allow them to advance as conditions warrant?"

"Sir, unless the Germans sabotage our efforts, I'm confident that we will be able to support the movement of artillery along the front to Morhange very soon. If we begin today, I believe that we can have forces in place for attack by no later than the day after tomorrow. All I will need from operations is the desired location and troop roster to be deployed in each selected location. If I can have that by early afternoon, we can begin the process immediately."

"The staff has the details nearly finalized, and they should have them available to you by no later than one o'clock," Foch replied with a certainty that gave Robert confidence for the conduct of the coming attack.

Pointing to the large map in front of them, Foch continued. "We will be attacking into the mouth of a funnel that descends through this valley and ultimately ends in front of Morhange. I plan to launch our attack along a broad front, with the artillery initiating and then supporting all movements of the infantry. That is why their mobility is so key to our success."

"I'm excited for the opportunity to help facilitate our success, General."

"Very well, Robert. Now let's get about our business. I will have the final plans of attack brought to you as early as possible and will expect an update later this evening as to where we stand in the deployment process."

With that, both men set out for a day of intense preparation for the first great engagement of the war.

———

Two days later, after seemingly endless hours of work, Robert found himself on the crest of the hills in front of Nancy, coordinating the movement of various units as they began to take their positions in the forming battle line. Everything around him seemed to be in motion, which at times seemed to border on chaos. He had commandeered a car and driver to help better coordinate the actions of his engineers in close communication with Colonel LeBlanc, who oversaw the artillery battalions. Artillery had long been the mainstay of the French Army; Napoleon ascended the ranks as an artillery officer using it as the basis for much of his subsequent success. The present army was dependent on a weapon that was believed to be the very apogee of that long tradition, the 75 mm fieldpiece.

Robert quickly appreciated that this weapon was as mobile as claimed. On level ground, it could be moved short distances by the gun crews, which allowed them to quickly change the position and angle of firing to optimize its effectiveness. The seventy-five, with its mobility and recoil design allowing for rapid reloading, made an ideal weapon for an attack relying on speed and the concentration of overwhelming force. Robert watched as the guns were brought into position by motorized and horse-drawn transports, taking comfort as their gray silhouettes soon filled positions judged optimal for the opening bombardment. All of this was given dramatic emphasis by the combined symphony of animals straining against their leather tact and the bass vibration of heavy weaponry as it rolled into position.

No sooner had the caissons fallen into place behind the artillery than the cavalry units, dressed in polished breastplates over bright blue and crimson uniforms, with their helmets flourishing long, flowing horsehair plumes, came into position from their livery areas among the hills before Nancy. Their arrival in the early-morning hours was heralded by the sound of massed hoof beats and the commands of their riders. With brightening daylight, their movement was visible to all as they moved into a position in front of the artillery in preparation to screen the infantry advance. Robert could not help but thrill at the spectacle of the events unfolding before him as the great army moved into position, giving dramatic confirmation of the magnitude of the events to follow.

Through the early-morning hours, the infantry progressed forward, led to their arranged positions by officers of varying ranks, all seemingly engrossed in their duties. Robert and his men moved through these swelling numbers to ensure that all final measures were in place to provide adequate support for the subsequent attack.

By late morning, the entirety of the Twentieth Corps had been deployed from the great crown of hills in front of Nancy. In the bright sunshine of a summer day, they stood poised, looking out over the vast terrain of well-manicured green fields stretching before them. Every man was held rapt by anxious anticipation. Robert, sitting near the vanguard of the attacking troops, was keenly aware of the challenges to be faced yet was strangely moved by the beauty of the land in front of them and calmed by the collective presence of the assembled forces. He smiled, thinking how Thomas would no doubt liken this to the tribes of Israel looking over their promised lands after years of wandering in the wilderness. He also hoped for the same good fortune that was the lot of Joshua and his legions.

Then it began. All the relative tranquility was shattered by the seventy-fives, which in near unison began their initial planned salvo on prearranged targets to be attacked by the advancing infantry. Robert had never heard such a cacophony in his life, even though he had often been involved in military exercises in which artillery was frequently used. Those weapons near him emitted a high-pitched wailing when fired, which, when amplified by the additional sound of cannon farther away, was like some wild banshee cry.

The sound was accompanied by the repeated bright flash of shells and soon by visual proof of their effects, as wide tracts of the land before them seemed to explode, hurling dirt and vegetation into the air, marring the terrain with the pockmarked evidence of their destructive power.

No sooner had the shelling begun when the cavalry began to move out in front of the great line, stretching as far as the eye could see. Then suddenly the lines of infantry began to advance in coordinated groups at a pace that was as much a trot as it was a march. With their royal blue coats and scarlet pants lit brightly in the morning sun, they only added to the spectacle of battle. Robert sat transfixed by the events unfolding before him, until he was summoned by General Foch to return to corps headquarters.

For the next few hours, the French troops advanced with little if any resistance. Despite this, Foch had been insistent in ordering that all members of his staff refrain from frontline participation unless dictated by unforeseen circumstances. The battle was now in the hands of the advancing troops and their commanders. His staff would be of little use near the lethal proximity of the battle line.

In the early afternoon of that first day, Foch's warning took on real meaning. The advancing French Army began to encounter ever more resistance, but despite this, their progress continued. Then suddenly the afternoon was interrupted by a sound that Robert had never heard but one that would become terrifyingly familiar in the days ahead. He heard first a low-pitch groan intensifying as it came closer to the French lines, before it climaxed in a high-pitched wail, terminating in a dull thud followed by the deafening explosion of a large-artillery projectile. This terrifying sequence was to be repeated at varying intervals over the afternoon, but for those such as Robert, removed from the zone of immediate impact, it was difficult to tell with certainty what effect the shelling was having.

As the afternoon turned into evening, widespread reports of success and confirmation of the French advance were flowing back to headquarters, gratifying the planners of the offensive. As darkness fell, Robert moved forward with one of his adjuvant captains to be closer to the front lines to assess the day's progress and to get an appreciation of the terrain now immediately in front of them. Along a quiet country lane, he encountered for the first time trains of wounded returning from the battle. In the dimming light, he saw the grizzly site of bodies rent apart, giving stark testimony to the horrific force of the cannon blasts heard earlier. The recent excitement so evident in headquarters was nowhere to be found here where the pastoral quiet was frequently dispelled by the groans of the wounded. All of this quickly dampened what pleasure Robert might have derived from the day's triumphs, although he consoled himself with a grim acknowledgment that such human collateral was the necessary price for the land taken.

———————

Following a somewhat fitful night's rest, Robert rose early to find Foch in an ebullient mood and anxious to add to the gains of the previous day. From the very beginning, however, this day would be different from the previous. Robert soon appreciated this when reports came back of sabotaged roadways, culverts, and bridges, all designed to impede or relocate the invading army into areas more advantageous to the defenders. Much barbed wire had been deployed along their course, which was particularly bothersome to the flanking cavalry, impeding not only their movement but the timely flow on intelligence that came with their advance. Despite Foch's warning, Robert found himself drawn closer to the front to better ensure proper support for any necessary countermeasures.

As he and his associates worked, Robert sensed a difference from the previous day, with the noise of fighting more dispersed both from the French seventy-fives and the sporadic bursts of small arms fire. The bright summer sky, so remarkable yesterday morning, was now shrouded in a thin veil of white, smoky fog, produced by the enormity of gunfire from both sides. The effect of the subdued light, the cacophony of sound, and the acrid smell of gunpowder had transformed a beautiful landscape into one that was now surreal and foreboding.

After returning to headquarters, Robert could better appreciate the full scope of the battle and began to sense a rhythm to it, almost like the tide coming to shore. In some areas, the advancing wave would be slowed by impediments, but eventually, they were washed aside as if by the power of rushing water. He concentrated on those areas where the advance was meeting the most resistance, in case further support might be needed.

With the arrival of darkness, the collective din began to subside. Once again, those in the back lines were confronted with the awful reality of the day's wounded and the more somber evidence of those killed. Robert had been spared the sight of the collected bodies from the day's action, but the casualty numbers as they came in could not be ignored, giving vivid testimony to the lethality of the day's action.

Even Foch seemed sobered, no doubt weighing in his own mind the benefit of the ground captured with the cost in human lives spent in obtaining it. Despite such feelings, the order for the next day would remain unchanged. The corps would press the attack. That night, Robert found it hard once again to sleep, dozing intermittently until wakened by the sound of caissons moving forward toward the battle.

That day's fighting resumed with even greater intensity. Then it was over, as the collective fury of the Twentieth Corps finally broke the enemy, and by late on the afternoon of the third day, the Twentieth Corps stood in full possession of their first objective of the war, Chateau Salins.

The mood in the ranks that night was one of elation mixed with pride of accomplishment. Foch too seemed genuinely moved by their success, realizing that it gave credibility to his many years of championing a doctrine of attack. To further heighten their elation, word came from Second Army headquarters that General de Castlenau had ordered the Twentieth Corps to hold the ground of Chateau Salins. The remainder of the Second Army would continue the assault forward toward Morhange, while Foch and his corps had the luxury of resting on their laurels for the immediate future. It was an opportunity Robert accepted gladly, and for the first night in many, he slept well.

5

To Comfort Always

THOMAS D'AVILLARD HAD RETURNED TO STRASBOURG from Paris at the urging of his bishop. His bishop had always valued Thomas's skills as a mediator, and no doubt his return had been motivated by the hope that they could be used to lessen tensions in the city as the crisis in the aftermath of the assassination of the Austrian heir intensified.

Since the German occupation of Alsace in 1870, there had always been hostility for the occupiers from the many French inhabitants that had remained in Strasbourg. The francophone population still was the largest group in the city and surrounding province of Alsace, but through the years, many Germans had migrated into the region. Their influence had been disproportionate to their numbers, as many had occupied key jobs in the government or obtained favored treatment from the new German ruling class.

In the past year, Thomas had been encouraged by a more conciliatory stance by the German ruling class, with various reforms being undertaken to try to give the French population greater participation in the governance of the province. Before he had returned to Paris for the summer, Thomas had been encouraged by an ever-greater sense of cooperation between the city's two principal factions, but now upon his return, he noticed a dramatic change. Everywhere there was a sense of worry and suspicion, including the university.

The one area in Strasbourg that had previously given Thomas hope was the university. Its diverse student body was comprised of the major nationalities of Europe. Nurtured in the spirit of a modern liberal curriculum, these same students had been exposed to scientific and political thought that spoke to the benefits of cooperation, rather than conquest, as the best means for constructive progress. Much of Thomas's work aside from his studies centered on teaching and often counseling the many students that he met. Given his likable character and the persuasiveness of his arguments, it was only natural that in his time in Strasbourg, he had accumulated many young protégées from various national backgrounds and political beliefs.

He had enjoyed the give and take of their conversations through the years, just as he had with his old friends in Paris. He was especially gratified when he could have some positive influence on his young student associates, instilling in them greater respect and tolerance for those with differing ideas. Now the whole community seemed on edge and suspicious, even those Thomas had viewed in the past as being more accommodative in their beliefs.

As the crisis continued to deteriorate, Thomas felt it his duty to stay in Strasbourg regardless of the risks should war break out. He had been comforted by a letter from the bishop to all priests in Strasbourg of non-German nationality, emphasizing the historic tolerance granted by civil authorities in past conflicts if the clergy strictly avoided any actions judged to be seditious. Given the accepted precedent of the church as a haven for the disenfranchised in times of war, Thomas had been content to trust his safety to God and the bishop.

His time was now consumed counseling the many students who were coming to him, asking what they should do in the event of war. For some who had strong objections to taking another man's life, his task was relatively easy; he recommended that they return to their homes and seek asylum with the church, seeking a position providing comfort to their fellow citizens while avoiding actual combat.

The real difficulty came with those who were undecided about volunteering for their country's army. This group often had questions regarding conflicts between their military obligations and the teachings of the church, specifically how certain acts might affect their future life and even their salvation. Such questions regarding the conflict between obligations and morality had long been of interest to Thomas, but with a war looming, they became even more relevant and problematic.

He had learned in the past, when confronted with difficult problems, to rely on the discipline of his training. Now it seemed at times that he could hear the voice of Aquinas speaking softly to him, saying, "It is right to use all your reason and intellect to address such weighty problems, but even for the best, it will often not be enough without the grace and wisdom of God. When you seem lost, look to the scriptures and the testimony of others to find what you alone cannot."

Though he knew what Aquinas had written was true, as he looked through the biblical texts, Thomas became frustrated by his inability to find the inspiration needed for such important guidance. In such matters, the texts were often ambiguous, with even Christ directing his own flock to render unto Caesar that which was Caesar's. The question for Thomas was, what was Caesar's and what was God's? How could obeying your obligation to the state be reconciled with the commandment to not kill? A satisfactory answer eluded Thomas, and, lacking it, he found dealing with the questions the earnest young men brought him increasingly unsettling.

Fortunately for Thomas, as the crisis escalated, the number of students seeking his advice diminished, since many of the foreign students had already left, leaving only a small contingent of Germans and Alsatians. His reprieve would be short-lived, however, with the declaration of war.

Thomas learned of the declaration of war in the peaceful surroundings of a library where he had spent many hours in days past searching for insight and guidance. The news had elicited a great sense of foreboding as well as profound disappointment in the failure of his efforts and those of countless others who had worked mightily to maintain peace among the tribes of Europe. He was unable at first to focus his mind or move from the desk where he was sitting, paralyzed by his dark emotions. At last, he rose and, barely conscious of his surroundings, walked slowly to a small nearby chapel to pray. Even there, he was uncertain in his supplications, sensing the enormous looming tragedy that would confront him and virtually everyone on the continent.

In the days that followed, Thomas felt rudderless and seldom ventured outside of the protective shell of his room or the library. The bishop had already informed all priests from hostile lands to confine themselves to clerical grounds, but in Thomas's present mental state, even that universe seemed too large.

It was just as well, as the entire complexion of the university and Strasbourg itself had been radically transformed. Virtually all the students were gone, effectively bringing classes to a halt. The city had been changed by the huge influx of military personnel and equipment into a virtual armed camp, making day-to-day commerce increasingly complicated.

Within days, word came of actual combat around Mulhouse, precipitating an immediate increase in the pace of troop movement into and out of the city. Soon this was accompanied by the first of what would become an all too familiar sight, the return of trains laden with soldiers too severely wounded to be handled in the field. At first, these numbers were not significant. As word spread of increasing conflict, however, in Alsace and especially in Lorraine, the number and frequency of these trains increased to a point where it was rapidly taxing the limit of the town's medical facilities.

Unfortunately, this wave of casualties did not abate but seemed to increase daily. Soon the support staffs in the medical community and clergy were finding it difficult to keep up with the enormity of the demands that this population of wounded and dying was placing on their capabilities. The situation would soon provide an opportunity for Thomas and other foreign-born priests, when the bishop obtained permission from the military governor to allow them to minister to the wounded in the receiving wards and hospitals throughout the city.

When Thomas heard of the opportunity, he welcomed it as a way to escape his confinement in the narrow realm of his clerical world. He had quickly become restless with the truly monastic lifestyle now imposed upon him and was excited by the prospect of more tangible involvement with the people affected by the war. He immediately dispensed with his morning's task of writing a commentary on a Christian's responsibilities in war to inform the bishop of his willingness to volunteer. He learned shortly afterward that he would be working in a receiving ward in a makeshift hospital and welcomed the chance to act on his responsibilities rather than simply comment on them.

His introduction to this new world came as a shock. The facility, although seemingly large from the outside, seemed crowded and somewhat chaotic when Thomas and several of his newly assigned colleagues were led into the central reception area. A host of personnel of various descriptions seemed to be buzzing in various directions all at the same time.

The group was given a brief introduction by an army officer who stressed that even though they were expected to conform to the clerical hierarchy, in this setting, ultimate authority resided with the officer in charge. The physicians and nurses had been briefed about their arrival and in practical terms would guide their duties predicated by the circumstances of the moment. They were then led to a new makeshift chapel and turned over to a senior priest who had previous experience in such circumstances from a recent ministry in Croatia.

After Father Peter introduced himself, he outlined a plan for their daily work. They would all meet in the chapel at six o'clock in the morning for prayer and then would be assigned their daily duties. The usual routine would be for each of the priests to be assigned to a ward where they could administer to the needs of those soldiers arriving or being held there. It would be important, Father Peter emphasized, to develop a working relationship with the medical staff, as they were most aware of those patients in need of holy sacraments. He warned that there might be days when the demands for their work might not allow for sufficient time to provide the counsel they might think appropriate, but in such circumstances, priority should be given to the most critically wounded.

All this Thomas listened to attentively, hoping for any information that might lessen the stress of adapting to his new responsibilities. Then, within minutes after Father Peter had finished, he found himself being directed to Receiving Ward C, a space recently converted from an office that had housed municipal workers.

It was an environment like nothing he had ever experienced. Even before he arrived in the actual ward, he was greeted by the pungent smell of alcohol and other disinfectants. He would come to associate forever that smell with the world that would now consume most of his waking hours. Thomas would soon learn that it was an altogether new and strange world, one in which horror mixed with heroism and where all were forced to confront suffering on an enormous scale.

Arriving on the ward, Thomas was impressed by the transformation, with former office cubicles being used as areas to house patients. Despite this, the space was seldom adequate, so at times there would be so many men arranged on cots or beds in each of these rather cramped spaces that it was difficult to stand among them. He noted larger offices and meeting rooms, which he would later learn had been converted to triage stations, where large volumes of patients could be seen on their arrival and evaluated as to their needs for further care. He would also learn that the upper floors contained facilities for surgery and other specialty services, such as the setting of fractures. What most impressed him from the first moment he entered the ward was a near constant sense of urgency that hung over the facility and its many employees. He also would come to understand that it was due to the volume and challenge of meeting the seemingly unending needs of the newly arrived wounded.

Soon Thomas was introduced to a young doctor, Doctor Rasmussen, and two sisters, Sister Ruth and Sister Teresa, who were on nursing duty. They all had a demeanor that gave them a stature disproportionate to their relatively young ages.

Sister Ruth told Thomas that things had been quiet thus far, but they knew that a train was due to arrive at any moment filled with casualties. Then, as if on cue, the receiving doors burst open, ushering in a long procession of wounded. The doctor and two nurses were quickly transformed as they gathered among the new arrivals, adding further gravitas to their presence.

What followed would be a pattern that would consume the rest of his days in Strasbourg. The medical staff would quickly assess the patients as they arrived. Some required immediate attention, and they were directed to appropriate areas as quickly as possible. At times, the urgency of the situation demanded that the doctor and staff attend to the matter at hand in the receiving area. Other patients, less critically wounded, were moved to rooms where they could be attended to at a less hectic pace. There were always several, however, for whom little could be done. For them, one of the nurses would appraise their wishes for religious support and would go to Thomas, asking for his help. The intensity of all this seemed further transformed by the bright light rebounding off the pale green walls and the unremitting smell of alcohol and disinfectants.

Thomas was thus introduced to another presence, that of death. It was a presence that he and most were unfamiliar with. In his lifetime, he had administered the last rites to the critically ill, but he had seldom been present at their death. For most people, death was only evident in the rites of the funeral mass. Here in this ward, however, it was a frequent specter that would focus Thomas on his priestly duties regardless of how tired or distressed he might be.

In this often-frantic maelstrom, he would attend to young men with little knowledge or experience of life. For some, their lives would end too quickly, while others would be doomed to a future of disability and deformity. With each passing day, the awful reality of this war was made ever more apparent. The pain and agony that he witnessed refuted the notions of the political theorists and philosophers espousing the glory of dying for the fatherland. The deformed faces and limbless bodies were powerful testimony to the costs of conquest and empire advocated by the warlords. Here there was little glory but much that was squalid, with fear in some form possessing all.

Though these men came from different regions and backgrounds, they all shared a common experience of suffering. They shared as well concerns not only for themselves but also for their families and loved ones. As the scope of this suffering became ever more apparent, Thomas came to detest those who had been responsible for this horror.

The reality and demands of these days were so great that they forced Thomas to focus on the moment rather than dwell on philosophic or religious uncertainties. He realized that whatever his beliefs might be or whatever conclusions he might have formed, they were to be sublimated to his present responsibilities. Here he was not to debate the purpose or even the morality of the war but to comfort those who suffered from it.

6

Pressing Forward

AS THE ENGAGEMENT WITH GERMAN TROOPS IN Lorraine continued, more information began to accumulate at the headquarters of the French Second Army about the nature of the enemy force in front of them. The picture that emerged was becoming clearer with each passing day. The majority of the troops they faced were Bavarian under the command of Grand Duke Rupprecht. To date, the French forces had encountered at least one corps, but there was no doubt they were simply a vanguard of an entire army that was concentrating around the fortress city of Morhange, blocking the way to Metz and the German heartland.

Word was soon received that General Castlenau now planned to commit the remainder of his army to attacking Morhange. Robert and the men of the Twentieth Corps were to be given a respite, while the remainder of the army would launch the initial assault. Despite the likelihood of increased resistance, the morale of the army was high after the initial success of the Twentieth Corps, which had further emboldened their commanders, believing the enemy to be vulnerable to the assault tactics of the previous days.

It was in front of Morhange where these offensive tactics would be tested on a larger scale than before Chateau Salins. From the very first, however, despite the élan of their well-executed attack, the first lesson about the terrible realities of modern defensive tactics was unfolding. Well-prepared German parapets in front of Morhange allowed them to return fire despite heavy artillery assault on their position. Moreover, the Germans in such prepared defensive positions were not confined to the use of rifles but could instead use emplaced machine guns whose rapidity of fire made obsolete any French calculation regarding the rate of return fire from German defenses.

As the men of the Second Army raced forward, they were met by waves of machine-gun fire and artillery even more violent than that directed by the mobile French seventy-fives. At the end of that first day and the many to follow, despite brave and spirited attacks, the will was simply no match for the physics of modern armaments. The fields in front of Morhange were littered with thousands of dead, some in rows, others isolated in gruesome poses attesting to the sudden and violent nature of their ends. In the afternoon light made gray by the smoke of incessant cannonade, German gunners had no trouble distinguishing the target presented by the bright crimson pants of the attacking French Army. The resulting carnage gave first proof of the lethality of present French tactics based as much on will and glories past as aggregated firepower.

The sight of vast waves of a French Army being shattered by the power of his defensive position now brought out in Prince Rupprecht a predator's desire to shatter and kill a weakened victim. Seeing the effect that his massive artillery assault had inflicted on the French, he now sought permission from the supreme command to launch a major counteroffensive. He was aware that plans called for his army's role to immobilize any French attack and serve as reserve strength for the planned primary assault through Belgium to the north. As he saw the French attack deteriorate, however, his instincts told him that an opportunity lay in front of him that could not be ignored.

Robert had witnessed the attack on Morhange along with Foch and other members of his staff from a protected ridge far from the battle. He was at first amazed and then horrified to see the devastating effects of the German defensive fire on the lines of advancing French. He watched helplessly as wave after wave of infantry battalions threw themselves at the German positions, only to be stopped by the combined effect of artillery barrage and machine-gun fire.

Suddenly, commanders were confronted with the dilemma of retreating troops impeding the forward progress of fresh units surging forward. Now the roads were being hopelessly clogged by the coalescence of both retreating and advancing units. This only added to the disaster, as the congestion and confusion allowed the Germans to concentrate their artillery fire there with devastating effect. In the end, the only solution was to halt the advancing forces in these pockets and even, at times, to withdraw to regroup.

This was to be the pattern across the entire front, with troops being turned back by horrific firepower, thereby limiting the advance of any further units coming in support. By late afternoon, the attack seemed to crest and then was turned back by the violence and intensity of the German resistance.

By nightfall, little if any ground had been gained, and the entire staff seemed stunned in contemplating what options might be available to change the course of this day's failures. For Robert, his observations of the day's battle coupled with some trigonometric estimates made clear to him the dilemma they faced. In noting the site of fire of the large German artillery placements, he calculated that they were out of range of the French seventy-fives as they were now deployed. Unless the front could be pushed farther toward Morhange, allowing for neutralization of these sites by French artillery, the infantry would continue to be exposed to the murderous fire of the German cannons.

That was the great dilemma as he saw it, because as this day had shown all too painfully, massed assaults, however well led, could be effectively disrupted by heavy enemy artillery and machine-gun fire. The murderous reality of the force of modern industrial weaponry had today proven far more lethal and effective than the combined élan of the French troops advancing against them.

That evening, Robert saw how Foch had been sobered by the day's events. He seemed unusually restrained at their evening meal, expressing the opinion that if Morhange could not be taken quickly, their entire offensive thrust toward Metz was doomed. Though he recognized the efficacy of the German defense, he expressed a belief that the French failure was in great part due to lack of coordination and focus in their attack. He left shortly after the meal to confer with Castlenaugh, who had called him to Second Army headquarters.

The following day saw Castlenau's army assault the enemy in a more orderly and restrained pace from the often-frantic assaults that had characterized much of the previous day's battle. During the first hours of the day, this tactic seemed to be more effective, with advances being made at many points before Morhange. Late in the morning, however, an ominous change in the character of the German resistance became apparent.

The nature of German artillery fire changed with the addition of numerous smaller-caliber cannons to the heavier weapons that had been used to target the advancing French from afar. Their added higher-pitched shriek to the deeper roar of the larger cannons combined to produce a cacophony made more terrifying by the extent of the destruction delivered.

In short order, a sight that would dominate French planning in the coming days became apparent. Emerging from the smoke and gunfire came massed forces clad in the gray-green uniform of the German infantry. These hoards, now supported by their own artillery fire, began to break across the French forces before them. The fury of the collision of the two armies was immense, and over the ensuing hours, a battle of horrific violence played out, with each side seeming at times to gain advantage only to then be held in check. By nightfall, however, large tracts of land had been lost by the French, especially in the southernmost sectors.

These losses placed the Twentieth Corps in danger, as their position left them farther advanced, endangering their flank to German counterattack. As darkness descended, Foch, increasingly aware of his vulnerability, issued orders for his troops to dig into more fortified positions to counter the threat of a nocturnal attack. Soon, Robert and others found themselves accompanying Foch to a hastily called war council.

Upon arrival at Second headquarters, Robert sensed the staff's somber mood. That very afternoon, word had come that Castlenau's son had been killed, which only added to the pessimism. Castlenau looked both saddened and severely fatigued. Nevertheless, he received Foch warmly, with deep appreciation for his expressed condolences. Shortly afterward, with the arrival of all of the corps commanders and their staffs, the group was ushered into a large conference area and seated around a large oak table. Robert and other staff officers were seated behind the gathered corps commanders.

Once seated, Castlenau came quickly to the point.

"General Foch, the army positioned on your right has taken a severe pounding today, and many of the units have found it difficult to hold their present positions. There has been much discussion about withdrawing to positions more suitable to defending against this enemy counterattack. Before any measure is taken, I want to hear your assessment of your present position."

"What is the overall status at this moment?" Foch asked.

"Fortunately, we have been able to withstand the first thrust of their counteroffensive without any breakthrough. This has been accomplished by valiant effort all along our lines and has required that we use virtually all our reserve units. As it now stands, the line of engagement is so deformed, and along with the casualties that we have suffered, I don't believe it possible to continue the offensive on Morhange. What is left is a planned withdrawal that will preserve our resources for the critical days ahead."

"What orders have been issued?" Foch asked.

"None so far, as I felt that it was imperative that I discuss with all of the corps commanders their assessment of their present status."

"What have you learned so far?" asked Foch.

"Some units are in better shape than others, but I believe it is safe to say that there is a unanimous opinion among the other corps commanders that a strategic withdrawal is necessary."

"What will that entail?" asked Foch.

"If we are to withdraw for defensive reasons, then the strongest position would be to fall back to the corona of hills before Nancy."

"That would mean essentially ceding all of the ground that we have taken so far. Would it not?" continued Foch.

"I am afraid that it would."

Foch paused for a moment to study the map before them that gave the most up-to-date positions of the Second Army and the enemy deployed in front of them. The headquarters was in a requisitioned farmhouse, and at this hour, the light was dim, forcing him to often rearrange the map to better appreciate certain details. Slowly, he recognized that already much of the ground previously occupied on his right had been lost, and the peril of his present position became apparent.

"I can see little that can be gained in our present positions. I agree that prudence would dictate a controlled withdrawal to the hills here before Nancy. Having done so, however, we should not cede any further ground, regardless of the costs. These hills provide us a strong position to take advantage of any possible mistakes on their part."

"What are you suggesting, General?" asked Castlenau.

"Their troops have proven their competence in defending a position, but we have no evidence to testify to their offensive abilities. Perhaps we could surprise them. If the troops on our right flank and center can be strategically withdrawn to a position before Nancy, we can return the favor of their greeting before Morhange. My Twentieth Corps would lie somewhat advanced from this position and could add greatly to their problems.

"Robert, remind me again about the gap near our position at Toul," Foch said as he nodded for Robert to come forward to the map.

For a moment, Robert too had trouble orientating himself in the dim light of the meeting room. "You can't see it as well on this map as you can on one of our topographic maps, General, but here between Toul and Epinal is a natural ravine that will force any advancing German Army into a narrow front."

"The Trouée de Charmes," added Castlenau, pointing to an area between the soon-to-be fortified positions that flanked it in on higher ground.

"Yes, that's it," Robert quickly confirmed.

Foch resumed speaking rapidly, as was his custom in addressing difficult matters. "I propose, General Castlenau, to see how well these German troops fight in the open in this trough. The following days will tell us much about our enemy. If he is foolish enough to challenge my corps in this area, then he will be canalized, and we can attack him on both of his flanks. We will then see if they are an able match for us."

"You are always the eloquent advocate for an attack, Foch," said Castlenau. "If we are successful in the withdrawal of our right and center to these hills behind us, then I am more comfortable in the margin of safety in the counterattack that you suggest. I will notify Joffre and GHQ of our intent to proceed with this planned withdrawal. It will not make General Dubail happy if our withdrawal puts his left flank at risk, but I can see no other reasonable option at this time."

"Perhaps General Dubail will be relieved to know of a counterattack that might ultimately strengthen his position," Foch suggested hopefully.

"Given the futility of our continued assault against their present fortifications, I think that it represents our best means to neutralize them and, if possible, retake the initiative on our front," added Castlenau.

"Now, unless you have anything else that you need from us, General Castlenau, I suggest that we should attend to the pressing business before us."

With that, Foch gave a brisk salute to his commander and departed to ready for a new fight in the coming days.

On his way back to Twentieth Corps headquarters, Robert reflected on the implications of the brief gathering. In the span of roughly twenty-four hours, it seemed to him that the entire foundation for the army's reliance on offensive tactics, if not undone, had been reshaped by the day's events. Now it remained to see how Foch and Castlenau would adapt to the new circumstances.

In the days that followed, the Second Army proceeded to fall back to positions of increased strength before Nancy, fighting all the while fierce battles with the advancing German troops. Castlenau was able to keep his army from major calamity during this time, although the casualties mounted higher each day.

Robert watched much of the battle from various vantage points, often in the company of Foch and other staff members. Despite the fact they were witnessing events from a safer distance, the ebb and flow of battle could readily be discerned. It was often a horrible yet fascinating spectacle. In some ways, it seemed like some strategic game in the war college designed to test their capabilities in managing ever-changing conditions. Yet his senses told him all too well that this was no mere exercise but an altogether more deadly and consequential enterprise.

On the evening of the second day of fighting, after the withdrawal had begun, the German advance seemed to take on a new fury, with more troops and artillery being brought forward from the army headquartered around Morhange.

At the makeshift Twentieth Corps headquarters, Robert watched the events closely with Foch and his other staff members.

Then late in the afternoon, Foch suddenly interjected, "He is now concentrating his forces, and if I'm not mistaken, he is headed straight for our positions along the Trouée de

Charmes. If that is so, then they will be concentrated before us by tomorrow afternoon.

"We have much to do tonight to prepare for the morning. By daybreak, I want nearly all our artillery in position, flanking this passage to greet them with a barrage like we received before Morhange. If they can survive that and remain in place, then we will see whether they can sustain the fury of our counterattack on both of their flanks."

Increasingly animated, he spent the next few minutes dictating a series of orders that were delivered throughout the entire corps.

Robert spent the night ensuring that the artillery units as well as the infantry could be deployed in the critical locations called for in these new orders of battle. He had little time to sleep except for brief catnaps caught at opportune moments, yet despite this, the urgency of the situation and the tension surrounding the assembling troops kept him fully awake and focused on his responsibilities.

The early dawn soon proved Foch right, with the German forces concentrating on the gap between the long ridges now heavily fortified by French artillery. Robert, still in an advanced position overseeing troop deployment, watched closely as the Germans drew closer to the newly fortified gap. At an appropriate moment, a massive artillery barrage was unleashed, making the French presence evident and clouding the early-morning sunlight in a fog of smoke.

Convinced there was nothing further that he could do at this time, Robert set out on foot for headquarters. His path led upward through a well-rutted road. A gigantic barrage of French seventy-fives on his right halted his advance in a copse of trees below the crest of the hill above him. From this vantage point, what he saw amazed him. Along both sides of the surrounding hills, waves of deadly cannon fire were being poured into the valley below. His feelings vacillated between concern and pride as he saw the effects of this combined enfilade devastating large segments of the advancing German lines.

As the guns came to a temporary halt, Robert resumed his upward climb, but the woods hid the first bright discharges coming from many locations along the German lines. Then he heard the shriek of incoming shells and saw gaping holes being torn in the terrain around him. Fully aware of the danger he was now in, Robert set out for headquarters, skirting behind the artillery line at a jog. It was then that he heard an incoming shell whose high pitch and volume froze his movement. He recovered in time to throw himself to the ground before the impact and the following concussion spewed earth and shrapnel in a wide circle around it.

Robert sensed only a huge hollow sound, like some gigantic bass instrument, and felt himself being thrown into the air. Then everything went black.

7

Distant Thunder

THE LAST SEVEN DAYS HAD BEEN GRUELING FOR General Joseph-Simon Gallieni. He had recently retired from the army, but the maelstrom that was the rapidly evolving war had forced War Secretary Adolf Messimy to once again seek him out. Previously, Messimy had offered him the job of army chief of staff, but weakened by a chronic medical condition, he had refused. Now Messimy returned, describing the dismal state of war readiness that now existed in Paris, and appealing to Gallieni's sense of duty, he offered him the job as military governor of Paris.

Gallieni's inclination was to dismiss the offer, but as he listened to Messimy describe conditions in the city, he realized that matters there could not be ignored. Much-needed work required to fortify the city and its environs had been delayed by political infighting or had been poorly implemented. He now realized that the city could offer little resistance to a German Army should it succeed in reaching its gates. He also fully agreed with Messimy that the loss of Paris, given its industrial and psychologic importance, would be lethal to the French cause.

Therefore, despite the increasing pain he was having in his spine, he reluctantly accepted Messimy's offer, if certain conditions could be met. These included full access to all military intelligence available to the war minister and a pledge that if the city was seriously threatened, he would be given the necessary troops to defend it. This was no small measure, he realized, given the control Joffre now held over such forces, but Gallieni needed such a guarantee should Joffre give less emphasis on defending the capital in the face of a forced retreat of the army.

Gallieni took up his position within hours of his acceptance. He came to his post with certain advantages that allowed him to quickly adapt to the circumstances he faced. He knew the city intimately from his many years of assignments and residency, including knowledge of its infrastructure and the surrounding terrain that would be vital in the event of an approaching invader. What he lacked was a thorough knowledge of the present staff and the strength and capability of the present garrisoned forces. Those first days, he spent much time reviewing his personnel and the senior staff he had inherited from General Michel, his predecessor. He also spent much time reviewing intelligence coming in from the frontline sectors.

His last position prior to retirement had been as commander of the Fifth Army, and from that duty, he was aware of the vulnerabilities and strengths of the northeastern regions in front of the city. He knew that they lacked easily defensible terrain and existing defensive infrastructure. Given these vulnerabilities, he searched carefully for any information pertaining to German intent in Belgium that could ultimately threaten vulnerable French territory northeast of the capital. What his trained eye was seeing did not make him comfortable.

What he was most concerned with were indications of a German buildup west of the Meuse River in Belgium. Though the conventional wisdom of the general staff said such an extension of the German lines was not likely, as it would place untenable demands on the remainder of their forces, Gallieni distrusted theories. He knew that the easiest way to Paris was from this more northerly direction, and if new intelligence refuted Joffre and his staff's present notions, he intended to call them out.

Focused by his fears, he began to cull from the stacks of incoming intelligence bits that served to only heighten his anxiety. What most concerned him were Belgium intelligence reports that reserve troops were being widely integrated into regular units of the German Army. If this was true, it would destroy French assumptions that the German professional army would never use reserves in any primary action. He now recalled previous intelligence indicating that for several years, college students had spent their summers involved in army exercises. If these exercises had been fruitful, then an infusion of competent reserves would dramatically change the calculus along the front lines by giving the German command the numbers needed to extend their lines without diluting their forces elsewhere.

As his concerns mounted, Messimy urged him to make a visit to the front to better assess the situation. He therefore requisitioned an automobile and proceeded with haste to meet with General Lanzerac and his staff of the Fifth Army.

His arrival at Fifth Army headquarters, which was within kilometers of the Belgian frontier, only served to reinforce Gallieni's concerns.

Upon entering, he sensed an air of deep concern, with the staff intently involved with the day's affairs. Everywhere there seemed to be haste, with aides coming and going from various locations within the complex. After a moment, he was recognized, and Lanzerac's chief of staff, General Hely d'Oissel, came out to meet him.

"General Gallieni, I'm pleased to see you once again. We heard that you were appointed as the military governor of Paris but certainly did not anticipate seeing you so soon in this region until we were notified of your visit. General Lanzerac sends his compliments, but at present he is tied up with General Belin from General Joffre's staff."

Gallieni's quickly replied, "You may wonder what my visit is about, General, so I will get to the point, as I can see that you have important matters to attend to. Since I have taken charge of the Paris garrison, I've been very interested in any intelligence that might have implications for the city's defense. Some recent observations concern me not only for Paris but also for your situation, which I know well from my previous posting."

"What's worrying you, General?" asked Hely d'Oissel.

"My concerns relate to a German buildup farther to the northwest than previously thought feasible by many of our strategists. If that is the case, then your army and the British will bear the brunt of a German offensive, which, given their usual thoroughness, I suspect will be launched with massive firepower."

"General Gallieni, I believe that your concerns are not without justification. Yesterday, we received news that at least ten thousand cavalry troops had crossed to the west of the Meuse at Huy, which raises the distinct possibility that a large infantry force is behind them. As we are presently deployed, we are ill positioned to defend against that contingency."

At that moment, General Lanzerac arrived, showing the frustration of his recent meeting with Joffre's chief of staff by a dark scowl.

"I am sorry to keep you waiting, General Gallieni, but I was delayed trying to convey to General Joffre's staff the serious nature of the threat that is developing on our flank."

"That's exactly what I'm here to talk to you about," replied Gallieni. "From the intelligence that I have seen, coupled with the intuition of an old soldier, I suspect that the main German offensive will come through the Meuse Valley, right at you and the British."

"I have been telling Joffre that for the last two days, with little effect," said Lanzerac, with a vehemence that belied his frustration. "They are so focused on their offensive that they think any German deployment in that direction will only make them more vulnerable at our proposed point of attack. While we throw ourselves at the German center, our extreme left flank will be increasingly isolated and vulnerable."

"What is your situation at present?" asked Gallieni.

"We have at last gotten some concession from General Headquarters to move one of our corps to the northwest in front of Dinan, which was done yesterday. The remainder of the army is still deployed in conjunction with the Third and Fourth Armies aligned for the coming offensive. Once engaged, it will be difficult to relocate them toward Dinan if they are needed, which I fear they will be."

"Have you had any contact with the British?" asked Gallieni.

Lanzerac seemed to redden perceptibly. "We met with their staff for the first time two days ago, although I'm not sure how many troops they have at present, as we have seen little activity in their assigned sector."

"We have been reassured in Paris from British intelligence reports that at least seventy-five thousand British troops are on the continent," said Gallieni.

"That may be, but there is little evidence that they are being pressed quickly into the line. Even if they do get into position, I'm not sure their commanders are sufficiently motivated for anything more than a token show of support, followed by a hasty retreat to the channel, where they can extricate themselves in case of disaster."

"You are not impressed with General French and his staff then?"

"General French seems almost an embodiment of a Gilbert and Sullivan modern general. He has complete command of the perfectly obvious, but beyond that, it is difficult to tell if he has any clear understanding of what terrain or enemy might lie in front of him. I got the distinct impression that any cooperation that might come from him and his men would be only insofar as it met their particular needs."

"What makes you say that?"

"General French seems typical of the British ruling class, believing the world exists for the benefit of their empire. In his mind, he could no more take orders from a French general or even agree to coordinated actions unless he felt himself suitably consulted and assured that British interests would be of the foremost importance. If he thinks that his troops are in jeopardy, it will be difficult to keep him from withdrawing to safety, regardless of our concerns or needs."

"What can I take back to Messimy concerning your situation at present?" asked Gallieni.

"Tell the war minister that I believe we may soon face a very large force of German troops in a major offensive through Belgium. At present, we are ill deployed to meet them, nor should we expect any significant help from the British in the immediate future to face such a contingency."

"You sound pessimistic, General Lanzerac."

"I'm just realistic, General. If we can't get a significant realignment of my troops to face this threat, then I will have real cause for pessimism."

Gallieni mulled over his discussion with Lanzerac as he proceeded to Joffre's headquarters. He was not interested in the politics of the matter; he was too old for that. His responsibilities for the defense of Paris and the threat of the German buildup before Dinan compelled him to discuss the situation with Joffre.

As he approached Joffre's headquarters, Gallieni noted the congestion of vehicles and weaponry surrounding it. It had the appearance of a small city, with numerous buildings and tents providing accommodations to the staff's needs. Upon entering, he was struck by the contrast with that of the headquarters of the Fifth Army. Here, everything and everyone seemed in place, with a quiet, almost sleepy atmosphere. Nowhere was seen the frenetic activity widely noted at Lanzerac's headquarters. Instead, numerous small offices served to segregate various bureaus into self-contained enclaves, which existed to supply Joffre and his staff the product of their labors.

He was greeted almost at once by Joffre's assistant chief of staff, General Berthelot.

"Welcome, General Gallieni," greeted Berthelot with a voice that belied his indifference to Gallieni's presence. "We received a communication from the war minister earlier that you should be expected sometime today. Unfortunately, General Joffre has found it necessary to make last-minute preparations with the commanders of the Third and Fourth Armies and consequently will not be back until much later this evening. What can I do for you, General?"

A convenient absence, Gallieni thought before responding.

"Well, General, as commander of the Paris garrison, I am sensitive to threats to my jurisdiction. As I have studied intelligence coming in from Belgium, I have become concerned about a German buildup there that has implications for our northern flank."

"I'm afraid you have been listening to General Lanzerac," Berthelot replied in a reassuring tone. "We have considered that possibility from the very outbreak of the war and conducted a large cavalry reconnaissance throughout the area. While there is evidence of German involvement in and around Liege, we believe at present that is primarily to secure the bridges and other strategic locations to protect their own flank. To date, we have seen no evidence that a large force has moved beyond those areas in a manner that would threaten our left flank."

"The Fifth Army staff reports evidence of a large cavalry movement along the Meuse toward Namur and Dinant," Gallieni interjected.

"We are aware of that and recently shifted one corps of the Fifth Army to the northwest in front of Dinant to engage those forces if they continue to move toward our lines. At present, however, we do not have further evidence those forces are large enough to disrupt our final plans for our coming offensive."

"What can you tell me about that?" Gallieni asked.

"General Joffre is finalizing preparations as we speak with the commanders of the Third and Fourth Armies. The German forces have elected to counterattack in force along our right flank in front of Nancy. This has stalled the First and Second Armies in their advance, but it has also demonstrated considerable German troop strength in the area. These numbers suggest to us that the German center is vulnerable along the French-Belgian border, and it is where we plan to concentrate our offensive."

"How will the Fifth Army will be deployed?"

"Despite General Lanzerac's concern, we believe that until unequivocal evidence arises to support a real threat to his flank, given the critical importance of this offensive, the intent is to commit the bulk of the Fifth Army in coordination with the Third and Fourth to add further mass to the offensive.

"As to any further buildup of German forces in the northwest, I would welcome it, as it will only weaken their position along our proposed line of attack," Berthelot said smugly.

"I hope you are right, General Berthelot, but there are reports coming into Paris that temper my optimism."

"What are you suggesting?" asked Berthelot.

"We are getting reports from the Belgians and even from the British of large numbers of reserve units being assimilated alongside regulars throughout the German Army. If that is the case, then that could allow for a strong German buildup to the north of the Meuse while maintaining troop strength elsewhere."

"It would also significantly dilute the fighting qualities of those forces, General Gallieni. We will see how the German clerk and farmer respond to the sounds of our incoming seventy-fives and the fury of our attack."

After a pause, Berthelot continued.

"General Gallieni, your concerns are well noted and will be considered in the coming days. What is most important now is timing and audacity. While the Germans are assembling north of the Meuse, we plan to attack as soon as we can be assured of support on our left flank from the British and hopefully the Belgians. The time is near to strike the enemy."

"I am very sympathetic to that strategy; my major concern was that, in our focus on the coming offensive, we do not leave our left flank vulnerable. You must understand, General Berthelot, that as military governor, I must thoroughly understand future risks to Paris."

"We can fully understand your position, General, but unless the conditions that you suggest become more apparent, then I am of the firm opinion that the best defense of Paris is to attack and destroy our enemy."

"To your success, General Berthelot," Gallieni replied with a nod. "I know that you have many things to attend to, and I appreciate your time. Good luck to you and the army in the days to come."

With that, Gallieni saluted, leaving to return to Paris. As his car gathered speed, his surroundings seemed to pass unnoticed, his mind now occupied with the implications of his day's visits.

It was evident that the stress of his present command had made Lanzerac more irritable and excitable than he had ever seen him. It was possible that his frame of mind had miscolored his analysis of present conditions. On the other hand, he was well respected as having one of the best analytic minds of the general staff, and therefore his opinions could not be easily dismissed. That his conclusions coincided with his own made Gallieni sympathetic to his concerns. His description of the British command was certainly unsettling, and regardless of its ultimate accuracy, Lanzerac's antipathy unfortunately promised further difficulties with them in the future.

Although Joffre was conveniently absent, Gallieni could read from the demeanor of his adjunct a staff thoroughly in accord with, if not intimidated by, their commander. Joffre had always been aloof even when he had served under him, but Gallieni noted that, with supreme command, he had used his manner to discourage discussion and intimidate opposition. That his command was focused on the coming offensive was to be expected. All that could be hoped was that it would succeed in time to remove the threat to Paris that Gallieni was now convinced was building along the Meuse River in Belgium.

As commander of Paris, Gallieni knew that he could not rest upon the certainty of that coming French offensive, however. His trip had given him enough to further motivate action, so by the time he arrived back in Paris, he was even more determined to initiate drastic measures to enhance the capital's defense in the coming days.

On the following day, Joffre issued Order No. 13 instructing the Third and Fourth Armies of Generals Ruffey and De Langle de Cary to ready for an imminent attack. A second corps of the Fifth Army was now ordered to move to the northwest, positioning the brunt of that army near the confluence of the Meuse with the Sambre. Dependent on the strength of the German forces moving toward Dinant, General Lanzerac was ordered to attack them or redeploy his forces to aid the French offensive on his right.

That same day, large numbers of German cavalry were engaged in front of Denant. Later that night, reports indicated a large contingent of German infantry moving behind them to the northwest of the Meuse, heading directly toward Lanzerac's two corps and the British Expeditionary Force entrenching around the Flemish town of Mons.

8

Recuperation

MARIE HEARD OF ROBERT'S INJURIES FROM A telegram sent by his mother, who had passed on the details that she had received from the army messenger. She had come to know Robert's mother from past visits and found her to be quite proper with a shy reserve. Her message to Marie was therefore made more poignant by her request that Marie and her mother act in her place to oversee Robert's needs, as the war made it virtually impossible to get to Paris from Provence at present. For Marie, the shock of the news was made worse by her recent experiences with other wounded men. Now she shared painful common ground with the many families she had met in the hospital trying to deal with the sudden intrusion of fear and uncertainty into their lives.

For a moment, she seemed almost paralyzed. Then, almost subconsciously, Marie drew on the mental discipline she had developed in performing and slowly began to regain her poise. First she realized that before she could grasp what responsibilities might be entailed by the request of Robert's mother, she would have to know Robert's present location and actual condition.

She was soon helped by the arrival of her mother, and the pair quickly set out to locate Robert's whereabouts. From these inquiries, the women discovered that Robert would be arriving on the following day, and as luck would have it, the hospital was within walking distance of their home.

Marie and her mother arrived early the next day, hoping to see Robert as he was brought in, but the hospital staff quickly squelched such a notion. They were able to take up a vantage point near the entryway of the receiving ward, where they might get a glimpse of the wounded as they arrived, but their position precluded any direct interaction. What they saw that morning was a long train of wounded being brought in and quickly triaged to the most appropriate location for care. It was hard, given the nature of some of the injuries, to make out the features of many of the men, but late in the morning, Marie's mother gave an audible gasp, recognizing Robert as he was brought in. He was asleep or unconscious at that time, but more disconcerting was his pallor and appearance, with his hair disheveled and his carefully maintained uniform replaced by a wrinkled cotton gown.

For the remainder of the day, the women made numerous requests to various staff members to visit Robert but were repeatedly rebuffed. Finally, their persistence seemed to have some effect, as a kindly, senior matron appeared to take notice of them.

"Excuse me, but I want you to know we are aware of your concerns, but it is our policy to limit visitation, even for family members, until patients can be fully assessed and stabilized. I am pleased to report, however, that the officer you have referred to seems to be making progress. The effect of the pain medicine he received during his transit to the hospital seems to have worn off, and he is now more alert and able to communicate his needs. There is no point in you staying here today, but if you return tomorrow morning, I am hopeful his condition will allow you to visit with him."

Marie's relief was immediately evident with her features brightening with the news, although it also seemed to have made her momentarily dumb, requiring her mother to reply.

"Thank you so much for your concern and the wonderful news. I'm sure we will both rest more comfortably now. We will certainly return tomorrow."

"It is the least I can do, madame. You will have to excuse us, as we have so many wounded here that it is sometimes difficult to find the time to adequately deal with families. We will expect you tomorrow, and if his progress continues, I am optimistic that he will be able to visit with you then."

———

Late in the afternoon of the following day, Marie and her mother were finally allowed to visit Robert. A nurse came up to them shortly after lunch, informing them that they would be allowed to see Robert at two o'clock. She warned he was still quite weak and that they should keep their visit short. She also told them that he had sustained a concussion as well as a broken collarbone and fibula and multiple contusions.

Upon entering Robert's room, the pair found him asleep. How different he appeared to Marie. He seemed so thin and pale. His leg was in a cast, and his shoulder in a splint. It was as if he had been stripped of all the essential elements that gave vitality and meaning to his life. For a long while, Marie and her mother sat silently at his bedside, neither daring to talk for fear of disturbing his sleep. At long last, Robert stirred and awakened. At first, he seemed confused, but slowly a sense of recognition came over him.

Then miraculously, on recognizing Marie, a smile came over his face. As she bent closer to him, before she could speak, he clasped her hands with his free hand and whispered, "I'm so thankful to see you, Marie."

Her heartfelt reply may not have fully registered, as shortly thereafter, he closed his eyes and was back asleep.

In the days that followed, Marie was ever thankful for her volunteer work in the hospital, which gave her experience in dealing with the realities of wounded soldiers. She drew on that experience to help comfort Robert's family when they finally arrived in Paris and to reassure them of the remarkable healing powers that these young men possessed, if given appropriate medical care. It was a reassurance Marie no doubt needed as well, as she knew optimism would be essential in facilitating Robert's recovery.

At first, Robert spent much of his days dozing on and off, and for those periods when he was awake, he rarely communicated in anything more than brief sentences. Only with close attention could one discern remnants of his old personality manifest in brief phrases and gestures. Marie, as much as anyone, was aware of the significance of such actions and grasped them as proof that Robert would recover fully. Seeing them also gave her added determination to do what she could to help further expedite his healing.

Fortunately, Robert's recovery accelerated as the pain of his injuries subsided. Marie was at first surprised and then thrilled to see him reply to her questions with longer and more complete sentences. She laughed heartily when Robert answered a nurse's question with a play on words that was typical of his former self.

As his improvement continued, Robert was transferred to a nearby ward where there was less need for the intensive care that he had first received. Here he was more dependent on himself to get around and to eat. He also received therapy twice daily to help strengthen his weakened muscles; their improvement seemed to also improve his mental acuity.

It was during these days that the long-planned offensive of the French command embodied in Plan 17 was initiated. The offensive of the First and Second Armies in the Lorrain, at first so promising, had been checked and reversed by a violent German counterattack. Robert had related details of this to Marie and seemed pleased to learn through discussions with other soldiers and hospital staff that the audacious counterattack by his Twentieth Corps had helped to stabilize conditions in that sector. Now the news indicated that Joffre was initiating a new, larger offensive somewhere to the north of the German center with most of the remaining French forces.

One afternoon, Marie was disappointed to note a change in Robert's demeanor. Though he smiled when she walked into the room, he seemed more withdrawn than he had been in recent days. The change in his appearance was alarming, pushing Marie to try to discern its basis.

"Robert, you seem very preoccupied this afternoon. Do you need any pain medication?"

At first, he seemed to dismiss her concerns as being nothing more than fatigue from a poor night's sleep.

Marie, however, was unwilling to accept this explanation without further discussion.

"Robert, I know that what you are going through must be quite difficult. I have talked to the nurses and the doctors, who have tried to help me understand what to expect in your convalescence and how I might help you improve. You shouldn't get discouraged, Robert, and furthermore, I want you to know that I will be here to help you, even if it means simply sitting quietly by to give you someone to talk with."

"Marie, you don't know how much your being here every day has meant to me. You are a reminder of the life that I loved so much. Unfortunately, all that is gone and can never be replaced."

"Don't be so pessimistic, Robert. I have seen you improve so much each day that I'm certain you will recover fully."

"It's not simply my recovery that I'm worried about. Even if I had never been wounded, it would still not change our circumstances. Already this war has disrupted so much that is important that I fear for the future."

"That may be, Robert, but pessimism won't help in fighting the Germans."

"You may be right, Marie, but as I recall more of what happened in those days before I was wounded, I find my memories to be very worrisome."

"What is worrisome?" Marie replied, with evident concern in her voice.

"As my memory has come back, it has been like a curtain being drawn up, with each day revealing more of what I have forgotten."

"Please go on," Marie encouraged.

"I first recalled several days before my concussion, but it seemed like there was a blockade that prevented me from recalling events closer to the morning I was wounded. Only now can I recall some of what occurred that day, and by tomorrow, I may remember even more."

"Tell me what you can remember, Robert," Marie persisted, with a look of relief in such tangible evidence of Robert's recovery. If there was a curtain rising, then she hoped that soon all would be revealed.

"Just before the start of the war, we spent long days assembling our units and bringing them into position for an attack against German positions in front of us. Those were exhausting yet exciting times, as everyone was aware of the task before us and our individual responsibilities. When the order came to advance, it seemed like all fatigue was swept away.

"In those first days, our advance was everything that we could have hoped for. The Second Army advanced rapidly, sustaining fewer casualties than we had anticipated. Within days, we had taken Chateau Salins with a well-executed assault that gave us all confidence for the days ahead.

"From there, we were forced by the geography and roads to funnel our subsequent attack on Morhange along a narrow front. With each hour, that phase of the battle seemed to intensify and came closer to their well-prepared defensive positions, which employed large cannons with a range far greater than our own seventy-fives. Anyone who has heard those cannons will never forget their sound. It starts as a low rumble, increasing to a loud shriek as the shell falls toward you."

Sensing his discomfort, Marie's demeanor changed, and she quickly suggested, "Robert, if this is making you uncomfortable, we don't have to continue with this any further today."

"It's all right, Marie. I feel that it's important to talk about it, as it seems to help draw out my memory."

Reassured, Marie offered no protest as Robert continued.

"After the first day of heavy battle, I tried to mentally block the sound of the artillery shells out of my mind, hoping to build up some kind of mental fortifications, as I had done in the colonies when I first came under fire."

Once more seeing the stress in Robert's face evident, Marie again interjected. "Robert, please take a break for a moment at least. Let me get you some water and straighten you up in bed, since you seem to be slumped to the side."

Then for a while, they both seemed content to just sit quietly, and what conversation they had skirted the details of Robert's recollections. Then, as if compelled to talk, Robert suddenly resumed his narrative.

"You know, Marie, I now recall vaguely the moments after the shell exploded. It seemed like there was a suspension of reality, almost as if I was in some transition from the horror around me to some better place. I can even remember the soldiers transporting me and a young nurse in the ambulance to the aid station. I seemed to sense my level of consciousness vacillating from moment to moment, but I recall one instant when the nurse seemed to be an angel."

Marie took this all in with obvious empathy and grasped Robert's hand. Hearing his recollections unfold in such a vivid description seemed to draw her into the maelstrom of that awful day. She at last replied.

"I'm afraid, Robert, that your experiences have had a far greater effect on you than you may understand at present."

"That may well be, Marie, but regardless, I remember enough to make me very concerned about this offensive that I read about in the papers today."

"Robert, please try and rest for a while. You are in no position to help those men or the army now," Marie pleaded.

"I know that, Marie, and that's very frustrating. Here I am, still alive, with a clearer understanding of what must be done but am helpless to do anything about it."

"Have you considered for a moment that you might be wrong about what you have remembered?"

"Unfortunately, the more details that I remember, the more certain I am of my conclusions."

"Robert, you should be careful about any conclusions you have reached, given your recent condition, especially if it makes you so upset."

Yet Robert seemed compelled to continue, as if the flood of thoughts was too much for him to resist. "The battle that I watched was based on years of theory that implied that success would depend as much on the will and attitude of the men as it would on weapons. To that end, there was no room for caution or hesitancy. The belief in this notion was so widely accepted by the general staff that little dissension was tolerated.

"I saw the intrusion of reality all too well before Morhange. Though we knew that the Germans had made defensive preparations, we were confident that the speed of our advance, along with the courage and preparedness of our troops, would allow us to overrun their positions.

"In that battle, I saw firsthand how wrong we were in many of our assumptions. It was as if God Almighty was dispensing lessons to show us the magnitude of our folly; I must tell you, Marie, that they were very painful and poignant."

Marie's pained look mirrored the emotions she was feeling in hearing Robert's poignant and frightening conclusions.

For a moment, she felt relief as Robert paused and sipped from a glass of water. Then suddenly, he resumed.

"The awful potential of modern weapons was all too evident. The sound of their artillery and the enormous destruction it produced along our lines was but the first of these brutal lessons. As we neared their lines, there would be others equally severe.

"There, we saw all too well the lethality of their machine guns, protected behind fortified placements from destruction by our artillery, even at close range. Despite our best efforts, the rapidity of their fire overwhelmed even the most rapid advance. Our folly was made even more evident by the insistence on attacking in our traditional uniforms, whose red pants stood out in the smoke of battle, making our infantry an even better target. It was a heroic and utterly disastrous exercise, demonstrating the futility of nineteenth-century tactics against twentieth-century weaponry.

"Now as I think of our men being launched toward the German lines once more, I'm afraid I know all too well what they will face. If the Germans are fortified like they were before Morhange, our offensive will be doomed; courage and audacity are no match for concentrated steel and lead, regardless of our valor."

As Robert related his story, Marie's mind raced furiously to keep up. This was all more than she had anticipated in encouraging his recollections. Now she seemed frightened by their destructive capacity on Robert's mental health. For a moment, she remained silent as Robert paused, but before she could speak, he resumed.

"Perhaps, as you suggest, Marie, I might be wrong; I pray that I am. Perhaps we may find a weak point in their defenses that can be exploited to great advantage. This is all unknown now. What I do know, however, is that in the coming days, our soldiers will face horrible challenges, and if we do have the good fortune to prevail, it will only come at enormous cost."

Unable to allow Robert to continue, Marie at last interrupted.

"That is enough of this for today. We can't know the outcome of these battles, despite your fears, and it does neither of us any good to brood over matters that we cannot control."

Robert seemed to welcome Marie's suggestion and relaxed visibly. For the remainder of the day, he seemed content with her helping him walk around the hospital when they were not concentrating on assembling a puzzle of a lovely spring meadow scene.

The pastoral scene, however, belied future difficulties that both anticipated—Robert with the fate of the army, and Marie with the difficulties posed by the doubt and anxiety that had wounded Robert's spirit.

9

Deliverance

WITH THE OUTBREAK OF WAR, THE STRASBOURG that Thomas knew ceased to exist. The university where he had devoted so much of his time seemed like a dying man. Gone was all the vitality imparted by the numerous students with their idealism and boundless energy. What few people remained were mostly older men involved in some form of research judged vital to the war effort. Now as he passed through the area on his way to his duties at the hospital, the stark contrast between the present circumstances of the university and his many remembrances only saddened Thomas further.

Strasbourg itself, with its location so close to the front lines, had been transformed into a military center. Its rail yards were in constant use, carrying large numbers of men and materials to the front, returning with spent and broken equipment as well as increasing numbers of wounded. It was an exchange that provided a painful reminder of the cost of the war now raging around them.

The makeup of the city's population also created major problems for the Germans, due to the large francophone population who harbored loyalties to France. Almost overnight, a state of near marshal law had been established by the military governor, making it necessary for the citizenry to have proper identification documents in their possession. For some judged to be potential risks to the security of the region, a more elaborate regimen was established in which they were required to routinely report their whereabouts and activities to an interior officer. Strict night curfews were in place, which limited what remained of social activity, reducing life in what was once one of Europe's most delightful cities to a struggle for existence.

Thomas was far more fortunate than most in that his work in the hospital gave meaning to his days, lifting him from the dreary existence that many in Strasbourg had now been forced to accept. His new role was to intercede when called upon to administer holy sacraments or, when time allowed, to council the wounded. In theory, his role in the hospital was governed by the church and its hierarchy, but Thomas soon recognized that many of the most senior priests had little experience and often less insight into how to deal with the many crises that inevitably arose in those stressful days. Thomas's experience in counseling students provided some understanding of how to deal with the many young men he now encountered and made him someone to turn to in uncertainty or crisis.

Soon Thomas found that much of what he was doing in the hospital dealt with crisis counseling. He prayed for the wisdom and means to comfort the wounded, but all his previous experience and study had not given him an understanding of how to deal with the scale of chaos and suffering now so much a part of his daily life. Always in the past, he could sense God's purpose when addressing the problems that were brought to him. Now, try as he might, he could not begin to explain to a frightened soldier or family member the reason for their suffering. At the end of a long day, he would search in vain in scripture and through meditation for some answer as to God's purpose in this catastrophe; his continued failure to find a satisfactory answer only served to rob him of much-needed sleep.

Thomas took his doubts to the hospital each day, dreading some encounter where his lack of insight might enhance the pain of a soldier or family member. Fortunately, he had come to realize that his mere presence as a priest and all it embodied provided comfort to many, a blessing Thomas ascribed to the power of the Holy Spirit far more than his own actions. This realization instilled a reserve in him that had seldom been present in the past. Often, he simply listened quietly and, when necessary, answered in practical, supportive language devoid of theology, except where specific rites or requests were clearly indicated.

This posture gave him a different perspective from his previous counseling and made him more aware of the many ways a man could express his needs. At first, most of the men he attended were German, but recently some French soldiers had been brought in as well. Thomas was gratified to see many instances where the wounded acted with courage, often sacrificing their own immediate comfort so that another more critically wounded could be attended to. Such behavior transcended nationality, with both French and German soldiers demonstrating actions that were inspiring in their nobility.

As important as such acts were to Thomas, others were a source of great disappointment and concern. One recent episode had been particularly unsettling.

One afternoon, several trains bearing wounded had arrived, taxing the capabilities of the existing facilities. Thomas had moved closer to the triage points to be available if needed to minister to those most critically wounded, and as he finished reassuring a young corporal about the prognosis of his wounds, he glimpsed out of the corner of his eye a French lieutenant appearing to have some type of convulsion. Quickly moving to the man's side, he saw that he was not convulsing but instead was shaking from fever. His face was flushed with features that Thomas had come to recognize as common with bacterial sepsis.

As the man's rigor decreased, he became aware of his surroundings, and seeing Thomas at his side, a look of relief came over him. He tried to speak to Thomas in halting German, only to be interrupted by Thomas replying in a French dialogue that clearly indicated the young priest's nationality and social class.

"Try and rest, my son," Thomas replied. "You will be in good hands here. The doctors and nurses are as good as they come."

The lieutenant paused for a moment, looking flustered, then resumed. "Father, I thought you had left, but now I can see you better."

"I am with you, son. You need not be afraid."

"I'm afraid that I'm too far gone for anyone to help me."

"We will do our best, Lieutenant."

"Father, I have no right to ask this, but I know that I'm nearing my end. I am Jewish, Father, and I know this may not be possible, but if you could please remember me to your Holy Father."

"Hear O Israel the Lord your God is one God," Thomas intoned into the young man's ear. "Your God is our God, Lieutenant. I know that his peace will be with you."

"Thank you, Father. It's surprising I'm not afraid, but still, you have given me peace. The only thing that I might ask is if you could tell my mother and father and fiancée that I was thinking of them and that I love them."

"I promise that I will do my best. What is your name, and where does your family live?"

"My name is Samuel Myerson, and my father's name is Isaac. He lives on 77 Rue St. Cloud in Paris. If you write him, he will know where and how to contact my fiancée."

"I will do all in my power to get word to him, Samuel."

"Thank you, Father; you have given me great comfort."

Bending over the young French officer, Thomas recited, "The Lord is my shepherd … He leads me by still waters … and even though I walk through the shadow of the Valley of Death, I fear no evil … and I shall dwell in the house of the Lord forever." Finishing, Thomas added, "Samuel, he will guard you today from the gates of Sheol. Peace be with you."

As he finished, Thomas saw the young man smile briefly and then close his eyes in peaceful acceptance of what was to come. Thomas then rose and, moving silently so as not to disturb the French officer, turned and scanned the increasing numbers of new arrivals for those most in need of his help.

Later that evening as the influx of new arrivals lessened, Father Klaus, who was charged with overseeing the clergy in the hospital, came up to Thomas and asked to speak to him.

From the early days of his work in the hospital, Thomas had an uneasy relationship with Father Klaus. Klaus, Thomas felt, was one of those people who enjoyed the power that came from authority and actively sought it. Early in their relationship, Thomas sensed a tension between him and Klaus, which he suspected arose from the older man's jealousy over Thomas's wide acceptance by the staff of the hospital.

"Father, now that it appears we have a chance for a break, I need to speak with you," demanded Klaus, indicating that Thomas should follow him to a quiet room off the main hall.

"What can I do for you, Father?" asked Thomas warily.

"Thomas, you know how limited and valuable our time is when there are so many new patients arriving. I have spoken to you before of the need sometimes to limit our actions with individual patients so that we may do as much good for as many as possible."

"Yes, I remember your words well."

"I wish that you would pay closer attention to them then, Thomas."

"What do you mean?"

"Early this afternoon, I saw you spend a very long time with a French officer. I know that you meant well, but we simply don't have the time for such ministry, especially to a Frenchman."

"Why should we not provide comfort to a man because he is French?"

"The unfortunate facts are, Thomas, that this is a war, and this is a German hospital. Our position here is ultimately at the dictates of the German authorities. We cannot afford to jeopardize our work by showing favoritism to their enemies."

"There was no conscious attempt of my part to show favoritism, Father."

"That may well be, Thomas, but I am sure that it could not be seen by the Germans as anything but that. Even worse, when I inquired about the man in question, I learned that he was Jewish. We simply don't have the resources to spend in such times like this on a race of people responsible for the death of our savior. There is a Jewish rabbi that could have been made available to him."

"Father, he was a man near his end, crying out for help. Do you think that Christ would have turned away from him under such circumstances?"

"Thomas, we are not Christ. What will become of that young man is between him and his God. It is all that we can do to meet the needs of the true believers. You may like to believe that your morality places you above such actions, but the reality is that we must be guided by what is politically expedient so that we can be allowed to serve those that deserve our ministry. There is no point in continuing our discussion. I must insist that in the future, when we are pressed in our commitments, you confine yourself to the German wounded first. Now, if you will excuse me, we both have our work to attend to."

His exchange with Klaus weighed heavily on Thomas's mind for the rest of the evening and over the next day. This war had created so many moral dilemmas that it made it difficult at times to act. The work he was doing was now being challenged not on moral grounds but from the standpoint of political expediency. Thomas knew his actions could not be governed by political considerations, and he had made no attempt to hide his beliefs. He was therefore not surprised when he received a note from the bishop's secretary stating that the bishop wanted to see him.

Thomas arrived at the bishop's study, finding him in a somber mood.

"I am sorry to call you on such short notice, Thomas, but I received information from the Red Cross I wanted to share with you as soon as possible."

Thomas asked, "What is it, Monsignor? You seem concerned."

"Thomas, in my present capacity, I am the first person contacted by the Red Cross when they have information pertaining to the family of any of the members of our diocese. This morning, I received news that your cousin Robert had been wounded in fighting in Lorraine."

"Do you know the severity of his wounds?" asked Thomas anxiously.

"The details of his present condition were not extensive, but the communiqué reported that he was being transferred to Paris for further treatment and convalescence. It listed his condition as serious but stable.

"I know how close you are to him, Thomas, and I wish I had more complete information to share with you. If it is of any consequence, in my experience, the wording is far more somber when reports come for family members in more dire conditions."

"This only makes my position here more difficult and frustrating to deal with."

"I am truly sorry for your condition at present, Thomas, because I know that if it were not for me asking you to return to Strasbourg when you did, you would not be in this predicament."

"It was necessary and proper at that time, but now I feel all that I have been familiar with and loved is gone," said Thomas. "The students are off to fight, possibly against their old schoolmates. My other work is increasingly irrelevant in a world where violence and near anarchy has usurped rationality and goodwill. At times, I wonder, *What is this all for?* The only thing that sustains me now is the sense of purpose in attending to these men who, like my dear cousin, have been victims of this madness."

"From what I have seen, Thomas, you have adapted to this new challenge well. Your ministry has been remarkable for so many that have been wounded."

"I appreciate your saying that, Father, especially since some of our own seem to take exception to my actions."

"In what way?" asked the bishop.

"Just the other day, I was severely admonished by Father Klaus for showing what he felt was partiality in attending to the needs of a gravely wounded lieutenant who had the misfortune of being both French and Jewish."

"That may explain the letter that I received from Captain Neuhaus, who is the liaison officer with our clergy at the hospital where you have been. He explained that a senior priest had called to his attention his concern in the manner certain enemy combatants were being handled by some members of his staff, and he wanted to underscore the need of the clergy to give priority to the German soldiers most in need."

"I am afraid that Father Klaus is more concerned with his relationship with the German officers than he is with his Christian duty," said Thomas sharply.

"That is for God to judge, not you, Thomas, but with prayer, we can hope that he will better recall how Christ dealt with the misfortunate and modify his ways accordingly.

"This letter, however, gets me to thinking. Since the outbreak of the war, there has been a policy of exchange between dioceses in France and Germany. The first exchanges involved the most infirm or elderly, but those are now nearly complete. I am thinking that this complaint from Father Klaus can be utilized to our advantage. I doubt if Captain Neuhaus or his superiors can be happy with a French priest in their ranks showing favoritism to the enemy or unwilling to conform to their demands."

"Meaning?" asked Thomas.

"Meaning I believe, with a carefully written letter using all of my diplomatic skills, I may be able to place you high in the priority list for exchange. That would accomplish several things. It would get you home to see your cousin while freeing Father Klaus from having to worry about your behavior or comparing it to his own."

"That would be extraordinarily good of you. I could not ask you to do that, however, if others are worthier than me."

"Nonsense! None are as worthy as you, and besides, it will soothe my conscience for getting you in this dilemma in the first place."

At the end of their conversation, they departed with an even deeper respect for each other.

Two days later, Thomas received notice that he should be ready to depart that evening at seven o'clock on a special train for repatriation to France. With so little time, he was barely able to gather up his few essential possessions and his most valued books and writings. He arrived just in time to catch the train that would deliver him from Germany.

10

To Feed an Army

IT HAD BEEN MORE THAN A WEEK SINCE SARA LEFT Berlin with Aaron Heilman in two slightly weathered lories. Aaron drove the largest, often accompanied by Sara or his niece Sasha. The other truck, which was smaller and older, was driven by his brother-in-law Frederic. The smaller truck had a trunk where they kept their personal belongs and other supplies, including two small tents that allowed them to camp if they could not find adequate housing.

Sara was amazed at how little civilian traffic there was on the road, even in the immediate vicinity of Berlin, an absence that seemed to confirm the high priority the army gave to their work, as indicated by their travel passes and petroleum rations. Their journey to date had been remarkably free of restrictions and frequently provided a firsthand glimpse of the vaunted German Army.

In passing through Berlin, Sara saw how the city was being transformed in its new role as the center for the war effort of the Central powers. She studied intently the areas surrounding the many large factories where, much to her disappointment, she saw little evidence that the daily routine had been significantly disrupted.

What was different, however, was the pattern of daily life in the city. The number of civilian vehicles passing through the streets was severely reduced. Aside from commercial trucks and the occasional taxicab, there were few passenger cars about. In their place were large numbers of military vehicles of all sorts, shuttling troops through the city and officers to planning sessions along the Wilhelmstrasse.

The shops themselves seemed to have fewer goods evident in their windows as well as fewer shoppers. The markets showed this trend as well, with long lines forming to purchase what few vegetables and other produce that were available. Despite the apparent deprivations, Sara noted that the people gave little evidence that these new hardships were discouraging them in the least.

In leaving the crowded districts of Berlin for the flatlands of Brandenburg, there seemed to be a more normal appearance to daily life throughout the small towns and villages. The farmers responsible for the produce that could potentially fill the army kitchens were where Aaron would focus his efforts. For many small producers and others outside of the major metropolitan areas, no liaison to the army existed at this time. Aaron's purpose was to entice them to redirect their produce and livestock from their traditional customers to facilities being designed to supply the large and growing needs of the army.

Already in the short time she had accompanied him, Sara could see Aaron had many assets available to him to accomplish this end. His long history as a dealer gave him invaluable contacts throughout the regions, and his reputation was such that the army had come to him to help fulfill their growing needs. In their travels, Aaron had related to Sara the many advantages that such a relationship provided. Now, in dealing with his old contacts, he had the resources to outbid any other buyer to help ensure the necessary supplies to meet the army's needs. As in the past, care had to be exercised to protect the rights of his clients by insisting on only the finest stock for such premium prices. Early on, Sara sensed that Aaron had the experience to recognize the quality he was demanding, while his reputation with sellers would command their respect.

Soon, commitments for livestock in Brandenburg were increasing so rapidly that visits from the officer assigned by the quartermasters' headquarters in Berlin became ever more frequent. Major Heinrich Shrieves was trim and well groomed, with an efficient manner characteristic of an officer in such a position. Sara was pleased to note, however, that he was also polite to civilian contacts, showing little of the arrogance so common in many of his peers. Perhaps it was his Bavarian background that gave him a more sociable disposition, but whatever it might be, Sara sensed that Aaron appreciated that he could speak comfortably with Shrieves and believed early on that he was someone he could do business with.

It was Shrieves's job to facilitate the collection of the livestock that Aaron's suppliers agreed to deliver in large stockyards that existed or were being constructed, and then to coordinate their processing and delivery by rail to the army as it advanced westward. It was apparent that Shrieves had some previous experience in logistics on a large scale, which no doubt contributed to his confident demeanor. Nevertheless, as the number and quality of animals coming from Aaron's efforts became more apparent, Aaron seemed to gain even more autonomy and respect from Shrieves, who increasingly sought out the older man for opinions relating to the overall management of this large undertaking.

Soon the two were meeting almost daily to coordinate their activities. Later, these meetings would expand to include many of the officials overseeing the receiving depots. It was a necessary part of the job but one Sara knew Aaron resented since it robbed him of the time that he had to deal with local suppliers.

In those early days, Sara asked many questions of Aaron. She was pleased that he took the time to respond in a patient and informative way, and these sessions ultimately led to a mutual recognition of a collective competence that could prove valuable in the coming days.

One afternoon following a long meeting with Shrieves, when Aaron's exasperation was particularly evident, Sara offered a suggestion to allay some of his frustration in the future. Explaining that his own efficiency would be improved by her presence, Sara suggested that Aaron obtain permission from Shrieves to allow her to accompany him to future meetings.

It was a suggestion Aaron welcomed, as he would do anything that might free up time from long meetings. Subsequently, Sara learned that, after some grumbling, Shrieves agreed to her joining Aaron in future meetings.

Sara approached those first meetings by taking pains to avoid any appearance that might suggest that she was overreaching her expected role. What input she might have was given to Aaron in the most discrete manner possible. Soon, however, all present seemed to accept her presence, including the military officers who begrudgingly admitted the value of her insight and suggestions.

After one of these meetings, Sara asked, "Aaron, how well do you know the territories to the west of Thuringia?"

"Well enough. I've traded in and out of them all the way into eastern France for many years."

"Do you think you could organize your network of suppliers in these areas as well?"

"With the appropriate time and support from the military, I would think it could be done. Tell me, why I would want to add more complications to what we already are doing by expanding farther to the west?"

"The simple answer is that it will give you more leverage with the military, and I believe if we structure this right, it won't involve all that much more work. More leverage will give you more prerogatives and more margin for profit."

"I'm listening. What do you suggest?"

"I have observed the way the system of delivery and transportation is presently structured, and it strikes me that much of it is functioning as if each of these areas is an independent principality. In Brandenburg, you are required to meet certain requirements, and the date of transportation is well spelled out. In Anhalt and Saxony, the requirements differ, and they are different in Thuringia as well. You are dealing with a confederation in which local authorities make it difficult to organize and coordinate large-scale deliveries."

"That is the nature of this part of Germany. Bismarck may have unified the Reich, but much of the old confederations still exist in day-to-day commerce."

"You are wasting time and opportunity through all of this inefficiency."

"You are speaking like a true capitalist rather than someone who is supposed to be so sympathetic to the workers," Aaron replied with a sly smile.

"Whatever you call it, I think it makes sense. The only sure means that you have of gaining more leverage for yourself and even those working with you is to build an ever larger network."

"How do you suggest I do that?"

"What is needed is a Prussian solution for this problem. I have no doubt that they have worked out all their military problems in this manner. Now they will have to apply them to more mundane matters, such as getting the necessary hogs to butcher to feed their troops. It is plain to me from our dealings that either they have not reached that conclusion or they have been unable to implement it."

"What would that solution be?" Aaron asked with evident curiosity.

"What is needed is someone to organize and oversee a process that overcomes the existing inefficiencies by providing a uniform method for acquiring and processing livestock and grains. Until that happens, bureaucratic pronouncements and local regulations will frustrate everyone.

"Your advantage, Aaron, is not to spell out the problem that they already sense but to offer a solution. Then, all that remains is to prove it on a small scale and then get someone to champion its ultimate adoption."

"Go on," Aaron said, with evident growing interest.

"Major Shrieves has seen how valuable you have been in arranging suppliers in this region. Suggest to him that with the right support you could standardize similar arrangements all the way to the western front. The value of such a large and coordinated network should be obvious to him. I have been carefully evaluating our present army and government contacts, and it seems to me Major Shrieves would be a good first contact. He knows his business and will understand the value of what you're proposing; he also will recognition the reward that will come his way if you succeed."

"You suddenly seem awfully interested in helping the kaiser's war effort, Sara."

"I detest this war and those responsible for it, Aaron, but I look at the faces marching by and see that most are young men who have been coerced into this war. No doubt the majority are from the working class. If they are going to be sent to the slaughter to benefit the rich, at least they should be given decent provisions.

"Even more important, Aaron, is the power that you will hold over the military if you can establish a near monopolistic position in their supply chain. Of course, you will have to be deferential in your dealings with them and no doubt concede a larger share of the profits than you might initially wish, but if you are successful, it will be you who has the upper hand in dictating terms for both you and your suppliers. If we have to participate in this war, it should be on our terms and not theirs."

Sara also knew but did not say that any expansion of Aaron's business to the west would bring her closer to the French or Swiss border and a possible escape to freedom.

"I'm impressed with your analysis, Sara. Your time around Karl Gold seems to have taught you a few things. I think you're right about Shrieves as well. He is known to be someone with relatives in higher places, whom he no doubt is trying to impress. I also concede that your arguments make sense even if our work might be increased. With any luck, my old friends in the west can be enticed to join our cooperative, and then the kaiser's army will become very dependent on a group of old Jewish livestock traders. How very interesting life can be!

"I'll speak to Shrieves tomorrow about this after I have had the night to think it over."

That next morning, when presented with Aaron's proposals, Shrieves quickly recognized their potential to increase order and reliability throughout the network, outcomes dear to a German's heart. If implemented successfully, logistical planning would be measurably improved, an outcome that Shrieves knew would have significant implications for him as well.

After some slight modification of his own, Shrieves presented "his" proposal to his superiors, who quickly approved the means for an initial effort. If the early trial proved successful, more resources would soon follow. Plans would be drawn up for a network of stockyards and collecting areas, as implied by Shrieves's proposal, that could ultimately serve as key locations to coordinate collection and delivery as far as the army advanced.

The following day, Aaron was apprised of the previous day's agreement. By midafternoon, he and his entire contingent were on their way to Thuringia, where they hoped to speak with many old associates before a subsequent meeting with his army handlers. As their journey unfolded, the overwhelming presence of the army was evident everywhere except perhaps the small, quaint medieval villages. In parts of many cities, it seemed as if civilian life no longer existed, replaced by the apparatus of an army on the march.

Finally, after sitting impatiently waiting for a seemingly endless train of soldiers to pass, Sara could no longer restrain her emotions. "I have never seen anything like this." Staring at the movement of a massive cannon in transport along the rail lines leading westward, she said dejectedly, "I could never imagine weapons this size or an army with so many men."

"They are led by Prussians," said Aaron. "They were weaned on war, and their lives are centered on it. Now they have inflicted their obsession on the rest of the Germans, which only makes their destructive potential even greater."

"Where are all the good Germans I've known who have spoken out so strongly against such an awful catastrophe?" asked Sara, with evident frustration. "The factories seem as busy as ever. Where were the strikes we were promised? Instead, the ranks seem endless, made up of vast numbers who no doubt have traded factory bosses for new Prussian masters. Now they are all being marched off to kill their like kind in France so the wealthy and privileged can prosper."

"There are still many Germans who sympathize with you, Sara," Aaron replied emphatically.

"I certainly don't see much evidence of it here or anywhere we have been in the last week. It seems to me that all this country is dedicated to making war. The conformity is frightening. How could a country with such great traditions of learning and so sympathetic to the cause of its workers be so transformed with the first sound of battle?"

"Well, for the moment at least, that is the reality, and those who disagree will just have to keep it to themselves until matters change."

"It will be hard for me to do that, Aaron, but I know what you're saying is best."

"Patience is a difficult virtue, especially for young people, Sara, but in times like these, it is more important to cultivate than ever."

"It will be a challenge, I concede, but I will try."

"Trying is not enough. We now have too much work for you to do anything but your best, Sara. I have confidence you will succeed."

"Well, if that's the case, Aaron, I won't let you down."

11

Once More into the Breach

ROBERT HAD BEEN CHECKING THE EXTENT OF HIS recovery by drills designed to test his memory and analytic capacity, and with each problem solved, he gained confidence in his ability to resume mentally challenging work. What remained, however, was the challenge of his broken leg, which still required him to use crutches to walk however slowly for short distances. As his strength improved, arrangements were made for him to leave the hospital for the home of an aunt who had been forced by the war to return to Provence. He had also dutifully noted his progress to his superiors in Paris, who welcomed the news and promptly assigned a young private to serve as his orderly during the time of his convalescence.

Despite the added help, Marie continued with her daily diligence, a task made easier by Robert's evident progress. This afternoon, she found him in the solarium, where he was resting from his exercise routine.

"You seem to be getting stronger each day, Robert."

"It hardly seems that way when I try to get up with these crutches. At least I still have my original leg to push around, which is a lot better than many others."

"You have not only your legs but your intellect as well. I believe in time both will be as good as new."

"I'm thankful for that, but the reality is that I will never recover my naiveté and optimism."

"You won't with that attitude, Robert. My advice would be to learn from your experiences and try to make something positive out of them."

"Spoken like the true optimist you are, Marie."

"It may seem optimistic to you, Robert, but if we are to emerge from this war with something meaningful, people like you must not give up on trying to improve on the mess we are in."

Returning to the solarium, Robert seemed nearly exhausted by the time he reached the couch facing out on the courtyard. As he was regaining his breath, Eloise, his aunt's longtime maid, came in to announce a visitor.

"Monsieur Robert, a distinguished man is here to see you. He gives his name as General Gallieni."

"Show him in by all means, Eloise," replied Robert, with a note of surprise in his voice.

As Robert struggled to his feet, he could see the unmistakable bearing of Gallieni standing tall and ramrod straight, outlined in the bright afternoon sunlight. How different it seemed from his days as the general's adjuvant several years ago. Then, Robert visited Gallieni in his rather dark and spartan office at Fifth Army headquarters. Now, Gallieni was visiting him in the sunny informality of the solarium, with a demeanor that suggested that their roles had somehow been reversed.

"Good afternoon, General," said Robert, trying to salute awkwardly while leaning on Marie for support.

"Good afternoon, Robert. I am pleased to see you up and about. No doubt much of your recovery owes much to the excellent care you are receiving," replied Gallieni, with a smile acknowledging Marie's presence.

"General, this is my friend Marie Bonneau."

"It is my great privilege to meet you, Miss Bonneau."

"For me as well, General. I have heard so much about you from Robert in the past that it seems we have already met."

"Robert, I hope you don't mind my visiting? If you are indisposed, I could come back later."

"Not at all, General. Marie and I were just sharing our thoughts on my progress. If it weren't for my leg and some annoying soreness in my collarbone, I would be as good as new."

"That is what I had hoped to hear. When I heard of your injury and your hospitalization here in Paris, I made it a point to follow your progress through my various contacts."

"That was thoughtful of you, General."

"It had more to do with my own selfishness as much as any thoughtfulness, Robert. You may have heard that I have been appointed military governor of Paris, which, with its many responsibilities, also has prerogatives. One is access to much critical information, such as the condition of some of our most gifted wounded officers like yourself."

"Why is it that I have the feeling your visit is more than a simple social one, General?" asked Robert.

"You have always been very perceptive, Robert. That is one reason that you are so valuable and why I was anxious to visit with you when the doctors gave me permission."

"I could leave if you would prefer, General," said Marie.

"That will not be necessary, Marie. What I have to say I'm sure will be held in strict confidence. Besides, it may be as important to you as it will be to Robert."

"Thank you, General. I have come to trust Marie's judgment as much as my own."

"Well, then I know the two of you must be wondering why I'm here, so I'll be brief.

"Robert, in my present position, I have been charged with the defense of Paris, and it has been made clear that if the Germans threaten the city, I am to defend it without quarter with all the means available to me. To do this, I have insisted on many necessary resources, including all available military intelligence.

"What I am going to say is not well known, nor is it a certainty, but the information I am receiving raises the risk to Paris from a German offensive developing in Belgium to our northeast. Robert, you know the importance that the army has placed on its present offensive, which is now underway. While it may be too early to know the outcome at this point, it appears we are already encountering effective German resistance. At the same time, intelligence confirms a large German buildup in Belgium north of the Meuse River, which could threaten our left flank.

"If our offensive sputters, then the weakest part of the Allied lines could be facing what appears to be the principal German offensive. I need not belabor the implications of such a situation to you, Robert; you know that territory very well from your previous work and know how vulnerable we are from our northeast if the Germans broach our lines in Belgium."

"Thanks to you, General, we have made a great deal of progress in improving our defenses in that region."

"That may be, Robert, but if I am to protect Paris, I must consider all contingencies, including the worst, which now seems increasingly probable. To face such a situation, I am also trying to assemble a staff of the most capable men available to me and enough troops to effectively defend the region. That is why I have been watching your recovery along with some other talented men who, like yourself, are now stationed in Paris for convalescence. If Paris is attacked, a superb engineering officer will be invaluable. There will be much work to do in reconfiguring our old battlements and engineering new ones.

"Prior to your injury, I had no doubt that you would be an ideal man for such a job, Robert. Upon hearing of your injuries, however, I was uncertain whether they would limit your effectiveness. Now, in talking with you, I believe what limitations still exist may be compensated for by judicious use of your time and the support of strong, young soldiers such as that young private presently helping you."

"I assume then, General, that you are offering me a position on your staff as an engineering officer?"

"As soon as you feel fit enough to walk around an office, a position will be available to you. I know you must feel a loyalty to your former command, but your infirmary makes you conveniently unfit for such frontline combat. You can fight your war from more supportive surroundings here in Paris than in the hills of Lorraine. Besides, if the worst happens, your old comrades will be drawn to Paris soon enough."

"General Gallieni, I have, of course, been thinking of what I can do when I am more fully recovered. Until you arrived, I was resigned to some backwater assignment. It would seem present circumstances dictate a more appealing prospect. Given what you have told me, I see little alternative than to accept your offer. Of course, I must get final approval from my medical doctors and further details of what I'm allowed to do until I recover fully." Glancing at Marie, he continued, "I would also like to discuss it with others if possible."

"Certainly, Robert, all this must be done. It will also give us the time to approve a transfer from your previous unit. I look forward to hearing your decision as soon as possible."

After Gallieni left, Marie was the first to respond.

"Well, I guess that pretty much decides what you will be doing in the next weeks."

"Are you disappointed?" asked Robert.

"Before all of this began, I would have been. I recognize now how much things have changed. Presently, we are all soldiers in some way and must do what is necessary when able."

"Hearing you say that is a relief. It has been frustrating trying to imagine where I might be of help, and now, out of the blue, I get this opportunity. There are few men in the army as competent as General Gallieni and certainly few places on earth worthier than Paris to defend."

"This war makes it necessary for us all to reevaluate our priorities, Robert. Only weeks ago, I had given you and Thomas a pledge that my mother and I would abandon Paris at the first indication of threat. Now, with my work in the hospitals, I've realized how much I can contribute here. To run away to some supposedly safer location now is no more acceptable to me as would abandoning your post be to you."

"It's good that your work is important to you, Marie, but sometimes there comes a time for caution. You have not enlisted to be a soldier."

"Now is not a time to be cautious, Robert, especially when I feel there is so much more that I could do."

"What more could you be doing, Marie?" Robert asked with a perplexed tone.

"I have a friend from school that was doing the same volunteer work as me. Do you remember Georgette LaSalle? I'm sure that I introduced you to her at least once."

"I remember Georgette well. She seemed to be one of those people with enormous reserves of nervous energy."

"That is certainly Georgette," replied Marie with a knowing smile. "She has adapted to her new surroundings better than anyone I know. Recently, she told me about a new assignment that I have been thinking more about since your injuries. Through the sister of a friend who is a nurse, Georgette found out about an opportunity to assist in dispensing dressings and other material to the front lines. She says she leaves Paris on a train toward the front and helps oversee the delivery of our sterile supplies and then returns later that night or the following day, helping wherever needed in attending to the wounded being brought back to Paris."

"No doubt there is a need there, Marie, but the closer you are to the front lines, the greater are the risks."

Before Marie could reply, she was interrupted by a knock at the door. Both she and Robert were startled to see none other than Thomas appear, looking more exhausted and disheveled than either could remember.

12

Journey's End

THOMAS D'AVILLARD'S DRAMATIC APPEARANCE WAS enhanced by the bright light of the solarium, whose glare increased the pallor of his face and better delineated the wrinkled condition of his clothing.

"My god, Thomas, is it really you?" Robert asked incredulously. "How did you ever get here?"

"It's a long story that I'm too tired to tell right now, Robert."

"Sit down, Thomas," Marie urged. "You look exhausted."

"I am, but the sight of both or you already makes me feel better," Thomas said with a hopeful tone in his voice.

"Well, sit down while I get you something to drink or to eat."

"I'm fine, Marie. Surprisingly, we were well fed on the journey home, and I ate just three hours ago."

Unable to control her excitement, Marie blurted out, "You must tell us how you escaped Germany, Thomas!"

Before he could continue, Thomas took time to settle in a comfortable chair, with his back to the bright sunlight. He paused a moment, then replied in a soft voice, "It was nothing as dramatic as an escape, Marie. It was all very organized, an exchange of noncombatants and select prisoners."

"How were you able to arrange a place on that list?" asked Robert.

"I'm not completely sure of the details, but no doubt much had to do with the bishop in Strasbourg. I believe that he felt responsible for asking me to come back before the war broke out, and then after I was stranded there, he began looking for a way to get me back to France."

"From the weight you've lost, it looks like you got out just in time. Are you sure that you don't want something to eat, Thomas?" Marie persisted.

"I'm fine, honestly. With the war, all of us including the clergy have had our rations reduced, so I'm used to eating less."

"Were you able to continue your old duties like before the war?" asked Robert.

"All of that has changed. Few of the students remain, so traditional classes for the most part have been suspended. This left me more time for my writing and research, but now so much of that seems irrelevant."

"What have you been doing then?" asked Marie. "I can't imagine you just sitting around doing nothing."

"I have been involved in an altogether new and difficult challenge. It's one that I could never have previously imagined or ever wished for. This war has forced us to deal with indescribable pain and anguish, and consequently, I was asked to minister to the wounded in a hospital in Strasbourg. There, all too often, it was my duty to minister last rites to young men dying before they even had time to truly experience life. For many others, it was my task to try and provide comfort."

As Thomas began to relate these recent experiences, a bank of dark clouds blocked the bright sunlight, adding a further note of gloom to his recollections.

"That must have been terribly stressful," said Marie.

"It is the hardest thing I have ever had to do. Often I did not know what to say, as nothing I had studied or done prepared me for what we all faced daily."

Robert, abandoning his usual reserve, replied, "I know all too well what you are saying, Thomas. It is a world almost impossible to imagine, let alone understand."

"It is the understanding that concerned me the most, Robert. I have always been able to counsel people, confident that by knowing God's intent, I could suggest a means to fill their needs. Now I'm at a loss to understand what that purpose might be."

Thomas's confession seemed to shaken Marie, who blurted out, "Thomas, no one I know has an answer for this. You should not be so hard on yourself."

"Every day, Marie, I prayed for God to give me the wisdom to provide some comfort to those many suffering men and their families. Some days would be more difficult than others, but the hope that in some way I might provide them a moment of peace kept me going."

"Thomas, you have spoken to me often of trying to understand something that is inscrutable to reason alone. Give yourself time to recover from all you have been through, and knowing you as I do, I am sure you will find your way."

"Marie is right, Thomas. I was in bad shape when I was brought back to Paris, and with excellent support, I have regained much of what I thought was lost."

"You both give me hope, which is something all of us need right now."

Their discussion was interrupted by the maid, who, upon seeing Thomas's condition, had taken it upon herself to have a pot of tea prepared along with a tray of accompaniments.

As they gathered around an ornate walnut table often used for such occasions, their conversation paused only long enough for Thomas to gain a second wind. He then resumed somewhat hesitantly.

"There is so much running through my head now. I can't seem to process it. It was not simply the condition of the wounded, as bad as that was, that disturbed me but the actions of other priests. Those most senior in the hospital made it clear that our job was to attend to the German wounded first, giving them priority over all others.

"My conscience would not allow me to discriminate in my duties. How could I justify treating one man's suffering differently from another? My actions inevitably led to conflict with those in power in the hospital and to the attention of my bishop. Ironically, I believe that it was that conflict with the priest in charge in the hospital and those of his army masters that facilitated my exchange for a German priest held in France."

"So, you were involved in a prisoner exchange?" asked Marie.

"An exchange of priests officially. In the end, the bishop who throughout this remained my devoted friend was able to place my name on the list of exchanged priests without significant protest from many of my peers, who viewed me as a potential troublemaker with the military authorities."

"How were you able to leave then?" asked Robert.

"I was told rather suddenly that I was to present myself at a certain location at the main train station at seven o'clock the night before last. When I arrived, I was gathered in a restricted area while my identity was verified and then was allowed to enter a train that was being kept well removed from all others, as if it and its passengers were being strictly quarantined. I was given a seat assignment in a small compartment, which I shared with two others, one a priest and the other a diplomat.

"We were instructed to remain seated unless we got permission from one of the guards stationed in each car to travel to the lavatory. The drapes on the windows were tightly shuttered, and we were forbidden to open them until the train came to its destination, which we were informed would be somewhere in Switzerland. At last, the train departed from the station, but it was some time before we gained any speed.

"The trip that night was one of the strangest and most eerie I have ever experienced. We were confined to our seats, and all lighting was kept at a minimum during our passage, since we at times would be close to the front lines. The two men with me were soon able to doze off, but the excitement of the moment coupled with the strained circumstances of my departure kept me from going to sleep.

"Just as I was dozing off, I was awakened by the sound of what I first thought to be thunder. When I became more fully awake, I realized that the repetitive sound was not thunder but must be coming from large cannons. For some time, as the train passed, the sound of large guns continued over what must have been several miles of the front. Though the shades were tightly drawn, at times the sky was light enough from the firing of the shells or their explosions to cast a visible light through the curtains.

"I had the sensation of being isolated in a strange craft surrounded by a terrible, unknown world. It was as if I was floating adrift in darkness on the River Styx, blind to the details but fully aware of the hell that must be around me. The noise and the flickering light against the curtains all persisted for some time. To imagine the unfortunate souls so close while

I remained separated by the safety of my conveyance only seemed to magnify the eerie horror of it all.

"At long last, the sounds fell farther to our rear and gradually disappeared. Shortly thereafter, the window lightened with the rising sun, and before long, we came to a halt at the Swiss border. In a matter of moments, the guards came through, telling us to gather our belongings to transfer to a waiting train that would take us into Switzerland.

"As we departed and passed through the quiet, efficient customs office, the thrill I had when I realized I was safe was indescribable. We soon were served a wonderful breakfast upon boarding our train. We proceeded to Geneva, where we were greeted by members of the Red Cross who took us to a gathering spot at a large and comfortable hotel near the train station. There, arrangements were finalized along with our paperwork for departure the next day.

"Last night, I slept soundly and then was awakened early to catch my train for Paris. When I arrived, I dropped off what few effects I had at Grandmother's, where I confirmed your location, Robert, and here I am, after two of the longest days of my life."

Marie sat silently, her face transformed by the concern she felt for his ordeal. As he finished, she asked, "What are you going to do now, Thomas?"

"Right now, I have little energy for doing anything, Marie. No doubt my superiors here in Paris will find something useful for me to do over the next days, but for the present, I am too exhausted to be of use to anyone."

Then, as if suddenly recognizing Robert and Marie's presence, Thomas said, "How rude of me. How are you doing, Robert? The bishop notified me that you had been wounded."

"Aside from some residual pain, I seem to be doing better than I could have hoped for. Today has been a remarkable one for me as well. Before you made your blessed reappearance, I was visited by General Gallieni."

"I suspect he was here to offer you more than good wishes," said Thomas.

"He has been appointed the military governor of Paris, and without saying as much, I could tell by the tone of his conversation that he knew a great deal about the status of the war, and what he knew was worrying him. He is looking for men to help prepare the city to defend against an attack, if or when it might come. Apparently, he had known of my hospitalization for some time and was waiting until I had improved to reach out to me."

"It is truly a blessing that you have come so far, Robert. What about you, Marie? How have your piano studies been going?"

"They have been put on hold for more important things, Thomas."

"Very important and potentially risky things," Robert interjected.

"What are you talking about?" Thomas asked worriedly.

"What Robert meant to say was that before he was wounded, I had been spending the bulk of my time volunteering for the Red Cross and in some of the hospitals here in Paris. I have recently heard of a possible opportunity that would give me more responsibility, but Robert worries it might be too risky. I have not decided on anything yet, and given what the both of you have been through, this is not the time or place to discuss it further.

"Today has been a blessed one for us all and deserves to be celebrated," Marie said with a determined note of optimism.

"No more serious talk for the moment. I will send out for some champagne so that we can toast it in the manner it deserves."

By the time the champagne arrived, Thomas had fallen asleep in a large, padded chair, and a heavy rain had further darkened the surrounding solarium.

13

The Fog Lifts

THE VAST MASS OF THE GERMAN ARMY WAS NOW making its violent presence felt along its western frontiers. The urgency of Robert's transfer directing him to the headquarters of the military governor along Rue St. Dominique indicated the threat this buildup was having throughout the military.

Having obtained medical clearance and with much help from his orderly, Robert dressed and was helped into a cab, which delivered him to his new posting in a large building conveniently located within sight of the National Assembly.

With little in the way of formalities, he was introduced to several of the staff by a young lieutenant whom he learned would be his adjutant and shown to an office with a pleasant view of the Parliament building and the Seine. He was pleased to note his office was on the first floor and easy to reach even with his crutches. The lieutenant, one Etienne Marceau, gave Robert an introduction to the usual daily routine, which he cautioned, aside from the daily morning briefing usually conducted by General Gallieni, had little that was routine about it.

The briefing was held promptly at nine o'clock, which gave them just about fifteen minutes to get to the large conference room adjacent to Gallieni's office on the floor immediately above them. Robert, insisting that he was able to manage for himself, struggled to make it on time to take a place that had already been assigned to him at the main table close to where Gallieni would sit.

The room itself was large with a huge oak table flanked by chairs along its length, with the seat at one end reserved for Gallieni or his designate. The table was arranged in a manner so that a large map suspended from the wall could be readily viewed. That map itself was a focus of constant attention, with several assigned staff members plotting the most recent confirmed locations of the armies now enjoined across the length of a frontier ranging from Switzerland across the breadth of Belgium.

The combatants were represented by various colored icons signifying armies, corps, and, when indicated, divisions. It was a sterile model of the violent reality it sought to represent, but the information it conveyed was of pivotal importance in shaping the subsequent day's actions for Gallieni and his staff. Even more importantly, Robert would learn, were the implications of the changing positions of these icons over time as harbingers of future events.

With little fanfare, Gallieni arrived promptly at nine and, after taking a moment to introduce and welcome Robert, began the morning session.

His routine was to review the information from the previous day and then compare it to the present location of the existing forces in the various sectors. Often, these changes had implications that would shape the subsequent meeting, but Gallieni preferred to keep the summary short so as not to limit further discussion.

Robert sat with rapt attention, as for the first time he could see the entire scope and status of the war nearly in the present tense. It was a view altogether different from those first few days of combat, during which he saw the war from the narrow but more lethal perspective of his Twentieth Corps. Here this quiet, almost clinical setting provided an environment that allowed for a more deliberative approach to battle planning, in contrast to the charged atmosphere at the front. He only hoped that conclusions reached here would prove advantageous when translated to that more lethal world.

Robert understood at one level the implications of those symbols on the map from the countless hours of theory and planning he had been involved with in the war college. Now, however, this was not some make-believe series of problems but a very real application, shaped by the awful reality of a building German presence to their east that added a gravitas never present in any peacetime simulation.

Robert's eyes were first drawn to the area where he and his comrades had launched forward in those first battles in mid-August. The territory they had taken in those early days had been reclaimed through counterattacks of the Bavarian Crown Prince Rupprecht and his troops of the German Sixth and Seventh Armies. After several days of desperate fighting, the front had been stabilized by a successful counterattack by General Foch and his Twentieth Corps in the gap between the French fortifications on the hills before Nancy. Now, well entrenched in strategic positions, the Second Army had weathered several assaults by Rupprecht's forces. Robert had been vaguely aware of the travails of his former comrades, but seeing the present situation so explicitly detailed gave him both pride in their accomplishments and deep respect for the many sacrifices necessary to achieve such ends.

The subsequent discussion showed how much the weight of the war had shifted to the northeast around the angle where

France, Belgium, and Luxembourg met the German border. Colonel Houget, in charge of the intelligence bureau, took the floor to update the status of the main French offensive unfolding in this area.

"We are now beginning the third day of the coordinated offensive that has been the focus of Plan 17.

"The general headquarters is closely guarding any information as to the status of this attack, claiming concern about critical information being inadvertently leaked by civilians in the government and the War Ministry. Despite this, we have been able to piece together an indication of the status of the battle from communiqués from the three engaged armies.

"We are also paying close attention to information coming from our scouting planes to supplement what information we are receiving in Paris secondhand from the field commanders."

"I suppose you are now going to apprise us of those findings?" asked Gallieni.

"I am, General. I believe the information the pilots have given us over the last few days is of great interest, given our responsibilities here in Paris."

"Please go on, Colonel," Gallieni continued.

"The Third Army launched their offensive from Verdun more than forty-eight hours ago. Their orders have been to drive toward Metz and Thionville to envelop the enemy and gain control of the Briey region and its large resources of iron. Before the attack, there were conflicting reports of the strength of the enemy before them. The estimate from general headquarters was no more than two corps of troops in the immediate path of the attack, but General Ruffy, based on his own estimates coming from locals, indicated far larger numbers of troops in the vicinity.

"Last evening, after nearly thirty-six hours, what seems clear at this time is that there has been intense fighting concentrated around the fortress at Longwy. Preliminary reports indicate large numbers of Germans were killed both by coordinated bayonet charges and particularly from our artillery shelling. Many casualties, however, have been sustained by the Third Army, and yesterday after a formidable German counterattack, the army was forced to shift its deployment northward."

"Has there been any confirmation of the taking of Thionville or Metz?" asked one of the officers seated to Robert's right.

"None yet," replied Houget.

"If the Germans are launching a counterattack, it suggests that they are opposing Ruffey with more troops than were first estimated," suggested a major across from Robert.

"It would seem so, but the weather conditions have made it difficult to know with certainty. What intelligence has discovered is that most of the troops engaged against the Third Army are Prussians under the command of Crown Prince Wilhelm, with at least one corps of reserve troops actively engaged in the fighting."

"Do we know how many reserves troops are with this army?" asked Gallieni.

"It is not known for certain, but some of the captured reserves had different identifying logos suggesting several different divisions. Some of the intelligence people for Ruffey think that there may be at least two reserve corps along with the regulars."

"What is their estimate of the total German strength of this army?" asked Gallieni.

"Third Army intelligence estimates, with the reserve divisions, at least four and probably five full corps. I did not get the sense that that estimate was shared by general headquarters when I spoke with General Belin last evening, however," said Houget.

"We will no doubt find out soon enough," Gallieni interjected. "What about General de Langle and the Fourth Army?"

"Unfortunately, we have a clearer picture of their condition as of late last night," continued Houget. "It has now been more than forty-eight hours since they launched their first series of attacks directed at Neufchateau. From the very beginning, they encountered brisk resistance, which increased yesterday. Successes were reported the first day at Virton from heavy artillery attacks on German positions, as was noted yesterday morning. Yesterday saw severe resistance in front of Tintigny, where large numbers of French troops were forced to retreat at the end of the day.

"Last night, word was received that at Rossignol, the Third colonial division lost both of its commanding generals and had losses so great as to virtually destroy it as a fighting unit. General de Langle's communiqué to General Joffre described the retreat at Tintigny and reported no satisfactory results throughout the remainder of the region. He implied the disorder caused from the scope of their losses made it impossible to carry out an organized attack for today."

Robert took all this in with deep disappointment and sadness. This was what he had feared most. He knew from his own experience what these men were going through and what they would likely face in the coming days.

"What did Joffre suggest in reply?" asked Gallieni.

"He encouraged General de Langle to persist. He believes there are no more than three corps of German regulars before him, and therefore, if the offensive is carried out with appropriate vigor, there are enough troops in place for it to succeed."

Gallieni then turned to Robert. "Robert, you are the only one at this table with firsthand experience along the battle line. What do you think of the situation as Colonel Houget has described it?"

"Unfortunately, General, it reminds me all too well of our experiences in Lorraine. What we encountered were German troops in well-established defensive entrenchments. Despite the use of artillery, often in coordination with infantry assault, we were beaten back by machine-gun and artillery fire at enormous cost in terms of casualties. The colonel's description of the destruction of that colonial division is consistent with what I observed with open field assaults against such positions, regardless of the manner they were carried out."

"Do these early results give any indication of the German troop strength?" asked Houget.

"Not completely. There are too many variables to say with certainty. If these German troops were well entrenched, then, in my experience, smaller numbers could have a far greater effect than we previously thought."

Gallieni nodded in recognition and then continued. "Colonel, please update us on the Fifth Army. Have they moved across the Sambre yet?"

"This, General, is quite interesting, as the situation in this area is quite fluid." Houget drew his finger along the course of the Meuse River toward its intersection with the Sambre.

"We know General Joffre saw fit to shift much of the Fifth Army out of line with the attack of the Fourth Army to redeploy along the Sambre to counter the threat of this large German force coming from the northeast. The Fifth Army is now deployed in an inverted V between the Meuse and Sambre, with the First Corps facing to the east, adjoining the Fourth Army. The remainder of the army is facing along the Sambre to the north. As of last night, despite evidence of an increasing German buildup in the area, General Lanzerac had not moved his troops across the river but has remained along its south bank."

"You seem to imply that some change is imminent," suggested Gallieni.

"This army has been in a quandary as to whether to support the attack through the Ardennes or to attack the German forces building up to their north along the Meuse," continued Houget. "General Lanzerac has chosen to wait until the British have come into position to protect his left flank along the Mons Canal. We know from General Wilson that the BEF as of last night is now in position to support a French advance across the Sambre."

"Many of us, including General Lanzerac, have been concerned about the size of the German buildup in Flanders. What do we know currently?" asked Gallieni.

"According to general headquarters, they estimate the entirety of German troop strength at fourteen to sixteen corps. These troops previously were held in reserve near Liege, but as of yesterday morning, there were several reports of German crossings of the Sambre below Namur and to the north of the Meuse. Even more revealing is confirmation made by aerial sightings yesterday afternoon as the weather cleared enough to fly over the area, showing two large concentrations of German forces moving toward Namur. One of these groups is following the course of the Meuse and is approaching our forces from the east. The other, which seems even larger from the aerial sightings, is moving to the north of the Meuse through Flanders toward Mons.

"When the British presence along the Mons Canal protecting our left flank is confirmed, then General Lanzerac will have the leeway to cross the Sambre and move toward Charleroi to engage these advancing German forces."

"Very good, Colonel Houget. Thank you for the update," Gallieni said in a manner indicating his intent to take charge of the meeting.

"Each day seems to give us a clearer understanding of our duties here in Paris. Currently, we have two main contingencies to ponder. The first relates to the success of our offensive playing out at this moment to our east. I am now and have been a proponent of such a tactic as the best means to bring this war to a quick and victorious end. If our efforts are successful, then any vigorous actions we take in Paris now might be judged harshly as being wasteful and unsettling to the civilian population.

"My own experience and instincts make me uneasy about complacency at this time. I know how vulnerable we are to an attack from our northeast from my command of the Fifth Army. If the Germans come through Belgium in force north of the Meuse and can push into France, then our army is at a distinct disadvantage. It is that understanding that has made me wary of the troop buildup described today around Namur. From my conversations, I know that General Lanzerac, whose Fifth Army must face such an onslaught, shares my concerns.

"Therefore, we need to prepare for a scenario where our offensive is checked and a large German counterattack succeeds in dislodging our army from Belgium into France. This threat seems to increase every day, making it imperative to act rather than merely speculate if we are to be successful in our duties.

"To date, we have accelerated plans for remaking the city's defenses, but those efforts will need to be intensified. Robert, I am glad you are here, given your knowledge of the terrain to our northeast. I want you to begin drawing up plans for defensive fortifications well to the northeast of the city. We have been promised by the government the troops necessary to defend Paris. In the meantime, we must develop the infrastructure to give these troops the means to succeed if the times comes when invaders are once again on our outskirts."

Shortly thereafter, the morning meeting concluded but not without a list of actions to be addressed as soon as possible.

From this single session, Robert learned far more than he had suspected. He now clearly understood that his new role would be demanding and perhaps vital to saving Paris. Despite his infirmaries, he welcomed the opportunity to face such a challenge.

14

Tending the Home Fires

MARIE HAD PURPOSELY NOT SEEN ROBERT OFF THE morning he reported back for duty. She feared that her concerns for his readiness to resume duty would be too apparent, adding an unwanted distraction from what no doubt would be a difficult day for him. She realized that what concerns she had for Robert's health seemed insignificant compared to those of others whose loved ones were on the front lines, but she still could not dismiss them lightly. The best she could do was to sublimate her anxiety to the imperative of the moment. This war was forcing everyone to revise their lives, and now without the need to care for Robert, she could resume her duties attending to the wounded, work far less sublime yet far more compelling than her musical studies.

If anything, Robert's injuries made the work that she had been doing ever more relevant. The fear that the many wounded she saw might someday be Robert had now materialized into reality. In returning, Marie was determined to assume more responsibility if afforded her. She was also anxious to hear how Georgette was as well. Yet before she could accept any new opportunity, Marie knew there was another factor that had to considered—Thomas's health.

What a revelation his reappearance had been! Coming as Robert had regained his independence, Thomas's sudden arrival had been startling and unsettling. Just as Robert had been changed by his wounds, it was apparent that the war had taken its toll on Thomas as well. He looked thinner and paler than she could ever remember, but even worse was his manner. Gone was his natural vitality and confidence, replaced by a somber, unsure manner. His speech, which was normally so fluent, was hesitant and textured with doubt and apprehension.

She also sensed her feelings for Thomas, which had been quiescent during those first horrific weeks of war, return with a poignancy that seemed enhanced by his absence. Reappearing in her thoughts were images of those last days before the war and their shared emotions on his departure for Strasbourg. She now knew that her feelings for Thomas had not abated but had simply been awaiting his return.

What Marie did not know was whether, with all that had transpired, Thomas still had similar feelings for her. How much of what he had expressed to her remained, given how clearly the war had affected him? Marie understood that, despite her feelings, the bond that the two once had could not be easily resumed if Thomas had been irreparably changed. It would be important therefore to know his mental status and to do what might be necessary to help him regain the spirit that had drawn her to him. These were the tasks Marie now faced.

Since that first day back, Marie had not had an opportunity to converse with Thomas alone. On this afternoon, she had scheduled her first visit with him, after learning from the staff at his grandmother's apartment where he had been residing that he was able and willing to meet with her.

As Marie approached the residence on Rue de Bac, it was all she could do to control her emotions. She knew this elegant residence only as the Parisian home of Thomas and Robert's grandmother. The entire building contributed its part to the accumulated architecture of a quarter whose refinement testified to the importance of those fortunate enough to live there.

Upon her arrival, Marie was impressed and a bit intimated by the apartment as she was led by the grandmother's maid to Thomas, who seemed out of place sitting in a beautifully finished reception room. She was pleased to see his general appearance had improved now that a well-pressed set of clothes had replaced his disheveled travel attire. The fatigue so evident on his return now seemed to have been resolved, giving his face more color and animation.

"Marie, I'm so glad to see you." In Thomas's warm greeting, however, Marie thought she detected a hesitancy in his voice that belied some uncertainty.

"Thomas, I can't begin to tell you how happy all of us are to see you safely home. Now that Robert has mended, I have more time to deal with other issues, including any matters you might have."

Marie was happy to see Thomas brighten in hearing her proposal.

"Marie, you perhaps more than anyone know my vulnerabilities, and you've helped by letting me share them with you in the past. Now that burden may be more than you or anyone else can bear."

"Thomas, I'm stronger than you realize. I know you have been through a lot while you were away, and much of that may be difficult to deal with. You need to know that I have as much time and patience as necessary if you need me. With time and God's help, I'm sure you will recover, just as Robert has done."

"I hope you are right, Marie."

"I know I'm right. Now tell me what you have been doing these last few days."

"Blessedly, very little except sleeping, eating, and small visits with the bishop."

"What did he have to say?"

"He thanked me for my service in Strasbourg and then suggested that I take as much time as needed before resuming any duties. He said he intended to visit me frequently to check on my progress and to offer any support that might be necessary."

"He seems to be a wise and perceptive man, Thomas."

"He is, Marie, and like you, I know he is concerned about me. I truly appreciate both of your thoughts, but I realize that they would be more effective if I was in a better state of mind."

"What do you mean?" Marie asked worriedly.

"I have no idea what recovery for me might be. All my thoughts seem to be colored by a gray mist, and even things that I love can't seem to draw me back into sunshine. I want to believe what you say, but any improvement will be hard while the workings of my mind seem mired in some mental sludge."

"Thomas, you are in no more position to know what you will be like than Robert when he first returned. I know, as does your bishop, that recovery will take persistence and hope, and I intend to help you with both. You can't let your experience in Strasbourg discourage you. You already look better to me today than you did when you first got home, and the staff here think you have made improvement as well. As things are now, it is important for you to get better, Thomas, but none of us can help unless you believe in yourself."

"I understand, Marie."

After pausing for a moment, Thomas changed the conversation entirely. "Marie, tell me more about the work you mentioned the other night."

Though somewhat flustered, Marie answered, hoping to keep Thomas engaged on a topic other than his dark mood. "Well, as I mentioned, I have volunteered with the Red Cross and at first was involved in the processing of sterile dressings. Lately, however, I have spent most of my time distributing them to hospitals throughout the city. It is work different from anything that I have ever done, and at first it was intimidating and a bit frightening. Then as I saw how important these supplies were to the wounded men, my anxiety disappeared. To know that you are helping these soldiers is truly gratifying and makes it possible to bear up with long hours and a great deal of stress.

"When you talked about your time in the hospital in Strasbourg, Thomas, I could relate to it in many ways."

"It is ironic and sad, Marie, but I have never seen any place where so much good could come from so much misery."

"The problem is, as much as we try, there is only so much we can do. Thomas, you need to understand that even the best fail at times in these circumstances. That may be difficult to accept for someone like you, but it is a painful truth."

"At some level, I know that, Marie, but what is frustrating to me is to understand how to better relate to these men who deserve only the best that we can give them."

"Don't be so hard on yourself, Thomas. You have only been at this for a brief time."

"Robert said that you were thinking of doing something more dangerous?"

"More important perhaps, Thomas, and with importance comes risk. There is an opportunity that would allow me to accompany trains carrying sterile dressings to the frontline stations to help oversee their distribution and, if necessary, care for wounded on the return trip to Paris."

"That is a long way from preparing for a recital in Saint Sulpice, Marie."

"We're all a long way from those days, Thomas."

"I didn't mean to sound judgmental but was merely thinking out loud. No doubt Robert is right to worry about you. It was not that long ago that you and your mother promised to leave the city if it became too dangerous to stay."

Thomas's mild reprimand gave Marie more pleasure than discomfort, drawing her back to a time before so much had compromised that pledge and to sweet memories of her former relationship with him.

"That's true, Thomas, but now that pledge seems naive given the circumstances we face. It is certainly not reason enough to abandon important work. I could not live with myself if I allowed some small consideration for my safety to prevent me from doing what I know to be important. Being in the hospitals and afterward helping nurse Robert has reinforced my commitment to caring for these wounded men."

"You should be proud of what you've done already, Marie, but it can be easy to get caught up with excitement and lose perspective on what you might be facing. Promise me you won't do something rash."

"Thomas, all those old logic lessons of yours will help keep me centered. Besides, until I can be sure that you don't need my help, I plan to stay close to Paris."

"At least my infirmary has some use then."

For a moment, both were silent. The quiet of the room whose elegance seemed so discordant to the substance of their conversation increased Marie's uneasiness. Then she was thrilled to sense a spark in Thomas's eyes.

"Marie, I have been truly blessed to know you."

"Thomas, don't sound so fatalistic."

"I'm not being fatalistic but truthful. Your visit today has been a dose of the tonic that I needed."

There was something in his reply that belied Thomas's present uncertainty yet also sounded a note of resolve. For a moment, Marie was overcome by her emotions, but she quickly regained her composure and replied, "I'm getting comfortable around patients because I know with the right care they can improve. I know that will be the case for you, and I intend to do what is necessary to help you fully recover."

What Marie did not say but clearly felt as she left Thomas that afternoon was that despite his many frailties, she had seen enough to give her hope for him and their future relationship. Hope was a true blessing in times like this.

BOOK II
THE WIND BUILDS

15

Checked

WITH THE REQUEST BY GENERAL LANZERAC TO withdraw his Fifth Army from further engagement with the German force advancing on his left flank, Joseph Joffre was forced to acknowledge the failure of the offensive that had been the central tenet of his plan to quickly and decisively defeat the German Army. Joffre had initiated Plan 17 by ordering two armies and a portion of a third to advance toward a region he deemed most vulnerable near the enemy's center in the Ardennes area. It was an action that embodied the ancient French prejudice for the glory of attack as the surest means to triumph.

Now after several days of bloodletting on a scale never before seen, reality was imposing harsh lessons that were quickly dispelling such naive notions that valor could singularly trump the overwhelming power of strategically deployed modern weaponry. Joffre had thrown his Third, Fourth, and portions of his Fifth Army against the well-prepared defenses of the German center and had achieved no significant advance despite horrific losses. The road to Berlin remained closed. Worse yet, his entire army, as presently deployed, was ill-suited to handle what appeared with each passing day to be a major German buildup on his extreme left flank.

As the French offensive waned, the brunt of Lanzerac's Fifth Army along with the British encountered this force in front of Charleroi and Mons and were overwhelmed by the strength and numbers of the German advance, forcing Lanzerac to disengage. This withdrawal and subsequently that of the British forced Joffre to face the enormity of the threat now facing the Allies. As much as Joffre detested the thought, he conceded that Lanzerac had no choice but to withdraw westward or otherwise face annihilation, much like the French forces at Sedan in 1870. To survive, his army and the small British Expeditionary Force would now have to suddenly pivot to the defensive. Joffre knew this would not be an easy task, history being replete with failed attempts to transform a failed offensive into a coordinated tactical withdrawal, but it was the only option that remained.

Most men, when confronted with failure on such a scale, would be shaken, losing confidence in their capacities and hope for the cause that they championed. Joffre gave no indication that the failure of an offensive that so much depended on affected him in the least. Despite the crisis boiling around him, he remained calm, laconic, and aloof, insisting on his usual routine, which included the sanctity of his mealtime.

Joffre was an engineer by training and focused on process and outcome. It was a training that would serve him well. When outcomes proved unsatisfactory, it was imperative to identify the causes of failure and fix them. He was also a soldier and knew it was his responsibility to adapt to the circumstances of the moment. Let others worry about what was past; his job was to find and fix the shortcomings of the present.

Now, with the fate of his country in the balance, Joffre would need all his analytic skills and confidence to win the time necessary to change the present circumstances of his army. In the ruins of Plan 17, he believed he could see the root causes for failure and more importantly the means to remedy them. What he needed was time and space to extricate his army from its present dilemma so that he could address the lessons he believed he had learned from the recent failings.

He immediately issued new tactical directives that aimed to address the lack of coordination between artillery support and the rapid, often frantic advances that the infantry units had made in their zeal to attack the enemy. What ground was held or taken in the future would be consolidated using defensive entrenchments that had originally been forsaken to expedite a forward advance that had proven illusory. Stricter directives with regard to the use and range of the artillery were issued, and recognizing the advantage that aerial reconnaissance had provided German gunners, he drew up plans to better coordinate such reconnaissance from his own air service.

Joffre believed that much of the failure for the offensive was not due to tactics or planning but severe inadequacies on the part of many of his commanders. He believed that most of their failings came from a lack of martial spirit, which led to hesitancy and poor execution during crisis. He now became a one-man tribunal, dismissing commanders where evidence indicated their failure to perform to his standards. The number of critical failures by such standards was large, and given the gravity of the present situation, Joffre believed that there was little time for the luxury of redemption. In the coming days, he would devote as much time to reorganizing his leadership in the field as he would in managing the logistic of the battles.

He also resigned himself to the painful task of informing Messimy, the defense minister, of the present situation. He hated politicians and found them to be more trouble than they were worth in peacetime. Now they were simply a drain on his time, which was all too precious to waste under these circumstances.

In a terse statement, he informed the government through the defense minister that there had been setbacks that would necessitate the change of the ongoing offensive and would require that portions of his forces adopt more defensive tactics in the immediate future. This would be necessary until a reorganization could be accomplished to provide more effective commanders and better-positioned forces for an effective counterattack. Until then, it would be necessary to draw back to fortified lines and wear down the enemy while waiting for the appropriate opportunity to regain the offensive initiative.

Despite all the unwelcome news he was now forced to digest, Joffre had received encouraging reports from the Russians, who were advancing in force into Eastern Prussia. Such an invasion, he suspected, would force the Germans to withdraw troops from their western front to protect the vital Prussian homelands and thereby relieve some of the pressure on his own lines. Nevertheless, as he stared at the map showing the location of the present deployment of his troops and the enemy, he realized that much would need to be done before he could hope for any reprieve from the tsar's armies.

His immediate concern was shoring up his left flank along the northern extreme of the lines of engagement and in apposition with the British forces. The advancing German forces were threatening to flank the British on the extreme northwest of the Allied lines, which would deny them access to the coast and separate them from the Belgian forces that had withdrawn to Antwerp. The situation on the other extreme of his lines to the south was still fluid, but the First and Second Armies had succeeded to date in stopping any further advance of the Germans into Lorraine.

Joffre had little option now but to draw units from these armies in the south to stem the German threat on his northern flank. What soon followed was his second directive of the war to the French Army, ordering them to fight in retreat while yielding ground when no other option was available. At the same time, he brought General Maunoury out of retirement to command a new Sixth Army comprised of troops that would be drawn primarily from the First and Second Armies and rushed to the northern flank to help neutralize the emerging German threat. His hope for France rested on his northern flank holding long enough for the Sixth Army to arrive. He knew the following days would be challenging, demanding the best from his army. Joffre intended to do what was necessary so that the army would meet that challenge.

———

For several days, General Gallieni had intently watched the symbols on the large map in his operations room marking the known positions of the armies engaged to the east of Paris, and his trained eye saw in these bloodless representations a major threat to Paris arising from northeast of the city.

Gallieni knew that the French Army had risked much on its opening offensive designed to quickly overwhelm the Germans, and with each passing day, more evidence of its failure accumulated. The French Army had thrown themselves at carefully prepared German fortifications, with little to show for their efforts except the horrific butcher's bill of wanton slaughter.

Gallieni knew only too well the consequences of such a failure. Now the French lines were concentrated and misaligned to face a huge German offensive comprised of three armies. If these lines were flanked or widely broached then the Germans could advance on Paris across broad, poorly defending tracts of northeastern France.

The intelligence he reviewed that morning was so disturbing that he felt it imperative to meet with the defense minister that morning. Before he had time to compose a memo to the minster, however, his orderly brought a note from Messimy himself, requesting a meeting that very morning.

———

When Gallieni arrived at the War Ministry, he found Messimy to be nervously pacing around his office while dictating to a secretary.

On seeing Gallieni, he quickly dismissed his secretary and walked to his desk, where he produced the recent communiqué from Joffre.

"What do you make of this?" asked Messimy, handing Gallieni Joffre's dispatch.

Gallieni took some time before replying. His mind was caught up by the implications of the tersely detailed facts and what he could now envision was the very real face of a massive German offensive that threatened the city.

Gallieni, in reluctantly accepting the position as the city's military governor, finally did so when he learned from the head of the Army Engineering Corps how little General Michel had done to prepare the city's defenses. Now he could see how critical that delay had been.

"Monsieur Minister, I have always believed that the Germans would have to launch a massive offensive in the first weeks of the war either toward France or Russia to quickly resolve the problem of a war on two fronts. From this report, it is now clear that that offensive has been directed to our northeast through Flanders. I have no doubt that they are proceeding with several armies toward us from that direction. It is an area that I know well from my past duties, and of all of our frontiers, it is by far the most vulnerable."

Messimy blanched visibly.

"Then the capital is truly in danger?" he asked. "How long before we can expect the Germans to be near enough to attack the city?"

"This is a large force, as it appears that it has been supplemented with reserve troops, but even conceding the uncertainty surrounding the adequacy of reserve forces, I believe you may expect the Germans before our outskirts within two weeks," Gallieni replied with the cold detachment of a professional.

Messimy looked dumbfounded. After a moment, he asked, "What would you propose to relieve this threat, General?"

Gallieni paused for a moment to organize his thoughts before speaking, then replied with more passion. "I believe that we must do everything that can be done to defend Paris. It is the hub of our railroad system and industrial production. More importantly is its symbolic meaning to our people and our enemies. I'm afraid General Joffre and his staff do not see Paris in the same way. I suspect that they view it as a strategic location primarily, and any consideration of its defense should be secondary to the overall strategy of the army. It is very likely that they would be willing to abandon the city or at least give it less priority if they could gain an advantage elsewhere in so doing."

"You know I share your belief in the importance of defending Paris, General. How can I be of help?"

"It is important that we prepare the city for attack regardless of how many trees might be felled or how much private property must be requisitioned and demolished. That alone, however, will not be enough. I believe that Paris cannot be defended from its interior like a fortress; we have already seen the failings of that strategy at Liege and now Namur. Paris must be protected by striking the enemy well before it gets to our walls. As I mentioned to you when I accepted this post, the time may come when it will be essential for the military governor of Paris to have an army at his disposal. I believe that time is now. You give me an army with threes corps, and I can and will defend the city well. If we sit back and wait for their arrival, then I'm afraid we will only invite the kind of looting and destruction that we are hearing about in Belgium. We cannot allow that to happen here."

Messimy stepped forward and grasped Gallieni's hand as a drowning man would a rope and shook it vigorously. "I agree wholeheartedly with your proposal, General. The difficulty will be in getting those three corps as things presently exist."

"That may be, Monsieur Minister, but I'm sure that if you and the government value Paris, you will find a way to get the troops needed to protect it.

"There is also one other important matter that must be done immediately. Paris and the surrounding twenty-five kilometers must be declared in the zone of the army if I am to have the authority to prepare the city's defenses with the speed that is necessary."

After a moment of hesitation, Messimy replied with less enthusiasm, "You can be assured, General, that I will do everything I can to help you in the challenges ahead."

"Including the three corps?"

Messimy could only sigh. "It no doubt will be difficult, but I will do all that is possible to deliver them to you as soon as possible. General Gallieni, I cannot tell you how much your advice means to me. Now, if you will excuse me, we both have much work ahead of us today."

16

Fortress Paris

AS GALLIENI RETURNED FROM HIS MEETING WITH Messimy to his office along Rue St. Dominque, his mind was abuzz with plans that would need to be initiated immediately. In the brief time he had to study the present status of the city's defenses, Gallieni realized how little his predecessor, General Michel, had done to implement plans to ready the city to withstand an overt assault. He also realized that not all the fault could be blamed on Michel.

He had spoken at length with the chief engineering officer, General Hirschauer, a man he respected for his honesty and competence. From him, he had learned of the countless delays caused by government officials when attempts were made to requisition property for strategic destruction. Some claimed that such actions were premature and would only serve to alarm the populace. Hirschauer believed that, in many instances, these delays were motivated by the proponents of an open city more concerned about their property rights than the defense of the city itself.

He also knew that defense would require more than the efforts of the army alone. The citizenry would have to be involved and made aware of the dangers they faced. To this point, he felt that the politicians had not served the populace well, often trying to hide the reality of the military situation from them. He had a great deal of confidence in the average citizen, however, and expected that they could be depended on to act constructively in the face of approaching danger if they were honestly apprised of the facts. That Gallieni intended to do.

Upon entering his headquarters, his staff was already assembled in the large conference room. The morning planning meeting that had been delayed by his conversation with Messimy soon convened. The room seemed more crowded than usual and far more animated, no doubt due to the stir that had been caused by the receipt of various communiqués from Joffre's headquarters. It took Gallieni a moment to quiet the assembled staff, and then he proceeded directly to his point.

"Gentlemen, I have just had a lengthy conversation with Monsieur Messimy, where I had the opportunity to review the latest information from General Joffre pertaining to the situation of the army, especially along the Belgian frontier.

"We all know of the offensive that has been engaged through the Ardennes and the new fighting around Charleroi and Mons. It is clear from General Joffre's report that we have been checked all along the line of attack and that now our three northern armies are being forced to make strategic withdrawals. These withdrawals, if they have not done so already, will force the army back onto French soil and place increasing amounts of French soil in jeopardy.

"I have seen the positions of our troops as reported by General Joffre and the combined intelligence reports pertaining to the position and strength of the enemy. From that information, a serious threat to the city is emerging.

"I believe the intent of the enemy is to direct the brunt of its attack at the northern flank of our armies, pushing to envelop our forces from the north and west. I have no doubt that the enemy forces are large, capable, and well armed. It is conceivable that despite the efforts of our army and that of the British now opposing them, the Germans may be able to threaten Paris within two weeks. If that is the case, gentlemen, we have no time to spare in our efforts to defend this city."

By now, the room had fallen into near silence, even more apparent as Gallieni paused for a sip of water. He then resumed in a succinct manner, leaving little doubt that he was clear as to what needed to be done to address this threat.

"We must now go forward with the seizure and, when indicated, destruction of critical properties and bridges that have been identified as key to the defense of the city. General Hirschauer will be made my chief of liaison in dealing with these matters with the civil authorities, as he has done in the past weeks."

"General Gallieni, I hope the news of this threat will help to expedite these projects, but I suspect that some will still be against the destruction of parts of the city," Hirschauer replied with a note of skepticism in his voice.

"I appreciate your concerns, General Hirschauer, but we can no longer tolerate such actions that frustrated your past efforts. I have given this much thought and now believe with this crisis I have the moral and legal authority to immediately intercede to rectify this situation.

"I cannot defend Paris when people want to put their property rights above our military concerns. Paris will not be an open city. Tomorrow morning, I have requested that the defense minister include Paris and the surrounding countryside for twenty-five miles on both sides of the Seine into the zone of the armies. I have no doubt that he will comply with my request shortly. Such an act, when authorized, will bring the municipal authority under the military governor.

"When that authority is granted, a meeting will be held with the principal civil authorities to discuss plans to reorganize the city administration and to present plans for reworking the city's defenses. General Hirschauer, you will be present at that meeting as well. I have begun working on the draft of documents that I hope you will have a chance to review this afternoon. I plan on having them signed by all at the meetings tomorrow, after which I anticipate that you will no longer face any legal or bureaucratic delay in implementing your duties."

Hirschauer nodded, acknowledging the implications of such an arrangement.

"It will also be necessary to involve the citizenry in much of the work of preparing our defenses in the days ahead, due to the shortage of available military manpower. To get their cooperation, they must be made aware of the possible situation that we all now face. Colonel Rabette, I will want you at the meeting tomorrow as well and subsequently to establish a bureau of information to help better communicate to the public the risks and their responsibilities in the coming days. We should not allow unsubstantiated rumor or fearmongering, but we should keep the populace honestly apprised of the situation that exists."

Rabette, the officer designated as information chief, nodded while frantically making notes. Then pausing, he stopped and asked, "General, what makes you so sure that you will be able to implement your plans tomorrow when we have had so much trouble getting things done before?"

"It's quite simple, Colonel. When Paris and its surrounding territories are declared in the zone of the armies, then all authority is ceded automatically to the military governor. At that moment, I will plan to have a brief conference with the previous civil authorities, appraising them of the situation and their prerogatives, which are to obey the military governor at penalty of treason if they do not. I will then ask them to sign the document that I have alluded to, which dissolves their responsibilities until the emergency has been declared over. They will no longer have any civil authority and consequently will be dismissed until their services are requested."

A knowing smile settled over the assembled faces in anticipation of the effect of this declaration.

"What happens if Messimy fails to designate Paris in the war zone as requested?" asked Rabette.

"Then I will resign as military governor. The defense minister understands what is at stake, and he is a patriot. I am certain that he will honor my request.

"Robert d'Avillard, I trust that your wounds are healing well enough to get around with some help from your staff?" asked Gallieni, looking at Robert with a questioning gaze.

"I will be able to do what is necessary, General, although it may take me a bit longer to get to where I might need to go," Robert replied confidently.

"Good. We can plan accordingly. In the coming days, General Hirschauer will be in many ways acting as city manager and will have little time to oversee the work that is essential to prepare for our defense. You, of course, will report your progress to him, but I am relying on your oversight to accomplish what will be necessary in terms of strategic demolition and the construction of appropriate fortifications."

Robert said, "I have restudied the present proposals for the necessary changes to the existing city, particularly in the north and western sections, and feel that they still are sound and well prioritized. I don't believe that this clumsy leg will interfere in any work that might be necessary there."

"That is all well and good, but we cannot defend the city by waiting behind fortified walls for a force as large and well armed as this German Army will be. If we do that, they will bring up heavy artillery and destroy much of the city and our fortifications, just as they have done to the cities of Belgium. We must instead extend the ring of our defenses well outside the old walls that protected our medieval ancestors and confront the enemy far from the city itself.

"At present, we do not have the troops to deploy in such defensive sites, but they must be prepared and ready when the Germans arrive. Paris will be an armed camp at the center of new fortifications that must extend for many kilometers outside of the suburbs. As of today, the defense minister has promised the garrison three corps of troops to defend Paris. We must and will be prepared for their arrival.

"Robert, I will have much more to say about this matter in the coming days, but you should be thinking of plans to construct fortified trenches and earthen battlements far to the northeast of the present city fortifications. Suffice it to say that with the change of authority, you will be given the tools and manpower to accomplish your objectives.

"I was a close observer of the first Balkan war and before that studied the wars in Manchuria," Gallieni continued. "If you pay attention to what worked rather than what was postulated, the information can be quite valuable. Defenders using narrow, deep trenches protected by earthen battlements and barbed wire, coupled with machine guns and other modern weaponry, proved virtually invincible.

"Robert, your task will be to enlist every able-bodied male in the regions and outskirts of Paris to construct those trenches and battlements. You will supplement them with wolf pits filled with upward pointing spikes. With three army corps filling such installations, the Germans will not get close enough to barrage our city into submission."

"How will I be able to obtain the civilian manpower I will need for such construction other than on a voluntary basis?"

"As it now exists, you do not have any authority to get civilian help other than by volunteers. That will change with the documents that are being prepared. Tomorrow I will authorize ten thousand picks and shovels to be delivered within twenty-four hours to your authority. I will also request any other tools that you might need to be delivered in the timeliest manner possible.

"As for the civilian labor that you will need, I will have the authority, and orders are being written to require all qualified males regardless of age in threatened areas to participate in labor battalions under military control to build these fortifications.

"Gentlemen, that is all for the present. We all have much to do in preparation for tomorrow and the days ahead. If you will excuse me."

With that, Gallieni turned and left, bearing himself in the composed and erect manner that they would all come to know and respect in the frantic and crucial days that would follow.

17

Georgette's Tale

MARIE HAD SPENT LITTLE TIME IN HER VOLUNTEER work during Robert's convalescence, but with his recovery, she felt free to return to her duties. On her first day back, the effect of the vast struggle being fought to the east was dramatically evident throughout the large complex of facilities designed to care for the war's casualties. Each day, hospital trains coming from the battlefronts would bring vast numbers of wounded to the medical facilities scattered across the city. To deal with their needs, additional medical facilities were converted from former residences and commercial buildings that bordered upon the existing medical centers and hospitals.

It was easier to find space than it was to find qualified personnel capable of handling the number of severely injured men. The supply of doctors and previously trained medical personnel, such as nurses, was barely adequate to deal with the tragedy. To compensate, volunteers and others with less formal medical training were being pushed into positions to help with some of the less critically wounded. The routines of the hospital established during peacetime had been profoundly altered as well. It was as if new procedures and methods needed to be developed daily to handle the changing circumstances of the moment. The uncertainty and turmoil also provided opportunities that would never have previously existed for people of skill and initiative.

Marie did not recognize many of the people she encountered that first day back in the sterile processing site. She was greeted as if she were a long-lost friend by the supervisor, who clearly was having difficulty coping with the demands that the numbers of casualties were causing. Before the day was half-over, Marie had received a battlefield promotion to replace a woman who had taken a leave of absence to help attend to her recently wounded husband. She was put in charge of overseeing the final distribution of freshly prepared dressings to the receiving facilities of the main medical complexes throughout the city.

From experience, Marie knew that to do the job well involved not only the delivery of the critical supplies to the hospitals but also to inventory the personnel there as to the number and types of dressing they would likely need the following day. This would require establishing a personal relationship with key physicians and nurses to more effectively gauge future needs. What Marie feared was the demand for their supplies would soon overwhelm the capacity of the present system to supply them.

Late that afternoon, she made it a point to accompany the deliveries to the largest hospitals in their network and to refamiliarize herself with critical staff members there. At the end of the day as she returned to the dispensary with some paperwork unfinished, it became clear to Marie that she would not be able to leave at the hour she had anticipated. She sent word to her mother that circumstances at work had necessitated a change in her plans and would prevent her from returning for dinner that evening. She then retired to a small office area, making careful notes of her afternoon's activities, which included the number and type of deliveries to the various hospitals and comments made by the medical staffs. When all of this was finished, she finally allowed herself the time to seek out the small canteen associated with the dispensary for something to ease the hunger that was an uncomfortable reminder of how long it had been since she had last eaten.

As she settled at an empty table near the back of the dining area, Marie reflected on all she had done that day with satisfaction. She not only had returned to work but had also been given new and more demanding responsibilities. As she lingered over her coffee, she saw her old friend Georgette from the music conservatory arrive, looking every bit as tired as Marie felt. Marie knew that Georgette had been working in many of the same medical facilities she had visited today and could tell from her appearance that she too carried weighty responsibilities.

Marie nodded to Georgette and was greeted with a broad smile when she sat down next to her.

"Marie, I hoped that you would get back before too long. I've been dying to talk to you."

"Georgette, I was wondering if I would see you today. I thought I might miss you if your work had taken you out of the city."

"That's one of the things I want to talk with you about, but there seems to be so much that has happened since I last saw you that it's hard to know where to begin. How is your boyfriend? I heard that he was getting better."

"Much better thankfully. That is one of the reasons I have been able to come back to work."

"Are you spending any time at school?"

"Not really. With Robert's injury, I haven't had the time or frankly the inclination to practice as I should, and besides, the school is so different now."

"I know. It's depressing to see," said Georgette ruefully.

"In a way, it makes it easier to concentrate on work like this, which seems more important now than our music studies," Marie said.

"I'm not completely sure about that, Marie. It seems all of us could use a few moments to step back from this and enjoy something beautiful. With things as they are now, I'm afraid few of us will have the chance to listen to a concert or even a small recital."

"The dispensary and the hospitals seemed to be almost frantic with activity today. How long has it been this way?" Marie asked.

"For several days, but it seems much longer than that. People here say our troops have launched a large offensive, but whatever the reason, the fighting must be awful."

"You mean from all of the casualties coming into Paris?"

"Yes, that certainly, but there is more. I have been going out with the hospital trains like I told you the last time we talked. Recently, I have been going to Verdun and some areas nearby that are the main receiving facilities attached to the Third Army. As hectic and intense as matters are here in Paris, they are doubly so there.

"I've now made several of those trips, including one that just returned earlier this afternoon. We usually go out at night to avoid congestion if possible. At Verdun, the supplies are downloaded to trucks, and injured soldiers are transported back to Paris. This is usually a daily occurrence, but at times I have stayed over for a day to oversee the distribution of the supplies and instruct on their proper usage in various way stations closer to the battlefield."

"What is it like near the front?" Marie asked.

"I would not mention this to just anyone, because it seems to have some bearing on the fighting. With you, Marie, I know that whatever I say will be between the two of us."

"Certainly, what you tell me stays between us."

"Well, if you listen to what is in the papers or heard on the streets, we're led to believe that it is just a matter of time before we break through and rout the Germans. Even in our hospitals here in Paris, however, you can sense that there is more to it than that. The closer you get to the front, the more evident the true reality is."

"And what is that?"

"The truth is that the fighting is incredibly violent and we are suffering enormous casualties. I know from what I see at those forward stations how many severely wounded men are there and how many will never be stable enough to return here. There are others who, even if they do survive, will take months to recover and will be consigned to spend the rest of their days severely disabled.

"In being in these areas, you, of course, talk to all of the medical personnel and even from time to time to the wounded. Looking at the wounded can be frightening, especially at first. Some of their injuries are horribly disfiguring, with arms and legs and parts of their faces destroyed. Worse yet is the look in their faces. Many seem stunned and don't seem to recognize your presence.

"I have heard also that many others died before they could be transported to the rear."

"My god, Georgette, it sounds horrible. How can you stand to keep going back up there?"

"People must think that I'm a ghoul to continue with this, but there is more to it. As frightening as it first seems, you can endure it when you see how much good comes from your efforts.

"I have been at these receiving stations when the wounded have come in so quickly and in such numbers as to overwhelm the staff. I know something of first aid, as you do from instructing the staff in the usage of our dressings. I have seen how much my help is appreciated during those hectic times when there are not enough personnel to deal with all the wounded. To those men, it doesn't seem to matter that I am not a doctor or trained nurse but only that I can help them.

"For all of our lives, it seems women have been relegated to the backstage. Now suddenly, by necessity, we are every bit as worthy as anyone else. At the end of one of those rides back to Paris, you see things differently. For all the nightmares, I also have memories of the times when my presence helped a man to hold on to life. Those memories give me hope of better things in the future."

"It's time that both of us go home and get some rest, Georgette. It sounds like we will need it for tomorrow."

"I expect you're right, Marie, but remember what I said. Whatever we do in Paris I believe can have even greater benefit closer to the front. As perverse as it may seem, all of the horror of this war gives people like us new opportunities to do something important."

That night, Marie struggled to get to sleep. All that she held dear seemed to be threatened if not yet destroyed. She hoped that Georgette was right about the opportunity for good that now existed amid all this turmoil, but she feared, even with such efforts, it might not be enough.

Slowly, Marie came to understand the course before her. She had been trained to work hard and persevere from her earliest years. What she now sensed was that these traits would have to be applied not in the music studio but in an even more demanding environment to help those most affected by the war. Doing anything less would be an admission of defeat, and that was something that she refused to acknowledge.

18

Belgium

SARA HAD EXPECTED WHEN SHE LEFT BERLIN WITH
Aaron Heileman that they would face many challenges along
with possible danger, especially if her identity was discovered.
She had been both surprised and deeply thankful that Aaron,
along with many people she encountered since she first sought
asylum, had been willing to help her, even at the risk of their
own safety. Each day that she was free from internment added
to her sense of gratitude but also served to increase her respect
for Aaron and others who were risking their freedom for Sara
and others like her.

From the very first days after their departure, Sara was
thrilled by the danger and excitement of what she recognized
as the greatest adventure of her life. This journey was nothing
like she had experienced, with the comforts of the city replaced
with long days traveling by truck, sometimes sleeping on a
rough bed of straw in the barn of an acquaintance of Aaron or
even in the back of the vehicle itself. The meals she ate were
rustic and, though no doubt nutritious and often even quite
good, were nothing like the fare that she was used to in Berlin
and Paris. That urban world she was so familiar with had been
transformed into rural villages and small cities that made up the

farmlands of central and western Germany. In all this, Aaron was like a guide, giving her not only instructions as to how to behave in this new environment but also insight into the people and society in which she now spent the better part of her days.

One afternoon, Aaron drew Sara aside to inform her that a meeting had been set up with Major Shrieves.

"What does he want this time, Aaron?"

"I'm not certain, but it seems like it's more important than usual, as he sent a sergeant to track me down with the news."

"I may never fully understand these farmers and traders that you deal with, Aaron, but I have a good sense for a man like Shrieves. His distaste for working with a Jew was evident from the first, but he, like many of his type, is quite willing to forego any prejudice he might have if it furthers his position. The more success you have, the warmer he seems to be."

"The German Army planners in their usual way have been working furiously to develop a network of sites where stockyards and collecting areas can be built to process the livestock necessary to support the army. Like most German planners, their work has been thorough, but they neglected the most important aspect of the process," Aaron said with a tone of smug certainty.

"Which is?"

"They had and still have virtually no understanding of the suppliers of the livestock that their system was designed to process. Their model is devoid of the human elements that are sometimes simple and at other times complex when it comes to motivating farmers and livestock dealers. They at least had the sense to recognize the error of their ways and to seek out people who could help them relate on a more personal level.

"I am here because those many suppliers and farmers that you have at times criticized were unwilling to blindly line up for some army quartermaster unless they got guarantees that they would be treated appropriately. Many of them have dealt with the army in the past, and they have long memories. They remember being forced to sell at prices well below the market and to guarantee a greater share of their herds than they felt reasonable. The army does not know how to motivate cooperation except by coercion, which will not produce the results they desperately need at this time."

"So, what makes them think these farmers can trust you, Aaron?"

"The smarter ones know better than to trust anyone. The rest know me as someone who has dealt fairly with them in the past and who has been honest. My word, I suppose, has been my best reference. Even the most skeptical know that what I have told them is true."

"What is that?" Sara asked.

"I told them that with this war, they have leverage over the army like they have never had before. The army desperately needs what they are supplying, and if the British naval blockade is successful, as I suspect it will be, then shortages will emerge, which will place the army's needs in competition with the civilian population. All of this means soaring prices for the producers. When I agreed to help the military procure livestock, I made it very clear what would be required to guarantee the supply that they needed. Now when I speak to my old friends and new acquaintances, I can quote them a price that will make it very worthwhile to comply with the army quartermasters.

"Most of the men that I deal with have been involved with livestock all their lives, as were their fathers and grandfathers before them. Most are Jews like me. We have seen in our long history many powerful men and armies come and go. It is wise to respect their power but not too much. Many of the powerful have failed, but our tribe, though it is far from our old lands, has survived. I suspect that for those of us that understand our traditions, we will survive once more."

"You better get on your way, Aaron. It's near time to meet with Shrieves, and you wouldn't want to keep him waiting," Sara admonished with a sardonic tone in her voice.

On arrival, Aaron noted that Shrieves looked more somber than usual and even deferential. After a few pleasantries, he quickly broached the subject of their meeting.

"Well then, Aaron, I will get to the point. Last night, I received a communiqué from headquarters highly complimentary of the work that we have been doing. I would be the first to thank you for your efforts in helping us achieve these recent successes.

"It seems that the planners in Berlin believe that the situation around Liege is stable enough that it would allow for exploring the possibility of building receiving depots for supplies somewhat like we have been doing in Germany. There is no doubt that we have the manpower in place there to expedite the building of any structures necessary. The question is, what can we expect, if anything, from the Belgians in terms of cooperation in procuring their livestock? Have you had any dealings with them in the past?"

"Major, you can't have been in the business as long as I have without some dealings with some of the Belgian traders. I also have the advantage of having a few relatives there as well, which facilitates our dealings on both sides of the border."

"Where are your relatives?" Shrieves asked pointedly.

"My closest is a cousin who is nearly my age who lives near Brussels."

"How close are you to him?"

"We have worked together at times, but I don't have a large network of acquaintances there like here in Germany. I know many people there, but most of my dealings in Belgium have been handled through my cousin or one of his associates."

"You must have some sense of their willingness to cooperate from those experiences."

"What I have observed is that the Belgians had as much trust in the Germans as they did the French or the Dutch; that is very little. They have enough trouble dealing among themselves, as the Flemish don't like the Walloons, and the Walloons don't trust the Flemish. In the past, I had far more success in dealing with the Walloons since they seemed more disposed to the Germans and Dutch, possibly because we don't speak French."

"Aaron, I would like to ask a favor of you."

"If it is reasonable, Major."

"I will need someone to help me with the Belgian dealers as you have done here in Germany."

"As I mentioned, Major, I don't have as close a group of contacts as I have here in Germany."

"You have more contacts there than likely any other German. I can guarantee that you will receive the same commission you receive here for finding willing suppliers."

"Major, what I know about the Belgians is enough to tell me that they are not going to welcome us with open arms. I suspect that my cousin may laugh me out of his house while he gives me a push through the door. If that is the case, I will have wasted a great deal of valuable time that could have been put to better use here in Germany."

"Well, Aaron, I suspected you might be concerned about such a possibility, so I received permission from Berlin to offer you a per diem salary of one hundred marks as well as a bonus for any contracts providing over one hundred head of livestock weekly."

"What about the facility at Aachen? There is much to be done there."

"I would be able to give you two days to work in the area. From what I have seen from your associates, they could handle much of what is needed until you returned."

"If possible, I would like Sara to go with me. She speaks excellent French, which could be of great help in dealing with the Belgians, and besides, she would be the most expendable in sustaining the operation here while I'm gone."

"That would be quite reasonable, Aaron. If there is nothing more, I suggest that we get on the way to Aachen as soon as possible."

After two days of intense work near Aachen, Aaron felt convinced that he could leave his brother-in-law in charge until he returned from Belgium. Early on the following morning, he and Sara set out with Shrieves and two of his associates by train to Belgium. Their departure was delayed so that they might take a military transport train rather than proceed by automobile as originally planned. No reason was given to Aaron for the change, but it would later be apparent that it was impossible for an individual car to proceed safely through Belgium. They were assigned their own travel compartments, with Shrieves and his aides in one compartment and Aaron and Sara in another. By nine thirty, the train slowly pulled from the station.

There was much delay at the Belgian border, as if the requirements of peacetime still existed, but at last all was deemed in order, and the train passed into the first occupied territory that Sara had ever seen.

At first, the Belgian countryside on the frontier and for the first few kilometers thereafter appeared very much like she had remembered it from her past trips through the area. As the train made its way toward Liege, changes began to become more apparent. The first was the absence of the normal number of people evident in the towns and villages along the route of their journey. Even the countryside seemed strangely vacant of activity. As the train approached Liege, the features of war became more dramatic. Approaching the fortress town of Archon, Sara was struck by a cloud of what appeared to be smoke suspended around the hill of the former fortress.

What she could see of the fortress was masked by this apparent cloud, but as the train approached closer, she could tell that much of it had been reduced to rubble. She sat staring through the train window, amazed at what she was seeing. This fortress was one of the many that had ringed the city of Liege on all sides, and because of their design and construction, they were considered nearly impregnable prior to the war. Soon she would see from the other side of the train the approach of Evegnée and a similar appearance to the citadel on its heights.

Hidden in the smoke and what she would come to realize was the dust that now enveloped the destroyed fortresses, Sara saw clearly the destructive capacity of modern warfare. These forts and all of those that had ringed the city had been reduced to smoldering dust-strewn rubble by terrible new weaponry. What kind of guns could do such damage she could not imagine, but the proof of their efficacy was clearly apparent. The twelve forts that had been believed to be virtually impregnable had been reduced in days, and with their destruction came the fall of Liege, opening a path through Belgium for the advancing German Army.

After crossing the Meuse as their train eased up the long incline that led to Liege's central train station, Sara could not take her eyes off the cityscape that passed. She had been to Liege before. It was the leading center of steel production for a country that had early on been transformed by rapid industrialization in the nineteenth century. Liege was not only a major industrial center but also a major center for socialism. Now that she recognized some of the buildings, it was apparent that much of the city had been transformed.

The city center was spared much of the damage she had seen around the fortresses surrounding the city. As Sara and Aaron departed the train, few if any Belgians seemed present. There had been an eerie absence of the native population as they entered the city, but here their absence was even more apparent. As she and Aaron progressed along the train platform, it was as if they were in Berlin. Everywhere were German soldiers and nonmilitary Germans dressed as if they were in a bureau in Munich or Hamburg. Sara had to look hard to find the occasional Belgian, who was often inconspicuously placed behind a bureau or sales counter.

Shrieves quickly met them along the queue, and together they hailed a cab that took them to a large nearby hotel virtually transformed by the presence of the German Army. Aaron and Sara waited while Shrieves spoke with the desk personnel, and then returning, he drew them aside.

"Here is your room key. I'm sorry, Fraulein, but there was only one room for the two of you. I'm afraid you will have to adapt your modesty to the situation."

"War makes for unusual circumstances, Major."

"Now you have your German passports, but I have had other military papers drawn up that will provide you with special privileges in case you are stopped when I am not with you.

"I would suggest that you take the rest of the afternoon to orientate yourselves to the city while I attend to my affairs. We could meet here tonight at seven o'clock for dinner and plan our day for tomorrow."

"That will give me some time to check on some of my old acquaintances that I know in the city, Major," Aaron said.

"That would be helpful but be sure that you have those papers I gave you. From everything I'm told, there is much uneasiness at present between our troops and some of the populace. The last thing we need is you getting mistaken for a hostile by one of our own."

"You may be sure that neither of us will go out without them, Major."

"Very well, Aaron. I will see you both this evening."

The room that Shrieves had procured for them was much nicer than Sara could have expected. It was a room with a separate bedroom opening on to a sitting room. She smiled at their good fortune, for such rooms were no doubt in short supply, and for a moment she felt new warmth for Shrieves in obtaining it for them.

Aaron, after storing his travel valise in a large closet near the bedroom door, readied himself for an afternoon of exploring the center of Liege.

"The major did well with this room. I haven't been in a place like this for some time. It will be nice to have a hot shower for a change. Sara, I will take the couch tonight in the sitting room so that you may have your privacy in the bedroom. Now I'm going out for a while to see what I can find out in some of the old neighborhoods that I've visited in the past. I suspect it will be best for you to stay here until I get back."

"You be careful out there, Aaron. I have never seen anything like the way the Belgians look at these Germans; it's as if they are trying to ignore their very presence while at the same time wishing them only the worst."

"I don't need a lecture to remind me to be careful, but thanks to the major, I now have a pass from the German Army itself to snoop around. It would be too bad to waste such an opportunity.

"In case I do get into trouble today or at any time that we are here in Belgium, you have those names that I gave you?"

"Yes, safely committed to memory, Aaron."

"If need be, you can likely find out the whereabouts of the second name from any of the synagogues here, as his whereabouts will be well known."

"I trust that I will not need them today, Aaron, as long as you use good judgment."

"You can count on that, Sara. I'll see you tonight."

After Aaron left, Sara sat at the window overlooking the street and watched him disappear in a crowd of officers arriving at the front of the hotel. As she settled into the large leather chair in the sitting room, she could not help but note the irony of her current situation, a foreign national under the protection of the German Army, an institution that she had opposed all her years in Berlin. If she got truly lucky, she might even use her good fortune to escape from their clutches while in Belgium.

From the time she had left Berlin, Sara knew that it would be virtually impossible for her to escape Germany without organized help. She could not have asked for any more than the help she had received from the friends that she had met since the war broke out. Aaron was certainly a prime example. Last night, he had shared his views of their coming trip to Belgium, which he thought had only a fair chance of success in meeting the needs of Shrieves and his handlers. Nevertheless, he no doubt understood that as the Belgian and French resistance collapsed, the German Army would move closer to France, where she might have a good chance of escape. In anticipation of such an opportunity, he had given her a list of locals in Liege and Brussels that she might contact in case she became separated from his protection. On that list was his cousin's son, who owned a business in Liege and who no doubt Aaron was trying to contact at this very moment.

As Sara waited, periodically peering out the window, it required all her concentration to keep her thoughts focused on productive ends rather than let them run off in wild speculation. Finally, as the long arc of the sun passed behind the buildings across from her, Aaron returned.

Perhaps it was due to the half-light in the room at this hour, but Aaron appeared more somber than Sara could ever remember. His face seemed locked in a scowl, and seemingly caught up in his thoughts, he sat for a moment before he at last spoke in reply to her questions about the success of his afternoon inquiries.

"I found the men I was looking for where I thought they would be, but I also found much that I was not expecting. Major Shrieves may have suspected as much, but I can see no chance at present that any Belgian with a conscience will cooperate with the Germans unless coerced to do so."

Sara's curious expression prompted him to elaborate further.

"There is so much that the German people don't know regarding what has taken place here that I hardly know where to begin. It all began with the hope that the Belgians would step aside and let the German Army pass unmolested as part of an ill-conceived and poorly written accord dictated at gunpoint. If they rejected cooperation and chose to resist, it was felt that they would offer feeble resistance. The German general staff, not surprisingly, has a timetable for their offensive that did not allow for protracted Belgian resistance.

"Unfortunately for both parties, the Belgians resistance was fierce and initially quite formidable. During the first days of the war, many German troops were lost in front of the forts here at Liège, which increased German frustration with the setbacks and their anger at both the Belgian Army and the native population. As the first days went by without success and the strength of the resistance increased, the Germans became increasingly hostile and suspicious of all the Belgian citizenry.

"In Liège, the end was reached with the arrival of massive siege cannons brought in by rail. No one had ever seen such weapons. Their size was unimaginable, and their firepower would prove to be lethal. The forts were subjected to an incessant barrage from these guns, whose noise was intolerable to even those safe within the confines of the city. The combined effect of the power of these weapons with the destructive psychological effects that the bombardments had on the defenders led to a rapid collapse of the city's defenses.

"Since that time, the Germans have proven themselves to be legitimate heirs to their Hun ancestors. If the story gets out of what has happened here, all of the progress German civilization has made in recent years will be shattered."

"What do you mean?" asked Sara apprehensively.

"I mean atrocities on a scale unimaginable. The Belgians were not supposed to have the courage and will to resist the German invasion across their territory. That they did effectively stunned and then infuriated the German command. Now surrounded by a hostile population, the Germans imagine themselves constantly under attack by civilian snipers and saboteurs. They have concluded that the only way to deal with it is by severe reprisal. I have spent the greater part of the last two hours listening to stories about things they have done. For anyone who associates German culture with Beethoven or Goethe, the stories I heard would seem unbelievable.

"What has happened is that in response to acts of resistance by civilians, the Germans have carried out mass reprisals; in some instances, entire villages have been burned, and all the adult men have been murdered. There is ample evidence that whole families, including women and children, have been summarily murdered, as well as numerous priests accused of harboring civilian resistors.

"The message that was sent to the Belgians is absolutely clear. Any attempt to resist German occupation will be met with severe reprisal and destruction," Aaron said contemptuously.

"So, a new dark age is beginning," Sara said.

"It would certainly appear so," Aaron replied, with a sadness that underscored his concern for the present situation.

"What do you plan to do, Aaron?"

"I plan to be honest with Shrieves."

"What do you expect to gain from that?"

"Shrieves knows by now that I will have heard something about these atrocities and no doubt suspects that there will be little willingness on the part of the Belgians to cooperate, at least in the short term. If this war persists with a protracted German presence in Belgium, then the reality of the situation may change. The Germans will be able to coerce the population to supply their needs or at least part of their needs, but coercion is never efficient. It distorts matters, leading to hoarding and a black market.

"Such a relationship between supplier and consumer is destructive in many other ways as well. By insisting upon conditions that make the Belgians little more than serfs to their German masters, the seeds will be sown for constant political instability, resulting in sabotage and clandestine attacks against the occupying forces. This is a costly and inefficient way to manage a country. Shrieves is a practical man, and if left to him, I believe he would be willing to forego any ill-chosen use of force if he could be assured that by doing so, it would make his life easier."

"How do you expect to ever get your relatives and their friends to work with the Germans after what you heard today?"

"There will always be people who are willing to compromise for the right price. Our major knows that. He also likely knows that such people make bad partners. They cannot be trusted. What he wants are reliable contacts like he has been getting in Germany, who have long and established reputations and can be good partners in return for excellent prices and some discretionary control over their wares."

"How do you know that is what he wants?" Sara asked, with a note of skepticism in her voice.

"I know from my conversations with him. He is not a Prussian but is from Bavaria, where they respect their farmers. After all, the Bavarians have had to sublimate their own lifestyle to that of a greater Germany, so why shouldn't the Belgians? Shrieves sees the new face of Europe in mercantile terms, with relations based on economic exchange rather than political power. He would like nothing more than to put his vision into practice here in occupied Belgian."

"Is that your vision as well, Aaron?"

"You mean a Europe as one big German marketplace, serving red-faced burghers and plump housewives? It is a vision fit for the Grimm brothers and almost as naive. These old European tribes won't give up their sovereignty that easily, though it might be to their benefit if they acted according to Shrieves's vision. I am much too cynical to imagine such a convenient solution to emerge from such chaos.

"Instead, I believe this provides an opportunity for men like me who can supply high-quality goods in high demand. It is not simply about profit but influence. The Germans may not like dealing with a bunch of Jews, but unfortunately for them, they may find doing so to be their best option. Puncturing their arrogance is almost worth as much as the marks we are making."

"Which brings me back to my question. What are you planning now?" Sara persisted.

"I need to talk to my cousin, preferably without Shrieves but with him if necessary."

"I thought he lived in Brussels."

"He does. Unfortunately, the German Army is now in Brussels, as of two days ago, which may complicate matters. Still, it is important that I speak to him."

"Why?"

"He is a person I trust implicitly. In times like this, that is a rarity. He and I have known each other for almost all our lives. He will know if there is any hope of dealing with Shrieves. Perhaps he might even agree to talk with him. If he feels that it will be impossible to work with the Germans, he will no doubt know who would. Whichever way, Shrieves will come away with a list of people that he can use as suppliers, and I will have fulfilled my end of the bargain. I spoke at length with my cousin's son, who is strongly against any agreement with the Germans, but he has promised to make his father aware of my presence here in Belgium.

"One other thing. Emil, my cousin, knows the territory around France better than anyone. If there is one person who can get you there, he would be the one."

"Well, it's getting time that we meet Shrieves for dinner," Sara said, looking at the clock. "You have enough to talk with him about that we shouldn't keep him waiting."

19

Hopeful News

AS EVENTS ON THE FRONT DETERIORATED FOR THE French Army, Robert's responsibilities increased dramatically. His were far different from in the past. No longer would he have the luxury of concentrating on a single problem and the satisfaction that came with its completion. His job instead had rapidly evolved to become problem solver and chief allocation officer for managing the limited resources necessary to build an effective infrastructure to confront the advance of the German Army on Paris. What little time he had was divided by his work in the field and the demands of planning and coordination, best met at headquarters.

At times, it seemed as if he were balancing several balls in the air, much like the circus jugglers he had so admired as a boy. No sooner would one threat be addressed than others would arise to take its place. Now he was being forced to make rapid decisions based on the priority of problems and often to create new or modify existing solutions to address them. This process was made immensely more difficult by the dynamic of the battlefront, which forced Robert frequently to reevaluate his initial estimates and plans. Far from being frustrated or discouraged, however, he seemed to be invigorated by the enormity of the challenges facing him and the urgency of producing satisfactory solutions.

A great part of his day dealt with the status of the build-out of defensive fortifications to the north and northeast of the city. This was a project that amazed him in terms of its scope and the nature of its participants. Its design was by no means complicated. Much of the work consisted of building deep trench works with surrounding earthen fortifications. While this work could be done by heavy machinery, in many instances, such equipment was not available, requiring that much of the trench work be done by hand if it was to be finished in time. With each passing day, it seemed the size of the labor force was increasing exponentially.

Now to the north and northeast of Paris, stretching for more than twenty-five kilometers, the soil of France was being upturned not by soldiers or excavators but by the men, women, and children populating the countless villages and small towns. Fueled by their memories of the Prussian invasion of their earlier years or by the horrific descriptions of German atrocities coming out of Belgium, they were highly motivated to contribute their efforts. Others had less apparent motivation, but whatever the reason, from the moment that plans for excavating fortifications in these areas became known, there was no shortage of civilian labor to help carry them out.

Yet despite the need for him to often be in the field, the desperate nature of the situation often required that he be at staff headquarters. It became apparent early on to Robert that if he was to continue his frequent inspections, he would have to have an efficient means of transportation. He quickly found that he could not depend upon military transportation, which was seldom available on short notice. Since his job often necessitated frequent changes in his daily plans, it was virtually impossible to block out a specific time to requisition scarce military vehicles. One of his lieutenants provided the solution when he suggested that Robert simply call a taxi when he needed transportation and bill it back to the army. After a brief conversation with General Hirschauer, the plan was approved, providing that the cabs were used strictly for military purposes.

So authorized, Robert sent an aide to inquire of the availability of Karl Gold or one of his appointed drivers to serve as needed for transportation in the city and into the surrounding areas. The aide returned with a message from Karl that it would be his privilege to serve the major and he need only notify him, regardless of the hour, and someone would be dispatched quickly to attend to his needs.

So it came to pass that very afternoon, Karl arrived to drive Robert to Chantilly to inspect an area where he was considering new excavation. It was the first time the two had seen each other since that night that now seemed so long ago when Robert had come to pick up Sara for their last evening together.

"Good afternoon, Karl. I'm pleased to see you once again and appreciate you offering your expert services to an invalid greatly in need of such help."

"It is good to see you once again, sir. I'm very pleased to see that you're able to be up and about. When we heard of your injury, we were very concerned."

After he was wounded, Robert, when able, had sent a communication to Lydia informing her of his condition, hoping in doing so that word would somehow reach Sara Morozovski. Despite all that had occurred since, seldom did a day go by in which Robert did not think back on their last night together.

"How is your wife, Karl? I hope that she is well."

"She is doing as well as conditions allow, Robert—if I may call you Robert."

"Of course. I had written to her about my injury, knowing that she would be able to pass the information on to Sara. She had written to tell me that she had learned that Sara had been caught up in Berlin at the time of the outbreak of the war and had subsequently learned that she had been hidden by some of her German friends, one of whom happened to be an old acquaintance of yours. From that information, she felt that there was a good chance that she was still safe. Have you heard anything else since then?"

"We have gotten bits and pieces of information communicated to us through a series of mutual contacts we have with Aaron Heilman, a man I have known for a number of years. Aaron is involved in some way with sheltering Sara. I know that his wife has long been associated with the Socialists, which may well explain their connection to her. I first met Aaron when we were both young men, and I have worked with him through the years. He is someone that can be relied upon."

"That's good to hear, Karl."

"As long as we know that she is with Aaron or his people, then Lydia and I feel encouraged that all will be well."

As the men spoke, Karl expertly navigated the narrow streets through the northeast quarters of the city and was now approaching its outer limits.

"For some time, that is all of the news that we received. It is strange how this has worked. Through the years, we Jews have developed our networks to trade goods, and from our experience, we have found people that we could trust. These relationships have been remarkable in many ways. They have not only enhanced our businesses but given us people we could turn to for help or information across many countries of Europe.

"A few days ago, one of my men brought me a letter that he had been handed by one of our Belgian contacts in an area still free of Germans. By some miracle, this letter had been passed along a chain of trusted handlers passing from Sara through Germany and Belgium back to me here in Paris."

By now, the surroundings outside the taxi seemed to fade from Robert's consciousness, with his thoughts now concentrated on what Karl was saying.

"In the letter, Sara said that she was well and was helping Aaron in his trading activities, which have brought the two of them to the west of Germany and near the Belgian border. She was purposefully vague, implying that she did not want to compromise the people who have helped her should the letter fall into the wrong hands. She noted that she had seen much that had been discouraging, but she still remained hopeful of getting back to France someday."

Robert sat silently as the speed of the car picked up in the countryside, now nearly free of any other transportation aside from occasional farm wagons and military vehicles.

"Did your man know anything else besides what was contained in the letter?"

"He said he was told that both Aaron and Sara had subsequently gotten into Belgium under the auspices of the German Army and had been in contact with people we know there. It is from them that the letter ultimately was passed to us."

Robert's head was spinning from the implications of Karl's revelations. For Sara to have gotten as far as she had seemed a miracle, but somehow to have co-opted the German Army for her purposes seemed almost preposterous. Whatever her situation, knowing her as he did, Robert had new optimism that she would somehow prevail in managing her hazardous journey.

By now, they were pulling up on the southern outskirts of Chantilly, where a series of rolling hills sloped toward the east away from the city itself. The surroundings looked timeless with the rolling fields arranged in their medieval pattern around the surrounding villages. How discordant all this construction seemed among this background. As he directed the car to a stop, he paused before stepping out to ask one more question.

"Did Sara say anything else in her letter, Karl?"

Karl seemed to hesitate a moment before replying.

"She did, Robert, though it is somewhat embarrassing to speak of. She said that she loved me and Lydia and was thankful for all that we had done to help her throughout her life. She also asked that we pass on word of her situation to her parents. In closing, she asked that you be told that she is thinking of you always, and those thoughts are what give her the strength as she tries to get home to France. You will have to excuse me, Robert, but it's awkward for an old man to tell you such intimate things. Lydia had tried to get word to you the other day but could not get through your security."

"Tell Lydia that I appreciate the thought nevertheless."

After a moment's pause, during which Robert tried desperately to wrestle his mind back on the real problems now facing him, he stepped out of the car and began his evaluation of the ongoing work before him.

As Robert made his inspection of the ground near Chantilly, his trained eye took in all the subtle changes of contour that might give benefit to defensive fortifications. He carefully made notes and compared his findings to topographic maps that he had with him. In many ways, this was a routine he had done so many times that it was almost rote. What was different this time was the urgency of these projects. He was thankful that he would not have to oversee the actual build-out of projects, as he had done in the past, but simply would design and coordinate their completion.

The most recent intelligence suggested that this area was of increasing importance, making it necessary to see firsthand the state of the fortifications being constructed. His inspection fortunately took less time than he had anticipated, and soon he was back in the cab for his return to headquarters.

On his way back from Chantilly, Robert focused on finalizing his thoughts and recommendations so that they would be nearly completed by the time he returned to the office, speaking to Karl only episodically. By the time he had crossed the Alexander Bridge across the Seine to the long esplanade before Mansart's great gilded Dome of the Invalids, his work was nearly complete. As he prepared to leave the taxi, he once again turned to Karl.

"Karl, I want to thank you for the excellent service today. I doubt if anyone in Paris could have gotten me out and back as efficiently as you did."

"It has been my privilege, Robert. In the future, if you need my help, you have only to send word or phone our location."

"I certainly will.

"And, Karl, thank you for the information about Sara; it's been some of the best news I have heard since the war began. If you hear anything more, please let me know."

"I hope I will have an opportunity to do so soon."

20

Decisions

WORD OF THE SETBACK OF THE FRENCH OFFENSIVE was already getting back to Paris even before the dramatic announcement of the incorporation of Paris into the zone of the army. The news quickly was contorted by rumors that soon made it difficult to separate fact from innuendo.

Gallieni, stationed at his headquarters in the center of the city, had a firsthand view of the mood of the citizenry as the bad news regarding the status of the war intensified. He had feared that the civilian population, shielded from disconcerting news by the previous city government, might react adversely to the more somber information that they now were receiving through daily announcements from his communication officer. The information was unembellished and terse, purposely avoiding speculation or unconfirmed information. Its purpose was to inform in a way that gave each citizen facts that they might use to best meet their own needs.

These messages proved to have differing effects on various segments of the population. Some, in fear of the unknown, set about leaving the capital as soon as they could make reasonable arrangements. Others, motivated by a desire to see the crisis through, took on new resolve to face the challenges ahead.

Many now came forward, including many women, to offer their services in whatever capacity the authorities might find useful. Their cooperation gratified Gallieni, who had predicted such a response from a people he had long respected for their ability to function under stress.

Regardless of what decisions might be made, the recognition of the approaching German threat served as a clarion call to action for all, including Marie and her mother.

———

For Marie and her mother, a decision to leave for Lyon could no longer be postponed. For Madame Bonneau, the decision was obvious. If it were not for Marie, she would have left for Lyon some time ago. It was only Marie's insistence on being close to Robert during his recuperation that had kept her there. Now with Robert mended, Monsieur Bonneau was insisting that she return home along with Marie.

The problem was that Marie, despite the risks involved, was refusing to leave Paris. Upon hearing the news from the military government, Madame Bonneau had informed Marie that she intended to leave Paris as soon as arrangements for the two of them could be made to return to Lyon. Marie would not hear of it, claiming that it was her duty to stay and help attend to the wounded. Madame Bonneau had tried to turn to Robert to help persuade her daughter to leave, only to find that the present crisis made it virtually impossible to get through to him. Desperate for support to help argue her case, she turned to the only person remaining in Paris who she felt might help reason with Marie, Thomas d'Aveillard.

She was surprised with Thomas's prompt reply, given what she had heard from Marie of his difficulties in Strasbourg, and was relieved at his promise to meet her that very afternoon. As expected, Thomas arrived at the announced hour, eliciting a warm greeting from Madame Bonneau.

As the pair settled into a comfortable pair of chairs in the large drawing room looking out on the courtyard below, Madame Bonneau could not but help but note the change in Thomas's demeanor from the last time they had met. He not only was much thinner but also seemed to lack the usual vitality that she had long admired. For an instant, she regretted asking him to meet with her. Yet knowing there was no other alternative, after some hesitation she began.

"Thomas, I'm so happy to see you. Marie is not back from the hospital yet. She went in early this morning, and heaven knows when she will return. The hours she has been working lately are staggering."

"When I got your message, I came as soon as I could get free, as I know how much concern you have for Marie's safety."

"I can think of little else right now, Thomas. If it weren't for her being here, I would have gone to Lyon at the beginning of the war. Now all I can think of is another siege and possible occupation by the Germans. I have heard far too many horror stories of what happened during the Prussian War. No fit mother would be able to stand the thought of her daughter alone in such circumstances."

"Why has she refused to leave with you?"

"She seems intent to remain at her post, as she puts it. She believes that this crisis is coming to a head and that she is clearly needed here. She tells me that she couldn't live with herself if she left for Lyon and abandoned those wounded men who seem to be the focus of all she does these days."

"I have had the good fortune to know your daughter now for several years and have watched her mature in front of my eyes. Before this war, she was a young woman of exceptional talent and immense potential, but I often sensed she resented much about existing conventions and the limits they placed on her achieving the goals she might have in mind. Who could imagine that Marie would forsake her piano lessons to attend to wounded men? Unfortunately, I too have had similar experiences recently, and I know dealing with those problems trivializes virtually everything a person has done before."

"If this is too difficult for you to speak about, Thomas, I apologize," Madame Bonneau replied with concern in her voice.

"It is difficult to speak of but also necessary, because it might help the both of us understand how to deal with Marie.

"Before I returned to Paris, I spent many long hours in a hospital in Strasbourg, attending to young men like those Marie is now involved with. It is like no experience I or anyone could imagine. It is so far removed from the life Marie led just weeks ago; those hospitals are filled with unimaginable sights, tension, and life-and-death responsibilities. It is work that draws on your inner being and requires real strength to persevere. I must honestly tell you that I was severely affected by my experiences and am still trying to deal with them.

"It's for that reason that I was hesitant to come here today when I received your request, but I knew that I could not refuse, given all that you must be going through."

"Thomas, I appreciate you being here now even more," Madame Bonneau said with obvious sympathy.

"As I said, it will be worth it if I can help you deal with Marie.

"During the time we have been acquainted, I can honestly say that I know few people who have matured like she has over such a short lifetime. She has a deep moral sense of what is right and proper, which should make you and your husband very proud."

"We are, of course, very proud of our daughter, which makes it more difficult to think of her coming to harm."

"Madame Bonneau, Marie is a remarkable person, and I have no doubt she can admirably address challenges even of this magnitude. I also have no doubt in the sincerity of her concern for those young men. No undertaking, even one so sublime as her music, can compare with the emotion of helping another when so much is at risk. I have seen men suffering great pain act unselfishly toward others with such divine nobility as to give hope that if we can somehow survive this senseless killing, better things may follow. Believe me when I tell you that experiences like that are not something that one can easily walk away from."

"I don't doubt the need for many nurses and other women to attend to these tragic young men, but those women have come from different backgrounds than Marie. It seems to me that she could use her musical talent she has worked so hard to develop to help in other ways than what she now feels compelled to do."

"From our perspective, that would seem a logical thing to do, but these are times where logic has little place. I have been trying to deal with that reality since the war has started. No, I suspect that in the faces of these wounded men, Marie has seen more immediate use of her talents than refined salons and concert stages.

"You should also understand that she must have great skills in dealing with these young men. The work is too demanding and at times frightening to persist without a calling for it. Knowing Marie like I do, no doubt she is viewed as an angel by so many men in need. It would be hard to turn your back on such an avocation."

"As difficult as it is for me to accept, I know that there is much to what you are saying, Thomas. The question is, What should I do to help and protect her? She insists that I return to Lyon as soon as possible."

"Your daughter is wise beyond her years. She is right; your place is with your husband now."

"That may be, Thomas, but how can I ever be free from worry if I leave her here alone?"

"Regardless of what we might do, none of us will be free from worry in the coming days. These are times when the best of each of us is demanded. I happen to believe that Marie has earned her right to perform on this new and difficult stage. The question is, What can be done to support her? I'd like to suggest a possible solution if I might."

"Please do," Madame Bonneau said encouragingly.

"I know that I could never truly take your place, Madame Bonneau, but at present, I could provide support to Marie on short notice. If it would give you peace of mind, it would be a responsibility I would gladly undertake."

"I could not ask you to assume such a responsibility, Thomas."

"It would be my privilege, if it would help reassure you in any way. I too have great concern for Marie and consider myself her friend and hopefully someone she can confide in. You know full well that you should return to Lyon. Realistically, with Robert indisposed, I am the only one left to represent your interests here. You can be assured that I will do everything in my power to balance her needs with our concerns."

"Thomas, are you sure that you are up to this?"

"You have reasons to be concerned no doubt, but it is just such a responsibility that I need to shake me out of fruitless ruminations and to reengage in something worthwhile."

"Knowing you as I do, Thomas, and hearing the sincerity in your voice, I believe you still are the only person I can trust with such a task. I will still need to think more about this and discuss your proposal with my husband and, of course, Marie."

"Of course, but I would urge that whatever you and Marie decide, you do it as quickly as possible."

"I have train tickets in hand for Lyon that will ensure just such action, Thomas. I will contact you as soon as Marie and I have made a decision."

"Then I look forward to hearing from you soon."

"One other thing, Thomas; in the future, please call me by my first name, Margarite, if you would.

"It would be my pleasure, Margarite."

As Thomas departed, Margarite Bonneau felt both a sense of relief and gratitude to have found someone to help protect Marie from dangerous impetuosity. She also had concerns, however, that Thomas's present condition might compromise his effectiveness. She seized on Thomas's sincerity to help allay those worries bolstered by the prospect of a long overdue reunion with her husband. Regardless, she now understood that the specter of worry would no doubt be an unwelcome companion in the coming days.

———

Since control of the city and region had been effectively placed under the army, Robert and all the staff had been working throughout the day and long into the night. When he was not compelled to leave headquarters, Robert found it convenient to stay close to his office, which was just down the hall from his makeshift quarters, dubbed the walking wounded wing due to the number of rehabilitating officers quartered there. One such man was a Colonel Girondon, who roomed next to Robert and was assigned to the intelligence bureau. Conveniently, these offices were next to the walking wounded wing, and with its large map room, the bureau proved to be a convenient place to quickly assess the present state of the war.

Robert had begun to show up in the map room whenever he took a break from his work or before he turned in for the night. He inevitably found Girondon there, limited by a shattered leg, perched at a desk nearby to the large map. Here Girondon could carefully monitor any changes in the affairs of the battles represented in the position of the various colored icons. Such observations, along with the information flowing into the Second Bureau, formed the basis for Girondon's often keen analysis, which Robert had come to use to plan his own day's activities. When news came suddenly that as part of a governmental shakeup Messimy was being replaced as war minister by Millerand, the first place Robert went was to Girondon.

"What do you make of this, my friend?"

"We have had a good sense this was coming since late yesterday. The government has been in a state of panic, made worse by Viviani's near-constant hysteria. Poincaré has decided that for the sake of a responsible and credible government, something had to be done. That something was a cabinet shakeup in which reliable and proven former cabinet members were brought in to offset Viviani's incompetence."

"Why get rid of Messimy? He was one of the few members of the government aside from Poincaré who seemed to have any idea about what to do."

"Politicians always need a scapegoat to blame when things go bad. They would like to fire Joffre as a gesture, but Gallieni squelched that immediately. Messimy was the next best thing. Joffre was his choice as army chief and responsible for the doctrine emphasizing the offensive and attack. Now that the great planned offensive has been repulsed and the country is at risk of being overrun, who better to blame than Messimy, who promoted this scheme.

"Also, President Poincaré needed someone he could rely on as war minister. If Messimy was going to get the boot, Poincaré felt the best qualified man to replace him was Millerand, Messimy's predecessor. Millerand would agree to join the government only on the condition that he get his old job back. Thus, Millerand is in, and Messimy is out."

"I hope to God that he can get us those three corps that Messimy promised General Gallieni. We are building trenches and fortifications day and night on our north and northeast, tearing down whole blocks of buildings in Paris, blowing up bridges, and even guarding the access to the sewers. None of that will amount to anything if we don't get those troops."

"Millerand is a politician, but he knows the army," Girondon replied. "He also is in accord with General Gallieni with regard to the need to defend Paris at all costs. There will be no fall off in his support for obtaining those troops. If it is any consolation, we have en route from the south a reserve cavalry division along with three divisions of territorial troops who will be arriving by train tonight. Unfortunately, Joffre has also pulled three divisions from the garrison to be stationed to the north between the British and the ocean."

"My god, doesn't he know how badly we need those troops?" Robert replied plaintively.

"Look at this map, and you can see why he did it. The latest aerial photos are very helpful in giving us an understanding of the status of the front, and what they are showing is not encouraging." Girondon gestured as he limped from his desk to point out features on the large map before them.

"I was afraid of that."

"Well, my friend, it is becoming very clear what is in store for the country to our northeast," Girondon continued as he pulled up a chair in front of the wall map.

"The main German offensive, as we feared, has crossed Flanders and, due to the present configuration of our forces, now has a very favorable route to Paris in front of them. Unless Joffre can get more troops from the south to confront them, our work here will soon get very interesting. There are other things they have going for them as well."

"Such as?" Robert asked with concern.

"First off, the scale of their attack is much larger than many thought possible. Secondly, these are the more elite elements of their combined forces, being comprised of two Prussian armies and a third of Saxons. They are engaging our Fifth Army and the British on the extreme left of our lines and vastly outnumber them. Lanzerac is a professional and will do what is necessary to protect his army, but unfortunately, what is necessary is now being dictated as much by the British as the Germans.

"They are falling back without any attempt to engage the German forces. It is strange, because they fought so well in their first engagement at Mons. Now it seems that their troops have a greater appetite for the fight than their leaders. Joffre has tried to get their General French to stand in line with the Fifth Army to stabilize the withdrawal, but the only thing he has gotten from his efforts seems to be a more rapid withdrawal of the British, forcing Lanzerac and the Firth Army back with them to prevent a gap forming in the lines."

"Or losing contact with the sea," said Robert. "If that happens, the Germans can easily flank us."

"Exactly. That is why Joffre is drawing three corps from the south to form the Sixth Army to bring into position on the left flank of the line between the BEF and the sea. That is also why it is so critical to engage and delay the Germans long enough until those troops arrive.

"I just returned from a meeting with some of my contacts in British intelligence," Girondon continued. "They seem dismayed at the lack of resolve that is now evident with General French and his staff. They tell me that the field commanders, especially Smith-Dorrain and to some degree Haig, remain committed to carrying the fight to the Germans, and I am told by British intelligence that the troops themselves still have high morale and resolve."

"That is some cause for hope at least," Robert said with more enthusiasm in his voice.

Girondon added, "Apparently, General French was given instructions on embarking to France to maintain autonomy of control of his troops and avoid the destruction of the army. He and his staff now seem possessed by the idea that the French have lost the war, and consequently they are taking measures to ensure British troops are able to escape the continent intact should disaster befall their allies. Their recent actions have been such as to make a stand on the Somme, as Joffre had hoped impossible.

"What my friends in British intelligence called me about was word of French's newest directive."

"Who are you dealing with there?" asked Robert.

"Several people, but my most reliable contact is Colonel Phillip Marks."

"I know him," exclaimed Robert. "We met during a strategy conference before the war in Britain. He seemed then to be a reliable sort."

"He and many of his associates make little effort to hide their distaste for what French is doing. That is why they called me over today. It seems that the field marshal has written London, describing his intention of withdrawing the British forces completely out of the line with the French behind the Seine. Such a withdrawal could clearly presage another to the west of Paris."

"If he does that, the French forces will be compelled to collapse back to Paris or even farther to the west."

"Exactly! That is why I wanted you and all of the staff to know about this as soon as possible.

"There is something, however, that Marks told me that holds out some hope for the situation. It seems that there is significant resistance to this idea of withdrawal in London."

"From whom?"

"Marks says that shortly after French's directive was forwarded to London, the British embassy here received word that Lord Kitchener would be making an unanticipated visit to Paris to confer with General French. He will be arriving by special train late this evening. A conference is to be set up with French and his staff for early tomorrow morning. In the interim, any action implied by the directive will be suspended until further consultation with the war minister."

"We can only hope that Kitchener is here to supply some backbone."

"Well, that won't be an easy task if you listen to General Lanzerac, who has nothing but contempt for the fighting qualities of their command."

"Well, let's hope Kitchener lives up to his reputation and gets the job done. Otherwise, we will have to drastically change the orientation and breadth of our defenses."

That prospect sobered both men as they stared quietly at the wall map, seemingly searching for some way out of the dilemma they seemed to be in. It was evident that in the event of a full-scale British withdrawal, the time left to ready Paris to face a German assault would be far shorter, a possibility that added even more uncertainty and worry to a task already straining the capacity of everyone charged with defending her.

21

The Extended Family

AARON AND SARA'S TRIP TO BRUSSELS WAS IN MANY ways a shorter version of their journey to Liège. During the morning's journey, the panorama that unfolded provided much to think about. Along the Meuse on the outskirts of Liège, the destruction around the various citadels was enormous, and evidence of recent fighting persisted for some way toward Brussels, until finally giving way to a zone where most of the villages and cities remained unscathed.

The German Army was an ever-present feature throughout, spread out in long lines of marching soldiers accompanied by horse- and motor-drawn transports laden with soldiers, supplies, and heavy weaponry. The number of troops seemed only to increase as they progressed farther to the west, and by the time they arrived in Brussels, they found the central city transformed into a virtual German metropolis. What remained of the Belgian populace seemed to be marginalized to areas away from the train station and central city.

Soon the entire party was transported to a rather pleasant hotel a short distance from the station, where Sara and Aaron were now each given their own room, albeit spartan in nature.

After checking in, Aaron soon set out to find his cousin. Winding his way through the streets near the train station, he passed through the Grand Place, now filled with German soldiers laughing and taking photographs as if they were on holiday. After several minutes of walking in a quarter of old and narrow streets, he arrived at a plain brick building with only the simplest of signs indicating the nature of the premises. He entered through a small side door, and in a small, well-kept office, he found his cousin Emile.

Emile rose quickly from his desk to greet him.

"Aaron, we've been expecting you. I'm happy to see you again, even though I suspect Paul thinks you have become an agent for the German Army."

"It would be easy for him to think that, no doubt."

"Sit down, Aaron, and make yourself comfortable," Emil instructed while nodding to a small chair near the desk where he was sitting.

"What brings you here, Aaron? If it's to advocate for the Germans, I must tell you that after all they've done, there is no way I can have anything to do with them."

"Emile, the Germans like to think that I am working for them, but they are actually working for me and my associates. I have come here to offer you something that you and those who depend on you need."

"Which is?"

"Business! Good, stable, and profitable business."

"If it's with the Germans, it can't be good."

"Hear me out, Emile. As it exists now, the Germans have the power to control what you sell and the price that you will get. If you do not accept this reality, you will no longer have a market for the livestock that you and your suppliers need. You are fooling yourselves if you think that you can deal in the usual manner with your old customers. They have the means to control your market and, unless I am mistaken, will continue to have for some time."

"What makes you so sure of that?"

"I'm not sure, and believe me, I hope that I'm wrong, but the German Army is clearly building up across the north of Belgium and shows no signs of drawing away from this area. Unless there is a dramatic reversal, their presence will continue, and the longer it persists, the more power they will have over everyone's affairs. If unchecked, they will control all aspects of Belgian life that they view most important, which most certainly will include supplying their army."

"If what you say is true, Aaron, what option do we have but to cooperate or go out of business?"

"You have many more options than you think, Emile. Think about it for a minute. You have access to one of the things that they need most: a supply of quality livestock. That gives you significant leverage over even the most brazen invader.

"You can enhance your leverage by joining a large group that will guarantee the number and quality of supply that the Germans depend on. Then you will be in position to dictate to them. Already in Germany, men like you are coming together into an ever-more powerful alliance. Going forward, the German authorities will have to provide favorable terms to us or risk the immediate disruption of their supply chain, which they cannot withstand for any length of time.

"With your contacts and reputation, you have the capability of controlling the trading operations with the Germans here in Belgium, as I hope we are on the way of doing in Germany."

"That is the problem, Aaron; we would have to deal with the Germans. Even if I could rationalize such actions in business terms, I doubt if I could get many of my associates to go along."

"Then ultimately, I am afraid you will all be marginalized. The German I'm working with, Emile, is one of the better ones. He sees the future of Europe in terms of a cooperative economic union in which Germany will be the first of equals. In return for access to a reliable supply of quality livestock, he will be happy to oblige the sellers with a fair price and the leeway to sell their products beyond their agreed-upon quota to whomever they choose."

"How do we know that he will keep his word or not be overridden by some superior?"

"I suspect he will keep his word not just because he is trustworthy but because he cannot afford to alienate good suppliers. I also have a good understanding of their needs, and there should be enough supply remaining for you to sell locally."

"For now, but they would have the authority to change their demands in the future."

"They could, but if you represent a large and dependable group of sellers who they have come to depend upon, they would do so at risk of alienating you, something that would be costly for them to do. What is being offered, although I am not sure that they readily understand, is an opportunity to establish a cartel. Once that is in place, the cost and effort it will take to dismantle it will not be easy to justify as long as the war is in doubt."

"I see what you are saying, Aaron, and it's beginning to make some sense. Somehow, I expected as much of you all along, despite Paul's concerns. Our people have had to deal with many other undesirable buyers in Europe throughout the centuries to survive. This is no different. I just wish there was a more palatable way to sell it to my associates."

"There is one possibility I have been thinking of. If you were not to agree with my proposals, I was going to ask you for the names of other people who would be willing to work with the Germans. I believe we could use one or two such people to our advantage. I suspect that the Germans would be willing to pay a small premium to them for nothing more than acting as some form of final transfer agent. In that way, your sellers could obtain the benefits of pricing and flexibility without having to suffer the embarrassment of dealing directly with the Germans themselves."

After a moment, Emile replied, "Yes, I suppose something like that could work. The man or men in question should probably be somewhat respectable. Yes, I can think of two brothers who might work out well for all of us. Let me talk with some of the others, and then I will get back with you tomorrow morning."

As Aaron got up to leave, Emile added in parting, "Aaron, it is good to see you again, and I do appreciate what you are offering, even if it means helping the Germans. Under the circumstances, I can see few better alternatives to what you are proposing."

"Emile, there is one other thing."

"Yes?"

"There is a young woman with me who is a friend of my wife."

"I suppose she is one of her political cronies?"

"She is a Socialist but not one of the wilder ones that come around from time to time. I doubt if you would ever catch her blowing up some office or threatening some official's life. In fact, I find her remarkably intelligent and practical."

"So, what is she doing here with you now?"

"There is a slight problem with her in Germany at present. She's French."

"French?"

"Yes, I'm afraid so. She was the head of the Berlin bureau of a Paris socialist newspaper."

"Why didn't she get out of Germany before the war started?"

"Young people are blinded by their idealism and by their seeming invulnerability. Don't you remember being like that?"

"Reality quickly shook some sense into me, as I'm sure it has for this young lady. I hope she understands how vulnerable all of us are now. Dealing with her situation is far more difficult and dangerous than dealing with trading livestock with the Germans," said Emile plaintively.

"I am not as young or as spry as you, Aaron, and since this war has started, I have made it my point to stay as close to home as possible. I have also tried to keep as low a profile as possible and to avoid any contacts with the Germans unless I have to."

"You're saying you don't know if you can get her to the French?"

"I don't know for certain, but Paul and his friends might be able to help. He has taken this invasion very hard and, along with many of his close friends, has become very bitter toward the Germans."

"I know. If the stories he told me in Liège are even half-true, he has a reason to be bitter."

"I hope that his hatred doesn't make him do anything rash for his own sake, but I know that he is cooperating with a number of other young men not only in Liège but throughout the country to try and organize resistance to any German occupation."

"He is a bright and idealistic young man, Emile, but it is a very dangerous business."

"I know that all too well, Aaron. Nevertheless, if there is a way to get this young woman out of Belgium, he or one of his friends would know as well as anyone."

"There is something that might help this matter, Emile. The Germans, or at least the German that I work with, has come to trust Sara. He thinks she is my niece and has come to appreciate her contributions to my work. He has given us a letter identifying us as designated associates if we are stopped by the German authorities here in Belgium. I suspect he could modify that letter to continue such protection if I could convince him that it is necessary for her to stay here to help organize efforts while I return to Germany."

"No doubt it would be very helpful if you can get such a letter. Paul is scheduled to return to Brussels tonight, as he does every two weeks, to discuss our business operations around Liège. It would be a good opportunity to bring up your French woman's difficulties to see if he has any ideas about how to get her back home."

"It seems, Emile, that I have brought quite a few distractions with me for you to worry with."

"Distractions are sometimes worthwhile. Let me work on these to see what can be done, and I'll get back with you tomorrow."

By the following afternoon, Sara and Aaron were gathered in Emile's home, where they were met not only by Emile but by his wife, Maude, and their son, Paul, as well. After Aaron introduced Sara to the gathering, Emile looked at her with a mixture of curiosity and pleasant surprise. Paul appeared much more reserved, as if suspicious of this unusual guest.

Emile quickly said, "Sara, Aaron has told me a little about your situation. If I might ask a rather simple question, why is it that you want to get back to France now?"

"The obvious answer is that in Germany, my presence as a French national is now illegal and is certainly not welcomed in occupied Belgium. In Germany, not only was I in danger, but so were many others like Aaron and his wife, who risked their own safety to shelter me. I worried more for them than for myself, and this gave me even more impetus to try and escape to the west."

"You are in Belgium now," Emile said. "We are all living here as hostages in our own country. Your situation here is not much different from our own."

"What you are saying is true unfortunately. If there is no other alternative, I would prefer to stay here rather than to return to Germany, if there is a way of doing so without compromising Aaron. There are many other reasons why I would prefer to get back home, however."

"Possibly a young man?" suggested Maude hopefully.

"There is a young man, but I'm not sure if he is even alive, as he is a major in the French Army. There are other things as well. If I stay here in Belgium, I will be forced to live in fear of being detected by the Germans, which will significantly curtail my activities."

"In what way?" asked Emile.

"Perhaps I should give you a brief understanding of what I did before I arrived at your lovely home today. Before the war, I was involved with the peace movement in Germany and throughout Europe. I did everything I could to oppose this war, knowing what it would bring.

"At that time, however, I could not conceive of the scale of damage that has already taken place, and seeing it makes me even more determined to fight against this war. This war must end for all our sakes. What I now understand, however, is that it cannot end with the Germans winning and controlling our lives either here in Belgium or France. We must all fight a Germany led by militarists who are now behaving like their barbarian ancestors. It is not enough to merely exist here in Belgium; I must go somewhere where I will have many more options to oppose them."

For the first time, Paul spoke more than a perfunctory sentence. "Sara, you are not alone in wanting to fight these people. The war came so suddenly that many of the men that I know were not able to fight along with our comrades in the army. Now with Liège overrun, we face the reality of having to fight them in other ways besides on the battlefield. You may be French, but I can assure you that a place could be found for you here in Belgium to fight the Germans, if that is what you want."

"If that's what I'm left with, then I would be willing to do what I can to help you, Paul. I believe that I could do more in France, however, if the French remain free and the war continues. I have more resources available to me at home than I would have here, where we must act covertly."

"What do you think, Paul?" Maude asked. "Is it possible that Sara could get through the German lines into France?"

"Under the usual circumstances as things exist now, it might be possible, but it would be difficult and dangerous. Father mentioned a letter that Aaron has that gives him immunity with the German authorities. If Sara has a similar letter, then it might improve her odds of success considerably."

"How is that?" asked Aaron.

"We are now many miles behind the advancing German front, which is moving westward nearly every day. To even get close to this front without a document allowing for travel into these regions would mean that she will have to travel essentially by foot, as obtaining a seat on a train without such a letter would be virtually impossible. I could not get here from Liège until the military situation was stabilized."

"I am sure that your father must have discussed our present relationship with the German authorities, Paul," Aaron interjected. "I think it very likely that I could get some type of travel permit from my German contacts that would allow Sara, along with other companions, the means to travel for purposes of organizing more forward supply chains."

"That would be very helpful," Paul replied with increased interest.

"I agree with Paul," said Emile. "I have also had some frank discussions with my associates since our conversation yesterday, Aaron. Not all of them are completely convinced, but all are willing to explore your proposal further by setting up a meeting between us and your German contact."

"I have spoken to him already, Emile, and have told him of our discussions. I have emphasized the importance of confidentiality and have already explored the terms of payment and quotas that they would be looking for. You will have to judge for yourself, but I suspect that the terms will be agreeable to you, with some modifications to meet your specific needs. He knows how important it is to get and keep reliable suppliers and is willing to do what it takes to cultivate such relationships."

"If what you say is true, then we have grounds for further discussion. My associates want some guarantee that we will be able to supply our own people."

"I think, Emile, that with sufficient numbers, you will have the leverage to readily negotiate such a prerogative."

"I hope that what you say is correct," Paul said hopefully. "I am beginning to see how this relationship might give us many advantages, not the least of which is to exploit the Germans from the inside. If we can get some type of preferred travel pass, this could prove invaluable in many ways, not the least of which would be to get Sara closer to France."

"As I mentioned, I think that could be arranged if there is no unresolved military issue in the areas where you might be going," Aaron said.

"At present," continued Paul, "those issues are along the Meuse and the surrounding areas. As of now, the Germans have not had the inclination to swing farther to the north. That is Flemish territory in these regions and well known to us. Perhaps it would be wise to travel there to meet with our friends, and while there, we might just find a way for Sara to cross into France."

"I always wanted to see Ghent," Sara said with a smile.

"Then it's toward Ghent and our new venture," said Aaron.

They all took up their glasses and boisterously toasted the proposal.

Over the next hours, Sara was caught up in the pleasure of the evening as Aaron and his family shared a meal and old memories. The effect seemed to boost the spirits of all present, providing a new sense of optimism for the coming days.

22

Leaving

AS THE MONTH OF AUGUST NEARED AN END, EACH day seemed to bring some new understanding of the threat posed by the collective menace of the German Army. Marie watched as the city was buffeted by unwelcome news from the front—or worse yet, rumor. She realized, like everyone remaining, that this was an August that Paris had not faced since the Prussian War in 1871.

August was usually the month in which many Parisians with the means to do so escaped the heat of the city for family vacations in the south or on the seacoasts. In their place were countless foreign visitors. Paris summers in the recent past were characterized by the mixture of many different languages and cultures, which the French to varying degrees tolerated as the necessary price for living in the world's most beautiful city. This summer, except for the occasional diplomat or Allied soldier, the entire city was left to the French.

That population had changed dramatically. Those with the resources who were not required to remain in Paris had been escaping to more distant areas of the country less threatened by the advancing German hordes. Now Paris was increasingly comprised of those who were required to be there and those who had no other option but to stay. Neither Thomas nor Marie fit these categories, and despite the increased peril to the city, neither regretted being there during this most remarkable time. For Marie's mother, however, the time had come to leave for Lyon.

Thomas had accompanied Marie and her mother to the train station to help transport her belongings. The Gare de Lyon was crowded with similarly dressed men, women, and families, looking almost like a painting of Pissarro depicting some scene of Parisians setting out on their August holiday.

As Marie and her mother said their final goodbyes in the crowded queue beside the train, Thomas hung back. Then he stepped forward as the older woman prepared to enter the train.

"Margarite, I wish that we could part under more normal circumstances. I know there is little that I can say that will ease your concerns, but I believe you are doing what is right for you and your husband by leaving today.

"Only God knows what lies in store for us now, but you can take comfort knowing that your daughter is doing important work in staying here."

"I know that, Thomas, and it does make me proud to think of her in this way. Still, it will be impossible not to worry about her while I'm in Lyon."

"Margarite, I will try to do everything possible to act in your place, if that is of any comfort. You can be sure that I too am concerned for Marie and certainly don't want her to take any undo risks."

"That is the best that I could ask for, Thomas. Marie and I both are fortunate to have you here in Paris."

She then turned one last time to Marie for a final embrace before boarding her train, whose conductor was whistling its imminent departure. Thomas once again withdrew to give the two women as much privacy as the crowded platform would allow. Then Marie joined him, waving feverishly to her mother, who was pressed against the window as the train gathered speed and left the station.

For a moment, Marie grasped Thomas's arm in hers, trying to suppress her sobbing. Then composing herself, she began to walk slowly, leading them from the platform.

For some time, they walked silently arm in arm, perhaps not daring to break the solemnity of the moment with ill-chosen words. Then as they entered the great atrium of the Gare de Lyon, the bright lights and alluring aromas of the Restaurant Blue captured their attention, providing a welcome spot to recover from the distressing chores of the morning. Almost without saying a word, they paused before the colorful décor and then entered, finding a small table near the back of the restaurant. For a moment, they sat silently. At last, Marie spoke.

"I cannot tell you how much I appreciate what you told my mother this morning, Thomas. I know your presence helped to reassure her."

"It was a relief to see her return to your father, so I'm pleased if I helped make her trip less stressful."

After a short interruption in which a waiter took their order, Marie resumed.

"I suppose we need to discuss what each of us intends to do now that I have been given responsibility for my own affairs."

"I intend to do just what I told your mother—that is to be available for you any time that you might need me and to provide advice that your own parents might offer. I told your mother the other day that you have earned your independence, but in her absence, I would try to present her concerns whenever necessary. You need to understand that any such advice comes only with your best interests at heart."

"Thomas, it upsets me to hear you talk like my father. I remember the old times where you taught me lessons far more sublime than those we are now trying to master. I also recall even more vividly our feelings when you left for Strasbourg. There seems to be little place for the old notions of love and hope now. Yet if that moment still means as much to you as it does me, I believe that our relationship must change by being honest with each other and discarding the conventions of student and mentor."

"Marie, you have to understand that I have no intention of dictating your actions. I only intend to keep your mother's concerns in mind. You have earned the right to your independence. As for our relationship, I have no desire to return to those student days either."

"I do not intend to have this war destroy us, Thomas, but it's difficult for me to think too much of the past right now, as it's too painful and takes my focus away from what needs to be done now."

They paused for a moment to enjoy their first course as it arrived, appreciating this moment of reprise provided by the small luxury of a meal that they might have taken for granted not long ago.

After a moment, Marie resumed. "Thomas, I truly meant what I said about your words with Mother this morning. Even more important was the way you said them. I was so worried after seeing you that day you returned from Strasbourg. Today, with Mother, I saw a bit of the Thomas I knew before."

"Marie, before I left for Strasbourg, I often tried to share my belief with you in the importance of reason and spirituality for living worthwhile lives. Then when I saw firsthand the carnage of the war, the reality brought me to a place I had never been before.

"When I returned to Paris, I was searching desperately for some reminders of those peaceful days past. When I first saw you and Robert, it gave me a feeling of hope that I had not felt for some time. Yet that feeling did not last, and as I roamed my old haunts, even this beautiful city failed to lift me as in the past.

"No doubt, much of this had to do with how so much has changed from what I remembered and loved. Many places, such as our old backroom gathering spot at the Bièvre, have disappeared or have been dramatically changed. Paul, the owner of the Bièvre, has tried to keep track of the many old regulars that were an important part of my life then. So many have been wounded or even killed that his accounts gave finality to any hope that those days would ever return."

"I'm so sorry to hear of their losses, Thomas," Marie said with genuine sincerity.

"As you know, Marie, that awful reality is what we now face, but at least more are alive than not, although there is one of our friends whose whereabouts remains unknown. Sara Morosovski, who was a friend of Robert, was in Berlin when the war broke out and has yet to be heard from."

"I don't think that I know her or even heard Robert mention her name."

"I doubt if you ever had the opportunity to meet her or any of our old group for that matter. She was one of the more remarkable members or our informal circle. She was studying law, and although she came from a wealthy Jewish family, her greatest concern was for the working class and the poor. She was working for the Socialists, heading the Berlin branch of their newspaper, *L'Humanité*."

"Well, at least there is no confirmation of anything serious, and without that, you can still hope that everything might work out for the best."

"To work out for the best. That is the hope that we all used to live by, Marie," Thomas said wistfully.

"Perhaps it still may be someday. I at least have escaped the daily stresses of attending to the wounded and am around people that care for me and have tried to help me deal with my imaginary pains."

"I have seen you, Thomas, and know your pain was real. You have no right to think of it in any other way."

"Regardless of how I might think about it, Marie, with God's help, I now seem to be getting better. My mistake was believing that I could reason through my problem, just as I had done so many times in the past. Fortunately, the bishop is a perceptive and kind man. He could see how distraught I was on returning from Strasbourg. He perhaps had been forewarned by his colleagues there, but he quickly took pains to see that I was given the time necessary to deal with my feelings. Also, my uncle proved to be an immense help."

"Your uncle the priest?"

"Yes, when the war broke out, he was still in Italy but returned to Paris, given the uncertain alliance the Italians had with the Germans at that time. When I talked to him, he quickly sensed the difficulties I was having in trying to reconcile my beliefs with what I had seen. He rightfully pointed out how in the long history of mankind, violence and destruction were an all too frequent part of history. Even as we were walking, he showed me the spot where the bishop was killed by members of the communard on the grounds of Notre Dame itself.

"He reminded me that at times, even for the best, reason alone cannot provide understanding. Good men have often wrestled with the same fearful questions when confronting a world disfigured by violence and war. At some point, you realize some questions remain unanswerable and understand that faith in God and his omnipotence provides a way to deal with the many uncertainties we face. My healing started when I realized that I could not explain the presence of evil but should instead concentrate on how I needed to act as a child of God."

Marie, clearly sensing the pain that Thomas's doubts had caused, asked, "Thomas, why didn't you come to me before?"

"How could I come to you, Marie, when everything told me that I was no longer the man that you had known before?"

"Oh, Thomas, don't you realize how little that meant to me when I could so clearly see the pain in your eyes?"

"Marie, your support is more than I could ever hope for. You have to understand, however, that I am still nursing myself back to where I once was, despite my reassurances to your mother."

"That I can respect and understand, Thomas, but I will not stand by passively, especially if I see you returning to the state you were in."

Thomas's features seemed to brighten in hearing this, and he said, "I would welcome your help as always, Marie, especially since I am determined to provide the support that I promised your mother. For both our sakes, it would be helpful to know what your plans are for the next few days."

"Well, if anything, Thomas, my work seems more important than ever, given how the war seems to be going. The conditions through all the hospitals that I've been in the last few days have deteriorated as the sheer number of wounded has overwhelmed their capacity. More doctors and trained medical personnel have come into the city from the provinces, but it never seems enough to deal with the inflow of those who need help.

"The army is requisitioning suitable facilities throughout the city that can serve to house the wounded, but the more specialized facilities, such as receiving wards and operating rooms, take time to set up and staff. Lately these conditions have forced a change in my work. Due to my recent training and experience, I'm now more involved in dealing directly with the medical staffs and, when needed, even the patients."

"What of your old job?"

"I have trained others to do what I did previously. There are several other women that I know to be capable and who can be relied on. If something unusual should come up that pertains to my old job, they all know where to find me. Given all that is going on, it seems that most of our roles are in constant flux, determined as much by our skill and willingness to work as much as any formal training."

"Are you planning to work every day this week?"

"I'm not sure what my schedule will be. We are so overwhelmed I feel that I need to be at work every day, unless I'm too tired to show up."

"I know all too well, Marie, from my own experience that you must make time for yourself. If you do, you will work with more efficiency and be better able to endure the stress that comes from it."

"That is easier said than done some days, Thomas, as you know. How can you turn away when so many need help, even if it means working extra hours?"

"It's hard, Marie, but for the sake of not only your health but any soldiers that you might be caring for, you have to try and be in the best condition possible."

"I will try, Thomas, but perhaps I should be keeping track of you as well, given what you've told me today, because you will try to overdo as soon as you feel better."

Thomas could not help but smile at Marie's suggestion. "I see now how quickly things have changed, Marie. You really have come a long way from that girl I met years ago.

"Marie, this meeting has been very productive. It has given me confidence and determination to resume some of my previous duties."

"Are you sure you are ready for that, Thomas? After what you have been through, I don't want to see you in the shape you were."

"I am truly thankful for your concern, Marie, but helping your mother has already given me a renewed sense of worth."

"I know you too well, Thomas, and despite what your bishop might think, if unsupervised, you might get ahead of yourself in what you take on."

"That is a risk I'm willing to take, Marie. This talk makes reclaiming my old life very important to me now."

"Thomas, I don't have the time to lecture you, as I need to get to my shift at the hospital. This discussion makes it very clear, however, that I can't leave you to your own devices, despite what you say about your bishop's oversight. For your sake as much as mine, we need to make time at least every other day to meet."

Marie's tone of voice was softened by a smile lighting up her face, which was quickly reciprocated by Thomas.

His broad smile, long absent since his return from Strasbourg, seemed to further inspire Marie to continue.

"Thomas, I want you to know that I would not have been able to insist on staying here in Paris, despite the brave face that I put on, if I had not known that you would be here to help me. It is hard to deal with things as they are now but would be almost impossible to face alone."

"You will not be alone while I'm here, Marie."

"Nor will you, Thomas."

23

Retreat

GENERAL JOSEPH JOFFRE HAD COME TO DEPEND ON and even relish his frequent trips from his headquarters to the front. In moments of crisis, he felt it necessary to get closer to the battle to better appreciate how his commanders and their men were dealing with the circumstances of the moment. His driver was a famous grand prix racer, whose expertise in handling the big touring car while coaxing the maximum allowable speed from its powerful engine further added to his journeys, infusing even the routine with an element of excitement. He had also come to appreciate the moments of isolation that these trips provided, allowing him to reflect on what he might have seen and learned on the day's visit.

What he learned from these trips was vital to managing the war. From the very first engagements, he had paid close attention to the actions of his field commanders, and his observations gave him information about their competence that he could not gain at a distant headquarters. As the great offensive upon which so much had been gambled faltered, he knew that it was imperative to reorganize his field command, and his accumulated observations made it easier to rid himself of commanders that he felt vacillated or failed in their duties.

Very quickly, he had removed many division commanders, and soon he would reach higher. General Ruffy, who had been highly excitable and lacking the evident self-control he felt essential for a commander of an army, was dismissed and replaced by General Sarrail as commander of the Third Army.

The Fifth Army was a more difficult matter. There, General Lanzerac, despite his quarrelsome manner, was clearly competent, having recognized the German threat early on and initiating measures to avoid the destruction of his flank during the height of the battles around Charleroi. Lanzerac was always difficult for him to manage, given his independence and volatility, and his intellect as well as his standing among his peers intimidated him. All of this had made it more difficult to make a command change, even though he had seen warning signs that Lanzerac was no longer capable of managing his command. Recently, despite Lanzerac's objections, he had to insist that the Fifth Army counterattack the advancing Germans at Guise and Saint Quentin. Remaining at headquarters to oversee the battles, he could not help but notice Lanzerac's apparent exhaustion as the afternoon progressed, sprawled in a chair and staring passively as messages came in from the battlefield.

That night as he thought over the day's events, he dwelled on that image of Lanzerac. By morning, he made his decision; after further inquiries, he returned to Fifth Army headquarters and, without much formality, simply drew Lanzerac aside and told him that he appreciated what he had done, but as things now stood, it was time for him to step down.

He was relieved that Lanzerac did not challenge his decision openly, instead accepting the news calmly, as if relieved from the burdens of dealing with the present situation.

What both men knew was that for France to survive, its army must not be dealt a lethal blow. That they had lost the initiative in their offensive and had sustained enormous numbers of casualties was apparent. What was not apparent to the pessimists was that these losses had not been fatal. Both also knew that the tactics necessary for the immediate future were straightforward. In the coming days, the French Army would have to engage the enemy in violent defensive battles, ceding territory only when it was necessary to preserve the integrity of the army. To that end, Lanzerac was ill-suited and had to go.

Joffre realized that he alone would be accountable for managing this difficult transition, but given the appropriate help, he felt confident that he could save France from the threat it now faced. To that end, he had relieved Lanzerac and in his place had elevated Franchet d'Esperey the commander of the First Corps. Franchet d'Esperey had little of the intellect of his predecessor or his introspection. Instead, he was a man of action, with a demanding if not violent temperament in the heat of battle. For all his faults. he possessed what was needed most at this time: unflinching courage and the will to take the battle to the enemy. Before dismissing Lanzerac, Joffre had asked Franchet d'Esperey about his fitness to lead an army. His acceptance was short and direct.

Now with the change at the top of the Fifth Army completed, Joffre felt a brief sense of disappointment as the powerful Citroen slowed, knowing that this usually presaged their arrival at headquarters. Indeed, as he looked up from the maps he had been studying, he saw the road leading to the French GHQ come into sight and began to mentally prepare for the barrage of information and concerns his staff would bring him.

The anticipated onslaught came almost immediately upon his arrival. The usual order and calm of the large ground floor was now less evident, with staff officers moving between various offices or huddling in discussion groups in the hallways. Expecting his chief of staff, General Belin, Joffre was instead met by his chief intelligence officer, whose worried expression further enhanced his unease. He was therefore relieved to find that Belin's absence was due to a call he was having with government officials in Paris and not related to worsening military developments.

As was his habit, Joffre made for the large map room adjacent to his office, now followed closely by his intelligence chief. Here the iconographic representations quickly made clear the problem confronting him. As he stared at the position of the advancing German forces on his left flank, for a fleeting moment he had a sense that all his recent efforts in the reorganization of his command might be an exercise in futility. Then he forced himself to clear such thoughts from his mind.

On further examination, he was relieved to find that there had been no change along his right flank to the south where the First and Second French Armies were holding tenaciously to their positions against a German assault, even though men had been taken from both armies in forming the new Sixth Army. This army, which he intended to deploy on his extreme left flank, would be crucial to a successful confrontation of the huge German contingent now clearly composed of three armies pushing into France from Flanders.

Joffre now grudgingly recognized that he had initially underestimated this threat. The Germans had skillfully employed reserve forces to fortify their numbers to neutralize his offensive, allowing this northern force to attack the undermanned British and French Fifth Army across ground that gave little advantage to the defenders. At some level, he admired the execution of his adversaries, but they had not yet accomplished their aims, and he intended to do all that was possible to prevent them from doing so.

While his efforts had been focused on the crucial French offensive, this large and powerful compilation of elite German troops had advanced through Belgium, driving into the British Expeditionary Forces at Mons and a portion of the French Fifth Army to their southeast. For three brutal days, the Fifth Army confronted the Germans. Then the British broke and, retreating westward, forced General Lanzerac to withdraw the Fifth Army as well to avoid another debacle like Sedan in 1870. The memories of that debacle haunted every French soldier and cast its shadow over the present situation.

Joffre knew that history well, but he was determined to resist letting his planning be dominated by the fear of a similar outcome. He knew that his army would have to fight on the defensive now, a painful recognition for someone who believed so passionately in the primacy of the offensive. Yet if his army and France were to survive, this was the only option that remained. The transition to a defensive mind-set must be flawlessly executed, defending French soil fanatically and retreating when no other options remained. He believed he now had commanders like Franchet d'Esperey in place for such a fight, which, if successful, could provide the time for a saving counterattack. Unfortunately, as the map on the wall in front of him indicated all too well his plans were subject to the twin threats of German might and British intransigence.

Lanzerac had had to deal with the British command from the beginning and had given ample warning as to the reliability and competence of General French and his staff. In his recent visits to British headquarters, Joffre had realized the validity of

Lanzerac's often bitter criticisms. There he found Field Marshal French often flustered and shielded by an overbearing chief of staff unable or unwilling to listen to his arguments. How bitterly ironic to have cashiered so many of his own generals, only to find the commanders of his chief ally now occupying vitally important ground and consumed by fear of defeat. In trying to explain the necessity of coordinated resistance, he had been met with looks of indifference if not overt hostility, and he was informed that the British troops were exhausted and needed to be withdrawn to an area free of the daily battles that were decimating their effectiveness.

The British were now indeed withdrawing, forcing the French Army to follow, thereby undoing any defensive stand on the Somme River. The British retreat was drawing ever closer to Paris and if unchecked might continue toward the channel in preparation for fleeing the continent. Unable to persuade the British command to fight, Joffre had turned in desperation to President Poincaré to appeal to the British government for help. Fortunately, word had come back that Poincaré's outreach had been well received and that Lord Kitchener, the war minister, was to make a trip to Paris for further consultation.

As Joffre studied the map in front of him, his thoughts were interrupted by the arrival of his chief of staff, General Belin. Joffre noted Belin seemed much more composed than some of his subordinates as he advanced bearing a stack of papers, announcing, "We've received a communiqué from President Poincaré with an accompanying letter from Lord Kitchener. I just got off the phone to confirm certain details."

Joffre studied the messages, including the terse directive from Lord Kitchener, which read, "British troops are now engaged in a fighting line with the French, where they will remain conforming with the movements of the French Army."

"It now only remains to see if they will be allowed to fight," suggested Belin dryly.

"Their troops will fight very well if their commanders allow them," said Joffre. "We saw what happened to the Germans at Mons when they engaged with those Enfield rifles of theirs."

"Well, it's a relief that we now have some understanding of where their position will be in the coming days and that it will not be on the way to the channel," Belin said.

"That may be, but given the German advance of the last two days, all our positions will likely be drawn much closer to Paris. Their First Army has made the most of the British withdrawal and may soon be near Compiegne," Joffre replied, his voice uncharacteristically reflecting concern for the rapid enemy advance on his left.

"Their Second German Army has not been so active recently," Belin said. "Our Fifth Army stung them badly at Guise. Franchet d'Esperey's counterattack there threw back some of their finest divisions. Whether they were significantly weakened or whether they just received a blow to their morale is not clear at present."

"Well, at least General Lanzerac can take pride in the last action he directed," said Joffre, with some evident pleasure.

There was a silence as the men seemed transfixed by the map in front of them.

Joffre subconsciously reverted to his engineering training as he analyzed the information in front of him. A portion of the enemy advance had indeed been slowed, but much more time was still needed to bring new reinforcements and armies into place to adequately confront the German strength. Two new armies were being formed, using remaining reserves and troops drawn from the First and Second Armies. Already he had appointed General Foch to head what was now called the Ninth Army to fill a gap that had developed between the Fourth and Fifth Armies in their uneven withdrawal from the Belgium frontier. He was thankful that the transportation system, despite the burdens placed on it by the necessity of moving so many troops so rapidly, had held up well, and by now, much of Foch's new army was coming into place.

The most critical piece was the new Sixth Army, which would be led by General Maunoury, who had been asked to come out of retirement. He too had a reputation as a fighter, much like Foch and Franchet d'Esperey. Many of these troops were still in transition and had not yet been deployed on the left between the British and the sea. The question was how far to the north of Paris that deployment should be.

Joffre said little, focusing on the map in front of him. He knew all too well from Gallieni's near daily demands for the three corps of infantry promised him by the war minister that the Paris garrison had been preparing defenses to the north and northeast of the city. Envisioning the confluence of these forces, his thoughts now crystalized.

"Notify General Gallieni that as of this moment, I am assigning the Sixth Army to the territories to the north and northwest of the British," Joffre announced with a sudden yet assured declaration. "Their location places them in the area designated as the Paris garrison, and as of now, until further ordered, they will be under his command."

General Belin looked at him quizzically.

"You can relax. General Gallieni will know what to do with those men."

With that, Belin seemed more at ease, then offered up another detail from his discussion with Paris. "One other item of good news for a change. Intelligence has confirmed that the Russian attack has forced the Germans to withdraw two full corps to the east. At least one of them has come from Kluck's First Army."

"That is good news. Let's hope we have the time to turn those numbers to our advantage."

With his mind now eased, he said, "Well, General Belin, I think our work here is finished for now, and if you don't mind, I think it's time for dinner."

Business finished or not, Joffre rarely refused to honor the hour for his dinner punctually. This evening was no exception.

———————

Robert was now routinely working eighteen hours daily, pausing to eat whenever feasible and to sleep only when mentally exhausted. Yet in some ways, his work had been easier than expected. Gallieni, in his capacity as military governor, had taken measures to ensure the participation of all able-bodied citizens, invoking the ancient decree of arrière-ban employed by medieval kings when a threat to the state was more than the knighthood could handle. The subsequent participation of the general population had been invaluable in the building of vital trenches and fortifications, which, if ever manned by the troops, would provide a potent deterrent to any approaching army.

This afternoon returning to headquarters, he found Girodon in unusually good spirits.

"You seem unusually bright today, Girodon. Good news, I hope?"

"You haven't heard, I take it?"

"Heard what?"

"We have received word that Maunoury's Sixth Army is to be dispersed in the fortified areas to the north of Paris, rather than proceeding farther to the northeast as originally planned. In other words, that army is now under control of the governor of the Paris. We now have our three corps to fill out your fortifications."

It took a moment before Robert could speak. "It seems almost surreal, Girodon. After all the worry, we will have actual troops to man all the fortifications that have been built. Now it remains to put them in the right place. No doubt you might have some opinions about that?"

"Well, if you ask, this is what I think. Much still depends on the movement of the three northernmost German armies, especially the First Army of von Kluck. At present, they continue to push westward, which is consistent with what we know of the plan that their old chief of staff, Shlieffen, drew up before he stepped down in 1905. That plan calls for the power to be concentrated in the advancing northern flank in order to envelop the city from the north and northwest, thereby cutting off access to the channel and entrapping our army. The farther to the west they push, however, the more extended their lines become, making coordinated movement ever more difficult."

"So, we should plan on them maintaining that bearing?" asked Robert.

"It's too early to say for certain, but for now, at least their First Army on the extreme flank maintains its westward heading," Girondon said, with some equivocation in his voice.

"It would appear that at least one of Maunoury's corps needs to go toward the Oise fortifications behind Chantilly then?"

"At present, that would be the prudent move, Robert, but I would not completely abandon construction efforts farther to the east. This plan of the Germans is complicated and is dependent on long supply lines. Already those troops have had long, forced marches over great distances. To date, it appears that they are quite formidable, but we are starting to get a sense that there may some cracks in their plan."

"In what way?" asked Robert.

"Their Second Army has been slowed in its advance by the counterattacks of our Fifth Army at St. Quentin and Guise, potentially disrupting coordination with the advance of the First Army. We are also getting some reports that their Second Army is at the limits of their supplies, which may also be contributing to their slowing."

"Well, you are a bearer of good news today, Girondon. Right now, wherever our troops are finally deployed, I feel confident that we can provide them fortifications to give whatever German Army they confront a very rude welcome. Thanks for the information on the Sixth Army. It's the kind of news we could use more of."

"I aim to please, Robert. I hope this optimistic trend will continue."

24

Barbarians at the Gate

AARON MET SHRIEVES TO DISCUSS HIS MEETINGS with Emile in a quiet room at the hotel that was previously used for informal business gatherings. It's brightly striped walls and ornate lamps seemed out of place for the more somber business of feeding an army.

"Good morning, Aaron. What news do you have from your cousin?" Shrieves asked expectantly.

"As things exist now, Major, it will be difficult to get immediate cooperation from the Belgians. To be frank, the behavior of your troops in many parts of the country has stirred up much bad feeling."

"I can assure them that those measures were necessary to counter widespread civilian attacks against our troops," Shrieves answered defensively. "I can understand, however, how those actions might be perceived from their perspective."

"I have spoken at length with my cousin and some of his associate who are interested in some future working relationship, but the timing at present makes it very difficult."

"Do they have any real intention of cooperating, Aaron, or are they simply looking for an excuse to go their own way? I can assure them that would be a risky proposition going forward."

"They understand that fully, Major. That is why they didn't dismiss my proposals until they could talk with you personally. Their basic concerns pertain to fair prices and some leeway to supply their own existing customers. I believe that you would easily be able to meet their expectations in that regard. I know many of them and can assure you that they would be reliable future partners, like what you are now seeing in Germany."

"What's holding this agreement up then?"

"At present, it's the worry of being perceived as primary suppliers to your troops."

"The day that they will have to choose between working with us or suffering the consequences is inevitable, whether they like it or not, Aaron."

"I believe they understand this but need some kind of cover to undertake any agreement now."

"Do they have any suggestions?"

"One thought would be to establish a Belgium company that could act as a subsidiary for that purpose. They have several locals who might well meet your needs as managers for such an undertaking, if you would be willing to support the cost of maintaining the business. I believe those costs would not be significant and would provide you quicker access to reliable sources of products."

"I don't see a problem with such an arrangement as long as a fair price can be worked out, but I would want to talk to them before returning to Germany."

"They would be very receptive to that, Major. There is one other point that they wanted to raise."

"Which is?"

"If something is to be established quickly, it would be wise to start out in areas that have not been disrupted by the war. At present, that would be nearer the coast in Flanders. Perhaps to facilitate matters, we could begin to explore that region even while we are holding discussions. Sara and my nephew might be ideal since he knows the territory and she can speak French."

"I am willing to do anything reasonable if that will expedite matters."

"Excellent. One last item. Perhaps to help matters further, you might issue another one of your letters identifying Sara and any accompanying associates as agents of the German Army, to help them avoid any unnecessary complications in Flanders?"

"That will be made ready by the time of this meeting."

"Fine, I will get back with you regarding times and places for tomorrow if it can be arranged."

"I will make it a priority to be there, Aaron. Thank you for your help."

By the following afternoon, Shrieves had his first meeting with Emile, Paul, and Aaron. After two days of difficult negotiations with a taciturn and recalcitrant Emile, an agreement was finally reached, facilitated by Aaron's willingness to accompany his Belgium relatives and Shrieves to Namur to help establish the foundation for a collecting and distribution center there.

At the end of the process, Emile and his associates were given more than generous terms and more leeway than expected to supply the needs of their Belgian customers. Shrieves conveniently allowed for the establishment of a front corporation, giving Emile and his associates appropriate political cover. To maintain that cover, Emile would remain behind in Brussels, while Paul accompanied Aaron, Sara, and Shrieves to Namur.

———

The following day, Shrieves and a young lieutenant, along with a driver and accompanying guards, set out in a large staff car and small lorry, with Aaron, Sara, and Paul following in a truck belonging to Emile. They set out toward Namur, where Shrieves had arranged a stay at a makeshift military base to serve as a center for inspecting the area. By agreement, Aaron and his group had arranged to stay with a relative of Emile who lived in a nearby village across the Meuse.

From the beginning, their progress was slow, with the primary roads crowded with military transports and personnel. At many intersections, there were traffic jams due to the unwillingness of various commanders to cede the right of way to other similarly minded officers. As they neared Namur, the evidence of the recent fighting was still fresh. Whole blocks of buildings in the approaching villages and on the outskirts of Namur had been destroyed. Left in their place was a picture of utter dissolution, with only partial walls and masses of strewn rubble blocking heretofore orderly streets. Few if any of the previous inhabitants of the areas could be seen, and those that were present seemed to be dazed as they picked through the rubble of what previously had been their homes or businesses. The destruction that Sara had seen around Liege was confined primarily to the fortresses surrounding the city. Here the war had moved quite literally into the villages and had fallen on the civilian populace as well as the combatants.

To make matters worse, there was a pall of dust that coated all the remaining structures and hung in the air, making it difficult to breathe and to see clearly. The closer they came to Namur, the more dramatic was the damage and accompanying destruction. An even more disagreeable sensation was noted as they approached the massed forces of the invading German Army—the smell. Now for the first time, Sara encountered the smell of the thousands of soldiers massed for battle who had neither the time nor the luxury to bathe. It was a smell that she would never forget.

Sara was relieved when at last the group stopped just short of the Meuse crossing. Shrieves came back to inform Aaron that he was going on toward Namur, so if they were still planning to reach their destination before evening, they could separate, meeting in two days at the large restaurant on the square of the village they had just passed. With that, the group parted and went their separate ways.

Sara felt almost giddy in being free from the German Army after countless days of close contact. In that time, all her notions of Germans had been shattered. The face of the German nation that she saw all too well in the masses of ill-shaven, foul-smelling soldiers clad in their gray-green uniformity was both frightening and repulsive.

Their leaders seemed to relate to one another by coarse language and complex actions, which, like male animals in a herd, seemed designed to show their importance and authority. There seemed to be a terrible sense of urgency in everything they did, regardless of its importance. Each day, if not each hour, had a designated goal, with all their being dedicated to reaching that end, only to find it replaced by another the following day. Surrounded now by an increasingly hostile population and the certainty of dangerous encounters with an enemy to the west, the mental strain coupled with the fatigue of endless marching and fighting was eroding what remained of their individual humanity.

Sara had watched the enlistees and common soldiers most closely because she knew that their ranks were made up of workers and farmers rather than career army men. What she saw was even more unsettling than the behavior of their officers. Many now marched with their features transformed by a blank stare, masking any individuality they might once have had. Gone was any spontaneity of expression or show of emotion. It was as if the combination of horrors and deprivations that they had already witnessed had stripped them of their being, replacing it with the soul of automatons. She searched in vain for someone who might be a father or lover or one of the many workers who she once thought would oppose such a war. On they marched, as if compelled by some mysterious power, often singing in remarkable unison the marching songs of the fraternity of warriors, creating a chorus of terrible beauty.

This was what repulsed her the most. It was not simply the terror and misery that this huge army had forced on the unwilling populations of Belgium but how the process itself had taken control of nearly all involved. No doubt this transformation of the country into a focused, monolithic horde was what the warlords had hoped for. Such reality, however, seen up close could easily dispel any false notions promulgated by the prophets of national glory. Sara saw in this collective might a betrayal of the most decent instincts of human behavior and grieved not only for those who had already suffered but for so many of her German friends who would be compelled to answer for the actions of their fellow citizens at some future day.

After a drive of approximately an hour, their truck pulled off the road down a tree-lined lane to a farm surrounded by fields that seemed out of place in their pastoral peace and loveliness.

The farm belonged to the Rosens. The wife, Golda, was the sister of Maude Brande, and Sara suspected that her husband, Joseph, was related in some way as well. As she gazed at the farm and buildings around her and watched Paul reunite with his relatives, it dawned on her how much this society of farmers and traders held more in common with medieval society, dependent on the products of the land, more than it did on industrial production. Yet this industrialized world, having spawned modern warfare with all its lethality, still was reliant on the practices of the old, a reliance that had proven beneficial to her.

That evening as the guests settled into their places for dinner, Sara knew well the protocol of the meal that would follow. Joseph and his son, Dierk, sat at one end of the table with Aaron and Paul. Aside from some snippets of conversation at the beginning of the meal directed at Sara and Golda, there would be little effort to include the women in their conversation thereafter. Instead, Sara was seated with Golda and her two daughters, Sylvia and Camille. The girls were said to be seventeen and fifteen years old respectively, and aside from their heights—Sylvia, the older, being much shorter than her sister—they were remarkably similar in appearance. Each of the girls had light brown hair and was quite attractive, having beautiful jade-colored eyes.

The two younger women were immediately drawn to this mysterious female visitor who had suddenly appeared in such an unusual manner. Sara by now had become adept at sharing information about her background with new acquaintance within Aaron's sphere to avoid disclosing too much information that might put them at future risk, should her identity be revealed. Slowly she took the two younger women into her confidence and was rewarded by increasing frankness on their part. On hearing of Sara's wish to venture into France, Sylvia began to share her insight into their current situation and how that might impact any attempt to escape Belgium.

"During the last week," Sylvia noted, "enormous numbers of German troops have moved through here toward the Meuse or Mons. Fortunately, it now seems that most are farther to the west, leaving our area more peaceful and hopefully safer."

"Did they cause much trouble here?"

"Only to the extent that they filled the main thoroughfares, which made it impossible to travel unless you used very small back roads. Unfortunately, the same could not be said for so many others living in the towns and villages."

"What do you mean?" asked Sara.

"The Germans," Golda interjected, "have become very uneasy in the presence of the Belgians. They see everywhere a population that is armed against them. Their response upon first entering any town or village is to take local officials hostage as deterrents against hostility directed toward their forces. In many cases, this tactic has not been the deterrent they hoped for, and unfortunately, the reprisals have been immediate and harsh. I know firsthand of civilians being killed, including some women, priests, and even children. These are not the acts of a civilized nation but those of an army of barbarians."

"They have even burned down entire villages," Camille added.

"I have heard that," replied Sara.

"Have you heard of Louvain?" asked Golda.

"What about Louvain?"

"We have been told that the entire city has been burned, including its great library and cathedral."

"That can't be true! Why would they do such a thing even in war?"

"I'm afraid it is true," answered Golda. "We have heard this from people whose credibility is beyond doubt."

Sara sat for a moment, so caught up in her thoughts that she was unable to speak. She thought of Stein and Frau von Suttner and her many beloved German friends. How could their people do such things? These were some of the most enlightened and educated people she had ever known, and their country had given the world so much through its artists and writers as well as its scientists and engineers. What madness could have come over them to burn a city with all its great treasures and to wantonly murder its civilians? She knew that she could never reconcile that collective evil with what she knew of the many individual Germans that she loved, and that realization weighed on her even more than the acts themselves.

As she reflected on what Golda had told her, Sara could hear the men engaged in a conversation that reflected the ambivalence of their position as well. Golda, with the timeless instincts that mothers possess, finally spoke up.

"Sara, it's time that you get some rest. There will be much for all of us to face tomorrow, and we can do it better with a good night's sleep. Those men will not realize it till much later, but they cannot undo what has been done. By the time they stop, we will all have gotten several hours of rest. Come with me. I will show you where you can change and your bed."

The following morning seemed to Sara unusually pleasant and even peaceful, with a bright sunrise promising a warm and sunny day. The setting in the countryside far removed from the clamor of the moving troops that had passed through in recent days only served to increase the sense of peace. Sara had risen early, at the first morning light, to help Golda prepare the morning breakfast.

During the evening, the men had decided to spend the following day talking with the various farmers and suppliers who were Joseph's closest associates. Aaron had made it clear to the Rosens that they or their associates were under no obligation to participate in any agreement that they did not feel morally able to comply with. Dierk, like his cousin Paul, had voiced significant concerns regarding any arrangement with the German invaders, but his father, like Emile Brande before him, had recognized the importance of such a relationship if the Germans continued to dominate the country in the future.

Before leaving, Aaron had spoken with Sara, telling her to remain close to Golda. He reassured Sara that contacts were being made with some of the locals to help get her back into France, but until such arrangements could be made, it would be best for her to remain as inconspicuous as possible.

After the men left, Sara helped the women clear the breakfast table and volunteered her help in any of the necessary morning chores. She soon found herself helping the sisters gather eggs, milk the cows, and clean up the stalls.

As the morning progressed, Sara had an opportunity to become better acquainted with both young women. Camille, the younger, was energetic and given to easy and open conversation. It was apparent to Sara that she had been spared from the details of the more atrocious behavior of the invading armies, as she still had a naive optimism about her immediate future and that of her family. Sara was sad to think that Camille's life, filled with seemingly banal insecurities regarding her looks and her relationship with certain young men, would be changed forever.

The oldest sister, Sylvia, was altogether different. Where her sister was open and a bit gregarious, Sylvia was reserved and quiet. At first, Sara had some difficulty in striking up any meaningful conversation with her. As the two undertook the disagreeable task of cleaning out stalls, however, their shared misery seemed to make Sylvia more willing to share some of her more intimate thoughts.

Sara sensed that the young woman was more aware of the tragedies surrounding the German invasion of her region.

She knew of many young men who had suffered in some way from the German invasion, and being bright and sensitive, this knowledge had already affected her greatly.

While they took a short break from their labors, quietly resting in the morning sunshine, Sylvia suddenly interrupted their conversation and pointed toward the chicken coop, where her sister had gone to gather eggs. There, coming seemingly out of nowhere, were two young German soldiers. The men were ill shaven and poorly dressed in a manner that suggested they were deserters from a combat unit.

They were at first startled and then pleased to discover Camille laden with eggs leaving the hen house. Seeing the two men and the look on their faces, without saying another word, Sara and Sylvia left the cattle barn, so as not to be seen, and moved in to help the younger woman.

As they reached the back of the hen house, they could hear Camille speaking in a loud voice to the Germans, who were demanding that she step aside and let them enter the building. Soon, one of the men struck Camille, then dragged her in with him as she tried to resist his advance.

The eggs that she had been carrying in a large basket had fallen to the ground, and the other soldier had stooped to gather them up while his companion occupied himself with Camille. Intent as he was on gathering the eggs, he did not see the shadow of a woman approach or sense the blow of a pitchfork that was delivered to the side of his head with all the pent-up fury that the atrocities of the recent days had provoked. The blow resounded with a dull thud, as if a large melon had been struck, and the soldier fell immediately to the ground unconscious.

The other soldier was not aware of what had become of his colleague, blinded as he was by his lust, and he also failed to notice the approach of the woman through the door. Sara, now unwilling to strike the attacker in the head for fear of injuring the struggling Camille, struck him with equal violence, driving the tines of the pitchfork deep into his chest. As he collapsed, releasing Camille from his grip, the younger woman bolted out of the hen house into the comforting arms of her sister. She did not see Sara take the pitchfork from the chest of the soldier and then strike it repeatedly against the head of the attacker until he was lifeless.

As she left the building, she saw Camille huddled against Sylvia. The latter, while holding her sister, looked contemptuously at the soldier lying at her feet. He lay motionless, with a large pool of blood collecting around his head

"You struck well, Sara. He is dead."

"So is his bastard friend," Sara replied.

For a moment, they said nothing. Then almost simultaneously, they moved in unison, intent on straightening up the area and hiding the bodies of the intruders who had brought the unwelcome presence of war on this beautiful morning.

25

A New Impulse

AS THE MONTH OF AUGUST DREW TO ITS END, FEW Europeans could doubt its historic importance. The optimism of the early days of the war was soon tempered by conflicting reports of battlefield success and by the swelling ranks of wounded being returned to the city for care. As the news from the front became more pessimistic, the population of the city became ever more anxious, with overt hysteria gripping those less suited to deal with dark prospects.

Unfortunately, many members of the government fell into this group, conflating fears to reality and making them ill-suited to confront the problems that the advancing German Army now posed to the capital. What was desperately needed was someone with his wits about him who could take charge in such a desperate hour. Fortunately for Paris, there was someone in position to realize that need, General Joseph Gallieni.

Gallieni had not predicted the exact circumstances he now faced, but upon accepting the position of military governor of Paris, he was fully aware of such possibilities. Early on, he set about remaking the city to better resist an assault. He knew war was an iterative business that presented varying opportunities that could best be addressed by a process that required accurate empiric information. Beyond that, discipline and focus were required to utilize such information to deal with the frequent situations where events of the moment did not conform to expectations. Only in this way could decisions be made that would have the best probability of ultimate success. Despite the problems he now faced, he was determined to remain focused, even as others got caught up in fears that paralyzed their usefulness.

He sensed it was this evident sangfroid and discipline that had attracted Messimy and some others in the government to him earlier, and he was not surprised, therefore, to receive an urgent request from the new war minister, Millerand, for a meeting early that afternoon.

Gallieni had had dealings with Millerand before and had far greater respect for him than most of the ministers that comprised the cabinet. He tried to keep Millerand appraised of his thoughts, just as he had done with Messimy, his predecessor, hoping to facilitate communication with the government in a manner that would meet the army's needs. From their recent conversations, he had learned that Millerand was spending much of his time trying to reassure other cabinet members of the need to maintain a presence in Paris. There was something in the manner of this recent request that suggested that very topic was on Millerand's mind.

When Gallieni arrived at the War Ministry, the scene was one of near chaos. Crates were being moved along with boxes of records, while others were being burned. On entering the minister's office, Gallieni found Millerand pacing, his manner reflecting his evident distress.

"Good afternoon, Monsieur Minister. What is it that I can do for you?"

"Well, General, I fear there is very little good about this afternoon. We have received this morning a communiqué from General Joffre, who has suggested that circumstances are now such that he is recommending that the government move from Paris to a more secure area."

"I had heard discussions of that sort were going on. What does the government wish to convey to me, Monsieur Millerand?" Gallieni asked somewhat hesitantly, fearing that he might be ordered to declare the city open to prevent its destruction during any ensuing combat.

"General, documents are being prepared to be signed by the president shortly to put you in charge of all authority, civilian and military, in the city, beginning at midnight tonight."

"Will there be any officials from the Foreign Office should the need arise to speak officially with our allies or with the Germans?"

"It has been decided that all members of the government shall leave the city for Bordeaux. In case diplomatic discussions are needed, Ambassador Herrick of the United States has graciously volunteered to act on behalf of the government in its absence. He is a man of great integrity who can be relied upon completely."

"What instructions does the government have for the military commander of Paris, Monsieur Millerand?"

"It is the government's wish that the city be defended by every measure available to you."

Gallieni hesitated for a moment then resumed. "Sir, I want to be clear on this point. If I am to defend Paris as you suggest, that may well mean the wholesale destruction of historic buildings by the enemy. Such a defense risks the destruction of the city itself."

Millerand paused with an expression that showed both great sadness and regret. "General, it is the government's order that you defend the city to the death."

Gallieni was both relieved for Paris yet sobered in hearing Millerand's unequivocal confirmation of his responsibility.

"Thank you for clarifying that matter, Monsieur. It is a responsibility that will be taken seriously and to which we will apply all our efforts."

With that, the two men shook hands, as if to confirm the imminent transfer of power soon to be consummated. Whether Paris would survive or be destroyed was no less clear than whether either man would live to know the outcome. Each now had come to accept uncertainty as a condition of their lives. For Gallieni, he had too much to do to waste any time worrying about it.

The following morning, September 2, was ushered in by a rain that had been falling throughout the night. It was Sedan day, but unlike that day more than four decades previously, the population of France awoke with their army having been severely battered on many fronts but still not vanquished. They also awoke to find that circumstances had now become so serious that the government felt it necessary to withdraw to Bordeaux. For those now remaining in Paris, the implication for their own future safety was apparent. Also, widely disseminated was a tersely worded poster hung at virtually every major intersection of the city, announcing the intentions of the military governor.

Army of Paris. Citizens of Paris.

The members of the government of the republic have left Paris to give a new impulse to the national defense. I have received a mandate to

defend Paris against the invader. This mandate
I shall carry out to the end.

Military Governor of Paris
Commander of the Army of Paris
Gallieni

BOOK III

TEMPEST

26

Resolution

THE PARIS WHERE BOTH THOMAS AND MARIE HAD chosen to stay was now but a strange embodiment of its former grandeur. Gone were the tourists and many of its citizens who had the option of fleeing. What merchants remained faced an ever-dwindling supply of wares but also fewer customers demanding their services. Instead, the city had taken on a distinctive marshal air, dominated by the comings and goings of the army through its streets and rail centers. Even more sobering was the ever-increasing number of wounded whose needs were taxing what space was available to accommodate them. It was to this last group that Marie and Thomas had concentrated their attention in recent days.

Thomas was pleased to feel new energy as he faced not only the responsibility entrusted to him by Madame Bonneau but also from further encouragement from his bishop. That encouragement came from the somewhat unique relationship between the two, which allowed the bishop to share frankly his concerns not only for Robert but also for the city's population that he viewed as an increasingly vulnerable flock. He had told Robert what troubled him in that regard was not simply the physical toil of wounded and dead soldiers but the psychologic toil it produced for them and their families. With God's help, the nurses and doctors could address their physical injuries, but what of the doubt and uncertainty that must be haunting their minds and souls? It was like a dark, unmentionable shadow that hung over much of the city, and if not addressed, it could have significant consequences.

The church both men knew had long served as a gathering place to address physical and emotional insecurity. The pain they were now suffering might make some reluctant to come forward, but the bishop had insisted to Thomas that the word must go out that the church stood ready to minister to the needs of those broken in spirit or haunted by fear.

What had encouraged Thomas and further lifted his spirits was a recent conversation where the bishop had told him that he was thrilled by signs of his improvement, as it was an answer to his own prayers. He had asked God for help from his clerical brethren to address the crisis of the war and then confessed to Thomas that, among his flock, he at his best was his most able. On seeing him regain each day some measure of his former self, the bishop had asked Thomas to take a greater role in counseling the wounded and their families.

Thomas had accepted this offer just as he had done the one from Madame Bonneau not only out of sense of responsibility but also from a rising optimism in his own mental faculties. What remained was to see if they were truly improved enough to sustain the demands of what might be asked of him.

After her mother left for Lyon, Marie returned to her medical duties, resolved to challenge herself by accepting the opportunity to accompany the trains laden with dressings to the delivery stations located close to the front. She had already begun to transition from her previous duties, allowing her to concentrate most of her efforts in the hospitals. She was confident that as things stood now, a two-day excursion to the front would be possible.

What Marie discovered on her first trip was a revelation. On the journey out, she took pains to organize her supplies so that they could be efficiently dispensed at each anticipated stop. The logistics were such that the train would stop at smaller stations first and then overnight at a major receiving area. At each stop, her dressings were thankfully received, and Marie carefully answered any questions before departing.

At the large facility where the train stopped for the night, after her initial duties were finished, Marie found herself with time to help the staff in other ways. She was asked to help oversee actual patients to free up other staff members. Marie was both frightened and amazed at the responsibility afforded her.

Now, instead of dressings and instruments, her charge was actual men. No longer shielded by a veil of sterility, she was now forced to speak and touch men whose suffering and fears were all too evident. How far she had come on this journey from the sheltered confines of the conservatory. Instead of beauty and sublimity, she now confronted sordid misery.

Then, by some miracle in this maelstrom, a wave of quiet resolve came over her, and what fears she had seemed to magically dissipate. She seemed to sense by instinct what these men needed, acting at times without a word to rearrange their pillow or bring them water, receiving in return a smile or look of deep gratitude.

She had done similar work in Paris but never in so intense an environment, where a man's grip on life was so unstable. She witnessed around her men suddenly deteriorate before her eyes.

Her first response had been to run for help, but she realized that it might not always be readily available. She therefore drew on her experiences in Paris, managing as best she could until further help could arrive.

The following morning, she was still energized by her work in the hospital. When the train departed for Paris laden with wounded, Marie felt a sense of both exhaustion and elation. She sought a warm sunlight seat to curl up in and watched as the surroundings outside slowly shed the trappings of war for the more blessed normalcy of undisturbed villages and verdant farmland. Then her exhaustion overcame her, and she slept until the train slowed in the outskirts of Paris. Her sleep, however, was far from peaceful, with thoughts of imaginary medical crises disrupting her dreams.

Upon arriving in Paris, the elation of her accomplishment seemed to outweigh any tiredness. As she was finalizing some routine chores, preparing to leave for the day, Marie was approached by one of the senior nurses that had been on the return trip to Paris with her. She was surprised that the nurse, Sister Nicole, sought her out to compliment her on her efforts, noting how much she had helped the staff at the front. Such help, the sister noted, was very much needed at this time, and she urged Marie to think of more permanent duty near the front line, where her efforts might have far more benefit than they would in Paris.

Marie had never considered such an opportunity, due to her lack of formal nursing training. Now she was being told that her actions had more than demonstrated qualifications that were badly needed in this unprecedented time. The heady sense of accomplishment was still fresh in Marie's mind, but before she yielded to impulse and accepted such new responsibilities, she knew that she would have to discuss them with Thomas. It was an acknowledgment that she in part resented, but her regard for him and her family made it essential nevertheless. Marie thanked the sister for her kind words, promising a reply after she had time to think the matter over.

Marie also understood that a discussion of this matter with Thomas would deal with more than a change in her responsibilities. Despite their recent discussion, Marie sensed there was much that remained unsaid in their relationship, and the implications of this duty in terms of the risks involved and the geographic dislocation from Paris could bring any concerns Thomas might have into the open. Fortunately, she would not have to wait long for such a discussion, as they had a prearranged meeting for the following afternoon.

———

They had agreed to meet in a small building near Saint Sulpice, which was serving as an office for Thomas and when needed for counseling wounded soldiers and their families. Thomas's office was large, with a window admitting a cheery note of sunlight, while a sturdy oaken door provided the quiet and solitude needed for counseling and personnel study and reflection. The afternoon had been warm with frequent sun breaks, which added to Marie's optimism in seeing Thomas smile and greet her with much of his past enthusiasm.

"Thomas, you look to be making progress each day that I see you."

"At times, I almost feel back to normal, if there is a normal these days."

"None of this would have happened if you had not pushed yourself to get better, and for that, all of us can be thankful."

"Perhaps, Marie, but whatever the reason, I'm thankful that I can actually be of use to someone. When I first came back to Paris, I was so confused and mentally exhausted I feared that I had little left to offer."

"We have been over that, Thomas, and it's not fair for you or anyone to be able to understand all of this and even more unrealistic to imagine you could provide meaningful solutions on intuition alone. We are all confused, trying to find ways to deal with situations we hoped we would never face."

"For me, Marie, I now realize the limits of relying on reason to help understand all this. As I floundered about, trying to find some explanation for this suffering, the words of Aquinas came back to me. When I gave up the delusion of my infallible rationality and turned back to the holy scriptures, I began to find what I had been looking for.

"In those books, man's many failings were noted in stories of war, conquest, and sin. Even God's chosen people suffered famine, plague, and subjugation. Yet in the Gospels, there is little discussion of specific events or our collective responsibility. Instead, our individual relationship to God is of paramount importance. The long biblical narrative suggests a basic truth; if we concentrate on our relationship with God, all other matters will fall into place.

"Now when I talk to the wounded men and their families, I can deal with their pain more effectively. In better times, God's presence may seem like a soft breeze on a sunny afternoon. Now his spirit is like a lighthouse in a storm, if only one pays attention to his signals. Many times, I have seen and heard of instances where the wounded have acted nobly, giving up for others what was rightfully theirs. How else to explain such kindness and nobility in the face of such awful circumstances than the workings of the Holy Spirit? That presence gives us hope for something better, if we can be sensitive to it and act in accordance with its divine inspiration."

"Thomas, I have had similar experiences recently in a field hospital where I saw people act in remarkable ways."

With that, Marie related her recent trip to the front and the subsequent request that she had received from Sister Nicole.

Thomas remained silent throughout her narrative and remained so for some time afterward. At last, he spoke, almost hesitantly. "Marie, what would you have me do? To let you relocate to the front even on a temporary basis would violate the trust your mother has placed in me."

"Why do you say that, Thomas?"

"Marie, you are the daughter of a proud family. What family would want their unmarried daughter left unchaperoned in such a location?"

"Thomas, you are trying to judge me by the standards of a society that is now under assault, if not already destroyed."

"Much could be accomplished here in Paris without the risk of being so close to danger."

"Thomas, when I am helping these poor men, all of my musical training seems so far away and insignificant. To see their suffering and be able to help in some small way brings me closer to that Holy Spirit you speak of. The wounded we see here in Paris are different from those near the front. There, despite my lack of formal training, I could be of far more help than here in Paris."

"What would I tell your parents or Robert if, God forbid, you were ever injured?"

"Thomas, I am not worried about my parents and exonerate you of any such blame or worry should anything happen to me. There is too much that needs to be done now to let worry paralyze us. Besides, my mother is stronger than you suspect. As for my father, I think he has always been somewhat disappointed that I was not his oldest son. If that is the case, what could give him more pride than his daughter sacrificing her safety for the cause of the republic?"

"And what of Robert?"

"What of Robert indeed. If there has been any benefit from this war, it has been that I now see things more clearly than when we lived our lives by the script of an old play. Even then, for all my respect for Robert, I had concerns for both our futures if we were to marry. Now this war has only confirmed my suspicions."

"What are you trying to say, Marie?"

"It is something I have tried to tell you before, yet it never seems to come out right. When Sister Nicole suggested this opportunity, the only thing that stopped me from accepting her proposal was my concern for how it might affect you, Thomas."

"That was wise not to accept something as serious as this on an impulse."

"It has nothing to do with wisdom, Thomas."

Thomas looked at Marie with a quizzical expression.

"Thomas, how could I go off and leave you in the condition you've been in?"

"You said yourself, Marie, that you can see how much I've improved."

"For that I am truly thankful, Thomas, but my real concern is how this assignment might affect you in the future."

"Marie, if you aren't worried about your parents, why should my feelings matter?"

"Thomas, are you really that dense? Despite all that has happened, I can never forget that day when you left for Strasbourg. I have no idea what your feelings are for me, given all that you've been through, but, if anything, I love you now more than ever. That is why your feelings matter, Thomas. I could not accept this new assignment if it would harm you."

Thomas took some time before daring to reply.

"Marie, I was in no condition to know my true feelings when I first got back from Strasbourg. Now, as much as I try to deny it, I cannot escape my love for you. It's that realization that causes me so much worry. How can I ever resolve my feelings for you with my vows and obligations?"

Marie's smile and flushed face reflected her feelings better than anything she could say.

"Thomas, how complicated things are now. Perhaps it would have been easier to work out such problems just a few months ago, but now so much is changed. The faces of those wounded men haunt me. Even for you, how could I ignore them, knowing that I might be able to help in some way?"

"I understand. That hope that I could help those soldiers in Strasbourg was one of the few things that sustained me.

"Marie, I have no doubt that you are one of those rare people who lift the spirit of others. I understand that I nor anyone else, including your parents, has the right to deny those wounded men your help. I also believe that this opportunity has come to you for a reason.

"Expediency is the enemy of greatness. I guess I'm sounding like a professor once again, Marie, but it is my way of agreeing with you. What kind of future would we have if we compromise for momentary gratification? If our love is to have meaning, we cannot let it blind us from doing what we both know is right. I believe some day these terrible times will pass, and then we will be better and stronger for having faced them with the best that is in us."

Marie did not reply, but Thomas could clearly see in her demeanor her feelings for such a shared future.

"Thomas, what you say is beautiful, but can't we allow ourselves something for the present? I'm not strong enough to live solely for a time that may never come."

Her plea was more than Thomas could bear. He cast a furtive glance at the hallway and immediate surroundings. Finding themselves alone, he closed the door and lowered the blinds to his office. Then Marie drew him toward her, aroused by weeks of suppressed love.

27

Hope

DURING THE FIRST DAYS OF SEPTEMBER, PARIS WAS filled with troops arriving from locations in the south to be deployed to the north and northeast of the city, to confront the coming German assault. Some showed the fatigue and wear of several weeks of incessant fighting in Lorraine. Their tattered, ill-kept appearance was alarming to those civilians who remembered how proud and assured they had been just weeks before. Others, such as a fresh contingent of Zouaves, resplendent in their bright blue tunics and scarlet pants, gave hope to those who watched, knowing that the survival of the city would depend on their collective success.

September was also a month when France, in its last great war with the Prussians in 1870, had suffered terrible humiliation under the inept leadership of Emperor Napoleon III at Sedan. Now, forty-four years later, that memory hung over the city as once again the threat of the German invader loomed to the east.

Nowhere was this threat sensed more keenly than at the headquarters of the Paris garrison where Robert d'Avillard was now spending the bulk of his days trying to facilitate the deployment of the various divisions of the Sixth Army to locations deemed critical by Gallieni and Maunoury, the newly appointed commander of the Sixth Army. Fortunately, his task had been greatly aided by his knowledge of the existing rail system, allowing him to prioritize the movement of troops from key locations near Verdun and Nancy into Paris.

Following an early-morning visit to the Gare de l'Est, he had returned to headquarters for a quick lunch, which he took in a corner of the large situation room of the intelligence bureau. Here, the large map that seemed to encompass the entire south wall of the room, provided a timely update on the present status of the conflicting forces. The informal gathering of officers, who, like himself, would come and go throughout the day, also provided Robert with further information. Now as he studied the position of the German right wing, he tried to project its future path in light of its most recent movements.

Recently, that advance had slowed everywhere but on the extreme right flank of their lines. If this continued, a major engagement somewhere to the north and or perhaps northeast of Paris could be expected. The crucial question for the deployment of French forces was where.

To answer that question, Robert once again turned to Colonel Girodon.

"Girodon, am I wrong to think that their Second Army is lagging behind the First in the last few days?"

"Not just their Second Army but those damn Saxons in the Third Army as well. They have been particularly destructive in our occupied territory, but Foch has brought his Ninth Army into position with the Fourth Army, and between the two of them, they are exacting a great deal of punishment on the bastards. This, by necessity, has slowed their Second Army for fear of opening a gap between them.

"Von Bulow, it seems, has some other issues with his Second Army as well," Girodon continued. "We are now beginning to understand how much damage our Fifth Army did to them at St. Quentin and Guise. That was very risky business, with Joffre having to virtually force Lanzerac into ordering very complicated troop movements, but it was done very well, with satisfying results despite the level of casualties."

"It didn't appear all that successful when the Fifth Army withdrew afterward," Robert said.

"The British withdrawal on their flank necessitated that. What is proving interesting is how slowly their Second Army has been in pursuit. We believe the damage they took at Guise makes them unable or unwilling to keep up with von Kluck's movement on their right."

"Possibly giving us the time to put troops in place to confront them?" Robert suggested hopefully.

"I hope that's the case, because if not, Robert, things could get pretty difficult in Paris in the next few days.

"There is something else that you might be interested in. For some time, in interrogating their captured officers, they clearly felt that our armies were beaten and all that remained was to get close enough to Paris to deliver a final blow. Now, however, after their beating at Guise, there seems to be less certainty among them. For many, that was their first time being turned, forcing them to recognize that we could break them in the field."

"I like the thought of a chastened enemy on their morale and effectiveness," Robert said. "Thanks for your usual insights, Girodon, but I've dawdled long enough and no doubt have a driver waiting to take me out toward Pontoise."

"Keep your head down out there, Robert."

"I plan to. One time getting bounced around by their artillery is enough."

Robert was pleased to see that Karl Gold was waiting this afternoon to take him to visit sites nearing completion in anticipation of the arrival of troops from the Sixth Army. Karl's own schedule had been busy, requiring that he attend to many other items rather than devote his time to Robert. This afternoon, however, he was there and assured Robert that he had time available. Robert appreciated the luxury of having Karl as a driver, because his knowledge of many alternative routes helped to facilitate any trip. He was subsequently gratified to be able to finish all that he had set out to do and return to Paris at a reasonable hour. Karl, seeing his more relaxed manner, broke the relative silence.

"Robert, I didn't want to bring up this subject earlier, because I knew that you had many important matters on your mind."

Robert had a sinking feeling fearing that Karl had received news of Sara.

"Is it about Sara, Karl?"

"Yes, it is. I promised to let you know of any information that I might receive, and that is why I made it a point to drive for you this afternoon."

"What have you heard?" Robert asked anxiously.

"The information I've received is only secondhand, so I cannot be certain that it is completely accurate. Nevertheless, Lydia spoke with the son of an old acquaintance yesterday afternoon while I was out on business. This young man had brought in a herd of cattle to the pens at the Bois de Bologna and had stopped to leave a message with us afterward.

"We have done business with his family for as long as I can remember. They are in Champagne near Rheims but also have many acquaintances throughout the region. His father was told that Sara had made her way to Belgium and was nearing the French border."

"Did he add anything more?"

"Only that the people she is with in Belgium are people that I know as well, and they wanted word to get back to me if possible. If she does succeed in getting into France, Sara knows other old acquaintances in that region from a trip she took with me when she was younger."

"That is encouraging, but I hope she is not trying to do something foolish and get to Paris. She will have to dodge a million Germans who are not in a mood to coddle anyone they think is a threat.

"Think about it, Karl. Have you ever known Sara to be afraid to do something she believes necessary? That's how she got stuck in Germany. If I know her, and I think I do, she will try to go where she thinks she can be most effective. If Paris remains free of German control, it will be her objective."

"Unfortunately, what you're saying is true, Robert. Ever since she was a young woman, she seemed compelled to do what she thought necessary, regardless of the risks or consequences."

Both men smiled as they reflected on their experiences with her through the years.

"In some ways, I feel kind of sorry for the Germans," said Robert. "They have no idea of the trouble they could be in if they get in her way."

"I would give anything to see her survive that matchup," Karl said.

After a moment of silence, Robert seemed to relax, saying, "There is nothing more either of us can do for the present, Karl. Nevertheless, this news is very encouraging."

Soon they arrived at headquarters, and before parting, Karl said, "If you need something, Robert, you and your staff know where I can be reached."

"Thank you, Karl, for all your help. Let's hope the next time we meet, the news will be even better."

Since the beginning of the war, Robert had little time to dwell on Sara's fate and tried to suppress any thoughts of her, given what little he could do to help. Now suddenly he was aware that by some miracle she might even be in France. Now he was unable to control his pent-up feelings, even though they were taking his focus away from the critical demands of the German advance. Yet such pleasant thoughts were a reprieve from all that he had been facing and a reminder of how important his work would be in the coming days, especially if it could improve the chances of seeing her once again.

28

Westward

STUNNED BY THE APPEARANCE OF THE TWO marauding Germans and their subsequent response, it took Sara and the Rosen sisters some time to recover from the shock of their actions. The younger sister, Camille, was at first irreconcilable, sobbing loudly until her sister grabbed her by the shoulders, shaking her gently until her crying was reduced to intermittent sobs.

"Camille, we don't have time for this. We all have to pull ourselves together," Sylvia admonished.

"Sylvia, help me get this man into the barn, out of sight, and straighten up this area," Sara demanded while looking intently for signs that might give evidence of the recent violence. "Camille, I know that you must be terribly frightened, but Sylvia is right. Go and get Golda and tell her to come and help us."

The younger woman, after a moment's hesitation, seemed to regain control over her emotions and ran to tell her mother of the day's misfortunate events.

Shortly afterward, she returned, following her mother, who was walking rapidly with a grim and determined expression on her face.

"Where are the two men?" she demanded.

"We hid them in the back stall under some hay," Sylvia replied.

"Hook up the team of horses to the wagon, and we'll put them in there and cover them with hay. We can then take them to the back pasture near the stand of willows where the old cistern is."

Little needed to be said as the women hooked up the horses and quickly put the bodies in the wagon, concealing them in a heavy blanket of hay. They then brought the wagon carefully in place near the old cistern. While Camille began to fork the silage out, as if preparing the area for cattle, Sarah and Sylvia quickly dropped the bodies, listening with satisfaction to the sounds they made as they fell into the dark depths below.

The women forked the silage into the area to justify their presence in case they should encounter unwanted visitors. Then, without wasting time, they returned to the barn, where Golda inspected the area again to look for incriminating evidence, while the sisters unhooked the horses. Satisfied that all was in order, the women returned to the house, where they washed up and set down to discuss what further needed to be done.

Golda began. "Camille says that she was surprised by the first man, who seemed to sneak out of the woods from behind the smokehouse. Did either of you see anything else?"

"I didn't see them until I heard Camille talking with the first German, and then the other came out from the wooded area," said Sylvia.

"They were not on the open road. I'm sure of that," said Sara. "The second one appeared to be rather cautious when he first came out of the trees. The way that he behaved makes me suspicious that they were deserters trying to forage food rather than a detail of the regular army."

"I hope you're right, because if they were sent as part of a coordinated effort to gather food, then they will be missed, and someone will be sent to look for them. If that happens, the Germans have a nasty way of extracting information from the locals," Golda said.

"For that reason, I don't want anyone, including any of the men, to know about this until we are sure that the danger has passed. If they know nothing, any story that they give to the Germans will be more plausible."

"It is now clearer than ever that I must try to get into France as soon as possible," Sara said. "I have always been afraid that if my real identity were discovered, then Aaron and anyone associated with him might be subjected to some form of reprisal. The German Army has made the occupied areas so unstable that, for everyone's sake, I cannot stay here any longer."

"We have been in danger, Sara, since the Germans occupied our lands," said Golda. "What happened today might happen at any time in the future. All we can do is keep alert for danger and pray that we can escape it just as you three did today."

"I have been studying the map," said Sara, "and from what Paul has told me, it seems the German Army has been concentrating its movements to our southwest into France. There may be stragglers and small units displaced to the north, but if they are trying to destroy the French forces as quickly as possible, little can be gained by diverting significant numbers of troops in this direction."

"Even so, it would be difficult for you to get into France without someone guiding you through the countryside," Camille said. "How will you get there, simply by walking?"

"I think I know a way to do that," Sylvia said softly.

"Camille and I have our bicycles, and both of us know the roads to the west into France and people that we might turn to for help if needed. Sara could use Dierk's old bicycle, which he recently repaired, and the three of us could fall in with the streams of refugees that have been displaced to the northwest from the war zone."

"I could not ask you to risk your safety in that way," Sara replied.

"Sara, how safe were we today?" said Sylvia emphatically. "As long as the Germans remain in control here, there will always be danger."

"Sylvia is right. What guarantee do we have even here on our own property that we will be safe from Germans? Sara, if you could get my girls to France, where there is still a chance that they might be safe from some arbitrary act of the Germans, I would be eternally grateful to you. As a woman, I understand the hazards we face, but as a mother, I'm unwilling to risk them if there is any way to get my daughters to safety.

"Sylvia knows the area near France well. She also knows where our friends are located. She would be as good a guide as you could get. She could also help you look out for Camille."

Sara had taken in Golda's proposal at first without comment. She had hoped to proceed, once she got close to France, by herself to lessen any risk to those who had helped her and to be more flexible in her subsequent travel. The prospect of taking Camille with them was not appealing, as the girl was young and had been clearly shaken by the day's events. She had been impressed with Sylvia, however, and believed her presence would improve their chances for escape.

There was something in Golda's eyes and her voice that made Sara hesitant to dismiss her proposal. How could she leave the younger girl here alone? How could she not make some attempt to help her escape, if for no other reason than to give her mother some relief from fear for her daughters?

"Camille, you have heard what your mother and sister have proposed. What do you have to say? Do you feel that you could leave here for France, knowing that the journey will be dangerous and might separate you from your family for some time?"

Camille sat silently for a moment and then seemed to compose herself.

"I know what Mother says is true about the risks here. The thought of that man's face will be impossible to forget if things are unchanged here in Belgium.

"Sara, if you agree to take me with you to France, I promise you that I will not be a burden to you or to Sylvia."

Sara sat silently for a moment while she gathered her thoughts. When had she ever done anything simply for herself? Now these women, who had shared the awful trauma of the day's events, were asking nothing more than a chance to escape from such terror, regardless of the risks. Sara now clearly realized how much of her life had been spent chasing dreams: the just treatment of the working class, a world at peace, a nearly hopeless relationship with the only man she had ever loved. What would come from her travails even if she was able to get back to Paris, knowing she had abandoned these girls she had shared so much with on this day?

Yet, who knew if France would still offer a refuge—and if so, for how long?

"Camille, if you and your sister really want to risk this journey, and if you, Golda, are sincere in wanting them to accompany me, then I promise that I will do all that I can to find them a safe place in France, as long as such places exist."

Despite the magnitude of such a decision, each woman readily agreed with near simultaneous nods of their heads.

"It seems that we are all in agreement then," concluded Sara. "Let's get our things in order, because I believe we must leave as soon as possible."

The women spent the rest of the afternoon preparing satchels of clothing with an attached role of bedding that could serve them well if they were forced to sleep out of doors. Each included a jacket for foul weather, and a small tarpaulin was wrapped in Sara's bed role. Provisions were also carefully packed to minimize space and weight yet provide them with a source of nourishment if needed. They were finishing their preparations by early evening when the men returned.

They arrived with tired and forlorn expressions. Only Aaron, who by now was used to dealing with the realities associated with the German invasion, seemed relatively unaffected. They must have been surprised to see the women distraught and ill prepared for their return. While Dierk spoke with his sisters, Golda quickly took her husband, Joseph, aside for a quick, hushed conversation.

When Golda returned, she announced to the men that in their absence there was an occurrence that had made it necessary for them to rethink the timing of Sara's return to France. She was quite forceful in her refusal to elaborate further as to what those events might have been, saying only that when the time was right, they would find out. Until then, it had been decided that both the girls would help guide Sara to France and if successful would stay with her there until conditions improved in Belgium.

Joseph, having been forewarned by Golda, voiced little protest except to ask if she was sure that there wasn't some better alternative. His wife gave him a withering glance, suggesting that there was nothing further to discuss in that regard, but before she could reply, Dierk interjected with a string of objections of his own.

Adopting a posture and tone of voice that suggested a long and familiar dominance in such family matters, Golda proceeded to inform her husband and son that all their objections had been duly considered. However, a matter of such importance had come up that underscored how vulnerable the family and especially the two girls now were, if the Germans were free to act without responsible oversight. Given that the present conditions might last for a long time, the women had concluded that the safest thing was to try to escape from German control as soon as possible.

The men, already drawn out by the strain of the day, seemed too stunned to protest further. Afterward, all of them gathered in the dining room for a supper that was as somber in mood as it was spartan in content. When the table had been cleared and the dishes washed, the women set about finalizing their preparations for their departure, which they planned for early the following morning.

With the first light of the summer morning, all were up to attend to the usual chores, as if this was a routine day instead of one of dramatic change. While they were eating, each seemed to make a concerted effort to avoid discussing the imminent departure that all now dreaded.

At last, with the table cleared, they assembled in the barnyard, where the tone of their discussion became focused and serious.

"Paul and I spent a great deal of time yesterday gathering information about the German whereabouts and activities in our discussions with other farmers and suppliers," Dierk began.

"They are concentrating their actions on a drive into France, leaving only enough troops to neutralize their Belgian holdings. I believe from our discussions that their army is for the most part no farther north than Mons, and the brunt of it has been moving away from us to the south and the west."

"Time is critical to them," said Paul. "That is why they have ruthlessly tried to put down any resistance here in Belgium, although it has been more than they anticipated. They had not counted on this much resistance, and it has caused them delays that they were not expecting. Now that they have finally seized the areas in Belgium that will allow them access to France, they will focus on their objective, which no doubt is Paris. That suggests that France can be reached from here without a significant detour to the north. You still must be cautious, however, as there may be stragglers or advance elements of their troops directly west of us."

"If you can avoid their forces," Dierk said, "I'm confident that you can get into France. What you do there is the next big problem, especially if you insist on trying to get to Paris." He made this latter point while looking specifically at Sara.

"To get to the French lines, you will have to get in front of the German advance, which will not be easy, as they have several days' advantage on you."

"What are you trying to say, Dierk?" asked Sara.

"I am suggesting, for the safety of my sisters, that you consider carefully the risk of trying to outrace the German Army to Paris. Once you are in France, you should seek shelter in the north away from the fighting until the outcome is determined."

"I have already promised Golda that I will do everything that I can to place your sisters in the best position possible for their safety. If keeping them to the north is best, then that is where they will go. If the Germans are repulsed, however, they may fall back onto these northern regions as well as northern Flanders. For that reason, if there is a way that we can arrive at a location behind the French forces, that will be my objective."

Little needed to be said further, and each seemed to realize that the time for the girls to leave was at hand. They then broke into small groups, thereby leaving Sara and Aaron alone as they made their final farewells.

Aaron was the first to speak.

"Well, Sara, we both knew or at least hoped that you would get this opportunity someday. I just wish I was there to see you arrive in Paris."

"You will be in spirit, Aaron, and I promise to get word to you when I do."

"I must confess that when we first set out, I had my doubts that either of us would get this far, but here we are. Do you know the real reason that we have been so successful in getting here?"

"It was due to a wise old Jewish merchant from Berlin who knew many people and knew how to use these contacts to his advantage," Sara replied.

"That is the least of it. If I hadn't been challenged, I would never have ventured much farther west than Brandenburg. More importantly, if I had not discovered how talented you are and how much I could rely on you, I would have quickly passed you on to someone else to shepherd you homeward. You have been a remarkable partner in all of this, Sara, and your confidence and courage have made me better."

"It seems to me that you have always had the courage, or you would never have agreed to take me in the first place."

"I may have had courage, as you say, but until we set out together, I had lost much of the audacity that I had when I was younger. Being around you has rekindled that. How else would an old man end up in such a position of power and responsibility?

"No, without you, Sara, I would never have felt it necessary to do what we have done. I am going to miss you very much, but it's an absence that I'll be able to deal with, knowing that you'll be in a better place to exercise your considerable powers to help end this war."

"How can I ever thank you enough for all you have done for me, Aaron? To end up here on the doorstep of France is simply incredible. That you would risk your life for someone you had never met is a testimony to your goodness. I don't consider myself a religious person, but I believe that God has favored us on this journey."

"If that is the case, we're both the better for it. As for me, I'm thankful he has given me the opportunity to learn from being with you, Sara, and what I have learned makes me certain you will get home, wherever that might be.

"Now, I have said enough. The time has come for you to get on your way. When I was in Brussels, I was able to get a map, which gave a very accurate representation of the roads to France from here. There is even some representation of the eastern regions of France as well. The war may have affected the access and quality of many of these routes, but it is wise to understand what lies ahead, especially if Sylvia might lose her way."

With that, he slipped the map into Sara's backpack and gave her a final hug and kiss on the cheek, being careful to hide his face so that she could not see his emotions.

"Aaron, I will see you again soon when all of this has passed and when we can reflect on our adventures and smile."

"Shalom, Sara."

"Shalom, my beloved friend. When we meet again, we might even consider resuming our partnership, which—even if I do say—has been very successful."

Then she hugged Aaron, carefully turning her head to avoid him seeing her tears. Afterward, she turned briskly, gathering herself and her belongings, and she and the two sisters mounted their bicycles for the day's journey ahead.

As Aaron faded from sight, a profound sadness came over Sara. Too often in these last weeks, she had been torn from people she had grown to love. How she hated this war! Then as she pedaled to keep up with the sisters, the rhythm of her exertions drew her back to reality and the demands of the present.

29

France Rejoined

WHEN SARA AND THE ROSEN SISTERS REACHED THE main road, they found it to be lightly traveled. Sara was pleased, fearing the crush of refugees that Sylvia had noted in recent days might slow their passage. After riding a few kilometers, Sylvia stopped at the crest of a hill that provided a panoramic view of the region to their north and west. Withdrawing to a secluded spot off the road, they paused for a drink of water while they studied the vista in front of them.

Nearby was Aalst, a town that the Rosens knew well from its proximity to their farm. To their south, they could see in the distance the smoke that marked the fires around the battle sites near Charleroi. The day was remarkably bright, with only a few large cumulus clouds hanging in the sky, so that the haze hovering in the distance could only be coming from the aftermath of the savage battles. The women were sobered by the clear demonstration of their proximity to the war's destructive presence. That direction, while no doubt the shortest route to Paris, was clearly one that posed risks too great to chance.

As their gaze swung to the northwest, they could see the variegated landscape of canals leading toward Mons, where reportedly a large battle recently had been fought between the

British and Germans. Almost due north was the great Flemish town of Ghent, for the moment safe from the German forces that were pushing toward the southwest, concentrating their efforts on their offensive into France. The women could no doubt pursue a route toward Ghent and then the coast and Bruges, with little likelihood of encountering Germans, but the distance would make their journey long and time-consuming. In the present circumstances, Sara knew that each day that passed made it more difficult to flank the German Army and get to Paris.

Ideally, their route would be farther south from Ghent. As they looked toward the horizon to the west, the distant spires of the ancient town of Tournai were barely visible. If they could reach Tournai, they would be nearly in France. It was clear to all three of the women that this was their best route, if only they could avoid any German stragglers or regular units. As they surveyed the region ahead, they could see no evidence of military activity, which, coupled with the relative light traffic that they had encountered, gave them some hope that the Germans were confining their efforts farther to the southwest. If that was the case, the distance to France was such that, with good fortune, they might expect to reach the border later that day.

Refreshed, they set out westward, using smaller roads known by Sylvia when they were available. Through strenuous effort, they made excellent progress, bringing the spire of the cathedral of Tournai ever closer. Now, the risk that Sara had taken in bringing the two Belgian women began to pay dividends. Near Tournai, Sylvia indicated that they should turn on a smaller lane that angled to the northwest from their present route. Soon they were progressing through the Tounai Valley, and after more than an hour of vigorous pedaling, they came to a rise where they could see clearly the French towns of Lille and Roubaix.

There, in a small glen of poplars, the women stopped for lunch and observed a bridge where several small wagons and two trucks waited to cross into France. As they watched, they saw a small group clad in uniforms none could recognize. Likely, they represented some local Belgium militia or government customs officers, but hesitant to be subjected to an unknown process, Sylvia suggested an alternative approach.

After finishing their lunch, Sylvia led them away from the bridge along a small lane that ran parallel to the river, away from Lille. They were still in the country, but now the population along the roads was more extensive than it had been earlier in the day. To remain as inconspicuous as possible, they slowed the pace of their travel for the next half hour, until once again Sylvia took an even smaller gravel-covered lane. It led to a broad, quiet stretch of river relatively uninhabited on either the French of Belgium side. It was a ford that she had learned of one summer while camping with classmates. After a quick appraisal of the situation, the women drew their skirts up, tightening them around their upper thighs, and placed their provisions on their shoulders to better negotiate the relatively slow current of the river.

Within a brief time, they were engulfed by the cool water, which deepened as they progressed toward the middle, threatening to soak all of them above their waists. They leaned the bicycles into the current for added stability until finally the depth as well as the current lessened, making their passage easier and hastening their pace to the opposite side. Within minutes, they were ashore. Quickly gathering their things, they found a path from the water leading to a small lane. Caught up by their efforts, it was some time before it dawned on them that they were now in France.

The lane that they were on was narrow and filled with ruts, which made it necessary for them to walk their bicycles for most of the time it took them to reach an opening in the dense forest. There the route seemed to lead to a larger road. As they neared the road, there was more traffic appearing through the canopy of leaves than they had seen throughout most of their journey to date. Pausing to assess their present situation, Sara, now free from the worry of being discovered as an enemy, gave silent thanks for Sylvia's expert guidance.

As they emerged from the canopy of the woods, they proceeded cautiously, searching for any potential danger that might necessitate a hasty retreat to the cover of the woods. Seeing no evidence of the German Army, they fell in with the traffic that was moving toward Lille. As they progressed, Sara began looking for a route from Lille that would take them to the southwest toward Lens, where she knew people she had met from past visits with Karl when she was younger. The intersecting roads that they encountered gave little promise of an easy route toward Lens, however, so until something more promising came along, Sara seemed content to follow the stream of traffic heading toward Lille.

Uncertain where they were after another half an hour, Sara consulted the map given to her by Aaron and afterward began to look for the occasional passerby coming from the opposite direction to help confirm their present position. At first, she was hesitant to approach these strangers, but hearing the old Picardy dialect that she knew from the past, she became emboldened by its familiarity to be more forward in seeking out information from the travelers they now were encountering in larger numbers. Many of these people were either unable or unwilling to give more than cursory information to a group of three strange women, but when Sara persisted, she often succeeded in prying out valuable details that she hoped would prove helpful.

What she learned was that the Germans were passing in a concentrated force moving rapidly to the south of where they were presently located. Tales of German savagery in Belgium had not been lost on the French, many of whom had abandoned their homes and possessions to flee from the invaders. Already stories of brutal reprisals against French citizens were being reported much in the same manner as had occurred in Belgium. For those fleeing toward Lille, it seemed better to relinquish some possessions rather than risk one's life.

The women also found out from a group of frightened elderly sisters, who had been all too close to elements of the German First Army, of a suitable road to Lens that intersected their present route. Sara was told that, as the road they were now on approached a gathering of buildings, including a women's school with a distinctive green cupola, there would be an intersection with a route that would lead toward Lens. From that intersection, Lens might well be reached by dusk if all went well. Encouraged, the women pushed onward, and in reward for their efforts, the dome of the school appeared in the distance by late afternoon.

As they turned from the road to Lille, they took a brief break to eat some cheese and bread along with some thinly sliced ham and drank water from the village fountain. Refreshed, they set out, determined to get as far along the road as conditions would permit. The road they were on was similar in size to the road toward Lille, but as they progressed farther toward the southwest, away from their original route, the number of refugees entering from the numerous smaller roads intersecting their route seemed to increase. At these intersections, traffic slowed due to the congestion of walkers and other vehicles trying to merge in the ever-larger flow of traffic. At these times, the women found that the only way they could proceed was to dismount their bicycles and walk with the crowd until they found a convenient opening to escape the congestion.

This was to be the routine for the remainder of the day— periods when they would break from the congestion allowing them to proceed at a more rapid pace on their bicycles, followed by the inevitable slowing that came with any substantial intersection. At times, Sara had an almost fatalistic sense that she was being carried by a wave whose power she had little control over. As the afternoon wore into early evening, there was little sign that the congestion would lessen.

The northern latitude at this time was to their advantage, as the daylight hours were still long. As the sun began its descent in the west, the traffic along the road mercifully began to lessen. Now with a less congested road in front of them, the nervous energy pent up through the afternoon was released, and they struck off on their bicycles at a rapid pace with renewed energy. Just as dusk was falling, Sara began to recognize familiar features of the countryside near Lens that she remembered from her trips with Karl. When at last she saw the road rise to a small village and saw the Romanesque church dominating the hillside, she knew that their long day's journey was coming to a successful conclusion.

At the top of the hill, she turned down a smaller road. At the outskirts of a village, she came to a tidy farmhouse surrounded by several barns and stock-holding pens that she recognized at once as the home of Karl's old colleague Albert Massard and his wife, Colleen. She was excited to see lights on the first floor, signifying that someone was still occupying the house. Shortly after knocking at the door, she was greeted by Albert Massard, whose suspicious countenance turned to pleasant surprise upon discovering the identity of his late-night visitor.

After a few preliminary questions, the Massards welcomed the young women in, and Madame Massard quickly went about preparing a snack of cheese and fruit. Afterward, they were shown to a comfortable upstairs room, with sleeping facilities for the trio, and another where they were afforded the luxury of a warm bath. Sara, surrounded by the sisters in a large bed, quickly fell asleep, awakening only with the first morning light and the cry of a rooster in the barnyard outside their window. Though she had every intent of getting up early, the fatigue from the previous day's travel was such that she quickly rolled over and went back to sleep until Madame Massard awakened her and the sisters, offering breakfast.

30

The Massards

THE YOUNG WOMEN WERE SLOW TO CAST OFF THE fatigue that had enveloped them during their peaceful night's sleep. When at last they arrived downstairs, they were greeted by Madame Massard and a large breakfast of cheese, meats, bread, and thick jams along with strong black tea. It seemed that the Massards had purposely set out to compensate the women for all the hardships of the previous day. Shortly afterward, Monsieur Massard arrived to join them and naturally asked about their plans for the day.

"We had hoped to inquire about the status of the country ahead of us before we departed, if that would not be too big an imposition?" Sara replied.

"Sara, you may all stay here as long as needed," Madame Massard quickly interjected.

Sara, knowing the Massards from her past experiences, was not surprised by such a generous offer but was appreciative of the gesture all the same.

"Colleen is right to urge some caution," said her husband. "In the previous days, the Germans have been moving to the east of us, although several cavalry units have brushed the outskirts of Lens. These uhlan detachments are scattered through the area, but the brunt of their artillery and infantry have been to our east around Le Cateau, purportedly moving toward Amiens."

Sara realized that if the Germans were nearing Amiens, they were moving at a pace that might bring them near to Paris within the week.

"The three of you need to remain here until I can at least get some more information about where the brunt of their army is heading. In fact, you are welcome to stay here as long as you need to, just as Colleen said."

"That is extremely generous of the both of you, Albert, but if possible, I need to get back to Paris. Nevertheless, we could all use a day to rest up and would be happy to help around here in any way possible to lessen the burden on you."

Sara knew the Massards from her past experiences to be both kind and responsible. They no doubt would welcome the help of the two Belgium girls for work around the farm, and now that she was in France, Sara would have little further need of their guidance. After breakfast, she approached Colleen Massard.

"Colleen, I can't tell you how thankful we are for the opportunity to rest here."

"It's our pleasure to have you here, especially in light of all that's going on."

"It must be hard for you and Albert to manage without your usual help."

"We have had to make do as best we can, but most of the able-bodied men, including our son, have joined the army or are working for them. We have been relying on our daughters and their children, who are not old enough, for much of the work that needs done."

"It sounds like you could use some help."

"All of us here are needing help, Sara."

"In that case, I want to talk to you about the Rosen sisters. As you know, they have grown up in Belgium and are very familiar with the work necessary to manage an operation like yours. They escaped with me to France because Camille was assaulted by German stragglers one morning while doing routine chores. Fortunately, Sylvia and I were close by and helped to rectify the situation, but all of us, including their parents, felt that given the German presence in Belgium, it would be better if the sisters could escape to France with me."

"I'm so sorry to hear that, Sara. We have heard many bad rumors about the Germans in Belgium and just pray that we can turn them out of France."

"Colleen, I promised their family that I would look after them and try and find a safe location for them in France. If you have need for help and could shelter them here, I can promise you that they will be very welcome and productive guests."

"I will talk this over with Albert, but I'm sure that he will agree with me. These girls would be a godsend."

"Thank you, Colleen. I would not have asked you this if I didn't think the four of you would make a good match."

After talking with Colleen, Sara approached the Rosens, finding them in the bedroom, pacing restlessly as they stared out the window.

"What did you find out, Sara?" Camille inquired.

"Not too much regarding the Germans, but I think I have some good news for the two of you."

Sara then proceeded to discuss her recent conversation with Madame Massard.

It was Camille who first replied. "Sara, if it is all the same to you, I would rather go on with you to Paris."

"It's not all the same with me, Camille. We have been lucky to get as far as we have without running into trouble. In the next few days, the German Army will be ever closer, making our journey far more dangerous. I had a long talk with Madame Massard just now. I know her and her husband from times past and know them to be fine people. Not only would they look after you, but your presence here would be a major help to them."

"I like the two of them very much, from what I've seen," said Sylvia. "If we could be of help and earn our keep, then I would be comfortable here."

"I think it is a situation that will work out well for all of you, Sylvia. I remember what your brother said about putting the two of you at risk. I can in good conscience leave you, knowing for the present you will be far safer here than following me toward Paris."

The remainder of the day was excruciatingly long for Sara, but it was also very productive. Word was slowly coming back that the German Army had not violated Amiens but had passed to the east of the city. If that was the case, then Sara realized she could take a more direct route toward the capital. Late in the day, other accounts began to come in that large elements of the German advance had been sighted on the roads to Compiegne. That information reinforced the plan Sara was evolving for her travel, which she was now determined to undertake the following day.

Sara awoke with the early-morning light streaming into the bedroom. The two Rosen sisters were still asleep, and she chose not to wake them to allow her some time to think. She left the house silently and walked to the crest of a nearby hill that provided a clear view of the sun rising in the east over the flat landscape toward Amiens. Stretching beyond into the distant horizon, she knew Paris lay less than one hundred kilometers to the south.

Under normal circumstances, the morning would have been beautiful, with a clear, pale eastern sky promising a sunny day for travel. Sara had become adept at reading the horizon for signs of trouble, much like a mariner looking out over an expanse of ocean, searching for clues to an approaching storm. Now as she looked out from her secluded vantage point, she could see unmistakable evidence of the proximity of the German Army, marked by a fine cloud of dust hanging in the morning sky east of Amiens, indicating the perturbations of thousands of marching boots and horses' hoofs. The proximity of this malevolent cloud underscored the risks that awaited her if she planned on beating the Germans to Paris.

Upon returning to the house, the Rosens were awake, and they and the Massards put on a brave face while Sara finished her packing for the day ahead. After a hearty breakfast and enduring the now familiar melancholy of leaving beloved companions behind, she set out once more. Her mood was made even worse this time, knowing that for the first time since the war began, she would now be alone.

Travel that morning was even more difficult than the approach to Lens, with the roads filled with large numbers of displaced civilians. The crowds often made it difficult to bicycle, especially when she encountered intermittent crowds traveling in the opposite direction. It was well past noon before she neared Amiens. With each subsequent kilometer, Sara became more alert for any indication from the south or southeast that might indicate the presence of the combatant armies.

From all that she could see that morning, with the distant flashes of gunfire coming well to the southeast, she sensed taking a more direct route to Paris, south through Amiens toward the old cathedral city of Beauvais, might be possible. From Beauvais, Paris would only be some forty to fifty kilometers beyond. She was further encouraged by the lessening of traffic on the road as they approached Amiens, making it easier to pedal unimpeded by denser traffic.

Then, without warning, there seemed to be a sudden commotion ahead of her. As she proceeded farther, she saw a group of riders emerge from an intersecting road and begin to block any oncoming traffic. At first, she had trouble recognizing them, but at closer range, the large lances many were carrying made it apparent that they were German uhlan cavalry, men with a well-deserved reputation for ferocity.

Now Sara saw a large group of green-clad soldiers, some mounted on horses and others riding in wagons, filling the road and pushing to the south. Now there was little she could do but hope the soldiers would pass without causing any harm. Matters were soon complicated by traffic being turned away from the advance of the Germans. To free herself from the gathering crowd, Sara withdrew to the side of the road.

A group of riders soon approached, with one of the men shouting to Sara in a brusque, demanding style.

Unable to hear clearly, Sara approached them, saying, "What is it you are saying? I can't hear you."

The soldier was clearly surprised by her fluent German, but before he could reply, an officer appeared, demanding to know the reason for the holdup.

"This woman speaks as if she is Prussian, wanting to know what we intend to do."

The officer turned quickly toward Sara, stating in a commanding tone in German, "Fraulein, you are not in Germany now, and we have no time for polite discussion. This unit is moving to engage the French to the south, and we cannot be responsible for any civilians proceeding in that direction."

"Herr Lieutenant, it is essential that I get to Beauvais for an urgent family matter."

"That is impossible at this time, Fraulein. Your matter will have to wait. Anyone going beyond the signs we are now posting risks being taken for a partisan or spy and will have to suffer the consequences. I regret the inconvenience, but there is no time for such routine matters on days like today. You will need to turn around immediately, as no one except the German Army will be allowed beyond this point until further notice."

With that, he tipped his cap and gave a look that clearly indicated that the matter was finished. He then turned his horse to rejoin the mass of men moving toward Amiens.

Sara slowly returned to the roadway and moved away from the German troops until she had passed the crest of a hill, out of their sight. She withdrew to the shade of a nearby grove of trees. There in quieter surroundings, she tried to compose her thoughts, weighing what options remained for the hours ahead.

31

Paris Readies for Battle

IN PARIS, THE FLIGHT OF THE FRENCH GOVERNMENT seemed to further amplify the threat of the approaching German Army to the remaining citizenry. As military governor, Gallieni now had virtual control over the city, with the police, fire brigades, and court system as well as all private enterprise subject to his and his chief subordinates' authority. Large areas of the city were shorn of trees and vegetation, with many buildings razed to provide necessary lines of fire for the artillery and infantry. Private homes and businesses such as hotels were requisitioned for hospital space or necessary military usage.

Gallieni was careful to maintain close communication with President Poincaré and various cabinet ministers to update them on the status of the city and, where circumstances dictated, to obtain tacit approval for actions that he had already initiated or was contemplating. At no time in these communications, however, did he intend to surrender one bit of his authority, intending to maintain his prerogatives to defend Paris as he saw fit.

There was one remaining civilian authority that Gallieni remained in close contact with, both from respect and possible need—the American ambassador Myron Herrick. Against the advice of some of those in his own State Department and despite the threat from the invading Germans, the ambassador chose to remain in Paris and was placed in charge of diplomatic responsibilities for the city. Herrick was of that group of Americans who, from the earliest beginnings of their national sovereignty, held the highest regard for French culture. Should the German Army succeed in surrounding the city, a situation in early September that Herrick believed likely, he was determined to negotiate with their commanders or even the kaiser himself to protect the great museums and cultural buildings from wanton destruction.

Robert d'Avillard remained at the center of all this as he helped to coordinate the ongoing construction of defenses and the complex logistics that were necessary to redeploy large numbers of troops from the south to critical areas around Paris. His duties frequently brought him into contact with the civilian populace, and like Herrick, they too sensed the power of the approaching enemy. What Robert had come to admire in those that remained was their resolve to resist the invader regardless of the risks or the chances of success. He believed the city had been transformed for the better with the departure of those most prone to hysteria and panic, leaving a far more stalwart population.

Now with the departure of many who had previously obstructed critical projects, defensive preparations were going forward rapidly. Robert's trained eye was beginning to see more and more reasons for hope. The work of the previous days had built out an extensive infrastructure of battlements and trenches that, if enhanced with troops possessing modern weaponry, would pose a formidable deterrent.

Now the dynamic of the French retreat had fortuitously delivered those troops in the person of the newly created

Sixth Army into Gallieni's control. These troops were being transferred from Lorraine, but most had yet to arrive. It now fell to Robert to ensure they would populate those battlements in time to confront the German advance.

He knew in this critical hour that the coming days would be the ultimate test for much of the work he had done since entering the army. The French lines were stretched from the Swiss border in the south to the northeast of Paris in an arc, with its center being Paris. By design, rail lines and significant roads had been deployed like spokes of a bicycle wheel from Paris to areas judged to be of high priority in a war with Germany. Now, after establishing a small office in the Directorate of Railways, Robert could keep close track of the status of those critical troops in transit to the capital.

At least four Army Corps had been transferred in the first days of September toward the north. Already more than one hundred trains daily were being choreographed along rail lines to bring many of these units to Paris, where they were then to be deployed to the Sixth or Ninth Armies. To anyone watching such an operation, the constant coming and going of troop-laden trains was no doubt impressive. To Robert, who had spent much of his working life planning such operations, each successive wave of arriving troops was a gratifying confirmation of the value of his past efforts, giving tangible evidence that the French Army had prepared well to meet the logistic demands that were now required for this most unforgiving moment. He could only hope that time would allow the crucial confluence of these troops that his plans had set in motion.

This morning had been encouraging, with the final troops assigned to Foch's Ninth Army either having arrived or in transit. Of greater importance from his standpoint was the confirmation that the first large transfer of troops bound for

Paris would depart by late afternoon. Satisfied that his work at the rail center was completed, Robert returned to headquarters, noting that the calendar indicated the day as September 2. Somehow, with all the recent demands of his work, he had lost sight of the fact that August, with all its challenges, had passed. He promptly headed for the intelligence bureau, where he was greeted by Girodon at his usual location near the large wall map.

"Robert, what news do you have from the field?"

"There has been a great deal of progress over the last twenty-four hours on the battlements on our northeast, and at least one corps of regular infantry is scheduled to arrive this evening to man them."

"It seems then that we might have a ruder reception for the Germans than they envisioned if they choose to come our way."

"What makes you think that they won't?"

"This is a funny business, Robert. You sit and stare at the positions of these armies from hour to hour and day to day, and you formulate what's in their heads. Then as those positions change, you are forced to constantly revise your conclusions. Yesterday, we got some indication that their flank was turning slightly away from Paris, south toward Compiègne, and today that movement has been confirmed and is even more apparent."

"What does that mean?" asked Robert.

"It may mean very little. They might be moving to the southeast to better align with the Second Army to resume a coordinated assault on Paris. On the other hand, it may mean a great deal. There is a report that papers have come into Fifth Army intelligence from a dead German officer showing a map with the anticipated marching orders for Kluck's army over the next days. If that information is to be believed, the First Army will continue heading southeast away from Paris."

"How soon before we know if that is the case then?"

"It depends, but if we can see evidence that the majority of First Army troops have shifted in this more southeasterly direction, and not just a few divisions or a corps, then I believe that we can be certain that that is their intent."

"Well, it doesn't sound like we will know for sure before tomorrow," concluded Robert.

"What I can say with certainty is that whatever planning is in the works now may not be all that relevant by this time tomorrow."

"I could deal with that if it means we won't have to defend such an extensive perimeter around the city. Thanks for the encouraging news, Girodon. I hope you'll have even more tomorrow morning."

———

As Robert entered his office to finalize some details of his day's work, he was stopped by his aide.

"Sir, the driver Karl is here. He says that it's about a matter that he believes is important, and he says he is willing to wait until you can see him."

"Show him into my office then if you will."

As Robert was taking his seat, Karl entered the room with an expression on his face that was hard for Robert to read.

"Excuse me, Robert. I know that you have many responsibilities to attend to, but I have some news that I know you'll find important."

Given the spate of unwelcome news since the war had started, Robert braced himself to hear the worst.

"Please go on, Karl."

"Well, Robert, when we last talked about Sara, I promised to let you know if I heard anything that might relate to her condition. That is why I'm here."

Robert had an awful sense that what he was about to hear would confirm his worst fears. It was all he could do to listen further.

"It's been difficult recently to get news from the areas threatened by the German advance, but the lines of communications that we old traders have established still seem to function. This afternoon, we heard from the nephew of one of my old associates who arrived in town on business that Sara arrived at his uncle's house near Lens, along with two Belgian women."

Robert could scarcely believe his ears.

"Near Lens?" Robert asked incredulously.

"That's correct. Apparently, Sara was still there when he left, but his uncle says she is insisting on setting out for Paris as soon as she knows the conditions in front of her will allow it."

"What foolishness!" Robert exclaimed. "What is she trying to do, get herself killed?"

"Well, she apparently arrived reasonably provisioned, riding a sturdy bicycle. As you are aware, Amiens and the areas south of it have not been overrun."

How Karl knew with such accuracy the German position Robert did not know, but he could only admire the information that came from his network.

"Knowing Sara as I do, I'm convinced that she is determined to get to Paris, and if the way is still clear, I would bet on her getting here," Karl said, trying to lessen Robert's concerns.

Robert knew that there was nothing more that Karl or he could do now but wait, as hard as that would be.

"Well, Karl, I appreciate this information. I will do what I can and reach out to an old friend in the area and ask for help."

Karl nodded silently and left, promising to keep Robert informed of any further news that he might hear.

The news from Karl was possibly the only thing that could take Robert's mind off his present duties, yet in a strange way, the two seemed to be linked. At present, both Sara and the German Army were in a race for Paris, with far more at stake than a medal. As if he didn't have enough on his mind, Robert would be keeping close track of the two participants, gauging the progress of one by the great map on the wall and the other by an imaginary one in his mind. As difficult as it was to bear the uncertainty, it was made worse by his realization of how little influence he had on that outcome. Despite his concerns, however, Robert knew that many races were ultimately decided by the spirit of the competitors, and that realization gave him confidence. In such matters, he would never bet against Sara.

Now all that remained was to retard her competitor.

32

The Edge of the Cauldron

DESPITE HER FATIGUE, MARIE WAS HAVING TROUBLE getting to sleep. This was only her fourth night removed from Paris, yet it seemed during that brief span of time, she had been transported to a different planet. Her mind kept racing back over the days since she left Paris, and the poignancy of her memories made it difficult to sleep.

Thomas had accompanied her to the station the morning of her departure. As the time came for the train to leave, both sensed the uncertainty of the coming days, and that shared anxiety seemed to draw them closer. This had made it easier for Marie to bear the sight of Thomas waving frantically as he disappeared from her view.

It seemed extraordinary that their relationship amid so much chaos had been strengthened. Absurd as it might be, Marie was thankful that the war had so reshaped expected norms as to make a relationship that might have previously been scandalous now seem possible. It was not yet clear what would emerge from all this, but there certainly would be change, and it likely would be enormous. Marie intended to co-opt that change to make a future with Thomas.

Shortly after the train had left Paris, Marie began to ready herself for the tasks she might face in the days ahead, knowing how demanding the work would be. Instead of addressing the precision of her music studies, she would now confront the fluid chaos accompanying the arrival of wounded men. There, everything was immediate. Men's lives could pour out before your very eyes. In such circumstances, what mattered was not absolute precision but an instinct for understanding problems and doing what was needed to address them. Here a person would not be judged by critics and arbiters of taste but by tangible outcomes relating to life and death itself.

Now, not only would Marie accompany the train to oversee the delivery of critical supplies, as in times past, but she would remain at the front in much longer intervals to help meet the grueling demands of the wounded. This was to be her new and formidable challenge, one she approached with excitement and trepidation.

After attending to the supplies, Marie had little to do but wait for the final arrival at the front. During that time, she half dozed off as her conscious mind mingled with her subconscious, producing a mixture of thoughts relating to her sheltered past and uncertain immediate future. All of this came to an abrupt close as the train slowed amid drastically changed scenery.

As the train stopped, Marie looked out on surroundings with little evidence of civilian activity, replaced instead by the presence of the army, with countless trucks and heavy wagons bringing equipment and men seemingly from many directions at once. Much of the activity centered on the hospital grounds, housed in a former monastery now converted to the more secular task of ministering to the wounded.

Within minutes of the train coming to a halt, their equipment was being unloaded under the guidance of some of the resident nuns, and Marie and those staying on were led to their quarters, which although cramped appeared neat and comfortable. Afterward, they were led to an orientation session and dined on a lunch of warm vegetable soup and bread. When their meal was finished, the new arrivals were taken to preassigned work areas to meet the personnel that would be responsible for their transition into their new duties.

Marie was familiar with the general layout of the facility, having watched the transformation of many buildings throughout Paris into hospitals and nursing facilities, made necessary by the number of wounded arriving throughout the month of August. This facility had the scope and design to meet the demands of large numbers of wounded, with its large central building surrounded by smaller structures of assorted sizes that would allow for care of a wide range of patients. The makeup of the wounded, however, was critically different from that of Paris, influencing the services provided and the facility's configuration.

In Paris, significant triage had already occurred, with the sorting process starting on the battlefields. Those with the most severe injuries died before they could be brought to the attention of the medical staff. Those who survived would arrive at facilities such as this often in far more serious and unstable condition than the patients transferred to Paris. There being a gradient of severity from the battlefield to Paris, Marie now was much closer to the critical extreme than she had ever been.

She was surprised to see how much had changed from the early days of the war. All was new and uncertain in those first days, with the medical staff being limited by the existing structure of the hospitals, which made it difficult to readily accommodate the huge influx of wounded. The structures built in response to this acute need already showed changes based on early battlefield experience. Here, almost the entirety of the rectory and surrounding monastery had been converted into a modern factory concerned with the handling and processing of human lives. Large areas designated for triage and secondary support areas such as operating rooms and cast areas had been well positioned and, to the degree possible, well equipped. More importantly, a serious attempt had been made to use the medical staff more efficiently, hopefully sparing them from too much fatigue.

In Paris, Marie had witnessed the effect on the various personnel from long, unceasing hours of work. In those early days, the personnel would be used until the crisis could be stemmed and those most critically ill could be attended to. As the numbers of wounded increased, the limitations of such a policy became evident in the attrition of the medical staff from fatigue and subsequent inefficiency. Now, work was more carefully allocated, with increasing numbers of personnel, such as Marie, being recruited to help alleviate the burden of work for all.

Much to Marie's relief, she learned that she was to be assigned as a triage assistant, entailing many of the activities that she had some familiarity with. She was taken to her duty area, oriented by the head nurse, and afterward assigned to a series of exam rooms where she and several other young women would assist in the initial evaluation of newly arriving patients. It was made plain to the new women that there would be a senior nurse or physician available should they need help or consultation.

Soon a new group of patients arrived, and the examining cubicles quickly filled. Marie's anxiety increased as she stepped forward to meet her first patient, but she soon was reassured by a sense of the familiar, acquired during her days in Paris. Though the intensity and gravity of the wounded men's problems had increased, Marie's collective experience had taught her to read the severity of a man's condition by how he appeared and what he said as well as by his apparent wounds. There was, she realized, an intuition about this work but an intuition that could be sharpened with experience and careful guidance. Such a mastery could not be acquired simply by rote repetition but required a natural aptitude that Marie now excitedly sensed she possessed.

From the beginning, she was engulfed by waves of newly arriving wounded, and all notion of events outside of her immediate surroundings was lost. The world was reduced to a concentrated intimacy between her and each wounded man in her care. Their numbers, however, demanded rapid assessment and action, seldom allowing Marie the luxury of time to dwell at length on a problem. Yet it was part of her gift that she was able to do what was needed for each of the men she encountered. For some, it would be a quick referral, and for some of those close to death, it was taking the time to see that his spiritual and personal needs could be answered. It was to this group that Marie felt the closest, as she could sense how much her presence meant to them.

Later, during breaks or at meals, the reality of the outside world became more evident. Formal news came from various publications that were heavily censored and often dated by the time they arrived. A clearer picture seemed to emerge from the stories related by soldiers or the locals who were charged with supplying the hospital with food and other necessities. What was becoming clear was the French forces were falling back to the west. How long this withdrawal would last or how much territory would be ceded to the invaders was anyone's guess. The soldiers all seemed to have a sense that there would come a time when the retreat would stop, and they would turn once more to the attack in one last great battle designed to drive the Germans from France. It was this hope for an hour of vindication that gave everyone reason to persist, and this spirit served to inspire Marie as well.

Despite the attempt to lighten the burden for the staff from those first hectic days in Paris, Marie found herself mentally and physically exhausted at the end of a day's work. At night, she had little difficulty in falling into a deep sleep that not only proved restorative but allowed a blessed escape from the intensity of her daily responsibilities. Her exhaustion-induced sleep would prove a blessing, as it was remarkably free of dreams or, worse yet, recollections of the day past. It seemed the best possible tonic to steady nerves and fortify constitutions.

During her third day, as Marie came off her shift, she sensed a new urgency among the personnel throughout the complex. Word had come that the German forces were advancing toward Chateau-Thierry from the north and east, increasing the risk that their position might be overrun if the advance continued. There had also been unconfirmed reports of troops moving directly toward them near the Marne River. As these rumors swirled, they were magnified by large contingents of French troops pouring into the region on troop trains from Lorraine.

That evening as their increased vulnerability became more evident, a meeting was called by Colonel Lafontaine, the surgeon in chief, to discuss the current situation and what options were presently available to the medical staff. It was clear to all of those assembled that the need for the facility was now even greater, given the prospect of a final culminating series of battles. Such fighting would no doubt result in even greater numbers of critically wounded, for whom this facility had been specifically established. The obvious difficulty was the risk to the patients and attending staff should their present position be engulfed by the advancing German forces.

Colonel LaFontaine, in discussions with the staff of General Foch, was told that the Ninth Army, which was now closest to the facility, could not guarantee its safety in the coming days.

He therefore had decided that all patients who were capable of being moved would be evacuated to the rear toward Paris as soon as arrangements for their transportation and housing could be arranged.

For the patients who were not capable of being moved and to provide for continued care for the newly arriving wounded, the colonel elected to keep the facility open as long as possible. At present, no decision had been made as to the disposition of the staff until it was known who wished to volunteer to stay. It was decided that those wishing to remain should submit their intentions to their superiors within the next two hours.

When she accepted her assignment to the front, Marie had hardly considered that circumstances would force her withdrawal within a matter of days. She had come here to help those who were most deserving of care. Returning to Paris would in many ways be abandoning the very men whose needs were the greatest. These men did not have a choice to retreat to safety but had stood and suffered the consequences. Having traveled this far, Marie was not yet willing to abandon a duty she believed was vitally important. She quickly made her intent to stay known.

It was this decision that now made sleep difficult; the elation of past accomplishment was dampened by the increased threat of real danger. The gravity of their situation was enhanced by the ominous sound of heavy artillery to their northeast, a sound that seemed to draw closer by the hour. Only after she imagined the pride Thomas and Robert would have in her staying did Marie achieve an equanimity that allowed her mind to escape the maze of recurring concerns and fall asleep. It would prove a blessed reprieve.

33

Opportunity

THE MORNING OF THE THIRD OF SEPTEMBER CAME
early for everyone throughout the headquarters of the Paris
garrison. Robert, like almost all around him, had worked
late into the night on various contingency plans to engage the
advancing Germans. After only a few hours of sleep, he quickly
ate breakfast and used recently installed field telephones to
check the status of several crucial positions. He was pleased
to find the connections working and much of the work near
completion. Another call to the Directorate of Railways
confirmed that during the early hours of the morning, several
units assigned to the Sixth Army had arrived from the south.
Furthermore, there were other reserves units scheduled to
arrive within the next days.

The staff meeting that morning included updates from the
night, but information from the morning reconnaissance flights
was inconclusive. The bright, clear morning, however, promised
that more complete information would follow, which, given the
rapidly changing situation, would no doubt prove valuable. It
was remarkable how quickly the airplane, whose first primitive
iterations were barely a decade old, had transformed military
intelligence. When weather permitted, near real-time estimates

of enemy positions could be obtained, which were now being used to direct artillery fire as well.

What was clear from the meeting was the few units of the Sixth Army already in place had not yet contacted elements of the advancing German First Army. Gallieni, never one to waste time, dismissed the meeting under the condition that those present be prepared to reassemble at short notice upon the receipt of more critical information.

Afterward, Robert took a brief time to tidy up some unfinished details and then wandered back to consult the situation map in the large staff room of the intelligence bureau. The room was even busier than usual, with intelligence staff being joined by others such as Robert hoping for some new information to better formulate plans for the morning. Soon, all gathered got their first glimpses of the mornings air reconnaissance reports. One pilot had reported large columns of German infantry moving on a clear southeastern heading, a course that would take them away from Paris. The implications of such sightings created an immediate stir among those assembled in the map room.

Colonel Girodon was, as usual, positioned on a couch, strategically placed to better take in all the information that was being posted on the large situation map on the main wall. Robert overheard his reply to a question from one of his subordinates.

"Very interesting tidbit, I admit, but let's not get too carried away by this report yet. Kluck may be moving some of his army, but we don't know just how many of his units yet. This report suggests at least a corps, but that is by no means a majority of his force. Until we know where all those troops are going, we cannot be assured that Paris is safe from direct assault."

Within the hour, more aerial sightings confirmed the movement of the German Army to the southeast. Moreover, each subsequent sighting clarified the magnitude of this movement. The excitement engendered by these sightings seemed to draw in even more observers, including Gallieni's chief of staff, General Clergerie, who, like Robert, seemed transfixed by the flow of information he was seeing.

There soon followed a British officer excitedly bringing information just acquired from their reconnaissance flights of the morning. After an animated conversation with his French colleagues, the icons representing the German position were moved to reflect this most recent data. With that, it was now clear.

Girodon and Clergerie were the first to recognize what this deployment meant.

"They are turning away completely from Paris," shouted Girodon. "They are exposing their flank to us."

Such findings were a revelation to those assembled who hours earlier had planned well into the night the means to confront a frontal assault on the city that many felt to be inevitable. Now the Germans were not only turning away from such an assault, they were doing so in a way to expose their entire right flank to attack. Within the span of several minutes, it became clear that the battle in the coming days would be changed profoundly. What role the Paris garrison would play was unclear, but unless matters drastically changed, they would not be confined to the battlements that Robert and so many others had labored over the last weeks.

Before any significant discussion could be had regarding the possibilities such an opportunity might present, word came down that General Gallieni was requesting that all members of his present staff reconvene in thirty minutes. Robert, from his first dealings, had come to admire much about Gallieni, including his ability to take resolute action when conditions demanded. He did not know what might come from this meeting, but he felt a rise in confidence that something positive would soon follow.

———

By the time the meeting convened, the large staff room seemed more crowded and certainly more animated than earlier that morning. The room was abuzz with numerous conversations, all of which were brought to a halt when Gallieni entered the room exactly at the specified hour. He quickly turned to General Clergerie.

"General Clergerie, you are absolutely certain from the intelligence gathered that the Germans have turned their entire right flank away from Paris?"

"We have gotten recent information from our pilots confirming what the British reported earlier—that is, the entire German First Army has now turned from a course toward Paris, southeastward in the direction of Compiegne. They likely have covering units of cavalry guarding their flank, but our aerial reconnaissance confirms that all of their infantry corps have changed course."

"This is extraordinary," replied Gallieni. "The German is thorough and takes great care in both the preparation and execution of strategy. There can be no doubt that their initial plan was to envelop our forces from the north and west of Paris. This change therefore raises several questions."

"Perhaps it is simply a momentary shift to the east to bring the advance of the extreme right wing in better alignment with their armies to the south?" suggested Clergerie.

"I doubt it, General," Gallieni replied. "It would be better for the original plan to hold the position of the army on their right flank and let the mass of their Second and Third Armies move toward them to regain better alignment. This shift suggests something more."

"I suspect, General, that the tyranny of numbers that we have wrestled with is now coming into play for them," Clergerie said.

"Several units assigned to this advance have been withdrawn to oversee positions in Belgium or meet the threat of the Russian invasion. Not only is their strength diminished, but we are now seeing evidence that their long and relentless march has degraded the fighting quality of those troops that remain. Intelligence confirms worsening supply shortfalls not only for their troops but especially for their animals. This no doubt relates to the length of their supply lines, which makes it more urgent for them to finalize their campaign."

"That may very well be," said Gallieni. "Increased urgency, however, cannot explain all of this. Their commanders are not amateurs, yet they have offered their flank to Paris. They are either unaware of the strength of our forces or are trying to draw us out to engage us in the open."

Gallieni paused for a moment and silently stared at the situational map that had been posted on the wall for all to see.

Colonel Girodon now said, "General, we have been gathering much information from their captured soldiers and documents, which suggests a great deal of confidence on the part of many of their commanders. It is quite likely that the commander of their First Army thinks our forces are practically defeated and all that needs to be done is to finish the envelopment of the troops they have been confronting outside of Paris."

Gallieni halted any further discussion by a slight raise of his right hand.

"I think that we now at last have the information that we need. For those of you who might think that the city has now been saved, I can only say that is a wishful delusion. Paris can only be saved when the Germans are driven out of the country. The defense of the city rests on this premise, leaving us only one course of action for the days ahead. If the enemy is intent on destroying our Fifth Army, then we must abandon our fortifications and attack his flank. This is how Paris can best be defended. It is only a question of timing, and if left to me, I would attack this afternoon. The longer we wait, the more opportunity for the Germans to discover our strength and counter our advantage. Realistically, however, we must coordinate our efforts with Joffre and the British.

"General Clergerie, what is the status of the Sixth Army?"

"Nearly all of their units have arrived and are available for deployment."

"What reserves do we have available to us?"

"There are still the original garrison troops as well as the Twentieth Corps, which is en route from Lorraine."

"When are they expected to arrive?"

Clergerie looked at Robert, who replied, "There are three corps coming from the south. Two are designated to support the Fifth Army and will arrive in the next two days. The Twentieth Corps will be the last to arrive, and I expect they could be deployed no later than the seventh."

Gallieni paused for a moment before resuming. "It appears that the Germans have given us a great and unexpected opportunity. It is an opportunity that I fear will be gone if we don't act swiftly. It is therefore imperative, General Clergerie, that you meet with the tactical staff and bring me a plan by no later than three this afternoon detailing an attack on the German flank.

"I will then confer with General Maunoury so that we can begin the actions necessary to get his troops in a position to attack."

"What about Joffre?" Clergerie asked.

"I will also notify General Joffre of our intentions so that we can discuss a coordinated counterattack with all of our remaining forces."

"General Joffre may have other ideas about such a counterattack," suggested Clergerie, knowing all too well how the commanding general might view such a crucial plan that did not come from his own staff.

"His most recent directive indicates the continuation of withdrawal to the Seine. It may be difficult to change his mind, especially if the condition of the Fifth Army could not sustain such a counterattack at present."

"That is always a possibility, but you forget that General Joffre was on my staff many years ago. I know him to be a capable soldier, and he will recognize the importance of the opportunity being given to all of us by the German command. The real question, as you suggest, is not the opportunity but whether the rest of our troops are capable of counterattacking and whether the British will cooperate in such an action.

"No, General Clergerie, I doubt General Joffre will reject such a counterattack simply because the idea did not originate with him. He will reject it if we cannot get support from the remaining Allied forces. Therefore, it is important that we have a plan ready for our Sixth Army to advance against the Germans by early this afternoon so that I can begin to consult or politic if necessary with Joffre and the others as soon as possible. If there are no more matters for discussion, I suggest that we adjourn until those plans are ready."

34

The Touch of an Angel

WITH THE DECISION TO ABANDON THE FIELD HOSPITAL, the staff was quickly assigned a variety of tasks to help expedite the arduous process of evacuation as quickly as possible. Care was taken to save as much of the valuable supplies and equipment as feasible, while a careful triage of the patients was made so that those most critical or in need of special attention during transportation could be identified.

The schedule of the various medical personnel was altered to manage the transition quickly and safely. Workers were placed where needed, often finishing one job and subsequently moving to a different undertaking and location. The work driven by the urgency of the move was intense and required a near continuous effort of the staff working longer hours and irregular shifts.

Given her preference for staying on, Marie was not assigned her usual job but to a role involving more direct patient care. She was given triage duty but with more personal responsibility to prepare her for the ensuing days where there would be less help available. Already the pace of the work seemed to have increased from an incessant flow of newly wounded arriving.

Later that evening as she was finishing a brief dinner, Georgette hurriedly approached, taking a seat opposite Marie.

"Marie, I heard you are staying on. Is that true?"

"It is."

"I don't know what to say. I never imagined staying, and yet here you are on your first real assignment, and you volunteer for duty that only weeks ago would be limited to very experienced personnel. I only wish I had as much audacity and courage as you."

"Someone had to do it, and when I volunteered, they didn't turn me down. Besides, I have been assured that we'll pull back when we're told that our position is untenable."

As she finished her meal, Marie said, "Georgette, I don't know when we will see each other again, but I want to thank you for encouraging me to come here."

"I can only wish you and everyone left the best in the next few days, Marie. Leave word for me at the Hospital Neckar when you get back to Paris, and we can have a grand reunion then. In the meantime, take care of yourself."

"You take care of yourself as well, Georgette," Marie said as the two women embraced one last time before parting.

Seeing Georgette depart, Marie realized more than ever how completely she had broken with her past. Georgette, who had been with her at school and been responsible as much as anyone for her being here, was now gone. She had anticipated that her work in the coming days would be challenging, but the sense of isolation seemed to give her pause. Then, as she had done in the past, she steeled herself, giving a short prayer for the strength and courage to meet her responsibilities.

Marie worked late that evening and finally dozed off near midnight. By the following morning, most of the patients, staff, and equipment had been moved or were in final preparations to do so. There now remained a limited medical staff, including two surgeons, several nurses, and some support personnel such as Marie. Space was reduced to a large receiving ward and several surgical suites, along with an area to observe postoperative patients and others who for assorted reasons would not be suitable for transportation. The railway was located close by so that patients could be readily evacuated to Paris as needed. For those members of the staff who remained, their reduced numbers virtually assured that the coming days would be a severe test.

The priory where the medical complex had been located was near Montmirail on the north bank of the Petit Morin River. It had been selected originally due to its location central to the Third, Fourth, and Fifth Armies. Now, as the battle had shifted, the facility was much closer to the front line, with the Fifth and newly formed Ninth Armies the hospital's primary shield against the advancing German forces.

The situation in front of them was becoming ever more violent, as the German offensive was now being opposed by French troops who were contesting every foot of their native soil. The medical personnel thankfully were soon augmented by withdrawn forward medical units that provided a welcome addition to Marie and the others who were confronting a flow of casualties that was making no concession for their reduced numbers.

By necessity as much as from any explicit skill, Marie's duties had escalated in their intensity and demands. The number of wounded and the severity of their injuries demanded not only an initial assessment but often some immediate intervention on her part. She was now seeing soldiers so unstable that often they would demand her undivided attention. In this often hectic and noisy environment, Marie marveled at how she and her colleagues were adapting to the many demands at hand. It was as if all her senses had been reset to facilitate her actions when a man's life depended on them. The grizzly sight of terrible wounds and the anguished countenance of the wounded flashed by her in rapid images that required Marie to suspend her emotions to provide for more objective assessment and prudent action. No time was available for reflection or subjectivity. So intense were these moments that only afterward did her mind seem to return to a more normal and measured pace of perception and thought.

It was in those infrequent moments of quiet that she would reflect on what she had seen and done. The immediacy of dealing with a life in the balance was both thrilling and frightening but always demanding of her best. She fought always not to be overcome by any one situation, knowing that the outcome required her being detached and observant. Nevertheless, she could not help some fleeting elation when her efforts were successful. Such moments gave further impetus to persist despite circumstances and fatigue.

Those reflections increasingly were filled with poignant memories embellished by the image of suffering. Many soldiers were so critically wounded that it was apparent that little could be done to save their lives. These men drew Marie's sympathy in a way unlike the others, because she sensed that in their last minutes, the presence and touch of someone sympathetic to their condition was more valuable than anything else that could be provided.

One man remained fixed in her thoughts. She had seen him being brought in on a stretcher and immediately recognized the severity of his condition. She motioned for his bearers to bring him to her, where in his pale, grim-covered face she saw the inevitability of his death. His gaze quickly caught hers, making a means of communication possible without the use of words, which often were lacking in such circumstances.

For men like this, Marie tried to note any wishes they might share as accurately as possible and to make sure that a priest be notified to attend to their last rites. In response to her questions, the man nodded to a pocket in his vest that contained a letter and further personal information. Her inquiring look was met with a nod of affirmation, allowing her access to the man's letter to his wife. What she read almost caused Marie to lose her composure, yet in the intimacy of what would be his last thoughts to his beloved, there was a universal elegy for the loss of life's best moments now being stolen from so many in the springtime of their lives.

Marie composed herself and assured him that she would be certain that this would be delivered, and then as she was rearranging his pillow, he gave her a look that erased any previous fear and uncertainty. In their place was a warm aura and a smile that spoke of content and gratitude.

Moments like these in the face of ever greater responsibilities gave Marie growing confidence in her abilities. She was thankful for the discipline instilled from her studies in the pleasant world of her past, but in the most difficult moments, she would draw on Thomas's counsel and spirit for further resolve and comfort. Whether it was from Thomas or the power of his beliefs, Marie seemed able to grasp some inner strength when most needed and sensed the transformative power of kindness to the victims of a world seemingly gone mad.

Yet to experience this made it easy to understand how Thomas or anyone might have difficulties in dealing with the psychologic trauma that such suffering inevitably produced. If one dealt with unanswerable questions and blindly apportioned blame instead of focusing on the needs of the many victims, it would be all too easy to be consumed by despair. Marie could sense how Thomas must have wrestled to understand this terrible calamity, and in the angst of his failure, the horrors must have taken an ever greater and darker effect on his mood. Being here, she now felt closer to Thomas and sensed their shared experiences would be a source of strength in a more forgiving future.

In some strange way, this cauldron of suffering taught powerful lessons; life was too unpredictable and fragile to postpone the essential. Now, old norms and expectations that had forced decisions based on expediency were losing their power to stifle others based on passion and conviction. As Marie saw the lives of so many young men ebb before her eyes, she resolved to stand fast in her beliefs and passions and reject the empty dictates of the past. If she and Thomas survived this awful ordeal, she vowed to do everything possible to see their love fulfilled.

Late on the afternoon of the third day after the partial evacuation of the hospital, the sound of the ongoing battles to the east became more prominent. Not only were the discharges associated with cannon fire more numerous, but they were louder and easier to hear. Marie tried at first to ignore the sounds, hoping they might simply be due to a change in the atmosphere or the wind's direction. As the afternoon wore on, however, the noise became ever more prominent, making it clear that the awful interface of the warring armies was moving in their direction. Shortly after seven o'clock that night, a major on the staff of the Ninth Army visited the facility and spoke with the doctor in charge. After some minutes, the doctor emerged from the meeting grim-faced and called together the staff not immediately occupied with the care of patients.

The major had been sent to warn that the German advance was coming ever closer to the hospital. It was the intent of the Ninth Army to resist this advance, but they might still be forced into strategic withdrawals until further reserves arrived. Any such withdrawal would endanger the position of the medical facility, and the major had come to suggest that all personnel as well as those patients that could be moved be withdrawn to the west as soon as possible. For those patients that could not be moved, army corpsmen would be assigned their care after the medical personnel had left.

So once more, what remained of the staff began processing the patients and medical equipment to be loaded into ambulances and a train that would be arriving that evening. Marie was spared the task, as she had insisted in working an extra shift to help deal with the incessant flow of wounded. It would be work every bit as frantic as that associated with the logistics of the move.

There seemed to be few men with trivial wounds. Instead, she was confronted with a succession of soldiers who would need significant surgery to deal with mangled limbs and head wounds. Her job was to stabilize broken bones and to help compress hemorrhaging, all in the hope of affording a reprieve that might allow for further intervention. It was an atmosphere so charged and grizzly that at times it was like a slaughterhouse awash with blood and flesh rent into deformities barely recognizable.

Finally, in the late hours of the night, a blessed decrease in intensity settled over all, allowing Marie to escape for some sleep. As she departed, she became aware of her bloodstained smock but, now hardened by her experiences, thought little more of it, except to discard it as soon as possible to get to bed.

Marie slept until daylight awakened her and was surprised by the changes that had taken place during the night. Many of the patients had already been evacuated to the waiting train or other motorized vehicles. What remained was the transfer of the most critically injured patients to ambulances that were being specially outfitted to better care for them. Their departure was dependent on the present military situation, which the commander of the hospital had been closely monitoring through contact with the staff of the Ninth Army. Shortly after breakfast, it was decided that conditions were now such that the more direct route to Paris might be endangered by advancing German forces. Instead, it was decided that the convoy should proceed toward Montmirail, where a large bridge could convey them across the Petit Morin River along a safer but more indirect route to Paris.

Marie and a nurse were assigned to a truck outfitted with four cots suspended like beds—two on each side, and what space remained was filled with valuable supplies. The truck in convoy with some twenty others lurched slowly along the rutted roads to the sounds of near incessant artillery to the east. The drive along the route to the bridge at Montmirail some six kilometers away seemed to take an eternity. The road was now clogged by both military as well as fleeing civilians, making progress both slow and intermittent. At long last, the bridge that would convey them to the south and away from the combat came into sight, much to everyone's relief. From her vantage point, Marie could see the first ambulances following the lead vehicle cross the bridge slowly. The line that followed began a slow progress toward the crossing as well.

As she drew near to the crossing, Marie heard for the first time the high-pitched wail all too familiar to the many soldiers in this procession. The terrifying sound ended with a huge concussive wave of energy as the cannon's projectile crashed to earth. From the corner of her eye, Marie saw a cloud of earth and the shattered pieces of what appeared to be a building along the access to the bridge. Soon, a second shell was heard incoming and landed at the opening of the bridge itself.

That shell made a direct hit on the truck in front of Marie, destroying it instantly. The force of the blast caught the truck Marie was in, lifting it from the ground and tossing it on its side. Marie was caught by moving cargo and then watched as the bed above her tore from its mooring, falling toward her. Her attempt to avoid it was futile.

Those in the remaining vehicles behind them rushed out in hopes of rescuing those trapped in the wreckage. As they clawed frantically at Marie's truck, hoping to get inside before the flames engulfed it, they found her lying unconscious inside, buried under the weight of a dead soldier.

35

Journey's End

DESPITE THE WEEKS SHE HAD SPENT IN PROXIMITY TO the German Army, accompanying Aaron and Shrieves, Sara's encounter with the uhlans had been unsettling. Afterward, she had composed herself away from the main road where she could better think through her next step. Remembering the map Aaron had given her before leaving for France, she took it out and was gratified to see that the roads in this area were included. From this, she could see that a road that she had passed no more than three kilometers previously angled to the southwest in a direction that presented a far better chance of avoiding the present German advance.

Now as matters stood, Sara had two choices: return to the hospitality of the Massards and give up trying to reach Paris or accept the risks and continue along this other road to the southwest. Unwilling to give up a goal that she had invested so much time to achieve, her choice seemed obvious.

After a small snack of bread and cheese, Sara set off, determined to travel until daylight held out. She paused at a nearby village to inquire about the status of the road ahead and was encouraged that no one had heard of the German Army being in force to their west. Studying Aaron's map, she noticed an intersection several kilometers to the west, with two other roads coming together in a six-way interchange. At that point, two roads led to the south; one headed for Beauvais, and the other in a more southwestern direction toward Normandy. Using some of her French francs that she had been carrying with her all the time she had been on the journey from Berlin, she bought a bottle of wine and some bread and cheese for her evening meal from an elderly couple who were still selling provisions from a small shop along the main thoroughfare.

Sara resumed her journey, determined to make as much progress as possible, given her late start. In the waning twilight near a small rise was a clearing near the edge of an old forest. It looked out to the southwest toward several villages scattered across the horizon. Seeing no evidence of German troops and discovering a small stream nearby that would serve well as a source for water in the morning, she decided to make camp for the night. After a meal during which she finished the bottle of wine, she spread out the blanket in her travel bag, and with the coming darkness, she fell quickly to sleep.

With the first light of morning, following a brisk wash in the stream and a quick bite of bread and cheese, she set off once again in hopes of avoiding German patrols during these early-morning hours. By the time the sun had gotten above the trees, she had already traveled some distance. Consulting her map, she now believed that she was nearing the six-way intersection she had targeted the previous day. At this hour, there was little of the traffic that had slowed her progress yesterday, but when she passed the intersection of a road to Rouen, Sara noted a poster affixed prominently along the side of the road, written in bold, large German with an accompanying French translation printed more discretely. She stopped to examine it more closely, and what she saw rekindled her awareness of the risk that had been made apparent to her yesterday.

The poster stated in unequivocal terms that the traveler was now entering territories considered under the protection of the German Reich. Sara had seen posters of this type in occupied Belgium as well. The poster cautioned that any actions carried out by the population against the German Army or authorities would be considered acts of war and would be punished in the harshest manner. She knew all too well what such punishment might entail from the fate of countless civilian hostages who had been shot in reprisal for real or imagined incidents perpetrated against the invading German forces.

It also stated ominously that anyone out after eight o'clock at night or traveling without appropriate papers would be detained and would be subject to discipline by the German authorities. Sara was thankful that she had left the Rosen sisters in the care of the Massards; explaining her own presence might be hard enough, but with the Rosens, it would have been impossible.

Sobered by the poster's warning, she moved forward cautiously and paused at the top of a hill that revealed the intersection of the roads she had been looking for. She saw little evidence of any military presence at this hour. Reassured, she struck out, proceeding at a more rapid pace on the road toward Beauvais. Soon, however, her elation was dispelled by the sudden appearance of a German motorized vehicle comprised of two soldiers in the front seat and an officer in the rear. It entered the road from a concealed country lane and was coming toward her. Before she could take evasive actions, she was spotted and ordered to remain where she was and dismount from her bicycle.

"Where are you going alone at this hour?" the officer demanded in a threatening tone. "Haven't you read that this area is now under the protectorate of the German Army?"

Sara was at first hesitant to reply, trying to quickly compose her thoughts.

"Where did you get that German satchel you are carrying, Mademoiselle?" asked the officer suspiciously. "You French have been duly warned about the consequences of stealing German property."

Sara suddenly realized that one of the bags she was carrying had been brought with her from Berlin, and recognizing its German origin, the officer had further reason to be suspicious of this lone rider.

Jolted by the tone of the officer's question, Sara quickly replied, "Lieutenant, it would be wise that you find out the circumstances before you begin threatening people and accusing them of acts of sedition against the German forces."

The officer sat in stunned silence, hearing the tone of Sara's reply issued in fluent German, and he subsequently allowed her to continue without interruption.

"I am working along with my uncle as contractors assigned to Major Shrieves and the German supply corps charged with obtaining agreements for stocks of grain and livestock from dealers in Belgium and France. If you will permit me, I will show you a document attesting to my relationship with the German Army."

"By all means, Fraulein, I would very much like to see the document that you refer to."

Sara produced the document that Hahn had given her in Belgium.

"This document is now several days old, Fraulein, and was written in Belgium. How is it that you are now so far from there in France?"

"How is it that you are now so far from there, Lieutenant? Do you think that all the army must do is advance, and all its needs will automatically be taken care of? Or am I mistaken to believe that you and your men have more than enough food and provisions for you and your animals?"

The officer paused a moment before replying almost absentmindedly, "Of course, we don't have enough food, Fraulein. That is one reason I'm on this road this morning."

"So that you can commandeer enough provisions to feed an army, Lieutenant? That is no way to win a war."

"What do you know about winning a war?"

"You've not grown up on a farm, have you, Lieutenant?" Sara asked.

"No, I'm from Dusseldorf. I was a manager at a small machinery plant," he replied tersely.

"Well, Lieutenant, you must know then that your machines cannot be built without the right raw materials. The same could be said of an army. You might have thought or been told that all it would take for the army to succeed would be to have the right weapons and discipline, but now no doubt you have discovered otherwise."

"What do you mean?" he asked suspiciously.

Recalling the appearance of the horses in the cavalry unit she had seen earlier, she quickly said, "Think about it for a moment. When horses are without the proper forage, they can only function at a fraction of their peak effectiveness. The same is true for an army. Without proper food, they are not the same army that they were when their bellies were full. Think what you will, Lieutenant, but our job is now as vital as any in the army. If we can establish relationships with producers here in France, as we have in Belgium, then there is a good chance that we can acquire far more of what the army needs than in all the private raids and forays through the countryside that are now being done in the hopes of obtaining food."

"I hope you're right, Fraulein," he replied with a markedly softened tone.

"I know that I'm right," replied Sara with her characteristic confidence.

"These farmers are smart, and they have heard what has occurred in Belgium with the German Army. They have already taken measures to hide much of what's valuable from you. What you will be able to get by force and episodic raids is a mere pittance of what is available."

"How do you plan to get it then?" asked the lieutenant with some incredulity.

"It's not likely that we will be able to reach any agreement in the immediate future here until it is apparent that the German forces have control in this region. Then, as in Belgium, we will work with the producers to craft agreements that are mutually beneficial to them and you. Failing that, Germany will be forced to coerce the necessary resources in those areas that are now in their possession. Unfortunately, such policies will not be productive or conducive to satisfactory long-term results."

"What you are saying makes sense. My company has worked with the French for many years before this war, and it was profitable for us all. Now all of that has changed, and heaven knows what will follow. For any of it to be any good, we'll all have to get over killing each other and recognize the mutual benefit you speak of. Right now, I don't know of too many people on either side who can think beyond what it takes to survive the next day."

After a moment, the Lieutenant added, "You know, Fraulein, I'm still not convinced that you are who you say you are or that you are doing what you say you have been sent to do. There is no chance that with conditions as they are in France, that even the almighty himself could work out a deal to supply food to the German Army. Right now, I really don't care about what your business is if it doesn't threaten me or my men.

"I will make a deal with you. If you share some information with me, I will try to do the same with you. Then, if there is nothing else to discuss, we can both depart peacefully."

"What is it that you want to know, Lieutenant?"

"We heard that a large contingent of Russian troops landed in Normandy and are at this very moment being deployed toward Paris. We have been sent to verify their presence. Have you seen or heard anything about them?"

"I haven't seen any evidence of their presence nor heard even rumors that would suggest their impending arrival. You must understand, however, that I'm not privy to information of that kind, so you should not rely too heavily on anything I say beyond my observations."

The German nevertheless seemed pleased by what she had said. "Thank you, Fraulein. I appreciate your help."

"You're welcome for what little it might be worth. Lieutenant, I believe, according to the information that we have, that the German Army is to the east of us at present. I have old family contacts about six kilometers to the south of us I'm trying to reach. How many more troops can I expect to encounter going in that direction?"

"Aside from reconnaissance units and possible deserters I know of, no significant German force immediately to the south of here. As for the French, I cannot say with certainty, although there is at least a division of troops that have been positioned between our forces and the coast ever since our armies have entered France."

"Then within the limits of what we know, it seems we can each proceed safely," said Sara.

"That seems to me as much guarantee as there is at present, Fraulein. Now if you will excuse us, we have some further inquiries to make ahead. I wish you well and hope to see you in Berlin someday."

"In Berlin someday, Lieutenant, in better times when we all can enjoy our friends and a return of a more normal world."

With that, the lieutenant nodded, and while the soldier in the front passenger seat kept a suspicious eye on Sara, the car turned back on the road and proceeded toward the west.

After the car passed from sight, Sara once again set off, soon arriving at an intersection where two other roads converged, one to the south toward Beauvais and the other to the southwest toward Normandy. Buoyed by the information she had received from the German lieutenant, she took the more direct route toward Paris through Beauvais.

Now alert to the prospect of German soldiers coming from the east, she proceeded, keeping a close eye in that direction while picking up the pace of her pedaling. As the day lengthened, the number of travelers on the road increased, which slowed Sara's progress, and by early afternoon, it was becoming apparent that she would not reach Paris or its outskirts before nightfall.

Emerging from a line of trees on a slight rise, she noted a large village below whose fertile fields spilled out in all directions from the medieval grid of streets surrounding a single spired church. How beautiful this image of the timeless fecundity of her country, and how welcoming after so many months of wandering in the foreboding landscapes of a Europe torn by the ancient curse of war.

What Sara could not know was how much this setting had been disturbed by rumors of German troops and cavalry moving in the environs. Indeed, there were great fears that the mass of the German invasion might be directed to the northwest of Paris, placing this idyllic setting at risk of being engulfed by enemy hoards. French cavalry units were now probing these regions for any signs of German intent in the area.

Warned of the possibility of infiltration by German agents, the sudden appearance of a lone and unknown rider approaching from the north of the village triggered suspicion in the soldiers charged with defending access to the village. As Sara approached the outskirts of the village, she was suddenly stopped by two soldiers emerging from beside the roadway. She was first surprised by their sudden appearance but then realized that they were not garbed in the pale gray-green of German troops but in blue and were issuing commands in French.

Before Sara could speak, one of the soldiers demanded her knapsack and began perusing its contents. She realized from the look on his face that he must have discovered the document from the German Army and silently cursed herself for not hiding it on her person.

The soldier quickly demanded that Sara dismount, and when she tried to speak, she was promptly silenced by a gruff command of the elder of the two. While this man held the women at gunpoint, the other entered the house, presumably to notify his superiors of the situation, and before long, a small police van appeared. Without further ado, Sara was taken into the village to what appeared to be the headquarters of a military unit in the area. Soon, an officer appeared. Clutching the papers that had been removed from the satchel and then pulling up a chair, he began questioning Sara in halting German.

When Sara replied in perfect Parisian French, he seemed somewhat surprised but resumed his questioning in a cool and accusatory manner.

"What, might I ask, is your purpose in riding alone under the present conditions, carrying papers that identify you as working for the German Army? Don't you know that your compatriots are not here yet?"

"Lieutenant, please allow me to show you my papers." Then. in a careful manner so as not to alarm the guard who was watching her closely, Sara reached into her stocking and produced her French passport. Handing it to the officer, she continued.

"Lieutenant, I admit that you have reasons to be suspicious, but as you can see, I am not German but French. My name is Sara Morozovski, and I am originally from Paris, where my father, Joseph, is the president of the bank Morozovski and Sons."

"If what you say is true, what are you doing with these German documents identifying you as working for the German Quartermaster Corps?"

"It's a very long story, Lieutenant. At the outbreak of the war, I was a correspondent in Berlin and avoided detention by going underground with the aid of many German friends I had made before the war. It was one of these friends that gave me cover by employing me in his business of supplying livestock to the German Army. In that context, I was able to get to Belgium, where, with the help of others, I escaped into France. Over the last several days, I have been making my way toward Paris."

"All of this seems a bit farfetched, mademoiselle, if not outright preposterous," the officer noted suspiciously.

"Excuse me while I check with divisional intelligence to see if they can help verify your story."

Only now did Sara realize the dilemma she faced. After the journey she had taken to get here, how bitterly ironic it would be to face the consequences of mistaken identity. Given present circumstances, it was a situation that could prove very difficult. She knew all too well what German captors might do in such circumstances.

The moments spent waiting did not help ease her concerns, but finally after what seemed an eternity, the lieutenant returned.

"Corporal, it seems Mademoiselle Morozovski must be telling the truth, as hard as it is to believe. When I called Divisional, I was told that one of Gallieni's staff officers had notified us of the possibility of Sara Morozovski coming into our area. It seems that she or this officer is some big shot and we are to facilitate her return to Paris as soon as possible."

Sara was stunned by her unexpected deliverance.

"Excuse me, Lieutenant. Might I inquire who the officer was that you referred to?"

"Certainly, mademoiselle," the officer replied with much greater deference than before. He took a moment to look at the papers he had brought with him. "The officer's name is d'Avillard, who I'm told is an old friend of our commander."

"Robert," gasped Sara, uncertain as to how he could have known about her presence. Then, realizing she was safe, she began to sob. Her former interrogator quickly came to her aid by offering his handkerchief in such a reassuring manner that, in her relief, Sara mixed short bursts of laughter with her sobs.

36

On the Marne

IN MORE THAN FORTY YEARS IN THE FRENCH ARMY, General Joseph Gallieni had acquired substantial insight into the craft of making war. His mastery was abetted by his considerable intellect, which made it easier to draw lessons from his experiences and those of others. From all this, he had been able to distill a set of principles that helped to shape his actions. One of these was never to prejudge the intent of an enemy to a degree that it would blind you to reality. A corollary was to never be surprised by the actions of your opponent.

Even before assuming command of the Paris garrison, it had seemed to him that the logical course of the German invasion after violating Belgian neutrality was for their armies to continue across the flat, less fortified lands of northeastern France to envelop Paris. In the latter days of August and early September, all indications seemed to suggest such a plan. When word came of the dramatic change in the direction of the German attack away from Paris, Gallieni was at first skeptical.

With subsequent confirmation of the shift in the advance of the German First Army, he welcomed the news but also realized the need for an effective response. As much as he would like it, however, he knew that the Paris garrison alone could not win an engagement with the Germans. Cooperation from Joffre and the rest of the French Army would be essential. Therefore, in conjunction with developing his own plan, he also began to reach out to Joffre and his staff.

As his chief of staff, General Clergerie, had suggested, convincing Joffre to support a counterattack would not be a given. From the very moment that he became chief of the army, Joffre had zealously guarded his prerogatives in shaping tactics and war plans. When the war came, one that he had long expected, he became essentially a military dictator controlling virtually all aspects of French life.

Gallieni knew the military protocol well and knew he would have to get through directly to Joffre to accomplish his ends. Nearly every general in the army disliked presenting a plan to Joffre, who would sit passively with an inscrutable demeanor while listening to a presentation; then afterward, often without further discussion, he would announce his intentions. The impassivity of his bearing and his dictatorial style intimidated and irritated his subordinate commanders. Gallieni, however, due to his previous relationship, was not intimidated by Joffre.

As his former commander, Gallieni knew that any plan that he brought to Joffre could not be dismissed casually without a great deal of concerted thought. He also knew that Joffre had a sound military mind, and he felt certain, given the circumstances, that he would support a coordinated attack with all the remaining forces of the French Army. After a briefing with General Maunoury to assess the Sixth Army's readiness to march as early as that evening, Gallieni initiated a call to General Joffre at army headquarters.

At general headquarters at Bar-Sur-Aube, where Joffre had been forced to withdraw near the end of August, the staff was also beginning to understand the implications of the shift in the orientation of the German right wing. When word came that a phone call had come from General Clergerie stating that General Gallieni wanted to speak with the commander about plans for an attack by the Paris garrison on the enemy's flank, Joffre refused to accept it, leaving his chief of operations, Colonel Pont, to deal with matters. Joffre was aware of Gallieni's abilities but also resented his former commander suggesting too strongly a course of action that he should follow. He believed there was room for only one commander, and he was determined to maintain the prerogatives of his position.

If he was to talk to Gallieni, it would not be over the telephone, an instrument that he distrusted, believing it all too easy for someone to mistake his intentions from a phone conversation. Furthermore, Joffre understood intuitively such communications degraded his ability to search another officer for visual clues as to his understanding and willingness to carry out his orders. Any future talk with Gallieni would be in person, where their conversation would be more secure, and any conclusions made more concrete through a written communiqué.

It was therefore left to his staff to intermediate the process with Gallieni's. Upon hearing of the plan for an immediate attack by the Sixth Army on Kluck's flank, Colonel Pont quickly grasped the implications for the remainder of the army if that strategy was launched prematurely. He also realized that he was in no position to give Gallieni's staff any approval without first getting it from his superiors. Before going to Joffre, therefore, Pont presented the proposal to his immediate superiors, launching a full-scale debate that was only interrupted by Joffre's arrival in the conference room.

As Joffre entered the room, he found his staff divided into two camps. One group argued that the army was in no shape at present to exploit the situation that the Germans had presented them. Others believed that the German vulnerability would be fleeting, but an attack by the Paris garrison could only be successful if coordinated with a wide-scale counterattack by the remaining French armies.

Joffre, as was his manner, said little but took in the various points of view, weighing them quietly and carefully. Today he would hear out all the information and viewpoints he thought essential and then make a decision that would be his alone. He was comfortable with this method for no other reason than he was supremely confident in his ability to make the right decision. It mattered little to him that he alone would be held responsible, as he had no intention of failing. Now, for some time, he listened carefully, interrupting only to clarify some point of contention or to request some additional information. Then satisfied that he had heard all that was necessary, he withdrew to his office, indicating that his chief of staff, General Barthelot, accompany him.

"What do you think of General Gallieni's proposal?" Joffre asked.

"It would require a complete change of direction for the army to suddenly turn and launch a counteroffensive. Such a maneuver is not simple even with fresh and veteran troops. The condition of the army is not good, with significant attrition due to casualties and fatigue. Even if they were better rested, many of these units are reserves."

"One of the most surprising aspects of this war to date has been how well those reserves have fought, especially here in France. I have no doubt that they will continue to do their duty," said Joffre.

"Even if we can shift quickly to the offensive, Gallieni's proposed counterattack will place enormous stress on our lines, potentially opening gaps especially between the Ninth and Fourth Armies. Some of the troops that could fill those gaps are still in transit from Lorraine. If we are to have the numerical superiority that would be preferable for such a counterattack, we should wait until those troops get here."

"And when will that be?"

"It will take at least two days for them to get into line and possibly more. In the meantime, I would suggest we wait and draw them deeper into a sac so when we are ready, we can turn and bag them."

Joffre paused to look at the large wall map and for several minutes sat in silence. At last, he spoke.

"General, I must clarify with Franchet d'Esperey some points pertaining to the Fifth Army. Until then, I want you to hold any further withdrawal toward the Seine."

"What shall I tell General Gallieni?"

"Tell him that it is my desire that he get his forces into position to attack on the south of the Marne within two days. By that time, we may well have the numbers to ensure turning the entire German Army."

With that, Joffre left a message for Generals Franchet d'Esperey and Foch, inquiring whether their armies could join with the Paris garrison and the British in a full-scale counterattack in as early as two days. He then took leave of his office and sat in a wicker chair under a large oak tree to contemplate his options and wait for their replies.

As difficult as his relationship was with Gallieni, Joffre knew that he was correct in his plan to attack the exposed German flank. He also knew from his experience as his subordinate that Gallieni's military instincts were sound and his judgment reliable. If France was to undo the damage suffered from the German advance, this opportunity provided by Kluck's turn away from Paris was tremendous if it could be exploited expeditiously. The arguments of the doubters all had merit, but in virtually all great enterprises, there are great risks. What mattered were not the doubts but the combined will of his army to overcome such obstacles and rout the invaders.

It would be tempting to postpone the action under the hope that time would improve the conditions of the troops and bring numerical advantages at the crucial time of the counterattack. He instinctively knew that it was a temptation that had to be resisted. Postponement would waste the likelihood that Kluck's troops would still be in a position of maximum vulnerability to attack from Paris. Postponement also increased the likelihood that the discordant movement of the German lines could be realigned, increasing their collective strength and decreasing their vulnerability.

Delay would also make certain that more French soil would fall into the hands of the invaders. With each passing day, new stories came into headquarters of atrocities committed in the many French towns and villages that had fallen into the hands of the Germans.

Joffre also sensed in the turn of the German advance dramatic confirmation of their vulnerability, something that he had only suspected. He knew all too well how difficult it was to coordinate an attack of such a magnitude, and these difficulties only intensified the longer the lines of communication and supply became. Joffre had agreed with General Wilson's assessment in a recent visit to British headquarters that the German attack was too hasty and overdone, making it likely that they would make a mistake that would provide the chance for the hour of reprieve. Could this be the mistake and the time? Joffre was beginning to think so.

German success ultimately depended not simply on taking French soil but in destroying the French Army. Despite all the setbacks to date, the French Army was bloodied but still intact. Joffre respected the spirit of Gallieni's bold call for action; what remained was for his battered army to seize the opportunity and prevail.

As Joffre sat alone in the cool shade, his thoughts began to crystalize into conviction. In the end, it would all center, as it inevitably did, on who was able and willing to sacrifice the most and fight the hardest. His troops were not in the best condition, but he felt certain that the German forces were in no better shape. What was essential was to regain a mental advantage. It was easy for commanders to become discouraged with the degradation of the fighting quality of their troops, faced with incessant battle compounded by continued retreat. Some commanders had come to view the Germans as invincible. This mind-set had to be quashed. What was now needed were troops with the willingness to fight and, more importantly, officers who would not only lead but refuse to accept defeat.

The awful crucible of the battles leading to this day had shown him all too clearly who could be relied upon to fight, even in the worst of circumstances, and who might equivocate. Now he felt far more confident in his field commanders and their chief underlings. He had brought Maunoury out of retirement and promoted Foch to command the Sixth and Ninth Armies, and he had replaced a spent Lanzerac with Franchet d'Esperey to command the Fifth Army. It was Franchet d'Esperey who, as commander of the First Corps, had saved the Fifth Army by his decisive leadership at the Battle of Guise. It would be these three commanders and their armies that would determine the fate of France in the coming days.

As the afternoon shadows lengthened and just before the time of his dinner, Joffre decided on a course of action.

Returning to headquarters, he stopped to confer with Berthelot.

"Have you heard anything from General d'Esperey?"

"Nothing definitive yet. His staff says that he has left for a meeting with the British and has yet to return."

"Well, keep pressing them for a reply as soon as he gets back. In the meantime, get with operations and make sure that all the command is notified that any further withdrawal to the Seine is to be on hold. Also instruct them to begin drawing up plans for the army to support the attack as outlined by the Paris garrison. All such actions should be made ready for an attack to begin the morning of the seventh."

"I will let you know when any word comes from Franchet d'Esperey or Foch as soon as it arrives. In the meantime, the Japanese officers are waiting for you."

Joffre recalled with some regret his having invited a Japanese delegation to dine with him that evening, in hopes of convincing them to persuade their government to support the Entente. Reluctantly, he left to join his visitors. Early in the meal, word came that a message had arrived from d'Esperey. It was all that Joffre could do to maintain decorum with his guests, but at the earliest possible moment, he excused himself to attend to pressing matters.

He took d'Esperey's message in Berthelot's office just off the operations bureau. The message was in keeping with d'Esperey's character, short and to the point. He informed Joffre that his troops were not in brilliant shape but could be ready to fight by the sixth. He then outlined a plan of action for the Fifth Army and included highlights of his discussion with the British, which indicated their willingness to cooperate in such an action if the Sixth Army was in position to protect their flank.

In seeing Joffre finish reading the message, Berthelot inquired, "The news is what you hoped for, General?"

"It seems we have a fighting general commanding the Fifth Army at present. He not only believes his troops to be ready but has included an exact timetable and place for their deployment. He even suggests that he has gotten the British to participate if the Sixth Army is in a prescribed position to protect their left flank.

"I know General Gallieni and was not concerned that he would have the Sixth Army in position to attack as soon as possible. What I feared was that our other commanders and especially the British would not have the audacity to support such a counterattack. General d'Esperey has dispelled my concerns, and I have little doubt that General Foch will as well.

"If the British can be persuaded to support the Fifth Army, as General d'Esperey's communiqué suggests, then I feel certain this is the time and place for our counterattack. We shall not fall back another step, Berthelot, and we will not fight along the Seine but here on the Marne.

"Please have operations draw up battle orders in accordance with the times and places as outlined by General d'Esperey."

Having given that order, Joffre felt better than he had all day, and shortly thereafter, an air of calm determination settled over the entire general headquarters as all realized that the days of the long, agonizing retreat were over. The second great offensive upon which the very survival of France was dependent was now imminent and would require all the collective effort of the Allied forces to succeed.

37

Forming the Battalions

BEFORE JOFFRE COULD ISSUE ORDERS FOR THE GREAT counteroffensive, events had already forced a change in his original plans. Now with a commitment that his counterattack would be supported, and worried that further delay might lessen its success, Gallieni elected to ignore Joffre's suggestion and proceed on a more direct path of confrontation north of the Marne. This would likely result in an engagement with German forces a day earlier than planned by Joffre. On being appraised of the news, Joffre accepted what amounted to a fait accompli, reluctantly advancing the date for beginning the coordinated offensive by one day.

Joffre knew that, despite all efforts to ready his forces and those of Gallieni, the outcome of the coming battle could well depend on the British Expeditionary Force. As fate would have it, they were now critically positioned between the French Fifth and Sixth Armies in a vital strategic position. In prewar planning, the British were positioned at the northern extreme of the Allied lines, as it was thought this would be the quietest sector. Therefore, another early policy error would have to be corrected, making it necessary for him to go directly to the British to try to convince them to act in coordination with the

French armies in the coming days. This was a task he did not relish.

Joffre knew from experience that dealing with the British command would not be easy. His intolerance for many of the traits that had so bedeviled Lanzerac in his dealings with them would have to be tempered for this occasion. Diplomacy had never been his strong suit, and what skills he had had atrophied with the increase in his authority. Yet he would have to rise to the occasion, for without British support, his plans were at a severe disadvantage. He only hoped that Lord Kitchener's recent intervention in ordering a halt to further British withdrawals would serve to stiffen their resolve, something hinted at in Franchet d'Esperey's communiqué stating that the British command had told him of their willingness to assist in a counteroffensive.

Yet as he began to present his plan to French and his staff, it was all Joffre could do to control his temper while the field marshal sat impassively, allowing his chief of staff, General Murray, to interrupt frequently with questions suggesting doubt in the feasibility of the proposed counterattack. Sensing that his presentation was gaining little, Joffre dropped any further discussion and instead turned to a less reasoned appeal that had proven effective in planning military encounters in the past.

"General French, I will not belabor the point further. The enemy has presented us with an opportunity that we have been waiting for. The fate of the war now depends on this upcoming battle. History will judge the outcome critically, but we cannot succeed without your help. Much will depend on your troops in the coming days. If we succeed, then France and indeed all free men will have cause to further honor the proud history of the British Army."

Before he could say anything more, Joffre noted a change come over his British counterpart. Gone was his stoic countenance, replaced by a face flushed and eyes filled with tears.

Despite General Murray's objections, Field Marshal French quickly assented to British participation in the battle ahead. During times such as this, great peril can dispel hesitancy and focus conviction. Joffre only hoped that this would be the case for Field Marshal French as well as all the troops under him.

As he left British headquarters, Joffre's relief gave way to a momentary sense of elation. All was now in place to issue final orders for the climactic counteroffensive. What followed was his Order #6. Its wording and the subsequent communiqué accompanying the battle orders was terse and somber.

"Now is the historic time to profit from the most recent position of the German invader and concentrate the Allied forces on the left for the long-awaited counterattack against the enemy." He added a stark admonition that "this battle will decide the fate of the country, requiring the ultimate effort from everyone involved to throw back the enemy." Now there was to be no retreat; each unit was to hold its ground at all cost rather than yield another inch of French soil. The meaning was clear to all that read it; all was now to be risked in this last great battle.

By the time Joffre's directive arrived at the headquarters of the Paris garrison, Robert and his fellow officers had been engaged throughout the previous afternoon and much of the night coordinating the Sixth Army's advance toward what they believed to be the exposed flank of the German First Army. It had fallen to Robert to ensure that the troops were transported by the fastest, most efficient means possible. He knew the roads and rail lines into these areas intimately but also recognized there were many unknowns that might disrupt even the best planning.

The demands of the moment forced any anxiety for the coming battle out of his mind. It was late in the evening when his aide reminded him that he had not eaten since early in the morning, and only then did he seem vaguely aware of his hunger. Much later, well past midnight, the pace of demands finally slowed enough to allow him to get some sleep.

By five thirty the following morning, he was fully awake and listening to Girodon relay what information had been received during the night. From all reports coming in, the route of the German advance seemed still to be heading to the southeast toward Meaux, where plans called for Maunoury's troops to engage in a major attack the following morning.

Robert knew the terrain of this countryside well from his many previous visits. It was bounded on the south by the Marne River and to the east by the Ourcq. There were numerous small tributaries and streams in the region, generally flowing in a northerly direction and bounded by sharply rising hillsides that often were heavily wooded. The valleys were heavily cultivated, and there were many small villages and towns throughout the region. There were also frequent bogs that made difficult terrain for battle. The area northeast of Meaux, however, was more suitable than most for an offensive.

As Robert crossed from his quarters to the new headquarters located in the old school concealed behind the Invalids, he was pleased to note the bright, cool morning air, which signaled a welcome departure from the unseasonable heat that had been present for much of the previous two weeks. As hot as it was in the city, the heat had made conditions even more miserable for the troops who had been in near constant action during those days. He looked on this change of weather as perhaps a good omen for the days ahead, certainly one that should improve the lot of the fighting men.

The morning progressed with little information coming in that might change the planned route of advance or the pending attack. Early-morning cavalry reconnaissance had indicated little German troop buildup along the day's prescribed route. Robert's close monitoring of the advance of the various units of the Sixth Army indicated that all were proceeding on schedule. Shortly after noon, however, reports began to come in of resistance coming from the high hills around the village of Monthyon, northwest of Meaux.

Within the following hour, reports arrived from two of the advanced infantry divisions as well as from a brigade of Moroccan troops stating that they were under heavy artillery fire that had forced them from the road to the shelter of the surrounding woods. As the afternoon progressed, it became increasingly clear that the German resistance was more than trivial. Fierce artillery battles were being fought, with the French firing from behind farmhouses and copses of tress at the elevations from which the German artillery continued to issue deadly and incessant fire. The progress that Robert had noted with satisfaction earlier in the day was now brought to a halt while the gathering French troops fought to force their way through the resistance toward the valley of the Ourcq River.

Robert and all the staff in Paris waited through the afternoon with increasing concern and frustration as conflicting reports came in of French successes, only to be countered in short order by other reports indicating a lack of progress. With each passing hour, it was becoming clear that the German force that they had encountered was substantial. The optimism engendered by the reconnaissance reports of the early morning had now been replaced by a growing concern brought on by the unexpected and fierce resistance that the Sixth Army was now encountering.

By nightfall, the terrible reality was apparent. The French had still not been able to advance appreciably since early afternoon and remained short of Meaux, where they had anticipated launching their attack the following morning.

The mood in the hastily assembled staff meeting later that night was somber. There was little more than a table and scattered chairs to support the assembled staff, who showed fatigue from a long and stressful day. The collective mood was as somber as the room was sparse. Gallieni himself showed the strain as well, with his features flattened and dark bags showing under his eyes. Despite this, he began the conference almost immediately after his arrival.

"Colonel Girodon, what is the nature of the forces opposing us on the Ourcq?"

"We believe, General, that it is the Fourth Corps of the First Army, commanded by General von Gronau. He is said to be an artillery specialist, and his handling of today's battle would certainly support that claim."

Turning to Robert, Gallieni asked, "Where are we with regard to our troop disposition now, especially here where the Germans have held us up?"

"Unfortunately, we are still far from our objective at Meaux. The brunt of the attack today fell on the Fifty-Fifth Infantry Division. By the morning, the remainder of the Fifty-Sixth Infantry Division and the Moroccan brigade will be in place to support the advance."

"I see," continued Gallieni. "At first daylight, the entire offensive will be initiated. It is imperative that we try and sustain the advance with the units coming forward. Unfortunately, the day's events have not only put us behind schedule but have alerted the Germans to our presence. They may not know the full extent and position of our troops, but they are now certainly aware we are here. As I see it, their First Army that we are now confronting is left with two alternatives.

"The first is, knowing now as they do that forces have been launched from Paris, to withdraw from their extended position, drawing into closer contact with their Second Army and consolidating their lines.

"The second is that they will turn and counterattack in hopes of destroying us and the threat we pose."

"What do you think that Kluck will do now?" asked General Clergerie.

"It is difficult to say with certainty," Gallieni replied. "If he swings his forces to attack us, he widens the gap that already exists between his army and the remainder of their forces. It is a risky gamble that threatens to expose both their flanks to our Fifth Army and the British, a situation that if properly exploited could be disastrous for them. I know how the Prussian mind works, however, and this general is every bit a Prussian. Usually confronted with such a choice, they will favor audacity over caution. I suspect therefore that, despite the risks, he will not withdraw but turn his forces on us and attack.

"If that is the case, then we will likely know from tomorrow morning's fighting. If we meet heavy resistance, then they are turning on us. If so, we will advance where we can, but it will be critical to hold our ground at all costs. It is therefore essential that the troops of the Fifty-Sixth Infantry Division and the

Moroccan brigade be pushed into the battle line by first light tomorrow, as no doubt every one of those men will be needed.

"General Maunoury asked me earlier what our contingent position will be should the Germans succeed in pushing us back. I told him that we have no fallback position behind Paris. We must, as General Joffre states, hold our ground at all costs. If we must, we will fall back into the defense works that we have built around Paris, but we will not retreat any farther."

With that, Gallieni brought the meeting to an end.

The cool, bright air persisted in the early-morning hours of September 6. On that morning, the scope of the battle characterized by the slow and fierce withdrawal of the French forces as they retreated westward ended. In response to Joffre's order of the previous day, the left flank of the Allied lines had turned to not only face their pursuers of the last weeks but to counterattack.

By early morning, the question that had been raised the previous evening in Gallieni's headquarters had been answered. At daylight, the elements of the French forces stalled before Meaux resumed their attack, aided by the arrival of the full contingent of the Fifty-Sixth Infantry Division and the Moroccan colonial troops. Through the early morning, they found themselves not only encountering resistance from the troops dug into the hillside above the valley but also increasing numbers of German troops arriving in support from elsewhere. By late in the afternoon, much of the French advance was halted by an enormous, lethal artillery barrage launched by these newly arriving forces. It was now apparent that the German commander, von Kluck, had chosen to try to destroy the French forces arriving from Paris.

Through the day, Maunoury continued to push the troops available to him into position to attack the Germans. Kluck, however, like a bear attacked by a pack of dogs, was turning on his pursuers, with his position being strengthened each hour by the arrival of more of his army. By evening, the French were still stalled before the Ourcq, while Kluck now had three full corps coming together.

For Robert and those at headquarters in Paris, their sense of the battle was hindered by the delay in accurate information coming from the units of the Sixth Army engaged at the front. What concerns Robert had increased with the arrival of a messenger bringing a note from Thomas. Robert immediately sensed news of a serious nature in this unexpected communiqué. Hastily, he opened and scanned its contents.

Robert, I pray that this note finds you safe.

I am writing to inform you that Marie was brought to Hospital Laennec after sustaining injuries during a withdrawal in the face of the German advance. At present, she remains unconscious and has injuries to her leg and arm. The medical personnel say it is too early at present to estimate her prognosis.

I wanted you to know this and hope that your thoughts and prayers can be added to my own for her recovery.

I am also praying that God will protect you and guide you in the coming difficult days.

All my best wishes,
Your cousin Thomas

The news coming at this most trying time sent a chill of apprehension through Robert. His focus on the ongoing battle had now shifted to concerns for Marie's tenuous condition. He had usually been able to rationalize the deadly nature of war as the collateral of necessity. Now, however, with this news, the awful, encompassing reality of what they all faced became too much to simply push away by mental sleight of hand. Marie's condition now clouded his thoughts with a sense of pessimism and futility. For the rest of the evening, he struggled to regain the cold, objective focus that was essential to do his job. His struggle continued as he tried to get some vital sleep, finally yielding to exhaustion well past midnight. His reprieve was cut short by morning sunlight heralding a new and challenging day.

38

Taxis to the Marne

AS DAWN BROKE, MEMBERS OF GALLIENI'S STAFF began to file into the conference room of the intelligence bureau with their gaze drawn to the wall map detailing the latest known positions of the forces coalescing northeast of the city. The pas de deux of the opposing armies traced by the sterile imagery of icons on this map during the last month was coming to an end. The retreat westward of the Allied armies that had brought them to the gates of Paris had been stopped by the combined directives of Joffre and Gallieni with the Fourth, Fifth, and newly formed Ninth Armies, along with the Sixth Army based in Paris turning once more to the offensive.

Today, the large wall map had taken on a more intimate character for those trying to foresee the day's events, as every man present had come into direct contact with many of the officers and men of the Sixth Army in the previous weeks. Indeed, some of these units represented on the map had passed through Paris in the last two days. The success hoped for in the initial French attack on the seemingly exposed German flank had been frustrated by a strategically placed vanguard of German troops, whose artillery tactics stopped their advance, allowing von Kluck to respond to the attack from Paris. Now it was clear that they would face the full might of the First German Army in the day ahead.

As Gallieni opened the staff meeting that morning, Robert clearly saw fatigue in the face of the old general. Nevertheless, he drew himself straight and seemed transformed as he began the meeting.

"Colonel Girodon, could you give us an update on the present situation?"

"General, it is now apparent that Kluck has turned his entire army to the west to attack the Sixth Army. Yesterday's fighting gave a clear indication of that, with Maunoury's advance encountering ever stiffer resistance throughout the day. By evening, the German advance had forced one reserve division to retreat into prepared defenses. We are now receiving reports that the Sixty-First Reserve Division is under heavy German fire threatening our northwest flank. General Maunoury has ordered Colonel Robert Neville's artillery to direct a concentrated attack on the German advance and is bringing the Forty-Fifth Infantry Division in place to support the position."

"What is the situation further to the right, Colonel?"

"As the map shows, this pivot by Kluck has disrupted the German line of attack, separating him from Bulow's army on his left by at least thirty kilometers."

"What is the status there?"

"Our Fifth Army may now have superiority in troop strength against their Second Army, thanks to the arrival of forces from Lorraine. That could prove very advantageous, especially if the British advance in conjunction with them."

"Only time will tell in that regard, General," Gallieni replied. He then continued. "Colonel, what is the situation with the Saxon troops in front of General Foch?"

"Previously, their Third Army advanced in support of the Second Army on their right flank. We are getting reports, however, that during the night, they pivoted to attack General Foch's Army on both his flanks."

Gallieni replied in a matter-of-fact manner, saying, "I am confident that the Ninth Army will be able to handle these assaults, given their position behind that marsh. It is now apparent that this entire battle is centered on us. If Kluck can turn our flank and envelop us, Paris will fall, and the remaining army will be in grave peril. If, on the other hand, we can stand and resist their offensive, then a well-executed counterattack by Franchet d'Esperey could split their forces. The longer we can hold our ground, the greater that threat becomes to the German command, a threat that could force them to change their tactics to save their army from destruction.

"Robert, what is the status of the Sixty-Second Reserve Division and the Fourth Corps?"

"We are beginning to deploy the Sixty-Second Division, and some of the units are already in position near Meaux. The entirety of the Fourth Corps will have arrived by this afternoon."

"Good. Now, gentlemen, our day's work should be straightforward. It matters little what the British and our other armies do today or tomorrow. If we can't hold against the Germans, then all will be lost. Robert, I want you to do everything possible to get those troops deployed as soon as possible. The Sixty-Second Division is to be sent into the lines now, as will the Fourth Corps when they arrive. We do not have the luxury of holding any reserves in support, as every man will be needed in this fight.

"Please keep me posted of any significant developments. Now let's attend to our duties."

Robert and no doubt every person leaving the meeting understood that the day portended violent and desperate fighting. It would be like Philippi, Waterloo, and Gettysburg, where great armies came together with the fate of empires in the balance. This morning's meeting made clear how important each new arrival from the Sixty-Second Division and the Fourth Corps would be. Robert could see no other alternative now but to visit the train stations to better oversee the status of the arriving troops and coordinate their deployment. He was pleased to find that Karl had left word of his availability. and soon the two of them were off to the Gare de l'Est to attend to matters firsthand.

Upon their arrival, Robert noted that despite the large numbers of troop arriving and subsequently being deployed, the process appeared to be progressing in an orderly manner. Now as he went about his duties, he could sense the tension building. He was requiring continual updates on the status of the rail lines and roads leading from the capital toward the battle. What he feared most was at any moment his plans might be disrupted by German artillery fire hitting some vital rail line, but fortunately, such disruptions had until now been only temporary.

By early afternoon, it was apparent that a major crisis was developing along the northwest extreme of the Allied line when word came in confirming the withdrawal of the Sixty-First Reserve Infantry Division to previously constructed fortifications after being subjected to powerful artillery fire and infantry assault. This withdrawal, coupled with the failure of French cavalry units to provide additional support in the area, threatened a collapse of the extreme left wing of the Allied lines. What hope remained to counter such a disaster aside from the resiliency of the troops already fighting in the area was to deploy what reserves remained.

Those most readily available were the Sixty-Second Reserve Division, which was now being deployed out of Paris, as Gallieni had ordered early that morning. Despite reports of German attacks along the railway, Robert had at last received confirmation by midafternoon of the arrival of those desperately needed troops into key positions needed to stabilize the area. Now, all that remained were divisions of the Fourth Corps still arriving in Paris.

The first of the units of the Fourth Corps to arrive, the Seventh Infantry Division was already in Paris and was deployed shortly after the departure of the last units of the Sixty-Second Division. As the trains finished loading and proceeded from the city, Robert received word of more delays along the rail line. The trains contained engineering brigades capable of making expeditious repairs as needed if the damage was not extensive, but Robert knew that larger areas of damage could drastically slow matters. By late afternoon, it was becoming clear that the progress to the front was much slower than anticipated, confirming Robert's fears. At the same time, word came from headquarters urging that all remaining reserve divisions be forwarded as soon as possible.

Now, as Robert struggled to get the last of the 103rd and 104th Divisions into position to board trains that were being held in the station due to delays up the line, his frustration grew. He did a quick calculation in his mind to estimate the time that would be required to get the entirety of the corps forward if the rate of delays did not change. At best, it would be late in the evening or probably early the next morning. What worried him more was the threat that more extensive damage would stop rail traffic altogether.

Karl, seeing the worry on Robert's face, inquired, "Bad news, Robert?"

"It's not terrible, but certainly we could be in a better situation."

"In what way?"

"The German fire at points along our rail lines is causing some disruptions, to say nothing of the risk imposed on the troops trapped in the trains."

"Have the lines been shut down?"

"Only for small delays at present, and fortunately no major tunnels or bridges are near enough to provide a target that could, if destroyed, really gum things up. Still, enough of these disruptions will make it impossible to predict with certainty how long it will take to get the remainder of these reserves to the front. It may well be that more of them will have to be sent by truck transport to help get them to the front tonight."

"Do we have enough trucks to do that?" asked Karl skeptically, knowing full well that there had been few military transports in the city in recent days.

"We should be able to cobble together a few at a time for now, but I'm afraid that the numbers would not be large enough by themselves to get a sizeable number of troops forward by later tonight."

"Are the roads open to the area?" asked Karl.

"So far, there appear to be no major impediments, and even if we do encounter some damage in one location, there are several alternative roads that would make it possible to get through to most any area needed."

After a brief pause, Karl resumed somewhat cautiously.

"Robert, I have a suggestion that at first might seem preposterous, but I would ask that you think it over before you dismiss it."

"Well, I'm certainly open to any suggestion, preposterous or not."

"You know that my cab company alone has more than fifty cabs that are available at any given time. I know, however, that there are more than six hundred cabs licensed by the city."

"What are you saying, Karl, that we should cab these troops to the front?"

"Now hear me out, Robert. Of those six hundred cabs, I would bet that virtually all their owners would be proud to provide their vehicles for use by the army, and I know with certainty that we would have no trouble finding enough drivers."

"How many soldiers could be transported in one of your cabs, Karl?"

"It would depend on how much they would be carrying. If it's what I've seen today, then we could get four or five of them into a cab without much trouble."

"Could you get to the front before morning?"

"It's about forty kilometers by my estimate, and even given poor roads and lost drivers, I would estimate that if we started this evening, then there is a very good chance all of the troops will be in place by morning."

Robert paused for a moment, then resumed decisively. "I think, Karl, your idea may give us some needed insurance. I will need to get this approved with headquarters, but I suspect that can be accomplished soon. When that happens, an order will go out to the police to enlist all available cabs in the city. As you know, simply having cabs will not be enough. While I'm gone, I want you to contact your drivers and all the others that you can reach and inform them of the need for their services. When the call goes out, we will have them gather at the esplanade before the Invalids."

"Robert, it would be a great privilege to organize the drivers. I know how important it will be for them to help, and I am certain we'll have enough volunteers."

Granted such authority, Karl returned Robert to headquarters and then set out at high speed to assume his new duties in mobilizing the vast new civilian transportation army for the demanding journey they would be called upon to make that evening.

The plan suggested by Karl had been formalized in Robert's head during the ride back to his office. His presentation to Gallieni was brief, given the constraints on the commander's time, but Gallieni, adept at making quick decisions, readily gave his approval. The order soon went out to the prefect of police to take command of the city's taxi fleet and direct them to the vast esplanade in front of the Invalids as soon as possible. Soon, countless black Renault cabs throughout the city began to discharge their passengers, many in the very midst of their journeys, and turned, following their dispatch to a gathering point in front of the great gilded dome.

There the great green esplanade was being converted into a giant taxi stand. The driver's queue soon stretched from the moat in front of the Invalids to the Alexander Bridge crossing the Seine. At the head of the line, soldiers would enter the black Renaults in groups of five and would then roar off to battle in the evening twilight. Along the line of cabs, drivers chatted and smoked while sitting on their fenders until advancing to the dispatch point. There, instead of picking up some Parisian dandy, their clients were now young infantrymen, their fresh faces lined with anxiety and determination.

With the commencement of the taxi deployment, Robert's evening hours merged imperceptibly into the night. What followed was a constant repetition of the process, with hundreds of men and their arms loading into taxis and setting off in the darkness toward the front, now so close as to be a virtual suburb. Karl had long ago left with a cab filled with soldiers, leaving Robert to deal with the deployment without his services.

As the evening progressed, reports began coming in of disruptions due to poorly marked roads and lost drivers. Matters were further complicated by drivers trying to return over the same congested roads on which they had come from the city. All these difficulties were becoming apparent when Karl returned to give an insightful appraisal of the problems as related to him by returning drivers. He had shifted his passengers to an empty cab so that he could return to Paris and report back to Robert. After a brief consultation with Karl, instructions were modified for drivers waiting to embark, outlining alternative routes for their return to the city.

Robert also assigned one of his adjutant engineering officers to Karl and sent the two out to help correct the problem areas along the route while distributing new information for preferred routes of return to the city. Seeing the resolve in Karl's face in departing only increased Robert's gratitude for his efforts and those of the countless others who had volunteered their support this night when the fate of Paris hung in the balance.

Later, with further confirmation of troop arrivals by train and assured that the continued deployment of soldiers in the cabs was now progressing as planned, Robert sensed that little more could be done and caught a ride with one of the taxis back to headquarters. He arrived well after midnight and quickly headed to the situation room to see the status of affairs as represented on the large wall map. He was gratified to see that the feared envelopment of their left wing had not taken place. An extensive artillery attack by Neville's forces along with a counterattack by regular units had for the moment stabilized the area. Moreover, he was proud to note that the map reflected the presence in that very area, so critical to the overall success of the battle, the troops of the Sixty-Second Reserves and now some of the Fourth Corps. Reassured, he returned to his quarters for a few hours of sleep before the early-morning staff meeting.

He was awakened by his orderly in time to quickly shower and eat. It took a second cup of coffee to fully awaken, however. The meeting that morning was somewhat somber due to the fatigue of many who were present. Robert was pleased to see that Gallieni, unlike yesterday, appeared much more his usual self. His discussion was brief, but he took pains to acknowledge the efforts of not only the troops in the field but of those who had done so much to get them in place. Now with the transfer of the Fourth Corps to the front, Paris no longer had any significant reserves that could be put forward, and for all practical purposes, the defense of the city was in the hands of the forces fighting against the Germans some fifty kilometers away.

The news that morning suggested the line of fighting before the city was for the moment static. Success for the former Parisian forces likely would come more from continued resistance to German attacks than it would from any counteroffensive. Accordingly, Maunoury was ordered to deploy his forces to protect against any breakthrough, thereby providing time for the British and Fifth Army to exploit the widening gap separating the German First and Second Armies.

After the meeting, Gallieni drew Robert aside.

"Robert, you are to be congratulated on your work during the last few days. I know how difficult it has been. As things exist now, there is little more for you to do around here the rest of the day. Unless you hear from me otherwise, I want you to take the day off and catch up on your sleep."

"Sir, that is an order I am happy to obey."

"Well then, I suggest you get out of here before someone else finds something for you to do. We'll see you at the staff meeting in the morning."

Robert lost no time in obeying Gallieni, but before he could think of retiring to his quarters, he had one more important matter to attend to. He checked with his staff one last time, leaving them an address where he could be contacted, then located a taxi to go to the Hospital Laennec to check on Marie and to locate Thomas, who would almost certainly be there as well.

39

Vigil

THAT THE LORD WORKED IN MYSTERIOUS AND wondrous ways had been ever more evident to Thomas since his return to Paris from Strasbourg. His mood in those first days, shaped by the scale of the trauma he had seen and all the uncertainty it had provoked, had been the darkest period of his life. He now realized how naive and unprepared he had been to deal with all that he had encountered. How could he or anyone for that matter face such awful reality? Yet for the sake of those suffering men, he had tried to understand what was happening to provide them the hope and comfort they so desperately needed.

Since his return to Paris, Thomas began to note a change in his mood, which ironically contrasted with events around him. Everywhere there seemed to be uncertainty, yet gradually his own thinking became more organized, providing increasing clarity and insight, as if a great fog was lifting from his mind.

He knew that he had been fortunate in his return to Paris, where close family, loving friends, and a supportive bishop had provided a catalyst for his recovery. More than anything, however, as his spirits rose, he knew he owed his improvement to God's grace in answering his supplications for the strength and wisdom to contend with the suffering around him.

From the first days of his arrival in Paris, Thomas had been under the watchful eyes of his bishop. The bishop was a man who knew the priests in his charge well and was expert in recognizing the malaise that might at times bedevil that brotherhood. Thomas was thankful for the bishop's concern in recognizing the frailty of his condition and the subsequent guidance he had provided to help relieve it. From this guidance, Thomas had been allowed to gradually resume increasing responsibility, in the hope that it would not only improve his mood but also provide comfort to the ever-larger number of people he had begun to counsel who had suffered trauma from the war.

There seemed to be a tonic to his work, in that the more responsibility he shouldered, the brighter was his mood and the better his understanding of the challenges that were now the focus of this new ministry. He had begun to sense that far from being unique, the present circumstances represented yet another instance in a long history where people were forced to endure suffering and hardship, often from the sins and faults of others. This realization had provided Thomas greater comfort in dealing with the misery around him, trusting that a merciful God had some greater purpose for this all too frequent accompaniment of the human condition. Was it possible there was some better end to all these travails? Why should deliverance be for only the fortunate few spared from tribulation? Was not Christ's passion at the very heart of redemption?

What comfort Thomas might draw from this more sanguine view of suffering was soon to be challenged by his notification of Marie's condition and her impending arrival at a hospital in Paris.

————

When word came that Marie had been injured, at first Thomas did not know what to do. She had left his name as the contact person in case of accident or injury, but Thomas was stunned by the terse and impersonal manner that the young messenger informed him of her condition. In reply to his flurry of questions, Thomas was told that he would have to visit Marie at the hospital for any further information. He was scheduled to lead evening mass that night but realized that it would now be impossible. Leaving word with the bishop's office that an emergency would prevent him from attending to duties in the coming days, Thomas set off for the hospital, his mind racing with unknown and frightening possibilities.

Upon his arrival there, he was made to wait in a large room with the families of other wounded for more than an hour before anyone came to speak to him. The nurse, a sister, softened in her manner upon seeing Thomas and took him aside into a small sanctuary where they could talk privately.

"I know you are concerned for our sister, Father, but it is too early to say for sure what the future holds."

"What has happened to her, Sister?"

"She was in an ambulance that rolled over trying to avoid a vehicle that had been struck by artillery fire. Apparently, she was trapped under equipment, and it took some time to get her out of the wreckage. This was not an easy task, as the rescue was frequently disrupted due to persistent artillery fire."

"Where would we be without brave men and women, Sister? How badly has she been injured?"

"She received sedation before her arrival, which makes it difficult to know about her mental facilities. At present, she remains in a coma, but it is impossible to know now what future course her condition will take. She also has broken several bones to further complicate matters."

Thomas thought of Robert's condition and drew some comfort from his recovery, but he knew all too well not to base his hopes on Robert's experience.

"Would it be possible to see her, Sister?"

"Normally we prefer to have the family members wait to see a patient like Marie until she is able to communicate. In your case, Father, we can make an exception. I will come and get you at a suitable time."

"Thank you, Sister."

After what seemed an interminable wait, the sister returned to the waiting room and motioned for Thomas to follow. He was led to a large ward where, in a corner bathed with the afternoon sunlight, he saw Marie. She was resting peacefully as if asleep and did not respond despite his touch and kissing her hair. Her face had been spared from injury, and in the afternoon sun, she looked every bit like an angel asleep. Thomas wondered how such a person so full of goodness could have come to this. Then, conceding how elusive the answer to that question had been, he quickly refocused on ways to help Marie.

That afternoon and the following day found Thomas at Marie's bedside whenever the medical staff would permit. For him, the rest of the world had faded into the background; so focused were his thoughts on her. It was all he could do to write to Robert and Marie's parents, notifying them of her accident. He also sent a message to the bishop, telling him of the necessity of being at the hospital to attend to Marie. Beyond that, he knew that there was little more that he could do but pray and hope that his presence would somehow be sensed and provide comfort.

His vigil was seldom disturbed by the medical staff, as no doubt they saw in his quiet suffering an expression of what so many others were enduring. The sister he had met the day before made it a point to see if there was anything that she could do to help, a gesture that he greatly appreciated. Aside from an occasional bowl of soup or bread, there was little more that Thomas needed at this time but to be with Marie.

Later that evening, the bishop arrived to pay a visit. He had known of Thomas's long friendship with Marie and even sensed the depth of their relationship. He too had met Marie through Thomas and had a deep admiration for the young woman as well. On seeing Thomas, he merely nodded his head. After placing a comforting hand on his shoulder, he pulled up a chair and sat quietly by his younger colleague.

Finally, it was the bishop who spoke.

"How are you doing, Thomas?"

"I am not sure, Father. If anything, I'm numb. I have seen so much of this that as horrible as it may seem, this is not surprising or even unexpected. All of what I saw in Strasbourg was simply a preparation for this. The same questions and the same feelings are there, only they have been muted by repetition. In the past, however, they were the loved ones of others, but now it is my turn to suffer my own personal agony."

"I know, Thomas. That is why I'm here."

"Thank you, Father, for your concern."

"I only wish that there was more that I could do, Thomas."

"I do too, Father, but in truth, you have already helped in so many ways. You have always given me wise counsel and allowed me to develop as God saw fit. Most of all, you helped provide the support for me to heal. For all that, I am truly thankful, as it has better prepared me for this moment."

"It was God who did far more than me, Thomas. I am confident that with his support, Marie will recover as well."

"Those are comforting thoughts, Father, as you are truly one of his beloved."

"Thomas, I'm relieved to see the strength that God has given you to deal with Marie's condition. It's remarkable how far you've come since your return from Strasbourg. I know that this is not an appropriate time to raise this, but at some time your testimony about God's guidance and grace could provide comfort to the many who so desperately need it now."

"I would welcome such opportunities, Father, but it will have to wait until I can be sure that Marie does not need me here."

"When that time comes, and I pray it will be soon, I know your thoughts will be welcomed, Thomas. People here in Paris are under great stress. As we speak, a great battle is underway in the outskirts of the city, so I'm sure your thoughts would provide comfort to many as they face the days ahead."

"What would you like me to do?"

"If you are able, there will be a great mass at Notre Dame tomorrow night. Ideally, if you could participate in some way, it would be a great blessing."

"You know how much I respect you, Father. I will think about what you have said and pray for the strength and guidance to do what I can for Marie and the many others you're concerned for."

"I will certainly pray for both of you as well, Thomas. May God's will be done."

With that, the bishop gave Thomas a brief embrace and withdrew, leaving him alone with Marie, surrounded now by the silence of a hospital nearly asleep.

For a moment, Thomas simply withdrew into his thoughts and the compelling quiet around him. Then he slowly gave into his fatigue and lapsed into sleep. His sleep was so deep, despite the confines of the chair in which he was sitting, that he hardly realized what time it was until he was awakened by a tap on his shoulder. It took him several moments to fully awaken, but when at last alert to his surroundings, he was surprised to see Robert standing beside him in the gray light of early morning.

"Robert, I barely recognized you at first. Forgive me. What are you doing here at this hour? Is everything all right?"

"I suppose it's as right as we can hope for. It appears that I won't be needed for the next several hours, and General Gallieni sent me home to get some rest after spending most of the night working. The problem is that with so many thoughts about the troops we deployed yesterday, the coming battle today, and Marie, there is no way I can go to sleep."

"Have you seen Marie, Robert?"

"I have, Thomas. She seems more beautiful than ever, sleeping so peacefully, oblivious to all our worries."

"I know. It seems a blessing that whatever might be going through her mind at present, she does not appear to be suffering."

"Is there anything that I can do, Thomas?"

"The only thing any of us can do at present is to pray and trust that God will care for her in his infinite mercy."

"You know how difficult it is for me simply to wait without being able to do something."

"It's difficult for me as well, Robert. When Marie first came back, it was all I could do to keep my focus. I was trying to attend to so many matters, like contacting you and her parents, all the while thinking of what I could have done and should do now to help her."

"You can't blame yourself for what happened, Thomas. Marie is someone who will not easily give up on what she believes in. She has come so far from when we first met her. Both of us did all we could do to protect her, but she did what she thought was best."

"I know, Robert, but it didn't make it any easier to inform her parents of her condition. At first, all I could really do was to sit by her side, hoping for some sign that she might be improving. That was a terrible time, but gradually as I sat at her bedside, the peace that surrounded her began to calm my thoughts. Before she left for the front, she was remarkably frank with me. Perhaps she feared something, because she told me how much she loved me and hoped for a future together. If that is ever to be, then I must do all in my power to see that she gets the best care possible."

"I have no doubt that she is in the best of hands, Thomas. I can see how much you care for Marie and should have realized some time ago how much you meant to Marie as well. I spent countless hours trying to think of ways that I could be a husband to her while trying to reconcile my feelings I had for another."

"Sara Morozovski, no doubt."

"You're right as always, Thomas. I was too caught up in my own circumstances to see the best solution was right in front of me. Thomas, I have no doubt you are the one she truly loves, and there is no one better suited for her than you."

"That might be, Robert, if there weren't so many complications."

"Complications! Thomas, all our lives are now consumed by complications. Who knows what tomorrow may bring?

Yet that comfortable, settled world that we knew is gone, and whatever complications belong to it have lost their sting."

"That may be, Robert, but what can come from such a world if serious matters and vows are dismissed for the sake of expediency?"

"Thomas, I could never imagine you to compromise your values, but circumstances help reorder priorities. I would never tell you what to do, but as I see it, Marie should take precedence over anything else."

"Until yesterday, I might have argued with you, Robert, but the bishop paid me a visit last evening when my mind must have been unusually receptive to suggestion. He asked me to participate in a mass tonight at Notre Dame to try and comfort the many now caught up in this war. Given Marie's condition, I was hesitant to agree, but after he left, I sat alone with her. Just sitting and listening to her breath, I soon had the sense that she was communicating with me in some way. At first, I could not understand, but the more I sat and listened, the clearer her thoughts seemed to be.

"I know for someone like you, Robert, so grounded in empiricism, what I am going to tell you might sound like nonsense, but hear me out. I was so tired last night that I fell asleep in this chair and did not awaken until you nudged me this morning. It was a deep sleep but one where my conversation with Marie continued. Only this time she spoke to me so clearly I can only think it was real.

"In that dream, she said that she would be with me always, so I should never shirk my responsibilities or compromise my beliefs on her account. It was as we were talking over dinner, but her love appeared so sincere that I had no doubt as to what I should do."

"And what is that?"

"I will do what I promised and look out for her regardless of the circumstances, but for the present, I feel she wants me to speak at the mass tonight."

"Well, if it's of any consolation, Thomas, I should be free this evening and would be happy to take your place here while you go to Notre Dame."

"That would be a great blessing, Robert.

"It seems strange, but I feel uneasy leaving her alone with the hospital staff. Given that her family obviously cannot be here, it seems to me there is no one better than you, Robert, to take my place."

"Unless something should require my return to headquarters, you can count on my being here in time for you to get to Notre Dame."

"I can't thank you enough, Robert. Now, as tired as you look, I think it's time for you to obey orders and find a comfortable place to get some sleep. I will see you later this evening."

With that, Robert took his leave, but on exiting the hospital, he was surprised to see Karl Gold waiting for him in his parked cab. As he approached, he noted a passenger in the back seat, and then he gasped audibly in recognition as she leapt from the cab and raced to meet him.

40

Doubts Dispelled

AT FIRST, ROBERT AND SARA WERE SPEECHLESS, holding each other without a sound as the traffic near the entrance to the hospital surged around them. Finally, Robert said, "My god, Sara, I can't believe it's you!"

For a moment, Sara said nothing, drawing Robert more tightly to her. When she finally spoke, it was all Robert could do to understand as she gasped out her words in short, emotional bursts.

Karl interrupted from within the cab.

"Will the two of you please get in? I can't stay parked here forever."

As the pair settled into the back seat, Sara, now more composed, said, "Robert ... I can't believe ... I am so thankful you're alive. It took so much to get here ... Now all I want is to hold you."

"Sara, you're home now. That's all that matters."

"Robert, when Karl brought me here this morning, I was so afraid."

"Afraid of what?"

"I have been through so much that it didn't seem possible I would ever find you, and then knowing you were near, I couldn't shake my worst fears."

"Sara, you are safe now; your fears are nothing more than a bad dream. Even better, by some miracle, I'm free all day and can spend it with you."

As Sara started to reply, Karl interrupted her. "Sara, Robert is right. You are home now, with your own people who love you and will care for you. One thing we have all have learned from this war is how valuable time is, because we no longer can take it for granted. Robert says he is free today, which is extraordinary, given what we went through yesterday, so you both should use that time to the fullest."

Sara nodded, acknowledging the wisdom of Karl's suggestion, and then simply settled next to Robert, content to be held in his arms, while Karl set out for Robert's flat, so seldom used in recent days.

Once there, both bid Karl a most heartfelt farewell and then retreated to the privacy of Robert's quarters.

What transpired over those next hours was far more than a reunion of lovers. At first, they seemed paralyzed by their intimacy, after so much had conspired against them ever sharing such a moment again. Robert especially seemed maladroit, fumbling to open the door and to adjust the shades to block the bright light shining into the windows. It was Sara who finally took him by the hand and drew him into the bedroom, which blessedly was free of any glare. Instead, there was a soft golden aura that served to illuminate the couple in a sensuous light.

The memory of their past liaisons had been forever etched in their memories, providing a source for hope and courage under terrible and trying circumstances. Yet this was different from even those remarkable moments. It was as if all those recent and painful experiences gave them a maturity that enhanced their understanding of just how extraordinary this moment was.

Sara gasped audibly in seeing Robert remove his shirt, overcome by the long dormant image of his tapered torso. His smell seemed to unlock a flood of erotic memories that now claimed her being.

Robert too had been sustained by thoughts of Sara's rich auburn hair, often unruly but always sensual, and her large breasts whose whiteness was accentuated by dark brown nipples that pointed upward when exposed to his touch. He now fumbled to open a gingham blouse he seemed to remember from a time past and gasped as he saw Sara naked, more magnificent than ever.

Each would have difficulty remembering what followed, as all their sensations were now sublimated to a desire so powerful as to suspend the world around them. For the ensuing moments, they were in a world where all doubts and worries were suspended. It was if they were truly one with their senses, under a spell so intense that they had awareness only for each other. In those moments, the bliss of their shared intimacy excluded base and mean reality. What communication there was came in the moans of anticipation and mutual contentment as Robert first caressed and then became one with Sara's femininity, ending finally in the music of her first climax, which was so powerful that its notes for a moment erased all the hardships they had recently endured.

Yet even for the worthy, such a state is not long permitted. At last, as their ardor cooled from physical exhaustion, the gray, somber present began to once again intrude on their collective conscience. Sara now noted with concern the evident pain Robert had in moving his arm and the scars on his chest.

"Robert, what happened to you?"

"I did not have time to mention that I was nearly killed in front of Nancy during the first week of the war. Fortunately, as you see, I may not be as good as I once was, but I'm still alive and functional."

"Thank goodness you're more than functional, Robert. When I told you that I was afraid when Karl brought me to see you today, what I feared most was that you would be a very different person from the one I once knew. Despite your wounds, I see my fears were unfounded."

"How do you know that, Sara? Both of us have been through so much that we can't help but be changed."

"Call it intuition, Robert, but I knew I had nothing to fear the moment I first saw you today. Your every movement and glance showed me an honesty that said, despite everything, you still cared for me. Now I know without a doubt that is the case."

Robert said nothing but simply drew her closer to him, and once again the lovers were drawn into that magical place where such worries were suspended by bliss.

After the consummation of their lovemaking, the world of mortals once more claimed its place on their consciousness. For some minutes afterward, they were content to rest in each other's arms. Then Sara seemed to be drawn back into memories of her recent odyssey and quietly broke the silence.

"Robert, it was such a struggle to get home. At times, I nearly lost hope of ever getting back and feared what I would find if I did. So many of my dreams are gone. The only thing that kept me going was the hope of seeing you. Now, despite losing so much, it all seems worth it to be with you now."

"Sara, I can't begin to understand everything that has happened to you, but now that you're here, I hope to help you make up for all that you have suffered."

"Robert, there is so much to tell you about. I don't even know where to start. So many things have happened. Everywhere, people are frightened and suffering. I was even forced to kill two men! I could never have imagined doing such a thing, but I did it—and did it willingly at the time."

Robert drew her closer to him, trying to comfort her.

"My god, Sara, how I wish it was within my power to have protected you. How naive I was to hope that my work could prevent a tragedy like this."

"You and the army that I so long distrusted have not failed yet, Robert. Had that been the case, I would not have this city to come back to or the chance of finding you. I will be forever indebted to that general who talked you into becoming an officer."

"Sara, this world is in an awful mess, but despite it all, your persistence and courage gives me hope for something better."

"Someday I might be able to talk about all that I went through, Robert. I can only say every day seemed difficult and often dangerous, and then when I got closer to Paris, every risk seemed magnified, making every kilometer even longer.

"When I neared Paris, I was almost arrested but was saved by a directive from an officer named d'Aveillard asking the French forces to keep an eye out for me."

"I will never dispute the existence of guardian angels again, Sara."

"Nor I, Robert. I should have realized things had made a turn for the better then, but I had become so used to disappointment I could not suspend my worries.

"At least this afternoon, we have been given a blessed reprieve from them."

"The miracle is that we may have been given more than that, Robert. I came here hoping to find something left of what

I valued. Now I realize that what I most hoped for is still here. We both have seen too much to take anything for granted now, but knowing you're here in Paris, things have changed dramatically—and for the better."

With that, nothing further needed to be said, nor could it, as once again the lovers fell under the spell of their passion. It was only afterward that Robert looked at his watch with a note of concern.

"Is anything wrong?" Sara asked worriedly.

"To be honest, I have completely lost my sense of time, and I suddenly realized that I made a promise to Thomas and don't want to be late."

"You have to leave?"

"Only for a short while. Thomas has been keeping vigil at the bedside of a friend, and I promised I would spell him so that he could participate in the mass tonight at Notre Dame."

"The mass for deliverance?"

"Yes, just like in the old days when other barbarians were at our gates."

"Well, Thomas is certainly a good choice for such a task. Is your friend someone I know?"

"Not personally, but you know of her. She is that young woman that I have spoken to you about."

Hearing this, Sara visibly paled.

"It's not what you think, Sara. Many things have changed since the war. Marie, the young woman, has matured into a remarkable woman, giving up her piano studies to help attend to the wounded. Unfortunately, she was near the front and was seriously injured."

"I'm so sorry to hear that, Robert. It sounds as if you love her very much."

"What I am trying to tell you, Sara, in my own awkward way is that if I loved her, it was nothing like my love for you.

Our families and many others thought us to be an ideal match, but there was always something that made us both hesitant to commit to each other. I suspect Marie could sense that I lacked the passion she deserved, but struggle as I did, I could never tell her I loved another woman more than her. How could I be a caring and faithful husband when I loved you, Sara?" As Robert talked, Sara's concerned expression softened, replaced by a glow fueled by Robert's confession.

"Fortunately, my own indecision and hesitancy has been rewarded in a most remarkable way. It seems Marie has for some time had her own doubts about our relationship. As I said, she has matured greatly and, no doubt emboldened by the upheaval of this war, made her true feelings known. It is something that I should have seen long ago, since it was so obvious. How ironic that her doubts, like mine, related to her love for someone else. It seems extraordinary, but I hope and pray that she will recover so that she and Thomas can build on their love for each other."

"Thomas!" Sara exclaimed. "I simply can't believe it. She must be extraordinary."

"She is, but I'm very happy for her and for me as well."

"For you?"

"Yes. Don't you see? Marie made a choice that I was afraid to make. She has freed me to do what I really want—to be with the woman I truly love."

"Robert, I feel so blessed. Whatever happens to us, this remarkable day will help sustain me forever. Now take care that you are not late for your appointment, as I don't want to miss what Thomas has to say tonight. Afterward, you know I will be waiting for you."

41

Missa Solemnis

THE EVENING MASS DURING THE WEEKDAYS AT NOTRE Dame was often lightly attended, with those present usually being elderly from the neighborhood or working men and women on their way home from their jobs. In the summer months, the number increased with tourists attending. With the beginning of the war, the pattern of attendance at the great cathedral changed, with increasing numbers of people from all sections of society coming not only to the conventional hours for mass but also at odd hours throughout the day and night.

In the previous days, as word spread of the critical battle now being fought in the shadow of the city, the attendance at the religious services rose in proportion to the concern for the outcome of the fighting. On this, the third day of that very battle, now within earshot of the city, tensions had so increased as to be unbearable for many remaining there.

In the past when the survival of the city was jeopardized, Notre Dame, or its predecessors situated at the very heart of the city, had served as a rallying point where the population could gather to appeal for divine intervention to help repulse the invaders. Here was born the legend of Geneviève, who through the power of prayer and her indomitable spirit rallied the ancient Gallo-Roman descendants of Paris to repulse a previous generation of Huns. Now it was to the spirit of this saint and to another, the maiden Joan of Arc, that many turned to ask for intercession from the almighty, whose very presence always seemed so close in the limpid light of the great cathedral.

Perhaps no structure on earth was this great cathedral's equal for moments like this. It rose like a timeless apparition in the medieval heart of the city, with an architecture so resplendent that it gave tangible proof of humankind's enduring greatness when inspired by the divine. Its great stone edifice reflected the genius of buttressing that allowed its inner sanctums to be transformed by light, while the statuary adorning its walls provided lessons to the faithful as they passed before her doors. It was inside those doors where God's presence could be even better appreciated in the ethereal light streaming through the sublime glass windows and in the combined music of organ and choir echoing off the great stone nave.

Now on this evening, with destruction swirling about them, many of the city's remaining citizens descended on Notre Dame looking for hope and courage, much like their ancestors before them. Many came with the deep sorrow of loved ones lost or maimed, and all knew of acquaintances who had fallen in the terrible battles that raged that summer. Others came in hope of getting some insight into the madness the world had descended into. All came to reach out to God, acknowledging their own frailty and seeking in this ancient and historic gathering place new strength to endure the trials ahead.

For some, the soaring grandeur of the cathedral with its glorious art provided comfort. For others, the ritual of the mass with its familiar refrains and moving music, amplified by the acoustics of the great stone columns, brought them to a closer relationship with the almighty. For some, however, it was the testament of God's message through the power and grandeur of the spoken word that sustained them.

In times like this, with so much suffering and uncertainty, the routine would not suffice. What was required was someone who could add eloquence to God's message, providing a powerful antidote against fear while soothing the wounds of those who had suffered. The bishop had witnessed Thomas's recovery while the fate of the city became ever more uncertain. The bishop knew a recovered Thomas, moved by the power of the Holy Spirit, was the person to deliver that message. He was therefore relieved when Thomas agreed to lend his considerable presence for the occasion.

Robert, in hearing of the bishop's proposal, had done everything he could to encourage and support Thomas's participation. Even his miraculous reunion with Sara could not dampen his commitment to act in Thomas's place at Marie's bedside. Now with Sara at his side, the pair radiated an air of bliss and excitement, which to others might seem inappropriate for such somber times as they waited to rendezvous with Karl to take Sara to Notre Dame and Robert to the hospital. With Karl's timely arrival, they were off toward their destinations.

After crossing the Pont St. Michel, they encountered a large crowd that had already gathered around Notre Dame, long before the start of the evening mass. Their numbers were so large in the huge square in front of the great entryway doors that they obscured much of the western face of the cathedral. Realizing it would be difficult to go much farther by cab, Robert motioned for Karl to pull aside.

"Sara, are you sure you want to wade through this crowd alone?"

"This is nothing to what I have had to put up with to get here. I wouldn't miss hearing Thomas for such a triviality."

"Have you even been in Notre Dame before?"

"Of course, I have, Robert. I may not be Catholic, but I am French. It is so grand and yet so sublime that regardless of your beliefs, you cannot help but be moved. I have no doubt that Thomas will be equal to its grandeur tonight."

"Well, here is a key to my apartment. We can meet there when all of this is over. Take care of yourself till then."

After a last embrace, Robert helped Sara from the cab, watching her navigate through the large crowd, still amazed by the wonderment of her presence. When she was no longer in view, he and Karl set off for the hospital.

It took Sara sometime to reach the Place de Parvis in front of Notre Dame, given the size of the gathering crowd. The atmosphere was already extraordinary, with silent and grim-faced people streaming in from all directions. Falling in line with the crowd gathering in front of the great western doors, Sara slowly moved forward and at last gained entry to the great nave that was rapidly filling. The soft evening light filtered through the great stained glass windows and was enhanced by the bright candles throughout, focusing all of one's attention on the gilded base supporting the gleaming white *Pieta* looming above the altar.

Sara was guided by the usher to a seat close to the aisle of one of the middle rows and waited attentively for the opening refrains of the mass with a peace she could not have imagined just a few days ago.

With the first notes, all those present were quickly caught up in the majesty of the moment. As all the elements of the mass began to unfold, Sara felt all her senses arouse to their fullest, focusing on each strain of music and passage of Latin.

At last, all stopped, and Thomas strode forward. Sara was struck by how much he had aged since she had last seen him, giving him a bearing more appropriate for such a somber gathering.

Stepping to the high altar, Thomas began with a reading of the Old Testament not in the Latin text but in the melodic Parisian French, reaching out not only to the devout but to the common men and women whose attendance that evening filled the vast cathedral. It was this collective presence, with their combined sufferings and concerns, that gave even greater intensity and meaning to the moment. As Thomas's words echoed from the great stone walls, they were quietly taken in by the many sitting before him.

He continued with the biblical passage.

> But where is wisdom found?
> And where is the place of understanding?
> Mortals do not know the way to it, and it is not
> found in the land of the living.
> The deep says it is not in me and the sea says it
> is not with me.
> It cannot be gotten for gold or silver nor can it
> be exchanged for jewels.
> Where then does wisdom come from and where
> is the place of understanding?
> It is hidden from the eyes of all the living.
> Abaddon and Death say, we have heard of its
> fame with our ears.

Thomas continued. "It is fitting that this poem comes from the book of Job. You may well remember that Job was a man who was blameless and upright, fearing God and shunning evil of all sorts. Despite this, or because of this, he was marked by Satan for a series of plagues designed to test the strength of his convictions and the greatness of his soul.

"Yes, it is fitting that we should think of Job today, because in many ways, we are now all like him. Few of us might possess his character and virtue, but we all share in our own ways the sense of suffering, loss, and agony that he felt when the world he had known, along with his own health and family, was destroyed before his very eyes.

"We too have now experienced terrible losses of family and friends, widespread destruction, and a very real danger that we might lose much that our homeland represents. Yes, we are all like Job now.

"And like Job, we cry out in our present misery, trying desperately to find some meaning in the troubles that have fallen upon us. With each loss and each new horror, our fears increase along with our confusion. How like Job we are in that regard, but are we truly like him? Like Job, we are confused, but in our confusion, we try to find answers, trusting to our own reason and senses.

"How wise we all were merely three months ago when, in the glow of those early summer days, many of us felt we knew full well the meaning of the world and our place in it. How proud and pleased we were with the material progress that we shared: the fruits of applied science and industry. Surely such riches were too valuable to be jeopardized by a return to the ancient ways of war and wanton destruction. Surely men, many for the first time experiencing freedom from the fear of poverty and oppression, would not jeopardize their present condition to resume the old tribal fights of Europe. We were living in a new age of enlightenment where science lit the paths to future prosperity and the arts lifted our souls to a new awareness of our human potential. In those bright summer days, it was easy to imagine that we were living in a new Eden, with a future bright with potential for all of the many inhabitants of the continent.

"Now we see all too clearly how wrong and foolish we were. Now, every day, we see so many beliefs and dreams being shattered. Once more we are beginning to understand our insignificance in the long continuum of history. As bad as it is for the common man, it is far worse for the soldier who has experienced a deadly reality well beyond what the generals and military planners could ever have imagined. Their plans and predictions have proven to be woefully inadequate, with the terrible loss of countless young lives testifying to their enormous ignorance. These unfortunate soldiers were led to believe in the glory of their cause and the certainty of their triumph. Vast armies have been assembled and thrown at each other for what purpose? If it is merely to prove the superiority of one tribe over another so that in their triumph, they justify their place to rule, then all of this has been a horrific crime. If it is seen as a necessary step to evolve to a more robust mankind by a triumph of the strongest, then we have truly entered a new dark age.

"All of the questions that have come from these terrible trials call out for answers, and yet as the writer of Job tells us, that wisdom eludes mortal men. Some will say, how can it be that such a horrible condition has befallen us? Like Job's friends, they will point out our collective sins, suggesting that these plagues are due to our own past shortcomings. In some cases. that might be true, but I can assure you that many have suffered like Job who have also lived their lives righteously. I have recently spent much time with a young woman who is now grievously injured who previously led an exemplary life in all that she did. No, it is too simple to blame the faults of the worst among us for the suffering of far too many good and decent people.

"I hear frequently the voices of those angered and embittered by their losses, demanding to know how a God who is supposedly omnipotent and loving can allow such a plague. What good can come from such horror, and what kind of God would allow such things to happen? How arrogant we are to believe that we can discern God's purpose through the narrow prism of our own experience and reason. Have we forgotten that mankind, from the time of the Fall, has suffered through terrible times? History is replete with whole peoples displaced or eradicated by war and pestilence. What makes us think that simply because we exist, we have any greater claim to peace and prosperity than our ancestors?

"Some will now say that we are the victims of a fate that is beyond our control; we are powerless to effect what is and what will be. Such a view abandons the sublime basis for our individual existence and in so doing abandons the hope that sustains our lives. For these unfortunate people, such a view constrains their lives to mere existence looking only to satisfy their most basic needs. In that, they are little different from the humblest members of the animal kingdom. It is true that from the time of our births, we have had little control over many of the events that shape our lives. Who can claim credit for the circumstances of their births or their parents? Who can avoid illness and the inevitability of death? Since all of this will come to pass, should we simply resign to live without hope or distinction, or is there another way?

"I am no different from any of you gathered here tonight. I have suffered the loss of friends and have seen many others grievously wounded. I have done my best to offer comfort to many, while at times being uncertain of what to say. In the moments when I have had the time to meditate and pray, even while sitting at the bedside of my dearest friend, God's purpose in this and what he expects from each of us has become ever clearer.

"I believe that God is both omnipotent and his love for us profound, although in times such as these, it is as difficult for us to understand, as it was for Job. Through my own pain, I have come to better understand the role that suffering plays in our lives. We are destined to have illness and suffer trials and hardship because they are a natural part of the human condition. For every lovely summer day, there is also a fierce winter storm. The darkness of night is followed by the glorious light of the new day, just as new life comes from the suffering of the mother in childbirth. God himself suffered through his son made incarnate so that we all could receive his greatest gift. Mary, in her sorrow while holding her fallen son, did not know fully what glory would follow.

"When all is well and we are content in the golden light of a summer day with a roof over our head and our stomachs full, it is difficult to realize our fallibility. It is when we have the misfortune to live in challenging times that we have a much clearer understanding of our own frailties. God is now teaching us all a lesson in the limitations of our reason and ideas. In these dark days, we are finding out how wrong many of our notions have been. Fortunately, there is much that can be learned if we pay attention.

"It is during grim times that untenable ideas and unstable institutions are swept aside by the awful intrusion of reality. It is during times of crisis that we too find out what is real about our own beliefs and, more importantly, our character. Now we are forced to confront what is truly important and in so doing better appreciate what is insignificant, petty, and false. These times test us daily to see if we have the courage and strength to endure hardship and setbacks and to act to defend what we know to be truly important. The most fortunate will discover much about themselves and, if truly worthy, may be afforded the gift of true wisdom and an understanding of God's plan for their lives.

"I have come to accept that a reason exists for such times as these. I also believe that these trials require that we accept the challenges we face and not run from them. Contrary to the pessimism of the fatalist who views our existence as little different from that of a fern, I believe that we exist for a purpose. Life is too complex and God's love too great to have our beings reduced to simple chance and a random coalescence of molecules. It is now more important than ever that we act in a manner that gives meaning to our lives and defines our worthiness in God's eyes.

"It has been said that during our lives, we are like actors called upon to play various roles. We may be cast as a pauper, or king, a merchant, or soldier. We may live in sunny times or periods of great upheaval. It is not up to us to choose our station in life, our health, or the times we live in any more than it is up to us to tell the director the part that we want to play. Yet what we can control is how we play that role we are assigned. It is up to us whether we play it with indifference or with all the greatness that we possess.

"From our birth, we have been endowed with a sense of good and evil, an understanding of acting nobly or dishonorably. This knowledge conveyed through the Holy Spirit can fill our consciousness with a sense of what is right and good. It is up to us to live each day guided by that spirit. The great tales that make up the holy scriptures tell us how God wants us to act our role. In return for his great love and protection, he asked of the Israelites that they listen to the Holy Spirit within them to direct their daily lives. As the ancient writers said, to fear God. Man's great weakness, however, is told in a long history of great calamities that came from the failure to understand and comply with that covenant.

"What are we to do then as we deal with sorrow and face great uncertainty? If we have meaning as individuals, then we must act and focus on what is important. We must be content dealing with matters that we can control and ignore those we cannot. What good is it to worry about matters that are beyond our means?

"We must not be influenced by the opinions of others but from what we know is right. It is up to us to make our judgments and act accordingly, based on our understanding of honor and righteousness, shaped by the divinity within us. In so doing, we will honor God's wishes, ennobling our purpose to foster good and defeat evil.

"We must be careful, however, as evil is everywhere around us. Voices cry out, trying to find blame for our miserable condition. It is natural to blame the Germans for our troubles, and surely there are many among them who are evil and whose actions have been reprehensible. No doubt in Berlin the same is being said about us by many Germans. I can tell you, however, that while I was being detained in Strasbourg before being released back home to France, I cared for many young German as well as French soldiers wounded in the first weeks of the war. I saw in the faces of these young men the same pain and fears that I saw in the French soldiers. All had families that loved them, and many on both sides behaved with nobility in the face of their injuries and in their concern for others.

"The point is that we are all God's creatures, regardless of nationality, and in our humanity, we are more alike than different. Evil does not therefore originate with one nation or one tribe; it does not come from famine or war or pestilence but from our own hearts and thoughts. This is the challenge of these dark days. We must exert control of our emotions, steadfastly holding to what we know to be right.

"Evil triumphs when we allow our moral being to be compromised by expediency and the stresses and uncertainties of our times. If we are corrupted by hatred, bigotry, and envy, then we become complicit to the very conditions that have led to our pain and suffering. Goodness triumphs when, in the face of great troubles, we persist in acting as God would have us.

"Now when we leave this gathering and this great cathedral tonight, we will all be soldiers. We will be called on to make sacrifices, to accept risk, and no doubt in many cases to suffer personal hardship. For many, our roles have not been given us to choose. Yet we all can choose how we will carry out our obligations. Let us pray that through God's grace we are given the wisdom and courage to act as he would have us. If so blessed, then we, like Job, will triumph."

Thomas paused for a moment to reflect silently, his head bowed, then resumed the text, first saying, "The poet continues in answer to Abaddon and Death":

> God understands the way to it,
> And he knows its place.
> For he looks to the end of the earth,
> And sees everything under the heavens.

He established it and searched it out.
And he said to humankind,
Truly the fear of the Lord is wisdom;
And to depart from evil is understanding.

42

A Day of Marvels

THOMAS WAITED PATIENTLY, SPEAKING WITH THE many who came up to him that evening after the service. It was clear to him that his words had touched them, simply from the look on their faces. Those looks would have sufficed alone, but in their words, Thomas grasped even further how thoroughly so many had been traumatized by the events of the last month and how much they appreciated the comfort that he brought them. Struggle, pain, suffering, and the power of a transcendent spirit had motivated Thomas to produce their balm, and for a moment, he felt a great peace, as if enveloped by the spirit and the place that had abetted his efforts. Then, regaining his focus, he gave a silent prayer that such a power for comfort be provided him in the days to come.

As the crowd thinned, Thomas was surprised to see Sara Morozovski waiting patiently for him to finish his duties. He quickly excused himself from the priests who had gathered around him and with a broad smiled walked over to greet her.

"Sara, it's good to see you. I had heard that you were trapped in Germany, and we all feared for your safety. Fortunately, I see that our worries were unfounded."

"I can't begin to tell you how happy I am to see you as well, Thomas. Your words tonight were truly inspiring."

At that moment, both were surprised to see Robert hurriedly pushing through the crowd.

Robert paused for a moment to catch his breath, then announced, "I came here as fast as I could, hoping to catch you, Thomas."

The smile on Thomas's face disappeared, replaced with a concerned look. "Is there anything wrong?"

"Far from it. While I was sitting quietly with Marie, she awoke and almost immediately recognized me. At first, she smiled, and then she asked what I was doing sitting at her bedside. She still does not grasp the full details of where she is or what has happened, but she asked me questions about her condition. Most importantly, she wanted to know how you were and if you knew what had happened to her."

"I knew something like this might happen while I was gone."

"Everything is fine, Thomas. I told her that not only did you know about her condition, but that you had been with her nearly the entire time since she had returned to Paris. I also told her the only reason that you were gone was to be present at an important mass being held at Notre Dame. Although she did not say it, I could tell from the expression on her face how happy she was to hear that."

"I must get back to the hospital."

"It will be all right for a while yet. I told her that you would be returning later, which seemed all that she needed to hear. She smiled and quickly went back to sleep.

"The nurse said that, given all that she had been through, sleep was the best thing for her and that I should not disturb her any further. After hearing that, I left, hoping to share the news with you."

"Robert, you are like some herald from God telling me that he has answered my prayers."

Sara said, "Thomas, clearly since we have last seen one another, much has changed, but despite all the tragedies, I can tell something has changed you for the better. Robert has told me about Marie, and it is clear to me how much she means to you."

Thomas paused a moment, as if hesitant to speak. "You're right, Sara. You have always been one of the most perceptive people I have ever known."

"No doubt I was also one of the most outspoken people you knew as well. Well, you will have to excuse me, Thomas, because, if anything I've become even more so. You don't have to accept what I'm going to say, but all I've been through recently has made me even more impetuous.

"Thomas, you pointed out tonight how much this war has destroyed, but you implied that something better might follow. It seems to me that your feelings for Marie offer hope for that future. You also spoke of being steadfast to what is right. In your life as a priest, you no doubt made vows, never anticipating your love for Marie. Now more than ever, I believe love like you have for Marie takes the highest precedence over previous commitments and most certainly over what others might think of you."

Thomas said nothing for some time and then finally replied. "Sara, thank you for your advice. How could you know how much my love for Marie and my obligations to the church have tormented me? Even before Robert's great news tonight, I had made a decision to give priority, as you might say, to Marie over any other obligations."

"Thomas, I'm very happy for you; it gives me hope that something good might yet come from all this misery."

"No doubt something has already, Sara; it is apparent in seeing you with Robert."

"There is no time for further sermons on that topic, Thomas," Robert interjected. "You have more important things to deal with at present than your cousin. You don't have to concern yourself with us when Marie is waiting for you."

"I don't want you to think that I'm ungrateful for your staying with Marie tonight and then bringing me such great news, Robert, but if you'll excuse me, I think I will take your advice."

With that, Thomas quickly said goodbye to Robert and Sara and turned through a small side door, leaving the pair alone once again.

———

As the two watched Thomas disappear, their presence next to each other felt even more remarkable, as they now were nearly alone in the vast nave that had mostly emptied. For a moment, they remained silent and drew closer together, then hesitated out of a sense of propriety the surroundings demanded. At last, Robert broke the silence.

"Seeing Thomas now, Sara, it's hard to imagine his condition when he first returned from Strasbourg. All of us were worried that the war had changed him forever."

"It has changed us all forever, Robert, but perhaps if Marie has anything to do with it, for Thomas it could be for the better."

"What an incredible day!" remarked Robert.

"What a miraculous day and such a beautiful evening," said Sara. "I only wish it would never end. Where shall we go to see the night through?"

"I can think of no better place than the Bièvre. How many wonderful times we shared there, and it's close by."

"The Bièvre it is then," said Sara enthusiastically.

Taking her by the arm, Robert pulled Sara ever closer to him as the pair crossed the Seine and then ambled slowly through the old medieval streets of the Left Bank until the familiar outline of their old haunt came into view.

They paused in front of the large windows, as they had done so many times in the past, hoping to get a glimpse of Paul or even one of their old friends. That night, the old restaurant seemed crowded, especially given the circumstances of the city, and after they had entered, they waited patiently for someone to direct them to an appropriate spot where they could quietly reminisce while they ate.

As in the past, it was not long before Paul spotted their entrance and strode rapidly toward them with a huge smile. The smile, however, could not hide the changes that had occurred to their old friend in the time since they had last seen him. He looked thinner, with his drawn face and graying hair making him appear much older.

"What a remarkable surprise to see the two of you. I can't wait to tell Yvette that you are here. Just seeing you makes me feel better."

"Paul, seeing you and being here in this beloved place makes me forget for a moment all we have endured since those wonderful days. Do you have a quiet table for us where Robert and I can try to catch up on all we've missed since we last saw each other?"

"Follow me," said Paul, leading them into the back room that they were so familiar with from their student days. Its small size was compensated for by its relative quiet and intimacy. The large table that was the site of their many gatherings had been rearranged now, but Paul put them in nearly the same position at a table that gave them both space and relative privacy."

"This will be fine, Paul," said Robert. "Please bring us a bottle of your best champagne."

Shortly after, Paul returned with the bottle of champagne, accompanied by his wife, Yvette.

"I told you they were here, Yvette."

"I knew they must be, Paul, when I saw your face, but I had to see for myself."

"Yvette, how wonderful it is to see you again," said Sara. "It seems that it was just a few weeks ago that we were all here together."

"How I wish that was the case, my dear. How wonderful those days were!"

"And so many of the others are now gone forever," said Paul somberly.

Yvette looked at him sternly, trying to discourage such a conversation, but it was apparent from the looks of Sara and Robert that they were anxious to know of their old friends.

"What do you know of our old gang?" asked Sara.

"Painchaud was killed in the first week of the war in Lorraine. His old antagonist, Martin, along with those two young firebrands from Perigord who often sided with him were all killed near Charleroi. We heard sad rumors about several others, including you, Sara, but only rumors. We have learned never to accept those rumors, since to do so would be to give up hope. Now, Sara, seeing you gives us a reason for such hopes."

"Hope supports our courage, Paul. We need it to endure," Sara replied with evident empathy. "How is Jacques? Is he still here?"

Both Paul and Yvette's faces paled perceptibly at the mention of their nephew, who had often helped them in the restaurant and whom all the students liked.

"We heard last week from his commander that he had been killed near Guise," said Yvette.

"If it wasn't for the restaurant, I don't how we would have continued," said Paul. "Our old customers come in now even more than ever. When they heard of Jacques, they were a great comfort to us. I just wish that we could get the same quality of meat and produce as we did before the war to better repay them for all their kindness."

"Paul, you and Yvette may not realize it, but your customers care less about your food, as good as it is, than they do for all of the love and service that you have always given them," Sara said. "In a world where so much is wrong, you and your restaurant remind your customers of better times and a reason to carry on."

"Sara, you have always been so kind and considerate," Yvette said. "Come on, Paul. We have others to attend to, and they want to be by themselves. You two, just relax, and I will have the best that I have sent out shortly. Enjoy your evening, and may God protect the both of you."

Robert and Sara sat silently reflecting on Paul, Yvette, and their old friends. The news was made more poignant by these familiar surroundings where they had spent so much time together.

At last Robert spoke. "I would never have suggested coming here if I had known it would be so painful. So many gone already. I can still see them like it was yesterday. Painchaud, the merchant who believed that profits would pacify the lion, now destroyed by the beast. You know, Sara, for as much as he argued with you, he had a fantasy of being your lover."

"I know that, Robert. He once made a silly pass at me, which now seems far more tragic than absurd."

"And poor Jacques. There was never a kinder soul. How out of place he must have been in the front lines."

"What were they like, Robert? The front lines? I often saw the German Army from close perspective. I saw them marching in organized masses so large I could not imagine anyone or anything being able to resist them."

"I can't begin to describe what it's like there, Sara."

"Was it that bad?"

"It was, but it is impossible for me to describe the whole experience in words. From the first moment when you come under fire, you are immediately aware that you have entered a different world. All your senses are fully alert, which only serves to intensify everything that you see and hear. The colors, the glint of bayonets, and the flash of gunfire are intense and then later are masked by the dust and smoke. Above all, it is the noise, sometimes so loud that it seemed like your head would explode. It is remarkable that anyone could function in such a realm, but we did. Yet all civility was stripped away, with men everywhere reduced to their most primitive instincts."

"I've heard enough, Robert. Thank God I've been spared from that, but it only makes me feel worse that Jacques and all the others had such horrible and needless deaths." She paused and then asked, "Will you go back, Robert?"

"I will if I'm ordered to."

"I know you too well, Robert, to expect anything else. What I meant was will you be reassigned once more to the front lines?"

"As of now, that is very much in the air, Sara, as I'm afraid our future is dependent on the outcome of this battle."

"What are our chances?"

"I was able to get a thorough update from headquarters while I was attending to Marie. It seems that our efforts yesterday in getting reserves to the Sixth Army allowed our left flank to hold throughout the day, despite a vigorous assault by the German First Army."

"Is that good?"

"Well, it certainly isn't bad. The Germans have a certain arrogance that can get them into trouble. Until now, they have had their way in this war. The longer we are able to hold back their advance on our left, the more vulnerable they will be to an attack toward a widening gap in their lines, created by the movement of their First Army."

"What do you think will happen, Robert?"

"I have learned to be cautious with predictions, but I know the disposition of both armies, and we are in a strong position. The longer we hold on our left, the more vulnerable they are to a counterattack."

"Then you believe we will win?"

"Don't overestimate my analysis; the outcome is never straightforward. All revolves around the combined will of thousands of desperate men. Now, enough of what I will be doing. What are your plans?"

"Robert, when I arrived in town last night, I was like a survivor from a shipwreck cast on a familiar but uncertain shore. I came here on a bike that I had been riding from Belgium, hoping to find some familiar face.

"When I arrived at their home, I found that my parents had already left the city, but I was finally rewarded when I found Karl and Lydia at home. From the look on her face when she saw me, I thought that I might have shocked Lydia to death. When everyone had recovered, I was given a place to sleep in that same bedroom we spent our last night together, and for the first time since the war started, I had a peaceful and uninterrupted sleep.

"Today started early when, after breakfast, Karl and I set out to find you."

"Well, we know how that turned out."

"Yes, and that is far from the only thing wonderful thing that has happened this remarkable day."

"How so?"

"Robert, when I arrived here, I was exhausted mentally and physically. Worse yet, I was haunted by the memory of having killed two German deserters threatening the two young Belgium women who later guided me to France."

"Sara, you were forced to do what you did. There are thousands of others who have been forced to do the same. I know something like that cannot be easily forgotten, but what you did was a necessity, not a choice."

"I understand that much better now. I went to the mass tonight hoping to speak to Thomas about what I had done. Then, as he began his message, it was as if he was speaking directly to me. All of us now have experienced doubt, worry, and suffering; that is our unfortunate lot. I have no more reason to complain about my difficulties than anyone else. Yet all during my trip home, despite all the risks, I knew that I must not compromise my beliefs. I now understand how important that mind-set was. If we are going to prevail, we must not be compromised by fear. Thanks to Thomas, I have a better understanding of what we have endured and what remains to be done."

"He must have outdone himself tonight. I wish I had been there."

"His words gave me peace and transcended religious dogma. They had meaning even for Jews, heretics, and atheists. We will face a great deal more before we can hope for an end to all this. Our best hope for a kinder future is to act nobly and with principle. Only then can we hope not only to endure but to emerge at the end with something of worth."

"I hope that will be the case and that your optimism will be realized."

"There is so much about this day that convinces me it will, Robert. Thomas thinks he has found in his faith a way to confront fear and uncertainty, but I also saw something in him tonight that gives me even more reason for hope. It is the same force responsible for me being here in Paris tonight. Seeing you today was reminder enough, but in all that gothic splendor of Notre Dame, I remembered the lines of a converted Jew from Tarsus: 'At present we see only indistinctly, as if in a mirror. Yet faith, hope and love remain; but the greatest of these is love.'

"You asked me what my plans are for the coming days, and for once in my life, Robert, I don't seem to have any except to be with you. That thought has given me more peace than I have had in years and is the greatest miracle of this remarkable day."

Epilogue

IT WAS CALLED BY MANY, AND ESPECIALLY THE Parisians, the miracle on the Marne. The French victory was far from an episode of divine intervention but instead resulted from the coalescence of very tangible factors during those five epic days in September 1914.

The German field commanders, given the speed of their advance to the outskirts of Paris, had overestimated their own prowess and underestimated that of their enemy. Blinded by imagined triumphs, they were slow to realize the retreat of their enemy was more by calculation than panic. The effects of French counterattacks, such as at Guise, had alerted General von Moltke, the supreme German commander, as to the hollow nature of their victories, which coupled with his native pessimism would have bearing on the days ahead.

As Robert had surmised, the last-ditch infusion of reserves on the flank of the Allied lines would prove decisive. They had provided the margin that allowed the troops of the Paris garrison to withstand the attack of the vaunted German First Army and had provided British and French forces the opportunity to threaten the widening gap in the German lines. This gap had come to dominate the dour Moltke's thinking with each passing hour, and finally, unable to ignore the disaster it posed to his army, much to the chagrin of his field commanders, he ordered a widespread withdrawal to consolidate the German lines.

On September 11, Joffre wired the government in exile that the Battle of the Marne was a great triumph for France. What he did not say, however, was how close that triumph had been to disastrous defeat and how costly it had been. No doubt, Joffre had reason to relish this remarkable outcome, as his steady leadership following the collapse of the early French offensive had contributed to this day. Equally important had been Gallieni, who was first to recognize an opportunity to deliver the city from the invaders and had led the counterattack that had done so. Neither man could doubt that history would long pay them tribute.

In the end, however, it was the mystical élan, a notion responsible for much early carnage, that ultimately accounted for the triumph. It was the masses of French and British troops, exhausted by prolonged fighting and discouraged by retreat, who at the supreme moment turned to face their pursuers. Reenergized and ultimately triumphant, their sacrifice during those trying days was the true basis for deliverance and where honor truly belongs.

It would be an evanescent triumph, however. The initial optimism of the Allies in their exhausted pursuit of their beaten foes was soon dispelled when they found their enemy had entrenched along the Chemin des Dames on French soil. There, the war of the trenches began, along with the first bloody lessons of the utter futility of employing past notions of battle to confront terrible new weaponry enhanced by sanctuaries prepared by pick and shovel. What ensued were frantic attempts by both sides to flank each other on a long northward series of battles, which finally came to an end at the sea near Ypres in Belgium. There, after a horrific stalemated battle, the combatants faced each other across entrenched lines that stretched the length of the continent.

Another prewar folly was now becoming painfully apparent to men on both sides. They would not be returning home before the leaves fell, nor would they be home for the holidays. As the first snows fell across the trenches, all realized the awful truth—that there would be much more required before they would be able to truly return home. It was a truth that was painfully evident to Robert but also to Thomas, Sarah, and even Marie, along with virtually all noncombatants across the continent.

On that first Christmas of the war, there was a blessed peace that fell across the front lines for several days. In homes throughout the continent, the spirit of the holidays seemed for a moment to offer a small flicker of light in a darkened world. Chastened by the lessons of their folly, however, all too many feared that the days would be many before that light would burn brighter.

TRUTH

This week I found the Holy Grail and started a revolution; now I'm going to the Philippines, with Excalibur in hand and the Black Madonna shielding my heart—to buy my wife a Louis Vuitton bag.

My name is Feenx. I am the Lady of the Lake, and Genghis Khan has risen from the ashes and freed my soul...

Acknowledgments

Of course I have to start by first giving thanks to that wonderful Creative Energy that is the Universe in which we live, the Creator of all things and the inspiration behind all that I do. The Light that can be seen and felt in all of Nature. The Compassionate and Merciful Entity that brings to all mankind a message of love and hope. The Omnipotent Spirit that guides me and sends to me Angels to show me what I need to see and learn in order to move forward in my own personal quest for the Grail.

To my beautiful child who reminds me daily that the simple things in life like love and laughter are worth fighting for. To her father for giving me the most precious of gifts. To the family I have loved deeply and lost who taught me how to continue that fight before our Creator called them home. To my friends, all of whom I cherish and love for giving me the strength to keep fighting.

To my conqueror for leading me fearlessly to battle....

Finally to the people of the Philippines, for their lessons on compassion, family values and faith and for showing me that the most powerful weapon in that fight is love....

Preface

<u>No, seriously—I made it all up</u>

He asked if I was a writer, while he was hovering over my table, fussing with the glass. "I always see you here, sitting, writing—you must be a writer."

He is a sweet kid, really; been serving me for two days. Yesterday he told me I have very kind eyes. Today he wants to know where I'm from. When I tell him I'm Canadian, from Toronto, his eyes light up. "What's it like there in Toronto? I've always wanted to go to Canada." Like I said, he's a sweet kid, and I would love to brag about my country, but at the moment the only lame answer I could come up with is that it's different there, very cold.

I know, it's strange that I can easily sit for hours and fill pages with colorful script, yet I can't answer a simple question. Perhaps it's the jetlag; perhaps it's the shock of being here at all. Right now, though, I am thinking it is more my own personal shame over the fact that the people in my world have so much more than the people here, yet they are constantly dissatisfied—always wanting or needing more. I simply can't look this gentle boy in the eye and tell him that the place I come from is a wonderful place. I can't agree with his misguided notion that my world is safer, more prosperous, and therefore a more comfortable place to be. I can't tell him that he should want to go there, that he would be happier, because I would be lying. I flat-out refuse to insult such a sweet-natured soul by telling him an untruth.

Oh I know, you are no doubt thinking I have lost my mind, and it was not too long ago that I myself was convinced I had. I can't argue with you and insist on my sanity when I am hanging on to it by a very thin thread. Honestly, what am I doing here? I've spent fifteen hours on a plane, flown halfway around the world, left my job, friends, family, and *my angel of a daughter*—God forgive me that—to join a man I love and admire deeply and embark on an adventure of spiritual growth. I hope this quest will lead to enlightenment and inner peace.

See, there you go—I am nuts, after all. Hmmm… You are probably right, and, if not for all the crazy and unexpected coincidences that led me here in the first place, I would take the advice you are no doubt telepathically sending my way, get back on a plane, and head back to reality. Unfortunately, it is much too late to save me from myself, and, though the logical thing to do would be to listen to you, I will remain and see this through to the end. Besides, I would disappoint a great many people—all those friends and family who, after seeing the previous two weeks of what some claim to be mini-miracles, are convinced that this journey is probably the most important thing I've ever done.

I did ask them, you see. I questioned them, sometimes relentlessly drilling them about their feelings and thoughts. The answer was always the same: "This you must do. This is what you were meant to do." Hell, we should probably all be committed together. It is extremely probable, in fact, that, being crazy myself, I have unknowingly surrounded myself with—unwillingly drawn to myself—others like me. I mean unstable, unbalanced, unreasonable people who are unable to see past their imaginatively invented illusions.

Somehow, though, I think if you knew them you too would put faith in their direction. You, too, would be reassured and sheltered by their faith in you. You would wrap that faith around you like armor and plunge headfirst into the battle we call life.

You would not fear failure, nor would you fear the unknown, but rather thrive on uncertainties and unspoken possibilities. I swear you would. Their souls are pure, their spirits are strong, and their beliefs are grounded in the here and now while still having the uncanny ability to fly free on the wings of hope. They are, in short, the kind of friends that you yourself would wake up every day being thankful you had—the kind of friends that lift those they love to great heights, freeing them of doubt and enabling them to soar. Would you like to meet them? I know just where to start...

My most important living inspiration—my reason for being, my sole purpose in life—is eleven years old, with stringy blonde hair and beautiful hazel eyes. She has a sweet, not-so-innocent smile, which should be, but never has been, marred by the crooked teeth she had the misfortune to inherit from her loving English-bred father. Her name is Madison, a name picked out by one of my college roommates on the very same day she also picked out my wedding dress. I found out two years ago that Madison means "daughter of a great warrior." It remains to be seen whether that reference is to me or her father. I am not blind to the fact that it could be from the latter. He is a good man when you get to the heart of it, and he is a fantastic father. Human, yes, and prone to mistakes, but then you will see, if you choose to follow me through this adventure, that I, myself, am far from perfect. If I must be completely honest about the whole me/he situation, he has every right to be angry as hell at some of my past misdeeds. Yet he maintains the stance that our daughter comes first, and that, after all, is really all that ought to matter. I can honestly claim that if I *have* to have an ex-husband, I have probably managed to acquire the best ex-husband that a woman could be lucky enough to have.

Oops, I have gone off, haven't I? I apologize for that, but you will have to meet him eventually anyway, as he is one of the important influences that got me here in the first place.

We were, I believe, in the midst of an introduction to my daughter. I suppose her most remarkable and defining feature is her long legs. They are so long, in fact, that at present, with her being only a few weeks away from her twelfth birthday, her hips are a good inch higher than mine, though when she stands beside me she is a good two inches shorter.

I can't for the life of me figure out where her height comes from. I am only five feet, and her father is not much taller. I am pretty sure that his parents are not genealogically responsible, and my mother's side of the family could not have been much help in that area either. It could have been my father, Joseph, I guess, but as I don't remember much about him—other than the presence of a tall blonde lady named Christine and little brown bags of strawberry-marshmallow candies—I can neither confirm nor dispute the possibility.

Yes, physically, her legs are what stand out the most, but, if you can get past them and her quirky smile, you will eventually see the most magical part about her. I am blessed with a child who exudes a peaceful, gentle, loving nature. She is a kid, of course, and, being a kid, she has her less-than-perfect moments like all other children; yet, beneath the surface lies a strong sense of earthy connection. She abhors violence and pollution, is extremely uncomfortable with other people's suffering, and every once in awhile she comes out with a statement or observation about the world that would leave Socrates with his mouth hanging open. It is in these rare moments of profound wisdom that my daughter disappears, and I find myself searching her eyes for a clue as to who the ancient soul is hiding behind them.

Oh yes, I am the doting mother, aren't I—the one who spoils and coddles and is blinded by my love for my child. This time I will argue the point; this time I will openly argue with you and tell you that your assumptions are wrong. If I were that kind of mother, I would be bragging to you about her accomplishments, would I not? I'd be telling you how high her grades are, how good she is in sports, how talented she is in the arts, and how popular she is. I won't, not because I can't (she does have some talent in the arts, but academically she is prone to laziness), but because I do not believe those things define who she is. They do not define her place in the world—not in the present nor in the future.

I would also like to point out that if I were so deluded as to think my child perfect, or gifted well beyond the norm—and had no grounds for that belief—then I would not willingly admit that, in those moments when it seems that someone else is watching me through her eyes, I find myself slightly afraid. Not of her, understand, but *for* her. I don't believe that, at her age, having a more advanced perception of the world and the energies in it can do anything but ostracize her from her peers. I doubt that she can find much of a comfort zone when surrounded by other youth whose main focus is how many people they can win over with their charm and wit. Okay, maybe that is stretching it a bit. I suppose charm and wit probably fall second to stylish clothes, expensive toys, and financial status of family. Though you may disagree with me, I think we sell our children short. I am sure they see much more with regard to social interaction than we give them credit for. It is not a big stretch to believe that at the age of eleven or twelve they could be capable of using that understanding to convince, sometimes deceptively, both adults and peers alike to give them what they want.

If you haven't noticed it, take the time to observe the younger generation of today. Give over for the moment your belief that they cannot possibly understand the harsh realities of existence and venture into the unknown; try to converse with them on a higher, more direct, level. You may very well be surprised at what you find. Take, for example, a conversation I had with my daughter over a year ago when I was driving her home from school. She was not yet ten and she had obviously had a rotten day. When I asked her what was up, she went into a detailed account of an incident involving one of her friends. Apparently there had been a falling-out of sorts, but, though my daughter seemed concerned about damage being done to a friendship she cherished, she seemed to be more concerned about the possible damage being done to her friend.

It went something like this.

"My friend Kate and I had an argument today; I wanted to play with her, but she seemed to want to ignore me. I probably shouldn't have pushed it, but I was a little disappointed, and we ended up fighting about something that shouldn't matter."

I would like to point out here that, though I would have liked to question or comment, Madison never gave me the chance. By the end of her story, I remember my mouth was hanging open with no words coming out, something that happens far too frequently for my liking.

"You know how we've been friends for over a year, Mom? I mean, we play together all the time, and we have a lot of fun. We like to do the same things, play the same games, we even like the same kinds of pets, but lately she has been hanging out with girls that are more popular. You know I'm not popular, right? Really, I'm okay with that. I mean, I don't see things the way they do, and I'm not very good at being mean. I don't want to hurt people to make them look bad so I can look good. Kate wants to be popular though, and that's okay too. She is my friend, and I want her to be happy, but sometimes at school I miss her a lot. I know why she has to ignore me though, and when we are together, just the two of us, we have a really good time, so I try really hard not to get angry. But, Mom, I'm a little worried. I mean, doesn't she know we won't be in this school forever? I wish she could understand that when we graduate, when we go to high school, she will have to do it all over again. They don't really care about her, anyway. It is okay. I know she doesn't understand, but when she grows up it will matter more that she is a good person—but that's the thing. I know she's a good person, and I don't want her to worry so much about being popular that she forgets that she is a good person. Mom, what should I do?"

Once you close your own mouth and recover from the brief shock you are no doubt experiencing, you can picture in your mind my own stunned silence. I mean, what is a mother to say to that? What great piece of wisdom can I impart to ease the burden of her troubled thoughts? At the tender age of nine she has just explained in depth more about interpersonal relationships than the average young adult at the age of twenty understands. I had no choice really, and, again, I remember this all very clearly. I simply turned to her and asked, "What the hell? You're nine!" It was not exactly the encouraging reaction she was hoping for, but, knowing my daughter as I do, I doubt that she was put off by my lack of comforting words. I doubt that she even needed to be reassured, but I did, after recovering a bit, take the time to let her know she was very perceptive for one so young. I also remember telling her that those perceptions and understandings would probably cause her as much discomfort in dealing with her peers as it would ultimately help the discomfort it was causing. Now I realize that, given the fact that she was being so open with her thoughts, I probably shouldn't discourage her. I did feel the need, however, to point out that others her age might not catch onto or explore that kind of reasoning until much later in life. I am still her mother, and though I occasionally find myself in situations where I am forced to concede to the unexpected wisdom of an eleven-year-old, it is also still my job as a mother to protect her from adversity and condemnation at the hands of others.

When my daughter isn't delving into the deeper recesses of the human psyche, she is busy being a kid doing all the things kids do. She, like all of her generation (much to my personal disgust and as a result of the shortcomings of my generation), loves to play video games. She also has a small addiction to the computer, which is turning out to benefit me by allowing me to keep in contact with her while I am off traveling the world. She also loves music—not much of a surprise, as her father was in school studying radio when I met him. She has a good voice, as well, when she forgets to be self-conscious. She can nail pretty much any song she happens to be listening to. She also seems to have a natural rhythm and beat and is currently studying hip-hop and ballroom dance as well as being a member of her school's step team (like stomp, but a different name). I have been trying to encourage her pursuit in the arts and to get her past her insecurities regarding how others will perceive her. It is the result of that encouragement that sent me to the airport in pursuit of a career I had long ago pushed aside.

You see, when my opportunity to reexplore my writing career arose, it was a conditional opportunity. It was not self-imposed, but, rather, the conditions were set by the man I travelled to the other side of the world to be with.

His first request of me was to ensure that my daughter understood and approved of my plans, as they would over the next year take me away from her on several occasions and for extended periods of time. It was important to him that I have my daughter's support if I were to embark with him on this adventure. He is, I have to point out, a different kind of man, with strong family values. You will get the chance to meet him later as well, given the fact that this book is our story, and he plays an integral role in the whole crazy adventure. I conceded to his wishes, of course, because they were both reasonable and touching. I took the time to have a heart-to-heart with my little girl. Her response? Keep in mind, please, that she is not yet twelve.

"Mom, you're always telling me to believe in myself and follow my dreams, but how can you expect me to listen to your advice if you won't follow it yourself? If you want me to do these things, shouldn't you set an example and do them yourself?"

Yet again I am left staring at my child with an open mouth, but, as I am now more accustomed to these little mature outbursts, I recover more quickly. This time I had the grace to thank her and let her know just how lucky I am to have a daughter who encourages me in such a selfless manner.

After you hear my side of the story, I am thinking that you may again be of the opinion that my mental capacity became impaired at some point in the past. Allow me to attack that fear from two opposite angles. You may latch on to whichever belief makes you most comfortable. Then we will be able to continue this journey together without the dangerous prospect of insulting your integrity or your sensibilities.

First, let's assume that everything I say in the previous and following pages is true. Fairly appropriate, wouldn't you say, given the title of the book?. Given that assumption, you would have to be wondering how I could possibly remember a conversation I had with my daughter over a year ago and share it with you in a manner that seems to be quoting her word for word. Realistically speaking, a word-for-word quotation at such a late date would seem to be nearly impossible, unless I had at the time enlisted the assistance of some kind of recording device. It's not likely that I happened to be carrying one in the car with me that day, or that I knew in advance that she would have something important to say when I picked her up, and therefore I was prepared in advance. A far more probable explanation is that I have a photographic memory and can somehow tap into past events by tuning my mind rather like you use a DVD player to track back to a place in the movie that you missed while getting your snacks. I, however, feel that is dangerous ground, as it suggests that I am far more intellectually advanced than I would like to believe myself to be. I fear both the complexities and responsibilities that a feeling of superior intelligence breeds, preferring merely to be a student of this life. I am not willing yet to breach the boundary between pupil and teacher. This leads me to suggest to you a safer and more reasonable manner in which to perceive what I am sharing with you, the reader.

I propose to you that this story be absorbed in the spirit in which it is being written—as a story, a tale, if you will—a fabrication that is perhaps occasionally interspersed with some very real observations. If you were to delve into these pages with the understanding that most of the adventures contained within are merely the result of an overactive imagination or even the unrealistic mental wanderings of an overly adventurous mind, then we might in the end come to an understanding. I get to safely share with you an interesting tale, and you get to read it with an open heart and open mind. After all, if it is *not* as the title indicates, then the contents and experiences throughout these pages hold no threat to you or your own beliefs.

It is, of course, up to you. It is not my place to tell you what to perceive as real; reality, after all, is subjective. Take, for instance, the Christian who believes that Jesus was crucified, died, and was raised again by a God who loves all his children unconditionally. That, to them, is reality, and the contents of the Bible are viewed as fact. Now, explore for a moment the Wiccan belief that the power of the world comes from the very earth itself and connects every living thing. To them, it is the manipulation, or, rather, controlled usage of that interconnected energy that allows what others perceive as magic to become a very real and very useful tool to maintain a comfortable and peaceful existence. To each individual, each situation, though coming from different ends of the spiritual spectrum, is very real. As such, reality becomes subjective, depending solely on one's fundamental needs and personal experiences. Before you ask, I will not share with you which belief system I myself follow. You will in time get to know me and will figure it out yourself. I merely wanted a way to illustrate my point, and I'm hoping that in doing so I have sparked in you, the reader, a little curiosity.

Here I seem to have hit a wall, which I assume for the moment means we are finished. But I leave you with one question: Fact or fiction? I know which I prefer, but I am curious what exactly it is that you find yourself wanting to believe.

Chapter 1

Out of the Fire and Flames is Born a New Life and a Renewed Hope

It's a crazy world in which we live, when two weeks ago I could be happily living out an average ordinary life in the city of Toronto, and then suddenly I could find myself uprooted and halfway around the world. I guess I would be exaggerating slightly if I said *happily* living, since, though I had a job, was surrounded by friends, and was living with a boyfriend who very obviously adored me, I, like many others living in my city, was completely dissatisfied with my current place in the world. Thing is, the unhappiness was never based on my need to attain a higher material status. I don't really want a bigger house or higher-paying job to pay for the bigger house. I can't imagine two things in life more likely to bring stress into my world, so I have very pointedly, for years, been trying to avoid both. No, if I was unhappy, it was lack of balance more than anything that was causing my distress. I had momentarily lost sight of the part of me that makes me whole. In ignoring that side of my nature, I had quite effectively managed to make myself sick. A weakened soul breeds a weakened body, and, as I had neglected to feed my spirit for far too long, my body had decided it, too, had had enough.

It was in the midst of my futile attempt to find help for my physical ailments that the cure for my spiritual ills accidentally (at the time I thought it was accidental) stumbled into my life. It is funny, you know, because when we met, there was no indication that we would have any kind of connection, much less alter the direction of each others' lives. Revo was a young, soft-spoken Asian who was studying to be an actor. He had just moved back to Toronto from New York, where his girlfriend was eagerly awaiting his return. My co-workers and I took him under our wing when he came to work with us. Although he had no experience, he obviously had a desire to learn. He managed to win us over with his friendly, open personality.

Our talks centered at first mostly around work, as I am one of those people who believe that I get paid to do a specific job, so I might as well get on with it. After we had worked a few shifts together, idle chatter turned to hobbies, and, in a brief exchange of words, a path was laid out before us that we would not initially recognize, but would ultimately end up walking down together. He discovered that I like to draw, and, after inquiring if he could see my portfolio, quite innocently asked if I would be willing to sketch up a logo for his band. When he told me the name of his band, I admit I was slightly intrigued, but I had not yet made any connection between my own personal quest and this sweet young musician. I told him I would, of course, be willing to do so, but as often happens in cases like this, life got in the way, and the idea was unceremoniously shoved to the back of my mind.

It wasn't until two months later, when he returned from a trip to New York on a casting call, that I was reminded of my promise. When he came back, he told us he had decided that he was going to give his notice at work so he could concentrate on his acting and his music. He claimed it was partly because of the encouragement of a few choice staff members that he had decided it was time to follow his dreams and stop worrying about the immediate effect on his wallet. I was apparently one of those encouraging voices in his ear. Yet, for the life of me, I cannot possibly see how, being stuck in a rut myself, I found the time or energy to inspire somebody else. Upon his return, he asked again if I would do the drawing. As I was agreeing to get it done before he left, I looked into his eyes, and something became immediately apparent—something I had not noticed until the very moment his brief visit into my life was about to come to an end. I knew this man, not in the sense that we were friends who talked and spent time together, but in the sense that the soul behind the eyes was one I had had encountered before. It also occurred to me that I had already drawn the logo—three years earlier, when I had first moved to the city. It was strange that I had not recognized it sooner. While we perused my drawings, we had briefly discussed the meaning of the name behind his band. We had also discussed the meaning of the medallion I have worn around my neck every day since Baba's (my Polish grandmother's) death. Yet, even given our common interests in an obscure and clouded legend, it had never occurred to me to dig deeper.

The evening of his return to the city I went home and redrew the old sketch, adding to it several unique symbols that tied into the theme of the band. When I brought it to him the next day, he was surprised that I had managed to finish it so quickly. I explained that I had drawn it three years ago and had merely been waiting for him to come and collect it. He was silently staring at it while I was quietly explaining the meanings behind the symbols buried in the piece I had drawn. I looked down and noticed that his hands were shaking, and the hair on his arms was standing up. What I had drawn had obviously touched him, yet again it would not become apparent exactly how deeply until a few weeks later, when our stories began to merge. His response at the time was that it was exactly what he had wanted and needed without being able to picture in his mind what it should look like. He wanted to know how I had managed to represent his thoughts so precisely without him having verbalized them; I wanted at the time to tell him that I knew his mind and his heart, but as we were only passing acquaintances, I was sure he would think me a little unstable, so I merely shrugged and explained that I had been visited by a brief flash of inspiration. He was content with the piece, but he never made these decisions alone; he still had to present it to the band. We left it that he would show it to his boys and let me know if they liked it. We parted ways thinking that we would see each other the next day, but he never did come back to work. Though his name once or twice crossed my mind, I did not much miss his presence nor did it concern me greatly that I might not see him again.

A few weeks passed, and life was pretty normal. I went to work, came home, took care of my house, tried to take care of myself, and basically maintained a safe, comfortable, mediocre existence. Then the phone rang, and a voice singing in my ear brought me out of my sleepy state. It was Rev, phoning to ensure that I would be attending the staff party at work. He claimed he had something for me, and the band was very interested in meeting the artist behind the graphic that he claimed encompassed all the meanings behind the band's very existence. I assured him I would be there and hung up the phone thinking to myself for the first time in weeks that I had something to look forward to.

My boyfriend and I arrived later in the evening at the restaurant and settled into the typical staff-party routine, exchanging pleasantries and excitedly hugging and wishing well to the same damn people I saw every day. It was in the midst of this pathetic ritual of false niceties that my little Asian demigod again walked into my world—and this time irrevocably changed the course of my future. I remember that when I saw him that night I thought that he truly was a beautiful creature. As he was pulling me aside, I realized that somehow, in the course of his absence from my day-to-day routine, my perceptions of this boy, no, this *man*, had changed. He handed me a white gift bag after pulling me into a hidden corner of the restaurant so we could be alone. I admit his behaviour had me confused, but he explained that he and his band were only stopping by briefly and he had not bought gifts for anyone else. We fell into an easy banter about the band and the art. When I finally opened the gift I, much to my dismay and embarrassment, jumped up and down excitedly like a little schoolgirl. You see, it was impossible to hide my delight, as he had wrapped up for me a copy of the band's CD now labelled with my graphic and signed by the band. The other part of the gift was a very nice set of art pencils. The whole thing to me seemed to be a very straightforward message to not give up on my art. The way he smiled at my reaction made everyone else in the building for one brief moment disappear and turned an otherwise unbearably dull evening into the beginning of a magical journey.

When I was done making an ass of myself over this small, yet powerfully meaningful gift, I came to myself long enough to remember to give him what I had thought at the time a carefully prepared farewell gift. The drawing I had given to him earlier had been a copy of the original. When I am working on graphics for businesses, or tattoos, I never give my original sketches away. This time, however, I had decided that the original belonged with him and had rolled it up so I could safely carry it to him without it getting damaged. I handed it to him like that, rolled up, placing it in the palm of his hand, coincidentally upside down. He would later point this out to me as a sign that we had a journey we were meant to make together. This particular evening, however, we were both completely blind to the signs pointing the way, and, as the evening progressed, it played out naturally to a slowly building, yet extremely satisfying, friendship. I met his band and he introduced me to them as the artist. After I mingled a bit more, my musician friend pulled me aside once again, so he could show me something I had missed.

I hadn't noticed that something I had drawn, the Celtic-style image of a mother holding an infant, when turned upside-down took on the appearance of the hilt of a sword. It had actually been the band's bass player, Craze, who had been the first to notice. Looking back on it now, I am flabbergasted that I didn't see it at the time as more than mere quirky coincidence. I can only guess that had we forced the issue or connected too soon, then perhaps we would not have gone in the direction we were ultimately meant to go. Yet it is strange, again, for me to think that I did not see past the surface weirdness of the situation. After all, I haven't believed in coincidence for a very long time. it has been a very long time since I believed in coincidence. As I said, I was in a slump. I had hit a wall and needed to break it down before I could continue my spiritual growth. It seemed to me at the time that though the wall was one I had built myself, it would take a great deal of effort to find a way to destroy it; I was not sure I was up for it. Later in the evening, I felt I needed to sign the drawing I had given him. So I asked to borrow it briefly. I found a corner to hide in to commence writing.

To Rev

Thanks for reminding me why Grail seekers
seek and never give up the quest.

My heart to yours always,

Feenx

I signed it "Feenx" the name I use when signing my art. It was a name chosen for me by life and circumstance and represented rebirth and new life rising from the ashes left behind by a destructive, yet cleansing, flame. I suppose I should also point out that until three years ago, when I moved to Toronto after my house burnt down, the only time I had put pen to paper was to write.

Up until the very day I, for some reason, sketched out a Celtic style graphic design of a mother and child, I would have laughed in the face of anyone who suggested I turn to art as a hobby. I am, always have been, and always will be a writer—not because my blinded-by-love friends and family encourage me to be a writer, not because some self-absorbed critic justifies my work by claiming that in his superior expert opinion my work is worthy, and certainly not because you are reading this book. Rather, I'm a writer because, when life takes an unexpected twist or throws at me a challenge of seemingly insurmountable odds, I feel compelled to make sense of it all by writing it down. Eighty percent of what I have written in the past has been solely for my benefit. Writing has always for me been a way to heal any damage that has been done to my spirit during life's little annoying struggles. I went to school to become a journalist, and, though I both found myself giving birth and getting married during my fourth semester of school, I somehow managed to graduate and do it only a couple points below honours. I was told all my life that I was born to write by people who claim I had started writing poetry at the age of five years. Yet, through no fault of any one thing, I had forgotten, not that I am a writer, but, rather, what me being a writer meant.

So you see, when Rev gave me the gift that silently stated, "Don't give up on your art," it wasn't only in reference to the art of drawing. It awakened in me a realization that I had forgotten who and what I was. I had been drawn off-course by the day-to-day struggle of trying to maintain an existence on par with what society expected of me. Thus "Thanks for reminding me why Grail seekers seek." What I had really been saying was, "Thank you for reminding me to search out the truth of who I am, the truth of why I am here, and the truth of what I need in my life to keep me happy and balanced."

We met strangers and left friends, and though I was very careful this time to get his number, with a promise to myself not to lose it, I still felt a sense of sadness and loss at the prospect of this man no longer being in my life.

The evening was over, we were on our way home, and all I could think was that I was on the verge of losing something very special. I realized at the same time that I had been given a very precious gift.

I lay awake in bed that night, praying for guidance. It occurred to me that all I had dreamed was being overshadowed by my own personal guilt over past mistakes. My fear of losing the most precious thing in my life was holding me back from using my skills and my gifts to better myself—and maybe even better the lives of others. I continued my nightly meditation for over a week, before it occurred to me that, given what I was asking for, I was not offering a fair exchange. It was only several nights later that I opened myself up completely to the idea of change.

It is not natural or comfortable for me to think in terms of influencing others. I have always felt deep down that there was something more I was meant to do, although I was raised by my grandmother to believe in the talents I was born with. The thought of using those talents to make a difference in even one person's life was an extremely uplifting idea. It was just that, an idea—a dream that upon my awakening dissolved into reality and, day after ordinary day, was never realized.

No more, I thought, lying there in the dark. If there is something I am meant to do, show me what it is; give me a sign in which I can put my faith. Guide me in the direction I am meant to go, and if it is necessary to sacrifice my life here with my friends and my family, if it is important that I be willing to let go of my reality, then so be it. I am ready. I will let go of my fear, accept my mistakes, forgive myself for all my misdeeds, and open myself to the idea of a way to atone for them. I will accept both the light and the dark within me and embrace my humanity and all that comes with it. The pain, the anger, the fear, and the joy—even the lustful hunger I have encountered more than once when in the arms of a man—all of it I will accept and know that it is these things that make me human. I will accept the hate and love, and all the emotions in between, that keep my spirit connected to this earthly plain. It is that earthly connection that I am here to experience, to learn from, and to revel in, allowing my spirit to grow. These things I will accept. I will put my faith in the belief that I am here to *do* more and to *be* more. When I accept these things, a path will be provided for me to walk safely down. There will be signs along that path, and there will be guides sent to keep me from veering off too far when it becomes necessary to steer around obstacles in that path. These things I accept; these things I believe; and, in believing these things, I will find the strength to walk that path. I will be given a clear vision with which to see those signs and granted the grace and humility to accept and be thankful for any help provided me along the way.

This was my final prayer late one night before I went to sleep. It was my plea to the powers that be—whatever you choose to call them—and my way of making peace with both myself and those powers. It was with hope that I could move on as a whole person; the torn spirit I had been would cease after that night to exist. I would learn to be grateful that, regardless of where the road led, for one moment in time I had given myself over to a higher power. I was completely secure in my faith in that power and my belief that this time I would get those answers I was so desperately seeking.

I am a writer and therefore prone to flights of colorful fancy. I revel in exaggeration, as it allows me to expand on my thoughts and ideas while remaining entertaining. Here today I put aside those exaggerations. They are no longer needed. What is reality now is more than fanciful enough and therefore more beautiful and attractive than anything my humbled spirit could create. As I was lying there, a comforting warmth was building in me and spreading over me. It seemed to emanate from, or perhaps enter, the area of my chest. My heart sped up, and my lungs seemed to breathe in a burning heat; yet, I clearly remember that for a moment I felt so detached from my physical self that I'm not sure I was even remembering to breathe. I fell asleep that way: wrapped in that warmth and secure in the knowledge that in the morning I would be embarking on a new adventure.

The next day I woke up, gave my wife a call, and offered to give her a ride to work. I walked into my boss's office and promptly quit my job.

Chapter 2

<u>And Never the Twain Shall Meet... Not This Time</u>

Yes, that's correct: I picked up my wife, took her to work, and quit my job.

I would like to point out that my wife, who happens to be a stunningly beautiful Black Irish woman with seductive Asian eyes, took the whole thing in stride. When I announced quite calmly that I was intending to quit my job in order to pursue my writing career, she merely cocked an eyebrow at me and passively stated, "This should be interesting..."

Now that I have your attention, allow me to clarify a few things for you. I can guess that my usage of the term *wife* has you a tad confused. I assume you have already ascertained that I am female. I have also mentioned that I live with my boyfriend, and though in this day and age a woman being wed to another woman is somewhat accepted in Western society, I doubt very much having both a wife and a boyfriend would be anything but frowned upon in any culture. Please allow me to explain. The term *wife* in this instance can be used both symbolically and figuratively. In the casual sense of the term, she is considered by those I work with as my at-work spouse, in that we communicate and relate to each other on a level of comfort very much on par with most long-time happily married couples. We don't need to say much to each other to accomplish any task at work that requires cooperation. It is well known, in fact, that we are able to read each other so well through the use of body language that there are times when we never say a word at all. It is also well known that we can fight as heatedly as any married couple. Yet we have a mutual respect and understanding of one another's views and refuse to let those arguments come between us on a deeper level.

If you would like to explore the term in a figurative sense, you will see our relationship is one of mutual support and commitment to each other's happiness, again much on par with most long-standing happily married couples. We stand beside each other, support each other, feel joy at the other's success, and suffer as the other suffers. We keep each other strong by refusing to judge either past or present foibles. We back each other, defending each other if necessary, against the criticism of others. We also have an intense respect for each other's private lives, which allows us to have multiple friendships that do not interfere with our own personal bond. We do not believe it is necessary to invade each other's personal space, clinging to each other in order to maintain our friendship. If you were to go to either me or her for support or advice, and chose to do so in confidence, you could feel very secure in the knowledge that it is not in our natures to run to one another telling tales and sharing gossip.

She is, when you get right down to it, the one woman in my life who, if I were inclined to go that route, I could quite comfortably share a home and future with. We would, however, have quite the difficulty explaining our future together to her very sweet, very loving husband Adam. He, by the way, also refers to me as *her* wife and finds the whole situation rather amusing. He is as white as she is black and as short and round as she is tall and statuesque. They will both kill me when they read this but, given time, will find the humour in it as well. When I say she is Black Irish, I mean she is a person of Guyanese/Jamaican descent who just happened to marry an Irishman.

I think combining his red hair and freckles with her own stunning features will make for uniquely beautiful babies. This is something they are supposed to start working on very soon; as I told Sophia, I look forward to meeting her son (yes, I predict a boy, but I very much doubt they will stop at one).

As to her complacent reaction to my abandoning her to the vultures at work (her words), it is not in her nature to question any decision I make that seems to be moving me toward a happier life. So, as with every other odd decision or idea I have come up with, she took it upon herself to support me in it, reserving judgment for a later date. Her comment on me quitting being "interesting" relates to the fact that she takes perverse delight in the discomfort of our restaurant management team. Being very much aware of how many hours I put in, and how many times during any given month I agree to cover shifts for others, she was of the opinion that my announcement would cause some squirming in the office. If it did, I never got the chance to relish it. In fact, when I told my boss I wanted to work on my book, he encouraged me to take a leave, securing for me both my benefits during that leave and my position upon my return. It makes it much easier to stretch your wings and take that first leap into the unknown when you have the security of a safety net beneath you. I like to believe, though, that I would have done it regardless, as I was feeling compelled to move in that direction. I did notice that when my boss and I were finished talking he seemed to have a glazed look in his eyes, as if he were not sure he himself believed he was allowing it. The damage, as they say, by that time was already done, and I left work just a little more sure I was doing the right thing. Now for the shocking part: I still did not know for the life of me what I was supposed to be writing about. I had in my head an abstract idea, and I also had in my head a not-so-abstract title, but the actual content and the purpose behind that content had thus far eluded me. So here I was, a mere week away from three months off, with a laptop on order (something I had arranged the week before without knowing why) and nothing to go on but a title that in and of itself told me nothing.

I should explain here that it has always been my intention to write a book, and for the longest time I always thought I knew what it would be about. I had lived what on the surface appeared to be a fairly normal life. I was born, grew up, went to college, got married, had a baby, got divorced, and went to college again—nothing overly exciting to the casual observer; yet, to those who had shared some of that life with me, my stories and my experiences were both dramatic and entertaining. That, combined with the unrelenting belief and encouragement of my recently deceased Baba that I could someday be an inspiration to others, made it possible that my life story might just be worth putting on paper. There were, however, several drawbacks to the whole scenario as I saw it, and I was hesitant to explore that particular avenue. As I said before, I am uncomfortable with being responsible for other people's success. In order for me to inspire the general population, I had to embrace the idea that what I had to say might just be important; this was something I was not yet willing to do. Secondly, I would have to give up my somewhat-reclusive existence. I don't mean reclusive in the way that I was hiding myself away from society. I have a very outgoing personality with my friends and acquaintances. My reclusiveness was founded on the belief that the general public had no right to know anything about my personal life.

It is, as many have pointed out, practically unheard of for me to allow people into my life deeply enough that they can share my fear or my pain. Surface anguish does not count. Many people have seen me rant and rave; some have even seen me cry. Few, however, have been witness to the gut-wrenching emotional collapse that has occurred with each loss I have endured throughout my short life. As I have carefully built and surrounded myself with thick, protective walls, the very idea of breaking through them and sharing my inner self with the public was abhorrent. In saying that, I also knew that in order for anything I wrote to be inspirational those walls would have to come down. It was both a frightening and daunting prospect and, again, something I was unwilling to do. Lastly, I was not quite sure where to begin. I had tried over the years several times to start writing this particular story. Each and every time I would get a little way in and then get the feeling it was not yet time. Every previous attempt had begun at a different starting point and then been abruptly abandoned when the beginning ceased to flow toward a conclusion. It had been an exercise in humility and futility, and I was not eager to revisit such an emotionally draining experience.

I was mildly concerned about the effects such a story would have on the people in my life who are dear to me. In order to share my life story, I would have to expose as well pieces of others' private lives and essentially drag through the mud individuals I have over the years grown both to love and respect. My Baba, shortly before her death, had seemingly given me an answer to this dilemma. She reiterated a piece of advice she had given me several times throughout my life. She had told me over and over again that if I were ever to write my story that I should do it in the form of a fictitious tale, though she would never discuss with me exactly what she thought my story was. She would only say with certainty that someday I would write and publish a book. It was not until shortly before her death that she had given the advice with any sense of urgency. The last time she spoke of it, however, was the week before she died, when she made me promise—quite literally, on her deathbed—that I would never publish my story as fact. Having given that promise to the person in my life I revered above all others, I was now stuck on how to go about fulfilling her wishes. Nor did I realize at the time either the import or the implications of that demanded promise. I only knew I had to find a way to abide by it.

All these concerns combined to leave me pondering over exactly what I had left my job to write about. I was still somewhat secure in my belief that I would be given direction, but it would not be until several days later that I would experience the true meaning of the word *faith*.

Chapter 3

They Say You Do Not Find the Grail—it is the Grail That Finds You

While I was going my own way and doing my own thing, apparently, so was my musician friend.

Starting several weeks prior to my decision to randomly quit work, Revo and I were continuing to keep in touch via the computer. We had tossed a couple of emails back and forth, and he and his band had invited me to come to a show. The phone call began with *Hey Vicky you're so...* (This was a silly little song he had begun singing when we first met; it went to the tune of "Hey, Mickey.")

Okay, we gotta think of a new catchphrase. Hahaha

Dearest Feenx,

I've decided that I'm just gonna call you Feenx from now on... yes, the decision is made.

The show is on the 25th of January at Raq Lounge and pool hall.

I attached an invitation flyer and also the Raq Google map.

Ummm, what else?... Oh, Craze told me he got your text msg. The guys think you're "really sweet." :)

That's it; hope you had a good day at work today... how many guys hit on you? Lol

Heart u, Revolution

Throughout the days leading up to the show, Rev and I had tossed back and forth several emails, mostly pertaining to his band and my art and how the two seemed inexplicably connected. This leads me to the point in the story where it is necessary for a little background on both. I fear that without some explanation you may become lost in the imagery I will shortly be presenting. I will start with the connection between his band name and the medallion I wear around my neck. The name of his band is the Holy Grail, which is taken from the legend of King Arthur and the Knights of the Round Table. My own personal quest for the Grail had grown over the years from a different source. I wear around my neck a shield handed down to me by my grandmother. It depicts the Black Madonna and is representative of the shrine dedicated to her in Poland. The shrine itself is said to depict Mary, who the Polish people consider to be the rightful queen and protector of Poland as a free country. There are several legends and stories surrounding the shrine in Poland, as well as others dedicated to the Black Madonna, which are scattered throughout various countries on almost every continent.

Now, the story of King Arthur is pretty well known and really quite accepted in most cultures, regardless of their spiritual beliefs. The story of the Black Madonna, however, is much more controversial than a straightforward, albeit mystical, tale of a king and his courageous knights seeking the legendary Grail. For most people, the Black Madonna is simply a depiction of the Virgin Mary and child. Depending on what country you hail from, the reasons for her being black vary. Some believe that various paintings and shrines have darkened over the years as the result of age and exposure to smoke from candles burning nearby. Others believe her dark skin is the originally intended colour, though most of these paintings are exceptionally old and, in some cases, this can either be proven as fact or fiction. Some people believe the reason for the colour is to encourage acceptance of all races, creeds, and religions as children of God. They say the Black Madonna is an attempt to teach humans to embrace each other regardless of where they come from. I like the idea very much and support wholeheartedly the notion, though I myself am a member of a much more elite group of Grail seekers. After studying several of the paintings, as well as reading anything I could get my hands on, I have come to the conclusion that it is quite possible that the Black Madonna is not the Virgin Mary, but rather Mary Magdalene.

Oh yes, I know, you may think me a victim of Dan Brown's novel—though I support the idea myself, I am not sure I support the method with which he reached his conclusions. The truth is that it matters not, as I don't expect for one minute that you would alter your own belief systems to match mine. I am only clarifying a few issues of my own personal views, so that we can continue this tale in a manner that will not leave you lost and floundering.

Regardless of what you believe the Grail to be—either a magic golden chalice or the wife of Jesus and the mother of his child—the meaning behind the idea of the existence of the Grail remains the same. The Grail as a chalice was believed to contain God's light, his wisdom, and the truth of his existence. The Grail as the womb that bore and brought to life the direct descendants of Jesus was said to also represent the truth of his existence, thereby bringing light and wisdom to humanity. Either way, the Grail stands for truth. The Grail represents the truth of who we are, why we are here, and, ultimately, the truth of where we are headed.

My point to all of this is that both my musician friend and I had followed the Grail trail, down two separate paths, for most of our lives. As we discussed and explored each other's stories, we discovered a few things. I am a great believer in the meaning behind names. I think names come to us and that we are chosen by them, not the other way around. Out of curiosity, I looked up Rev's first name to see what it stood for. His middle name is pretty self-explanatory when you think about it, but that is a story for another time. His first name is Vincent, and I replied to his previous email with a reference to the meaning behind his name.

Dearest Revolution—(did you know Vincent means conqueror— what are you planning to conquer today?)

Hey, sweetie: Thanks for the info, and, as usual, for making me smile. You are really good at that. I'll run with you calling me Feenx. If u r a good boy I might even let you see my Feenx tattoo someday. I will try very hard to be there on the 25th, but since I am going in for minor surgery on the 21st I may not be feeling the greatest. Don't worry; nothing major. They just found something that might be causing all my problems and they want to remove it and see if it helps get rid of my headaches. I do, however, really want to see you play as well as just get to see you before you take off again on another journey. Someday, I swear, I'll go with you on one of these trips of yours, just for the fun of it, but for now I guess I should let the doc try to get me healthy first. While I'm lying around in a drug-induced stupor, maybe I'll get the chance to do some writing or drawing. I get a week off work to recupe, but I don't think it will take that long. Well, hon, gotta run—still silly enough to be going to work every day, and I would hate to be late. Take care, luv, and play safe. Say hi to the boys—xo.

Oh, I forgot—can I give your number to Sophia? She misses you...

He wrote this back.

My dearest Feenx of the West,

You deserve every smile you receive from everyone,

I'll pray that the surgery goes well. The show on the 25th was cancelled; the owner came back from LA and some logistic stuff. I'm trying to set up another venue for Feb 1st, so hopefully you'll be fully recovered and back up to your lively self.

*It would be fun to go on a bunch of adventures with you. And you have a Feenx tattoo?! Mmmmm … Okay, I'll try to be a good boy… *struggling* =)*

Someone once told me it means victorious, but I did not know Vincent meant CONQUEROR! Lately I've been conquering myself. As soon as I'm done that, the world is next.

And I swear… if I was ever a prince of the Grail in my previous life, you were surely my princess.

Greetings from the boys and yes, of course, Sophia can have my #. I miss her too. I've been pinching my own ass the past few weeks I'm missing her so much :)

Yours always, Revo

Shortly after my surgery, I sent a reply and took the opportunity to send him one more detail about my name that I had not yet bothered to mention. It was something another Grail-questing friend had pointed out several years ago as a joke and something I had forgotten about until recently. My last name, Norloch, means "of the lake." My rather large teddy-bearish friend had said a few years back that, given the fact that I am female, in a sense that meant I was also a lady (something I must point out here and now is a title I have categorically denied for years). He had finally gotten around to saying, in a convoluted and twisted way, that, in short, I was the Lady of the Lake—the very woman, in fact, who handed King Arthur his sword at the beginning of his quest for the Grail.

Dear, sweet Revolution,

I'm sorry your gig got cancelled; hopefully I will get to see you perform on the 1ˢᵗ instead.

The surgery seems to have gone well; my headaches are less intense, so that is a good sign. I would have written back sooner, but I have been on the couch sleeping for the last five day;, apparently my body decided I needed the rest. Overall, though, I feel good, so if you are playing on Sunday I will do my best to be there. (I work that night, but I can come up after work, so you will have to send me some info as to where and when and how the hell I can find it.

You know be good *is one of those terms that can be relative to whatever current situation you find yourself in, so don't try too hard. Being a good boy does not always mean you should follow the rules— try to keep that in mind.*

By the way, I know you said you were leaving again on another trip, but I can't remember when it is you said you are leaving, so drop me a line and let me know; that way, even if you don't have a show we can hook up for coffee and a chat before you leave. Very odd situation I find myself in; I already love and respect you, but I don't really know that much about you… strange to know so little about somebody I somehow feel so familiar with. I have no idea how often you check your email, but I am off work until Thurs lunch; if you get this and have time, give me a call. We can go out for lunch, and you can catch me up on all your plans to conquer the world.

Until then, my friend, play safe—and try not to give yourself too many bruises pinching yourself, because claims of self-mutilation will not save you next time you see Soph. She likes pain, lol. Say hello to the boys for me, and I will, of course, give Sophia a squeeze for you.

Oh yes, and here is your name info for today. One of my last names is Norloch, which means "of the lake," and, since I am a woman, it means I am the "lady of the lake" (coincidence is merely a sign on the road that helps us find our way).

My heart to yours ;) xo Feenx

Coincidences and colorful imagery aside, I am sure you can now see where I am going with this. Yet again, neither Rev nor I were putting any significance to these twists of phrase nor were we contemplating taking our passing acquaintance past a professional level. We both viewed the whole scenario as interesting, yes, as entertaining, certainly—but neither of us were allowing ourselves to read anything into it. I believed at the time, and so did he, that we were headed in two completely different directions. Yet the emails continued.

He sent me yet another invite to yet another new location for yet another new gig. I would have my daughter that night, and I had sent a message on Facebook asking if she could come with me. He answered immediately.

Hey, Viki,

I love reading your emails. **You are an inspiration to my heart.**

I'm glad the surgery went well. *I was looking for turmeric the other day, which is a natural anti-inflammatory, but I couldn't find the right extract. Canada needs to step up on the natural remedies* *stage; in the US you can find it at any local drug store. I'll look again today; there's this good herbal store downtown.*

I know; both shows got cancelled, but where 2 doors closed a window was shattered by a wave of wind that consisted of several TV producers, directors, and a record label. It's just in those times when we're down that God will give us a hand to get back on our feet, and—just like that video you sent—we have to on our feet again before we can start walking.

Thanks; now I know what you mean by "be good" =) hahahaha

I kinda felt the same way about you the first time I met you. In fact, people told me about you at the workplace, and it didn't seem like they were getting it entirely right. After a few conversations, there was this serendipitous feeling of knowing you.

Hmmm…. Lady of the lake… like the lady of the lake in King Arthur's quest for the Grail. The sword got lost and the sweet protective lady gave it back to King Arthur. Funny how that works out—smile—my band's name Holy Grail … you made that beautiful sketch years ago… and when you turn the sketch upside around, it's the handle of a sword… and as soon as you gave me the picture, I left Tucker's to continue the journey.

Did you know that your name means "Victory of the People?"

I talked to the owner of the gig, and it's no problem. Just let them know you're with the Holy Grail, and they'll let her in. It's a friendly crowd, and the people are nice. If she's anything like her mother, I'm sure she'll fit right in, lol.

Some producers will be there, so if you need me to introduce her to some engineers and other artists, I will. If she has the voice you say she has, maybe we can nurture that, and who knows. =)

At a time when I was beginning to lose hope, a time I felt I lost my Excalibur… you gave it back to me in one flash: maraming salamat *(thank you very much in tagalog-Filipino language)*

With love, Revo

It was only days now until his performance, and I had just that day gone to work with my wife in tow and taken my boss up on his offer of a leave of absence in lieu of me quitting.

Hey, Revo,

I'm glad my emails make you happy, and as for me being an inspiration, it works both ways, 'cause, baby, have I got news for you (no, seriously, I do—it is BIG NEWS).

I harassed Craze and sent him a text, 'cause I wanna tell you in person, but you no call. I be thinking you r phone shy, yes? On a side note, I feel great—no headaches, and we will most assuredly be there Friday nite. My little girl seems to be looking forward to it, and me, well, I can't wait to c u play.

I've got a business proposition for you. I know you are not going to have a lot of time Friday night, 'cause you will be pulled in a million different directions, so call me when you get this—I know u r a busy boy—but I'll keep it short and relatively painless.

I'm so very glad you found your way to Tuckers. I am sure they had lots to say. I try very hard to keep people at bay and keep them guessing; if they belong inside my walls, they will find a way in. Unfortunately, it seems to give people a lot to talk about; luckily I don't much care, and the smart ones, the ones that matter, see through the stories anyway.

Jean Victoria Norloch

Teehee—what can I say? Next time round, don't make me wait this long. I've been in this city for 3 yrs waiting for you just taking your sweet time about coming round lol. I tease, but seriously, something tells me we have a connection from another time and place.

If I have helped set you on a positive path—if I can somehow set your heart free so you can soar—then I have done part of what I think I came to this city to do.

Maddi will be fine on Friday, I am sure; we'll meet whoever you want, but I also know you are there to work. Call when you can— write when you want—and play safe till I c u again.

Love, light, laughter, **Viki**

He never did call but I got a response.

Viki, what's your phone #?!

Lol

I saw Sophia yesterday... awww... I can't find your #. My phone is shitty and can only store 100 numbers, so once in awhile it deletes random numbers when I put new ones in there.

I have been busy preparing for my trip to the Philippines: all the contacts there and getting ready for the show tomorrow and some recording. I'm so glad you're better. =)

So, Maddi is coming. Yeah... can't wait to see her in person; she's such a pretty little girl in her pic.

Um... yeah, sometimes I can be a little phone shy—I should get over it. Btw, got news too—will explain tomorrow at the show. xo

I wrote a very quick reply and then went on with my day.

Oh, u r such a bad boy, lol: 416-775-5575 (remind me to beat you later for losing my number) xo. I am home tonight and working from 11:30–4:00 pm Friday, but we will be at the show. She even made me take her shopping—having a girl is expensive. Love ya lots, Vik

I dropped by work the day of the show and took the opportunity to speak briefly to Sophia about a strange idea that had popped into my head—an idea I couldn't shake and the reason I wanted so badly to talk to Revo. I was having trouble bringing myself to write or create in my house. It was not a space that held much comfort for me. Rather, it seemed so steeped with negative energy that I felt it was draining me of my creative abilities. I told Sophia I had realized I had all this time off and I needed someplace magical to feed my spirit. As Rev was going to be taking a trip to spend a few weeks in the Philippines, I thought that maybe I could catch a plane and, using him as a guide, find some inspiration for my work. Crazy thought, eh?

I really felt bad asking Sophia what she thought, as I had been planning to take her and my daughter to Europe in the spring and could at the time only afford to take one trip or the other. I expected that maybe she would think me nuts, as I hadn't even spoken to Rev about the idea. Add to that the fact that I hardly knew him, then throw in an insecure and slightly jealous-of-his-prerogatives boyfriend—it was not, in general, the sanest of ideas. What did she say? Humph, I'll tell you what my grounded, down-to-earth, committed-to-reason friend said.

She said, "Okay, you can go, but only if you pick me up a Louis Vuitton bag while you are there."

I really do have the strangest friends...

The night of the show, I picked up a friend of mine and drove out with my daughter to the other side of the city. The friend in question is another person in my life who I have a very strong past-life connection with. We met through the same restaurant, which seems to me now to be a central meeting place for wayward spirits. When I first met him, I was slightly taken aback by this quirky little man. Honestly, he is shorter than me, and yet his self-assurance is so evident in the way he carries himself that at times he seems to me to be ten feet tall. He has a fantastically strange sense of humour, dresses to kill, and has a knack for getting out of trouble a split second after he gets into it—something that, thanks to his love of women, he manages to do frequently. When he isn't entertaining or challenging the world (depends on his mood), the quiet side of his personality emerges. He has a deeply buried and seldom-shared intellectual nature. Yet, when he does let it show, his confident advice and encouragement is often all that is needed to bring a friend back from the brink of despair. He always knows exactly what to say and when to say it—whether it be to lift up a friend or knock down an enemy; his words always hold a vast amount of wisdom, truth, and power.

He and his wife are both Jamaican, and when their youngest son was born they jokingly commented that he had my hair—near to impossible, given the fact that I am white and the new baby (my godson) is quite dark in both colour and origin. Yet, sure enough, when I finally saw him there it was: soft, wavy, medium brown hair.

I had recently asked my friend Conrad if he was interested in taking our baby (yes, my godson, my baby) home. I meant to Jamaica, to meet the family, something they have not yet had a chance to do. Conrad's answer was simply "My home is wherever you are, but, yes, I suppose some day we should take Deshaun to Jamaica." The answer was both touching and not that unexpected, as even his wife has commented that he and I have a connection that runs deeper than the here and now.

Again, I am only telling you these things so that later you can grasp each individual's part in this twisted tale—and if by the end of this you believe a single word, I will be absolutely amazed.

On arriving at the studio/lounge, we settled ourselves in, and I wandered behind the bar to teach the bartender how to properly make a Long Island Iced Tea. Rev saw me there and came up laughing, shaking his head and commenting that somehow I manage to make myself at home regardless of where I am.

Prior to the show, Rev and I had agreed to share our news after the band's set but instead spent the first hour together idly chatting. He played a visualization game or, rather, attempted to, but my answers were so twisted and far out of left field that he kept having to stop and backtrack. The most important part of the game turned out to be the part about a white stallion. I was to describe a horse, what colour it was, and use three words to represent the horse's personality. I chose majestic, powerful, and peaceful. He explained that the horse was supposed to represent my ideal mate, and the colour white, he said, laughing at me again, stood for purity. I found out later a deeper meaning behind the white steed, but we will in time get back to that. Eventually, the musicians had to go get organized, and I returned to my own table where Madison and Conrad were settled in ordering a late-night snack.

The first part of the show was a young drummer, a nine-year-old boy who could whale on a drum set better than several adult drummers I've seen. It was good encouragement for my daughter, who still held fast to the belief that, being young, it would be difficult to be taken seriously in the music industry. Yet here was a small boy who was being encouraged and applauded by a large group of adult musicians. Granted, he deserved it, but I could see the whole scene was having an extremely positive effect on my daughter's resolve to enter the world of music.

It is funny how the little things touch us in big ways. Here was this random guy I had met through work and who had no more than a passing interest in me—yet he was going out of his way to encourage my daughter to follow her dreams. It was touching, and it gave me a clearer inside view of who this man really was.

When the Holy Grail finally finished their set it was late, and Madison had her head buried in her arms, trying, but failing, to sleep through the noise. Rev and I still took the time to share our news, but, as the room was way too loud, we left Madison with Conrad and found a corner where we could talk. He told me to go first. So I told him I had decided to take some time off work and focus instead on my writing. He was very surprised, as he knew me as an artist, not a writer. Though he seemed pleased, he also had a slightly confused look about him. He asked me, "Really? You write?" Though I knew I should be getting Madison home, I stayed long enough to briefly explain my background and education in journalism as well as my ambition to write a book. He seemed a little more shocked than I had expected him to be. So I told him so. I also told him that, of all the people I knew, I would have thought *he* would be happy that I had decided to take a chance and follow a dream. He said, "No, no, that's not it," and he gave me a little grin. "It just seems quite coincidental that, given my news, you just recently decided to start writing."

Then he proceeded to tell me his tale. As he spoke, things began to fall into place. Apparently, his father had been a member of a revolutionary group before Rev was born. They had fought for the freedom of their people from oppression by a corrupt government. There was a legend taken from the time of the revolution that said someday a man would come to the Philippines and teach its people how to be free. The prophecy was made, during a large gathering of revolutionary soldiers, that the man's name would be Rebo, and he would be born of one of the men present. The only reason Rev knew about the tale was that his own father had been at that rally. He explained that his father had thought to Westernize the name, replacing the *B* with a *V*, and turning his name into the first four letters in *revolution*. Rev also pointed out that many children around that time had been named similar to him, and his own father had told him that it would likely be someone who had grown up to be a lawyer who would come forward to actively make change.

Rev's father was no longer involved, and, in fact, no longer even living in the country. Yet, for some reason, Rev said he felt himself being pulled back to his homeland. It was time to take a break from his music career and delve deeper into the meaning behind his given name. He also felt that somehow his people could be helped and inspired through the arts. Then he told me that the very same day that I had quit my job he had informed his band that he was going back to his home country and was not sure if he would ever come back. They had given up the lease on the studio, and he was preparing for an extended stay—when, up until only a few days ago, his intentions had merely been to have a short reunion with his family.

He had gotten it into his head to write a book exposing the corruption of the government, with the hopes that it would open the eyes of his countrymen. It was an idea he had been tossing around in his head for years, and then three days ago he had awakened with a strong desire to follow up on that idea. Now, here he was, on his way there, without any concrete plan for completing the challenge he was setting for himself.

He gave me another tiny smile. "You know, it is awfully strange that we both just happened to alter the direction we are going in on exactly the same day. I quit my band, and you quit your job. Now, I'm a musician, not a writer, and as I'm thinking to do some writing, I could probably use the advice of someone who is trained in that area. I think we need to talk more about this before I leave. Something tells me our time together is not yet meant to end."

It was my turn to look poleaxed, given my stop at the restaurant earlier to see my wife. I was also overcome with a panicked sense of urgency stemming from his decision to not return as intended. I happened just at that moment to glance over at Madison and realized that we had been talking a lot longer than I had originally intended. We made quick plans to meet before he left for the Philippines, and I gathered up my child. I left feeling both exhilarated and exceptionally confused. It seemed what I had suggested as a possibility earlier in the day was now turning out to be a very real and very scary probability.

It wasn't until Conrad made a comment to me in the car that I began to shake. Keep in mind, as I quote him, that while he was in the club with me, he was at the other end of the room and could not possibly have seen or heard a damn thing. I must also make it very clear that he and Sophia do not talk often. There is no way she would have breached confidence and shared our earlier discussion with him. Conrad was staring at me as I drove and, finally, after a few minutes of laughing to himself, he decided to share what he seemed to find a very amusing joke indeed. "I know you, Vik, and I know that look. You're going after this guy, aren't you? You are going halfway around the damn world to meet this guy." With my baby sleeping in the backseat, I tried to be reasonable about the whole thing. There was no way I could leave her for long. The whole idea was nuts. There Conrad sat, his smiling mouth split in an ear-to-ear grin, laughing his ass off at the fact that I was about to transverse the globe to follow a man I hardly knew. He was supposed to tell me not to do it. He is dedicated to his kids, and he knows how dedicated I am to mine. What he should have done while he had the chance was talk me out of it. Hell, until that night he had never met the guy. He had no foreknowledge concerning what type of person Revo was and no grounds to trust him. His love for me alone should have elicited from him the quite reasonable request that I at the very least think it through. Oh no, not him! When we finally got to his house, with him still giggling, his only comment on getting out of the car was: "Hey, have a good trip, eh?"

Chapter 4

Flying Cards, White Horses, and the Gospel Lady

It wasn't until I got home and had Madison safely tucked into her bed that I was willing to admit to myself that my story had found me. My instincts told me this was going to have an irrevocable effect on my life, and, though I hoped that in the long run it would be for the better, I was understandably afraid. Unfortunately, I have a bit of a wild side and—regardless of the impact to my safe, secure life at home—I found myself wanting to jump in: feet first, eyes closed, and hoping against hope the pond was going to be deep enough. I sent a quick text to Rev, then headed off to bed.

Hey, sweetie,

I forgot with everything else going on last night to tell you how much I love watching you play—you really are talented, and I hope you never give up that part of yourself. Listen, it occurred to me today that perhaps it is not my *story I am meant to be writing, and though I know I will be seeing you on Tues, I wanted to give you something to think on until then. I am very serious when I say I want to come to the Philippines—and, yes, I know it's way out of left field, but I want to learn about your people, and I am wondering if you would teach me about them and tell me your story, the whole story—not just the stuff you briefly highlighted last night but all of it. I am willing to come there and learn if you would be willing to take the time and teach me. I figure if you have not by now run away screaming for fear that I have lost my mind, then maybe there is more to this. Perhaps if we collaborated our efforts: your knowledge and the gift that I was blessed with (the ability to pour my heart and soul onto paper), then maybe we can bring your people's story to the attention of the world. I feel so strongly about this and am willing to take the risk and invest the time, if you will help me by leading me to the information I need. If you are interested, you know how to reach me or you can wait until Tues and we can talk then—and, so you know, my full name means "Yahweh's great victory of the people." Perhaps the people who named me had a premonition—I hope you are open to the possibilities of us working together, because suddenly three yrs does not seem that long to have waited after al. Love, light, laughter. xo, Feenx*

I didn't believe, of course, not at the time. I went to bed with all sorts of doubts in my head. Did the conversation we had really mean that this was a path I was supposed to follow? Did Rev really see it too, or would he take a look at my latest email and think *Man, crazy lady, got to get away.* What would happen if, by some off-chance, this was the road I was supposed to walk down? Where would it lead, and how many sacrifices would I have to make along the way? It was not a very restful night.

I still could not quite believe that I could write a book that would not only sell but would inspire the people who bought it. I'm not sure that even now I can reconcile the idea of me being anybody important enough to initiate change or affect the future of our world. My brother claims that it is the safe side of my personality keeping me grounded, so I can continue to do the work we are doing. I have discovered that as long as I am actively trying to help others, then the pieces just seem to fall into place, and answers are just sent to me as I need them. It is only when I begin to be concerned about my own security and make decisions based on those concerns that I find myself completely off-track and wondering how I got there. I can only guess that that is how it is supposed to work; I still haven't had the chance to sit down and ask God about it, so I will for the moment have to continue to draw conclusions based on what I've seen and been through. It makes sense, though, that if "the powers that be" want us to be selfless and compassionate, they would only actively help us when we are.

The next day Madison and I had an early morning hair appointment. When I attempted to wake her up, however, I discovered she was far too tired from the night before. So I left her sleeping and went on alone.

As per my now-usual routine, I quickly checked my email before I left and was pleasantly surprised to see a positive response to my email from the night before.

My Lady of the Lake,

Can we meet up at 12 instead of 1 on Tuesday? It's my last day and I have to be at the Airport 5 am Wed.

I'm home finally after 2 nights of late nights and music from Live Nights, lol.

I had dance this morning, then the gym, then the studio, then went to sell some equipment, then to my cousin's, then to Risa's and the guys, and I spent some bromance *time together. I want to leave on good terms with them; it's another long story. Maybe your words of wisdom can solve the dilemmas we've faced.*

Thanks! You know, I learn every time I go on stage, and the words never *and* give up *have kind of been exhausted in my vocabulary by people who prefer instead to use the words* believe *and* faith. *So, the way I see it, winners never quit and quitters never win. The more battles I can find myself in in life, whether win or lose, the more I will ultimately learn the lessons I need to learn to win the greater war. Each step on stage or film is a battle, and I can only hope that with every step and every breath I breathe, I learn and improve— until one day the whole world is watching.*

I think what the Philippines need is God's great victory of the people.

In high school, I was a pool shark and loved billiards. At this age, I hadn't read anything about the Arthurian Legends or the Holy Grail. I went out with my friend, and I bought a pool cue. When I went to the counter, the teller told me, "Nice pick, the Excalibur."

I said, "That's a cool name," and he told me I would never lose with it. I don't think I have to this day. It was only about 4 years ago when I discovered the tales of King Arthur and the Grail; soon afterward we formed the band.

Legend has it that the hilt had powers of its own. It was only when Craze turned your art upside down that we all saw what was clearly the hilt of a sword. And it was that night that you gave it to me, rolled up like a sword—and with it on my person, I felt all fear vanish. I'm thinking of that now, because I have it hanging on top of another picture in my room, and beside it is a card with the silhouette of Elvis that my mother got me for my trip to the Philippines. She wrote in it, "I hope one day you'll be like Elvis, only in popularity," as if to say: "but don't die so young."

Anyway…

I'm game with this entire scenario, with 3 conditions. And I guess we'll talk about them when I see you. That and ... I'm just wondering: where did you come from? And where have you been all my life?

One of my acting coaches always told me, "Don't take care—take risks." =)

1. It's what you sincerely want to do and where you want to go.

2. It will make you happy and wake you up every morning with a greater purpose to stay focused and finish your book.

3. Your daughter supports it. I can see now—she was the window God opened when doors and walls had closed in on you.

As I drove, I realized I had to go. Yet the idea itself was so far out in left field and so unexpected that even if the prospect of a trip to the other side of the world was exciting, the reality was scary as hell. When I arrived at the salon, my stylist, Victoria, immediately noticed a difference in my demeanour. I believe she said something along the lines of "you're glowing." Now, taken out of context, that could mean my appearance was one of lighthearted happiness. Coming from Vic, however, it took on an entirely different meaning. Vicky is a spiritual child of the new age. Her journey to enlightenment has taken a different path than those who use structured religion as their guide. She is a believer in karma. She also believes that the energies that make up our world are what tie together and define our existence. She believes in the power of healing energy being shared and manipulated by others for the use of mending both body and soul. She also believes, like many others, that mankind is on the verge of a spiritual revolution. She can neither define nor describe, however, how that revolution will manifest. She can only say with certainty that it is inevitable. She feels that it is a necessary step in human evolution and that it will lead humanity toward a more enlightened state. She studies healing arts, spirit guides, chakras, and meditation. She relies on the powers of plants and herbs that nature has provided for us and looks to spirit guides to give her direction and confirmation. She is aware of the importance of recognizing signs, what some refer to as coincidence, and their place among us as a tool of encouragement and direction. She also believes in auras, the energies that come from within us and extend past our physical beings to connect with the rest of the world. Believing in auras as she does, she quite literally meant that to her I was glowing. My auras or energies at the time were exceptionally strong and vibrant, which (to her) visibly made my body seem to glow. She, of course, wanted to know why. I figured it couldn't hurt to bounce the idea off her. So, while she was working to mix up a new interesting hair colour, I began to explain what had happened. The more I talked about it, the more animated I became, and the more the whole crazy scenario seemed to make a great deal of sense. I explained how this man had a twisted past, having been born in a world where poverty and oppression are a part of daily life. I told her a bit about his name, how he got it, and what it meant to him. I also explained that, given the current state of economic and political instability in his country, what he was proposing could be extremely dangerous if we were not extremely careful.

I went into detail about how he himself had been gathering information for years in the hopes of using that information to inspire and awaken his people, and that through the use of his art, both theatrical and musical, he hoped to reach the younger generation and set them on a course for change. With all his ideals and beliefs, really, all he had was a dream, with no defined way to turn that dream into reality. I explained that what I was proposing to do was to go with him and collaborate with him to create a story that would both awaken and inspire. It had occurred to me that I had been, in fact, attempting to write the wrong book, and that is probably why I was never able to finish it. I asked her if she thought I was nuts. She said she didn't. Of course, I would expect a positive reaction from her, given her own spiritual quest. However, I had to make it plain to her that I could not honestly say how this journey would affect my relationship with my boyfriend. The catch there was that he is how Victoria and I met. He is her friend, not I. Here I was proposing to fly to the other side of the world with another man. She asked if I had told him, and I explained that I had not, as I was not yet sure that I was going, and I felt no need to upset his comfort zone. I also explained that if I were to do this it would have to be with or without his support—something I neither expected her to understand or encourage. She did both. In fact, she discussed with me the spiritual cost to myself if I decided not to take the trip. She inquired if years from now I would regret not going. She encouraged me to follow my instincts and base my decision not only on reason, but on awareness of the signs that seemed to be pointing me in that direction. She suggested that we go in the back to do a tarot reading. While we were back there and I was shuffling the cards, she was telling me that the cards would choose me by either poking out or sticking out or, very rarely, falling from the deck. Just as she was finishing her sentence, one of the cards flew from the deck to land face-up on the other side of the room. I continued to shuffle as she went to pick it up, and I noticed that as her fingers touched the card they were trembling. I cocked an eyebrow at her, curious which card had set her so on edge. The card was an indicator card depicting a lady on a white horse and very pointedly saying that I was to embark on a journey.

The card also indicated that if I were to go on this journey, I would be provided with both direction and protection. What had left my good friend shaken was that she had never seen such a violent reaction from a deck of cards nor had she ever been witness to such an obviously straightforward message.

The next three cards also decided to fall out of the deck in rapid succession. The first card, the card that represented past issues, told us that I would need to let go of what was past; doubt, fear, and guilt were no longer welcome in my world, and I would not be able to embrace my future if I could not let go of the past. The card said the future was where I needed to be. The next card represented the present and also spoke of a journey, an adventure of spirit and awakening of self. The third card, representing the future, spoke of a peaceful end and a satisfactory completion of a spiritual quest.

Now, as I said before, it would do you, the reader, a great justice if you would take these words I write and believe they are a colourful, fanciful tale. I do hope you take my advice to heart, because, though the imagery contained within so far may seem to some rather mundane; to most it would seem quite fanciful. So I take this opportunity to once again implore you not to believe a word of it; it is a tale, a fabrication. It is an illustration of thought written only to intrigue and entertain you. I am certainly not sitting at this moment on the patio of a hotel restaurant in Pasay City, Manila. I am also not listening, as I write, to the animated banter from five Chinese businessmen sitting behind me. There are not several Asian children in the adjacent pool chattering away rapidly in their native tongue. I would also like to point out that yet another sweet young waiter here at the hotel did not just bring me another drink. I did explain to you before that it would be safer for you and for me if you would choose to embrace this story in that manner, and, as the tale is about to get that much more strange, I hope you are open to my suggestion. Now, I have to ask you: After all that Vicky and the cards had said, how could I deny that I was meant to take this trip? No, really. How could I doubt it? I did. It is in my nature now as I get older to second-guess every little thought and idea. I have in past years made too many mistakes that threatened to shatter the happiness of myself and others.

I was very excited, however, at the prospect of taking the chance that I just might be on to something. My apparent enthusiasm was enlivening my hairdressing friend. Our talk turned back away from the politics of the country in question and veered toward the prospect of a spiritual revolution. Vicky brought up the Mayan calendar and the fact that it ended in 2012. She asked if I thought that would be the end of the world, and I answered no. I have always believed, for my own reasons, that the end of the world would not be the catastrophic end of all things as predicted by many prophets. Rather, it is possible that it would be a shift in belief systems so monumental in magnitude that it would catapult humanity as a whole into a higher state of being. Books like *The Celestine Prophecy* and *The Secret* explore this shift from the point of view of each individual person. These books open people's minds to the energies that will eventually be required to attempt a shift that includes worldwide population. As to why the Mayan calendar stops in 2012, I have my own theory, which includes two reasons.

One: It is possible that in 2012 humanity will find itself at a crossroads and will either embark on a new enlightened path, and thereby reach a higher state of being (what some refer to now as *ascension*), or they will destroy themselves through greed and hunger for power. The Mayan priests had not been able to see past this fork in the world, as the choice had not been made. It would be impossible to tell what that choice would be. Humans are excruciatingly unpredictable in nature, allowing their thoughts and feelings to be their guides rather than relying on their inborn instinct. Knowing full well that it could end either way, it stands to reason that the priests could not be sure there would be a need for a calendar at all.

The second reason ties in directly with the first: If mankind went down the path to destruction, then they would cease to exist. Simple, yes? Okay, now following the reasoning I previously explored: if mankind actually found a way to attain that higher state of being, that ascension which New Agers tell us is possible, would they need a calendar? No one can say exactly what that higher state would be. Some predict a shedding of our physical shells and a return to our base state of energy. Some view it as *heaven on earth*, believing that we will maintain our physical form but will have accomplished spiritual oneness with ourselves, each other, and the nature that surrounds us. In doing so, we would shed our materialist needs and desires, living instead in our natural surroundings. If that were the case, would we need a calendar?

Please understand that I am not telling you these things are fact. They are theological ponderings that have been explored and discussed by minds much greater than mine for many centuries. These theories neither encompass all that I believe nor do they stem from a basis in proven fact. I do not expect you to alter your ideals and I do not wish to steer you away from your faith. I merely point out that these ideas exist and have existed from ancient times, all the way back to the pagans and their ritual worship of nature. I am not saying it is the right way, nor am I saying it is the only way. I do offer the chance, however, if you are curious, then, by all means, to explore the ideas yourself.

We do currently live in a world where information is readily available. God bless the Internet and its ability to put information at a person's fingertips. I caution you, of course, not to believe everything you read, but to read everything you can and take from that material only what you need to maintain a happy, balanced existence. I myself am still learning; as you will see, the beginning of this journey was merely an open door to a whole world of information. I am a curious being and, as such, am constantly asking questions—neither accepting nor denying what I learn. I continue to seek, to strive, and to grow from the knowledge I acquire, and I find that the more I learn the more questions I have. It is a continuous cycle, one I rather enjoy the experience of. If you, dear reader, can take anything from this book as fact, take this: knowledge is not power. It is not something to be used as a weapon against others, and it will not make you a whole person. The hunger and thirst for knowledge is where the power the lies. It is not a power that can be misused or misdirected; rather, it is a power that comes from within. It is the power to be able to open our minds, our hearts, and our eyes to new ideas, broadening our views and strengthening our resolve to be better people. It is in the *search* for knowledge, not the acquisition of it, that we achieve balance within ourselves and our surroundings.

This I know to be true. This I know to be real, and, if you learn nothing else from this story, learn this; the rest will fall into place, and you will believe what you personally need to believe and learn what you personally need to learn in order for you to be whole. As an aside, I do not know where you should start. The beginning of each person's spiritual quest is not something that should be guided from outside, it must come from within, and so I cannot be much help to you in that area. After saying that, I do advise that it doesn't hurt to ask questions and really listen to the answers. Again, you don't have to take each answer for fact; nor do you have to believe in everything you learn about, but it helps to be open to new ideas and to the views of others. They may have something to teach you, and, in turn, you may even have something to teach them. Think on it awhile as you read through the rest of my tale. Then, when you are finished, go out and explore the world. It is fun; really it is. When you get past the fear and the doubt you may even learn to enjoy it.

Back at the salon, we were wrapping things up when my phone rang. It was a number I didn't recognize, and, as I was in the middle of a conversation, I should not have answered. But I did.

The voice on the other end explained to me that her name was Sherry and she was inviting people to her church for gospel study. Um, no… you see, I have difficulty with believing in structured religion. It's not because the ideals behind it are unsound but because I find it very easy for people to abuse power they think they have secured directly from the hands of God. Consider the priest who tells you that in order to talk to God you must go through him. I am not sure about this, because I have not actually sat down with God and had a conversation over tea, but I can guess that he does not require the use of memos to hear and acknowledge our prayers. I am, as I said, not positive. I am no priest and so probably do not have the authority to make such a statement. Yet I can't for the life of me understand why a God who is all-powerful and all-seeing would not hear a prayer that was not first channeled through one of his chosen. I would like to know if I am right—and I intend some day to ask him—but it is my experience as a nondenominational spiritual pupil that my own prayers have been answered several times throughout my life *without* an intermediary or the use of idols.

I was very polite to this woman in my refusal and hung up the phone feeling only mildly guilty. I was on my way out the door when the phone rang again. It was the same number. Again, against my nature, but following my instincts, I chose to answer. I told this sweet little old lady, "Sweetie, you just called me, and I said I wasn't interested. Are you sure you have the right number?" She replied, sounding rather flustered, that she could not have just called me. She never calls anyone twice. Then it hit—maybe, just maybe, I am supposed to talk to this woman. So I tell her that I think for some reason I am supposed to talk to her, but, as I am in the middle of something, can she please call me back another day. She said she'd call me back the next day, and I hung up the phone. As I was now in a state of flux—should

I stay or should I go?—I pushed the phone call to the back of my mind. I told Vicky I should probably call an old friend up and get my chakra centred before I embark on this bigger-than-little adventure. I left the store with phone in hand, now sure that I would like to go, but not yet knowing why. I got in the car, got on the phone, and, when my Pops answered, I told him simply: "Okay, I'm ready; it's time."

Chapter 5

<u>Fairies, Horses, and Gifts from Heaven</u>

He was, of course understandably confused, my poor Pops was, but, before I get into the why and the how, I should probably give you an explanation of how Pops came to be my Pops at all. Pops is not really my father. My real father, my biological father, passed away when I was three years old. There is still a great deal of mystery and many unanswered questions surrounding his death, but that, I think, is an entirely different book. Pops is also not my stepdad. That title belonged to a loving, caring, and somewhat rambunctious man who passed away a day before my mother's own untimely demise six years ago. Lastly, he is also not the sweet, gentle, good-natured male half of the couple who upon my parents' unexpected deaths decided to take me under their wing and bring me into their family. It was an odd situation, to be sure, to be fostered at twenty-seven years of age. And yes, you guessed it; it is not yet time for that story either.

No, Pops is just another one of those random people who unexpectedly pop into your life, thus "Pops." Two years ago, I was working as a waitress in my united nations of restaurants, when I inexplicably felt a pull toward this little decrepit old man who was sitting in my section having lunch with his friends. I overheard bits and pieces of their conversation as I was serving them and the tables around them. Their animated discussion intrigued me, and I found myself repeatedly wandering past the table.

They were discussing the theory that coincidences are not just random occurrences, but rather signs that are meant to guide us down the road of life. What fascinated me so much was that this group of men, all well past the age of sixty, was having a very loud, very open discussion about this theory. I have seen this belief proven true several times in my own life, and I had often heard it discussed. The more spiritually advanced already know there is no such thing as coincidence and eventually get to the point where they don't feel the need to state the fact. The people who usually talk about such things were, in my experience, much younger, and they were also usually people who had just begun their journey to enlightenment. This was not a discussion, therefore, that I expected to hear from a group of men who were very obviously closer to the end of their personal quests. I also noticed that all three men were taking turns following me around the room with their eyes—none more so than Pops, who seemed somewhat drawn to the medallion around my neck (at least, I think it was the medallion he was staring at—it couldn't be my cleavage, as I don't have any). The lunch crowd eventually thinned, then vanished; yet, these three men stubbornly remained. They were well aware that the restaurant was well past closing time, and they had paid their bills what seemed to me eons ago. I approached the table one last time to offer more coffee before going off to cash out and wrap up my day. *Very strange little man*, I remember thinking.

I was rewarded with confirmation of that assumption by way of an offhand comment when I arrived at the table. "You know, you look like the daughter I never had... Yes, yes, I think you are. Would you like to be my daughter? I very much feel that you already are."

He stated this so placidly, yet with such conviction, I couldn't help but giggle—at which point he quipped, "Yes, my daughter would sound like that; hmmm... you must be her."

Normally a person's natural instinct would be to run, but I really wasn't feeling anything other than mildly amused. Realizing that he hadn't managed to scare me off, he asked yet again, "Are you my daughter"? His friends were rolling their eyes while attempting to crawl under the table. However, I couldn't let him win this battle of wits, so I merely arched an eyebrow at him and responded, "Sure, Pops, I am your long-lost daughter; you've been missing me, haven't you?" They were strange words coming from a little waitress girl, but it immediately put his friends at ease, and an odd, but educational, friendship was born.

It turned out Pops is an author himself and a healer. He has written and published books on metaphysics and, at the time I met him, was working out of his house as a spiritual healer focusing on the realignment of chakras. During a brief discussion that day, we discovered our birthdays happened to be one day apart, his being July 4, mine July 5. We agreed to meet for lunch on his birthday to celebrate them both and exchanged numbers with the intention of keeping in touch. As usual, time and circumstance got in the way, and in the next year we did not find many chances to meet. We did keep our birthday date, and when he had a hip replaced I dragged Sophia to the hospital to pay him a visit. We kept in touch by phone, and he kept trying to convince me to let him do a healing, something I continually told him it was not yet time for. My Baba, after being extremely sick for a year, finally succumbed to her illness, and in the spring of this year she had passed away. Pops began a vigil by phone, repeatedly calling to check on my well-being. Each time he called he offered healing, and each time he offered I told him, "No, not yet—it isn't time."

Well, now it was time. Though he didn't immediately recognize the significance of those words, I do recall him asking me where I was flying off to and explaining that he could feel the energy over the phone. He said an energy that strong indicated flight. We talked briefly, and I explained that I had this opportunity that I was contemplating taking a chance on, and, as I was going on this trip, I thought now might be the ideal time for a healing session. I also explained that I felt I would need as much strength and balance as I could get. Having him align my chakras would probably help with that. He emphatically agreed, and we set a date for a session the following Monday. I hung up the phone and headed home.

At this point I was figuring: *Okay, cool—game on.* I mean, as his earlier email had shown, Revo obviously understood my priorities and supported them. It suddenly felt like a very safe venture—not in a physical sense, but emotionally, which we all know can be the more damaging of the two. Still, I was not entirely positive I was going; Rev and I had still not met in person to go over details. Therefore, I didn't feel the need to broach the subject with my daughter just yet. Taking Rev's conditions to heart, however, I did decide to see if my cosmically connected little girl could find it in herself to approve without me having to voice aloud what it was that needed approval. One of my bosses, Alya (oops, that would be ex-boss), had given us a joint gift for Christmas, and I decided it was high time we tested it. In order for this to make sense to you, I must again present a bit of background on this new character. Our history centred around my job at the restaurant. It was Alya, in fact, who had hired me when I had chosen to wander in off the street, resume in hand. I would like to clarify a couple of things.

First: When I originally applied for the job, it was completely at random. I had just moved into the city and had been driving around aimlessly trying to decide where I wanted to work. I am not even sure how I ended up in the plaza where the restaurant is located, as it is both quite a distance from where I was living and well off the beaten path. I certainly did not know the restaurant was there, nor, for that matter, that it even existed. I had no foreknowledge as to what kind of restaurant it was, and I happened to luck out as far as getting in the door on that particular day.

You see, unbeknownst to me, the restaurant closed between the hours of 2:00 PM and 5:00 PM, and it just so happened that I stumbled on the restaurant and slipped in the door exactly at 2:00 PM, as the hostess was coming to lock up. I asked her if they took resumes; she gave me an application and told me I should sit and wait. The hostess, a young lady by the name of Sarah, told me she had a feeling that Alya would want to meet me and went off to find her, as I sat down and flew through the process of filling out the application. I needn't have bothered. Alya didn't look at it until several minutes after she decided to hire me. When she sat down to interview me, she said she had the feeling I belonged there. We talked a bit about ourselves and shared a bit of our experiences. Then we eventually turned our attention to the matter at hand.

Before she looked at my resume, she said, "Since I've already decided to hire you, I suppose I should see what kind of experience you have."

We talked some more, going over minor details with regard to uniform, dress code, etc. Then I left some thirty minutes later with a promise to return that evening to start training. It was without a doubt the most unique interview I have ever had, and I remain thankful to this day that I was lucky enough to stumble blindly into her world.

The three years I have spent there have overall been happy ones. The friendships I have built with the people there have been both a comfort and a blessing.

Alya herself is a vibrant, independent woman who hails from a strong spiritual background steeped in both Christianity and mysticism. Over the past couple of years we have fed, energized, and encouraged one another. We have watched each other grow and taught one another various lessons along the road. We have also clashed numerous times, both being strong personalities secure in our places in the world. Though it has been proven repeatedly that we do not always agree, our bond has remained strong. It was shortly before Christmas of this year that Alya decided that her time at the restaurant was done. Her last act as manager had been to hire Revo—something I recalled later as being another one of those coincidental occurrences. She had come to me on her last night of work and confided that she had been asked to do one last interview. She felt that as she would not be there to train this individual, she should not be the deciding factor in his obtaining the job. She admitted, however, that she felt compelled to meet this character. I encouraged her to follow her instincts, as they were usually pretty accurate. She did the interview, and, oddly enough, she hired him. The reason I say *oddly* is because the man had absolutely no experience in the restaurant industry—unless, of course, you wish to count dining out. Now, given that Alya takes her job and responsibilities very seriously, it is not in her nature to hire someone who hasn't got a clue what he is doing. It is also not in her nature to cease taking that responsibility seriously until the job is in fact complete. So it is not likely that she hired the boy simply because she no longer gave a shit. That is simply not an attitude she is capable of.

Sometime around Christmas, Alya had held a dinner for close friends. The dinner was for adults, but, as I believe that where I go, my daughter also goes, Alya was nice enough to invite her as well. She welcomed Madison with open arms, even going so far as to get her a small Christmas gift.

There were actually three small gifts, both tiny in size and momentous in meaning. The first was a small crystal charm pendant of an owl, which Alya had lovingly wrapped up for Mad and to which she had attached a small note. The second gift was for me, and it was a framed picture of a statue of Mary Magdalene that currently resides in the Louvre in Paris. The picture was one Alya had taken herself, and attached to it was a note saying: "Some gifts come from very far away and need no explanation." She was, of course, well aware of my fascination with the Grail and had, in fact, given me a card when she left the restaurant that thanked me for many long talks and wished me well in my personal quest for the Grail. It is with the opening of the last gift that we can continue our tale.

Alya had managed to find a tarot deck that depicted fairies as the guiding spirits and had included a card that read: "To aid in the mother-daughter bond that is the belief in magic." It was an especially touching gift in two respects. My daughter has for years collected fairies, and it was very sweet of my friend to acknowledge that hobby and include it in the gift. It was also my daughter's first tarot deck—something that I cannot in retrospect see coming from any purer source.

It was this very deck that on the Saturday afternoon after my hair appointment I decided to open and test. My daughter was playing once again on the computer, so I decided to cleanse the deck, tune it to me, and then do my own reading before bringing her over to teach her how. I shuffled the deck with the intention of doing a simple three-card spread, and again the cards decided to jump out. They were, of course, different in appearance, as it was a completely different deck—yet their meanings matched exactly the meanings we had read earlier in the day. I really wasn't that surprised but was most curious to see what would happen if the deck was instead tuned to my daughter. I called her to come sit with me on the floor and proceeded to instruct her on what to do with the deck. After I was satisfied that she had completed the ritual cleansing, I again began to shuffle the cards. Yet again, three cards leapt out in rapid succession, and yet again their meanings were crystal clear. This time, however, they were three different cards, but the direction they gave was the same as both the three I had done myself and the three from the salon. The thing that stood out, however, above all others was the fact that in every single card there was somewhere buried in the card a picture of a white horse. It wasn't until later that I would understand.

I was anxious to respond to the email I had read that morning from Rev. Once we were done the reading, I asked Madison if I might use her computer to check on an email that I was expecting from a friend. She said, "Sure Mom, say hi to Rev for me," and a big, goofy grin split her face. You know, you would think it would be easier to raise the smart ones!

My Holy Grail,

12 is fine my sweet—you do mean 12 noon, right? No matter if you mean midnight, it won't matter; I'll be there either way. Just let me know, okay (T-bones)? I am glad you are getting a chance to say goodbye; it is something I will have to make time to do over the next couple weeks. I figure it will take that long to get the passport settled and make arrangements for the flight and the million other things I'm probably not remembering I need to do. As far as your friends go, I have learnt that they will be your friends (no matter where you are and how long you happen to be gone for) only if they are meant to be in your life; if, on the off-chance your time with them is done, then you have already learned all you need to from each other and the memories and lessons will stay with you always, even if they cannot...

There are a million things we will have to talk about on Tues so perhaps I can answer a few of your questions now. It is not only what I want; it is what I need. I have known all my life that there was more that I was meant to do. I have prayed countless times for the wisdom to recognize the signs I was sure I would eventually receive to lead me down the path I need to follow. I can say with complete conviction that I have never felt so secure in any decision I have ever made—I actually feel at peace and free for the first time in years, and, though I look forward to telling you this all again in person so you can see the truth of it in my eyes, I know also that you need to know it's real—so have faith, and run with it, and we will both end up where we need to be...

As for Maddi understanding, I think she will support me only if she feels that I am content, and if it is something I believe in she will be disappointed only if I don't do it. It was Mad that did one of the tarot readings that confirmed for me that this is where I need to go—and she used the cards that Alya bought her at Christmas to do the readings—the connection being that Alya is the one who, three years ago, hired me at Tucker's without looking at my resume. I walked in, we met, and she told me she thought I belonged there, and that was that...

I have never been more at peace or so focused on a goal. I have absolutely no fear of where this will lead; my heart and mind are more open to this than I could have ever dreamed they would be, and I am so grateful that I finally get to start what is sure to be one of the greatest adventures I will ever have.

I will tell you this again in person when I see you—so you can see and feel the truth of my words...

I came from your past and, as to where I have been, I've been here: living, and learning, and waiting for you to find me and set me free.

It will be an adventure, don't you think?

I will see you soon—xo

I now decided it was past the time of trying to decide if I should go and well into the time I should start trying to figure out how to tell my family and friends that I was going. The next day went by rather slowly. Maddi was back at her dad's for the night, and I did not really want to broach this subject of my leaving with my boyfriend. I feared a negative reaction to my decision and was not looking forward to the conflict that I expected to come of it.

It was during this day of restless uncertainty that I decided to look up Genghis Kahn. Revo had told me that he had been informed a few years ago that his spirit guide was the Mongolian conqueror, and I thought it prudent at this point to find out exactly what I was getting myself into. I was entertained to discover that his wife, Borte, was often depicted in white and riding a white horse.

Chapter 6

Brooms and Broken Burdens—Honestly, I'm Working on It.

Looking back, I realize I should have been more open right from the beginning with my boyfriend regarding both my reasons for going and the feelings of dissatisfied restlessness that had built up over the previous months. It wouldn't be until after Rev left that I began to really be aware what kind of impact this trip was going to have on my current relationship.

My state of mind now, however, was one of clouded uncertainty, and I found myself looking to others for distraction. I had agreed to meet with Rev on his last day in Canada. We wanted the chance to say goodbye, and we still had not made any concrete plans as to what kind of work we were planning on doing. We had in our heads a very generalized idea, but nothing definitive. On the day of his departure, I had agreed to do some marketing work with my boss. I was willing to do anything that would keep my mind occupied, and, as a result, I was now spending the morning touring around the city with my manager, working to promote the restaurant. It was in the midst of this traveling around that Revo called and asked if I could find my way to his home rather than meet him at the restaurant we had agreed on. He was only hours away from leaving and still had not managed to pack for his trip. I agreed to go to him, thinking I would meet with him briefly and return to the restaurant later to continue my work with my general manager. I never did make it back to work, as we ended up spending almost the entire day together talking and discovering more about our history.

The whole thing started innocently enough, with me arriving to find him desperately trying to throw together things he would need to take. At first we only swapped idle chatter while he walked around his room tossing stuff into an open suitcase. He indicated at one point the drawing I had done, which was now hung on his wall, and he started explaining to me his girlfriend's reaction on seeing it. Now, you have to understand their relationship was pretty solid. They were used to being apart, and she had never shown any kind of insecurity or jealousy. In light of that fact, Revo had been extremely surprised when she had gotten angry over a simple drawing mounted on his wall. He had told her, "But, you met her, remember?—I introduced you at the restaurant," to which she had responded that she did indeed remember and that she very much did *not* want the drawing on his wall. We discussed the night in question, as I remember very clearly meeting this girl. He had been working late, and she had just flown in from New York and was sitting at the bar waiting for him. I was working that night as the bartender and thought that I would try to be friendly and make her feel welcome. I offered to get her something from the bar while she waited. She wasn't interested. Rev had come in a few minutes later and formally introduced us, at which point I again offered to get her something. Again she refused. He recalled that later in the evening she had admitted to feeling extremely threatened by me, though she could not understand why at the time. She had conceded that we did not seem to have any chemistry between us, and that, combined with the fact that I was quite obviously an older woman, led her to rationally consider that I was not a threat. Yet, for some reason, the whole idea of me talking to him had really pissed her off. The whole story reminded me of an incident that had occurred only days before Revo's girlfriend had flown in from New York, when my own boyfriend had been hanging out at the bar waiting for me.

Rev had walked by, and I'd thought I'd be nice and introduce the new guy. My boyfriend was well known by the staff, and, though he had on occasion shown jealous tendencies, it had never before been directed at the people I worked with. Rev made a comment to my boyfriend about how he must be doing something right for me to be so loyal. He said that I was always getting hit on by customers and that my first response had always been "Sorry, I have a boyfriend." Rev said that it must be nice to be in a relationship that was built so strongly on trust. Strangely enough, my boyfriend made some really condescending response (I can't remember what exactly), but I did remember that it had left Revo looking like he'd been slapped. I had questioned my boyfriend on it later, and he admitted that he couldn't explain why he had said it. He, too, had apparently felt really threatened, but could not understand why. Revo threw another shirt into his suitcase and joked that maybe they had seen something we had missed. Even with me sitting there alone with him in his room neither of us felt any kind of sexual tension, and it wasn't until much later in the day that we figured out why.

We sat there on the bed for awhile, continuing to talk, though our attention was now turned to the reason I was to join him in the Philippines. He explained that he had the desire to help his people, but he had no idea how to go about it. He told me about the research he'd done into the political history and that he had studied the historical whys and hows of the political corruption. The problem he was running into was how to present that knowledge to the people in a manner that would not only interest them but also inspire them to do something about it. Most importantly, he had to find a way to do it safely. He told me that is why he felt he needed to go back to his country to pursue his acting career.

He said actors there are sacrosanct, and they are in such a positive position in the public view that those in power are hesitant to openly move against them. He felt that if he could amass enough popularity then he could find a way to safely make a move against the corruption in his country. It was a bold plan and one I was not entirely sure would work. I did, however, see how his contacts there in the media industry could open the doors for both of us—but maybe not the way he thought. I did not immediately make any kind of proposal, and our talk eventually moved into the area of our childhoods. We had both been raised surrounded by oddities and strange occurrences and legends. We had also both been raised to believe we were meant to do something important. Neither of our families, however, had bothered to tell us what that was. We swapped strange stories about our younger years. He told me about his father's history and the revolution, and I told him about the high weirdness that occasionally went on around my family. The first story I told him was about a time when I was very young and my mother and I had been staying at her mother's house.

The grandmother in question was extremely entrenched in the Catholic faith, and though my own mother had left the Church shortly after my birth, she still tried to be respectful of my grandmother's views. I remember being asleep in bed with my mom (beds were not in abundance there) and waking up to my mother screaming. There my grandmother stood in the doorway, staring at me, saying nothing. My mother grabbed at me and was screaming at my grandmother that she would not allow it.

She kept repeating: "You can't have her. I won't let you use her."

It went on for a very long time, and, being young, I was absolutely terrified by the whole experience. Eventually, other members of the family awoke and made their way to the room. I was led away and tucked into bed with my godmother, but still my mother continued screaming.

I kept asking my godmom why, but all she said was, "Shush now; time to sleep."

I guess I eventually passed out, because I awoke in the morning and all was quiet. In fact, when I went down into the kitchen everyone was sitting around having coffee acting like it had never happened.

I tried to talk about it and ask what it was all about. I wondered, was my mommy sick?

My grandmother casually reached across the table and slapped my face hard enough to make my head snap back. She quietly whispered: "It did not happen, and you will not speak of this ever again. Do you understand?"

All I could do was sit there with tears streaming down my face and nod. I was only a six-year-old child and had no one to turn to for comfort or answers. It was never mentioned again, at least not within the confines of my family. I have told a few friends over the years and, other than agreeing the whole thing was supremely screwed up, they really didn't have any answers for me either.

The next story I told him was about a trip I had taken with my aunt (also my godmother). We had gone out of town overnight to pick up a new car that she had purchased. During the night I had woken with a sense of foreboding about the next day and our return trip. I was sixteen at the time and had learned already to follow my instincts. While talking to my dad the next morning on the phone, I had asked him to talk my aunt into staying an extra day. He agreed to try, as he had also grown used to relying on my instincts. Unfortunately, she didn't listen to him any more than she had listened to me. Shortly after I had hung up the phone, we were driving down the road, and, as it was winter, the roads weren't the greatest. I wasn't wearing my seatbelt—given my premonition and the driving conditions, that was, I admit, pretty stupid of me. About an hour into the trip, I got this very strong urge to put on my seatbelt. I heard a distant disembodied voice whispering in my head, "Do it now." I listened—wouldn't you? I mean, really, how often is it that voices in your head actually give you good advice? As my seatbelt clicked into place the car started to spin, and the next thing I know there was a rather large tire staring at me through the windshield. My parents later told me that she had lost control and broadsided a highway snowplough doing ninety kilometers an hour. I don't know if you have ever seen one, but they are very large pieces of equipment, and my aunt's car was only a little hatchback. It was completely written off. This is only hearsay, however, as at the time I saw none of it, and when I asked later, my parents refused to let me see the car. They said something about it being too much of a shock for me in my current fragile state. I do remember whispered conversations days later (they would exclaim, seemingly in awe of the fact that I had managed to survive) as we sat in the hospital by my aunt's bed waiting for her to give in to her injuries. She had been taken off life-support, after the doctors had declared her brain-dead and told the family there was nothing more they could do. Oddly enough, it was me to whom the family turned when they were confronted by the decision.

I was pulled into a hospital room three days after the accident by my grandmother (on my mother's side), and she sat me down and asked me what I wanted them to do. She explained to me that I was the closest thing to a daughter my godmother had had, and so the final decision was up to me. It was an easy decision to make. The first time I had seen my godmother after the accident had been in a long room with about ten beds lining the wall, separated by plastic. The whole scene was like something out of a futuristic horror movie—a long line of bodies, with wires sticking out of them, were connected to machines to keep them alive for whatever twisted purpose the mad scientists had cooked up in their warped little brains. I didn't think my aunt would like to live like that, and that is exactly what I told my grandmother.

She agreed and thanked me for being able to make such an adult decision. She apologized for having had to ask me, and I remember that even though I was at the time going through hell, it was one of the only times I would ever in my life really connect with the woman. For that brief moment we understood each other completely, and for that brief moment of understanding I am eternally grateful.

My godmother left us peacefully a few days later, surrounded by her family, and everyone in the room that night agreed they had felt her leave. My cousins and I had discussed it later, and they had agreed that there had been a sense of contented peacefulness in the room the night she moved on, but what I never told them is that I heard her whisper thank you. Perhaps it was a necessary delusion created by my own fragile mind to help me come to terms with the decision that I had made, but I like to think that I had done the right thing and she took the time on her way out to let me know that she would be okay.

On the day of the accident I vaguely remember crawling out the window and yelling at the driver that he had killed my aunt. I remember also that police and ambulance were on the scene almost immediately, but they seemed for some reason to be ignoring me completely. It was instead a passerby who took me to her own vehicle, saying that it would be warmer there. It was in the van that things started to get a little weird. She told me she was a healer and she had been sent to make sure I was okay. She said it wasn't my time yet, so I had to let her help me. It was an odd situation to be in, to be sure. I had just crawled out the window of a completely wrecked automobile, and nobody from the medical team or the authorities seemed in the least concerned about my welfare or my whereabouts. I stayed with this woman, sitting in the front seat of her van. Honestly, I was too dazed to argue with the woman, so I leaned my head back against the seat and let her get on with it. She offered up a little prayer, then began to run her hands up and down the length of my body. She never actually touched me—her hands stayed hovering about an inch over my flesh—but even from that distance I could feel the heat off them. I had a similar experience much later in life when I sought a Reiki healer to find a way to manage the pain in my back, but at the time of the accident I had never heard of Reiki, so I had no way to connect what she was doing with any kind of reality-based healing method. All I knew was that there was amazingly comforting warmth spreading through me, and, as she continued to whisper prayers while moving her hands around me, I felt this warmth starting to heal me, both physically and emotionally.

I left her van a few minutes later, feeling much of my strength returned to me. I wandered over to where the fireman were trying to get my aunt extracted from the twisted metal that had been her car. They asked me to talk to her, to reassure her that I was okay, and so I stood there beside the car for a long time talking to her, telling her I loved her and that it would be okay. I don't think I could have done it if I hadn't spent the time in the van with my mystery angel; she restored to me both my strength and my faith, and it was with her in mind that I managed to get through the next few days without completely losing myself to feelings of anger and guilt. I at one point looked back to where the van had been, and I couldn't find either it or the lady who had come to my rescue. Although I never got her name or found out where she came from, I know that she is probably still out there somewhere bringing peace to others in need. Maybe someday she will even get a chance to read this and know what an amazingly positive impact she had on me that day.

If you are out there somewhere… thank you.

I did eventually make it to the hospital, and they did eventually check me out and tell me I could go. But where was I to go? At sixteen years of age I had no money and was in a strange city far away from home. What could I do? My parents couldn't come for me, as the storm had gotten worse, and the roads were closed. So there I sat by myself in the hall of this massive emergency unit until a nurse approached me. Well, she said she was a nurse, but she was in jeans and a T-shirt, so, who knows? She told me I was to go home with her until my parents could come for me in the morning. I didn't sense any danger in it, so I agreed to go along as long as I could call my mother. This lady reasoned that it would be better to call from her house where I would be able to sit comfortably and take the time to assure my mother I was okay. Again, I felt no threat from this woman, so I decided to go. Looking back on it, I do not remember her name, what she looked like, or where she lived. I cannot picture in my mind her house or the face of her husband. I do remember that her husband had gone out and gotten me a toothbrush, some pyjamas, a robe, and some slippers. The clothes he had bought had fit so well that I naturally assumed my mother had given them my size. Not so; when I finally called my parents they were extremely surprised to hear that I was in this house. There ensued a very long conversation between said nurse and my dad. I was not privy to the conversation, as the nurse's husband had chosen that moment to insist that I go take a bath to help ease some of the bruising. If I had to do it over again, I would have been questioning every step of the way, but I was young, and scared, and felt very much alone.

When my parents picked me up in the hospital the next day, where the nurse had dropped me off, my mom went to the nurses' station to ask for the girl's name so she could thank her in person.

The hospital staff had absolutely no clue who she was talking about. It was only several years later, as I began explaining to Revo, that the full impact of what had happened that day really hit me. I had gotten an MRI to try to find the cause of back pain I was having. When the doctor pulled me into the office to discuss my results, he asked if I had been in an accident. I told him not recently, and he asked how long ago it was and how bad it had been. I wanted to know what this was about and told him I would not answer any more questions until he gave me some kind of explanation. He explained that I had a recent fracture in my back that was more than likely causing my current problems, but it was the evidence of old injuries in my body that had him confused. Apparently, there had at one time been multiple fractures throughout my body that had long ago healed. There was nothing in my medical record to indicate such a massive amount of damage. He said my accident at sixteen was recorded as resulting in only superficial bruising, but the injuries described to him by the technician who had done the MRI were extensive and would more than likely have ended with loss of life. He could therefore not see how the picture could be accurate, because on the off-chance that I had survived such an injury, then I would certainly have remembered it. He wanted to do more tests to confirm the results. He was now sure there had been a mix-up between patients, so back I went for more tests. It turns out the pictures *had* been mine—my back was broken, and my doctor now turned his efforts to finding a way for me to manage the pain until it healed. The other injuries were never mentioned by either me or him again.

There I was, sitting in this man's room, telling him this, and he didn't even flinch. Not a "that's crazy," not a "no way," not even a "yeah, right"—nothing. He just listened and nodded and stroked my arm, trying to comfort me, knowing full well that just telling the tale was bringing up some pretty negative memories. That's right; that's what I said—stroking my arm, something he had apparently been doing the whole time I had been talking. I also realized only at the end of the tale that I had been lying there talking to this guy with my head on his chest for over an hour. It had been so natural, so comfortable, that I had not even noticed. After my story we decided to get up, go out, have lunch—and more conversation ensued.

We got into a detailed discussion about God and our views on both his existence and his impact on society.

It was Rev who started it all by calling me on something I not realized he had picked up on.

"You know, I don't get it. You obviously believe in God; we've talked about him several times, but, for some reason, when I make reference to the Bible I can sense you flinching inwardly. It's not anything that you're doing with your face or body language, but something in your eyes says you have issues with the scriptures."

It would take awhile to explain, but I figured, as we were still waiting for our food, time was something I had.

"Oh, it's not God I have a problem with; it's structured religion I find myself questioning. Too much blood has been shed over the debate about whose God is the right God. Thing is, I've spend the greater part of my life exploring different religions and have found that they all teach the same fundamental life lessons that humans need to grow spiritually. So it angers me that instead of following those lessons and learning from them, people waste their time and energy on arguing about which teacher is right, without realizing that all those teachers are working off the same lesson plan."

He gave me a quizzical look. "So, you don't believe that structured religion has a place in our world?"

"No, that's not what I mean at all," I answered hurriedly. "Humans need guidance in order to know which direction to take for answers to all of life's questions. They also need something greater than themselves to believe in: something to bring them strength, encouragement, and comfort in times of sorrow. People just need to stop fighting over what to call their God and get on with living the life he wants them to live."

"So, you think that if there were one central religion that the world could stand behind, the fighting would stop, and the world would find peace?" He was starting to sound slightly put off. "I'm surprised at you; it sounds like a Nazi mentality: one race, one religion, one belief system. You're Polish aren't you—how can you, of all people, agree with Hitler—have you forgotten the camps? How can you bring yourself to think that way?"

"Again you are making an assumption based on only part of the story. You should know better than that—hell, you should know *me* better than that," I said heatedly.

"Oh I do," he laughed, "even if we just met. All I want is for you to be able to explain it, so you don't find yourself getting into trouble down the road—so, go ahead, explain…"

"Oh, I see…" And I did; he was thinking to help me get it straight in my own head before making the attempt to present the idea to the world. I got the sense that in the past he had always played the role of teacher, with me the willing pupil. I was a little more independent, though, this time around, and we would have to see how that would play out in the end, but for the moment I decided to maintain the status quo and bow this one time to his will.

"Okay, so you think that I have Nazi head because I want people to stop fighting over religion, but I am not saying that they should all follow the same religion. The idea is ludicrous; each person, each culture has their own needs, their own views on how life should be lived. The world is a vast place with different climates and living conditions. Each of the religions that exist have grown from a combination of those climates, the history of each individual culture, and the needs that those cultures have to continue to survive, grow, and thrive. It is not for me or anyone else to judge their way of life or their belief system, when I have never lived as they do, or learned as they have learned. My views of the world are different than theirs, and, therefore, so are my own personal needs for a faith to follow. My point is that I respect each individual religion and culture, regardless of what that is, because, as long as it is a positive belief system that teaches patience and understanding, it is a good thing. I don't much care what you call your God, as long as that God shelters you, protects you, and guides you to a better way of life—with emphasis put on respect for life and the need for spiritual growth.

My big problem lies in the constant battle between the leaders of these religions, who seem to think that it is necessary to insure the continued loyalty of their followers by proving to each other and the world that they are right. Their God is the only God, and if you do not follow their God's teachings you will no doubt suffer terribly. Depending on the religion in question, you will either go to hell, or you will be punished here on earth by having all of the good things in your life taken away. These leaders use threats and promises of Utopia to maintain their followers' faith instead of merely teaching those same followers compassion and understanding. They forget that we all have a right to live here, that we all must learn to live together. Their need for domination and control blinds them to the reality of the world being a diverse, complex organism that can only maintain its existence if there is a continued balance between the organisms that live here—which are, by the way, merely an extension of that central core that is our planet. We seek power and control and destroy the very world in which we live, the very world we cannot exist without. How can we justify the need to be right if that need comes at such a high cost?"

He leaned back in his chair, and, glancing down at the table, then back at me, said, "You know the world isn't going to change yet, right?"

I also glanced at the food that had been delivered during my one-sided dialogue. "Sure, I know that, but wouldn't it be nice if it could…"

I popped a piece of bread in my mouth and waited; surely he had more to say than that.

"Okay, so your own belief system stems from humanity's need to accept their own diversity and embrace and encourage that diversity while still maintaining their individual belief systems and cultures. Do I have it right?" He sat there staring at me with a little grin on his face after saying all those words, and I summed it up in one sentence: "Ha!" I sniffed, "Yup, that's about it, and I honestly believe that someday humans will get there; it is only a matter of time."

"Hmmm… yes, well, that is what we are supposed to be working toward then, isn't it, but not yet, my love, not this time…" He leaned forward. "Now, what about you—how do you see God, and how do you reconcile your belief for understanding with your obvious disdain for things like the Bible?"

"Okay, well, first of all, it isn't what is written in the Bible that I have a problem with," I looked him straight in the eyes, "It is a fantastic, wonderful, uplifting, and enlightening story that has brought hope to millions. However, it is a story, written by men, and—though those men were witnesses to some of the most incredible miracles that have ever occurred on this planet—they were still men, human men, and in being human they were fallible and imperfect."

"Ouch, you question the validity of the most popular and most widely published piece of literature ever created…;" cocking his head to the side, he looked at me and asked, "what gives you the right?"

"I don't question whether or not the content is valid," I said, laughing, "as I said, the very existence of and impact of that particular book is what makes it valid. What I question is the fanatical study of its teachings with a mind closed to any outside influence that may contradict those teachings. By all means, study it, learn from it, but, for God's sake, learn to take the lessons within and put them in context with the world in which we live. Open your eyes and see the people around you. Although they may not believe the same as you, they are still going out into our world and making a difference for the better by actively working to help others in need. Does the starving child on the street need to believe in God in order for a Christian to be willing to feed him? I do not think that is what Jesus taught do you? When a man is dangling from his fingertips off a cliff, do you think it appropriate to stop and ask him if he has faith before reaching down your hand to help him up? Come on, stop looking at me that way—you know exactly what I'm saying!"

"Oh, you are too cute when you're pissed—," he reached down for a bit of bread, "but you only answered half the question; how do you see God? What is God?"

"Well, you may not agree with this one, but if I were to define God as an entity then it would have to be the central core of a massive ball of energy that extends around and encompasses everything that exists. God is something akin to the brain that controls and manipulates this enormous mass of energy, and when a person feels like he is being guided or sent in a certain direction to do God's work or God's will, then it is very much like you stretching your arm out so you can pick up that piece of bread."

"So, every person, every living thing is like one of God's limbs that he moves around at will to help him accomplish any given task?" He smiled, "I couldn't have put it any better myself... you have learned a lot this time around, haven't you?"

"Yes, well, I've been through a lot, then, haven't I? It's kind of hard not to learn something when God is constantly ramming lessons down your throat, isn't it?" I looked down at the table. "You know, we have hardly eaten anything—too much talk—but we have to get going; you have a lot yet to do today."

"Very true," he agreed, calling the waiter over and asking for the check. "Let's get out of here."

As we were leaving the restaurant we were holding hands, and he gave me a little kiss on the lips much like the kiss a husband would give his wife on his way out the door while rushing off to work. We stopped by work so he could say goodbye to Sophia and let her pinch his ass one last time. I took the chance to corner her while he was saying goodbye to our boss, and I asked her: "Did you see this coming? I mean, I didn't see this coming. It's right, it's natural, but it's way beyond unexpected."

She gave her answer with a wink and a smile: "Sure, hon, but would you have believed me if I told you?"

I concurred that I certainly would not, and we left it at that. Next I took him up to his studio for one last jam with his band, and I lay there on the couch on my stomach listening to him pound away on the drums. The whole thing seems ridiculous when I look back on it. We were not dating, had never even discussed or (at least on my part) considered the idea—yet, here we were acting like a couple who had been together for months. His bass player finally arrived and seemed not all surprised to see me there stretched out on the couch. I told them I'd leave them to it, gave Rev a quick kiss goodbye, and told him to call me when he needed a ride home. It was on my way home that it really hit me.

What the hell was I doing? I had a boyfriend at home who loved me, and, though I already knew we would not likely stay together as a couple, I did still love him. I most definitely did not want to hurt him, and he certainly deserved better than this. Strangely enough, as much as I wanted to save, at the very least, our friendship, I felt uncontrollably drawn to this other man on a level that I couldn't explain or at the moment even attempt to understand. When I finally got home that night, I wandered around the house, very restless. I went on the computer and went out of curiosity more than anything over some of the emails that had been flying back and forth. They were all very familiar in nature. We were like two old friends bantering about common interests. There was one in which he asked me to look up Jose Rizal. I had, and had discovered that he had been a great hero to the Filipino people: a writer, a politician, a philosopher, etc. (accomplishments too numerous to mention). He had later in his life worked very hard at pulling down the corrupt government in power. He had failed in the end, but not before managing to win the hearts and support of a nation. His battle ended when he was executed by the political power of the time. Sadly enough, it had happened only shortly after his marriage, and he left behind a woman who had stood beside him throughout his brief battles. She had chosen to fight with him and was left a grieving widow. It was that small detail that I had casually passed over the first time I read it and that small detail that stood out now as being exceptionally large. I did not like the idea a bit. It was not the fact that it seemed so sad, or the fact that it seemed so familiar. I most assuredly hated the fact that I felt it was destined to happen all over again.

The whole process of revisiting these emails did not take very long. I soon found myself pacing the house, bitterly confused about what to do, so I did the only thing I could think of. I reached out to a friend, but the direction of my reach was perhaps odd in nature. I called my boyfriend's sister. We had, during the last year, grown close over many heart-to-heart chats, and I knew I couldn't tell her about this minor (well, really, I thought it would go away—I mean, it *had* to go away, because it was threatening to really screw everything up) problem of confused emotion.

I could, however, let her know I was leaving and why, and I could confide in her my fear of the reaction I would get when I finally got the nerve up to tell my boyfriend I was leaving. She was way beyond supportive, and, out of respect for our mutual high level of trust, I will not break confidence here regarding our talk. However, I will say that I hung up the phone reassured that regardless of what came of this I would remain close to at least one member of the family. I also felt comforted by the fact that if on the off-chance that my boyfriend did not take well to the changes that seemed to be forthcoming, he would at the very least have the strong support of his family. It was only a few minutes after I had hung up the phone that my boyfriend wandered in the door. While waiting for Rev, I had called Sophia and offered to give her a ride home from work, so I couldn't stay and talk for long. I did feel I owed him something, though, so I told him we would make time and have a heart-to-heart about what was going on. We had been seeing each other only in passing over the last couple of days, and, even though he knew something was up, he had no idea how big a something it was.

I promised to make time and then practically ran out the door. The truth about what was going on scared the hell out of me, and I was not yet willing to face it. I picked up Sophia at work, and as I drove her home I told her everything that was going through my head. As usual, she didn't judge, but she had some good advice to give.

We were sitting in the car in her driveway, when she looked at me and smiled. "Are you happy?"

Oh, hell, I couldn't help it; I answered quite frankly, "Ecstatically."

She then said, "Well then, if you are happy, that is all that matters, because when you are happy you can soar to great heights, but you must remember to always be honest in your happiness: honest to yourself and honest with others, because when we are not honest happiness gets taken away."

It is a hard lesson to learn this thing called honesty. Perhaps of all the lessons it is the most painful. It is the most damaging, and it is the one lesson that finally frees us to live the rest of our lives comfortable in who we really are. I abhor the process of learning this lesson, and I repeatedly fail the various tests given to me on it. I rail against the powers that be like a stubborn child throwing a temper tantrum. If I could only get it right this time, then maybe I will be done and won't have to come back and do it again. Something tells me this won't happen; regardless of how well I do this time around I will have to do it all over again anyway. So I stubbornly persist on bending some of the rules, and, having a rebellious nature, I choose the one rule that seems to be of the utmost importance. Being antagonistic in nature, I openly question the rule and the lesson attached. Is there not a time and a place for dishonesty? Are we not required, for the benefit of others, to stretch the truth just a little to soften the blow when reality strikes? Hell, we all do it—except for Sophia, who boldly proclaims, "I might be a bitch, but at least I'm an honest bitch."

Oh, I see her point, I really do, and, as I said, I am working on it—but I am more concerned at the moment about being honest with myself: about my nature, my core, what makes me tick. As she said, we have to be honest to be happy. I am learning (slowly, I might add) that if I am honest with myself about what I want and need it is a hell of a lot easier to find a way to get it. I am also learning that by being honest with myself it prevents me from having to be dishonest with others. They may not like the truth—in fact they may very well detest the truth—but then I do not have to force myself to make them happy by telling an untruth. I am not responsible for their happiness, only my own. With that realization comes the freedom to walk away from the presence of those whose judgmental attitude makes me essentially unhappy.

It is a vicious cycle, this need to belong. The more we bend ourselves to fit the expectations of others, the closer we come to breaking. I don't particularly feel like breaking just yet. I have way too much left to do in this life to waste time with breaking. So I am attempting to straighten. A few people have placed some weight on my shoulders along the way, but then I willingly bent my back, allowing them to unload their own burdens. Some of those burdens will, no doubt, hit the floor as I slowly rise, but with each determined stroke of the pen I come that much closer to standing straight. When I'm done, there may be a mess of broken burdens at my feet, but I will find a broom and help to sweep up the mess I have made. Somebody is going to have to hold the dustpan, though. They weren't all my burdens to begin with, so I think maybe I deserve a little bit of help.

Chapter 7

<u>Questions, Answers, and the Art of Arson</u>

I'd like to say I did the right thing that night (what you might think would be the right thing), but Sophia did say to be honest.

Revo called; I went. It was a simple decision that set us on twisted path of coincidental encounters and symbolism bordering on high weirdness. He hopped in the car when I picked him up, and, after a quick kiss hello, we sat and chatted for awhile. He told me more about what he was hoping to accomplish but admitted he had no idea how to go about it. I explained to him that the one promise my Baba had made sure to get out of me was that I would write my story as fiction. As every other piece of advice she had ever given me had been extremely beneficial, I figured maybe that's what we should do. He seemed to like the idea.

I had in my mind the idea that we could marry my idea of the upcoming spiritual revolution with his desire to see a more prosperous future for his people. I was proposing the story of two people on a spiritual journey, but if we based the story in the Philippines we could incorporate all the issues of the people there and in other Third World countries. I hoped to inspire people to work toward change. With slow, steady steps forward in a positive direction the worldwide population would slowly move toward a more positive future. Of course, I wasn't deluded enough to think one book or one story could change the world, but in my mind every little piece of individual inspiration was one more piece added to the big puzzle that is our undetermined future. I made the suggestion, he took it to heart, and we began hammering out a few more details.

We talked about the dangers of asking the wrong questions, and he seemed very much concerned about the possible threat to our safety. I pointed out that, as we were already acting like we had been together forever, it would be believable to the casual observer that I was just his Canadian girlfriend out for a visit. I also explained that it would be easier for him to access certain information than for me. He could easily steer conversations with friends or family toward politics in a noninvasive manner. I, on the other hand, would very likely end up shot if I even brought up the subject with the wrong person. We also agreed that any major information that we managed to find would not be put on paper until I returned to Canada. Again, he was concerned about safety and cited the execution of one of Philippines's greatest national heroes as an example of what happens to those in his country who question authority. At this point, I believe I mentioned not particularly wanting to lose him again when I had only now found him—which took our discussion in a new direction.

This time his concern was more passionate in nature, and he admitted to being very worried about the fact that it seemed too familiar. We had been down this road before, we both knew it, and we also both knew the outcome. The problem was he wasn't sure he could do it again. He was positive that he didn't want me to have to do it again. We could run with the idea that we had to follow the path we both saw as being chosen for us, but the price could be extremely high. We had paid it before, more than once, but although he was more than willing to suffer himself, he was not at all happy about the idea of me suffering at his side. It seemed I had a decision to make and not much time to make it.

He sat there looking at me with sad eyes, imploring me silently to walk away. He had to know; I doubt for one minute he believed I would, but what we want and what we are forced sometimes to accept are two entirely different things. To me, it didn't seem much of a choice, really: lose him now or lose him later. I went with later. There was no way in hell I was going to give up any of the precious time I could have with him. I had spent an entire lifetime feeling incomplete and hungering for that connection that would make me whole. In the space of a couple of hours I had found, recognized, and accepted that other half willingly into my life. I'll be damned if I was going to give it up. And that was exactly what I told him.

He was left feeling torn: knowing that keeping me away from him would keep me safe, but also knowing that we would both be completely miserable if I actually listened to him and let him go.

He gave up after several minutes of pained silence. He merely shrugged his shoulders, "So, you're coming home with me, and we are going to start a revolution."

I had to laugh; the whole situation was hysterical. Here we were, two reasonably responsible adults, sitting in a car, having a rational, open discussion about having shared our lives together several times in the past and our concerns over doing it all again. Seems completely crazy, doesn't it? I swear there were no drugs or alcohol involved, and neither of us would be considered by society as an unsound or potentially dangerous personality.

Of course, viewing someone as potentially dangerous is subjective. When you think of all the people you meet along the road of life and the effect they have on yours, you can see my point. Next time you are out in public, take a look around you, and, if any of the people you see are a threat to your safety, your happiness, or your way of life, try to run figure out why. Where you are in the life in time will drastically alter who you perceive as a danger.

If you are a young woman, then perhaps the well-built, muscular young thug standing on the corner is more a potential playmate than a potential threat. If you are a little old lady struggling home with a couple of bags of groceries, then that young man likely looks twice the size he really is and three times as dangerous. To the cop driving by in the cruiser, the young thug is probably more a potential nuisance than a potential threat. To the baby mamma staying at home awaiting his arrival, he is possibly her salvation. Think about it. To the baby mamma he represents the food and shelter he provides. The cop is wondering how the young man goes about providing that food and shelter, and the old woman is hoping that in his quest to provide food and shelter for his own family he does not take hers away. As for the young woman, she is not likely thinking much beyond the fact that he is a hottie, and if shelter crosses her mind it is only in relation to the bed that may found inside.

So, you see, it completely depends on you and what you perceive as the reality of the situation. Though I am willing to bet the average person might well find the conversation between me and Revo verging on insane, there are just as many others out there nodding their heads and thinking to themselves, "Sure, I can see it—I've been there myself." The conversation eventually died, and tension started to mount. We really could only stay there so long before we both got restless. It was either drive or jump each other, and, as having sex at the time was not going to accomplish anything, I chose to drive. We headed to a quiet place on the bluffs where we would be free for the moment from busy city life.

As we drove, I told him yet another story about my Baba, trying to explain to him why it was so important for me to heed her warning. In retrospect, the explanation really wasn't necessary;

he trusted me completely and took me on my word. At the time, however, it was a much-needed distraction from the looming shadow of fear that had begun to worm its way into our minds. Our hearts would stay true, but rationality and reason have a way of taking over emotion when that emotion involves danger to one's heart.

So, I drove and talked, and he listened, quietly, intently and openly...

I told him about a conversation I had had with Baba shortly before she died. It had been hard in those last couple of weeks to get any straightforward answers out of her. I had still not asked her everything I wanted to know about my father's death or my mother's crazy behaviour, and I was still very curious about how my stepdad fit into the picture. Yet, as her time drew nearer, I felt less inclined to trouble Baba with things that might upset her in her last days. Of course, it didn't help matters much that she had begun for some reason to speak randomly and fluently in German. It was a language I did not understand, and I was therefore not able to communicate with her in it. I had never heard her speak German before, and until two weeks before her death I had not been aware that she was fluent in more than one tongue.

It was during the last week of her life, in one of her rare, seemingly lucid moments, that she had told me two short tales. One began after I asked if she had been there when I was born. I was curious, as it seemed to me that she had both always been around and that she was more of a mother to me than my own mother had been. Her answer was not one I was prepared for.

She closed her eyes a moment while she spoke, leaning her head back against the wheelchair. "Oh no, I wasn't allowed to be there, but I was waiting for you. Yes, I was. They brought you to me straight away, as soon as you were born. You were only a day old when I first held you in my arms. I remember it so well. They brought you to my home and handed you to me. I was so happy. You were so beautiful, and I was so grateful for this gift. They left right away, of course, but we were okay, you and me. We didn't need them, we had each other."

I was a little confused by some of it, so I asked her, "What do you mean, they left?"

"Well they brought you to me, handed you over, and went away. It isn't hard to understand." Her eyes popped open, and she stared right at me. "They went away; they had to go away."

Now, I don't know if any of you have kids of your own, but the very idea of bringing a one-day-old infant to stay with Grandma while the happy couple goes off on holiday is completely foreign to me. I did not really want to think of the reasons behind it. In fact, being a mother myself, I am still not able to reconcile the idea at all. I had to know, though—that accursed human curiosity did me in yet again!

So, timidly, I queried, "Where did they go; I mean, how long were they gone?"

She reached out and laid her wrinkled, gnarled hand on my arm. "I don't know, child. They brought you, placed you in my arms, and then went away. It was a long time, a very long time, and that, as they say, is that."

Then, with a little twinkle in her eye, she smiled a lopsided smile. "I wonder if we are having rice pudding for dessert. You know they feed us too damn much rice pudding; every day with the rice pudding…"

The conversation was in her mind over, and I was not one to attempt to change her mind. So we spent the next hour playing cribbage and discussing rice pudding vs. tapioca.

On the day I told Revo about my crazy adventures in Baba Land, I was no closer to wrapping my head around the answers to the puzzle of my birth than I had been on the day I found out Ma and Pa had left me at Baba's. These things we discussed as I drove. In truth, I talked and he listened. It wasn't until halfway through my next story that he had anything to offer other than a smile.

As I was pulling in to park the car, I started in on the tale of a shopping adventure my Baba had told me about. Apparently, sometime shortly after acquiring for herself this little infant girl, she had needed to go to the mall to get groceries. It was a really mild fall day, with the sun shining and not a cloud in the sky. Baba had just parked the car and was in the process of getting me out of the car seat in the back, when she looked up to see a black car at the stoplights out front of the mall parking lot. For whatever reason, something about the car scared her, and she stopped a moment to stare at it. Suddenly realizing what was wrong, she went about the hurried, panicked task of getting me to safety. By way of explanation, she told me a week before her passing, "The car was still on the road, but I thought to myself, 'Oh my God, you're right, it's going to hit us.'"

Now, at this, Rev looked at me and said, "'You're right?' Hold on, *who* was right?" and I explained that Baba told me that I had somehow warned her that the car was going to hit us. He was sitting there looking at me, and he asked, "Vick, how old were you?"

I answer quite frankly, "Three months."

Again you would think again at this point he would be getting the urge to run away from the crazy lady and her stories, but no...

He just smiled and said, "So, was the car totalled?"

That's right, not "What happened?"; not "How does a three-month-old baby tell anybody anything, let alone see the future?"; and certainly not "Okay, can we maybe go home now? I... um... have to get some sleep before my flight."

No, not him; he just wants to know how much damage was done. Completely content to believe the rest, he is only curious about the outcome.

I explained to Rev that, according to Baba, she had had lots of time to get me out and we were well out of the way and standing in the mall entrance when this black car finally came barrelling through the parking lot ten minutes later. Baba told me the driver had later claimed to have lost control and that he had managed to get away with only a few bruises, but both the front end of his car and the back of my Baba's (where I would have been sitting) were completely obliterated. I also told Rev that it was minutes after hearing that story that I ceased to ask any questions of my grandmother pertaining to my past. The answers I was getting really only left me with more questions.

The evening was wearing on, but neither of us cared at this point if we got any rest. There was one more thing I had yet to tell him before I could let him go home—a secret part of my past that, in my eyes, threatened what was left of our time together. It was not a story I wanted to share with this man, but it was also not conceivable for me to keep any secrets from him either. He hadn't turned and run so far, but in light of what I had to say that didn't really mean anything. Unbelievable stories about strange occurrences and random coincidences were one thing. The truth about past decisions resulting in arrest and conviction were a different matter altogether.

It might, however, be our last night together for a long time, and I could not let him go without testing the waters of my newfound urge to be completely open and honest. So I told him that there was one possible problem with this whole scenario, one glaring oversight that I had neglected to mention. He was, of course, understandably curious, but he reassured me that whatever it was we could probably work around it.

So I blurted out rather abruptly "I have a record, a criminal record, and I'm not even sure yet that I'll be able to get a passport and, if I can, how it will affect the work we want to do."

He smiled and asked innocently, "Okay, what'd you do?"

I didn't want to tell him. Hell, I don't particularly want to tell you. I am not proud of my behaviour in the past, and though it is with time getting easier to face, the wounds are, as they say, still fresh. I could not, however, lie to this man, so I offered up a piece of my life I have worked very hard to hide.

Shortly after my parents passed away, I started dating this man who ultimately ended up moving in with me. At first I thought it a selfless act of love. He had left his home, family, and friends to move six hours away to a town he had not known existed. Things went well for the first few months. I went back to school for auto mechanics, and, as he was not working, he helped out by taking care of the house and picking my daughter up from school. Sometime during those first few months, however, my back had really started to hurt, and I was finding it more and more difficult to function. The less I was able to do, however, the more he helped out, and, in the beginning, I was very grateful. But time passed, and as my quest to find a diagnosis and cure for what was now crippling back pain progressed, so did his inability to find work. We were at the time living off my student loans and the small inheritance my parents had left me. As the savings dwindled, however, so did my ability to attend school. After being diagnosed as having a fractured spine and herniated disc, I was forced to drop out, cutting off my student loan funding.

Still he was not working, nor did he seem at all inclined toward the notion of finding a job. Several other factors came into play, of course. I had tried to financially help out a friend, who ended up screwing me over, thanks to her addiction to coke. Although my parents' house was now rented out, the money coming in was not even covering the expenses on the property. I soon found myself in a situation I had not seen coming. Something had to give. He was quite literally sucking me dry, and, on the verge of being broke, I made the attempt to kick him out. This is when the demon entered, and my sweet, supportive boyfriend turned into a manic-depressive suicidal maniac who refused to leave. Fights ensued, and I found myself standing at one point in my kitchen with a chair flying past my head. Thing is, I am only five feet tall and 110 pounds, but he was six foot four and all muscle. I figured I was screwed. So I called the police, and, though they did come, they ultimately ended up leaving him there. They did acquire from him his promise to leave, but only after I willingly signed over one of my cars in the presence of the officers into his possession. The idea was that if this man had a car he would have the means to drive away. The police told me I had not been hurt yet, so they couldn't do anything. So, all I could think of to do was give him the car so he would go away.

He did for awhile, driving out to Alberta to find work, but his hold on me was not easily relinquished. He started phoning daily and leaving ten-to-twenty-minute-long messages on my phone. Each message was a mixture of sobbing and begging me to reconsider, blended in with threats on my person. I called the police again, and they again said that he had not hurt me yet, so there was nothing they could do.

As all this was going on, I had been trying to find another source of income. With a broken back I was now technically disabled and unable to either work or finish school. I tried to apply for disability, but, as I owned property, I was refused. I tried to apply for welfare and was told I had to sell my parents' house. So I put my parents' house on the market, then went about the task of trying to be honest with my landlord: asking, hoping for a little understanding. He told me that I could grow or sell pot for him in lieu of rent. Big help he was.

Still the phone calls continued, and eventually my crazy ex began the habit of driving all the way back to Ontario on his days off. I would wake up at 3:00 AM to find him standing over my bed staring at me. Still the police said they could not intervene.

Desperation can, I have learned, cause temporary insanity, and it was not long before I became a victim of the human weakness of mental deterioration. Luckily this whole time my daughter had not been affected. She had neither witnessed any of the violence nor been exposed by me to the reality of our desperate situation. A phone call that threatened to change that finally prompted me to act.

It was yet another message on my machine, but this time it was a very calm, self-assured voice that spoke: "You honestly have no idea what it's like, do you, to have everything, then lose it—just like that it gets taken away. Well, you will know very soon what it is like. You will know what pain is. You think you've suffered before? No, only after I have taken away everything you have, only after I take away from you the one thing you cannot live without, only then will you know what it's like to have your life stolen from you."

"Hell no, you didn't—oh hell, you did!" That was the thought I had immediately after hearing that message. He was coming back, and he was coming back to take my baby. I had to do something, but, as the police had thus far refused to help, I took the road less traveled and went to the one person I trusted to make it right.

Now, all my life I have managed to fit in with almost every available social circle. It is well known by my friends that a large part of my youth was centred around criminal activity. I had grown up and gone clean the moment I felt that first tiny spark of life inside of me, but even after the birth of my daughter I maintained my contacts with those I had worked with in the past. Honestly, you never know when either someone in leather or someone connected to someone in leather will come in handy. The price for any assistance they give may at times be high, but they do have ways of accomplishing seemingly impossible tasks. So, instead of bringing the recorded message to the police, I travelled instead into the bushland hills of northern Ontario to meet my fate. After hours of discussing my options, we came up with a plan to torch the house, collect the insurance money, which I would then take to relocate, and lose myself in one of the bigger cities.

The offer was at one point made to help my ex-boyfriend disappear altogether. Something about it being very hard to locate a body in the northern parts of Ontario bush country. The offer was also made to do the drive out to Alberta, hunt the asshole down, and give him a warning beating that would leave him contemplating, while fighting for his life, whether harassing me all this time had been worth it. I could live with neither. I may have a criminal mind at times, but my heart far outweighs the power that mind has over me. I do not like to see others suffer, and, regardless of what he had done, I could not bring myself to go that far. I couldn't bring myself to ask a close friend to go that far.

As much as the world may think that what the man did was wrong, it was done out of love for me. It was his way of trying to help when nobody else had, and it was an action taken with great risk to himself. I have not seen him since, but someday I hope to get the chance to say I am sorry for putting him in the middle of a situation he had no business being in the middle of. I hope also someday to face his family and tell them he is a good man, with a good heart, and though at times it may be a little misdirected, his loyalty to his friends and family is far beyond what the average person is capable of. My friend's name was Jacob, and he did, in the end, live up to his name. May God bless him for his sacrifice.

We settled on the fire. It was my way of sacrificing a little to gain my freedom and safety for my child. To the flames I would lose almost every material object I owned, including all of my parents' furniture, some of which held great sentimental value. It was a small price to pay, however, and as I now felt that I was very much on my own in this, I agreed to the requested price and we set about planning.

The time came, the house burned, and the insurance company paid up. We moved and settled into a life in the city, and though I felt deeply shamed by what I had done, I was, for the moment, free. Karma, though, has a way of catching up with you, and, as a result of my firebug friend pissing off another criminally minded individual, we got ratted out. Police picked me up while I was visiting friends in my old town, and there I stayed, trapped by my bail conditions, awaiting my day in court.

Strangely enough, in the end it all worked out. I explained to the detective why I had done it, and he admitted that in this case the cops had really screwed up. He might even, he added, have done the same in my place. So, between my lawyer, my confession, and a detective who sincerely believed I did not deserve to be in jail, I ended up serving an eighteen-month suspended sentence— much shorter than the twenty-five years to life that I could have gotten. I was instead released into the community with strict conditions and curfews and allowed to maintain a somewhat normal existence with my little girl. I was even encouraged by my parole officer (a very kind and gentle man) to pursue the art I had discovered on escaping to the city. Instead of serving my community service in the usual manner, I instead did a painting representing life and hope that was later sold at an art auction, with the proceeds going to the Hospital for Sick Children. All that I really had left to do was come up with the $120,000 to pay off my debt to the insurance company—a debt I do fully acknowledge and accept as mine and a debt I wholeheartedly intend to pay.

Throughout the entire story, Rev had once again sat silently listening, not uttering a sound—until at the very end he broke into laughter. I was not sure how anything I had just said could possibly be perceived as hysterically funny, but I let him laugh himself breathless and patiently waited until he was able to speak.

"Too funny" he said, still snickering. "Here I am thinking it is something horribly bad, and here you are thinking I will think it is something horribly bad, and it turns out we are more alike than I thought. I am an arsonist too." With that, he went back to losing himself in a fit in laughter, and if not for the fact that I was already sitting down, I probably would have fallen on the floor laughing myself.

Chapter 8

<u>Linear Life Lessons and the Cost of Acceptance</u>

Okay, so maybe we shouldn't have been laughing about it, and I just know you are thinking we are a couple of sick, twisted individuals. In our defence, we were only laughing at the discovery of yet another unexpected parallel in the lives of people from two entirely different worlds. We did eventually sober up, and he looked at me quite seriously and said, "But I never thought to do it for money."

Argh! "But—" I protested, with my face starting to flush, "I was not—"

He never let me finish. "No, that's not what I meant," he laughed, giving me a little grin. "You had your reasons, and I will not begrudge you those. You do what you have to do to protect your own. Children's safety always comes first. "No," he said, shaking his head, "What I meant was: I did it because I am really fascinated by fire… I like watching things burn."

I wish I could have seen my own face. I must have looked funny as hell, because I was totally shocked by his admission.

He laughed at me again. "It's okay, really; I have it under control now," and he started to quietly explain that while he was younger he had accidentally set two separate fires, destroying both the back room of his home and a school bathroom. He never went into much detail about the first, but he did tell me the story of his bathroom adventures at school.

Apparently his friend and he had been playing with lighters in the boys' bathroom, using them to burn toilet paper and a few other things they had found lying around. The bell had rung and they had had to hurry on to class, so Rev tossed the last piece of paper in the nearest garbage can and left. Of course, burning paper tossed into garbage containing more paper is going to eventually turn into a large quantity of burning paper. Fire spreads and takes on a life of its own when left unattended. It was that very principle my friend had been counting on when he torched my house. Of course, kids don't think of these things. They think along the lines of "Shit, gotta get to class, so we don't get in trouble."

Long story short: the bathroom got torched, and the school authorities went in search of the culprits. Rev and his friend ditched their lighters and agreed not to tell a soul, but as the day went by Rev overheard comments by other classmates, which led him to the conclusion that his friend had a big mouth. Too many smirks in his direction left him feeling extremely uneasy, and when he finally did get called into the office he knew in his heart he was most definitely busted. He was a stubborn one, though, and had no intention of 'fessing up. He knew if he did it would be guaranteed expulsion, so, when confronted by a very irate principal, he categorically denied his involvement. The head of the school produced the lighter belonging to Rev's friend and asked Rev to whom it belonged. Loyalty outweighed reason, and Rev answered that he didn't know. After what seemed to Rev to be hours of interrogation, the principal finally switched tactics and tried to cajole him into confessing. He explained to Rev that if it were an accident, and if he would own up to it, perhaps they could come to some kind of understanding. Eventually Rev conceded defeat and took the high road. He admitted his crime, and, instead of being expelled, he was rewarded for his honesty by the chance to remain in school and work at redeeming himself. He was put into counselling, but, as he wasn't really a firebug, they soon let him discontinue his sessions. The counsellor concluded that he had learned his lesson and really had no need of further assistance.

I was dumbfounded by the similarities in our stories—not the cause so much, but the effect. In both cases we had been handled with gentle, compassionate understanding by those who had been in a position to irrevocably destroy all our future hopes and dreams. Both of us had begun by stubbornly denying our mistakes with the intention of protecting the other person involved, and, finally, in both instances, because of our willingness to live up to our mistakes and accept the consequences, we were given a second chance by some remarkably understanding individuals. The only major difference was in the timing, but then we had led essentially different lives and taken two entirely different roads to get where we now were. I thought at the time, *It will be very interesting to see how these two roads will end up merging.*

I honestly couldn't help thinking that the whole situation was funny as hell. I picked up the phone while we were still sitting in the car, and I gave Sophia a quick call. At first Rev was asking me what the hell I was doing; it was one of the rare times he seemed to be completely caught off-guard by anything I have done or said. When he heard her laughing hysterically on the other end of the phone, he understood. She is one of those rare people in my life who completely understands where I am coming from, and, as she has the same sick sense of humour as me, I figured I would take the time to share a giggle with her. After all, given all that she does on a daily basis for me and others in her life, the least I could do is put in as much effort as possible to make her smile. Before she hung up the phone, she told me to remind Rev to take me shopping for her Louis Vuitton bag, adding that she needed one for her niece as well. Letting her go, we turned back to our own conversation.

We talked a bit about our younger years, trying to discover any more similarities between them. We ended up on the topic of pool halls and found we had both put in a fair amount of time in these when we were teenagers. He never told me much about actually playing. I myself had partnered up with a boyfriend at the age of fourteen and embarked on a year-long, highly entertaining adventure in hustling.

Every time we would enter a new pool hall, the boy I was with would "teach me" how to play pool. He would lean over the table with me, directing the cue and openly giving me pointers. There is a sucker born every minute, and eventually another male of the species would wander over and offer to play a few friendly couples' games, enlisting the help of their usually less-than-enthusiastic acquaintances. It would only take a couple of games with both girls sucking and the boys cleaning up for the newcomers to get bold enough to wager a bet. My partner and I would lose one more, and then, suddenly, beginner's luck would kick in, and I would accidentally either hook my opponent or just have a short lucky run at sinking a few balls. It was more than enough to tip the scales and allowed us more than once to make a killing at the tables. It wasn't obvious enough, however, to get us in trouble, though I suppose it helped that I always played in low-rise jeans and a low-cut top. The point is, we never got busted (not for that, at least) and it turned out to teach me a thing or two about human nature and the power of female flesh over men. I am a lot older now, and my body is admittedly not what it once was, so I do not use those tactics in battle very much anymore. I do still, however, rely on men's natural instinct to underestimate the intellect of a cute girl. Though I am now usually fully clothed, it is still fairly easy to get what I want without giving anything up.

As I said, all Rev would tell me was that he had spent a fair amount of time playing pool, but he gave no gory details on how he had learned to play or why. He had already told me about his pool cue Excalibur. He thought it was pretty funny considering he had discovered King Arthur later in life. He mentioned that he wanted to bring it with him, but he didn't have a lot of room left. He was bringing presents for his family, as is the tradition in the Philippines. I offered to pack the cue up with my stuff, if he would trust me with it, and he laughed again. "So, the Lady of the Lake is going to bring me my Excalibur. You know, it seems to fit, doesn't it?"

We again broke into peals of laughter, both agreeing during brief rest periods that the whole story was indeed turning out to be a strange one. We eventually came back to the topic of us and how comfortable it felt just being together. "You know, you realize that we have been sitting here talking for hours like two people who had known each other their entire lives," he said, smiling. "There is still so much about your life that I have to learn, but I already feel like I know exactly who you are."

The thought warmed my heart, if only because I knew he was right. It seemed that all the other surface day-to-day crap didn't really matter. There was a deeper connection, something warm and comforting about being together. There was no urgency or need to explore the future, because with him I was perfectly content to be in the *now*.

I agreed wholeheartedly, telling him, "We have time, I think, to explore all that other stuff; I'm just glad I finally found you." Jokingly, I added, "Just don't make me wait three years next time. I'm a very impatient person."

He smiled at that. "Sorry, I have always believed in being fashionably late."

Oh, stop it—we are not nuts, and, if you ever get the chance to meet someone you connect with on that level, you will more than likely find yourself having the same conversations. I have, in fact, had chats very similar to this with several different people I have met along the way. So, instead of sitting there grinning inwardly at our inability to accept reality, open your mind to the idea that you, too, have been here more than once. Then, next time you meet someone for the first time and it feels when you look in their eyes that you have met them before, open your mouth and say, "I know you." Maybe, just maybe, you'll discover a long-lost friend who will gladly and willingly come back into your life and make it richer and fuller with his or her presence.

It was getting late, and the time to let him go was coming close. As we drove back to his house that night, we continued talking. "You already know I wrote that song three years ago," he mumbled, half to himself. "I just never knew who I was writing it for. I thought maybe I was writing it for myself, you know, knowing that I wasn't really where I needed to be."

He looked at me then, and there was a hint of sadness in his eyes I couldn't understand. "Maybe I was writing it for both of us; maybe I knew there was someone out there I was meant to find…" His voice trailed off, and in the silence that followed there was a brief moment of pain. In a flash it was gone, as he continued his tale. "The guys insisted on recording it. You know, it was the first song we put on CD. I didn't think it was the one. I didn't think it was good enough, but the guys made me do it anyway." He was smiling again, "I am glad they did." So he had rescued us briefly from an uncomfortable moment, but the thought lingered in my mind: *Why is he so damn sad about all of this? What is he seeing that I am not?*

I couldn't bring myself to ask, and I didn't want to ruin our last few minutes together. I left it alone, preferring to steer the discussion back to safer ground. I asked when the flight was, and, as we pulled up to his house, we were safely back to talking about mundane topics like the weather and jet lag. I was grateful for the rest. It had been an emotionally draining day. The problem was that as surely as I felt the connection between us I also felt the inevitable severance of that connection. It seemed to hover there just out of reach like a shadow in the corner of a brightly lit room. It was a darkness that was at once out of place yet also had every right to exist. It didn't threaten for the moment to spread out and consume the light, but just by its presence the promise remained unspoken that it would eventually come forth.

I ignored it, as I am wont to do in situations that I do not approve of. I wasn't ready to accept it, so therefore it could not harm me. I never told him that I saw it too. I wasn't prepared to have that discussion. I still don't want to face it even now, but then I have discovered recently that I am not much in control of what happens. The only thing I seemed to have any power over was how I dealt with each new situation or challenge as it arose. So even though I maintained my state of denial, I was aware of the threat that shadow posed and I could acknowledge the price it will finally ask me to pay when it comes forth into the light.

Our night together was over. He had a plane to catch, and I had a life here I had to continue to live. After he ran quickly into the house to grab his cue, he placed it carefully into the trunk, saying, "Take good care of it please; keep it safe."

I assured him I would and then turned to him, burying my face in his chest. "Please be safe," I whispered to him. "I'm not ready yet to lose what I just found."

He held me for a moment, stroking my hair, trying to reassure me that he would and that he would see me soon.

Then he was gone, and I was left to drive home alone, trying very hard not to allow the shaking in my hands to spread. I knew I'd see him again; that wasn't my fear—it was the fact that I recognized how much damage our chance meeting would cause to some of the people in my life that I had grown to love. I knew I was being slowly pulled away from the life I now had and that, for good or bad, I would allow myself to be led. I didn't think it was all about him, however, and that bothered me as well. It would be nice to have the comfort of having somebody else's presence at the end of the road, but for the moment I did not see that as being possible. We had been brought together for a reason; we would use each other's love and strength to accomplish what we had to do, and then he would be gone.

He had foreseen it, and it saddened him. Even knowing the outcome I was willing to try, and as I lay in bed awake that night I prayed he would find a way to take the risk. I knew even if our time together was brief it would be beautiful—if, and only if, we could let go of tomorrow and find a way to live for today.

I had asked Rev to send me his info—where he would be staying and where I should be heading, so I could begin to make arrangements for my flight and hotel. As was my habit, though it was late and I was tired, I made the time to check my email.

After I had dropped him off he had apparently taken the time to leave me a message.

Pasig City Metro Manila

That is where my aunt is. Remember the writer I told you about that was on the 5-dollar pesos? Whose book inspired a revolution? His name is Jose Rizal—Pasig City was the Capital of Rizal province before Metro Manila was formed.

So, we're staying in the capital of the revolutionary writer who stirred shit up. Isn't that great? =)

I hope to see you and ex very soon.

My lady of the lake, a wave of inspiration has come upon us. I just pray we have the discipline, strength, and wisdom to hone in on this great power.

Yours always

R

I wrote back quickly just to let him know I was going to try to get there as quickly as possible. I never bothered to tell him I already knew about Jose, it was a topic for another time. For the moment, he was mine and that was all that mattered. I figured he would not get the chance to read it until he arrived, but I needed to let him know I was with him; it wasn't much, but I would learn later it had been enough...

Rev,

Thanks for the info—I will book my flight tomorrow. I will keep your sword safe, my heart, until you and Ex can be reunited. I think it will be an honour to stay in the same city—perhaps senior Rizal will pay us a visit some night and lend us his wisdom and his vision. If we keep the faith, my love, we will find the strength and the wisdom to see this through—play safe, xo

Always yours, Vik

Sleep was a long time in coming that night; I lay awake for hours trying to come to terms with the emotions raging through me. I was ecstatic that he had found me and terrified of him being taken away; yet, there was a certain peace to be found in the feeling of faith I had in what we wanted to achieve together.

I felt him fly away that night as I drifted off to sleep, and, though he was gone, I could still feel him with me. It was an odd sensation, this entity hovering near, but it was comforting, and I knew then that even when the time came to let him go he would still always be with me.

As a side note, because my first real acceptance of the possibilities that life was presenting had largely been due to that first tarot reading at my hair salon, I was now (more out of curiosity than anything else) checking out my daily tarot online. The cards continued to coincide with my daily activities, and checking my card at the end of each day was becoming an entertaining evening ritual.

Today's card was the *Ten of Wands*. It suggests that my power today lies in conscience. "He ain't heavy, he's my brother." I own responsibility for the baggage I have chosen to carry, but I am ready to lay the weight of a burden or secret I have been hiding behind, where it belongs, in order to reconcile my conscience. Do I want to be right or be alone? I am empowered by blind faith in fulfilling my purpose or greater good to "just do it," and I transform through passion or direction in principle.

Chapter 9

<u>Fear, Faith, Flight, and Wisdom in a Child's Eyes</u>

When I got up I headed straight for the computer and discovered a little secret about my newfound long-lost love: the man hardly sleeps…

He had left me yet another message.

Tomorrow you need to read up on Jose Rizal. Sometimes my relatives joke about how I look like him. He was taken from his sweetheart when the Spaniards persecuted him for his book. This isn't the first time we're doing this. I have a feeling we've done this before… many times over and over.

Now I understand what you mean by "I was taken away." I was… I wasn't careful enough last time. One of our last journeys might have been with Rizal, only this time, we'll be more careful.

Goodnight, so much to talk about… so much to say…

Xoxo

What does a woman say to that? What would you have said in my place? There it was in black and white (and by now you know I much prefer colour)—everything I felt, everything I feared, staring at me from my computer screen. It was an unreal reality looking me straight in the eye and challenging me to take it on. I never have been one to back down from a good battle, so I wrote back, knowing this time there was no way he'd get the message before he landed.

I know sweetie,

I feel the same way: we have done this before, and it feels like every time you have been taken from me it was for a greater good but the pain of it has lingered. I've always felt like I was born missing a part of me but at the same time knowing that you would find me again eventually. I had to learn patience and faith, but it will be worth it in the end; as I said, I will take whatever comes, as long as it comes from following the path we were meant to follow. I thanked the gods again today, and I will continue to do so every day, for finally bringing you to me. You are right—there is so much for us to talk about and explore, but I feel safe in the knowledge that we will be given the time we need and the strength to believe in this when obstacles are presented. I was thinking that since I had already offered to take Soph to Italy, perhaps it was because I knew that was one of the places I would have to go. I'm hoping you will think on it; I think it might be safer to do some of my research there after I learn about your people and live among them, and I would love it if you would come with me. I know it is one of the countries she feels pulled toward, and I would like to give her the chance to see it before she starts building her family—a way of saying thank you to her for keeping me grounded and sane. I'm not scared anymore—all my fear and doubt have disappeared, and this feeling of contentment and peace has taken over me. I will be leaving very soon to go make arrangements to join you, but for now I am going to do some research and read up on Jose Rizal. I already started writing this morning, and I think I will have to do a bit each day whenever I feel the need to put pen to paper. If you get the chance to write down some of your thoughts and feelings in the next few days, do it—the book will flow really well if it can come from both sides of the story as it unfolds. Please stay safe, and, like I said in the text, lie low—all will come in time, but we need to be very careful. I do not want to lose you yet... my heart to yours, xo

After sending it off, I gave myself a moment to gather my strength, then set about the task of finding out what I needed to travel to the other side of the world.

As much as I have always been a free spirit who suffers from wanderlust, I have not had the opportunity to travel. Both a commitment to my daughter and responsibilities to my ailing parents had kept me grounded. I had also been very aware in previous years that my time with my beloved grandmother was short. I was hesitant to stray far from her, as I felt I had yet much to learn from her strength and wisdom. I do not regret what some would view as restrictions on my freedoms. Through my commitment to my family and my desire to stay close to them, I have learned much about myself and my own limitations. I have also learned through my mistakes, and as those mistakes creep into and meld with this tale, I will be more than happy to share them with you as well as the lessons learned along the way. Let's face it—after the last few chapters there aren't very many secrets left for me to keep.

Besides, if you can accept where you have been and find a way to use the knowledge you've gained, it becomes easier to see where it is you are supposed to go. It's like a boxer training for a fight—every swing that life throws at us, every time we are either hit or manage to dodge the punch, our reflexes become faster. With each practice round our skills are honed, so that when the "big fight" finally arrives we are prepared for it. I am positive that the powers that be arrange these little challenges for us to train us for the real thing; we get knocked down, we get up, we wipe the blood from our eyes, and the next time we know when to duck and when to punch. I have learned to be thankful for all the woes that have befallen me and can say with all honesty that I am grateful for the times my soul has cried out in agony, "Please God, no more." It was by surviving those times that I learned compassion and understanding for others who suffer, and I built up the emotional strength to make it through my next personal battle.

I have a strong belief in looking for the good that always comes along with the bad. If you are aware that you need to look for it, it is only a matter of time before you see it. Unfortunately, one first has to be willing to accept the possibility that it is there to find. I, through my own experience, have learned how difficult it can sometimes be to see past the pain. I now feel quite blessed by all that I have been through, as it has shown me a clear view of the reality of life. Rather than hold me back, it has helped me build a strong foundation. From there, when the time was right, I could (as my friend Sophia says time and again) take flight.

I have a friend I grew up with who has told me several times over the years that each loss has been just another test. Her name is Chelsea, and she is a sweet-hearted girl, who, although she doesn't always agree with my way of doing things, has always understood the reasons behind my actions. I have decided when this is all done I will have to send her a copy and a note to say thank you. I need to let her know that she was right and that it is partly her faith in me that over the years has helped to keep me on my feet. Perhaps she saw that in time things would change, and eventually I would find my way.

Time did pass, and circumstances did change; I suddenly found myself able to explore the world and write about what I'd learned. The fact was, though, that I did not know how to go about it. I was flying blind, so to speak, and I had to rely on my more travelled friends for guidance. My first project was to get a passport, something I had never attempted to do. My criminal record could at this point completely destroy any hope of my pursuing this new endeavour. As much faith as I had that Rev and I were supposed to meet, I am still human and, as such, am prone to fear and uncertainty.

I discussed it with Sophia, and she told me that in her experience most countries were open to people like myself. She encouraged me to at least make the attempt, explaining that the only sure way to fail at something was never to try. Still it worried me, and it was with fear again in my heart that I made my way, application in hand, to the passport office. I got there late because I had made an impromptu phone call, and the lineup, of course, was absolutely horrendous.

I made another quick phone call while I was waiting in line. I called an old friend by the name of Natalie, thinking I would catch her up on what I was up to. Natalie and I had met six years ago, shortly after my parents had passed away. I had been staying in our family home after the funeral, trying to wrap up my parents' personal affairs. I was spending time with old friends, while I was working out the details of what I was going to do with a property that had suddenly been handed over me and at the time was over eight hours away from where I was living. I was trying to give myself time to heal surrounded by friends I had grown up with, friends who had known my parents and who could understand and share my pain with me.

My parents had been ill for a very long time, but their death was still a shock, in that they had passed away only a day apart. We were all having a hard time coming to terms with the reality of a married couple dying from two completely different, yet natural causes, in two different hospitals, in two distant cities. My dad had passed away on May 8 when his kidneys and liver had shut down, and my mother had passed on May 9 when her lungs and heart gave out. Coincidentally, May 9 that year happened to be Mother's Day—something I think my mother had purposely arranged, as I had managed for years to repeatedly forget her birthday. I can imagine she was determined for me not to forget this particular date. It was a very surreal experience for all of us, and the bonding between old friends had been absolutely essential to our survival. Natalie was a young woman to whom my friends had introduced me. I recognized immediately on meeting her that she had an absolutely beautiful soul. She was hardworking, intelligent, kind, and dedicated to her family—yet it seemed she was stuck in a world in which she didn't belong. She had dreams of getting away from the small town she was living in and finding her own way in the world. However, at the time she did not have the means.

I found myself touched by her plight and, surprisingly enough, in a position to help her achieve her goals. I offered to give her my parents' car. She was understandably shocked. We had, after all, just met, and the idea seemed to her to be a bit on the crazy side. She was concerned that she could not pay me, but I assured her that no payment was necessary. I explained that, as I already had a vehicle, and as my parents no longer needed their material possessions, that the car might as well go to someone who needed it. I asked only that she repay me by using the car to escape the life she was wanting to flee and drive to a better, happier place. My faith in this girl was much rewarded. She has since established herself in a small town in Southern Ontario; she bought a home and is currently engaged to a man who makes her exceptionally happy. He is, oddly enough, a Mexican Mennonite, who speaks five languages fluently, and who appears (though I have not met him) to be her perfect counterpart in that he himself is a well-rounded, earthy personality.

It was this young woman I now chose to call, and it was while I was speaking with her that I managed to regain a little of my strength. We were talking about her upcoming wedding and the honeymoon that was expected to follow soon after. She, however, also has a criminal background, and though she has never been officially convicted, she still has a few things left over from the past hanging over her head.

She was not so much concerned with the acquisition of a passport or her ability to leave the country. She was worried, however, about her return to Canada at the end of her trip. If she did, as she had been warned years ago by an officer of the law, still have unanswered charges in the system, then the authorities would no doubt pick her up on her way back into Canada. I asked her why she hadn't dealt with this sooner. I was quite confused as to why someone I viewed to be quite intelligent would be so blind to the fact that the problem would not simply go away on its own.

She assured me she was well aware of the fact, but as she had never had any desire to travel, it had not really been a problem—until now. I told her that if she wanted to get on with her life, she had better also get on with sorting out her shit. I spoke with her for a long time while I was waiting, and I told her repeatedly that she would not know if she didn't try. I was encouraging her to take the chance and find out what her issues with the authorities were and then take the responsibility and deal with those issues appropriately. The problems would not work themselves out. She would have to let go of her fear and face them head on. The more I tried to convince her, the more I managed to convince myself.

By the time my number was called, I was feeling fairly confident. I boldly approached the desk and declared to the girl behind the counter that I had a criminal record. I explained the ability to travel would be very important to my work and that I needed to know what, if any, restrictions would be placed on that ability. She very kindly did some digging and explained to me that for some reason or another she could find no record on file. She also explained that she was privy through her system to more information than customs agents would find available to them when looking at my passport. She concluded that if there was nothing for her to find then there would also be nothing for them to find. I got the information I needed so I could send my proof of flight to her later, thereby expediting the process. I also obtained the date my passport would be ready for pickup: February 11. As I was leaving, this very sweet young lady used a strange choice of words when she said goodbye: "So now you know you are free to fly, you better go find your wings." Her name was Angie.

The rest of the day went smoothly enough. I made my way to the travel agency and attempted to book the flight and hotel. Thanks to Revo's timely message, I could move quickly on getting my travel arrangements made.

All seemed to be going fairly well, given that I had such short notice for the trip. My agent managed to find a flight that thankfully didn't stop over in the States. Restriction-free passport or not, there are still some places I doubt I can go and chances I'm not willing to take. My agent also put a reservation in a hotel at Passay City; she did not recognize the name of the city that Revo told me he was staying in. Thinking that I had maybe misspelled it, we both made the assumption that he had meant Passay.

The flight was booked for February 12, with return flight twenty-three days later, and the ticket information faxed to the passport office. I was now well on my way to leaving. The hotel was on hold, and I would not find out about it till the next day, but I was far from worried. I figured things would work themselves out but decided to focus my energies instead on how to explain to my daughter that I was leaving the country. The only time I had ever been separated from her for longer than two weeks had been four years earlier when I had been arrested. I had been restricted in my travel, due to my bail conditions, and was not allowed to leave the small town in the Ottawa Valley that I was being detained in. As my daughter was in Toronto on the day of my arrest, I was not able to go to her, and, understandably, her father was hesitant to bring her to me. There ensued a three-week mini-adventure involving interfering family members, Children's Services, and outright miscommunication between everybody. The whole distressing process did work itself out in the end, and it was ultimately through the help of both Children's Services and my arresting officer that my ex-husband was finally convinced that he should bring my daughter to me.

It is strange to think that only after the system had failed me completely, and only after I had been forced to act out of desperation, that my faith in that same system would be renewed and made stronger. In this instance, it was either my ex-husband or a member of his family who had called Children's Services on me. It was also in this instances that Children's Services, after meeting me, apologized for intruding and then actively acted on my behalf to have my daughter returned. Combine their belief that I was no threat to my child, and the efforts of the detective who had arrested me in contacting my ex-husband and explaining that he was violating our custody agreement, and— voilá! My baby girl was once again safely in my arms.

I would like to point out that at the time I was disgusted and angered by the whole affair; yet, looking back on it now I harbour no ill will toward my ex-husband for trying to protect our child. It is, after all, his undeniable love for her that makes him such a wonderful father. I can be proud to say that my baby's daddy will always put his daughter's safety and happiness first. So, you see, we grow, we lose, we learn... It's a good thing, and for that gift we must learn to also say thank you.

This time, however, I would be leaving her by choice—not something I am comfortable doing. As I said, she is only eleven, and I thought it would be many years yet before I would be willing to leave her side. It was with much trepidation that I looked toward telling her I had to go. When I picked her up from school, we were intending to go directly to her dance class, but the instructor called asking if we could push the lesson back an hour. I agreed, thinking it would give me time to explain matters as best I could. As we were driving toward my daughter's favourite restaurant, the phone rang again. This time it was Sophia, wondering how plans were progressing.

We got into (with my daughter in the car beside me) an in-depth conversation about my upcoming trip. I at one point told Sophia that at least now I didn't have to find a way to broach the topic with my little girl, as she had inadvertently done it for me. My discussion on the phone was more than enough information for Maddi to base her yay or nay on. So when it was time for us to sit down and eat, I merely had to ask her if she had any questions. She had only one. How long?

I told her that it would likely be a three-week trip, but that I would be back in time for her birthday. She seemed heartened by the notion, but said quite pointedly that she would miss me. I agreed wholeheartedly and told her leaving her would be the hardest part. I did reassure her, however, that part of my reason for going was to secure a better quality of life for us both in the hopes that in the end we would be free to spend more time together. After dinner we went on to her dance class, and as she was partaking of her lesson I took the opportunity to call her dad. Again I found myself looking up at a rather large wall I myself had created. How would he take the whole idea? I needed his support in this. He would have to be willing to alter his schedule in order to accommodate three full weeks of child care. He would have to make arrangements to travel inconveniently to the other side of the city to accommodate her dance lessons. I was leery of asking this extremely large favour of him. He owed me nothing, really, and had every reason to be selfish and unaccommodating.

Prior to our divorce I had put him through hell, but I had been working very hard over the last few years to establish a safe, communicative relationship with him for the benefit of our child. I had repeatedly bent over backwards to make things easier for him in the hopes it would prevent confrontation. I had willingly signed off on child support so that he would have the money to go back to school. I had often altered plans with my daughter so that plans he had made at the same time could be realized. I had allowed my daughter (much to the disgust of my family and dad) to call his girlfriend Mom; that had cut very deeply, but I felt it was for my daughter to decide who she would allow into her life. I put my faith in my belief that my daughter would know me in her heart as her mother and that that bond between us could not be threatened. Even though I didn't believe that the woman not yet married to my ex had any right to be called Mom, I did believe and have faith in my own child's intuitive abilities. She would know in her heart who did and did not love and care for her. In my mind, any extra love given my child was ultimately a good thing.

My friends and family did not agree with my methods. Being, however, the black sheep in the flock, I continued to go my own way and ignore their advice to stand up to this man. It seemed my perseverance would pay off in the end. When I finally got up the nerve to call Saul, he encouraged me to take the opportunity presented and set about assuring me that we could work out the details as we went. He also gave me some good advice with regards to phones and using them abroad. He did not question me on particulars, for which I was grateful, but instead he put faith in the fact that I was being honest with my intentions. I was yet again shocked and amazed and extremely grateful to him for his understanding. I hope someday to get the opportunity to apologize and admit to him that my treatment of him during the end of our marriage was disgraceful. I could have found better ways to deal with the issues we had, but I was young and had much to learn. Our divorce, however, has taught me much more than I believe our marriage could ever have, and I am extremely thankful for going through the experience of both. I doubt very much that he has the same view, but then, I have never bothered to ask him. I suppose someday I should, perhaps on the same day I say thank you for helping me get this far.

After Mad's lesson I had a brief discussion with the instructor about the upcoming trip. I was fortunate that the mother of Mad's dance partner was also present and agreed to change the day and time of dance classes during the period I would be away. I very much wanted to make things easier for Saul. I owe him so much more, I realize, but at least I could start with giving him that.

We were on our way home, and I wanted to confirm that my daughter was okay with the whole idea. I explained that I was very concerned about her nonchalant attitude toward my upcoming trip. I made it very clear that I value her opinion with regard to the decisions I make, as those decisions ultimately affect her as well. Yes, I used those words, all of them. As I have already told you, she understands, as all children do, much more than we give them credit for. Her answer gave me strength, courage, and reassurance. I told you at the beginning of this story what she said, but when you put it into context it is that much more enlightening. Given all that we have been through as a family, both together and apart, it is remarkable to know that it took being willing to leave it all behind and follow my heart to find out just exactly where my heart was. God bless the unselfish wisdom that can be found in the eyes of a child, as it is through those eyes that we are able to see the true beauty and love that surrounds us.

The *Six of Wands* suggests my power today lies in validation. I rise to the occasion and am motivated or confident to take it to the next level by the recognition, admiration, praise, or accolades put on my achievements or personal success. I am newly aware of and proud of my sense of empowerment, and I transform through acceptance.

Chapter 10

<u>Black and White vs. Colour</u>
<u>Logic and Reason vs. Me</u>

My day started out with an average routine of getting up, showering, hopping in the car, and dropping by Tim's on my way to the next appointment. (I skipped over checking my email, as I figured he was either still on his way or having just arrived, had not had time to send me anything.)

This time it was the doctor I was off to see, a follow-up on a CT scan done three months earlier. It had been a part of a series of doctors' visits and tests ordered in a futile attempt to find the cause of blinding headaches I had been suffering from for over a year. I don't even know why I bothered going. I had finally had surgery, and the headaches were now gone. It had been a dental surgeon, of all things, who had accidentally stumbled on the probable cause and taken a long-shot chance at operating to cure it. He didn't even think at the time that it would work, but I had agreed to it anyway. I was long past caring how they took the pain away. I only knew I wanted it gone. I was now fully recovered and was having trouble remembering what it had been like to have a blinding headache twenty-four hours a day. Honestly, it was one of those things I didn't mind forgetting. Still, I thought I had better follow through with getting my test results, figuring that it would be good to know if there was anything else wrong with my head.

While I was on my way, I got a call from an old friend. I had given him a shout the previous morning, before I had wandered off to the passport office. That call to him had been the reason I had been late getting there; it was the reason I had been forced to sit waiting there for over an hour. I wasn't even sure why I had called him, except maybe I was still looking for a little confirmation that I was on the right path. Deacon is the one person in my life I can absolutely count on to play the devil's advocate, keeping me reasonable and grounded with his steadfast belief in logic. The man's very presence in my life is a paradox and therefore should not be; yet, he remains a huge part of my world, and I am very grateful for his honesty and his guidance. We had started dating shortly after the fire, while I was still living in the Ottawa Valley.

I still remember the first time we met. It had been a blind date set up by his sister, and his reaction to my appearance was comical, at best.

I had hopped into his truck, and he had taken one look at me and said quite bluntly, "I don't usually date girls with tattoos and shit in their face."

His reference was to the piercings I have, but even though he was blunt as hell, he was at least still smiling when he said it.

I told him that I didn't usually date people without, so we were both taking a chance. Right then, I knew if nothing else came of this I had at least made friends with someone I could respect. Respect him I do, and date we did. He stuck by me through my arrest, with much risk of condemnation by his peers, and we continued to try to make it work even after I moved to a city four hours away. It couldn't last, though, not in that way, and it was on one of my biweekly overnight visits that the romantic part of our relationship came to an end. I remember that night very clearly. We were lying in his bed talking about me leaving in the morning, when he decided for his own reasons to cut me loose.

"You know, Vick, it can't continue." He tried to say it gently, but gentle doesn't come naturally to him, and as he talked I was relieved to hear the strength return to his voice. "I can't take care of you there. I can't watch over you and protect you when you are so far away. You shouldn't be alone all the time. It isn't right for someone like you to be alone. You are never going to find someone else if you are still here clinging to me, and I really need to know that you are safe. I need to let you go so you can find someone who can take care of you... someone who will love you."

I could have argued with him, tried to make him see reason, but it felt wrong to do so. I understood him then as I understand him now, and I know that in this one moment of agonizing openness he was making an extremely difficult and selfless decision.

"I don't think this is what God wants for you. You are not meant to be stuck here. There is so much you can do." He did at this point manage to lower his voice. "Do you understand? Can you let me let you go?"

I did understand, and I couldn't tell him because I couldn't trust my voice, so instead I snuggled up to him and, putting my head on his chest, I slowly nodded my head as the tears started to flow. I laid there like that, silently crying in his arms until he fell asleep. Then I offered up a little prayer in the hopes I could give him one more gift.

For years he had been suffering from stomach pain that had at times disabled and distracted him from his very active, very passionate role as an adoring father to his two little girls. I lay there with my hand on his stomach and I concentrated all my energy into healing him of this affliction.

I prayed to the powers that be that he be allowed to be cured of this ailment. He is a selfless man and deserves the strength of body to go along with his intensely powerful soul. I never spoke of it to him, but I have often asked him over the past couple years how his tummy is. Every time we speak his answer is the same: "No problems, Vick; don't know why, though, I haven't changed any of my bad habits, but it seems to have gone away."

He would not believe it if he ever read this story. He is too strongly chained to the here and now. Thankfully, though, he never *will* read this book, so I won't ever have to explain my reasons for bringing him into the tale. He would be pissed at me, I assure you, as he very much values his quiet, humble existence. He would not welcome the intrusion of the outside world. It would cause him to flee and find a shack in the bush, no doubt, in which he could hide. That is why I say he will never read this book. He does not believe in mixing business with personal. Though he fully acknowledges and accepts my artistic side, he rails against the idea that he may somehow be part of or an inspiration to that art. This is also why I say that his existence in my life is a paradox.

He sees the world in black and white. There are no grey areas. Life is either truth or lie, no in-between. You either live that life in the right or you do wrong. He will not acknowledge or accept any choice that is anything but one or the other. The road of life for him is well defined by his principles and integrity. Every step forward is thought through carefully and analytically. He weighs the pros and cons of his decisions, picks apart possible consequences, and then makes his decision based on the ethics of those decisions. Ethics and morals are his signposts on the road of life, and there is not much room on his chosen path for deviation or drastic change of direction. He is, in all honesty, my exact opposite—and I love and cherish him deeply for it.

What makes our relationship so undeniably strange is that he seems at once appalled and fascinated by my view of the world. He does not understand how I can so openly attack life with seemingly no regard for the future. He does not understand the colourful spectrum that I see when I look at life and all its possibilities. He does not understand my distaste for reality— and not understanding is not something I think he is used to. I doubt very much, in fact, that he has ever encountered anything or anyone in his life who he could relate to less. Being who and what he is, his natural instinct should be to remove himself from anything that threatens to endanger or destroy his solid belief in logic and reason. Yet he remains in my life a close friend who is always there if needed. He seems unable to remove himself completely, and, though he refuses to read my work or see things my way, he continues to be an inspiration to me in a strangely detached way. He sees in me a goodness that I had ignored for a long time myself, and, through his faith in that positive half of my soul, he has constantly encouraged me toward being a better person.

The very thing he tries so hard not to be—my teacher, my guide, my inspiration—he manages to accomplish by his insistence that it is not his role. As our friendship has grown and strengthened I have found myself exceptionally grateful to have him in my life. Even if we are not meant to be a couple, I love him dearly, and he is one of the few men in my life who I can see myself growing old with.

I have a vision of us sitting by a lake in our later years thinking back and laughing at all the previous stupidity that was us. I can picture us both, beers in hand, lounging against the backs of padded chairs, swapping tales of "you remember when..." and "did I ever tell you the story of...?" It is a comfortable prospect for the future. Though he insists that he will never marry again, I doubt very much we will need any kind of vow to hold us together. They say you are supposed to marry and grow old with the man in your life who is your best friend, and I can quite honestly say I am content with merely the *growing old with* part. As I said, the two of us are happy to just be, and that by itself is a beautiful thing.

I would like to address one more remarkable characteristic that Deacon possesses, but, as it is of a sensitive nature, I will try to approach it gently. I would like to point out that I am merely making observations here, not judgments or condemnations. The world is the way it is for a reason; I support and embrace religious and spiritual diversity. Yet the issue I am about to tackle has to be mentioned eventually, so I will take the risk and hope against hope that you receive it in the spirit in which it is given. Now, Deacon is so special because he is a follower of God's law, although he views the law as merely an exceptionally respectable guideline for his own personal moral code. The man quite literally lives by the Ten Commandments; this to me is a remarkable feat for anyone living in today's society. If you don't believe it would be difficult, then look them up…

I can think of a few, off the top of my head, that the average person has trouble with.

THREE: You shall not take the name of the Lord your God in vain

I am sure I do not have to explain this to you. Don't claim you don't hear it that often, because I hear it all the time. Don't claim you don't do it; I do it, and many others in my world do it; hell I've even heard priests and ministers do it (oh, shocking, isn't it?). Now, I don't have any clue what the consequences for disobeying are but that is not my concern. The point that I am trying to make is that Deacon somehow manages to live his life by these rules, and I have to marvel at the discipline needed.

FOUR: Remember the Sabbath Day, to keep it holy

Oops! Does that mean we are not to be at work on Sunday? Hmmm… it sounds pretty straightforward, but then, maybe it just means we need to make sure we put aside a few hours on Sunday to go to a church and worship; then again it does say *day*, so…

TEN: You shall not covet your neighbour's house; you shall not covet your neighbour's wife, or his male servant, or his female servant, or his ox, or his donkey, or anything else that is your neighbour's

Well, now, all we do is covet, isn't it? *He has a shiny new car, so I want a shiny new car. He has a big, beautiful house, so I should have a big, beautiful house.* We are constantly seeing those better off than we are, and, instead of saying, "Wow, good for them," or "They must have worked really hard for that," we instead ask ourselves "Why can't we have that too?"

TWO: You shall not make for yourself a carved image: any likeness of anything that is in heaven above, or that is in the earth beneath, or that is in the water under the earth

Now, I can only take this to mean that we are not to have false idols… and, you know, this is one of those times when I am going to keep my mouth shut and let you figure it out on your own…

You will, in time, ask your own questions on this one, and you will find your own answers.

All I know for fact is that these commandments were in Exodus, in the Bible's Old Testament, and, though they are commonly known to be God's law, given by God for his people to follow, I have so far only found one man who does follow them. What he was doing with someone like me, I will never understand.

It was with all of this in mind that I had called Deacon on my way to the passport office the previous day. I figured if anyone in my life would have a good reasonable argument for me not to go it would be him. I told him about my three month leave from work, my intentions to write a book, and my crazy plan to go to the Philippines. He knew, perhaps more than anyone, the risk I was taking. I would be using money I had put aside to secure my child's future, and there was no reasonable way to conclude that I would ever get that money back. That risk was against all the fundamental principals he himself used to dictate his own life: safety, security, and structured planning for the future. I should have, could have, and originally intended to set that money aside for my daughter's education, and it was a huge leap of illogical faith in what I viewed to be my possible destiny. He knew all of this, and I half expected him to ask me where the hell I had come up with such a harebrained idea. Much to my confusion and delight, he did not. Instead, he joined me in my leap of faith and temporarily spread his own wings and jumped with me off a cliff into the unknown.

"Okay," he quipped over the phone, "So you have to go to the other side of the world to write a book. It sounds like something you would think necessary. In fact, it is very probably something you should do. It might be very good for you."

I was speechless. Here he was telling me to go for it instead of lecturing me yet again about how twisted my view of reality was. Perfect, I thought. The one person I can rely on to bring me back to the real world, and he decides now to join me in the twilight zone. Great, now what do I do? Hmmm... I guess I better go. All this had run through my head that morning, as he spoke to me over the line, encouraging me to follow my dreams. He did also suggest that I keep my eyes and ears open for possible problems along the way. He also mentioned that I should be prepared to pay a price for the freedom of exploring the world and the opportunity that had been presented.

"There is always a cost. You know that nothing in this world is free."

I promised him that I would indeed be careful, and when I hung up the phone I was thinking that I would next talk to him upon returning to Canada. Not so. As he had apparently taken it upon himself to at least make sure I made it there in one piece, he called me again while I was on my way to my appointment.

"Hey, how long are you going for?" he questioned me over the line, not even bothering to say hello.

"Nice to talk to you too," I shot back. "Not that it matters much, I'm thinking, but I am going from the twelfth to the ninth. Why?"

"Yeah Vik, that's the thing—it does matter." He sounded slightly exasperated. "If you are there longer than twenty-one days, you need a visa."

"What the hell?" I asked, "My travel agent didn't say a damn thing about a visa."

"Figures, good thing I called then, eh? Look, I can't talk long; I'm at work," he explained quickly "I went online yesterday and checked out the information from the consulate, and any visit longer than twenty-one days needs a visa."

"Well, what the hell do I do?" I asked, feeling a bit panicked. "How do I get one? How long does it take?"

"Relax, it can be expedited," he explained again. "You can get one in twenty-four hours usually, if you are willing to pay extra."

"Great, no problem; I can do that." I was now thinking I was in the clear, until he threw another curve at me.

"Yes, but you need a passport to get a visa. When did you say you were getting your passport?" he asked, again sounding rushed.

"Um, I think I'm screwed," I mumbled "I get my passport on the eleventh and I'm on the plane on the twelfth. So…"

"Yep, you're screwed!" he agreed with me, and then he started chuckling to himself. "It's a good thing I decided to stick around, then, eh? Look, I do have to go, but I'll send you the consulate number in TO and a link through your email, so you can check the site out yourself. Good luck, eh?"

Soon after he hung up, the number for the consulate came through in a text message, and as soon as the car was parked I started dialing. I figured there was no need to panic yet. I still had a couple of days, so I should be okay. I kept trying to call while I was waiting in the doctor's office. It was one of the rare moments when you are grateful that the doctor is never on time. I tried calling again after the good doctor had seen me and had given me a clean bill of health. I called again while waiting in line upstairs to make an appointment at the travellers' clinic for my shots and twice again on my walk back to the car. I had to leave it alone while I drove, but as soon as I was parked where I was picking up my new computer I tried one more time. Still nothing. The line was busy yet again. For the moment it looked as if I was not going to get anywhere.

Eventually, I managed to complete the few errands I had been running and found my way back to the house. I immediately went online and into my email to get the link to the consulate. I went to the site in question, and, as I started reading, my heart started to sink. The requirements were fairly well explained, but there seemed to be way too many for my liking. By the time my boyfriend Reynard arrived home at 6:00 PM, I was pretty convinced my trip was about to be cancelled. One of the things I needed was proof that I had enough financial security to stay for an extended length of time. It was a reasonable request, no doubt, but, as I had neither a credit card nor a large amount of money in the bank, I really had no way to provide the consulate with that kind of information. Yep, I was most assuredly screwed. When Rey walked into the bedroom, I was sitting on my bed with my head in my hands, trying to figure out what to do. I explained briefly what my problem was, and as I was verbalizing my needs I came up with an answer.

So I got on the phone to the travel agency, thinking I'd just change the flight and shorten my stay. Easy solution, right? Oh no, not for me. Turns out the office is closed, and the only person left there answering the phone is an unlicensed trainee left behind at the end of the day to clean up. To make matters worse, my agent has the next few days off. On the upside, the sweet young lady volunteers to try to contact the airport and make them aware of my situation. She explains that if she leaves a note in the office one of the other agents might be able to assist me. The young woman puts me on hold, and, as I'm waiting, I am wondering to myself if this might be a sign I shouldn't go. After about ten minutes of silence, a friendly familiar voice came on the line.

"Julia!" I exclaimed, "I thought you had gone home."

She explained that she had indeed gone home and had been almost to her door when she had realized she had forgotten something and had been forced to return to the office. She apologized profusely about the mix-up with the visa and promised to fix it immediately if I didn't mind holding a bit longer. I certainly did not, and I leaned my head back against the pillows on my bed and closed my eyes in relief. I didn't have long to wait. She was back soon enough with news that she had changed the flight and would have new tickets for me in the office the next day.

"Oh yes, and by the way," she added, "Your hotel fell through, but another one of much better quality had a cancellation and is willing to give you a room for only twenty dollars per night more than the original hotel. So, really, you'll be staying in a five-star for the price of a three-star. I tried to call you earlier, but your phone was busy, and, since they need an answer by tomorrow morning, I'm glad I have you on the phone now. I can call them as soon as we are done here. That is, of course, if you want to take it."

Well, hell yes, I took it, and I was yet again reassured that I'd be making my way across the ocean. Of course, the entire time I was on the phone, my boyfriend (is it fair to continue calling him that?) had been standing by my bed listening. We had finally had a chance a few days prior to briefly discuss my trip, but I had not gone into an in-depth explanation about my reasons for going. He was still confused over my quick decision to leave, but he had decided for reasons of his own to support me. Just as he was turning to leave the room, he made a suggestion.

"You know, life would be a lot easier for you if you had a credit card. These things would not be such a hassle." He smiled a little. "I know you can't get one, but I can get you a copy of mine. I would feel better knowing you had an emergency backup plan."

I started to protest, but he was already on the phone to his credit card company. By the time I had followed him into the living room, it was too late. He was already hanging up, telling me, "It should be here in a couple of days." The idea made me extremely uncomfortable. I was torn between feelings of gratitude and guilt. He was trying so hard to help me do this thing, even though he really had no idea what the thing was that I was doing.

It was time for me to sit down and be as honest as I could be. He deserved to know that this new path I was starting to walk down just might lead me away. To be honest, it already had, but it was one of those times when a gentle half-truth would cause less damage. I was concerned about destroying him. Although he was in his mid-thirties, he had never shared his life with another woman. He had had plenty of girlfriends, but never one he had lived with. We had struggled with the change to both our lives when we got together, but, though the road had been rough, we had both assumed that it was going to last. I had made it clear several times that I would not remarry, but it remained an unspoken presumption that this was indeed a long-term commitment, just with no legal paper required.

I knew now the change that was coming. I could not continue living the way I had and still move toward my future in the arts. I needed to be free to wander and discover the world, and it worried me that accepting that freedom would mean leaving certain parts of my life behind. A much as I would like to think I could still be myself and continue to play a domestic role, I was becoming more aware every day of the impossibility of balancing both.

It also occurred to me that there was no way I could give up even a remote chance that Rev and I could be together. I had spent long, lonely nights hoping and praying for that other half of my soul to somehow find his way to me. Looking into the eyes of my past, present, and future had awakened in me a burning desire to stand by his side. I could not— would not—deny myself. In my mind I already belonged to this man; heart, body, and soul, I was his. I always had been. I had shared my life with others, given them as much of myself as I was able, but I had never been able to bring myself to give it all. There had always been a reason to hold back, the knowledge that someday I would be faced with a choice. Someday a person would come to take me away from my world and pull me into his. I had never cared if it would be a man or a woman; I knew that when the time came I would go.

It was a painful realization, if only because I was desperate to avoid hurting Reynard, a man I had grown to love. I resolved to explain as much as I could to him. I sat down in the living room with him and started to talk.

"I am not sure that the card was a good idea; I am not comfortable with using your money to make this trip. It makes me feel as if I am being unfair to you."

He was surprised at that. "But, why? You need a safety net. Hell, I need you to have a safety net. Besides," he grinned at me, "It's not like I won't be able to find you to get the money back. I know where you live, remember?"

It made me sad to think about what I was about to do, but it was necessary, so I continued.

"You don't understand: this trip, this journey, it is something I have to do to save myself and get back to who I am. I don't know where it will lead or what kind of impact it will have on my future. I do know that it will lead to change, and in order for that change to occur I must give myself over to it with everything I have got. I can't hold back or be afraid about what might come of this. Do you understand what I am trying to say?"

He still looked confused. "Of course I do, and I said I would help in any way I can. Why are we discussing this?"

Poor soul, he wanted to support me, and, in the blindness that his love for me was causing, he was unable to see the possible danger to himself.

"Look, hon, what I'm trying to say is that I have to commit all of my time and all of my energy to this book and to this trip."

He grinned again. "I know that—I've hardly seen you for days, and you're not even gone yet."

In my mind I was thinking, *Oh, but I am, a part of me is already on the other side of the world…* I wanted to make it clear to him if I could.

"Try to understand this," I said pleadingly, "I no longer have the energy or the time to dedicate to you, this house, or our relationship. I need to harbour that energy and use it for my work."

His eyes flashed for one brief second of realization and then glazed back over. It appeared he had chosen to return to a state of denial. "Once you're back, it will be fine. Go do what you have to do, and then we will go from there. Okay?"

Stubborn, obstinate creature.

"I don't know when I'll be back," I mumbled with my eyes downcast.

"What the hell are you talking about?" he groaned. "Your flight is back on the fifth."

I looked up, forcing myself to look him in the eye, "I am talking about the fact that I do not know when or even if I will be able to come back to this on an emotional level. I am not sure anymore this is the life I was meant to be living."

"Oh," he said quietly and moved his body back on the couch. "Well, can we not just wait and see?" he said hopefully. "I mean, you go, do what you have to do, come back, and we'll deal with it then. Okay? You said yourself you don't know what's going to happen, so don't assume this trip will change anything. Keep in touch while you are there, and let me know you are safe. I'll be waiting for you when you get back. It will work out." He added angrily, "And take the damn credit card with you, so I will at least believe you are safe."

I realized I would have to accept his offer…

All I could do was sit there and stare in wonderment at this intelligent, reasonable man suddenly being reduced to a creature suffering from unreasonable denial of fact. I gave up the argument. I wasn't going to win. Part of me didn't really want to, but eventually the truth of our situation would have to come out—whatever that turned out to be.

I went to Madison's room and logged in to send Rev a quick message.

Hey sweets,

Hope all is going well over there and that u r getting settled in—I also hope u will be checking your email, since I don't wanna call you and wake you up if you are finally getting some rest. If you get the chance, give me a shout; I know the time zones are way off, but I don't care if you wake me up. I can always sleep later. Everything seems to be working out here; the flight is booked, the hotel that I had reserved at 100 a night which was a 3-star fell through, but then the 5-star hotel that we looked at yesterday that wanted 210 a night called my agent today and told her they had a cancellation and would give it to me for 120 a night, so all is well.

Thanks to my friend Deacons' quick thinking, and the random fact of the travel agent forgetting something at the office and having to go back, a possible problem with regards to me needing a visa was solved today—we changed my return date so I won't need a visa this trip—and now I have the option of getting a 58-day travel visa later if I need or want to go back (did you know they will only issue you one per person?) I am learning quickly.

I was just talking to Maddi online and she said to say hi to you so, "Hi"—she is being so totally supportive and selfless about this whole adventure—you are right, she was my open door. She has brought me back from many a dark dangerous place more times than I can count—I really am blessed. Well, hon, I will hopefully hear from you soon. I will be running around like crazy till I leave, but I'll check my mail at random times and my phone is with me always. See you soon, xo

I went to bed shortly thereafter to lie awake and ponder what would come of this. Before I went I checked out my daily tarot, and, as I read, I let out a little audible groan...

> The *Nine of Swords* suggests that my power today lies in realizing that I am not my mistakes. I can't do this alone or pretend anymore. The illusion of comfort in denial or sacrifice is no longer mine. There is no shame in my suffering, no healing in silent torment. It is here at the surreal crossroads of the "soul search," where dawning truth meets the anguish of overwhelming resistance in mind over matter, that I can finally wake up, change my mind, let go of what no longer works, or my own losses or choices. I am empowered by intense acknowledgement or epiphany, and my virtue is gratitude or relief in recognition.

Chapter 11

Eyeliner, Angels, and Backseat Drivers

Shortly after waking, once I had a coffee in hand, I took the time to check my email. I was glad to see that Rev had made it safely, but a little concerned about some of what he had written. I was pretty sure I did not want this piece of art I intended to create to become political; I personally can't stand politics and avoid the subject whenever possible.

Unfortunately, my other half has always somehow managed to immerse himself in the politics of whatever age he happens to be in, and, as much as the peaceful priestess in me would prefer to initiate change through positive spiritually based inspiration and enlightenment, it seemed to me that the two were interconnected. One issue could not be addressed without the other, a fact that irritates me no end—but then, I suppose that is why there are two of us. I can't imagine trying to tackle both at the same time without help; I think exhaustion would put an end to the battle long before the government or the churches even bothered to try. However, at the time I read the email we had only begun our journey together; there were several realizations yet to come, and at the time I knew very little about where we were headed. I did know that we had something we were meant to do, I knew that we were meant to do it together, and I knew we had been down this road before. I also knew that my instincts were telling me that becoming ensnared in politics could pose a threat to both of us, a risk I myself was not yet willing to take.

Jean Victoria Norloch

Vik,

It costs 210 dollars a night *at a hotel and I found out today it cost 250 dollars a* month *to* OWN *a condo. Because of the recession, real estate prices dropped so much. Well, it's 9 pm here, and I've survived day one and made it to the evening, so my body adjusted extremely fast. My uncle told me it would take me a week, but I think you're right when you said your body will tell you where you belong. After only a day, I've almost fully adjusted.*

Such a weird thing happened today. We were driving, and the traffic was just horrendous. My cousin's fiancé was driving, and we started talking about the corrupt government. I guess I got a bit enthusiastic and began talking about ways to improve the infrastructure. Then, out of nowhere, as a joke, my cousin yelled, "Vote for Revo!" and her fiancé told me to consider running for congress. I feel, however, there will be a new medium of power that will circumvent the use of politics. The people do not need a voice; they need an ear to listen to them.

So far in the last 3 days I've only had a total of around 11 hours of sleep, but my energy levels are extremely high.

I've written a bit. When I type it seems as if something takes over my hands and types away. The weather is so great here. I'm so lucky to be staying where I am. I'm being treated really well, and I know not a moment of it can be taken for granted.

Your dearest always,

R

I figured maybe I would get lucky, and he would stay on safe ground if he focused on his belief that he could inspire people through the arts—but there was no point in trying to give him direction. He would more than likely go his own way regardless of what I said. Besides, I had chosen to leave my life for the man—the least I could do was offer my support, regardless of how uncomfortable the idea of politics made me. I dropped him a quick line, then got ready to go. I had a long day ahead of me yet and much to do…

R,

It seems so crazy that a condo can be so cheap, when it costs so much for just one room, but I guess it doesn't really surprise me—the economy between nations is so far out of balance because there are too many different factions struggling for power and control of the almighty dollar. It's 3 pm here, and I have been running full-tilt trying to get all the arrangements made. I'm glad your body has adjusted so nicely and that you are not completely exhausted. Your family sounds like they will stand behind you no matter what crazy decision you make—which is an incredible feeling. I would know, because I am getting the same support here. I will have my hotel info for you later today, but I have my flight info for you now, so you know well in advance when I am coming. My flight leaves here at 12:15 am on the 13th with a 2-hr stop in Hong Kong, then on to Manila. My flight should touch down in Manila at 5 am on the 14th—so I guess u r right: I will be seeing you on Valentine's day. I was curious about the significance of the date, so I looked it up and found out that Valentine's day was originally a pagan celebration honouring life and fertility, but it was the Catholic Church that changed the meaning as well as the date—the original holiday was apparently on the 15th, so, hey, we have two days to celebrate life and love. Let me know when you can if you will be able to meet me at the airport—I'd feel safer with you there, but, like I said, I know you have a lot of things to do and people to see. Enjoy your visits and your adventures, but please stay safe—we still have so much left to do. Keep in touch.

Yours then, now, and always…

A quick shower, then back in the car with Timmies in hand, and on the road to another new and strange encounter. The fact that I was driving toward this particular destination at all was really rather odd. For some strange reason, I had gotten it in my head a few weeks prior that I should get my eyeliner permanently tattooed on. This was an extremely strange decision, as I am generally a low-maintenance type of girl. Even working in an industry where appearance can translate to dollars (if you look good, people tend to tip more), I had never been one to spend a lot of time on hair and makeup. Not that I don't want to be attractive, but I really can't be bothered with all the effort involved.

I am still, however, a woman, and occasionally it is expected of me to put a little effort into my looks. This had recently started to pose a problem, as the vision in my right eye was deteriorating rapidly. It was, as a result, becoming increasingly difficult to put eyeliner on without completely making a mess of things. Still, I am not one to turn to extreme measures to improve my outer beauty. I am, however, rather partial to the way my eyes look when they are lined in black. They are a unique hazel that tends to change to reflect whatever I am wearing. When lined in black, though, they cease being merely interesting and become darkly intense eyes, eyes that I have been told by many give people the impression that I can see right through to their souls. I rather like the idea of being able to enter a person so deeply merely by looking at them. It's not with the intent to invade their inner being, you understand, but I am fascinated with humans and spend a great deal of time studying them. I rely on my eyes to in effect hypnotize others into being more open and honest with me. They have always been my most striking feature, but with a little help in the makeup department they become a useful tool in my exploration of the human psyche, a tool I was now in danger of losing.

I had spent days looking online and questioning friends, trying to find out if the procedure was even safe. If there was too much risk involved it would be a "no go," but I had discovered that it was in fact safe, and I decided to go for it. I had searched several sites online for clinics that specialized in that kind of work. For some reason, I had put the number for the first site I came to in my phone. I then went through about fifteen more sites before returning again to the first. Something in the name drew me in, and I bookmarked the site and decided that if I ever got the urge, she was the lady I would call.

I had gotten the urge. Sitting outside the bank in my car one morning while waiting for Sophia to do her banking, I had one of those random spur-of-the-moment ideas that end up leading to an enlightening encounter of the spiritual kind.

Today was the day. As I drove, I went over in my head all the things I had done in the last few days. I had a good hour of driving to lose myself in thought: conversations I had had with friends, along with all the little signs and symbols that seemed to be pointing the way, ran through my mind. Several of them had been extremely strange and seemingly coincidental. It was during my reflection on these signs that I had a momentary loss of faith. How could I be sure I was doing the right thing in going? Even though I felt a sense of direction for the novel I was aspiring to write, my faith in my ability to actually finish it was dwindling. All the support I was getting was amazing, but I reasoned that the support was coming from the people in my life who were only in my life because they always *had* supported me. I also reasoned that I could have misinterpreted all the little signs and portents. Perhaps they meant something else, or perhaps they meant nothing at all. I had prayed for a sign of some kind, and it seemed I had been given many, but, again, how could I be sure? What if I went ahead with this, investing a great deal of time and energy, and then nothing came of it? How would I be able to justify risking my daughter's future security on the chance that I would be a success? Doubt crept in and soon threatened to consume me. Really, it wasn't too late to change my mind. Was it? I was completely torn in two. *Do I stay or do I go?* I was starting again to doubt my sanity, so, in a last-ditch effort to hold onto it, I offered up another prayer to the powers that be. I drove the car and spoke to the air. I started by being thankful for the opportunity, but explained that I was still suffering from uncertainty. Was there any way, and I realize I was asking a lot, that I could get a more definitive sign?

When I think back on it now, I feel I was being selfish, but at the time I really needed to know. I mean, let's face it, signs and symbols aside, though many of us talk to God on a regular basis, it isn't as though he is likely to talk back. He doesn't often lean over your shoulder and whisper sweet nothings in your ear, and you are not about to get the chance and sit with him over tea and ask his opinion on world issues. It just doesn't work that way. Guidance comes through more indirect means, and, unless our hearts and eyes are open, that guidance is easy to miss. Even with an open heart, even when we are able to see the signs, they are sometimes difficult to accept. This was the problem I was having.

I had recently acknowledged that I was now no longer driving the car that was taking me down the road of life. I was, it seemed now, in the passenger seat but was still trying to clutch at the wheel. I was hesitant to relinquish my control over my direction and destination. The problem is that a car is not meant to have more than one driver. Too many hands on the wheel can have disastrous consequences. Thankfully, I was blessed, and God took his eyes off the road ahead long enough to look at me and shout, "Let go of the wheel before you make me crash the car!"

I had not yet had the benefit of this warning, however, when I pulled up in front of the house of pain. I call it that only because, man, it really hurts having a bunch of needles rapidly and repeatedly piercing tender flesh. I knocked on the door and was greeted by a strikingly pretty woman by the name of Brigitte.

"Welcome to Auriel's Touch," she smiled. "Come on in; I'll be right with you."

The house/clinic had an extremely warm and inviting atmosphere, and I immediately felt my fears regarding the upcoming procedure melting slowly away. My other fears would not be far behind. She was right; I didn't have long to wait, and she was soon sitting with me going over options. Before I knew it I was on the table, and she was getting set up to begin adding a little extra colour to my life.

"Do you mind if I talk while I work?" she asked me, while she was leaning over my eye with the needle. "It makes the time go faster."

I told her I didn't mind at all; in fact it would probably be good to have something to distract me. As she talked and began to tell me a little about herself and her business, I began to feel an affinity with this woman. She and I had been through similar situations with our husbands and our divorces. We both had one child who seemed destined to follow us in the arts, and we had both had to struggle with our exes on the topic of allowing our children to pursue a career that was a little off the beaten path. She, too, had just reached a new level of comfortable communication with her ex and was in the midst of changing the direction of her career. The only difference, really, was that she was already successful and well established. That was probably due to the fact that she was also ten years older. Still, our stories were shockingly similar, and I enjoyed listening to her ramble on about life and love. She was also a very spiritual creature with a strong faith in God and his presence in her life. She told me repeatedly how she had been both blessed and challenged by him over the last few years.

Each time she had been given a test of strength and character she had also been taught a valuable life lesson. She, like me, believed that with every painful tragedy that befalls us there is always the presence of something good and positive. It is this balance that helps us grow and prepares us for our next challenge or lesson. She also believed, apparently, in acknowledging the gifts that God gives us and in being grateful for opportunities as they are presented.

"Oh, and by the way." She smiled an angelic smile. "I am supposed to tell you that when God opens a door for you, it is appropriate that you to take the steps forward to walk through the door—stop doubting, stop fearing, and start walking."

What? What? Now, wait a minute. I had not told this lady a thing past the fact that I was a writer and that I was leaving soon to go to the Philippines to visit a friend. No details about my life or my intentions had been discussed. In fact, I had not had much of an opportunity to talk at all, as I had been given strict instructions not to move. Here I was, lying on my back, staring through teary eyes at the face of this woman and feeling like I had been kicked in the head. I was for the moment completely numb, and my mind wasn't able to function. Well, I had asked for it, hadn't I? I had wanted some kind of definitive sign.

You know, at this point I am thinking that there is one very obvious lesson to be learned: when God kicks you in the head to send you flying through the door that he has opened, you would probably do well to smile and say thank you as you are flying by!

Brigitte didn't give me a chance to recover. She merely continued on with her work, as if she had not said anything particularly interesting. I couldn't say anything. I still wasn't able to move, but it was now more a paralysis caused by a giant shock to the system than one caused by fear of a misplaced needle.

She started in about an interesting tale on how she had acquired her business name. It was a story that stuck with me and one I would need to make use of in the near future. She told me that when she decided to move her career out of the area of artistic tattooing and into the field in which she now worked she had decided she needed a name that better suited the work she was doing. As she would be working to cosmetically improve the appearance of people like burn victims to help them be more confident and comfortable within themselves, she needed a name that had a nurturing connotation. She also believed that she was being given the chance to work with people like that so she could help restore their faith and give them back their trust that they would find their way out of the darkness they were currently experiencing. Her problem was that she had no idea what name to use. After weeks of pondering, she decided to simply go online and look on the business registry to get ideas. When she went to her computer, however, she could not get it to turn on.

Not having much spare time in those days, what with changing careers and all, she put the idea aside. She had intended to get someone to look at her computer, but she forgot to do that as well. Approximately a week later, she had been walking through her living room and noticed a piece of paper lying on the floor. She bent to pick it up and realized that it was a list of all the archangels' names. It was a list she had kept in her room by her bedside for years and had no business being on the floor in her living room. One of the names seemed to draw her eye. No matter how many times she glanced away and then back to the list, her eyes always seemed to fall on Uriel. On a whim, she decided to go to the computer she had abandoned a week earlier and see if it would work, so that she could look up the meaning of the name Uriel. Here's what the site she found read.

"To build self esteem and confidence, inner peace and tranquility; untangling knots of anger and fear and effecting peaceful resolution of personal problems, both social and professional; inspiration for

nurses, doctors, counsellors, teachers, judges, public servants, and everyone in the service of others. "

All these things tied into the work she would be doing, and she decided to use the name. She noticed that there was a variation available for the spelling, a variation which she chose to use for her business name. I am not sure at the time she realized what she had done by choosing to add the *A*, but I intend to go back some day and ask her.

As I realized later in the day, when I finally looked it up, there is also an archangel Ariel, and, when combined, the two names represent the very core of whom and what this woman is. One thing that did strike me immediately was the association with water. I am a water sign, Rev is also a water sign, and it was across oceans I would soon travel to a land surrounded by water in the hopes of finding out where it was I was meant to be.

Symbolism has a crazy way of creeping up on you, and, when it does, it is best to be wary. Sometimes the presence and the seeming insistence of the message the symbol represents can leave you feeling completely powerless and overwhelmed. Really, it was a bit much, and though I left soon after, feeling grateful for being given the chance to meet her, I was a bit shaken. It was very hard to accept the idea that somebody like me, with all the bad things I had done haunting my past, could be forgiven, accepted, and openly guided by God.

I was again humbled at the thought. I found myself crying as I drove home and praying that in the end he would find me worthy of his faith.

I arrived home in late afternoon and decided to look the angels up online. I found a site, as I mentioned earlier, and discovered both angels Ariel and Uriel. I looked to a site called *Angel Focus* and read the following.

Ariel means "lion of God," and is often associated with lions. When Ariel is near you, you may begin seeing references to or visions of lions around you. Ariel is also associated with the wind. Found in books of Judaic mysticism, and cabalistic, Ariel works closely with King Solomon in conducting manifestation, spirit releasement and divine magic. Ariel also oversees the sprites, the nature angels associated with water. Ariel is involved with healing and protecting nature, including animals, fish and birds. If you find an injured bird or other wild animal that needs healing, call upon Ariel for help. Ariel also works closely with Raphael to heal animals in need."

Uriel means "'God is Light," "God's Light," and "Fire of God." Uriel is considered to be one of the wisest archangels because of his intellectual information, practical solutions, and creative insight.

Uriel warned Noah of the impending flood, helped the prophet Ezra to interpret mystical predictions about the coming Messiah, and delivered the cabal to humankind. He also brought the knowledge and practice of alchemy, and the ability to manifest from thin air as well as illuminate situations and give prophetic information and warnings. All this, considered Uriel's area of expertise, is divine magic, problem-solving, spiritual understanding, studies, alchemy, weather, earth changes, and writing. Considered to be the archangel who helps with earthquakes, floods, fires, hurricanes, tornadoes, natural disaster, and earth changes, Uriel is called on to avert such events or to heal and recover from their aftermath.

In the eighth century, the Christian Church became alarmed at the rampant and excessive zeal with which many of the faithful were revering angels. For some unknown reason, in 145 AD, under Pope Zachary, a Roman counsel ordered seven angels removed from the ranks of the Church's recognized angels; one of them was Uriel.

On another site, called *Connecting with the Light*, I found the following.

Ariel—Name means "lion or lioness of God." Ariel is known as the Archangel of the Earth, because she works tirelessly on behalf of the planets. Ariel oversees the elemental kingdom and helps in the healing of animals, especially the non-domesticated kind. Call upon Ariel to become better acquainted with the fairies, to help with environmental concerns, or to heal an injured wild bird or animal.

Uriel—He is the wise angel who sheds light on all darkness. When you are feeling depressed, angry, victimized, or confused, call on Uriel. He will come and pour his golden light over you. He will help you release anger, unforgiveness, and any other negative emotions that may be clouding your vision and judgment. He will help you find peace and answers.

Well, perhaps, in my dazed state of pain with multiple needles penetrating my eyelids, I had misheard. Perhaps Brigitte knew exactly who both angels were. In fact, I am sure now she did, but I still intend some day to go back and ask her. For the moment though, try to picture me silently sitting in front of my computer, eyes flying across the screen, "Ask and ye shall receive" would not stop repeating in my head.

I couldn't help myself. I had to share this story with someone, and I was soon on the phone with Sophia. I told her the entire tale, as crazy as it seemed, and waited for her response.

"So, I guess you've been told." I could hear the grin in her voice. "Honestly, it takes you long enough sometimes."

"Really, Soph?" I moaned, "It's been a weird day, and I'm thinking you are being just a little harsh."

"No," she shot back, "I don't think I am. Jesus boots. What more do you want for proof? You are the one who has been saying for years that there is no such thing as coincidence. You've been getting signs and guidance for weeks. You've had the support of everyone you know since you started this crazy quest, yet you have the balls to continue to question it. You dare ask for yet another sign."

Her words were angry, but her tone was not, and I knew she was only trying to rekindle the fire that she feared might be starting to go out.

"But, for God's sake, Soph! I'm a sinner, not a saint." I was getting a little annoyed.

"You have the mind of a criminal, yes, but we both know that your heart is pure," she said gently.

The thing was, she was right. I shouldn't have doubted, and I made a silent apology to God for losing sight of what he was offering. "Okay, you're right. I deserve that. I really do."

Her voice was soft. "Everybody else has faith in you. Don't you think it's time you had a little in yourself?"

As usual, I couldn't say much in argument. She is almost always right in her interpretation of situations. I was being extremely ungrateful, and it was time to stop asking "Why me?" and start saying "Thank you." Still, I wasn't sure what I could possibly do to be a positive influence and initiate change. I told Sophia this, expecting to get another earful. I was surprised to hear her agree.

"I don't know either," she admitted. "But I do believe that God will let you know what you need to know when you need to know it. I don't think you are meant to plan ahead. Hell, I don't think at this point it would make a difference. He'll take you wherever he wants. It is your job to go along and watch and learn from what he has to show you." She started to laugh, "Do you think you can stop him if he decides to use you?"

"No," I frowned, "probably not."

"Okay, so just go with it, and stop asking who, what, where, and why. You're acting too much like the journalist, questioning and analyzing everything. Stop for awhile, and just let yourself live. Analyse later. It will all come together eventually. For now, just enjoy the moment."

"Okay." It was so true what she was saying. It all made a great deal of sense. I promised her I would heed her advice and stop trying to figure out where we were headed. After all, when God is driving it is a pretty safe bet that you will get there eventually.

I left a quick message for Rev and then went off to bed, content for once to let someone else do the driving.

Hey sweetie,

Here is all my contact travel info. Hotel: Heritage Hotel, Roxas Blvd., PO Box 454, Passay City, Metro Manila, 1300, Philippines. I am thinking all the info you need is there, if I missed anything, let me know. Hope you had a good sleep and pleasant dreams (very pleasant)—hopefully I'll hear from you before you run off for your daily adventures. Your emails make me smile—just knowing you are having a good time puts me in a happy place. Here's hoping my emails still make you smile too. Have fun wandering, but don't do anything too crazy without me. Hate to miss all the fun—Muah (see, I learn, lol).

xo to you, my baby, see you soon.

P.S. remind me when I get there to tell you about the sweet angel from God I randomly met today—it is a story that so needs to be told in person but one I am sure you will enjoy.

Oh, I almost forgot my daily tarot.

The *Knave of Wands* suggests that my power today lies in experimentation. I enthusiastically initiate new, extreme, or novel opportunities for adventures, fads, connections, or enterprises and am an active and image-conscious player in the game of life. I am empowered by signs of approval for my performance and transform through arousal and charisma.

Chapter 12

<u>Shots, Shopping, and Sweet Sophia</u>

… A new day, a new coffee, and a new chance to discover new things…

Of course, a morning would not be complete without checking the email.

Lady,

So far nobody is willing to talk. It might be too dangerous still, baby. I'm meeting up with a director, and my aunt asked me, "What will you say if they ask you where you got your name?" and I was silent, then said "I'll say it's from the revolution," and she cut me off and said, "Nooooo, just say that your dad picked it… don't say anything about a revolution or anything. Okay?" and I said, "Okay…" I have a strange feeling that my family knows EXACTLY why I'm back in the Philippines. Which is why I'm practically being treated like a king: fed, my clothes washed and ironed for me, driven around, I'm even given my cousin's room with its own private bathroom. It's so bizarre, baby… but none of them think I know the story… well, they at least know that I don't know the details of it. Maybe this is part of the plan, for me NOT to know all of it, so I can go about innocently without attracting too much attention.

Maybe to take the pressure off me…

Jean Victoria Norloch

It's quite unbelievable… I almost feel guilty sometimes at how good I'm being treated… maybe I shouldn't though, huh?

I got a meeting with a director today. I have a good feeling about it. Wish me luck.

I watched King Arthur yesterday, the movie. I think the latest one they made is the best version.

Mmmmmuah, xo

Anyway, off to my adventure for the day. Muah =)

I wrote a quick note back.

Rev,

Baby, you are sooooo stubborn—listen to your Aunt PLEASE!!!!!!

No more questions, no more investigating until I get there. I have an idea on how to get this done in a safe way that will have a very positive impact—maybe not in just the Philippines but in other countries as well. Try to trust that things will fall into place as they are supposed to, but we have to be very careful as to what direction we take this in, so again I am asking you to concentrate on your art and your contacts through art and for art until we have a more concrete plan. Your purpose is pure—I already know that—but I agree that this story is not meant to play out in a political arena. We are there to write a story, yes, but we are not there to upset the people who run the country—if we do, this story will never get told and we will have to go through all this again next lifetime and start from scratch. Behave yourself, my love, and stay low, stay safe, and wait for me. As far as letting people treat you well—if that is their wish, then let them do what they want, but do not let them lead you down a stray path. Enjoy your time there: get to know your people,

*their culture and spiritual beliefs, their hopes and dreams—the rest
will come…*

Have sweet dreams—I will be with you soon, xo

I soon found myself sitting in my car again, waiting for Sophia
to come up from her dungeon, so we could get on with our day.
Two things you can count on with this woman: she will always
tell you the truth, and she will always be late. She lives in an
apartment in the basement in her mother-in-law's house, and
I find myself envying the relationship the two of them have. I
consider Sophia to be a very lucky girl to have for a mother-in-law
a fiery, quick-tempered redhead who loves her unconditionally.

The old woman absolutely amazes me. She drives a little red
sports car, spends more time out of the house than in, and when
she is at home she can usually be found wearing a bathrobe and
holding a beer either in hand or within reach—crazy bird, she
is.

Sophia seems to take it in stride when mamma switches from
sweet little old woman to dragon lady in the blink of an eye,
something that happens daily. Though they are both opinionated
and stubborn as hell, it hasn't seemed to negatively affect their
relationship. I do have to feel sorry for Sophia's poor husband,
because, when the two women decide to join forces to convince
him to do something, it must be very similar to being trapped
between a ship and an iceberg: crushed, cold, unable to breath,
and with legs dangling in midair. I doubt he ever has much of a
chance to outrun their powerful will.

It was certainly taking Sophia long enough to get out to the car.
I was not willing to wait for long—we had way too much to
accomplish in such a short time. She came stomping out of the
house with a scowl marring that beautiful face of hers.

"Morning, I guess," she moaned as she dropped into the seat. "Why is it so damn early?"

"Oh, quit whining, and drink your coffee," I grunted, as I backed out of the driveway.

"Mmmm, caffeine, yes, that should help," she finally smiled at me. "So, what do we have left to do?"

I ran down the list. We had to be at the clinic for shots at 9:30 AM, had to hit the bank one more time, then head off to the mall to pick up the hotel voucher. I also wanted to tackle my growing list of essentials but was a little concerned about time. I still had to make it to my brother's for dinner, and, as he lived an hour away, I would be pushing it.

"So?" she asked as I drove. "You hear from Rev?"

"Sure!" It was my turn to frown. "He's running all over the damn place with his cousins, visiting people, and having discussions with everybody he meets about politics and the need for change. Hell, he even sent a message telling me that they were driving around the city when his cousin stuck his head out the window and called 'Rev for President.' Not exactly what you would call lying low."

She whistled through her teeth, then exclaimed, "Well, you did say he was pretty passionate about wanting to help his country."

"Yeah, yeah, I know, but I also recall saying he needs to be careful. He won't be able to accomplish anything if he gets killed." The thought made me really angry. "He has to find his place first, set down some kind of foundation, so these people can trust him. Besides, you know how much I hate politics. I just wish he'd focus more on his acting and his music, as he originally intended. His cousins are encouraging him to follow a more political path. I just don't feel it is the right way to go about it."

"Hmmm, sounds like you also have plans for him. Don't you think, though, that it would be better to let him find his own way?" She had a point...

"They are thinking politics, you are thinking spirituality and arts, and it is him who will have to make the choice. Let him go for now, see what he does, and if it starts getting dangerous then talk to him. Don't discourage him, though. You're the one who is so sure he needs to do this, so let him do it," she grinned at me. "Don't worry, hon, he'll be very much alive when you get there."

"I know, I know," I conceded. "I have to have a little more faith. It is hard, though, when he is so very far away. We had so very little time to make plans before he left. I honestly think we can create something special to put into print, but we have so much more to discuss about how to do it."

I know I was sounding pretty whiny and, given my experience the day before, I really ought to just let it go.

"I guess I have to work out some of my own issues, too. Besides, I have a lot to do before I can even get on the plane. I had better put my efforts into getting there. The rest will probably work itself out."

"There you go," she grinned, "You're learning. You know you saw it yesterday. You admitted it yourself. You've had your proof now. Put yourself in God's hands. Let him guide you. Rev will be fine, and you two will see each other soon. You'll lift each other up and soar to great heights together. Be confident, be patient, and let the book write itself." Laughing, she added, "In fact, after all you told me, I think it already is."

I had to agree with her there, but, even with all the interesting stories and symbolism I had already witnessed, I still had no clue as to what kind of conclusion I would make at the end of it all.

I supposed she was right, though. For the moment, it was the journey that mattered, not the destination.

We arrived at the clinic and, after driving around for fifteen minutes, finally found a place to park. We kept up an easy banter about mundane things like weather, drama at work, and how much I had left to do. While we were waiting for the doctor, she asked me about Rev's reaction to my criminal activities.

"He took it pretty well," I answered, "but then he doesn't seem much surprised by anything I tell him."

As I finished speaking, I realized we were in a very busy, very public, waiting area, not the kind of place one should be discussing these issues. Oh well, I shrugged inwardly: I am who I am. It's about time I stopped trying to hide from it.

"So," she arched an eyebrow, "Did you tell him everything?"

Hmmm, I was thinking, *Did I?*

"Yup, I think I did. You know, I don't think I could lie to that man if I tried. He knows at least as much as you." I winked at her, "and he, like you, doesn't seem to give a damn where I've been. He seems much more concerned about where I'm going."

"I knew there was something I liked about that man—other than his delightfully pinchable ass, that is." She smirked at me, then added seriously, "I'm glad you guys got past that so quickly. It will make things easier for you."

"Me too," I agreed. "If it was anybody else, I'd be concerned, but nothing fazes the man. You know, I told him a few of my crazy family stories and he never even blinked."

She laughed, "Well then, I guess if he took those in stride you have nothing to fear. Which ones did you tell him? Not that they aren't all pretty much messed up, but I'd hate to see you scare him off."

So I went over the stories I had told him already, adding that our time had been short, so I hadn't been able to tell him all of them.

"Too bad you never got to tell him about the three days you spent camped out in the kitchen with your mother and her rifle." She laughed as the woman beside her shot her a surprised look. "That one would be a sure test of his ability to accept the weirdness that has been your upbringing."

"Oh sure, I'm positive he would love to hear all about my mother keeping me hostage in the kitchen. I mean, it's not every day one's mommy decides that someone is coming to take her daughter away. Certainly I can see his amusement as he pictures in his mind my mother lying by the patio doors, rifle in hand, waiting patiently for the bad men to come so she can pop a cap in their ass. I shook my head, "No, I'm not sure he's quite ready for that one yet."

Just then I was called in to get several needles stuck into both shoulders. After I was done, we hurried out and wandered toward a store across the street, where my wife proceeded to pick out a few cute little dresses for me to wear on "vacation."

Once we were back in the car, she queried, "You know, you never told me how that ended. I mean, why did your mom put down the gun?"

"Oh, that," I shrugged. "Dad came home from wherever he had been for the last week and told her it was okay—they had taken care of it." I shook my head, "And before you ask—no, I have no idea what the hell it was all about or what it was *they* had taken care of or who *they* were. I was only nine years old and I wish I couldn't remember any of it."

"No need to get stressed about it now, hon." She shook her finger at me. "You've had years to get used to your messed-up childhood. Use what you can from what you went through, and let the rest go." She grinned at me, "There had to be a reason for it. You know God never makes us go through anything we can't handle even if we suffer for it at the time. Over time, and with the help of people who love us, we find a way to survive." She added while once again laughing at me, "The good with the bad, remember—it's what you're always preaching to people. Balance: it makes the world bearable."

Too true. Once again she had found a way to throw my own ideals back in my face without insulting me in the process. She was right (I realize I say that a lot). It was my religion—the one belief I relied on beyond all others to keep me from giving up, the one thing beyond all others I wanted my daughter to learn. I felt it would give her strength to make it through all the challenges life would present to her. I had been trying to both show it to her and prove it to her since the day she was born. Even when she was an infant I would talk to her about the need for the universe to maintain a balance. Every time something had gone wrong in our lives I would find the good in it and point it out and explain it.

My daughter had proved to be an apt pupil, and, as she began to believe, I could see it helping her come to terms with some losses in her life. Only this past spring when my Baba had passed away, my baby girl had come to me and tried to comfort me by saying, "It's okay, Mom, Baba isn't suffering any more, and we still have each other. Baba taught us that, Mom—that family takes care of family, right? Besides, now we have one more guardian angel to look out for us and to protect us so we will be happier, safer, and stronger."

With that, she had given me a hug and one of her lopsided little smiles, then run off to get back to her computer.

I was reflecting on this as I pulled into the bank parking lot. "You know, Sophia, you're right. There is always a light that shines through the dark. Sometimes it just takes a little wisdom from our family and friends to help us to see it."

"Of course I'm right," she said as she climbed from the car. "Look up the meaning of my name sometime; it wasn't given to me by chance."

We spent the rest of the day rushing around trying to get everything done. We picked up the tickets and Soph paid the balance on my hotel. We rushed through Sears picking through luggage until we found a set that met Sophia's requirements. We must have gone through every set in the department store before she settled on one. She insisted that it be the lightest we could find, explaining that I would probably be bringing some gifts back and had to take that into consideration. She also pointed out that if it was a mundane, common colour it could easily be lost. Of course this is what I rely on my friends for, it seems every time I get a crazy idea in my head to go off on a new adventure they find a way to make it work. We grabbed a quick lunch, did a quick look around the mall for sandals (impossible to find in Toronto in winter), then gave up and headed home.

On the way home, I popped in the Holy Grail CD. "I want you to hear something, but, before you do, tell me what is the one thing I've been saying since we met?"

"You?" she wrinkled her brow. "You keep saying that you are tired, that life has already exhausted you, and that you are more than ready to go home." She looked at me quizzically. "Why, what does that have to do with—"

"Just listen," I said, cutting her off and pushing play.

The song played out while we drove, and when the chorus came on, her eyebrows made a very good attempt at climbing off her forehead.

"Damn, chica, Rev wrote that?" She mumbled, "Girlfriend, you in trouble."

"Don't I know it?" I agreed as the words "Come home, come home, I'm coming home" played in the background.

"It just occurred to me—did you ever tell Rev about that dream you had six months ago?" she asked as I pulled into the driveway.

"No," I said, confused, "Why would I... Oh, shit!"

"Yes, dear, I know..." she said, shaking her head. "And all this time you thought the faceless person in the dream was Deacon." She laughed at that. "Surprise! So, you gonna tell him?" she asked me seriously.

"I dunno; I mean, the whole point to the dream was that he came for me on his own. If I tell him, doesn't that kind of negate the purpose?" I looked at her sideways. "What do you think? Should I tell him?"

"Sure, I can see that going well—how do you tell your newfound soulmate that you had a dream six months ago that involved you sitting on your couch watching a discussion between your current boyfriend and a faceless man you couldn't identify. How do explain that this faceless man came in to get you and sat your boyfriend down to tell him that you really didn't belong to him, that you actually belonged to him, the faceless man?" She arched a brow, "What was it this ghost man said?"

"Um," I looked down a little sheepishly, "That I was his wife, had always been his wife, and had only been on loan, but that it was time for Rey to give me up, so I could go home where I belonged."

"Oh yes, "she purred, "Now I remember: his wife, on loan, go home... right."

"But it was just a dream," I argued

"Oh no you don't," she answered firmly, "You're not getting away with that crap, and you said yourself, at the time, you knew it would happen." She added, giggling, "You just had the wrong guy!"

"Hmmm..." I admitted, "I guess I did at that. I didn't see that one coming."

"Well, now you know," she smiled, "But to answer your original question: no, I don't think you should tell him yet; see what happens first. There may be a time he decides to come back and explain this all in terms Reynard can understand, and, if not, it doesn't change the fact that the faceless man has finally come to claim his bride." She added sadly, "Poor Rey."

"I know," I pouted, "It really isn't fair to him, is it?"

"Well, chica, like I told you, you have to be true to you, or you'll never be happy," she grinned at me wickedly. "Besides, the man is hot, girl—you lucked out..."

I didn't have much time to get back on the road and headed to my brother's, but we took a moment more sitting in her driveway to say goodbye.

"You know, I'm glad you and your brother are back in each other's lives," Sophia reflected. "I think you are going to need him around to support you on this journey."

"Oh, he'll be around," I assured her. "Even in the three years we weren't talking he was still a part of me. After all, he was pretty much the only parental figure I had growing up, other than Baba. He provided pretty much my entire early education in life. Most of my personality traits are his fault. He apologizes all the time for giving me such a jaded view on relationships, but I keep telling him a lot of my strength and survival instincts are wrapped up in those views, so it's okay."

"What do you mean?" she asked. "We have a great relationship!"

"No, woman!" I laughed, "I mean the way I deal with the opposite sex." I gave her a long look up and down, "One of which you are most definitely not. No, he thinks I'll have a hard time finding a life mate who can both understand me and keep up with me. He taught me at a very young age to be free and independent. With Mom being a little off at times and Dad not being around, it fell to him to raise me during the winter months. He wanted me to grow up confident and able to take care of myself, so he drilled it into my head that the only person I could count on was me."

"Ouch, no wonder you are not good on crying on people's shoulders." She pointed out, "Yet, you have some really solid, safe friendships with both men and women. So, how does that work?"

"Oh, well, those people are in my life because they don't need to hear from me every day to know I love them. They let me go my own way secure in the knowledge I will always come back around." I reached over for a smoke, lit it, and blew a puff out the window, "But when you are in a committed relationship with one person, that changes. I mean, the average man isn't going to be comfortable with his girlfriend or wife constantly wanting to go their own way. I need to be with someone who knows I am with them in spirit even when I can't be in the flesh. Theo knows that and he very much fears I will never find that person."

"Do you think that it will happen?" she asked me quizzically. "I don't think such a man exists," she added, laughing.

"Who knows, but either I will find one who will set me free, or I will find one who I will finally willingly get in a cage for. Either way, if I end up happy, like you said, that's all that matters."

"True dat, sister, true dat." She gave me a quick hug. "Have fun, stay safe, and have a good flight okay? Oh yeah," she added, "Say hi to the Holy Grail for me, tell him to stay sexy, and pinch the rump!"

She got out of the car and then stuck her head back in the door. "You're going to experience a lot of things that many do not get to, so enjoy the people, culture, and, most precious of things, life. Your heart will be so full that you will soar above your wildest dreams past the clouds. Just save a little piece of it for me. You may be leaving the country, but know that you are always close within my heart."

With that she was gone, and I would not see her again until I returned weeks later a changed person. Her words, however, stuck with me—a lesson on life and love. As I traveled, she continued to send me inspirational words and encouragement. The emails she sent to me in the following days were full of light, laughter, and love, and they helped to keep me focused on the positive. I have been extremely blessed by her presence in my life. Most of what she tried to teach me to see, believe in, and have faith in, eventually did come to pass, though at the time I had no idea just how prophetic her words would be.

All I could think of that day as I watched her walk up her drive was, "Damn, I have the hottest, sweetest, most beautifully souled wife in the world."

I swung by my house to send a quick email to my boo, but he was one step ahead of me...

Jean Victoria Norloch

Hi, baby,

I had a good sleep. Actually had my first 8-hour sleep last night. Did you already pay for your hotel? That hotel is about 15 km from where I am, but that 15 km can turn into a 1-hour to an hour-and-a-half drive from where I am because of the traffic. I asked my cousin and he said there's Holiday Inn and Crowne Plaza that's closer. Crowne Plaza Galleria Manila, Quezon City or Holiday Inn Galleria Manila—these hotels are 30 minutes even with traffic.

We're going to the gym now. See you on Valentine's =)

I sent a quick note back.

Hey, babe,

Yup, hotel is paid for, but that's okay for this time around—it was such short notice and with no way to phone you to make arrangements I figured it wouldn't hurt just once to live it up a little. If we can find a place closer once I get there, I can see about getting a refund in a couple weeks—but I did get it for cheaper than the regular rate, and since it's a 5-star, it has a gym and Internet access as well as several other amenities that we probably don't need. But it will be fun, so no worries. I wonder if they have mopeds for rent—then 15 km won't be so bad—if you get time look into it.

I have been running full-tilt trying to get all the arrangements made—I got my shots today, just to be safe, and Sophia took me shopping; with everything else going on she still manages to bring me back to reality on a regular basis by making random mundane decisions like buying me a couple new summer dresses so I would have something to wear 4 you if we end up going out on a dinner date. She really is too sweet—wow, what else—um, I have my luggage and, though I still have a huge list of equipment to buy before I come out, I did manage today to get all the pads of paper and pens and all the non-techie writing tools I'll need while I'm there, so my to-do list is slowly getting cut down. I'm on my way to see my bro tonight and spend some much-needed downtime, but I'll check the comp again tonight or tomorrow and see what u r up to—miss ya, xo

I grabbed my stuff, jumped in the car and headed out.

Chapter 13

<u>That's Appropriate</u>

I completely lost myself in the music that was playing on the radio. Before I knew it, I was pulling up in front of my brother's house.

I let myself in and hollered down the stairs to his basement entertainment room.

"Hey, baby, I'm home…"

"Come on down, just playing with my toys," came his baritone reply.

I dropped my stuff in the hall and descended the stairs to find him sitting in this favourite chair toying with his remote. When I say *remote*, I am being a little flippant—my brother is a gadget junky and his idea of a remote control is a five-thousand-dollar computerized device that is wired into and programmed to control every electronic device in the house. He's a smart guy, my bro, and he has spent the last two years completely rewiring his home. He has speakers on the ceiling in every room that are connected to a master stereo that is controlled by his super remote. He also has an extra stereo upstairs that can be separated or linked into the system depending on whether or not he wants different things playing in different rooms. The crazy mini-computer he calls a remote also runs this extra sound system. His massive wall-to-wall screen and projector in his entertainment room, as well as his other, smaller TV (only 106") located in his workout room are also—yes, you guessed it—run by the same remote.

Now, don't get the wrong impression; he's not rich, just very handy when it comes to electronics. I remember the first time my mother brought home a computer—I was about six years old at the time, which make him sixteen—anyway, he took it apart to see how it worked and then put it back together again while Mom was at work. She never found out until years later, and by then it was much too late to punish him for it. He also, at the age of fifteen, wired a headset into his bedroom phone so he could tinker and talk at the same time. His love of electronics led him into the field of robotics, and he now happily (except when his bosses are ticking him off) works as a troubleshooter for a company that makes both electronic and robotic equipment.

As I said, everything he has done to his house by way of improvement he did himself—including renovating and designing my favourite room in the house.

It is my room, he says—designed apparently with me in mind during our three-year separation. Aside from the giant screen and kick-ass sound system, it also has deep burgundy walls with black trim. A floor-length black velvet curtain covers the one and only window. The coffee table is a beautifully carved stone dragon with a glass top, and the wall sconces are little gargoyles hidden in each corner holding little balls of dimmable light. In short, it is the most comfortable room I have ever been in, and it is so me!

He glanced up from his electronic baby and, after giving me an up-and-down once-over, commented, "Good to see my sister finally came back to me."

A little confused, I commented "I came back to you months ago—so what are you talking about?"

"So you did," he said, standing up, "but judging by the clothes you're wearing, the real you, the part of you that makes you *you* has decided to come out to play."

I glanced down at my long, brightly coloured hippie-style shirt. "I suppose she has at that." Then, laughing, I added, "You know, I never noticed…"

"You never do," he added. "Every time you go off down some new adventurous road you revert back to your natural tree-hugging state. I have to keep track of these things, you know; helps me to know which of your personalities I am talking to."

"Oh, yes, well I'm rather hoping this one sticks around for a bit. I think I'm onto something, and she's a big influence in a positive way. I'd hate to lose her halfway through and end up not finishing what I've started." I spread my arms and shrugged. "Besides, she's much more low-maintenance than that other one. It helps that I don't have to spend a lot of time on my hair and makeup—have too much to do."

"Right, well let's get out of here; you can tell me all about it over dinner," he said as he reached down and turned off his system. As I followed him up the stairs, he added "But don't put that other girl too far to the back of your head, you'll need her yet before this is over."

We hopped in the car, and, as we drove off, I reflected on what he had said. I did have two very different personalities.

One is an extremely bad girl who enjoys challenging and confronting the world by doing the exact opposite of what everyone expects. She is a strong, determined spirit who goes her own way, regardless of who it hurts, as long as it gets for her whatever it is she wants at the time. She usually keeps company with other criminally minded individuals who find warring against society as entertaining as she does. She has been known to take over completely at times and wreak havoc on my otherwise quiet existence. She wears tight jeans, tight tops, shows off her cleavage (what little she has), and uses her sexuality to persuade men to do what she wants. She is an extremely dangerous girl; if you threaten her or those she loves she will gladly slit your throat and not waste a second of her day on feelings of guilt. She is manipulative and conniving. She has a vengeful nature and is willing and able to expend a great deal of energy on plotting the demise of anyone who hurts her or gets in her way. All these traits are what have allowed her to survive the various challenges life has thrown at her. She is a nasty, hardened individual and is usually present when life is exceptionally difficult.

However, she can, like he said, come in handy. She knows how to take care of herself, and the walls she has built over the years provide an extremely strong protective shield. The problem is that with her domineering nature it is difficult at times to convince her that she is not needed at the moment. Even after she successfully gets us through whatever rough spot we are in, she boldly clings to her control, and it can sometime take months to talk her into letting go. I do need her, and I have learned over the years to even love her, but, quite frankly, she can be a real pain in the ass.

My core personality, the one who my brother was saying welcome back to, is a creative, spiritual entity who delights in exploration and adventure. She is a gypsy, an explorer of the world and all that it contains. She adores people, animals, and nature. She is an inquisitive little thing who constantly pokes her head into new places and asks way too many questions. Anything new is something to embrace and learn from. She, unfortunately, does not take being tied down very well. She suffers from wanderlust and cannot thrive until she is set free to venture forth into the world without commitments or responsibilities. She usually wears long skirts and baggy clothes. Her hair is almost always tied back, but occasionally, when she is not actually writing or painting, she lets it down.

Her strength comes from an open, honest personality that she uses to draw those to her who will help or support her. She has a gentle warmth about her that people feel very comfortable to be around, and they are therefore more than willing to allow her into their lives. She is an artist, a writer, and a free spirit. It is very easy to love her, but when the bad people come into her world, she runs and hides behind her counterpart. "Her Evilness" takes over, and God help the people who tried to mess with the "Gypsy Princess."

Now, please understand—it has taken me years to come to terms with and learn to manage these two completely opposite entities, and, no, I neither need nor want your damn medication. I have it well under control. The two of us have come to an understanding, and, now that we are no longer battling each other for control, we are quite balanced and at peace with each other. Using our individual talents and personalities and blending them together, we have managed to create a strong, loving, soulful individual who recognizes the need to break free of societal expectations and has the strength and willpower to do it—with the underlying desire to hurt as few people as possible along the way.

Oh yes, I agree it is an absolutely crazy concept, but then I already told you perhaps we should all be committed, and there you were, thinking I was referring to my friends and family. Oh, okay, you got me—I was at the time referring to exactly that.

Speaking of those very people, I would like to take the opportunity to say thank you to all of them for having the good grace to never throw it in my face that I do indeed have a split personality. They have learned over the years to recognize and embrace whatever side of me happens to be facing the world on any given day. I am sure they (friends and family, not my two me's) have had to face their own inner battles concerning my emotional issues. Yet, for some reason, none of them has ever confronted or accused me (apart from Saul, but then, who can blame a man for getting completely confused and stressed out over being married to a crazy lady?). They have never tried to make me be anything other than who I/we am/are—for which I am exceptionally grateful.

Oh, and by the way, I am thinking that you should not fault them for not insisting I seek medical or psychiatric help. Apart from the fact that being left to find my own way has allowed me to make my way here, I am sure the whole journey has been entertaining as hell to witness. I myself would not want to stop watching such a comical show. Laughter does make the world go round, and thanks to my idiosyncrasies my friends have had a lifetime of it.

It is interesting to note that my brother also has an alter ego, whom he refers to as Bob, but that is something we will no doubt explore at a much later date.

When my bro and I sat down at the table, I promised him I would hold tight to my dark side, though I admitted I don't think many people like her.

"What the hell do you care what other people think?" he asked, reaching for the menu. "There are people in your life, you know, who love all of you; as for the rest of the world… screw 'em."

"True," I agreed, "But it has posed enough problems over the years. Look at what it did to my marriage. Saul never could learn to accept what he often referred to as my double life. It's not easy for people to come to terms with."

"No, but that's not what wrecked your marriage, is it?" he asked, glancing over the menu. "What destroyed your marriage was that *you* never accepted it. The problem wasn't him, sis. It was you. Now that you have learned to acknowledge the existence of both of you, you aren't in danger of hurting anyone else through your denial."

Yes, I thought, as he ordered his steak. I suppose he's right. If I am aware of it I can manage and control it. I can also stop trying to run from it and hide it. If I am open with others, then no worries; either they accept me or not. If they do, that's perfect; there will be no surprises down the road and nobody will get hurt.

"Only one problem with that, hon," I said, pointing my order out to the waitress. "There's still going to be one more victim when all is said and done."

"True, true, but if you handle this right he won't get too damaged, and you can both get on with your lives." He glanced at a passing waitress and grinned, "Good view tonight! Listen, Rey's gonna get hurt, yes, but you can't help that now. Just be careful not to do it again—you keep trying to settle down like this, and it's just not what you were meant to do."

"I know." I glanced at another passing waitress. "You're right, the view is good tonight. I just hate the fact that he's going to get hurt at all, though, you know. He's a really good guy; he deserves better."

"Yeah, but you have to take care of you," he said, shaking his head. "I guess, though, that me trying to drill that into your head all these years is probably half the problem. Sorry about that, I really am, but you know, maybe there is a guy out there somewhere who's strong enough to handle being with you." Laughing, he added, "Being with all of you, as you, that is. No more denial, okay?"

"Okay," I agreed, "I will either marry Superman or die single— it's agreed."

He changed the subject. "So you gonna tell me what woke you up this time? Does he have a name? Or is it a she? No matter, really, fill me in on what's going on."

Over dinner I caught him up on everything that I'd been doing; it took the entire meal to do, then dessert, then coffee, and most of the car ride to Future Shop. I went over all the conversations I'd had with various people to give him a better sense of where I was headed. He already knew where I was coming from. I ended my tale with, "But so far the book seems to be writing itself."

As we pulled into the parking lot, he turned to me and smiled, "Well you certainly haven't made it easy for yourself this time, have you?"

"Do I ever?" I answered, grinning.

"Ain't that the truth. But we'll have to talk more later," he exclaimed, looking at his watch. "Shit, it's almost nine. Come on, they're closing soon. I hope your list isn't very long."

When we got into the store it was almost empty, but, given that it was two minutes before closing, that wasn't really a surprise. I had several things I needed, and I would need help finding them all. We finally found a salesperson and I briefly explained what I was looking for. It was very entertaining to watch the interaction between the young sales guy and my brother. The young man would look at my brother and ask a question with regard to the stuff I needed. My brother would shake his head, then gesture to me and say, "You're asking the wrong person—the lady is buying."

The kid would then ask me the question. I'd give an answer, and he'd go off and find what I needed. Yet, when he'd get back, he would direct his next question or comment to my brother, who would again chuckle and say, "You're asking the wrong person— the lady has the money."

This went on for a good twenty minutes before the youngster finally clued in and focused on me instead of my brother. I can understand the mistake; my brother is a rather robust gentleman at six foot two, with striking blue eyes and greying hair that gives his overall appearance an air of distinction. He certainly doesn't dress like he's out to make an impression (something he does purposely to keep materialistic personalities at bay). His quietly confident demeanour, combined with a handsome, distinguished face, has a way of giving the impression to strangers that he is somebody of importance, which of course he is to me—but I know him well enough to know that if he was ever viewed by the general populace that way he would probably fall down laughing.

I, on the other hand, am a very petite, hopefully young-looking female with (as Deacon says) shit in my face and tattoos. Not someone you would immediately recognize as having money, status, or possibly even an education. That's how I like it, though. Let them underestimate me. Let them underestimate me all they want; it just gives me more room to manoeuvre.

Once this young gentleman realized he had been focusing on the wrong person, we actually started to accomplish something. With a little talking, pretty soon I had four sales people running around the store finding me what I needed. My brother stood off to the side watching and giggling to himself, as teenager after teenager came running up with various pieces of equipment. He watched in wonder as one of the sales boys talked me out of buying a phone and instructed me instead to buy one in the Philippines, explaining that it would be cheaper.

I turned to Theo/Bob and laughed, "Did you see that?"

He sniffed, "Yeah, you realize what he just did, don't you?"

"Sure," I answered. "But to which part are you referring—him losing a sale or gaining a guaranteed return customer?"

The activity continued for a good half hour until I had everything I needed. Surprisingly enough, they even managed to find me a computer bag that looked like a hippy-style backpack. Good boys they were, but the biggest surprise was when we were cashing out.

"Listen," said the dimple-faced boy behind the counter. "You had to wait a bit, so I'm going to throw those flash drives you need in for nothing. Okay, we have three eight-gigabyte drives left, and you can have them—my way of saying sorry for the delay. Oh and there's a store wide sale on today so you get a discount, I guess you lucked out, the sale ends tomorrow."

Hey, who am I to argue? I ended up leaving the store with everything I needed, as well as having 20 percent from the bill and my free flash drives. Not a bad night of shopping.

As we were getting in the car, our young helper from inside came out, got into the car beside us, and off he went.

"You amaze me, you know that?" My brother put the car into gear. "You absolutely amaze me…"

"Me?" I asked innocently. "What did I do?"

"Hmmm, let me see," he said as we headed home. "You walk into a store at two minutes to closing, with a list of shit you need a mile long. You somehow manage to get the entire staff involved in helping you out. I mean, Jesus, Vik, they even went rummaging in the back room for twenty minutes to get your voice recorder. Then you get everything you need and go to cash out almost an hour past closing, and instead of the guy being annoyed that you just kept them all there way past closing, he for some reason feels guilty for making you wait, so he gives you free stuff." He was shaking his scruffy head yet again. "Do you not notice the effect you have on people? From where I was standing, it was pretty amazing to see. The funniest part about it is you're not even trying. You don't have to do a damn thing. People literally crawl up your little finger and wrap themselves around it."

"Oh," I admitted sheepishly. "No, I never noticed. I just thought they were being nice."

That sent him into peals of laughter, which he did not recover from until the car was in his garage and we were comfortably seated outside drinking coffee and smoking cigarettes.

"So, it would seem, as I said earlier, that you have set yourself a bit of a challenge," he said mildly. "If I get the gist of what you are telling me, you're proposing to travel alone to the other side of the world to meet a man you just met, but have a past with; not only have you chosen a Third World country, but you have chosen to broach the topic of political and spiritual independence in a country that is dominated by two very powerful factions. On one hand you have the Catholic Church, and on the other you have a politically corrupt government backed by an equally corrupt military. Now, if I get this right, you want to go in there, learn as much as you can from the inside, then come back here and write a book that will both expose the corruption and encourage the people to do something about it. But, wait for it; you want them to do it peacefully and without violence. Oh, yeah, and while you are at it, you want to toss in the idea that the world needs to learn a little religious tolerance and understanding if the human race is going to have a chance at moving toward its next step in its inevitable evolution." He put his smoke out. "Did I cover everything?"

"Yep, that's pretty much it," I said, grinning up at him. "You missed two very important facts, though."

"Oh yeah?" he asked. "What's that?"

"One, I intend to come back in one piece, and two, I have absolutely no idea yet how to pull it all off."

He laughed till he cried.

I gave him time to recover; then I added quite seriously: "I know exactly what I want to do, but I'm at a loss as to how to do it. My biggest challenge so far has been myself. Everyone else seems to have faith in me, but I am having trouble believing I can make any kind of impact. I am a complete unknown and without a good story to back me up I will fail. It's the story I need, the actual content and events that uplift and inspire." I shrugged. "If you have any ideas, don't hesitate to throw them out there."

"You said yourself that the book seems to be writing itself and, quite frankly, if all you have told me is true, then I agree that certainly seems to be the case." He lit another smoke. "So, maybe you should just go out there and see what happens. In this particular case, maybe no plan is the best plan."

"You know, I think Sophia's been trying to tell me the same thing," I realized. "I am thinking maybe I should listen to both of you and stop worrying about it. I have been trying just to concentrate on getting there and let the rest just fall into place, but it is hard not to overthink everything that's happened so far."

"Keep busy. If you are too busy to think…" he trailed off.

"I've been trying, but everything I do seems to be a reminder of where I'm going. I stopped at the bank, and the woman behind the counter, a lady I've never met, spent thirty minutes talking to me about the need for change and her hopes for the next generation. She wasn't Filipino, but her husband is, and they had lived there for ten years. Then I stopped at the drugstore to get a MedicAlert bracelet, and the guy behind the counter started talking about spiritual growth and his hope for the future generation. Hell, he was barely old enough to not himself be part of that future generation—and they didn't even have the bracelet I needed."

"I know. I get what you are saying, but maybe you were just meant to tuck all that information into the back of your mind," he grinned. "I mean, listen—really listen—to the tale that you told on how you got to this point. It is most definitely not your average story. I'm half expecting you to change water into wine at some point, and I'm fully expecting that you will finish, publish, and sell this book."

"You see, you all have faith in me that I can't justify." I looked down at my feet. "Even if what I have to say is important, who is going to listen?"

"They'll listen if they are meant to listen." It was his turn to shrug. "You know I don't go to church, and I don't go in for all that religious stuff, but it would seem you are being given a task, so I would think you should probably stop whining about it and get on with it."

"Okay, okay, enough. Can we maybe talk about something else? I'm getting tired already, and I haven't written a word," I said half jokingly. "How about the weather or maybe the economic crisis? No wait, I've got it. How's your love life?"

"Right, three topics that have been beaten to death verbally. No thanks." Scrunching his nose at me, he added, "How about we call it a night. Okay? You have a lot to do tomorrow, and I have some walls to rip open."

"Sure thing, but I want to check my email before bed, okay?" I said as I walked past him into the house.

Sitting downstairs in my favourite room, I read Rev's latest email.

Jean Victoria Norloch

Hi, baby,

Okay, if you're sure. I don't think you should ride a moped here. Once you get here, you'll know why, lol. The traffic is bad, a lot of people don't follow the traffic regulations, drivers are very aggressive, and the pollution is terrible 'cause half the cars use diesel. If you can talk to your travel agency and switch hotels, there might still be time. If you don't want to go through the hassle, then that's fine.

Sometimes the taxis here are shady, especially to tourists who don't know their way around town. If you want, you could get a car and a driver that my family knows and trusts. To rent a car + driver would cost around $400 Canadian for 3 weeks. What do you think? Just do it for 2 weeks or something. Saves you the hassle of getting a taxi every day. It's a fixed rate, and you can focus on other things while you're getting driven instead of the frustrations of driving around such insane traffic.

We can pretty much get anything we need here at its cheapest rate 'cause my family has been here forever and know the ins and outs. I was thinking of starting a business here that would just earn money immediately. Labour is cheap, and there could be an even stream of revenue.

Keeping my days busy. It's so great here. I drove by where my condo is being built.

So weird. I was hanging out with my cousin's girlfriend and her friend and my other cousin, and they got me talking again, and they told me I sound like I would be an honest president. They drove me to a few malls to get my pictures printed. I think I know where I can get the unlocked cell phone and SIM card, that shouldn't be a problem.

Yes, I'll see you at the airport; can you please give me all the details: flight #, local time of arrival, and airport. Also, can you buy products from online? Like amazon.com... wasn't sure whether you used a credit card or not.

I'm falling in love with this country more and more the more time I spend here.

A lot of the young people have such a passion to fight the corrupt system, but they feel hopeless in finding a channel that will bring back justice. Contacts are coming along well. My mother is hesitant to ask my father for information… I think maybe she's afraid it will jeopardize my safety. I'll ask her again. Hope everything is well; tell Madison I said hi as well. Did you give her the DVD? Xoxo

As my brother seemed to have disappeared for the moment, I took the opportunity to write a quick response.

Hi, sweetie—I am at my brother's right now, but as soon as I get home I will send you all the flight info. My brother and I have had the most incredible heart to heart, and he believes this is what I was born to do, and he's excited for me that I'm finally getting to do everything I've always dreamed of. He really believes life has been training me for this, and that's a really encouraging and comforting feeling. I went w/Sophia today to get some cash, with the intention of getting a prepaid Visa before I leave; I figured it would be good to have with me as an emergency fund. Why? What's up, hon? What is it I should be looking for online?

Let me know what u r thinking—I'm glad u r staying busy, but try to remember to lie low and not draw attention too much. It could be stopped in its tracks before it ever gets off the ground if we are not exceptionally careful, so behave yourself, my love, and try not to get yourself in trouble. When u r talking to your mom, tell her we can come to him and that I have ideas, methods, and contacts that will help get the information and present it to the world without putting a gun to our heads. Safety first—remember u r there to focus on your music and acting, and I am there as your girlfriend to visit you, support you, and learn about your culture and maybe meet some of your people. We r not there for any reason that would spook any locals. Stay grounded, stay focused, and stay safe—the potential of this is too important to both of us to rush it and take unnecessary risks.

We will talk about what direction to go in when I get there, but I have been getting some really concrete and positive ideas in the form of dreams, and I think, once I get to see you and sit down with you, if we combine our ideas, and we go about this the right way, we can take flight with this and really make some changes for the better. But you are right, I think, in your original thinking that first we must open the world's eyes through arts and the media; once we accomplish that, the rest will fall into place as it is intended to.

Can't wait to get there and share your passion for your people and your country—kisses to you, xo

I was checking my daily tarot, and I let out a groan as my big brother walked in with a tea for me.

"What's up?" he asked, setting down the tea beside his laptop. "You get bad news?"

"No," I shook my head. "Just more proof that I'm an idiot for doubting. Don't worry about it. I'll get used to the weirdness again soon. Things have just been too normal for too long. It will take time to adjust."

"Wrong, sis." he settled into his chair. "The only thing that's been too normal for too long is you."

"Right, because me going my own way has always worked out before. Come on, Bob, I always manage to get myself into trouble eventually. Who's to say I won't this time?" I sipped my tea. "I'm bound to make a mistake at some point."

"No doubt, but when you do you, will get back up and keep moving. It's when you let doubt and fear slow you down that failure can catch up to you and bring you to a stop." He looked down into his tea, "Speaking of failure, Vik, about three years ago when you called to tell me you needed me. I'm sorry, kiddo, I—"

"Couldn't handle one more thing?" I offered up a little smile. "I get it. Really, you didn't fail me, and I'm not angry. You'd been through enough yourself, and it ended up working out anyway. I certainly wasn't alone, so stop feeling guilty. I'm here now, and that's what matters, right?"

"Thanks for that—you're the only person I know who gets me. I really am glad you're back; I missed your crazy selves," he said, laughing. "Now, you ready for bed?"

We headed upstairs to the spare room and he got me settled in.

"Don't know if I'll see you in the a.m. I have to leave early, but you can let yourself out the garage, okay?" he spoke from the doorway.

"Sure, no prob," I answered while snuggling into bed. "Thanks for having me for the night and running around with me. The company was appreciated."

"Hey, no worries; besides, running around with you is fun. The way you do things when you are on a mission is amazing—going in a million different directions and somehow meeting in the middle." He turned to go, then looked back. "Organized chaos, that's you. Always has been, and, honestly, I hope you never change."

With that he was off, and I was left to think over my day. If enough people told me I could, I wondered, would I eventually believe? I doubted it, but then I didn't think I had to believe it to do it. It was the doing that was important. I closed my eyes and prayed for another day of good luck and strength. I fell asleep giggling to myself about my daily tarot.

The *Six of Swords* suggests that my power today lies in transition. I have what I need and am willing to trust the process in order to move on, seek refuge or new opportunity. I'm not willing to remain where my perceptions are invalidated, but, being vulnerable, I must rely on guidance to move in a new direction or trust that I can make it or be led to security and new hope. "Wherever you go, there you are." I am empowered by perseverance and my virtue is survival.

Chapter 14

<u>Really? You Name This One (I Don't Have Words)</u>

I would like to say that I woke up and had a normal day—one not steeped in symbolism and intense spiritual conversation. I would like to say that, but I can't.

It started out normal enough. I got out of bed, made tea, and took my time waking up while I wrote a quick note to Rev.

Hey, my sexy baby—I forgot I have not given the CD to Maddi yet, because I haven't seen her—but I did tell her about it and I spoke to Saul about it too. He used to sing in a band back in the day, and I asked him if he would work with her and the CD (he can sing—boy used to give me shivers, lol. His voice is solely responsible for me getting pregnant in the first place, lol) and he said he would do that and he would take good care of the CD, so all is well there—which makes my life a little easier, I have to admit, because it's one less thing for me to worry about. Still can't believe he's supporting me in this, but, hey, I guess maybe we've been divorced long enough that he realizes we don't really have any reason to fight anymore, so it's all good. Gotta go, 'cause I should really hit the road and get back to the city to organize some of my equipment and get to packing. Will talk to you soon, xo

After signing off, I jumped in the shower.

I have to stop a minute to tell you about the shower. Oh, I know, what can be so exiting about a shower? Honestly, though, until you've had one Bob style, you've never really experienced how beautifully relaxing a shower can be. Like I told you, my bro had spent a lot of time renovating, and one of his biggest challenges and accomplishments turned out to be the downstairs bathroom. Not only did he build an aesthetically pleasing environment, he also took the time to do a city-wide store-to-store search for the ultimate shower head. The thing is easily as big as a small plate, and I'm sure it is capable of many settings, but I never bothered to change it; the one he had it one is just fine. He had mentioned it to me the night before, but I thought he had to be exaggerating. I mean, really—getting all excited about a shower.

So, picture yourself standing in a pleasantly warm, fully tiled, big-as-most-closets shower enclosure. You turn on the water and this wonderfully created piece of equipment starts to…

Pour water over your head—come on, what did you think I was going to say? It's a shower—it can't rub your feet or give you a massage, or maybe you were thinking… I'm ashamed of you! Get your head out of the gutter, will you?

After my hour-long shower, I hopped in the car and headed home. I had a crazy busy day ahead of me, so I was in a hurry to get on with it.

As I was driving along, minding my own business, the phone rang. I glanced down and noticed it was the Gospel lady. Two things I should mention: I am horrible with names, so how I remembered hers is beyond me. Also, I have the worst time with numbers. I still have no idea what my social insurance number is, and, given that I am now in my thirties, you would think I have had it long enough to memorize it. How others remember things like bank account numbers, license plates, and friends' phone numbers is something that to this day amazes me. Oh, believe me; I've tried every trick I can think of, even translating numbers to words. I'm lucky if I can remember my new postal code six months after I've moved. Oh, I know what letters go where, but they just have to throw those stupid numbers into the mix, and I'm completely lost because of it. This particular day, however, I recognized the number, and I answered the phone with, "Well, hello, my dear. I've been waiting for your call."

"Allo dahlin'. Did I getcha at a bad time?" came this aged voice over the line.

"No, no love, just driving. Your timing is great," I answered quickly. "So, what can I do for you hon?"

"I'm a justa callin' to see where you at. We is havin' a Bible study, and I was a wonderin' if you is a comin'?" She really is the sweetest sounding lady on the phone.

"Oh, sweets, um, please don't think I'm putting you off, but I'm leaving town in a couple of days and I don't have much spare time." I was trying to sound as positive as possible. I was convinced I was supposed to talk to this woman and didn't want her to think I was putting her off. "How about as soon as I get back?"

"Sure, dahlin'; where it is you is a goin'?" she asked sweetly.

"Well, I am off to the Philippines to start work on a project. I am a freelance writer." I figured I might as well start believing it if I was going to be one.

I was confused by the silence on the other end. Had I said something wrong? Then I heard her draw a breath.

"That's a why you is supposed ta speaka ta me," she explained breathlessly.

"What do you mean, dear?" I asked, curious where this was headed.

She blurted out her answer all in a rush "I worka for CBC in Manila for twenty long. I keepa my people there. I talk to 'em; you go see; they help you … I say you is okay, they speaka to you."

Yeah, right—this was not happening. Okay, well, in case you missed it, let me explain. First of all, a reporter's lifeblood is her contacts and informants. Journalism can be an extremely competitive, even cutthroat business. The money is only in the breaking story. If you cannot get the news first, you do not get the money. Ergo, reporters do not go around handing out their contacts to complete strangers to use—no, not even retired reporters. Informants are usually handed down to a protégé or a younger friend who is still in the business. It can take years to build up a list of safe and reliable contacts overseas. Here was such a list being offered to me by a woman who I had not even met in person.

Secondly, I had never mentioned Manila. It was where I was headed, yes, but I had not told her. Now, one could assume, as it is a major city centre with a large international airport, that it was my destination. Manila is not a tourist area; it's for business trips, not vacation—too much smog and no beach. It is also, however, not a place one would go to learn about the native people and the native culture.

I was temporarily speechless.

"Is okay?" she asked timidly. "Mayhap you is too busy."

"No, no!" I practically shouted. "Not too busy for this. Are you kidding me? This is a huge help. It is amazing. I would be more than happy to make time. No problem."

"Okay, dahlin'" she said placidly. "When you be a leavin'?"

"On the midnight of the twelfth," I explained. "Not very far away, I'm afraid."

"Oh my, we meet soon, yes? Tomorrow? You be busy?" she enquired.

"Nothing too much; my daughter has a hair appointment at 5:00, dinner at my sister-in-law's at 6:00. Then nothing." It would mean a lot of rushing around the night before I left, but hey, that's okay—it would be worth it.

"Dahlin' you comma church 8:00, okay? I give you names and numbers; my friends they help."

She still sounded so sweet. How could I say no?

"Sure, but you'll have to call me later to give me the address. It's kind of hard to write while I drive."

We talked a little more, then agreed to talk again the next morning, and I hung up the phone thinking I was an extremely lucky girl. My phone rang again about thirty minutes later as I was exiting the highway.

"Hey, big bro. What's up?" I asked (gotta love call display). "Did I forget something?"

"Nope, just calling to see how your morning went," came his mild reply.

"Oh man, how did you know to call?" I said excitedly and then went into a brief account of my talk with the Gospel lady. "You know, bro, stuff like that does not happen every day."

"Humph," he snorted. "It doesn't happen to people like me every day, but you, on the other hand…" I heard him mumble something about water and wine, then, "Hey, I gotta know. How did you like my new shower?"

"Oh man!" I exclaimed. "That was so cool. Really, man, I have never had such an incredible shower. It was like being…" But I won't bore you with that, because we have already established what could possibly be exciting about a shower.

I did eventually get home. It was around 10:00 AM, and the first thing I did, as usual, was check my email. Of course he had left a message.

Expect a different world when you arrive. Traffic is crazy. But that will soon be fixed. The reason why I'm asking if you have a credit card is because you need to get a personal air ionizer. It's a state-of-the-art air filter that you wrap around your neck. Literally, if you don't use it here, when you blow your nose after being outside for a bit, you will blow out all black. The pollution here is insane. My cousin has allergies and it breaks out every day. I gave her my air filter, and now she's fine, but I don't have one for myself now and need you to get it online, 'cause you can't get it out here. This is a different kind of pollution than Toronto.

Where we're staying we'll need it. Driving, or flying to the beaches, the air is heaven, but in the city… without proper protection, it will age you like no tomorrow.

Here's the website for it.

http://www.amazon.com/Germ-Guardian-Personal-Purifier-PS-100/dp/B000J153UC/ref=sr_1_15?ie=UTF8&s=electronics&qid=1234048539&sr=8-15

There are plenty others when you search "personal ionizer"—some cheaper, some more expensive. But this one has its own rechargeable batter and I've used it and can attest to its effectiveness. This emits ozone, which can be good and bad. Good when in an area that lacks ozone (like most major cities in Philippines) and bad when there is too much ozone. It works, though; my cousin, who normally gets sick every day 'cause of her asthma and the pollution here in the Philippines, said it helps her a lot.

http://www.amazon.com/Personal-Supply-AS150mm-Clear-Shell/ dp/B000B6CMZ4/ref=pd bbs sr 4?ie=UTF8&s=electronics&qid =1234048539&sr=8-4

This one is probably the best one, 'cause the most research has been done with this one, but the only difference is that it doesn't emit ozone. Some people are sensitive to ozone (which the other one emits) and can get dizzy or have headaches.

My mother still keeps ignoring my question about the origin of my name. Maybe you're right, and we do need to travel to Italy, but we have to talk about that 'cause I'm still focused on getting settled here and making my connections.

I already have a meeting on Tuesday at one of the largest malls in the world, called Mega Mall—lol—Filipinos love their malls, beaches, and food. I wake up at 6:00 every morning, I just finished playing guitar and wrapping up this email... thinking of you a lot. I don't know what will happen either, but whatever does happen, I just hope and pray that our relationship stays strong.

I left him a message of my own.

Hey, baby,

So, I was going to try and save all these little crazy coincidence stories so I would have something to make you smile when I get there—but this one tale I have to tell you now, because it's just too crazy and off the hook to not share right away. You know, while you are over there and weird shit is happening to you, weird shit is happening over here too—random people popping up with ideas and lending a helping

*hand and words of wisdom or just encouragement, but this time it's
like the powers that be sent an active angel my way.*

*It started the day I got my tarot readings that confirmed for me I was
on the right path; I was at the hair salon (yes, I know, weird that my
hairdresser is also a spiritual guide, but, whatever), and right after
she did the reading (remind me to tell you about that, because the
card that made me decide to go to the Philippines literally flew out of
the deck) the phone rang, and it was one of those random phone calls
asking me to come join a gospel study, so, me being me, I told the lady
politely that I wasn't interested and hung up—I mean, it's not that I
don't believe; I just really have a problem with structured religion, as
I feel it puts a box around the true beauty of spirituality and limits
people from realizing their true potential.*

*Okay, so the phone rings again, and, instead of ignoring it (it was the
same number, and usually I would refuse to answer), I get the urge to
answer and take two minutes to talk to this lady. So I very gently tell
this woman: Sweetie, you just called me; I said I wasn't interested.
I asked why she called back, and she said there's no way, because she
never calls people more than once. Apparently, she believes that if
they are meant to talk to her they will; if they are not open minded,
then it's just not their time. So, me, I am thinking:* Wow, maybe
there's a reason I'm supposed to talk to this lady, *and I tell her
that I feel like we have been chosen to connect for some reason, but
as I am in the middle of a hair appointment, can she call me back
(keep in mind this is a random stranger who called me out of the
blue for a Bible study—not something I would normally be open to).
She agrees to call the next day—we hang up on good terms but not
with any set plan. She stayed in the back of my head, but I didn't feel
any urgency for her to call and wasn't worried—figured she would
when the time was right. So I am driving back from my bro's today,
and the phone rings. It turns out it's this lady again, and she invites
me to another study on Sunday night—I tell her that I still feel like
we are meant to talk and though am leaving for the Philippines in
a few days maybe when I get back we can meet up. She asks why I'm*

going—I tell her I'm a freelance writer, and she lets out this gasp, and I can literally feel the excitement over the phone—turns out she worked for the CBC (HUGE) for twenty years and still has all her contacts in Manila (haven't told her yet that's where I'm staying), and asks would I like it if she contacted them and set up a list for me before I go! Okay, so, really, now I am freaking out 'cause—oh my God—this is way too perfect, but also I am running out of time, but I'm driving and I can't write the directions down. So I tell her she is going to have to call me back yet again. Anyway, to sum it up, we are meeting tomorrow night and she is convinced that God sent her my way and that I am moving in a really positive direction and that we will have help along the way if we continue on the right course. So, baby, I hope this story gives you chills, and I hope the hair on your arms is standing up as you read this, because I know I'm getting chills writing it! Gotta run. Play safe, my love—stay safe, my love—I will be by your side very soon. xo

After I was done writing him a mini-novel, I got on the computer, looked up several stores in Toronto that supposedly sold the air filter thing, then started calling around. I only got hold of two stores, one close by and the other an hour away. I spoke to both people and ended up deciding to check out the store closest to me. Out of courtesy I called back the first store and told the very kind gentleman on the other end of the phone that if the store I was going to didn't work out I would get back to him in a couple of hours. He understood and said he would hold one for me just in case.

I jumped back in the car and headed over to Pacific Mall. It turns out the lady at the store had misunderstood what I had wanted. I called up the other guy, asked him what time they were open until, and promised to be there to pick it up before they closed at 8:00 PM. I figured I still needed a few things, so I would wander around and see what I could find. Pacific Mall is very confusing. It is really just a giant building with hundreds of little booth-sized mini-stores arranged in a grid. Half of the signs are in Chinese, so you never know exactly what you are walking into, and the map at the front is also in Chinese. Basically, if you don't have a translator you are screwed.

I began by going store to store. I reasoned the systematic approach would cover everything and I wouldn't miss a store that might have what I needed. It didn't work. I got through about twenty stores and had only managed to find one sweater that I had not been intending to buy. So I changed tactics and took my brother's advice to heart: organized chaos. I walked right past ten stores, then stopped and backtracked into a store two booths back. It turned out to be a jewellery store, and I thought, *Hey, maybe, just maybe, I can actually get my MedicAlert bracelet.* It was something I'd been trying to do for over a week, but everywhere I went they told me the same thing: it's a two week wait; this was not good. I would be long gone in two weeks, and I should probably have something on my body that said: No, DO NOT GIVE HER PENICILLIN—SHE WILL DIE! So I walked into the jewellery store and asked the girl if she had anything that could be engraved. I explained what I needed it for, but she apologized and said she didn't have any. Her sister, however, also worked in the mall, and her store had several such items, as well as an engraving machine. Brilliant! She gave me directions, and I wandered over. I started by explaining that I needed a bracelet that could be engraved and then told her why. So she told me that she could do one better. Apparently, someone had ordered a MedicAlert bracelet, but never came to get it. She and her co-worker had just been discussing whether or not they should send it back. No need, I assured her. I would take it. So they looked up the spelling of penicillin online and told me to come back in twenty minutes.

I went back to wandering the mall, thinking there was no way I would be as lucky with the sandals. It was the middle of winter (well, weather-wise, it was) and every store was filled with boots.

I continued to wander until I felt a pull in a certain direction. Following my instincts, I headed into a store that also appeared to only sell boots. It turns out the store happened to have a back room, where I found a single pair of bronze wedge sandals with rope-style tie-ups. Perfect! They matched almost everything I owned. Even better— that one and only pair just happened to be my size; and they were on sale. Well then, I guess that worked out. Oh yeah, I forgot. The girl working the counter—she wasn't Chinese; she was a Filipina.

Okay, so now I'm thinking maybe I should try to arrange the rose I want delivered to my daughter for Valentine's Day. It is a tradition that my daddy started years ago, since he was often gone from home; he started sending me and my mom a single red rose every year on Valentine's Day. It never mattered where he was or what he was doing, you could count on that rose saying, "Hey, remember I love you." I have kept up the tradition for my own daughter, ever since my dad's death, and I was not about to stop now.

I wandered a little more, randomly picked a flower shop, and walked in. I got lucky. They had this great basket all in purple and red with a giant purple teddy bear (my daughter's favourite colour) and filled with Ferraro Rocher (my daughter's favourite chocolate). Nice! And, yes, they would deliver.

"Oh? You're going to the Philippines? I'm from the Philippines. You'll love it there. Sure, I can throw in a long-stemmed red rose. No extra charge. Yep, we will deliver on Valentine's Day." Then the young man smiled, "Great, thanks a lot. Have a nice trip."

It was time to pick up my bracelet and get my butt back to the house. So far, the day had been a success, and it was only 3:00.

I got home around the same time as Rey did, and I figured, since I still had a few little things like toiletries and stuff, maybe he'd be up for a tour. He was all for it, as he needed to get a rat to feed our snake anyway. Henry is a rather large boa who can get quite cranky when he's hungry. We hopped into the car and headed over to the Scarborough Town Centre. It was 4:30, so we grabbed a bite to eat and tackled my list. As we walked around, we talked about whatever popped into our heads until…

"Did you just say you were talking to your brother last night about your writer's personality vs. your normal everyday persona?" He stopped walking.

"Well, yeah," I shrugged. "But I like to think my artistic personality is my main personality. That other girl can be evil as hell." I turned and looked at him standing there. "Why? Am I freaking you out?"

"No, it's just that," he started walking again. "Well, it's a little strange, because I was reading a short story last night written by Stephen King. It's about this author who switches back and forth between this crazy writer guy and an average, ordinary family man."

"No shit!" I exclaimed. "Really? That sounds pretty cool."

"Yeah, it's a good story, very good story. It's just weird that you were discussing it with your brother around the same time I was reading it." He glanced over at me as we walked, as if asking me to explain to him how that was possible.

"Look, hon," I said gently. "I know you don't believe the same as I do, but, honestly, stuff like that happens all the time. The only reason you are noticing it now is because you've been watching and hearing about everything I've been through in the last few days."

"So, you're saying because I see it happen to you it will start happening to me? No," he said, shaking his head. "I'm not you. I don't think like you do. I'm not connected like you are."

"Oh, hon," again I said it gently. "You're wrong there. We are all connected to the same energies. Some are just a little more aware than others. Actually, to be honest, I'm surprised it took me so long this time to see the signs. I've been a believer for years, but, in retrospect, my mind has been pretty closed since Baba's death, so I shouldn't be too hard on myself. What I'm trying to tell you, though, is that once your eyes are open to it, once you know what you are looking for, you will start to see signs everywhere you look.

"If you say so, but honestly," he asked disbelievingly. "What do they mean? How do you even know when it is a sign? Let alone understand what it is telling you to do?"

"They are only there as guides," I said, giggling. "It isn't like God is going to write a message in the clouds. They pop up most often when we are headed in the right direction. They provide confirmation and reassurance, so we are able to move forward without fear."

"Oh," he sounded dejected. "Well, like I said, if you say so, but I just don't think I can see the world the way you do. I'm just not there yet."

No, I thought, *you're not—but maybe at least now you have a chance of getting there eventually.*

There was no point in pushing it, though, so I dragged him into my wife Sophia's favourite store so I could get some cream for my skin. My wife had introduced a shop called Sephora to me months ago on one of our rare non-work-related outings. It is strange to me that we can be so close, but, for some reason, never actually spend much time together socially. Most of our discussions about love and life take place either on the way to or from work. We can go for months without actually spending "quality time" together. No matter—it works, so why question it?

Now Sophia, being Sophia, is exceptionally picky about what products she uses on both her hair and her skin. She refuses to cut corners financially when it comes to such things. It is not unheard of for her to spend a few hundred dollars on products to straighten her hair. She dragged me into Sephora one day while we were wandering around the mall. It was a shocking introduction into the world of upper-middle class cosmetics. The prices are ridiculous (something Rey did not hesitate to point out), but Sophia insists they are well worth the price. As I am still smoking, I seriously doubt any amount of magic serum will save me from the visible effects of the toxins I choose to poison myself with daily.

I now meandered into this store, dragging a reluctant Rey behind. It only took a moment to find what I needed, and we were at the cash counter in no time. While I was there, I took the opportunity to sign up for the discount card. Part of the application had a spot for my email address, and my hand hovered over the space for a moment while I pondered what I was about to write.

My email *eviloctopus* didn't seem to me to be appropriate any longer. It was the first time I had ever found myself questioning the use of it, but it occurred to me that if I was going to make the effort to write a book or novel with a spiritually uplifting message I should have an email account that had an equally uplifting meaning. So I was standing there, pen in hand, not writing anything, when Rey looked down at his watch and exclaimed "Shit, Vicky, it's twenty to six. We gotta go, if you are gonna make it to that store for the air thing you need."

"Damn! Okay, let's get out of here." I rushed through the form and paid. Then we practically ran to the pet store to get the rat. Luckily we live very close to the mall, so I dropped Rey and the rat at home and then jumped back on the highway and raced to the other side of town.

The traffic was practically non-existent, and I made extremely good time, even though I did get lost for a brief moment. I pulled into the parking lot at twenty to eight, with plenty of time to spare. Yet when I got out of the car and approached the front of the store, I noticed it was dark. The hours listed on the door confirmed what the gentleman had said, 8:00 PM closing. Weird. Oh well; I figured maybe something had happened, and I hoped it wasn't something bad like a family emergency. At least now I knew where the place was. So I decided to give the man I'd spoken to a call first thing in the morning and come back as soon as they opened. Of course, the traffic would be worse during rush hour, but I was more concerned about the really nice guy I had spoken to earlier. He had been so kind to me on the phone. I really hoped all was well.

I decided during my drive home that I would look online that evening and see what kind of email account providers were available. If I found one I liked, I would then worry about finding a more appropriate name to go with my new account. I got home, went into my daughter's room, and began by checking my email.

Hi, baby,

That is indeed a crazy fricken story. Lol—it's weird how God so often lends a hand when you're trying to help his people and are fulfilling your destiny. It seems to be falling into place so well here too. It's falling insanely well. It's crazy... I just know I'm meant to be here, and my studying in Toronto, New York, and everything else in my life has led to this moment. I've been thanking God all day for bringing me here.

I'm going to send you a gmail invite, and I want you to choose a gmail name that suits you. This will redefine your purpose, mission, and destiny in life. I think your eviloctopus *days are over... just a little disturbed every time I see* EVIL OCTOPUS *when I check your email. Hahaha*

Check for my gmail invite, which will allow you to create a gmail. com *account. I won't tell you or demand you choose a specific name. Just one that's the real you. Not one that someone else chooses for you. One that's the true you. The light that's inside you waiting to make a difference. Craving to go home. And persisting for change. Use the first thing that comes to mind. I trust you will feel it in your intuition.*

Your dearest and dearest always.

Apart from the way he signed the email, which even now threatens to make my heart leap out of my chest, I found myself struggling to catch my breath. It was strange enough that he had sent an email at all, given my thoughts earlier in the evening, but when I checked the time on the email I was forced to take time to recover before I could act on it. It was sent at 5:32 PM my time. Well, what's a girl to say to that? I clicked the link and found myself at the gmail site. Now all I needed was a name. I recalled the story Brigitte had told me with regards to her new identity. I decided to go back to the site I had previously found online explaining the meanings and purpose behind the names of the archangels. If one of the names leapt out at me, I would claim it for my own.

Out of the names that were listed at the top of the page, *Gabriel* really grabbed my attention. It was the only one that started with G, and I reasoned that as Rev had chosen gmail, maybe I should take a hint. So I clicked on the link and read about Gabriel.

Meaning: *"Strength of God"; "The Divine is my strength"; "God is my strength." The only archangel depicted as female in art and literature, Gabriel is known as the messenger angel and is one of the* *four archangels named in Hebrew tradition, and is considered one of the two highest-ranking angels in Judeo-Christian and Islamic religious lore. Apart from Michael, she is the only angel mentioned by name in the Old Testament. She is a powerful and strong archangel, and those who call upon her will find themselves pushed into action that leads to beneficial results.*

Gabriel can bring messages to you, just as she did to Elizabeth and Mary of the impending births of their sons, John the Baptist and Jesus of Nazareth. If you are considering starting a family, Gabriel helps hopeful parents with conception or through the process of adopting a child. Contact Gabriel if your third eye is closed and your spiritual vision is therefore blocked; if you wish to receive visions of angelic guidance regarding the direction you are going in; if you wish to receive prophecies of the changes ahead; or if you need help in interpreting your dreams and vision.

Gabriel helps anyone whose life purpose involves the arts or communication. She acts as a coach, inspiring and motivating artists, journalists, and communicators and helping them to overcome fear and procrastination. Gabriel also helps us to find our true calling. Ask for Gabriel's guidance if you have strayed from your soul's pathway and if you wish to understand your life plan and purpose. She can also help if you can find no reason for being or if changes are ahead and you need guidance, or if you are contemplating a house move, major purchase, or thinking of changing careers. Call Gabriel if your body is full of toxins and needs purifying and if your thoughts are impure or negative and need clearing and cleansing. Gabriel is also very helpful if you have been raped or sexually assaulted and feel dirty as well as being under psychic attack, or if you feel that you have absorbed someone else's problems.'

I am guessing I don't need to explain why, after reading all that on *Angel Focus*, I chose to embrace the name. I felt I had been given an incredible gift of a second chance. Keeping with the theme of *G*, I settled on gabrielasgift. Understandably, I was

Jean Victoria Norloch

not surprised when the name was available. As I clicked *send* to complete the process and acquire my new identity, I offered up another little prayer of thanks.

I sent Rev an email entitled "last email from evil o," explaining the entire story and including a link to my new address.

Hey, hon,

Wow—you need to stop reading my mind—or maybe it was your idea and you were sending me ideas I was picking up on, because, while I was out getting some more stuff ready for the trip, I was thinking that the days of eviloctopus *have come to an end—I mean, it's not really a good networking name, right? Funny thing was, I hadn't decided yet what email account I was going to go with, and I was going to come home and check out what's available. Instead, I got home and you had already sent me a link—all good, hon. I set it up—my new address is* <u>gabrielasgift@gmail.com</u>*—I actually got the idea from that other random lady I told you about the other day. I will tell you the story when I see you, but her business name is* Auriel's Touch*—named after the archangel Uriel, who is the bringer of courage to those beginning a new journey. I figured I would check out the archangels' names and see if one suited my purpose, and it seems that Gabriel would be fitting. I have always thought that it was one of the most beautiful names. Apparently Gabriel means "God is my strength." Gabriel is the angel of child conception or the process of adopting a child. Gabriel also helps anyone whose life purpose involves art or communication. She is the defender of the element of water and the west; the angel of resurrection, mercy and peace, and benefactor of* messengers! *Gabriel will help you with purity, rebirth, creativity, prophecy, and purifying your thoughts, bodily and emotionally. She is patron angel of all who work in the field of communications. I think you will agree that it fits.*

I guess I will be sending you email now from that account, so watch for the name. I will write again soon. xo

I sent the email and, before logging off and heading to bed, I checked my daily tarot.

> The *Queen of Wands* suggests that my power today lies in liberation. I radiate or communicate personal power, passion, and allure and am not dragged down by trends. I have a bold, magical flair and a spirit of innovation and pride. I am secure in my identity or performance and thrive on creating, designing, or fostering new or equal opportunities for aesthetic or personal growth, expression or awareness. I am empowered with gratitude, attention and reputation to go beyond the call, and I transform through exploring or initiating change.

This time I didn't groan. I smiled a satisfied, content, grateful smile. looked up at the heavens, and whispered "thank you" to the God who I was now completely sure was listening.

Chapter 15

<u>Mistakes, Miracles, and What it Means to Know God</u>

Should I bother commenting on my morning routine, or should I just jump straight to the email? Okay, email it is!

My Lady, very nice.

Yeah, I've studied the archangels a bit. Love the name.

Can you bring another ionizer? My other cousin has problems when he wakes up here, too. I'm thinking of just MASS importing a bunch of those here from China, I don't know how they would sell, though. I think if you educate the people on their benefits and educate them still on the side-effects of NOT using them, people would buy.

The meeting with the director went really well. So bizarre, because he's an inspiration to me through all his movies and the themes of them; yet, when I talked to him he told me that I was inspiring him. I have to watch two of his movies; then I'll meet him again.

If you see or talk to Sophia, tell her I already found a place to get her bags, hahahaha

I had a nightmare… but instead of dwelling on it like I used to, I got out of bed, shook it off, told myself it was just a dream, and converted the story to paper. Now I'll use it for my fictional story.

I found some hotels that are much, much closer. I looked at the hotel, though, and it looks nice... maybe you should stay there. Live it up, you know—you deserve it.

I have another meeting today. As long as you humble yourself to them and don't treat them any lower than you, they'll treat you like gold. They've been oppressed and repressed for so long... and still, in those living conditions, you see them laughing and with smiles. It's quite powerful.

I'll pick you up at the airport on Saturday. When you bring the ionizer on the plane, keep it in your carryon bag with your laptop. Keep it turned off until after the plane takes off and keep it on throughout the entire flight; it will help you with your jet lag. Put on your headphones, too, when u use it. Some airlines don't allow it, but if they think it's just an MP3 player, you're fine.

Always yours, R

Really? Well, I suppose I should be used to it by now, right? Wrong! If you are one of those people who, like me, can see the cause and effect of seemingly coincidental occurrences, then you will probably agree with me when I say that I honestly hope I never get used to it. If you cannot understand that statement, then let me explain. When you live your life in a manner that allows you to follow the paths laid before you, every new day is a new adventure, with wonders around every corner. Like a small child, I am able to look at the world with eyes wide with wonderment and see the vast power and beauty in even the tiniest, drabbest parts of this remarkable place in which we live. There is warmth and light in all the things that surround us: people, animals, and nature. Call it God's light, if you choose, or the power of Mother Earth; either way, it exists when you open your heart to it and will fill you with hope for a better, more peaceful tomorrow.

Don't get me wrong. I am also, unfortunately, very in tune with the pain and suffering that exist here. It comes from being a fairly strong "empath"; yet empathy breeds compassion, so, although the abilities I have can sometimes cause pain, I am grateful for them nonetheless. It is not easy to feel others' pain, anguish, or negativity. I certainly don't enjoy the constant struggle that comes with each new invasion of emotion. I am a bleeding heart, so every time someone hurts I tend to tune into it, hoping to draw some of their pain away. Of course, their pain really should not be able to hurt me, but, if there is enough of it, it can be uncomfortable. I also try to stay away from confrontation if I can (me not Evil she thrives on it). If you add an empath into the mix when two people are arguing, the negative energy tends to flow much faster and build much more quickly. The negative energy literally bounces off itself in a continuous cycle. It is rather like the starter in your car; the magnetic energy continues to cycle in on itself until it builds a powerful enough charge to start your engine. Of course, the process is exactly the same for two people who are not particularly tuned in or empathic, but it is a slower building charge, allowing time to avoid the inevitable explosion. The worst case scenario is two strong empaths who are not aware of their abilities, as awareness breeds caution, which allows the outcome to be controlled. If, however, there is no awareness, the results can be catastrophic in nature. I have actually had a few no-holds-barred fights with others like myself in my younger years, before I learned how important it is to pull back. These were memorable, and every single one of them led to irrevocable emotional damage. Even while I mourn friendships lost, I know those moments taught me lessons I would later need, so I cannot bring myself to regret them.

There is as always a positive side, for, as dangerous as the pain and anger can be, the joy and contentment of others can be an equally powerful experience. Those who are at peace with themselves and their surroundings can be like a soothing balm to my at-times-tortured soul. As long as I focus on the positivity of the energy being offered and make sure my own troubled spirit does not affect the giver, then I am able to make use of others' purity of thought to heal an injured heart. This is also reversible, which is why I have constantly exposed myself to others who are unbalanced, willingly putting my own peace of mind at risk in order to ease their torment. It is partially how healers work, drawing negative energy from a person and replacing it with the positive.

Next time you find yourself in a confrontation with someone, instead of continuing to feed them the anger you feel, focus instead on giving them love; you will be amazed at how quickly they come around to your way of thinking. They will likely never know, in fact, how it is you managed to get them to change their minds; they might even believe it was their decision. I caution you, however, not to do this merely to get your own way; it will backfire, as it is not a tool that selfish people can use effectively. You must be truly interested in not wanting to hurt the person you are fighting with for it to be completely effective. It is a learned skill in some, an inborn gift in others, and something the world as a whole should explore the use of. Taking in someone else's anger and feeding that person love and understanding is a potent, powerful way to maintain balance in both your own life and the lives of those you care for. Try it—I promise you will not be disappointed.

As for ever getting used to the ever-present magic that this wonderful indestructible energy brings to my life, I pray that I will continue to be amazed and grateful for every strange, mystical occurrence. I fear the loss of these things in my life; if they were gone from my world, as strange as they sometimes make my world seem to be, I would much prefer my holographic existence to the reality that society deems it necessary to embrace. I think if these things were ever stolen from me it would very likely destroy me; fortunately, I do not believe in "reality" any more than the average person believes in "magic," so I doubt it will ever be an issue.

As for all of you out there who know exactly what I'm talking about, look up to the heavens and shout it out with me: "THAT WAS SOOOOO COOL!"

This is, of course, exactly what I did; I looked up said to myself, "That was so cool," then I took the time to answer his email.

Hey, my baby,

So weird—I just got your email now about getting one more—thing is, I already drove all the way out there (it's at 400 and Rutherford Road, so long way), but, get this, I talked to the guy like 3 times today; he knew I was coming late last night; each time we talked he reassured me they would be open till 8 pm, so I leave early, take a wrong turn, have to double back, and still I manage to make it there for 7:40—but no guy—doors are locked. I guess when you want something you get it, eh, because now I am going back this morning, and I will be able to get an extra one. Things just seem to be completely out of our hands (well, mine anyway, lol).

I'll let Soph know about the bag—she is spoiled, eh? What was your nightmare about? You are supposed to be having good dreams— maybe u r supposed to use it in your story. Like I said, if we are able to change the hotel when I get there, we will—but if I keep this one we will also have somewhere to escape to if we want alone time. As much as I would love to be beside you every minute of every day, I doubt, with all you have going on, that it would be possible, even if I was a few minutes away—though I am not sure I am comfortable with doing any exploring on my own. Is all good? We can figure it all out when I get there, right?

I'll call the guy for the ionizers this morning—hopefully he has three. I am one day closer to Manila and one day closer to some adventuring with you—talk soon. xo

So, email sent, I went about the task of getting him his ionizer; funny that the second time I drove out there it was so foggy that if I hadn't already known exactly where I was going there is no way I would have found the place. It would appear my trip the night before had been not without purpose after all. When I got there, I found out the owner had indeed been indisposed due to some kind of family emergency, but the clerk assured me that all would be well and thanked me for my concern. After a brief discussion on how the ionizers worked, I left with yet another busy day ahead. Granted it was only 9:30 AM, but I would be picking my daughter up at 3:00, then be off to the sister-in-law's for dinner, and then finally go to meet the strange woman and partake in a Bible study. The whole concept, I must admit, was a little daunting for me. I remember studying the Bible when I was young, at my mother's insistence, and, of course, I had done my time as a Sunday school teacher while in high school, so I was more than familiar with its contents—but I was aware that the people I would be meeting were more than merely familiar, they knew its contents intimately.

Now, you may be mildly curious as to why, when I am so interested in spirituality and religion, I would not take time to read the Bible and learn its contents. As I said, I have read it, though it has been years since my last legitimate study of it. That little adventure was one undertaken in my later high school years, and it was done from the view of somebody not merely looking to learn from the words written but somebody who was also looking for the flaws. As I have said before, it was written by man and man is fallible. There are several instances in the Bible where the stories are not complete or consistent, and some of the stories are riddled with contradictions. Truth to tell, if one were to study it in that manner, they would no doubt find more than enough evidence to make them question the validity of the whole thing. However, in saying that, I believe in what its lessons stand for, and I do, without a doubt, believe in God and the strength that comes from knowing him. My views, however, do not always mesh well with the Christian community, and though I speak to God on a regular basis, I cannot quote scripture, and by no means do I lead a pure life. Admittedly, one could point out the last two weeks as an example of divine guidance and intervention, but, for every person who believes that I have been guided, there will be one who says that my flaws and lack of study of God's word put me in jeopardy of saving my soul. Regardless of your own personal views—views which I myself choose not to judge—you have to admit the evening will be an interesting one!

All of this was in my mind as I drove back to the house to make a last-ditch effort at packing. Of course, I could not go on with my day without a quick check of the email—even if at the moment I had no real time to answer anything he wrote.

That is pretty amazing lol.

Yeah, the nightmare is probably just something I can use in my book and script.

It only becomes reality when you dwell on it. The constant energy you feed your thoughts can materialize them, right, so... I'll just see it as fiction. My mother's dreams seem to materialize, but mine don't, and neither do my nightmares... now I know why I get them, then. =) They're so I can write realistic events and know the feelings of them without them actually happening. It's so weird—my mother's nightmares and dreams actually come true. She had a dream of me standing in front of millions of people and talking and also dreams of my face on billboards all over cities. Who knows! Lol—I don't know… they haven't materialized yet.

I got lost in the mall today, and my whole family got so scared.

Anyway… just finished watching American Idol *with my cousin, and it compelled me to practice.*

My cousin's fiancé said he would drive me to the airport. So, see you then.

xoxo

Interesting thought, that: speaking in front of thousands of people…

Glad to know it was him she saw… to be quite honest, better him than me. I rather like my quiet existence and do not enjoy the prospect of ever having to talk to a large crowd of any kind of people. The idea terrifies me to no end, so if God is kind (and I have seen evidence that he is) then he will never ask it of me. Of course, if it is where this strange path leads, then who am I to question? I will do as I am expected when the time comes, but if I can ask for one thing for myself, it is that I be left alone to wander and explore the world and the people in it without the interference of the public eye. Leave me with my quiet life; the world not knowing my name suits me just fine, thank you.

Oh, right—how can I hope to write a book, publish it, and still not have any kind of fame… Well, we'll get to that later, but I am hoping against hope that that is what I'll be able to do. I guess, as with all things in life, I will just have to wait and see how that works out…

The next hour was not really overly exciting, which was a very nice change. The trip to pick up my passport was quick, and

I soon found myself back at home, staring at my suitcases and wondering what to put in them.

While I was yet again wandering around my house, with a lost look in my eyes, it occurred to me that during the last two weeks I had not called the one person who would probably be most interested in what I was about to do—not interested, perhaps, in the writing or the reason for the trip, but more interested in the fact that I was taking a trip at all. And here now enters into the tale a woman who has stood by my side for twenty years, no questions asked. Regardless of what I have done, where I have gone, or who I have chosen to spend my life with, she has always stood by me. She was my tree, my strength—my Lina.

If home is ever to be found in the existence of another, then I have found home in Lina.

She is the quintessential redhead: she has a fiery temper and is willful, stubborn, strong, and independent. Yet, for all of those things—some of which people have viewed as flaws—she is also loyal, giving, loving, supportive, and honest—if she decides for at any reason to pass judgment on the actions or decisions of anybody in her life, she is more than honest about that judgment. She will quite openly tell you exactly why she thinks what you've done or are going to do is wrong, and then she will look you in the eye, smile, and tell you to do whatever you want—she will still love you in the end and catch you if your current stupidity happens to cause you to fall. She is a remarkable individual, really, and given all that we have gone through and done together, it is a wonder we have not yet managed to kill each other or ourselves. We're two strong-willed women, yes, who have managed through mutual understanding and respect to maintain a friendship that spans twenty years of life-changing experiences, moves, and personal growth. God willing, there will never be a day when the woman is not in my life. To me she is a tower of strength on a stormy day, the tree I seek shelter under when it pours or when the light of the sun gets too hot; but she is also my most entertaining friend, and it is for her I smile more easily than anybody else (apart from my daughter, that is).

Our relationship is twisted; at times she is an incredible tease, so when she found out a few years back that I have in the past had girlfriends, she made it a ritual to try to tease me as much as possible when I am visiting—not verbally, you understand, but physically. It was only after she discovered my weakness for the female flesh (oh, really, like you are surprised—honestly I have not had a girlfriend in years, nor do I intend to pursue that particular avenue again anytime soon. Truthfully, I much prefer the company of men, thanks, though the female body is, you have to admit, remarkably alluring). Lina got into the habit of changing in front of me, brushing my lips with gentle kisses rather than kissing me on the cheek, and hugging me, at times, in a little too—hmmm, how would you say it?—oh, *friendly* manner.

The thing is, she is straight as you can be, visibly shuddering at the thought of sleeping with a woman. It's funny, since she supports anything anybody else does and refuses to condemn anybody for their personal choices when it comes to sexuality, but she would not venture into that realm herself if her life depended on it.

Her teasing has gotten the attention of several others—friends who laugh uproariously when she gets going; it seems she doesn't much care who is in the room when she decides to test our friendship. I only refer to it as a test, since she is so straight; really, she has to know that I wouldn't ever dream of crossing that line with her, but she continues to offer unspoken promises of a physical relationship. Like I said, she is a tease, and the whole thing sends those who know us into uncontrollable fits of laughter when she takes the teasing to greater heights in public. Regardless of all of this, we will always remain extremely comfortable in each other's presence. There really is not much in my life she does not know about, and, as to those things I haven't shared with her, it is only because they are inconsequential or I simply haven't had time.

She still lives in the area in which we both grew up, refusing to leave the place, as it keeps her close to her family. Her mother is her main concern, and I can't blame her; the woman is hard not to love, really, and my friend's dedication to her is not unwarranted. Of course, it doesn't help that my friend is also terrified of flying, so, whether or not she will ever travel the world with me, it is an unspoken rule of our friendship that I will wander wherever life seems to take me as long as occasionally I make it a point to wander back her way into her comforting arms, to share with her in person whatever adventures I have had. And, no, you will never meet her—as much as she no doubt intrigues you, she also is an extremely private personality who would crumble from fright if she thought the public knew much beyond the fact that she exists.

She has plagued me for years with the question: When will you come home? (in reference, of course, to the town in which she now lives) and I have promised her many times that when the end is near I will find my way back there to live my last years out with her. I can promise her no more than that, and I dearly hope the powers that be allow me to fulfill that promise in the end. I have asked her many times to join me some day on my ventures, but still she refuses, which is not really a surprise, as she won't even spend more than an hour in a car; she claims it makes her too sick. Personally, I think maybe she just gets bored.

Really, there is not much else to tell about this incredible individual, except that we were hellions in our youth, both determined to get into as much trouble as possible, and we were arrested more than once for stupidity that should have never happened.

I remember one incident that resulted in both of us having to do community service over the theft of lawn chairs—yes, I know, who the hell steals lawn chairs? But, at the time, we needed them—no, really we did…

We were at a field party out near one of the local towns, and there was nothing to sit on, so my friend and I wandered into the closest settlement of new houses and borrowed a few lawn chairs from various backyards. Now I use the term *borrowed*, because we fully intended to return them the next day; however, we woke in the morning to the smell of burning plastic and discovered, much to our dismay, that the boys who had stayed up all night by the fire had run out of wood and were now contentedly stoking the failing fire with our chairs. Of course, since we had taken them, *we* took the blame for the whole thing and soon found ourselves having to go to court for theft of chairs. Stupid, really; we were both given community service and ordered to go to a class on the repercussions of theft and the effect it has on society. How embarrassing, really, to stand up in a group of people and admit you are here because, yes, you stole lawn chairs. Still, to this day it is a running joke with some of the people who knew us then, and my friend and I can laugh about it now; I mean, it's been years really—we were only fourteen at the time.

Lina tells people still that I was the ringleader then, and, I suppose I can admit it now, if trouble was found and we were involved, chances are it was my rambunctious brain that had thought it up. People grow up and they change, and, though I would not take back one single moment of time spent with her or take back any of the crazy silly things we did, I can't see myself ever having the desire to do any of it again. Still, I view it as the process called growth: we live, we steal lawn chairs, we learn.

I now chose to call this remarkable lady, just to let her know I would be out for awhile. I should have called her sooner, and I told her so on the phone, but she reminded me—without mincing words—that it really had no effect on our relationship, since I don't see her every day anyway.

"Oh, for…" Waves of exasperation and red-headed attitude came through in her voice, "What are you worried about; you hardly see me now anyway, and we talk maybe twice a month, not counting text messages. You'll be back soon enough; just do me a favour, and don't get killed, eh; you promised to come home some day and I'm holding you to that. Oh, and say hi to my goddaughter, eh; tell her I love her and you, too, so stay safe."

That's it really; she didn't have anything else to say—not *why*, not *when*, just: *don't get dead.* Again I make the claim that my friends *are* odd… but, again, I have to take the time to acknowledge how blessed I am by their presence in my life; it has become a daily ritual for me to look up to the heavens and say thanks.

Phone call done, I took a moment to drop a quick line to the man on the other side of the world.

Hey, hon,

I got the ionizers; I could only get two, as that was all they had, but when I leave I can leave mine behind for one of your cousins. I also picked up my passport today, so I am all set. I still have to pack, but at least my running around is done. It's so weird: everyone I talk to down here, even just random strangers at stores and the bank, are so excited about this trip. They always ask if I will come by when I get back and share some of what I've written. I've been telling them I will; I just hope I remember them all when it is time, but then, I suppose it will be hard to forget them, considering some of the crazy conversations I've had with them about this trip. It will make fantastic material and it's the kind of "No way, that did not happen" story that will suck people in.

I still have to pack, but I am sure I'll be as ready as I can be come tomorrow night. For now, though, I have to run; still so much to do. Sophia sends her love and her pinches, lol—can't wait to be there. xo

That done, I jumped in the car and headed off to pick up Madison. When she finally found her way to the car, she asked what our plans were for the night. I explained about the last couple days and my need to go the Bible study that evening. I asked her if she wanted to join me and realized she was very hesitant to answer. I reassured her she did not have to go if she didn't want to, but I made a point of asking her why she would prefer to stay home on our last night together.

"Oh, Mom, it's not that I don't want to spend time with you, really." She looked at me briefly and then turned her head back to the window. "It's just that, well, I don't go to church, and I've never read the Bible, and, well…" She paused here, as if gathering her thoughts, then blurted out in a rush, "I won't be comfortable there; I don't see things like they do, and I don't understand most of what they are talking about."

I could understand her point, but at the same time I was a little confused by one particular thing.

"But, hon," I asked gently. "You believe in God, right? So how is it you think that you don't see things the way they do?"

"Of course I believe in God." She shook her head. "I don't know how to explain it; I just don't think I'll be comfortable."

She paused again for a few minutes, and I was hesitant to push her; she might only be eleven, but give her enough time and she can put together some pretty well-thought-out explanations.

"It's like this, Mom; you know the story I told you when I was younger about what happened when I was born?" Her voice sounded a little distant, as if she were remembering something.

And I did indeed know the story, but thought perhaps it was one she herself had forgotten. The last time she had spoken of it had been when she was five years old, and I had never mentioned it since, thinking it was not something we needed to discuss. I am sure the idea of her telling me anything about the day she was born sounds a little unrealistic, but, as we have already explored my views on reality, you should not be surprised by anything I say. The story is indeed an odd one, and I will tell it to you briefly, as she told it to me at the tender age of five years. I can't for the life of me remember how the subject came up then, but, as you read the next few lines, try to keep in mind that this is coming from the mouth of a little girl who has been to church maybe a total of seven times in her short life and a few of those times were weddings not services...

The story she told me of her birth also requires a little back ground into the troubles that surrounded her birth. My body apparently does not like the task of bearing and delivering children, as we discovered much to our dismay while we were into my second day of hard labour. I could tell you the entire tale, but I doubt very much it is really pertinent to the issue at hand, so I will be brief. Basically, childbirth almost killed both me and my child, and though I was blessed after three days of labour with a healthy, beautiful baby girl, it would be weeks before my body would begin to recover. How my daughter managed to survive two days in the womb after the water had broken has never been explained to me by anybody other than my daughter herself. The doctors certainly did not have an explanation, and I can't seem to find anybody else who supports the notion that it is possible. Yet, by some miracle, it happened, and it was to this miracle and her remembrance of it that my daughter now referred.

At the age of five she had explained it to me in simple five-year-old's terms. Basically, she claimed that at the time of her birth she was scared that she was going to die. She remembers very clearly knowing that something was terribly wrong, and she also remembers not wanting to die. She claims also that shortly before she was born, God came and spoke to her, telling her not to be afraid, that she would be okay and that he would take care of her.

Seriously, that is what she told me, and, no, I do not question it. Would you? I mean, who am I to assume that it did not happen simply because she was only an infant? Who am I to assume that her recollections of this thing could not be real? To her they are very real, and it would be faithless and ungrateful of me to try in any way shape or form to sway her belief in this. How many five-year-old children can look you in the eye and say they talked to God?

Believe what you want; me, I choose not to doubt. She believes, and so I believe, and it was with that belief in mind that I now waited for her to finish her thoughts.

"Okay, so you asked me if I believe in God, right?" she again glanced over at me, "and you know I do, but you are asking the wrong question."

Oh yes, I know she's eleven; its okay, I deal with it all the time, really I do. I think maybe, in time, you will get used to it to.

"You should be asking me *why* I believe, not *if* I believe." As usual, she continued to stare out the window of the car as I drove, and, as it seemed she was waiting for something, I took the obvious next step.

Simply, I asked her, "Okay, why do you believe?"

"Oh Mom, that's easy, really; I believe because I know he exists." She turned to me and gave me an impish little smirk, and then her face became serious. "I have seen the proof of his existence; I have seen miracles happen; I was saved by a miracle, so I know he exists, and I am grateful to him for saving me. He let me live—how can I not know he exists?"

Okay, so you can picture me driving along, both hands on the wheel, eyes round as saucers, and eyebrows climbing up to my scalp, right? Nope, not this time; there was no shock on my part, just a mild curiosity as to where this was leading. I have to say, at times like these I am grateful for the long ride home after school; it allows for the most unique discussions.

"Alright, so, if you believe, why in the world would you think you would be uncomfortable around people who also believe?" Leave to me to ask the silliest of questions, assuming that I knew the answer.

"Oh really, Mom." She managed to sound patient and exasperated at the same time, quite the feat coming from a young girl. "You said that it's a Bible study; I've never read the Bible, so how can I study it with them?"

At this point she looked at me yet again, and her eyes were very clear and bright and the impish smile that I know and love so much had again returned to her face. "It's simple: I don't know the Bible; I only know God."

With that, she turned her head away and went back to staring out the window, lost in her own thoughts. The discussion, it seemed, was over for the moment, and I was left, not with a feeling of awe, but a quiet contentment about what she had said.

It occurred to me as I drove that if you have a question, and you really want to know the truth, you should ask a child.

Chapter 16

I Am Who I Am, and I Can Only Be Me

I will not bore you with the details of dinner with the family, except to say that it is good sometimes to take the time to appreciate the small things—like a casual spaghetti dinner with the people who matter most to you.

Nor will I give you a detailed account of all that occurred during the Bible study. I will, however, include the lesson that the gentleman who ran it prepared, so that you may see what was discussed. I will also highlight one particular discussion that stood out and the lesson it contained. First the lesson plan.

Observations about John 19

INTRODUCTION

- *"Behold the man!" "Behold your King!" (slides) Interesting parallel statements by Pilate. What did they see? Isaiah 53 tells us. Let's read it. So what did they see? (Click)*

- *And what do we see when we look at Jesus? Paul tells us what he saw in Hebrews 12:2: Let us fix our eyes on Jesus, the author and perfecter of our faith, who for the joy set before him endured the cross, scorning the shame, and sat down at the right hand of the throne of God. Consider him who endured such opposition from sinful men, so that you will not grow weary and lose heart."*

> *We see a PERFECT, GLORIOUS EXAMPLE of how one man endured incredible suffering and shame in the service of God.*

- *Every time we partake of the Lord's supper, our Lord Jesus is giving us the opportunity to LOOK at Jesus, to behold him at this ultimate moment of sacrifice, faith and humility, and endeavor to be more like him, to submit to our wonderful loving King.*

- *We will be using today the gospel records to behold our Lord in his time of suffering, along with Isaiah 53, Psalm 22, and Psalm 69.*

BEHOLDING THE MAN

- *Jesus "turns the other cheek," not even saying a word in his own defence.*

- *Finally, he speaks in private to Pilate, letting us in to his thinking process, the source of his strength: "You would have no power over me if it were not given you from above. Therefore the one who handed me over to you is guilty of the greater sin." Jesus acknowledges in word and, more importantly, in action that no matter what is being done to him, it is his Father's will, and therefore he can accept it.*

- *Lesson for us: HOLD YOUR TONGUE/ACTIONS WHEN YOU FEEL YOU ARE BEING ATTACKED/MALIGNED*

- *Being able to truly "turn the other cheek" when we are put down, physically or verbally, especially in public, is extremely hard, because of our selfish pride—we want to defend our honour amongst our peers. We feel, rightly or wrongly, that the other is trying to destroy our reputation in order to raise themselves up, and we want to fight against it in our self-righteousness.*

- *But Jesus, even though he KNEW he was in the right, encouraged us to keep the highest outlook: not to look at it as another person doing something to you, but to look at it in the light of faith: your*

Father is causing you to suffer so that you can be made perfect. Whatever you are going through, it is your Father's will you go through it.

- *In Psalm 22, Jesus says it is God who brings shame and suffering upon us, for his loving and righteous reasons, and God we must turn to to save us from it.*

- *Another hint as to how Jesus managed not to lash out at his attackers with his God-given power appears in the gospel of Luke. In addition to his God-centred perspective, it was his overriding care and concern for others that held his baser emotions in check. Jesus had an amazing ability to get outside himself, even during great suffering. How did he do it?*

- *Jesus said in Luke 23:34 "Forgive them Father, for they know not what they do."* FOR THEY KNOW NOT WHAT THEY DO. *Jesus demonstrated an* UNDERSTANDING *of his attackers—he put himself in their shoes and acknowledged that they didn't truly realize that what they were doing was wicked. In fact, a few of them probably did, to greater or lesser extents, but Jesus refused to judge them as having evil motives. He acknowledged that every one of us, even the ones that appear the worst, are fundamentally the same—we are all fighting hard internal and external battles in life. Jesus identified with the battle that raged within him as well as his attackers, and actually felt camaraderie with them, even if they didn't with him.*

- *Jesus' concern for others was primarily, but not solely, focused on their eternal well-being—he demonstrated concern for temporal and emotional well-being, also, when he provided for his mother and when he mourned for the coming terrors the citizens of Jerusalem would have to endure at the hands of the Romans.*

- *Jesus taught us through his example, many times in his life that, although we are ultimately concerned about the kingdom of God and human salvation, true agape love commands that we be aware of human suffering in this life, and let it affect our hearts, instead of remaining aloof from it—weeping with those who weep, visiting the sick, feeding the hungry, and providing water for the thirsty. And, regardless, how can we expect anyone to listen to a message about an abstract hope for the future if they are dying of thirst right now, or have not known the comfort of being loved in the first place? Providing for the material and emotional needs of our fellow man is not just being a blind, bleeding heart; it is the right and godly thing to do.*

- *But, of course, the ultimate concern continues to be people's eternal salvation, and Jesus' words on the cross bear this out as well.*

- *In addition to using the words of Psalm 22 to help him keep a divine perspective, Jesus used them to actually continue his ministry of proclaiming the kingdom of God right to the last. He kept his mind on his JOB, his LABOUR OF LOVE.*

- *Now we come to our Lord's last word on the cross, and we feel a tremendous sense of relief with the words "It is finished," and, in Luke 23:46, "Father, into your hands I commit my spirit."*

- *This is further evidence of the fanatical drive to see his task of loving service through to the end. But not only was this a relief for our Lord, to finally rest after three and a half years of pushing himself to the limit in service to his Father; these words should be to us a joyful victory shout, for with them our Lord put to death his sinful mind and opened the way of salvation for all mankind.*

- *Romans 5:12-21; Psalm 98, read!*

Now, whether or not you are a Christian, there are good life lessons to be learned from these scriptures, but it is up to you to explore for yourself your own truth. As I have said many times before, it is not for me to decide for you what you wish to believe. I offer a view of what is out there and offer the idea that the truth is out there for each individual to find—but how you find it or what road you choose to take on your journey is not for me to decide.

However, I also believe strongly in the base messages that Jesus taught: *love and compassion for your fellow man.*

If you take nothing else from all that I have written or will write, then I hope you can at least accept that as being the most important life lesson you will ever learn. Love and compassion— they will allow you to move forward in your life with a smile in your heart and a spring in your step and to acknowledge that all other humans are fundamentally the same as we are. They suffer as we do, love and fear as we do, have hopes and dreams as we do. Remember these things. Embrace the idea that all your fellow men wish is to also be happy and to not suffer. Do what you can to help them in their quest for happiness and inner peace. This does not mean judging them or trying to change their ideals; that, my friends, is not our job. It means simply finding within yourself the courage to love and respect even those who would harm you, the courage to feel the pain of others, and the commitment to working toward relieving that pain. Whatever path you must follow to learn that lesson, whatever messages you receive, in whatever form helps you to see that as being true—those messages are the ones you were meant to see, the lessons you were meant to learn, and they will not be the same messages from the same source for all people. Our world is vast and ever-changing, our beliefs are varied, and our backgrounds are different. Far be it from me to say which belief system is the right one or the wrong one—as long as it is a positive one that is based on mutual love and respect for your fellow man.

Now that I have said my piece, I will explain a bit about one of the discussions during the study.

As I listened to various people in the room speak, one thing came to my attention. It was that some of them felt an overwhelming sense of sadness at the idea of Jesus being sacrificed on the cross. I was confused by it, and I took the time to tell them so. I explained that though I could not quote the scriptures, I understood their content and the message therein. I also explained that I did not think it was meant to bring sadness to their hearts, but rather to lift and inspire them. I told them that the idea of Jesus's death was to free men of past doubt and guilt for their sins, so that they could move forward with love in their hearts and continue to grow spiritually. I do not believe that if a person dwells on past mistakes and therefore spends time wallowing in self-pity and self-hatred that he/she can look at the mistake objectively. We are human, and, being human, we continue to make mistakes—but we must learn from those mistakes and take the lessons learned from them, using those lessons to move us forward in life. Those lessons help us to grow spiritually, and it is those lessons and spiritual growth that encourages our evolution as humans. Yet, how can we possibly see the lesson if we are blinded by fear, anger, and doubt?

I asked the people in the room, "Can't you see that it was with a great amount of faith in humanity as a whole that God was willing to sacrifice his only son? How can the idea of that much faith and hope for humanity make you sad or despondent? Is it not a message of hope? Is it not meant to free your heart and allow you to heal yourselves through faith? How then can it make you sad?"

I was amazed at the discussion that followed and the response that came from these questions, and I sat back for awhile, shaking my head at the idea that those these people believed in the Bible's teachings and spent hours a day studying them, yet some of them did not see the positive message contained within. I admit, of course, that I am no expert, but when I read the stories contained within the Bible I find messages of love, compassion, and hope, and I see no reason to be saddened by the sacrifices made by others who were sent before us to spread those messages. They willingly gave of themselves for the sake of future generations, and their stories should inspire others, for if the message of love is important enough to die for, then perhaps it is a message that we should latch on to and listen to.

The discussion that followed included my belief that we ought to have love and respect for all our fellow humans, regardless of their personal beliefs, and I was surprised at the willingness of some of the members to hear what I had to say. I expected, I suppose, to be shut down the moment I spoke of the idea that it is really the same God sending the same message over and over in different forms. I also was very clear that I do not much care what people call their God, as long as that God shelters them, protects them, and guides them to love and have compassion for their fellow man. I expected quite honestly to be rebuked and accused of going against the content of the Bible, and I was prepared to stand up for my beliefs—yet, surprisingly, I was accepted in spite of what I believe, and there was a good hour of positive, open discussion with some of the members.

Again, I maintain that the same message has been sent to us through other means, through other faiths, and through other religions for thousands of years. It continues to be sent to us in various forms: in literature, films, music, and all forms of creative art. Again, I will not tell you which of these belief systems to follow, but I will tell you that when the message comes to you, in whatever form it is sent, it is for you to listen and explore the truth behind that message.

All in all, it made for an interesting evening, and I left the place feeling very uplifted and inspired. I took the time afterward to call both my brother and Deacon to share with them my experience and I couldn't help but giggle at their individual responses. Of course, my brother thought the whole thing tremendously entertaining.

Leave it to him to giggle at the thought of me standing in a room full of Christians and openly declaring my beliefs without regard to whether or not they will persecute me for them. Of course, Deacon's response was expected; he simply wanted to know what the hell I thought I was doing trying to convert a bunch of Christians. I laughed at that, really. As I explained to him and am trying to continue to explain to everybody else I meet and talk to, I do not wish to convert anybody to anything. I only want to open their hearts and minds to the possibility that there is a much greater power at work in our world, one that desires for us to learn certain truths and is continuing to send us messages to help us find those truths.

I feel I have to point out here for any Christians who may be reading this book that if they doubt what I say, then they should please read Romans 13:8–14, as well as Romans 14. For those of you who are not Christian, please do for me the favor of taking the time to partake with me in one minor experiment. Over the next few days, spend the time to consciously be aware of your thoughts and actions toward the people you share your lives with and the people you encounter on a daily basis. Do not look at them as you see them physically, but rather see them for what they are: fellow humans who wish only to find happiness and be at peace. Take the time to share with them as much positivity as you can manage, simply by showing kindness, understanding, and acceptance. Give to each new person you meet a sense of well-being and love. Smile as much as you can, and when you look around at your life, take notice of and feel appreciation for all the little things in your life that make you smile. Try it for a little while, and see where it takes you. As I have learned for myself, and, as I hope you will also learn, the more love you give out, the more you will receive; the more positivity you share, the more you will encounter. Do these things out of concern for all living creatures; do them with an open heart and open mind and see where the experiment takes you. See what comes of doing for others instead of yourself; perhaps it will open your eyes to the beauty that exists here and provide you with hope that that beauty will continue to flourish.

After I had shared my experiences over the phone, I also took the time to send Rev an email.

Hey, hon,

Hope you are sitting down when you get this one. I sent you the story of how I found (or rather how I was found by) the lady that worked for the CBC out of Manila, right? She called me today to confirm that I would go to meet her tonight at this Bible study group for her church—again something I would not normally do but felt compelled to follow through with. The meeting was at 8 and I got there early, but she wasn't there yet, so I got to talking to some of the people there and kind of getting a feel for them. The Bible study starts and still no lady—but, hey, I jump in anyway. Now I am surrounded by 15ish people of different racial backgrounds (white, Asian, Indian, black) and they are all over 50, but, as the study continues, I realize that the topic of the night pertains in a big way to both our (yours and mine) views on religion, spirituality, and the need for change—so I offer a couple comments, but I openly explain to them that I am not a denominational Christian and I don't know the Bible well enough to quote certain scriptures, but in light of my own personal experiences I can put what they are discussing into a more realistic and earthly context. (I will so explain this all in detail when I see you in person). As I am talking, people start to get involved in the discussion, and, rather than spouting phrases like "but the Bible says," they begin thinking more in terms of the stuff that happens to people every day and how it relates to the teaching of the Bible. Keep in mind I have already told these people I do not study the Bible the way they do, but rather have studied it in passing, along with several other religions over the years. So, the study session wraps up on a really positive note, and we are hanging out having tea, and people begin to approach me, asking questions about my views, and about my trip and about my (our) ideas for this story. So I'm explaining that I view religion as a conduit for the fundamental life lessons that people have to learn in order to grow spiritually, but that I do not believe that any one religion is necessarily the "right religion" and that given that we live in a society where (especially here in TO) we work and live shoulder to shoulder with others from different racial and spiritual back grounds and yet somehow manage to have respect for each other's beliefs—then is that a stretch to be willing to study other religions with an open heart and open mind and look for the common vein in all of them—the base teachings that are geared toward bringing spiritual growth to each and every student of all religious and spiritual back grounds? I point out that maybe it is time for the world to stop arguing about whose God is the one true God and focus on the meaning behind the belief in a higher power—and OH, WOW!—THEY LISTENED! It was incredible—here were these hardcore Bible-studying Christians opening their minds up and willingly wrapping their heads around the ideas I was presenting—not all of them, of course, but enough to make me sit back and really think about what I was doing there. They were making comments like "I wish I could see it the way you do" (that was an 80ish-year-old white granddad) and "what you say makes sense—makes the teachings we study more real" (again 80ish, but this time African woman) The gentleman who led the session asked me to come back when I get back from the Philippines, and more than one of them asked if I would be willing to go talk to their church group located in Manila if they sent me the contact info via email. One man offered to contact the group in Manila and let them know about me if I would be willing to go speak with them—I mean WOW—it was incredible—so crazy incredible, and not something I had ever seen myself doing until tonight. To top off the story, on my way home I got a phone call from the lady who had sent me there in the first place (she never did show up) and she told me her friend from the study group had called her and thanked her (THANKED HER, LOL) for sending me to them. She told me that right around the time she was supposed to leave for the meeting there was a power outage, and her entire street went black, and she felt safer staying at home, as she wasn't sure how widespread the power outage was or even if the subways were working near her area. All she knew was that her street and surrounding area were dark, and she felt compelled to stay home. She wasn't even able to call me until the power went back on, as her cordless phone would not work without power— her power went back on right about the time I was leaving the church, so she had gotten the call from her friend and then called me right away. I know the whole story is CRAZY, but, baby, what a strange, wonderful end to a really powerful two week. If you are experiencing as many crazy things there as I am here, then, baby, the book is practically writing itself. I so can't wait to see you and talk to you and explore all this (your stories and mine) in person, but, he, if I go to this church in Manila, will you come with me? Think on it; I think you should—I think maybe that is part of the reason you are there. They say God works in mysterious ways, but this past two weeks has been way beyond mystical for me—so much to do—so much to say—so much to share—so excited! See you soon, my heart. xo

Well, I guess that pretty much sums it up for you.

Of course, as you can expect, I went to bed feeling exceptionally hopeful and excited about the upcoming trip. The previous two weeks had opened my eyes to a whole new world of possibilities. I now neither worried about or feared where I was headed, but, rather, I was determined to enjoy the ride. I checked my daily tarot, of course, before heading off to bed.

The *Four of Pentacles* suggest that my power today lies in possession. I choose not to be bound, identified, or paralyzed by ownership, possessions, or means, in order that I may always have a free hand and room to grow. I am practical, responsible, and determined about protecting my purpose or advocating for my resources. I am empowered by the status quo and my asset is value.

Right, well, I think that's enough said for the moment.

Chapter 17

<u>Taking Flight</u>

One of my favorite numbers is seven, and so it is no surprise that it is the seventeenth chapter with which I end up taking flight.

I checked my email in the morning before I began packing.

Hi, baby,

Excited to see you, too. Manila Bay is close to your hotel; maybe we'll go check that out on Valentine's. I just finished watching my director's movie. It talks about foster children and the system here. I love his movies 'cause they're socially engaging.

Have a safe trip. That is pretty amazing. It's true; most people will respond to the truth that way—only some who are blinded by fanaticism will not see the true light. That accounts for a good chunk of the world's population.

See you soon.

Safe travels, my lady

That's it; that's all—a simple wish for a safe journey.

Was I excited? Hell, yes, you bet—but the day, to be honest, was completely uneventful, so rather than bore you with the "I packed this, then that, then the other…," I will instead use this as an opportunity to explain what you will be experiencing in the following chapters and how the letters you will be reading came to be written. Oh, but first my tarot for the day, in case I forget later to include it.

> The *Lovers Card* affirms my alter ego is a port key to a soul mate, or deal, whose superpower is compatibility in the midst of reconciling dichotomy to interconnect as a whole new entity or "color." To be or not to be: with ultimatum or rival tensions mounting, negotiating acceptable trade-offs validates our unique perspectives to reflect what each lacks for a balanced voice of truce. When we're together, I'm beside myself, so I concede mutual vested interest, incentive, or opportunity to my other half for valued consideration. For only by the power of self-respect in reciprocal vulnerability, need, and compassion do "me and thee consummate we." The rest is all a dance on the sidelines of Cinderella pandering, or prohibition, or around a Bermuda Triangle of bottom-line temptation to cheat by provocation, promiscuity, or shame. But here at the gate of impasse, I still have a choice and my pride.

Well, given where I was headed and how I felt about the man I was supposed to be meeting there, I guess it fits perfectly, doesn't it? So I feel I need not say any more about it.

Now, you have not met the person I will be referring to next, and I feel I need to explain why she plays such an integral role in this tale. She is another long-time dear friend with whom I share many mutual beliefs. I had visited with her for two days and explained about my upcoming journey. I enlisted her help as both a researcher and first copy editor. You need not know much about her, other than that her name and mine are the same. Her middle name is Rose. She is a Christian/wiccan (shocking, isn't it?) who has managed to marry the two spiritual beliefs and use from each the positive teachings she claims are very evident in both. If, in the future, you need to become more intimate with her, then I will accommodate. All you need know at the moment is that she is somebody whom I love and trust. She is also somebody I happen to have a great deal of respect for. She is an information magnet, and her abilities as a researcher have helped me more times than I can count as I wrote this book, so it only makes sense that she is in my heart as I wrote the letters you are about to read.

It was my intention originally to just write about what happened and include those experiences in the form of stories buried in chapters. What happened instead was that I ended up keeping a daily log (sometimes more than once a day) of my trip and the events that took place. All the letters are exceptionally personal and from the heart, as they are being written to her, so I ask that you please understand and have respect for the fact that this is a very large piece of my heart and soul I am about to lay at your feet.

I will ask only that you read them all with an open heart and open mind, given the content of some of them, and not take offence at what you read, but, rather, allow it to arouse in you the curiosity that I hope will inspire you to continue your quest for your own personal truth.

Honestly, there is not much more to tell at this point, and I might as well get on with sharing the actual trip with you; although, before I do, I suppose I owe you one more daily tarot. As I left on the twelfth and landed on the fourteenth, I spent the thirteenth in the air, and, since the tarot for that day is more than appropriate, I think you should be given the opportunity to read it for yourself. Keep in mind that it was written for the very day that I was on a plane flying toward my future. Though I had absolutely no idea of what that future would be, I made the trip with full confidence that it was where I was supposed to be at the time.

The *Star* suggests that my alter ego today is the Goddess, whose superpower for rising to the occasion lies in my innate ability for inspiration. I will pursue my dreams and what makes me happy—life's too short. I will allow time for me today. I may even get my fifteen minutes of fame by seeking recognition from others and striving to sparkle in the limelight. I am immortal! Sometimes it's better to burn out than just fade away. Find your cosmic groove, and go for it!

Well, my dears, it has been a great honor sharing these past experiences with you, and I thank you for being gracious listeners. The next time you hear from me I will have another viewpoint altogether. Although up until now I have been talking to you, the reader, directly, from here on out I will be directing my words to another. Remember that they are from the heart, and that I wrote them with the awareness that the reader would probably be listening in, so please do not feel left out. All I say in them, and all I share, I do willingly and with a heart I am unashamed to bare to the world. Godspeed, my friends, I will talk to you very soon.

"All major religious traditions carry basically the same message, that is love, compassion and forgiveness ... the important thing is they should be part of our daily lives."
Dalai Lama

"If you judge people, you have no time to love them."
Mother Teresa

"I believe in the fundamental truth of all great religions of the world."
Mohandas Gandhi

"The essence of all religions is one. Only their approaches are different."
Mohandas Gandhi

LETTERS TO BEANER

February 14, Hong Kong Airport

Hey, sweets,

Originally I intended to spend the flight out writing, but what can I say?—my body was screaming at me to sleep. Have you ever tried to sleep on a plane, especially flying economy?

Right now I'm sitting in the airport in Hong Kong, waiting to transfer. I already changed my clothes and freshened up, as it is twenty-three degrees here, but—go figure—the air-conditioning is on, so, even though I'm in the other side of the world in a tropical climate, I'm still freezing.

I'm trying to kill time, surrounded by Asians, and I can't understand a word they are speaking, but they are all friendly. I tried to get hold of you to tell you my crazy story from the night before I left, but you no answer. I could write it all out here, but I want (no, *need*) your feedback. When I called my bro to tell him he again mumbled something about changing water into wine.

The sun is starting to come up here; feels like a new life is dawning along with a new day. Did you know that 90 percent of the population in the Philippines is Christian? Considering my views and my hopes for this book, the next three weeks should be interesting.

I have made contacts in Manila through that random phone call, and once I tell the conclusion to that tale (maybe it is the continuation), you will agree, I am sure, that I am probably meant to meet some of them. I am thinking we will be boarding soon. It's almost 7:00 PM here, which makes it 6:00 AM there. I doubt we will be back in time to the hotel for me to call you today. I know Rev wants to try to get some time in together before we go exploring with his family.

We can't even let them know there might be anything more than friendship. Their traditions are very strict, and it would be seriously disrespectful to go against them. He says that in time, once they get to know what kind of person I am, they will welcome me with open arms, but for now, no public displays of affection allowed. It's too bad, but probably for the best.

Well, hon, I'm gonna get my shit sorted, put the book away, and hopefully I will be talking to you soon. Play safe. xo

February 15, patio of the Heritage Hotel, Manila, early morning

Hey, Beaner,

Okay, so now I'm sitting in the hotel restaurant, and it's been one full day since I arrived, and I am still in shock over actually being here.

These people, baby—wow!

They have so very little and live such simple lives. Okay, maybe not so simple (they are hungry, their city is dirty and polluted, and the traffic is insane)—but they are happy. I mean, living in TO we don't have nearly as much smog, our traffic is less, and we have so many more amenities—but we're angry and dissatisfied. Yet here there is a feeling of peaceful contentment and acceptance.

They have a saying here in their native tongue: *Bahala Na*—it means literally "leave it to God."

Strange to think that they could live their lives day to day with a constant struggle for survival hanging over their heads, yet they have no inner fear. Maybe it is because they feel they have nothing to lose, but I think it is more than that.

I've only been here for one day, so I know I have so much more to learn, but if and when I get a chance to talk to these people, I am positive it will only confirm for me why they live the way they do.

When I arrived I was picked up by Revo and his cousin's girlfriend. They were so incredibly sweet to me. They helped me get settled in; they wouldn't let me carry my own luggage or even open a door. One of the girls is named Alya—the same name as the boss who randomly brought Rev and me together. She told me when I first arrived that the Filipino people are the best hosts in the world, and I believe it. I gave them all the soaps and candles I had brought. They were very surprised but definitely pleased. I also gave one girl one of the cards you had made (the one with the man putting a ring on a woman's finger). The girl I gave it to is getting married in July. She had tears in her eyes. I told her I had picked it out without knowing who I was getting it for, but that I knew now that it was meant for her. She seemed very touched; even though they are upper-middle class (which is to say they are much better off than most here), she was still flattered by the gifts. I think because they were made by a friend they meant more than anything I could have bought in a store.

After the gifts and a quick chat, the girls left Revo with me and ventured off home. I unpacked a little and then had a shower. Revo went wandering off to the gym. At first it was strange to be here with him. As I said, out of respect for tradition he has not told them about us, but, even though we displayed no open signs of affection, I think the two girls saw something there. The first chance we got to be alone, we talked. Amazing—since he's been here for two weeks, you would think the physical would come first, but not him. He is very focused and open with me about his hopes and dreams, so, instead of a dangerous, lustful reunion we had a comfortable, communicative reunion. (Don't worry, princess, the passion is still there, but it is not a priority or even a need, and I can't remember a time where I was more content just to be in somebody else's presence—not male anyway.)

No matter. I am going far afield from my story. After my shower we went to a mall, located not far from my hotel. Buddy, this thing was *huge*! I mean you could easily fit three or four Scarborough Town Centres in there. We wandered around awhile before deciding to get something to eat. Revo insisted I eat local food, so we had two rice dishes made with cow's tongue and mushrooms, as well as this other dish (it is kind of a cross between a soup and a sauce) made with oxtail. Surprisingly, it was all very tasty. After we ate, we wandered around the mall some more and talked. Though we had both promised ourselves to quit smoking, we ended up giving in to the cravings and going in search of smokes. We could not find one store inside that wonderful massive complex that sold cigarettes.

After questioning the locals, we ended up making our way down toward the water. We found ourselves at Manila Bay (it was a place he had wanted to go, but he hadn't known where it was). It was a giant boardwalk down by the water with little restaurants and food kiosks every couple of feet. It was the weekend, and the place was packed with locals; apparently, it is not really a tourist area but more a spot where locals go to hang out. You could see the shock on some of their faces at seeing a little white girl wandering around aimlessly, but it wasn't the kind of shocked stare that makes you feel you shouldn't be there. It was more a sense of "What the hell?"

This place was packed with people, kids everywhere running around, and every few feet there was a guard with a machine gun. Rev explained that the mall was privately owned and so, by extension, was the walk down by the water. Since terrorism by revolutionaries is always a threat here, the guards are a necessary expense to protect the owner's investment. If people do not feel safe when they go shopping, they will simply shop somewhere else—simple concept, really. Again, though there was no feeling of being threatened, in fact the guards blended in so well with the atmosphere that I didn't even notice them until Rev pointed them out to me.

As an empath yourself, you can understand, I am sure, what it feels like to be in a situation where everyone is either angry or afraid. The spiritual drain from that kind of atmosphere is extremely damaging, and it can leave you feeling exhausted and weak. Now, imagine for a moment entering a world constantly threatened by violence and poverty but still feeling a sense of inner peace and security from all sides. It's a contradiction, is it not? I mean, it's not something you would expect, not even something you would think could be possible. Yet, here it is reality. While I wandered around down here, the only feeling I could pick up that could be considered anything close to negative was a feeling of confusion mixed with a little guarded caution from the locals when they glanced my way.

Don't get me wrong; on the surface they are very welcoming and friendly, but I can tell that they are definitely wondering what I am doing here.

Okay, for now, I am going to wrap this up. I will find another patio later today and complete the tale, but for now I have to work on finding my way around this hotel. Maybe I will get a pedicure (my feet look horrid, and this is most assuredly sandal kind of weather), so, my dear, wish me happy wanderings. I'll talk back at you soon. xo

February 15, patio of the Heritage Hotel Manila, lunchtime

I'm back; I spent a bit of time checking on my email and looking up a bit about St. Lucia. Now all I have to do is talk Rev into going.

I also booked a spa session, manicure, pedi, and facial and am now back on the patio having lunch. I'm thinking of staying around the hotel today to get my strength back and get centered and focused. I ordered a glass of wine, and, as it happens, their wine of the month is one of my favorites—life is good.

Okay, so I left off with our wandering the boardwalk. While we there Rev pointed out a building that one of their (Filipino's) previous corrupt leaders had begun construction on. The story goes that this particular leader was in such a hurry and cared so little for the workers that the leader pushed them well past the point of exhaustion. In their tired state (the workers), they began to make mistakes that resulted in the catastrophic collapse of one of the upper floors, which killed almost every worker on the site. The person responsible for these people abandoned them and the project, never even bothering to extricate and provide proper burial for the unfortunate victims. The building remains to this day unfinished; locals refuse to enter it for fear of the spirits that still linger there, trapped on our earthly plane by their anguish at their untimely demise. Now, please understand this is only as the story was told to me, and I pass no judgment on the truth of this tale, nor do I pass judgment on those who were supposedly responsible for these people's deaths. I was not there; I do not have all the facts, so, therefore, I cannot fairly judge. I do, however, feel deeply for the people who suffered the loss of loved ones, and I hope that they have managed to find peace since the time of the accident.

Rev was absolutely shocked when I asked to go there. As I said, he is young yet, and though he is very intelligent as well as intuitive, he has much to learn—but then, my dear, we all do.

I feel a need to explore the site, feel for myself what is there, and perhaps gain some guidance from who may still linger. It would also be nice to offer some kind of consolation to them and try to get across to them the hope for a better day. I would reassure them that they did not die in vain and that their memory lives on, and that the memory shall forever remain as a lesson to those that follow—a reminder of where greed can lead us.

After this, we wandered back to the mall, discussing politics and religion, expanding on our previous discussion about our hopes for this book.

I should point out that we have now agreed to focus on both the political and religious repression that overshadows Third World countries. We have also agreed to focus our attention on the lessons that repression and corruption can teach us and society. For now, though, I should be focusing on our adventures.

We did eventually find our way back to the mall. I was wearing heels (silly, I know), and though I had already promised myself I would not buy anything from the big department stores, my feet were killing me, so I really had no choice but to search out some sandals.

I told Rev though that in the future I would rather make my purchases at local markets, so that the money would go directly to the people and not to the larger corporations. He said he didn't know where to find one, but one of his many cousins would.

(As a side note: the club sandwiches here at the hotel kick ass in a big, big way—they are so good they are addictive!)

While we were at the mall, Rev told me that I can probably get some money for stuff by using my bank card. I hadn't had a chance to exchange my Canadian coin, and though Rev had been paying for everything so far, he flat-out refused to pay for the shoes. Too funny, really—there is apparently an ancient legend that is all about what bad luck it is for a man or woman to buy shoes for their other half. He could not remember the legend itself, as he heard it told at a very young age, so I cannot tell it to you; he did, however, remember the lessons behind the legend. Thanks to that story, though, and the superstition that is attached to it, I now know that if I get stuck I can access my bank account through the machines here.

I swear, every time I need direction or information it comes to me in the strangest ways. Even answers to little problems or needs seem to be provided before I even realize I actually am in need. Amazing how that works, really, when you think about it. I guess the trick is not to think about it at all but just believe that is the way it is, and the rest kind of falls into place.

We got the shoes and then headed back to the hotel.

We hung out a bit in the room, while he read one of the books I had brought with me. The book was on the Freemasons and the Solomon Keys. (Coincidentally, he wears Solomon Keys around his neck as well as carrying a templar symbol surrounding the two opposing triangles that represent man and woman)

Anyway, we eventually ventured back out. I wanted to get some snacks and drinks to keep in the room, and we had been told there was a store just down the street. So we went around a corner and, holy shit, wouldn't you know it—the market I wanted was right there in front of us. It ran for blocks, every single thing you could possibly want or need was being bought and sold by locals. Again, they seemed very shocked to see a little white girl wandering around in a hippie skirt. Given that it was very late at night, well after dark, and the fact that it was obviously a place tourists very rarely go, I'm not surprised at their surprise.

The people selling things were not wealthy by any stretch, and, when I asked Revo later if it would be there during the day, he explained that they probably all had other jobs during the day and only came out at night to try to make enough money to feed themselves and their families. And families there were: kids everywhere, mothers nursing babies, grandparents resting in chairs by the stands; some were even catching some sleep while people shopped around them.

Revo kept telling me to watch where I stepped; it was very dirty on the streets, and I had to constantly reassure him that I am not a porcelain figurine that will break the first time I fall.

The children, as I said, were everywhere; they were playing with each other in the streets, using empty cans and other pieces of refuse as balls to kick around and chase each other with. It could have been a sad experience: the children were very poor, covered in dirt, and barely clothed (I even saw one child sleeping curled up on the steps of a local store), but, even with all of that, they were very obviously not neglected. Not emotionally: the people here love and revere their young; though they cannot always provide for them in a material sense, they shelter them by giving them love and affection in an otherwise harsh environment. There is nothing more beautiful to a child than the comforting arms of a parent. As I said, it should have been sad, but it was uplifting; there is so much Western society could learn from these people about love and compassion. Their family values are stronger than anything I have ever experienced, and, if others could only think the way they do, perhaps we could learn to care for each other in a deeper sense.

We wandered for about an hour; I purchased some fruit and was swarmed by a group of very dirty little children begging for money. Rev explained they were probably working for the syndicate, the underground crime organization that runs the underworld in the Philippines. I didn't give them any money, because he told me it would just go back to the crime bosses anyway and the kids would not benefit from it. I guess in all places there is at least one organization that is not exactly interested in working for the greater good of the people but is more interested in working for itself. I sincerely hope the human race finds a way some day to get past that level of selfish indulgence and manages to find its way to being more concerned with humanity as a whole—but that, I am thinking, is a whole other topic…

I also bought a pair of shoes for Maddi, purple knee high convers, that I am sure she will love. While we were buying the shoes, I was approached by an elderly woman who claimed she was hungry. I asked her to wait while I got my change, then gave her twenty Php. She kept touching me, saying "God bless," and rambling about hunger, but at one point, while Rev was engaged in a conversation with the man running the store (can you call it a store—I guess it is really a booth), she wrapped her finger around my arm, pulled me to her, and looked me straight in the eye, saying quite clearly: " I see you, I know you; they see, they know… you are different, and you will be blessed for it… trust *him*; he will protect you." She cut off and went back to babbling and rambling on under her breath as soon as Revo started paying attention; then she wandered off into the crowd.

It is strange that I never felt compelled to give money to the tiny little bodies that were all around, but there was something about the way this woman had approached me that had drawn me to her. I looked for her many times as we walked, but I never saw her again, and I have to wonder, if she had had the chance, what more she would have said. It was a quick encounter, but it taught me to trust my instincts while I am here. I will probably need to go on instinct for most of my visit, as I do not think that everything here is as it appears on the surface.

Well, my sweet, my meal is almost done, so I should wrap this up—but, before I go, I should tell you something.

I will be writing to you every day. The original handwritten ones are going to be given to my brother to be kept safe in an unopened envelope until they are needed. Yet, even though they will be used in the book, be assured that every time I write I am writing to you, and my words (whatever they are and however they spill out onto the paper) are from the heart and are meant for you.

I will try to call again tomorrow. Right now you are no doubt sleeping, but I will probably write some more soon, though I can't say when, as I am only writing when my muse tells me I should. Keep the faith, my sweet, and believe we are not done here. In fact, I am positive this is only the beginning of a long, trippy journey.

Love much. xo

February 15, patio of the Heritage Hotel Manila, 4:10 PM

Hey, hon, me again…

Just a quick check-in; I went and had a pedicure and manicure that turned into a full-body massage. Now I am back on my patio, I think to do a little reading. If I think of anything to tell you, maybe a little writing as well. I'll get back to you. xo

February 15, patio of the Heritage Hotel Manila, 10:30 PM

Hello, guess who…

I went upstairs and probably passed out; I guess jet lag is finally catching up to me. I'm feeling very seriously dopey today. I got to talk to Maddi, though. When I woke up I went online to check my email, and she was on msn. I said hi to you, too, but you were in soak-in-the-tub mode. It's really been a quiet day for me: a lot of sitting on the patio resting. I did a really cool sketch earlier, though. It started with a stylized version of the Masonic compass, then ended up as a heart-shaped rose with an all-seeing eye in the middle (which is not a Masonic symbol originally, but one they use), then worked in an angel wing that has an infinity sign in it. I forgot, I also put in a yin-yang symbol as the iris of the all-seeing eye, and then, to finish it off, I added in a symbol of the Solomon Keys that represents Yahweh. It turned out pretty good; even though it was totally unplanned, when turned on its side it looks like the shape of the original mother and child I drew three years ago; cool, eh?

Honestly, though, that's all the news I have really. Revo's mom flew in from Italy today for some kind of reunion, so he will have to spend the next few days with his family for the most part. I did speak to him, and hopefully, I will be able to see him tomorrow. If not, it's okay. I might get some real writing done; for now, though, I'm going to read a bit more and relax a little while I still have the chance.

Love, light, and laughter. xo

February 16, patio of the Heritage Hotel Manila, early evening

Okay, so I'm back from another day of wandering—well, not really a full day, more like a couple hours. This may be one of the last times I write to you from the patio at the hotel. I was taken to a place today by Revo that I'm hoping will be like a new home base for me. It is another local hotel, but they have a huge back lawn that looks out over the water, and you know just how much I love water…

There are tons of lawn chairs and umbrellas in case you get too hot or it rains, palm trees everywhere, and you can actually hear birds, not traffic. It will be the perfect spot to write during the day—when I am not being toured around, of course, by Rev and his cousin's girlfriend. Alya is super sweet, and I am hoping we will get some one-on-one time. You know, it just occurred to me that no matter where I go, men can still be pigs, and that is funny as hell, given that I am halfway around the world. I will have to keep that in mind while I am here; it is really not that much different than being at home. Also, remind me to keep my business and thoughts to myself. I'll have to explain that when I see you again in person. Okay, so where was I? Oh yeah, I am hoping that Alya will take me to a few places while I am here as well as tell me some more stories of her life growing up here.

She is, as I said, upper-middle class, and she was raised in a safe, secure home, but her schooling and education here ensured that she learn about all the people in her country, rich as well as poor. She told me that when she was in school one of her mandatory assignments was what they refer to here as *immersion*. We refer to all French schools as French immersion schools; here immersion means to go to live another way of life, one not like your own (so if you are upper class they basically force you to live in poverty for a few days). She had options to choose from; for instance, she and her partner (no, they do not go alone) could have gone to an inner-city slum area and lived as the people on the streets do. They chose instead to go out to the provinces; she claims she wanted to see what the poor people in the country lived like and experience what it was like to try to survive without all the amenities she had grown up depending on. I guess I should have known they would make that part of their education system. It makes sense, and it is too bad we don't do something similar in the West.

She and her friend went way out into no man's land to stay with a family who really had nothing that could be referred to as a material possession. Their house was a one-room hut with a bamboo platform to sleep on. They had no running water or electricity, and Alya found herself wondering how they survived.

She asked them, of course (I mean, that was why she was there, right, and she wanted to know); how did they, for example, buy food.

The answer she got was pretty simple but not what she had expected. The mother of the house apparently looked at her a little confused at first but eventually came out of her shock and explained that they didn't buy anything. How could they? They had no source of income, so they had no money—but they also had no need for it, as they grew everything they needed. Simple, no? They grew what they needed, and they had continuous crops, so a continuous food supply. I'm sure it is a little more complicated than that—much harder to grow what you need and much more time consuming than going to the freezer and grabbing a roast—but, since they don't have to leave the house to go to work, they don't have to worry about extra time spent in preparation. Not much time cleaning either, I'm sure, when you live in a hut. I doubt very much you need to dust before company comes over.

Now, I know I seem to be making light of what again should be a sad situation, but the way she told it was that, as shocking as it seems, these people were extremely happy. She said they went to bed at night around 6 PM when the sun went down, and they got up when the sun rose in the morning. They spent their days together tending crops and animals, preparing food, or just playing with and loving their children. Not much excitement, perhaps, but they were content, and, after a day of adjustment, so was Alya. She was only there for a few days, but it had a profound effect on how she viewed the world and the people in it.

I sincerely hope, though I know they cannot stop their lives because I am here, that she will be able to find time to go out to the provinces so I can see for myself. I am also planning on contacting the people whose names I got through the strange encounter with the gospel lady. Perhaps they do missionary work, and they will be able to send me in the right direction.

Alya's story opened up a discussion about awareness and the imbalance that exists between the wealthy and the poor. She says that they all know it is unfair, but what can they do? She says very few people will openly voice their opinion about such injustice and that the average citizen is complacent about the problems they see every day. They are aware of them and would like to help but don't really know how to provide that help. It is easier, for example, for a wealthy family to donate to charities without thought as to where the money goes than it would be to actively seek out those in need and provide for them directly. I think it runs deeper than that. I think there is an underlying fear of the government and perhaps also the church officials. I am new to these people, so it is not comfortable for them to discuss these things in depth, but I am hoping that with time this will change. I know I planted a seed today. I could see it in Revo's eyes, and I also know that he—though, as I said, he is young—is starting to believe on a deeper level that change is possible—more importantly, that it is inevitable.

He is still hesitant to leave his comfort zone, but perhaps in time he will have a more adventurous spirit. It's strange to think that it was him and his openness about his ideals that led me here in the first place, but that he still hovers between being driven to make a difference and being afraid of the sacrifices making that difference might entail. I doubt very much that he will lose all his fears immediately, but then, he still needs time to know me and be comfortable in the idea that I do not have a hidden agenda. After all, what kind of crazy lady flies halfway around the world to stand by the side of a man she hardly knows, to embark on a personal mission—on such a grand scale, with nothing but the faith in a better future as her guide?

He is afraid of losing sight of what's important if he allows himself to feel too much, and he's scared of the effect getting too close personally could have on the success of any work we do together. He may be young, but he sees far. He wanted to know what would happen at the end of the three weeks when he is not prepared to let me go. He tried to tell me he was worried I would be the one getting hurt, but when I asked him who it was he was really trying to protect, himself or me, he conceded defeat and admitted to both. I told him that ultimately it would not matter; we would be together when we were meant to be together and we would not when it was time for us to be apart. I couldn't offer more than that, really, and what he was trying to get to but was failing miserably at was that that neither could he. Funny, eh? He makes me happy, lifts me up to a higher place, and inspires me to great heights, yet we both know that when I leave we will no longer be able to be together. I always said I would fight like hell to stay with the one I felt was my other half, and now I'm contemplating walking away because the only way to hold onto our time together and the feelings it awakens in me is to let it go.

I wish we had more time today to talk it out, but he is right about one thing. If we focus on that and the dangers those feelings present to each other, then we will lose sight of our reason for being here in the first place. As I told Sophia before I left: if nothing comes of this past my return to Canada, then I will still be able to look back on this book and thank God for the opportunity given to me.

Well, surprise, surprise…

I may just be running out of things to say—except that the staff here, after seeing me write seemingly non-stop for three days, are now beginning to be more open. They are now asking me questions about what I am doing here. One of the girls here has offered to sit with me and tell me more about her people, and one of the men has approached me several times to start idle conversations. I was hoping I could make my presence known here without seeming to be a threat to any of the locals. I was concerned, after several talks with Rev about the dangers here, that I would have a difficult time pulling these people out of their comfort zone. But it appears that, given time and patience, they will walk out of it willingly for better reasons than any persuasion on my part could provide.

I have to tell you, hon, they are a beautiful people, and they deserve so much more than what they have.

Okay, luv, that wraps it up for tonight, I think. I actually started writing the preface today and should probably get back to it, but I will be wandering around the city on my own tomorrow, so I am sure by tomorrow night I will have much more to share. Stay safe, my dear. xo

February 17, patio of the Heritage Hotel Manila, 7:30 AM

Good morning, sweetie,

I am sitting outside again having my morning coffee and was trying to relax and read a bit for once, but it seems that it is not to be. These overwhelming urges to put pen to paper are becoming quite distracting. Even when it is my full intent to sit and ponder or relax and read, I find at odd moments I am forced pull this damn book out and commence writing.

I get the feeling I'm supposed to drop you a quick note with regards to my plans for the day and maybe toss in some of my thoughts along the way. I spoke to you last night briefly so I could read you the preface I have written. Your reaction was extremely reassuring, as I remember well your own talent for the written word. I feel I have no more appropriate person to turn to when it comes to open and honest feedback on my work.

Manila is waking up, my love; the sounds of traffic filter through the walls, as the people of this great city embark on their daily adventures. I will hopefully be joining them soon enough, as I am headed out today with a couple of destinations in mind. I am planning to wander over to the Mall of Asia with the hopes of having my phone unlocked and getting a local SIM card, so I will have a local contact number to give to anybody I might randomly run into. It would also help when I email my contacts here in Manila if they have a way to reach me even if I am not in my room (which I never am, except to sleep). After that I am planning to wander over to that place Rev's friend showed me yesterday; there is a feel to the air today that is pulling me outside.

I was thinking this morning that I should try to get in touch with one of the Catholic churches here as well. I can't remember if told you, but Revo and I have often wondered how much of the natives' offerings are actually being fed back to the locals in terms of relief funding and education.

I am a little concerned that asking too many questions in that area may place me in an uncomfortable position, but, if I am cautious and approach the Church with the appearance of wide-eyed innocence, perhaps they will be more forthcoming. Besides, I honestly believe that I will be protected from harm as long as I stay aware of the possible dangers and do not veer off-course. Today is day four, and I would like to spend it laying the groundwork for the next couple of weeks, and perhaps, who knows, maybe I will run into somebody along the way who will guide me down the proper path.

I have also decided that my next stop after the Philippines will be St Lucia; it seems my gospel lady was sent as a guide of sorts, and I think it would be wrong of me not to follow where she leads. I know I mentioned it before, but I never did go into detail about the reason why I have just this morning decided to go (whether or not Rev wishes to follow). I feel it is time to explain why. This, however, we will discuss in person; it ties into my past and the trail I must someday follow to discover the source of certain truths.

Not yet, however—perhaps I will reflect on it more while I am sitting by the water today and have a clearer view of the energies around me. For now I will let you go, so I can make my way up to my room and get prepared for my day. I hope I have much to tell when I write you next, as I really feel things are going to start moving quickly once again. Luv ya. xo

February 15, seawall lawn out back of Hotel Sofitel Manila, 12:30 PM

Hey, sweetie,

Well, I am finally sitting down to write in a place that resembles the tropical paradise I am supposed to be staying in. There is a place here called Sofitel; it is an old hotel located on Manila Bay. It is the same place Revo brought me to yesterday and still as beautiful as I remember it to be (good to know I was not lying to myself). I am sitting on a chaise lounge facing the bay and surrounded by a vast expanse of lime green lawn. A slight breeze caresses my arms as I write, for which I am grateful, as the sun is extremely hot here even when the haze obscures its light. There is a small sprinkler only a few feet away, for which I am also grateful, as every once in awhile my body is kissed by a gentle, refreshing mist.

I keep expecting somebody to come kick me out. I mean, I don't belong here, really; my own hotel is a good fifty Php away by cab, but apparently it doesn't matter much to the people here whether you are a guest or not—or perhaps they simply don't realize I am not. I am thinking, while I am looking around, that this is most likely where the people with money stay, and, now that I know it's here, it is most definitely where I would like to stay when I come back (strange, this feeling that I will be back to the Philippines again, though I know no possible reason for my return).

It is very pretty and peaceful here, and the whole atmosphere is inspiring, but I find I get more inspiration wandering around among the poorer quarters of the city. I am becoming immune to the strange looks I get from locals. I guess they don't see many white people wandering the streets. The ones who are here stick mostly to the malls, restaurants, and hotels. Hell, there are hardly any white people in my hotel, let alone out in public.

It is so hot today, for some reason. Alya was saying yesterday the weather right now is very unnatural for this time of year, though I would think that since all weather is derived from nature it is completely natural—better, perhaps, to say it is unusual. She claims it should be cooler. I will try to bear with it (imagine me complaining about the heat—wow—we humans truly are never content to just be as are we). I am thinking, though, that unless I want a swollen brain I should probably go about finding some shade. Give me five; I will be right back, though I doubt you will even notice I am gone.

Hey, so I went to get up and move and what happened—the sun went behind the clouds; go figure. I guess I should have known, eh? I moved out to the pool, but it is not much more shady, and there is also not as much privacy. I think I'll take a walk, see if I can find some lawn to stretch out on, and then maybe I'll feel comfortable with staying here to write. Wish me luck, hon; hopefully I will have something interesting to tell you by tonight.

February 18, patio of the Heritage Hotel Manila, noon

Hey, it's me yet again; I actually managed to find a peaceful place to write yesterday and ended up finishing the first chapter. Yes, I know, it was a bit of a surprise to me too, but once I started writing everything just seemed to flow.

Today, though, I am feeling like things are off. I woke up with a cold, and it seems like I don't have much drive or ambition today. I don't think it's helping that the person I was counting on to show me around is extremely distracted by the unexpected presence of his mother. Her timing is quite remarkable, really, and it is most definitely testing my resolve. I have to remember that my purpose here is not centered around him and me. I can't rely on him to give me direction all of the time, but it is difficult to go it alone. I have decided to stick around the hotel today, partly because I am hoping to find a way to strengthen my resolve. When he is not around, it is up to me to stay focused; I feel there is much I have yet to learn from him, and I know I must be patient—it is not easy.

His mother refuses (much as my own family did) to discuss the circumstances of his birth or the significance of his name—which plays a large part in how we got here. He continues to question her, and she (wisely, I think) continues to shut him down. He says she is here for a high-school reunion, but my instincts tell me otherwise. Security has suddenly been tightened up here in the hotel, and there is a feeling of anticipation in the air. I am not sure exactly what I have brought myself into, and, as you know, I hate the waiting game.

I have emailed the local chapter of the church I discovered in TO, and I am still planning on making my way to a local catholic Church, but, until his mother decides to give him some time to himself, I will not get much help in that area. I have to admit I am slightly disappointed in that. After talking to Alya I was looking forward to meeting his outspoken cousin. I think we may have a lot to learn from each other as well, but I am not sure

Rev is anxious for us to meet. Who knows? Maybe I am reading too much into things, since he did tell me he had managed to slip some of my ideas about religions and the church into a few of their discussions. However, I believe that as Rev is preparing to stay here permanently he is now more concerned with securing a safe place among his family and social network before he takes any steps toward stirring up questions of faith and political position.

I was hoping to discuss this with him, as I have now resolved to go ahead with the book, with or without him, though I am concerned about the repercussions that might have on his life here. I understand why he wants to stay here, and I admire his desire to help his people. I am also constantly telling him to be careful about how he moves forward, but there is a fine line between caution and being fearful. Fear causes us to take a step back when threatened and often leads to loss of purpose and resolve, something I do not believe either of us can afford.

I know that if I were there, you would be telling me to let him find his own way, and you would, of course, be right. I try every day to think about what my friends would have to say by way of encouragement and advice. I also try every day to follow that unspoken advice. When you are on the other side of the world, however, and very much alone, it is extremely hard to maintain equilibrium. No matter; I believe that what is meant to come will come, and I will try to remind myself I am not really alone.

For the moment, I think I will let you go and again lose myself in a bit of reading. Later, perhaps, I will work on chapter two, and, in doing so, maybe I will get bit of my strength back.

Stay well, stay safe. xo

February 18, lying in bed in my room, Heritage Hotel Manila

So, I finished chapter three and I have only been here four days. Rev says that at this rate I will be finished before I leave. I sent back him a text telling him that I did not believe the story will end when I leave, so there is no way I can finish the book while I am here. He wants to read what I have written, but I told him that will be difficult until I put it into the computer, as I am sure there is no possible way he can read my writing (I can barely read my writing).

I am at the moment lying in bed waiting for dinner to arrive. I ordered a Caesar salad, because I am sure my body could use the garlic. This cold is making me miserable, though I am grateful I came down with it, as it has forced me to stay at the hotel.

Oh, hold up—dinner's here…

You know, I have to say I love these people. They are so sweet and they seem very curious about what I am doing. The young man who just delivered my food says he sees me downstairs all the time. I told him I am working on a novel, and the patio is a very comfortable place to write. I feel a little bad, though, because I did not sound very enthusiastic. My cold is making me unpleasant, but I will have to try harder to not be miserable; these people certainly don't deserve to be frowned at.

Their curiosity ties into why I am so glad I got sick.

Do you remember the young woman from the other night who said she was willing to share information about her culture? Well, she approached me today to let me know that Friday is her day off, and she could meet with me then. I told her I had a local phone now, so she gave me her number. Coincidentally (love the word, lol), her name is Angel. We ended up agreeing to meet tonight on the patio after she is done work, which I just realized is in only an hour and I am, as you say, slightly drained. I'll let you know what I learn, xo, but for now I should rest.

February 19, patio of the Heritage Hotel Manila, 5:00 PM

My sweet,

I have to say I have undeniably fallen in love with both this country and its people. So far I am only scratching the surface, I realize, but the reality of what occasionally peeks out from underneath is at once shocking and soothing.

Last night I ended up having a very intriguing encounter, and I hardly know where to begin.

I had agreed to meet with Angel, and, though I was exhausted physically, I dragged myself down here at midnight as promised.

I was concerned about meeting her here, as I know from experience the strict expectations the management at hotels such as this have with regards to staff-guest interaction. It seems my fears were well founded, as she was threatened with disciplinary action shortly before we left together. She had unfortunately tried to meet me wearing civilian attire. She is young, only twenty-three, and very obviously new to the service industry. She was not expecting that her innocent attempt at making our rendezvous seem nonchalant seemed to her boss to be an attempt at deception. I do not know even now if the encounter cost her the position here, but I can only assume the worst, as it is well past the time she was to start work, and she has not appeared.

It's strange to think that even in a society where their entire behavioral pattern centers around being welcoming and accommodating hosts that her attempts to befriend a foreign visitor could cause such problems—but then, that is the way of big business. Propriety is always at the forefront of their day-to-day routine, and any breach of that propriety, however innocent in nature, causes great distress among those who, as they say, write the cheques.

What amazed me most about the whole situation was not that it happened but rather her reaction to it. She did not seem to be concerned. Here, in a country where the people struggle every day to feed themselves and their families, this young woman, answering my inquiries about her possible dismissal, simply stated, "If it's God's will."

I would love to explore this notion further, but, as that is not where the conversation began, it would not be in line time-wise with the rest of our late-night adventure. I only mention it to explain why I can comfortably sit here writing to you, unconcerned with the notion that this sweet young woman might have lost her source of income as a result of trying to assist in my work.

I have to pause here briefly to point out that I spent the afternoon sleeping. We did not return to the hotel until after 4 AM; combine the early hour with this irritating little cold, and my body simply refused to give anymore. I am feeling much revived after hiding away for the day in my room and will be adventuring out again later this evening to meet Rev at a mall near his mother's hotel. It will be nice to see him, of course, as we have much to discuss after last night, and yet I wonder at his request that we meet in public. I am certain he's avoiding spending time alone with me because he's concerned about straying from our purpose.

I do, of course, realize that his intentions are applaudable, but it is still difficult for me to accept his fears. Angel seems to think the whole situation is rather sad; she believes that we could find a way to be together as a couple and still manage to accomplish our goals. It is funny that as I am sitting here I am feeling the same sadness myself; yet, it was only a few short hours ago that I was trying to convince Angel it is just simply the way it is. I almost managed to convince myself. My explanations on the matter certainly made sense to me at the time; yet, the unfairness of it all threatens to overwhelm me. I dread the inevitable discussion on the subject, which is probably going to occur this evening, and, at the same time, I feel reassured by the comforting words Angel chose to share with me last night.

Our talk began shortly after we arrived at a local outside mall. After purchasing a couple of bottles and finding a quiet corner, she openly began to talk about herself and her own personal history. I had to stop her long enough to explain my presence here, and it was the first time since being here that I have been completely honest about it to anyone but myself and Rev. I was more honest, in fact, with my explanation to her than I had been to myself. The explanation gave me an opportunity to clarify the situation in my own mind and provided a much-needed clearing of clouded issues.

I told her that I had unexpectedly found myself giving my heart to a Filipino man, who, though he has made it more than clear he cares deeply for me as well, is much more concerned about finding a way to uplift his people and give them a chance at a better way of life. I told her that given our age difference, the fact that I am a white divorced single mother, and, of course, that my life is in Canada, it is extremely doubtful that we will ultimately end up together. As I said, she was saddened by this, but I replied that if our work together made a difference in the lives of the people here, then our union, as brief as it may end up to be, would still manage to create a stronger, more powerful bond between us than anything a mere romantic relationship could accomplish or provide.

Oh, Beaner, I want to believe my own words—I really do—but this man wakens something in me I have never experienced, and I am loathe to give it up. Physical attraction aside, his very existence in my life has led me down a path I'd never imagined I'd walk. His strength of spirit uplifts me and makes me fly to new heights. I greatly fear losing that feeling of free and easy flight and have to constantly remind myself to be grateful for the mere experience of stretching my wings to take that final leap. It is not easy.

Oh yes, I know it is not meant to be. Constant testing of faith, however, is draining on the soul, and if I were not constantly surrounded by this feeling of hope, it would be very easy to falter and fall.

Before Alya continued to expound on her life here, she took the moment to thank me for taking such a selfless risk as to travel halfway around the world in the hopes of making even the smallest difference. I wish I could justify her faith in me, but I struggle every day with my own insecurities.

She reminded me, though, that it is the little changes that lead to big changes. There were several times throughout the evening where she seemed to feed my own thoughts back to me. Three weeks ago a conversation like this would have made me squirm, but I am becoming used to encounters with various guides who are being sent my way. It has become commonplace, and I am recognizing it much more readily.

After reassuring me that the book I am working on may, in fact, have a positive effect, she carried on with her own personal story. She is a graduate of the University of Hong Kong, but, not being able to find work there, she came back to Manila. Her job at the hotel was quite by accident, and she claimed it was possible that she had been sent there simply to meet me. Apparently she had applied for several secretarial positions around the city, and the Heritage had been the first to respond.

(You know, I just looked up and the sunset is absolutely incredible—white and red and deep purple streaks across a pale sky—it covers the first half of the horizon, leaving a soft, pinkish glow on the clouds overhead.)

The hotel management had told her that she would be working the front desk, but when she arrived they put her in the lower position of server in the restaurant. She said she was disappointed but figured there had to be a reason. You see, she is a born-again Christian (a girl who was raised Catholic, as are most Filipino people) yet found herself disillusioned by the idol worship that dominates the Catholic faith. Later in the evening she compared Catholicism to Buddhism, citing the former as a religion that centers around the worship of material representations of both saints and demigods. She seemed to believe that it was this worship of what she called false idols that distracted from the lessons present in the teachings of the one true God.

I still will neither agree with nor dispute her beliefs, as it is not my place here to judge. I was, however, intrigued by her views, as—regardless of what you choose to call the power that we are born from and the energies that protect and guide us—I do not believe those energies give a damn for material objects. Though it *can* be argued that if God creates man and man creates material things, then, in essence, it is God who is also creating those material things. I do not believe, however, that those creations by man are a necessary part of our appreciation of God's power. I figure, if you need to see or feel evidence of that power, you need look no further than the feeling of holding a babe in your arms. If we could take that feeling further and stretch it to encompass all people and all things in our world, then we would be one step closer to experiencing that sense of oneness with the mystical energy that humanity seems to be lacking.

Man, by his very nature, exists to create. It was the creation that concerned her—not the act of creation itself, but rather the usage of the objects created. She explained that Catholics spend a large part of their spiritual energy directing prayers to extensions of God rather than to God himself. This confused her, and she couldn't understand why—if, as the church claims, God is always with us—she could not just talk directly to him. She started to question as well the need for certain rituals and gestures used in Catholic worship. Why, for example, would it be more important for her to genuflect at the altar than to, say, show her love of God through her daily interactions with people? She could not justify in her mind her right as a Catholic to go out into the world and judge and condemn others in God's name and then be assured her actions would be forgiven simply because she went through the act of confession and prayer over a string of beads.

I must clarify that my explanation of her thoughts is not word for word. Her English was very broken at times, and it was a struggle for her to find the right words. I have included metaphors in order to clarify for you her ideas, and I do not believe she would fault me for it.

Her reasoning, as I said, was sound, and her own quest to come closer to that power had led her to find an open-minded Christian community. She said it had not always been easy for her; she had struggled daily with her own doubts and fears before she learned to put faith in something she could neither see nor touch. She explained that the Christians taught acceptance and forgiveness of self and others. She claimed that the longer she studied with them, the easier it became to find peace within herself and her surroundings.

When I asked if, coming from a largely Catholic society, she found it difficult to openly not follow the same faith, she assured me that the condemnation of others with regards to her faith was a test of character. It was how she responded to that scrutiny that allowed her to maintain her strength of purpose and her belief in a higher power. She asked me if I loved God. I told her as truthfully as I could that I loved the idea or essence of God but reminded her that my perceptions of god might not be the same as hers.

I explained to her my encounter with the Gospel group in Toronto before I came to the Philippines and told her that my experience there had been positive. I mentioned that I could not quote the scriptures, as I had not studied the Bible in depth in recent years, but that I could take the teachings in the scriptures and relate them to the here and now. I told her I understood the fundamental lessons behind those teachings but could not willingly believe that the scriptures themselves were the only message that God had ever sent to his people to show them and guide them to a better way of life. I feel it is the meaning behind the words that is meant to be the lesson, not the words themselves.

At this point, she brought up a very valid concern and taught me a lesson I needed to take to heart. She explained to me that people needed proof to believe in something. It is part of human nature to want to have something they can see and feel that connects their belief in a higher power to the physical existence here on earth. It is not the words themselves, as I said, that teach the lesson, but they do provide a weapon of sorts against doubt and adversity. She described the scriptures as a sword in hand (interesting description, given the imagery that got us here in the first place), a blade that could be used to cut through the fears and doubts of others.

She suggested that others I speak to might not be as open or accepting as the group I first met with in Toronto and that, though my purpose was pure in its intent, my methodology might be flawed. She asked me whether it would not be better to acquaint myself with the actual teachings, so I would have a weapon at hand when questioned or confronted. Her reasoning again was sound, and I found myself admiring the wisdom in one so young.

We talked at great length about her faith. She mentioned that sometimes it was hard to attend mass on Sundays in light of her job and her need to pay her bills. She said she felt guilty when she could not attend. I questioned her again and asked if she really believed that God cared one wit if she was in a church when she prayed. I told her about my grandmother who had suffered guilt and self-doubt for years about not being able to attend church on Sundays. I explained that as a result of her failing knees she could no longer climb the church steps, and though she had lobbied for a ramp to be built to provide wheelchair access, it was a good ten years before anything had been done. The whole scenario had been rather disappointing, as the Catholic Church has access to funding far beyond the means of other religious communities, and it was discouraging that they could not or would not use those funds for such a simple request. It was only after the ramp had been built that my grandmother commented that she no longer felt the need or desire to be in a church to pray. She had accepted the idea—after many years of self-deprecation—that God was listening anyway. My grandmother had asked how I had known the truth of it at such a young age, and I couldn't give her an example, except to tell her that it was what I knew to believe, so it was my truth. Now she believed, so it was therefore now *her* truth. I explained to my grandmother that I believed the energy that we call God is all around us at all times and that it stands to reason that those energies are in tune with our needs and fears, regardless of where we are. I also explained that perhaps it was the need for her to learn that for herself that allowed the failure of her knees and the delay in construction of the ramp. It simply took so long for the ramp to be built because it took so long for my grandmother to learn and accept the lesson being taught.

It was here that Angel imparted another much-needed form of wisdom. She explained that her need to go to church did not stem from the need to be in a place of worship. The idea, in fact, that the building itself was anything other than a gathering place was foreign to her. The purpose behind going to church at all was twofold.

First, it was a way to surround herself with those of like mind. She could spend time with people who believed as she did, who both helped to keep her grounded and lifted her up when she was feeling afraid or sad. She also stated that it gave her a chance to do the same for others. The actual act of going to church was centered on communal support and encouragement and really had nothing to do with the building at all.

Secondly, going to church was, in its own way, a manner of self-sacrifice. She said it seemed very little to ask to give up a mere three hours of her week and dedicate those hours to worship. The challenge, or sacrifice, if you will, was in putting aside worldly needs and commitments in order to give herself over to God for those three hours. It became a matter of choosing between, for example, her job and the paycheck it provides, and the spiritual rewards gained from that sacrifice. She pointed out that, by being willing to give up that paycheck in order to commit herself to worship, she was quite literally putting her worldly safety and security in God's hands. She strongly believed that he would provide for her what she needed—but only after she was able and willing to both see and accept what he provided.

The night was wearing on by this time, and the establishment where we were sitting was closing, so we decided to walk over to a store close by and try to find another place to sit. As we walked, she told me it was not so long ago that she had cried herself to sleep several nights from fear and despair. She knew at the time that something was missing from her life, but she was not able to grasp what it was. As we sat, she said it wasn't until God took everything from her that she began to search for answers in the direction of the church. Once she got past the bitterness and pain and opened herself to the idea that perhaps it had all been taken away for a reason did she begin to really open her eyes to what could be if she gave herself over to a higher power. She began to feel what she described as "lighter"—not so weighted down by her physical needs and desires. She felt more in tune with her surroundings; the more peace and kindness she worked very hard on giving to others, the more she received. She said it was a continuous cycle of giving and receiving God's light. What she shared with others she got back in turn.

In short, she was describing the same principle mystics and prophets from all ages and parts of the world have taught for centuries, yet she was relating it in terms she could understand and believe in. She had learned to embrace the idea through her introduction to Christ, and it had become her truth. In living by the very principal of getting back what you put out into life—a principal as old as time and a principal taught around the world in countless different forms—she had started to turn her life in a more positive direction.

As I continue to explore each new religion and belief system as it is presented to me, I am aware of the common vein that threads through them all. Will it become apparent, as I venture forth, that the indescribable energy that flows between all living things is in the end (or rather the beginning) the root of all faiths in a higher power? Will the theory of the give and take of that energy be finally proven to be the essence, the very spirit, of that higher power itself? What kind of possible effect could that have on the ultimate survival of the people who claim they alone have knowledge of the true path to connecting with that power? What, in the end, would happen if the average person realized that access to that energy is easily attainable? Would it be for the better? Are humans yet at the point in their spiritual development where the use and manipulation of that power will not become corrupt?

It concerns me that we may not yet be ready for that next step. Yet it seems to me, in light of all of my recent experiences and discoveries, that we humans are taking the first steps necessary to achieve that higher understanding. I can only hope that when the time comes society will be able to overcome its greed and lust for power and move forward together as one toward a higher, more peaceful state of being.

Fears and speculations aside, I still have much to learn here, and my story with Angel has not yet come to an end. We are to meet tomorrow, as she wishes to share more of her community and her church with me. I agreed to go with her to a gospel session, as I think I am not yet done exploring the Christian faith or their beliefs. I am eager to learn from these people as well as share my own experience—in the hope that we can benefit each other mutually in our own personal quests for spiritual growth. I have to wonder, though, where this particular branch of the road will lead. I do hope my idle curiosity does not ultimately end up being my undoing. I will have to put my faith in my purpose here and hope I do not get led astray.

I suppose, as I have been writing now for hours, I should give my hand a rest as well as my heart and mind, but I will continue to update you on my adventures. Until next time, my sweet, love, light, and laughter…

February 19, Starbucks patio, Gledhill Shopping Centre Manila, 11:00 PM

Well, this is different; I am on the other side of the city, by myself, at 11:00 at night. I'm here to meet Rev, even though he's always telling me not to go out alone at night, but it's okay, I'm not overly concerned. The people here—though shocked, I'm sure, to see me here alone at night—seem to be, for the most part, ignoring me. I wouldn't have bothered pulling out the book, but I have to wait anyway, and I have a short update for you.

I was sitting up in my room, after sending text messages back and forth to Rev all day, trying and failing to set up a meeting. I was feeling very alone and very discouraged. I was wondering yet again if I had lost my mind, travelling halfway around the world on a whim. I had sent a text to Angel earlier enquiring as to what had happened and asking her why she was not at work and if she was okay. So I am lying there having my moment of doubt when she sends me a text telling me she is okay and asking how I am.

I wrote back the following.

I am doing okay; just lying here trying to remind myself that I am *not* alone, but then you just proved it—really, are you okay?—I was a little concerned.

Her response started:

"Yup...I happened to ask for a rest day—that's the reason why I'm not around tonight. And, yes, you're right; you're not—" *message cut off*

Seriously, it *was* cut off, but I got the gist of what she was trying to say. I was crying silly tears and feeling very much revived, thinking to myself she really was an Angel, and I sent back:

I am not sure I got all your message, but I am sure I got the message.

I was halfway through sending my response when the rest of her message came through again, only this time it was the whole thing.

"Yup...I happened to ask for a rest day—that's the reason why I'm not around tonight. And yes, you're right, you're not alone; however, you're just being given more time to think things through. You're called for it—you're one of God's messengers. You can do it, I know. God bless."

I wish you could be here, buddy, and see these things with me. I honestly feel so overwhelmed at times by all these little messages and signs. It almost feels unfair that I can't share them with the people in my life. If for one day you could see this through my eyes, I think that you, too, would cry. Like me, you wouldn't know if you were crying tears of joy or sorrow, and, like me, you wouldn't care.

I guess that's why I was born a writer, so I could share this crazy trip with the rest of the world. Well, hon, gotta go. Rev's here, and the story must go on.

February 20, patio of the Heritage Hotel Manila, 1:24 AM

The deeper I delve into the mystery that is my trip to this country, the harder I find it to cope with the unexpected emotional ups and downs that result from my experiences here. Right now I am warring with myself over my uncontrollable and undeniable love for this madman and the also-undeniable fact that for the moment, at least, I have to keep my distance.

I mean, hon, if you could have seen him last night, you would have wanted to cry. He is so obviously confused by all of this: him—me—us—why we're here—what we're doing—I wanted to grab hold of him and tell him that I refused to give up on this feeling. Yet all I could do was distance myself and see if he could work it out alone. God forgive me my greed, but I so want to be allowed to be with this man—but somehow I feel that he will ultimately end up being my final sacrifice.

It doesn't seem fair in the slightest, and I am having trouble coming to terms with acceptance. I had the chance to tell him I need him; I had the chance to tell him I loved him—and I didn't. Instead, I watched him squirm like an ant pinned by a thumb, wanting desperately to get away and not knowing how.

Two more weeks is all I have left, and every day that passes I accomplish more toward my goal and cut out more of my soul. I have a memory of kneeling at this man's feet and I cannot bring myself to tell him about it. Again I ask forgiveness for my greed, for my selfish desires. In this world it is easy to give up a life. The real test is to be willing to give up your own wants and needs, to sacrifice that which you hold most dear. I thought I was finished with that part of my test, but now I feel like all the rest was only in preparation for this.

How can I look into his eyes, knowing that he is the very same man I have shared so many lifetimes with, and yet be willing to walk away from sharing this one? I wish you were here; I need some kind of guidance, some comfort, some hope…

I do not want to do this alone. I want to stand at his side; it is my place, my right. I have too much pride, perhaps, to think that at the end of it all I deserve for my prayers in this to be answered. We talked about my writing, about his dreams—always about his people and his hopes for them. I watched him, relished in the beauty of his presence and my faith that he will stay strong; yet, at the same time I wept inside for the loss of him.

I told him I would publish this and asked him if he was prepared. I told him the story had to be told and asked him if he was ready. I can see that he is; he harbors no doubts or fears for his own safety; he is scared, but not for himself. He says his time here is not yet over; he has too much left to do. He says that my time here is also not yet finished, and so, for the moment, I am safe to wander among these people. He says that God is not finished with us, that we will be protected—and yet he is scared. He told me the government would not go after him directly; he said they would threaten his family. He didn't want to finish the thought, struggled visibly to find the words. He said if they did, then he would dare them to try. He said that God allows vengeance for those who do not hate, that God allowed certain individuals the right to impose justice on those who do wrong. But justice, he said, would not save his family, and justice could not bring them back.

So will we make a choice. Will I stand with him and risk my most precious gift? Will he allow it, knowing that which I hold most precious could be threatened? Can we allow ourselves to continue this journey, knowing the possible cost?

The air seems very heavy tonight; despite the slight breeze that is playing across the leaves, there is a feeling of weight to the air, even as it causes the leaves to dance.

He smiled and said, "But your book it is just a story…what have I to fear from a story?"

Still, he asked the question, wordlessly (we are far beyond the point where words are needed), silently imploring me to make the choice.

Baby, I had no answer…

I still do not know what I will do when the time comes.

I fear I will soon have to decide. I will come back to you, of that there is no doubt, but will I leave my heart and my soul here with him when I go.

If he asked me today to be his bride, it would be my duty to stand with him. He will not ask. I can see it in his eyes; he cannot— not from lack of love or desire but because he does not want the sacrifice to be mine. I think he feels it is his to make and in making it he will protect me. Beaner, I think it is too late—not too late for us, but too late for me; the decision is, after all, mine to make, is it not?

I must resolve to tell him when I see him next, to reassure him I have thought it through, so that he knows I made the choice willingly. If it is what's meant to be, I will have one more chance. Whether or not he will accept is long since out of my hands, but I will have to make the offer. If I don't, it will be my life's failure and regret. Rejection I can live with, in light of the spirit in which it is given, but to never try or take the chance—that is unthinkable and therefore unacceptable.

Damn, I wish you were here; it would help a great deal to have a voice of reason whispering in my ear. But it is not to be; I will have to go it alone and hope against hope that I am doing the right thing. Maybe my dreams will give me the answers I seek.

I certainly hope yours are more peaceful in nature than mine. Stay well, my heart, until we speak again.

February 20, patio of the Heritage Hotel Manila, 10:00 AM

Well, hon, my dreams had no answers, not that I could see.

It is morning, and it is supposed to be a day when I get together with Angel. We are to go to a gospel session together tonight and maybe out for some social interaction. I don't feel the slightest bit excited about it. I have been writing for days, and both my spirit and my body are exhausted. I woke up this morning with little red dots all over my legs. It does not appear to be a rash; more likely it is little ant bites from my hours spent out here on the patio. I am tired though, so very tired and worn. I still feel a little lost.

My ramblings last night went far afield of my intended writing, but lately it does not seem to matter what I want to write or even if I want to write. There are times when the pen flies so quickly across the page that I do not see how the words flowing out can be coming from me. I don't even know half the time why I am sitting down to write—only that I am compelled to, and, regardless of how weak I am feeling, if I do not get out of bed and put pen to paper, I can find no rest. I did try one day to stay in bed, but I couldn't sleep. My body, though tired, was restless, and my mind would not stay silent long enough for me to get any sleep. Even today there are things I need to do, but I can't seem to put the book down long enough to do them—so I write.

I think I am only allowed to stop long enough to go learn or experience something new, and, when the lesson is learned or the experience complete, I find myself back here, unable to sleep until I write it down. I am sure that I was stuck at the table this morning because I did not tell you everything that we discussed last night. I was so concerned about my inner fears that I lost sight momentarily of the reasons we had gotten together in the first place.

When I got there, I wrote you briefly while I was waiting, and when Rev finally showed up, his smile lit up my world. He was so excited about an audition he had just gotten for a local show here. It is the Philippines version of Big Brother, and, unlike the one in the States, this show could make or break his career. I thought when I was still at home that it would be best for him to concentrate on his arts and push the political ambition aside. Now that I am here, I wonder if success as an actor would divert him from his purpose. Something tells me not; something tells me it will be a doorway for him to enter the public eye. He explained that famous actors here are virtually untouchable by the government, so it would also provide him with a safe haven of sorts. If successful, he would be protected from retribution from those in power. If he was known and loved by the people, then the government would not move against him. The situation here is unstable at best, and they cannot afford to have another uprising on a large scale.

I do trust that if he were put in that kind of position he would not walk down the path of corrupt power. I am sure his intent is pure; his eyes sparkle when he talks of his hopes for the future of his country. Still, he is young, and fame and money do strange things to the soul.

I suppose it is really my own impatience that is bothering me. I am well known for wanting things to happen when I want them to happen. You would think that after all these years I would have learned to accept what comes and not try to force situations to adhere to my own personal guidelines. I find it difficult, however, to sit and watch while an event plays itself out. The waiting game has never been my forte. It is odd how Angel pointed out that perhaps part of my reason for being here is to learn patience. She is probably right; every time I have sat back and let the "power that is" point the way, the road suddenly becomes smoother.

As I said, I asked Rev if he was worried about the repercussions from this book. He seemed annoyed that I would ask; in fact, his whole demeanour last night was one of restless impatience. He was continually fidgeting and shifting in his chair. He also was finding it difficult to meet my eyes—eyes that he has told me before are at times far too intense for comfort. I was having trouble understanding what had him so uncomfortable, but looking back, I realize he had recently poured his heart out to me and I hadn't had the courage to respond in kind. I shall have to remedy the situation, as I think only then will we be able to again find comfort in each other's presence. There are still too many things left unsaid.

While we talked, I asked him if he thought his people were ready to let go of their fears and latch onto the idea of freedom. I wanted to know if, given a leader to follow who truly had their best interests at heart, they would stand behind that leader. In short, I wondered, as I did in the spiritual sense, if these people were ready for change in the political sense. He says that though they still live in a world where fear overshadows their ability to move forward, that, given the right kind of leader, they *would* abandon their fears. He talked about the political infrastructure and explained that if the person at the top of that structure was corrupt then the corruption would ultimately trickle down and spread among the people. He doesn't believe that the people of this country need a leader who will tell them how to live, nor do they need a leader who will show them how to live. Rather they need a leader who will simply inspire them to want to live so they can work together for a cleaner, safer world.

Give a man a fish; feed him for a day. Teach a man to fish; feed him for a lifetime. It's a sound theory and one that applies both politically and spiritually. After discussing briefly my hopes that this book would marry the two ideals, we talked a little about the risks. That is when he explained his theory that God allows justice if and only if the reasons for that justice are pure. He questioned, for example: if God had frowned on righteous retribution, then how could a man like Genghis Khan be allowed to live to the age of eighty years? Surely if Genghis Khan's actions went against the natural order, then the powers that be would have stopped him. Rev cited names of conquerors throughout history who had tried and failed to destroy in the name of justice but whose underlying hate eventually destroyed them.

Men like Napoleon and Hitler, in an attempt to abolish religion and replace it with political domination, were thwarted and the world allowed to recover. Rev said that it wasn't until I came along that he found a way to accept the idea that anger had its place in the world. My idea that balance was essential for survival had awakened in him the realization that without anger we would become complacent. If we cannot feel anger at the unjust behaviors of others, then we have no reason to take action against that injustice. He said if we continue down a path of blind acceptance then we have no hope of initiating change. For too long we have allowed repression and starvation to run rampant, out of our belief that it is not our place to rise against it.

These ideals, however, go against the fundamental grain of the spiritual belief system here that seems to be at the core of these people's strength. I believe that the two ideals can co-exist, but it will take time for the general populace to make such a monumental shift in their beliefs. It's a shift that they would have to initiate on their own, not one they can or should be forced to.

Again I wonder if it is a change they are ready for. It would not be an easy one, and I cannot even say it would at first appear to be a positive one. "It is God's will"—the centre from which all hope in this land spirals out. How much would they have to alter their beliefs to achieve a state of "it is Gods will that humanity actively impose its own"? The idea that man was created to feel, dream, and think for himself—so he could take responsibility for his own actions and thereby take responsibility for his future— is one that has been around for centuries. Yet, even with that belief, man seems to need to put blame on an unseen force for all the wrongs in this world. It is a strange balance of complacent acceptance and an active desire to make change.

It concerns me still that man cannot find the balance, only because the two ideals are so seemingly opposite. I cannot see how humanity could embrace them as one. I suppose that is why I am actively seeking the common thread that underlies all religious and spiritual beliefs. I am curious whether the basic thread that is seemingly woven through them all can be safely acknowledged by the people of this world. If they are shown the possibility of its existence, would they begin to search on their own, or would they recoil in fear of the repercussions to their own faith? I would hope we are past the point of fearing knowledge. I could hope we are ready to seek the answers that are being made available, but we are human and thus we fear the unknown. We fear change, and we fear that which we cannot understand. Sadly, it is not possible to love or embrace fully anything we fear.

Someday, perhaps, we will learn; some day our eyes may be opened…

As I said, I have hope and faith that we may be moving toward that change. As a student of this world, I look forward to watching humanity take those first steps, but it will take men like Rev, with great sense of purpose and purity of heart, to lead us to it.

It is funny that even given his history and his family's belief in his future role as leader, he himself is too humble to see how much good a man like himself could do for this country. He understands what they need here, and he does not fear the dangers that would come with working toward fulfilling those needs. He sees a chance for change, and he believes his people ready for it, but he does not yet, I think, embrace the idea that he can be a powerful force to initiate that change.

We will see…

Time is the only answer to this particular question, and time, thankfully, has a way of never running out.

Well, my sweet, I must wander off again. I feel my time is done here for the moment, and I should probably get back to the reality of living. If I continue in this vein of ignoring the day-to-day essential requirements of this physical body, then I will not long hold onto my strength. Besides, the story can only go so far if I am sitting here writing—after all, it is not my story, it is theirs, and they are out there…

February 20, random coffee shop, South Central Manila, 8:00 PM

Okay—seriously…

I am yet again sitting in a random part of Manila, alone, waiting to meet somebody…

I wonder if these people are convinced yet that I am completely nuts. I am—convinced, that is. Damn, this city is BIG and loud and busy and dirty and…

Oh hell, I could go on listing shit for hours. I don't even know what street I'm on or how I would go about getting back to the hotel if I needed to. I mean, holy shit, this is certainly a test of Rev's theory that I am safe here no matter what.

Amazing culture…

I told the taxi driver he is incredibly brave to drive here for a living. You know, there are hardly any traffic lights, cars just go wherever the hell they want, and so far I haven't seen one accident. Incredible to think about, really. If our people tried to live this way, there would be blood everywhere.

February 21, hotel room, Heritage Hotel Manila, 10:36 AM

As I'm lying here in my bed trying to motivate myself to get up, I am having a hard time reconciling myself to continuing the work I thought I was sent here to do. Every time I think I have a clear picture of why I am here, I find myself facing another personal wall that I am forced to climb in order to continue. I don't suppose the whole trip is meant to be an easy one, but, as I told Rev two days ago, the emotional roller coaster that is this trip is turning out to be quite draining.

I must apologize for leaving you hanging last night. Angel arrived while I was in mid-sentence, and I was forced to quickly tuck the book away so I could join her.

Last night's adventure was a long one, with many discussions that I will share with you shortly, but, before I do, I must tell you that some of what we talked about has left me shaken. Not shaken in the sense that I doubt my purpose for being here but in the sense that I doubt my worthiness to pursue that purpose. I told Revo last night that I do not think it fair that I cannot be with him. I don't mean in the sense that I am here by his side always or that he is by mine, but that we will not be allowed to test the boundaries of our relationship. He says that as much as he does not want to lose what we have, in his heart and mind it is already over. He cannot see past the inevitable time when we will have to be apart, and he cannot see how it could possibly work with us apart. At the same time, he fears the threat to the core of our bond—not so much because of being apart physically, but having that physical separation cause doubt and anger between us.

He is worried that in the end I will hate him for not being willing to try. I attempted to explain that our inability to be together is situational and has no effect on how I feel about him, but I do not think he has much faith in my being able to separate the physical and emotional. When we are together like last night, talking to others and sharing our ideas, we feed each other. It would be nice to think that a year from now, when I come back, book in hand, we will still have that bond of shared energy.

He has admitted he is a lustful young man, and I have to remind myself to very careful about the lure of physical hunger. It is, after all, not the physical bond I am seeking, and though I know just how beautiful having both can be, I do not need more than the emotional to sustain me. Perhaps this is something I should discuss with him, though I am not sure he would believe me. I, like every other person I know, struggle with my own insecurities. I have felt jealousy and possessiveness in several relationships, and I know from first-hand experience the damage they can cause. Here with him, though, I don't feel the need to hold on. I do not need to cling to him to keep him with me, and I certainly don't feel any kind of desire to keep him to myself. I think he belongs to the world. I think he has the chance to make a difference here, and it would be wrong of me to want to keep him from that. I really feel that as long as I know he's with me in his heart it doesn't matter how many others he shares that heart with. I myself love deeply and passionately many people in my life, so why would I expect that he could love only one?

It makes so much more sense when I am able to put it on paper, and, even though I would rather discuss this with him in person, I don't think that he needs to see my eyes anymore to know that I speak the truth.

I'm gonna take a break, hon—as I said, I am not yet out of bed, and I need to look up a couple things before I do downstairs and commence writing. Our discussion last night was long and it will no doubt take hours to get it on paper for you.

February 20, patio of the Heritage Hotel Manila, 12:56 PM

Why do we pray?

Why do we doubt?

Why do we suffer?

I resolve from now on to ask these questions of each individual I meet who is willing to share his or her beliefs and faith with me.

I am done asking them of myself; I already know what I believe… yet I also know that beliefs change as new knowledge is provided and really all I desire is to continue to learn and grow.

I am sitting in my favorite spot on the patio and relishing the renewed energy that has been blessedly bestowed on me. It was only after I wrote to you, and then forced myself out of bed, that I received a message that confirmed my beliefs that I am meant to wander and explore. Deacon had sent an email explaining that his company is being reconstructed, and, as he refuses to move to and work out of Denver, they have presented him with an amazing severance package. He says he wants to spend the summer with his kids and then spend a couple months travelling the world, and he asks if I would come with him.

He wouldn't be ready to leave until fall, at the earliest, and in light of how quickly the book is progressing, I figure that I will have wrapped it up about then and be free again to journey on. The timing of both his email and his plans for our trip could not be more perfect.

As I said earlier, I have been struggling with the idea of finding my place and finding my mate, and it was only after meeting Rev that I felt like my lifetime search for my other half was complete. The thing was, it didn't make sense that I would have met my perfect partner and then have to leave him. I mean, the unfairness of it was overwhelming, and I viewed it as yet another test of strength.

When I met him, I was still searching for that final missing piece; there was still a void, an empty space that had to be filled. Yet, even with the empty space, my life has been very full. I have had the joy and sorrow of loving and losing many people over the years. Each time I met a kindred spirit, another piece of me was put back into place, another part of my spirit returned, and it was a constant roller coaster of intense emotion. Each and every person who has touched my life has given me direction, and every adventure with those people has been beautiful and enlightening. Each and every one of those adventures inevitably came to an end.

Somehow, someway, those friendships and bonds have endured. I have loved both men and women and shared my hopes and dreams with all of them. Yet I still felt incomplete, as if I were destined to be alone, because it seemed that in the end I always had to leave those people behind. Then, when I met Revo, I really felt that he was the one soul that I had been searching for, but I did not recognize that he was not the only one I needed to make my life complete.

People speak often of old souls reunited, of soul mates finding each other, and the beauty of the idea has an undeniable pull. Yet, it does not make sense to me that an ancient soul could have only one mate.

Looking at it in a larger sense, in terms of souls being extensions of the massive energy that is the foundation of our existence, you have to wonder at the implications of it. I have a theory which, of course, I will share, but in no way will I expect you to believe it—in fact, even if the theory seems sound to me at the moment, I might very well change my mind as this journey continues.

In the beginning there were the original explorers, the then-new but now ancient spirits that came to this world to learn and explore. Those beings have continued their adventures and returned times innumerable in the quest and thirst for knowledge and understanding—for the mere purpose of exploration and experience. Yet every generation and race expands in the physical sense, and each new body is inhabited by either an old soul or a new one. The question, then, is Where do the new souls come from? Does it not stand to reason that the older, stronger souls are able to shed a part of themselves and divide their energies to give birth to the new? In that instant of division they leave behind a part of themselves that is, as a result, incomplete. Does it not then also stand to reason that the more times that soul divides the more pieces of that soul are spread out among humanity? Following that line of reasoning, one could conclude that of those ancient souls there are many extensions stemming from their cores currently walking the earth.

Perhaps, the older the soul is, the more pieces of itself—or "soul mates," if you will—exist, and it is the quest for finding those lost mates that leads people to search for their perfect mate here on earth. As humans, however, we do not allow for the idea of having more than one life partner. It is unnatural to our conditioned beliefs to embrace the concept of more than one love. We do not share easily, especially the younger inexperienced personalities who, like children, are still learning to let go of what they have so they can gain something new.

Picture the infant who is grasping a piece of jewelry, say, a nice golden necklace, that the unknowing wearer has inadvertently put within the baby's reach by the simple act of picking up the child. The baby sees the shiny object and is intrigued by it so latches on by wrapping little fingers around the piece and refusing to let go. It is a mother's natural instinct to replace the infant's treasure with something new, thereby encouraging the child to release the grasp on the pendant. As the child grows, it learns through this experience, as it is repeated time and time again, that only by letting go of the object it currently holds can it make room in its hand for each new gift that is presented.

I liken this action to our search for our ideal mate—the one person who makes us whole, the one treasure we long to have with us always and never release. Yet, as I said, if the ancient souls throughout the centuries divided many times, then they would not have only one perfect mate, but many. It would seem that, regardless of how many of those pieces they managed to draw back to themselves during their current lifetimes, until they come into contact with that final piece they would continue to feel incomplete. They would continue to seek and hunger for that oneness, that feeling of wholeness that they know is available to them but which they have not yet attainted.

It wasn't until I took a step back and looked long and hard at the people in my life, both past and present, that I realized where this hunger was coming from. Though Rev might have been what seemed to be the final piece (we will see), he is not the only one.

By releasing me to explore further my own purpose, he ended my search by confirming for me what I already suspected.

I have been struggling with my own personal guilt for the effects of my actions on Rey. I have been trying to figure out how I could possibly explain to him and have him understand that our time as a couple is done. I am fearful of hurting him and destroying in him his willingness to love again. I mean, how could I possibly justify my actions here; how could I convince him that I was capable of loving and needing more than one person in my life? It is a concept not easily understood.

How could I reasonably expect him to accept the possibility, if I could not accept it myself—if I continued to struggle with the idea that I was meant to stay with one person, even when the very centre of my being denied that that was reality? How could I expect him to see it as I do—or even expect him to be willing to hear what I have to say and believe it as truth—when I do not understand the truth of it or believe it for myself? I do not think that in the end I am meant to settle. I am a wanderer, an explorer of time and this world. I cannot explore and learn from this place if I am not free to go where circumstance and opportunity take me. I do not think that, as an explorer of this world, I am meant to make a difference on a grand scale. It is not for me to lead these people to a better way of life. I have never felt that was my purpose, and I do not feel it now. Rather, I must inspire those who will make a difference—however, whenever, and wherever I can.

It would appear I am going backwards, from this morning's life lessons to last night's discussions, but I know of no other way to explain it and have you understand. I say again, if you could see through my eyes you, too, would find hope in what you had witnessed.

I would not have gotten the email if I had not gone online to look up the Age of Aquarius. I did this after a conversation we had last night about how the world is destined for change. Our dispute was over the how and the when—more so about the *when*—the *how* is, I think, for another time.

It was close to the end of the evening, and we had spent the night discussing religion and spirituality with Angel. We had explained our views and our beliefs and answered for her as many questions as we could.

At one point, after purposely antagonizing me and putting me on the defensive, Rev looked at me and said, "You know, you are beating a dead horse. The time has not yet come for this, and you are attempting to do something that these people are not ready for."

I argued that I realized that it was not yet time for a monumental shift in reality, but it was still my purpose to work toward that shift. I also argued that I didn't think I was the one to finish that particular struggle, but I was definitely meant to help move it along.

I have to point out that Angel seemed lost for the moment, but we will get back to that.

Rev said, "Why do you continue, when you cannot possibly achieve it in this lifetime? It is not meant for us to see this time around."

I know he was not trying to talk me down; rather, he was reminding me to stay focused on the smaller changes, but I was frustrated enough to respond quite selfishly: "I am tired; I do NOT want to do this again; I do not WANT to come back—I want to go HOME!"

It is something that you and others like you have heard me say many times, and, until today, it was how I felt. I was tired; I didn't really want to do this again. We have been here too many times before and seem to be getting nowhere; yet, when I look around now, I see how far humanity has really come. Our evolution, albeit slow, is irrevocably moving forward, for good or bad; we are advancing, and it seems to me we may finally be moving in the right direction.

Even with that knowledge, it is still exhausting to continue the fight when, as he pointed out, it is not yet time to win it. He is right, whether I like it or not. We are not done here, and it was my rebellious nature that led me to respond so thoughtlessly.

His eyes flashed for an instant, only the tiniest of signs that he was briefly annoyed, but they softened immediately. His voice was silken when he responded, and I was reminded yet again of how much I needed this man in my life to give me strength.

"You have to come back." He whispered it quietly, not wanting, I think, to share this moment between us with the world. "You—we—are not done...

After that he seemed to come back to himself and realize that Angel was quite openly staring wide-eyed at our conversation. He asked her if she believed in past lives, and she shook her head, no.

Babe, if you could have seen her eyes,—she was like a deer caught in the headlights: startled, afraid, and frozen in place by what she had seen. I quipped that she was young yet—she will learn. He nodded his acknowledgement even as he began to explain to her the theory of the ages. He went over it only briefly, explaining about Jesus coming around the end of the age of Pisces and the meaning behind the Age of Aquarius.

That is, after all, how the whole conversation started, with him asking if I knew about the Age of Aquarius. He had asked me if I knew when it was, and I had answered: now. He had begun to argue that it was not until around the year 3000, so we still had many more years to wait. I argued back that he hadn't asked me when it ended, only when it was, and, as we were currently in the development of that age, I stood by my answer of "now."

He rolled his eyes at me, as if to say that I was purposely playing games, but I told him that if he wanted a specific answer he should ask a specific question.

He went back to his argument that our next big step in evolution as a race would not take place until the end of that age, giving us a good seven hundred or so more years of struggle and strife. I have looked it up since then, and they say it ends in the year 2600; yet, that is only one theory, and, as you know, the calculations have not yet been proven to be precise. It is a comfort, I must say, to be able to write to you knowing that I do not have to go into long-winded explanations about the history behind these ideas. It's a comfort also to know that if I brush on a topic that you have yourself not yet explored, you will simply go look it up and find your own answers.

I still hate the idea of being responsible for someone else's education, and I abhor the idea of having to direct somebody toward one particular belief system. We discussed that, too, but I will get back to that as well. As I said, Angel looked somewhat poleaxed, not quite sure we were for real. We had, after all, been having a very open and animated discussion about God, Christianity, and religion. For us to switch over so quickly to reincarnation, old souls, and the passing of the ages must have been very disheartening for her. She is a very young soul, and, as such, fearful of concepts she does not understand. She does not like us to embrace the unknown, nor does she see the beauty in the unexplored.

Perhaps part of our reason for pulling her to us was so that we could awaken in her a thirst for knowledge. Only time will tell, but I do not think that it was accidental that she stumbled into my life. I felt mildly amused at her reaction; she is so secure in her faith that it occurred to me that she was not in danger of losing her way, and, if and when she decided to, she would search out answers to the questions we had inadvertently put in her head. So far, we had spent the evening working on encouraging and securing her faith while, at the same time, asking her to acknowledge and accept that ours was not identical in nature.

To be honest, the evening had begun innocently enough. I had agreed to join Angel in the gospel study, which turned out to be fortunate, as the group of Christians she studied with were all Chinese. As such, they were born-again Christians coming from a Buddhist background. It gave me the opportunity to meet some of these people and leave them my number. If Buddhism is something I am meant to explore and learn about, they will call. If they do not, then perhaps it is meant for another time.

Again, only time will tell, and I have quickly learned not to force the issue. I did, however, have a small run-in (if you can call it that) with a minister; I later shared this encounter with Rev. He later used this encounter to yet again try to antagonize me into backing down from my beliefs. I didn't, and he is quickly learning that the more he tests my resolve the stronger it becomes.

Angel had introduced me to the minister, and I talked with him about my book and my purpose behind writing it. I can tell you, he was not open to the idea that more than one religion could be accepted, but I tried to explain that, as long as an individual's god guided him or her to enlightenment, then it didn't matter what that person chose to call that god. He wanted to know what I believed. I told him I believe there is a higher power and that the power guides us, shelters us, and protects us. It is through knowledge and acceptance of that higher power that we grow spiritually and learn the lessons required to achieve a higher state of awareness and harmony within ourselves, the world that surrounds us, and the people in it. He wanted to know what I call that power. I told him: "You call him God, so today I call him God." He obviously did not like my answer, but then I did not expect him to either understand it or accept it. I left my number with him, however, and if he chooses to call, I will meet with him and learn what I can.

Rev was annoyed apparently at what I had done, and he questioned my right to try to alter the views of a minister of the Christian faith. This in turn angered me, and I shot back that I had the right to explain my own beliefs without fear of condemnation. He gave me one of his quirky little smiles and softly stated, "You're so defensive."

Unfortunately, I heard his words and not the meaning behind them and again responded in a very ungracious manner. I exclaimed, "If I am defensive, it is only because you accuse me of doing to others the very thing I so openly disdain and speak out against."

I argued that I was not trying to convert a Christian into believing what I believe but rather asking the Christian to accept me regardless of my beliefs. Why should I have to call my god by any particular name to gain acceptance, when I know, love, and respect that god on a personal level? Who, in fact, was he to judge or question my knowledge of that god on the basis of my name for that god?

Exodus 3:14

God said, "I am who I am. You must tell them: 'the one who is called I AM has sent me to you'"

Writing continued from the hotel room, lying down

At this point, Rev pointed out that I was setting myself up for failure if I believed that I could convince people to follow my beliefs. I told him yet again that I did not expect them to believe as I did and that I only asked for the respect and freedom from others' judgments to explore my own beliefs. I continually forget that I am surrounded by Christians, and he seems to keep a constant vigil out for anything I might say that will endanger me, yet he continues to question and challenge me.

I explained that I had been accepted and welcomed in several different communities so far in spite of my openness about my beliefs. In fact, the only time I had felt pressured was when being confronted by fanatical Christians. At this point, he quickly changed the subject by pointing to a monument in the distance and asking Angel what it was. In the end he apparently got from me what he had been looking for. I think he tests me at odd moments to be sure I will be able to defend myself in a manner that will not bring condemnation and retribution. He seems to have a great deal of faith in my writing, as I have faith in his work to provide his people with tools to create better lives for themselves. For each of us, our chosen paths contain apparent and unseen dangers, and we must shelter and protect each other from those dangers.

When Angel was preparing to leave last night, she asked Rev if he would see that I got home safely. She asked him to protect me, and he very quickly answered that we protect each other. It is when he is soft-spoken and gentle that he touches me the most; his quiet assurance is extremely comforting, and I need it for survival here. If I were not constantly sheltered by those moments of love and understanding, it would be easy for me to lose my way. He is such a blessing to me, and I am so very fortunate to have finally found him.

I apologize for bouncing around so much with regards to our conversation last night; it is not one that can be properly explained in a linear manner. If I attempted to start from the beginning, you might not experience or learn the evening's lessons in the intended manner. I understand that might make no sense to you, but, since you will be reading this long after it was written, then the timing of all of it is relative to you. As usual, I do not map out what or how I am going to write; I simply write and therefore cannot adhere to the restrictions of linear time. Nor can I attempt to create within a boxed-in ideal of someone else's expectations. It is not my nature nor is it my purpose.

I have faith that you are keeping up with me and my random ramblings; fortunately, you are an intelligent, inquisitive creature who can easily follow along.

I am sorry, sweetie, but I must for the moment take a break; my body is telling me to rest, and I am very much in tune with its current needs. If I do not rest when it is time, then I will eventually weaken. So, I am off to take a nap, but, before I go, I will tell you that my earlier reference to a box brings to mind a game Revo played with Angel last night—the same game he played with me the night I discovered I needed to go to the Philippines. I will tell you all about it when I wake. xo

February 21, patio of the Heritage Hotel Manila, 9:53 PM

Okay, so I was going to continue telling you about our story last night, but something came up. I wrote it down in another notebook, because at the time it didn't seem to have a place in this one, but it would seem the answer to my dilemma was, in retrospect, another part of the tale. I will, however, write my views down in the other book as well. I only wish to make note of it here, so, if and when I choose to incorporate it, I will know where it belongs. I will, of course, discuss it with you in detail, and we can decide together if it has a place in these pages.

Okay, so I just filled you in on everything, and we shall see what happens later, eh?

So, when last I left you, we were sitting on a bar patio in Quezon City, Manila, playing a game with Angel. It is a visualization game involving a series of questions that grow from each other. The answers are supposed to reflect one's personal beliefs and desires.

The questions and answers run as follows.

The subject is asked to picture in their mind a white room, an empty room with white walls, and then the questions begin...

REV. Picture a box in the room. What size is the box? Is it small, medium, or large?

ANGEL. Small box.

REV. Where is the box? Is it sitting on the floor? Is it floating in the air? What is the box doing?

ANGEL. It is on a table.

REV. What colour is the box?

ANGEL. It is red, yellow—all the sides are different colours.

REV. Now picture a ladder in the room. Where is the ladder? How big is the ladder?

ANGEL. Ten steps, and it is leaning against the wall on the right side of the room.

REV. Now, picture flowers in the room. What colour are they, and where are they in the room? How big are they?

ANGEL. One flower, a daisy, and it is on the table. It looks like a normal-size daisy.

REV. Okay, now picture a horse in the room. Where is the horse? What is it doing? What colour is it?

ANGEL. It is a rocking horse, like the ones children play on. It is brown, and it is on the floor in the middle of the room.

REV. Okay, now use three words to describe the horse's personality.

ANGEL. (looking confused) It is a normal horse. (At this point she struggled for words, but, as Rev prompted her, she came up with the following.) Harmonious, graceful, content, relaxed, and chillin'.

REV. Okay, now picture a storm in the room. Where is the storm? How big is it, and is it affecting the things in the room? Is it touching them or blowing them around.

ANGEL. (with an odd look on her face) It is on the left side of the room, across from the horse, away from everything. It is a letter storm, made of words.

Okay Beaner, are you ready to learn what it all means?

Well, before I tell you, take the time to ask yourself the same questions, write down the answers, and then compare them to our explanations.

"Nothing, it means absolutely nothing; it's an idle game to pass the time … I'm joking," he told her that, just as he had told me the same thing before he was kind enough to explain it.

I had written everything down, so it was easier to go through the explanation with her.

The box represents her pride; as she chose a very small box it showed she was a very humble girl. He couldn't explain about the table, and if I ever get the chance, I will ask him where he learned the game, so I can try to find the answer myself. The fact that the box was sitting on something, however, and was not floating, represents that she is not an artistic soul. Rather, she is grounded, logical, and rational.

The colours on the box indicate her personality and how others view her. If it had been clear or transparent, that would have meant that people could easily see through her. As it was multicoloured, it indicates that she shows many sides of herself, her personality, to different people, depending on the circumstances.

The ladder represents her life ambitions. As hers was approximately the same height as her, she has attainable ambitions. As the number of rungs on the ladder was very specific, her ambitions are also very structured and well thought out.

We came next to what the flower represented, and before she answered the next question I wrote down on my own paper the word God. Rev began to explain to her that the flower represents the people in our life who we love and cherish, but he was confused as to why there was only one. So he asked her who she thought that one person was. She answered God; the fact that it was a common type and normal size then indicates that God is a normal part of her day-to-day life.

Okay, now to the horse, of course…

It is meant to represent her ideal mate. Her horse was a rocking horse, so her mate should be fun-loving and love kids. He should be harmonious, graceful, content, and relaxed. Let's not forget chillin'! Though Rev was stuck on the colour, I pointed out that since it was brown it indicated an earthy, grounded personality, which is like Angel's own.

Well, hon, there's more, but again, I am tired, so off to bed. Tomorrow I think I will head off to Rizal Park and maybe find a shady patch of grass to work on the next part of my tale. I wonder if I will meet anyone along the way who can tell me more about these people. Rev seems to have withdrawn from the equation for the moment, so, as I said before, another guide should be popping up at any time. I'll let you know what happens. xoxo

February 22, patio of the Heritage Hotel Manila, 4:43 PM

You see—if I wait long enough the answers come. I quite literally only crawled out of bed an hour ago. I was so sick and so tired all day. I had no drive or ambition and was feeling quite lost as to which direction to go next. So I eventually pulled myself out of bed and decided I was going to come down and try to get some food into me. While I was here, something Angel said to me the night before kept popping into my head. She asked if I would like to visit a local orphanage with her and see the work that is being done there to help the homeless children.

The idea intrigued me. After all, the point of coming here was to bring the plight of these people to the attention of the world. I got sidetracked, of course, as I am wont to do. My curiosity about human behavior gets the best of me at times, I admit, but the idea itself was still buried in the back of my mind.

I wondered, though, who was sponsoring the organizations, and, as I was pondering, it came to me that my time here is running short; I have only eleven days left. If I aim to find out as much as I can, I can't sit and wait for Angel to take me around. She has her life to live, and I don't want to intrude on that. It also occurred to me that the fact that Rev has been unavailable is a very strong lesson in independence. I would have to learn not to rely on anyone's but my own intuition and intelligence to lead me in the right direction.

So I took a chance and asked the waiter if he knew of any local orphanages that cared for homeless children. He said yes—as a matter of fact, he could tell me two organizations off the top of his head.

One is government-run, called the DSWD, and another one is run by the local media network in Manila: ABS-CBN, which also happens to tie in with Revo's work in the entertainment industry. I took a few minutes out to go upstairs and look up a couple for myself online. I typed in orphanages, Manila, Philippines on a Google search and the first name that came up was Shepherd of the Hills Children's Foundation. Once I was back down at the patio, I asked the waiter if he had ever heard of that particular orphanage, and he informed me that the hotel that I am staying in happens to sponsor that organization. He did not, however, have any information on what they do, but he told me I could more than likely get the contact number through the concierge. He told me if there was anything else I needed he'd be more than happy to help me out.

It's amazing how open these people are when you show an interest or concern for their people. I guess I shouldn't be surprised by it, really; any interest from the outside in helping to alleviate the poverty here must serve to open their hearts a bit more to the possibility of a better future. They get quite excited when I tell them I am writing a book and am here to learn about them. Their eyes shine just a little more when I ask questions, and, instead of being cautious, they seem to want to jump at the chance to help. I am, I admit, still feeling drained, but at least now I seem to have a trail to follow. I will have to wait and see where it leads.

In the meantime, I will try to wrap up for you our previous night's discussion with Angel. She, like the minister, wanted to know what I believed, especially after listening to Revo and me arguing about whether or not my expectations were too high. I told her the same thing I tell everyone else who asks and reiterated that I did not believe I had to call that higher power by the same name as others, as long as my faith and knowledge of it was secure. Revo jumped into the conversation at one point and asked her if she knew what voodoo was. She replied, "Black magic." I shook my head, while Rev began an in-depth explanation of the basis of that particular spiritual belief.

He explained that the practice of voodoo originated in Africa and was, in fact, a religion that was headed by a dual god/ goddess, Mawu-Lisa, or, alternatively, a single divine creator, Nana Buluku, who embodies a dual cosmogonic principle, and of which *Mawu*, the moon, and *Lisa*, the sun, are female and male aspects. The religion is believed to be so old, in fact, that it dates back ten thousand years and is believed to have ancient roots in Mesopotamia, Egypt, India, and Asia Minor.

The word *voodoo (vodon, vodoun,* or *voudon)* means God Creator or Great Spirit. It is a belief founded in one supreme God, a very abstract omnipotent force. It is through worship and knowledge of that God that its participants strive to better understand both the natural process of life and their own spiritual nature. The art of *vodon* is one of healing, both within one's self and the world. Practitioners use prayer and ritual to celebrate forces of nature. They also honour specific deities or spirits who are believed to actively work as protectors and guides. Rev likened this to the Christian belief in angels, saying that they were extensions of God's power sent to shelter and protect. He also pointed out that a large part of their faith centered around the idea that the more positive action they took in their lives, both toward their own spiritual growth and toward that of others, the more positive energies they would in turn receive.

I pointed out it was very similar to the wiccan Law of Threefold Return, which holds that whatever benevolent or malevolent actions a person performs will return to that person with triple force, thereby ensuring that its users could only expect misery if that power was not used for the betterment of others.

Rev made it quite clear that only the Westernization of these arts twisted them into a religion that was believed to have negative connotations. When they didn't understand the belief behind the religion, people's views of it were prone to inaccuracy. I agreed and say that it is human nature to fear what we do not understand. It is also our nature to hate that which we fear—and what we hate we work toward destroying.

Angel looked rather taken aback by all of this. It seemed to her, I believe, that we were attempting to cloud her own beliefs and thereby lead her astray. We attempted to reassure her, and I hope we got through to her that we did not intend to threaten or belittle her faith. In fact, the opposite is true—we were merely trying to point out that there are underlying currents of similarity to be found in most major religions.

For example, *vodon* involves the search for higher levels of consciousness in the belief that we must open the way to God. Again, you can compare it to the Christian belief that through faith and knowledge of God we open the way to allow him into our lives.

Angel was surprised, I think—in fact, I am sure that would be putting it mildly—but it was heartening that she didn't immediately run from the idea. Rev pointed out that her body language indicated that she was feeling insecure and possibly threatened by the topic. She had, in fact, leaned back in her chair as far as she could away from him; her chin was also lifted as if in defiance, and her arms were folded across her chest defensively. When he mentioned it again, she said quite pointedly and fiercely that she believed in God and that she could not see voodoo or black magic as being a way to worship that God.

Rev replied that that was indeed the whole point he was trying to make: because she had not researched these things for herself and could not definitively say they were true, she could not then accept our explanations of them. He also said that her God teaches acceptance and understanding, not judgment of others. How could she claim to live out God's wishes if she was not willing to at least try to accept or understand the beliefs of others? Why, also, should she, secure as she was in her own relationship with God, fear knowledge of other faiths and religions? She did not have to change her beliefs in order to open her eyes to the possibility that the core of those beliefs could in fact be found in other religions.

Angel had mentioned black magic more than once, and Rev seemed to think the matter needed to be addressed. He explained that the "black magic" part of voodoo was, in fact, a twisted offshoot of the original religion. It is not what the true practitioners of that religion believe, and it has no place in their worship.

I pointed out that every religion has its opposite, evil side. Christianity has it counterpart in Satanism, and the wiccans also have their opposite in the dark arts of black witchcraft. As long as there has been religion there have been those who choose to follow the opposite path of that religion. The world revolves around balance, and so, for every good there must be an equal and opposing bad. Yet it is personal choice that dictates each individual's beliefs, not the foundation behind the beliefs themselves.

I do not advocate the belief or practice of these darker arts, but I do acknowledge the need to understand them. I do not believe that one can effectively defend against an enemy one does not understand. I also do not believe that the denial of their existence will in any way, shape, or form initiate the destruction of those beliefs. I think that it is for those who follow a more enlightened path to reach out and understand those who do not. Only through that understanding can we begin to call those who have lost their way toward a more positive direction. I also believe that in order to accomplish that task we must understand why they lost their way in the first place.

If, for example, you point your finger at someone who has stolen from you and loudly declare, "You are a thief—therefore you are a bad person!" then you are closing yourself off from an opportunity to help that person find a better way. You have not asked why the person has stolen, and, in not asking, you cannot know that he is perhaps trying to get money to feed his children. You cannot know, if you do not ask, that he has lost his job. You cannot know that, though he has applied for government assistance, he has been denied. You cannot know that he is perhaps the only source of income for his family, as his wife is ill, and you cannot know if you do not ask that his friends or family are in no position themselves to help him.

I do describe one of the worst-case scenarios, and I openly acknowledge that not all people who have committed crimes have any justifiable reason for committing those crimes. I only wish to point out that if we merely point our fingers and accuse, without first asking why, then we are ignoring one of the fundamental life lessons we have been sent here to learn. Empathy for others leads us to understanding, and understanding opens the door for positive action. We can continue to point and accuse, or we can seek the reasons behind behavior we do not understand. It is a personal choice to be made by each individual as they journey down the road of life.

I would like to think most people would be open to the idea that the question *Why?* is an important one to ask.

Why does that person believe as they do?

Why does that person act as they do?

Why does that person live as they do?

When we look for the answers to the questions of *why*, we open ourselves to a greater understanding of those we share the world with. Should we not make peace with those around us?

Our discussion, as you can plainly see, ran all over the place throughout the evening, but it kept returning to that base belief that part of learning about ourselves is opening ourselves to learning about others and the world around us. I don't want to tell others what to believe; it is not my place and it is not my way. I only want to understand why others believe as they do. It is a constant hunger in me that I cannot seem to satisfy, this curiosity of people's ways and reasons. There is so much out there to learn and so much that others have to offer.

I hope we didn't scare the little darling too badly. She is young, yes, but she is intelligent, and I have hopes that she can eventually get past her fear of the unknown. I think her strength of faith will take her far, and I am certain she has much to teach the world. She has taught me a great many things already, though I am sure she does not recognize the fact. I am very grateful for the opportunity to meet her and hope I have, in turn, given her some things to think on.

Well, hon, the evening is wearing on, and I have hopes that tomorrow will be a busy day ...

I sent Rev a text regarding my plan to seek out orphanages and organizations that fund them. I hope, since his mother is leaving in the morning, that he can find the time to tour around with me—but I also realize that he may still be more interested in protecting himself by keeping his distance. We will see what happens tomorrow, and I will keep you informed. Goodbye for now, beautiful lady. I will talk to you soon.

February 22, patio of the Heritage Hotel Manila, 7:30 AM

Well, darling, I may just have both found myself a new friend in adventure as well as a way out to the provinces under the protection of a fairly burly, yet surprisingly sweet, gentlemen from England. I hate to celebrate my good luck prematurely; I will tell you how it happened if and when anything comes of it. It may turn out to be another one of those "No #*! ##!* way—that did not just happen" moments—but it appears that yet again, as I need them, so they are provided. If in this case I am wrong, then I can't say I much regret the time spent, and I certainly will not consider it to be time wasted. It did turn out to be a much-needed distraction and release of tension.

I am, however, at the moment very much in need of a shower and a bit of down time. The shower, at least, I think I can manage; the down time is much more unlikely, as I still intend to see if I can gain access to some of the orphanages. I am not sure what I am looking for, and certainly I do not have an expectation as to what I will find; I just feel that I need to go.

It has just occurred to me that I have made a breakthrough here with the people who work in the hotel; they are finally beginning to call me by name, which is a huge step in the right direction with regards to open communication. Wonderful, only eleven days left, and I am finally getting them to see me as more than just another guest.

Man, it's early; in retrospect it's a very good thing I slept all day yesterday. I honestly can't tell you at what ungodly hour I actually fell asleep last night, or rather this morning, but, as I said, it was well worth it.

I met some new and unique individuals last night, on two separate occasions. One was a mild-mannered flight instructor from China, who was very obviously in need of a bit of company. He was mildly interesting and very nice, but I have the feeling his intentions were not exactly pure. I think his eagerness to buy me beer was a bit of a giveaway, but, as I was expecting a call from Deacon at 11:00, I had a good excuse to escape to my room.

It was on my way to my room, however, that I was stopped briefly by a much more intriguing personage. A sweet old guy who I have seen around the hotel several times over the last few days with his team of... hmmm... well, let's call them *engineers*, for lack of a better word. I've noticed him only because the fact that he bears a striking resemblance to my dad made him stand out from the continuously changing crowd of people who inhabit this hotel.

I was walking by his table when he called me over, and, as I felt I had time, I allowed myself to be pulled off-course. It turns out he is an Englishman here with his work crew preparing to install some fiber-optic cables out in the provinces, which will allow Internet and phone access out in some of the rural areas. Again we go back to communication; always it seems we are pulled back to communication and the use of it in bringing out world closer together. Novel idea, that...

He was interested, as I have discovered many here to be, in what I am doing writing every day. He wanted to know from whence I hail and what it is I am working on. At first I tried to give only a surface explanation, but he, being much older and possibly wiser, saw right through the façade and proceeded to ask questions meant to draw out more information than I was at the time willing to give. I was tied to the clock this time so had to excuse myself, but, as I left, I did promise to return and talk a little more with him about my book. After speaking with Deacon briefly on the phone, I made my way back down to the patio and partook in a glass of wine with both the elderly gentleman and a young man who had joined the table.

The young man, I will call him Hippie, was at first very quiet, and, in obvious deference to the other gentleman, kept silent while my fine English friend began to drill me for information. What was my book about? How did I come about the idea to write it? What was the purpose behind the book? What were my conclusions so far? Most importantly to him, it seemed: had I been published before and, if so, where and under what name?

The answers to most of those questions you already know, so I will not bore you with the details. As for his enquiries as to what I had previously published, I admit I was vague at best. I flat-out refused to give him the name under which my work has been published and I refused also to give him any solid information concerning the content of that published work. I was also shamefully misleading with regard to the type of work I had done in the past, but, as I explained to him later, the current topic is one that could in a roundabout way cause serious repercussions for those involved. Much to my dismay, I found myself being overly forthcoming about the how and the why of this particular piece of literature, and I sincerely hope that my openness will not, as they say, come back and bite me in the ass.

I blame his similarity in appearance to my late stepfather for my blatant disregard for caution. I am sure it had nothing to do with the beer and the wine.

It was only after he seemed satisfied that I was levelling with him that he ceased his relentless questions, and his young friend took the opportunity to speak.

It was the young friend, in fact, who I discovered had much more to offer by way of life experience than the unusual old gentleman I had first thought to gain some insight from. It turns out my young hippie is the son of a well-to-do entrepreneur who managed somehow, in spite of his wealth, to raise a selfless, earthy individual. It amazed me that this man, who had been sent to the best boarding schools in England and who at one point had thought nothing of purchasing things like Lamborghinis and yachts as playthings, had chosen to put aside his worldly possessions and go to live a much-less-materialistic life in South Africa.

Oh yes, darling, you read that correctly. His father is a self-made multimillionaire, an oil barren among other things, and yet he chooses to eke out an existence in a small community in South Africa. Without, I must add, the aid of his parent's not inconsiderable fortune to help pay his way.

Okay, I admit it—it sounds a bit farfetched and very much like a story fabricated to lure in an unwary female. However, as it did not come up until much later in the conversation that he hailed from a wealthy background, he had absolutely no reason to lure me anywhere; I was already there. We were thoroughly entranced in an animated discussion and he had already won my attention with his open and friendly demeanor. His story goes something like this.

He was born and raised in England by a well-to-do self-made oil tycoon. In his youth, he attended all the best schools money could buy and worked where he chose in occupations that allowed him to surround himself with all the toys a rich kid could want. His spending habits in his younger years were flamboyant, to say the least, and he himself had no regard for the people in this world who had less than he. He did, however, have the fortunate benefit of having two supportive and loving parents. So, when, at the age of nineteen, he found himself in a situation where he was forced with the very real probability that he was soon going to be a father himself, he was saved from self-destruction by the some very well-rounded advice from his father.

Rather than condemn him for his carelessness, his father encouraged him to embrace the idea that perhaps it was time to grow up. Hippie told me that his father never chastised him, only supported him unconditionally, and it was through that support that his views of his life and the lives of others began to change.

His father had apparently always tried to instill in him the belief that he was no better, regardless of his financial or social situation, than those who seemingly stood below him. He did have the benefit of growing up knowing that money and status were not what defined an individual, yet he was still complacent toward the struggles and trials of those less fortunate. How his attitude changed and his eyes opened is, according to him, a story in and of itself. I am therefore hoping to come back to it at a later date. I would like the opportunity to see him again and perhaps glean from him a more in-depth version of his tale—which I will, of course, share with you.

He did, however, have a few enlightened views that pertain to the material and topics discussed at various times throughout these pages. He seems to agree that the world could use a gentle nudge in the direction of acceptance and understanding of others, but he views the lack of these things as a lack of interest, not a lack of information. He pointed out quite readily that we all see the pictures of starving children on TV and in the papers, but, as it does not immediately affect us, it does not hold our interest for long. He says the world is very much aware of the plight of these people and others in Third World countries around the globe but that awareness is nothing more than a passing glance.

I argued that it is one thing to see or read about the child but quite another to feel and understand the child's hunger. He says it's true that they are two different levels of awareness, but he does not believe it is easy to attain the latter. People must first be convinced that they need to do more than simply stare blankly at the face of the child before they will be willing to take the next step and taste the tears of that same child. The problem and the challenge are: how does one convince anybody that empathy and understanding of others is an important part of our growth as humans? I have to agree; it is a dilemma, yes, but one I am willing to attack full-force, if I have to exhaust myself to do it.

I was surprised, however, at the eloquent explanation given the source. He is, as he openly stated from the beginning of our conversation, a non-believer in the spiritual and religious communities. This fact shocked me completely, as he had had such well rounded and grounded views of the world in which he lived. He amended the comment later, saying he simply refused to discuss religion and spirituality openly, as his views on the matter covered such a vast array of belief systems while adhering to none that it was impossible for the average person to understand from whence he was coming.

I am anxious to explore his ideas further with him, and, as we are meeting up later to wander around, I intend to get him to open up a bit more about them. It is strange that I have come halfway around the world and have encountered people from different parts of the globe and different religious backgrounds who believe all the same fundamental ideals. They only call them by different names and describe them as coming from different sources, but the end result seems, so far, to be the same. Humans, as diverse as we are, really are not that different when you get down to the core of the being.

Hippie also talked about the idea that living a simpler, less materialistic life is not one many people are ready to embrace by choice. They do, for the most part, enjoy their creature comforts, and it would seem unwise and unfair to expect them to give them up. He did, however, agree that we would do well to take a step back from technology once in awhile and get back to the basic one-on-one level of communication. For example, rather than come home and sit in front of the TV with your child and consider that quality time, get off the couch and actually spend time talking with that child. He agreed with me that children see way more and are much more perceptive than we give them credit for, citing his own experience of finding himself on the receiving end of profound wisdom coming from the mouth of a nine-year-old. He says he does, in fact, find himself basing most of his more important life choices on that wisdom, believing that his child's intuitions are for the most part more accurate than his own. And I thought I was nuts...

Realistically, though, we do share many of the same views and ideas, and I am greatly looking forward to talking with him further. It does surprise me that we could come from such different backgrounds and life experiences and yet end up coming to the same conclusions. I am beginning to see a pattern emerging in this, and, as it emerges, so, too, does the possibility that my very broad views on spirituality and reality might just have a basis in fact.

It is, I admit, the long way round to proving it, but I am up for the trip, which is, after all, why I am here. I wonder what interesting person I get to meet next. Yet again, the prospect excites me, and I look forward to my next unexpected encounter.

Well, hon, it was a late night, and I would like to get showered and work toward getting some info on the orphanages. I will talk to you soon. xo

February 23, patio of the Heritage Hotel Manila, 11:30 PM

Hey, sweets, just dropping a line to let you know I should not have dismissed my encounter with the pilot so soon. It turns out that one of the two things that he continued to bring up throughout our discussion has significance after all. He had mentioned Balacun several times, and I was under the impression that he was trying to get me to go there with him, because he kept saying over and over that I should go to Balacun, but you know, I was thinking about it the wrong way and didn't pick up anything until today when I went back online to look for more orphanages. This time the one I first found was not there (weird), but a new one did show up in the form of a link to the Precious Heritage Children's Home in Balacun, outside metro Manila.

I am going to run with the idea that I should go there and am about to call a lady who the concierge told me will be able to put me in contact with the various orphanages here in Manila.

The second thing he seemed to feel was vitally important was the terracotta army of China's first emperor, Qin Shi Huang. It was hard at times to discern what he was trying to say, as his English was very broken, but he was very definite and clear in one respect. The first time he mentioned it, his English became very clear and fluent and his eyes shone as he peered into mine and told me: "You know this place; you must go to this place; then you must know that you remember this place."

Honestly, the first time he said it I thought I had heard him incorrectly, but not ten minutes later he looked me square in the eye again and said definitively: "You must remember this place; you must remember the horses, the reason for the horses" (again with the horses).

The entire evening had been like that. We would talk, and whenever it was about his family or work, his English would be extremely difficult to follow. He tried to teach me a little Chinese, but again, he didn't know the English words to translate, so the conversation had been sporadic and slow—yet, every few minutes his eyes would brighten and sometimes in mid-sentence he would very pointedly insist that I go, that I remember...

It was a bit on the weird side, sure—especially since I had not discussed with him my interest either in history or religion, and I couldn't figure out why he was being so emphatic about it—but then again, I did not put any importance on it at the time. Now, however, I am thinking it is maybe something I should look into. I know nothing about the history and cannot therefore relate it to my current search for answers, but I think that somehow, some way it might also tie into the rest of this crazy tale.

I keep wondering where these many leads that apparently run off in many different directions are taking me—but I feel it drawing to a conclusion. Yet, for the life of me, I cannot grasp what that conclusion might be. There are no coincidences, eh, or so it would seem, but, again I am completely and utterly stumped as to where this one will lead. Wish me luck, my wiccan friend; I feel at this point I may need it.

February 24, patio of the Heritage Hotel Manila, 10 AM

Patience has its rewards. I took the time to stop at the desk this morning at Hippie's urging, and discovered some information I would not have found otherwise. The owner of the hotel personally supports an organization in the provinces that cares for orphans. In fact, the concierge and his friend have travelled there many times to make donations and help feed the children. He gave me the name of the place and said he will speak to his boss about arranging for me to go there. I do not think, though, that I should go out empty-handed and am wondering what I should bring. I will ask them when I go back in what an appropriate donation would be. As I visit each home, I will carefully collect information on how people can make donations to these organizations directly, so the funds donated will not be wasted on things like red tape and advertising.

These people are being so incredibly helpful to my search, and I look forward to any adventures I might have out in the provinces. I came out to the patio, as usual, for my morning coffee and was just treated to the most pleasant surprise. One of the young waiters here brought me out a plate of fresh fruit without my asking, explaining that he had noticed that when I am writing sometimes I forget to eat and he wanted to remind me to take care of myself or I would become ill. I have only been here for a few days, but they have apparently come to know me very well. I do, indeed, forget to eat when I am working; it's true, and if I am not prompted I can go for the entire day without remembering. My little guardian angels—that is what the staff here are to me. I am so glad I ended up in this hotel. I would have missed the chance to meet all these beautiful people.

People are very surprised when they hear I am financing this book and this trip myself. They seem to think that it is a long shot to go halfway around the world on a whim in search of a story; yet, as Hippie pointed out last night, if you believe in something strongly enough and your purpose is pure you will be rewarded in the end.

I've really been doing nothing but writing for several days, and it is time I got out of this hotel, but at the same time I realize that had I not stayed here and gained their trust they would not be so willing to help. The boys at the front desk are digging up a number for me, so I can contact the orphanage I intend to visit today. I do not wish to offend anyone there by just showing up unexpectedly, and, again, I would like to know if there is anything I can bring. The trip out will be expensive, but, as the hotel is providing me with a driver, I will at least be safe.

I sincerely hope that Baba is smiling down on me and approves of how I've decided to spend her money. I think she would...

I got a lecture of sorts from Deacon, and it reminded me that a large part of this particular learning experience is learning to help people, not in the way *I* think they need to be helped, but, rather, in the way *they* would like to be helped. If I can provide information on organizations that exist here and dispense with all the red tape that surrounds the funding of these organizations, then, maybe more of the money will reach the people those organizations are intended to help.

It is a novel idea, don't you think? I'd be giving those more fortunate the chance to be in direct contact with the people whose lives they would touch if given the chance. Crazy thought, I know; again, I say we will see what happens, and after I have gone out there, I will come back and explain more of my idea. It is not a path I saw myself going down—yet it is a path that I can be nothing but grateful for being led to.

Must fly luv, much to do…

February 24, patio of the Heritage Hotel Manila, 4 PM

Okay, so my day so far has been one of writing and waiting…

I managed to obtain more contacts form the hotel with regards to local orphanages, but other than the one meeting already arranged, I have not had any more positive feedback. This has turned out to be fortuitous, as I have managed to complete yet another chapter. I also met some of the crew that my new hippie friend is working with. They were very friendly, and they had a fair amount to say.

They asked me what the hell a little white Canadian girl was doing in the Philippines. I told them the book was based in the Philippines, so I was here to see for myself the people and the culture. They asked whether I had been to various places and whether I had partaken in certain local delicacies. I told them that I had not as yet had the opportunity, and one of them asked, 'How the hell can you write a book about a people and their culture if you don't expose yourself to it?' I was tempted to explain that the book was based *in* the Philippines, not *about* the Philippines, but I chose to keep my mouth shut. I did, however, explain that, given the fact that I am a single white female travelling alone, it was not wise for me to venture out too far from the hotel on my own. I did not bother to tell them that the man who had offered to be a guide of sorts had quite literally abandoned me to my own devices—a fact I am now coming to view as a blessing. I did tell them that as my evenings were free, and as they have actually been living here and working here for years, I was open to the idea of evening tours around the city. If there was a part of the culture they wished me to see, then I was more than willing to let them show it to me.

I am not sure they took me seriously, but they will be back for dinner, and we will see then if they have taken to the idea. They are burly, rough men, the kind I have always chosen to surround myself with; I have no fear of them. I have every faith in the fact that I would be quite protected and sheltered by their presence.

I also was bold enough to tell them quite seriously that when I needed things they were usually provided to me when the time was most beneficial. Therefore, I am completely convinced that when it is time for me to go out to the provinces and see some of the culture there, a way will be provided for me to do it safely. The crew are all atheists, and they didn't believe a word of it. They scoffed and said that the idea of me simply sitting and waiting for my next guide to show up, or for the path to that guide to be made clear, was a ridiculous way to get things accomplished. I am thinking if they hang out with me long enough their attitude just might change a bit.

They did ask me if I had been to Smokey Mountain, and when I said I had not, the biggest, nastiest of them (we will call him Bear, as his nature is one of a grizzly whose cub has been threatened, yet he can be quite gentle as well, so, grizzly or teddy—either one fits) decided to give me an education. According to him, Smokey Mountain was originally a dump that over the years built up to a massive mountain of garbage overlooking the bay. After years of this buildup, someone (the government, apparently) decided they should try to put the land to better use. So they levelled it off and proceeded to cover it with topsoil and build housing on it for the less fortunate. The problem is that every time it rains the toxins from under the soil rise up like a mist and poison whoever happens to be in the area. So the people behind the project had to abandon it, and they proceeded to knock down all the buildings, levelling everything and leaving behind only rubble. Of course, they never replaced the housing, so the people who had moved in there are again without a place to live. The whole thing ended up being a huge waste of time and effort, not to mention money, and it was all because there was this idea that housing should be provided for the people but they really didn't want to have to spend the extra money on better land. They told me that, to this day, when it rains the mist continues to rise from the ground and the massive pile of earth looks like it is smoking. That's how it got the name Smokey Mountain.

I can neither confirm nor deny this story, as it was handed down to me in the form of legend, yet behind every legend there is a lesson—but we'll get back to that.

The tale's end led to the next tales beginning, as often happens in these cases. The next guy, one of two twins living and working with the crew (we'll call him Blue Eyes, as his eyes are a striking match to the colour of a clear blue sky) began a story about a company that came here with the intention of striking it rich.

This company moved into one of the local communities and proceeded to hand out thousands of free phones. People were very excited and started using the phones to call all around the world. Keep in mind that many of the locals have family members who work overseas, where the money is better, so they can send money back to support their families. The people called everywhere: Canada, Europe, other parts of Asia (you get the idea).

Time passed, and the bills came in, and the people said, "What is this?" When the company people explained that the phones were free but the usage was not, the people said, "No, no, you said free!" Now, herein lies the problem: thinking these people simple and uneducated the company never bothered to get them to sign any kind of contract. The company just assumed that they could either pressure or outsmart the people into paying, but the people said, "No way! We no sign, we no pay—we know our right." Of course, legally, the company can't do anything— no contract, no money.

They were never able to convince the people and eventually were forced to give up the fight. As Blue Eyes said, "They had to shut down the entire operation and leave the country with their tail between their legs. Bloody fools lost millions!"

This story also is hearsay, but the lesson remains the same.

So the other twin (we'll call him Pale Eyes, as his eyes are the white-blue colour of the sky on a summer's day during a light misty rain) decides it's time to add his piece. He starts in about how everybody blames the government, but in reality there's a much deeper reason for some of the problems. He says the people are used to having things for free. For example, when they want power they simply tap into existing power lines and use what's already there.

He told another story about a project he worked where they were asked to go in and provide power for some new housing that was being built. When it came to the attention of the people who were supposed to be relocated to the new development that they would have to pay for power, they argued and said they wouldn't. The people refused to move, and the project was abandoned like the others. This time, however, the building was not knocked down; they were left with unfinished shells. Once the crews moved out, the people moved in. They tapped into existing power and to this day remain there living in incomplete buildings that amount to not much more than hovels. They do, however, have roofs over their heads, running water, plumbing, and, of course, hydro—they live quite contentedly there for free.

As Pale Eyes said, "Bloody fools keep trying to come in and make things better, to change things, but these people are happy the way they are, because, in the end, they are free."

I don't think I have to tell you this story is, again, word of mouth and therefore cannot be taken as fact. The lesson, however, in all of it is pretty clear. When you are an outsider looking in, it can be very costly indeed to presume you know what another person needs or wants.

They left shortly after that, and it was only after I had worked on chapter six that it occurred to me the lesson was an echo of what my friend Deacon had cautioned me about on the phone two nights ago. That was the very same night, in fact, that I met Hippie, and, by the long way around, met these interesting fellows.

I hope I get the chance to know these fellows; at the very least I would like to enquire whether they think I will learn as much by wandering around sightseeing and partaking of local cuisines as I will wandering around and partaking in conversation with locals. I doubt they will argue the point when I present it in such a reasonable and logical manner.

This, by the way, brings us around to my reasonable and logical Deacon—who made a point to connect via phone the other night regarding the possibility of us doing some exploring around the globe. While we were talking, he made sure to point out that I had to be very careful in my intentions to help people who I might not yet understand. He said he hated to play the devil's advocate, but he wondered whether it had occurred to me that these people might be quite content living as they were. I told him not to worry, that it was very much on my mind that I shouldn't meddle in other people's ways. I told him that was, in fact, what this whole damn book seemed to be turning out to be about. I do always advocate the open-minded approach to different belief systems, and it turns out I also see the need for that approach when dealing with people we see as less fortunate. I mean, really, if they want to be Westernized, fine, who am I to judge—but, at the same time, we as Westerners need to be willing to only share with them what they require, *not* what we think they should have.

I have mentioned before that I was immediately struck by the contented nature of these people, and I have come to the conclusion that neither I nor anybody else has the right to assume they need or want my help. It has occurred to me also that it is another one of those really big life lessons many of us have yet to learn.

Quite honestly, empathy and understanding tie into these both politically and spiritually. It is not up to us to decide when and how to help others; rather, we should be there for them if and when they decide they want or need to change or help themselves. As I said in one of my previous letters, I very much felt this whole affair drawing to a close, and the time for that is, in fact, very near. Yet, given that fact, I am grateful to the people of this country for allowing me in long enough for me to see and understand where they are coming from.

I am still going to continue my attempts to tour the orphanages and research the different charities that exist here, if only so that I can include them in my book. This will give the people who read my work a chance to donate freely and directly to the already abundant and active charities here in Manila and around the Philippines.

I came here with the intention of hunting down a story I had the enormous ego to presume I knew the truth of, and I leave here with a very humbled outlook on religion, spirituality, culture, and life.

From the beginning, when we were driven by the desire to help initiate change, to the journey itself that taught me the true meaning of that change and its possible repercussions, to the yet unfinished conclusion that indicates it is very much up to the people here to decide if they even want change, it has been an interesting and eye-opening journey.

I will continue to write to you and keep you updated on any new developments, but I will be surprised if anything profound pops up. I think I should now spend my days working on my chapters and my evenings relaxing and enjoying these people and their hospitality. I am sure there are more lessons to be learned, either here or on my next adventure, but for now I am quite content with where this particular road has taken me. I will for the moment bid you a good night and leave you with this thought: I have been blessed and am very grateful for every new opportunity to learn about life. Night night. xoxo

February 25, patio of the Heritage Hotel Manila, 8:00 AM

Well, darling, there were no profound philosophical quandaries to ponder in my adventures last night. As I predicted, the whole evening passed rather peacefully over wine and beer. The conversation, however, was interesting and the people, as always, intriguing.

I met a fish last night by the name of PH. He is a power horn who resides here on the patio at the heritage hotel, and he is much loved and revered by his caretakers. He is three years old, and I am very much hoping he will live out the fifteen or twenty years that are expected of him, as I would very much like to come back and visit.

He is very *maganda* (beautiful), with clever markings on his body that resemble Chinese characters—appropriate, since at the time of our introduction I was sitting out here on the deck having a beer and learning Chinese from my pilot friend. The markings mean "luck" or "good fortune" in Chinese—also appropriate, as this whole trip has turned out to be rather fortuitous.

The man who cares for and feeds my sweet little finned friend took the time to explain a little about the breed. They are extremely violent fish, much like the Japanese fighting fish, and cannot be put in the same tank with other fish, not even ones of the same breed. They are so confrontational, in fact, that in order to allow them to mate one must install a divider in the tank. The divider must allow the two fish to come close and smell each other but be strong enough to keep them apart. The female is then put into the other side of the tank and their courtship, if you will, ensues. The whole process takes about six months. He explained that for the first while they mainly ignore each other, then after awhile they begin to spend more time close to the divider. Eventually they make it a daily ritual to bump noses, and, once they get to the point when they are almost always swimming face to face, the divider can be safely lifted. Once they have mated, the female is removed before they start fighting (apparently pregnant fish get cranky too). It is a long, arduous progress from the viewpoint of the breeder, but I could see how humorous he thought the whole adventure actually was. In fact, my fish-keeping friend seemed to think the whole thing funny as hell. He kept bumping his hands together to mimic the bumping of noses and laughing his ass off.

Every time he grinned he showed off this odd little gap in the front of his teeth that on any other man might look extremely unattractive. Yet this quirky little fellow's smile was warm and honest and rather endearing; I simply couldn't help but love the guy.

Just to clarify what he was telling me, I asked, "So, essentially, what you're saying is they meet, they take about six months to acknowledge and get to know each other, then, after deciding they like each other, they have sex and he kicks her out?"

Again he laughed his ass off, and I pointed out while he was giggling away that if our youth today would take a cue from these fish and spend more time getting to know each other before hitting the sheets maybe there would be a lot less unplanned babies.

He laughed at that as well, but then he stopped long enough to smile down at me and say, "You see, there is a lesson everywhere, if you can only recognize it."

Strange little man, wouldn't you agree?

The rest of the night passed rather quietly; my Chinese pilot friend eventually went to bed, and I remained, making a valiant effort at reading and relaxing. One of the floor managers approached me, and we ended up having a long conversation about my writing, his life, and all the things we have both learned along the way.

He apologized for disturbing me and explained it was not usually his way to talk so openly with strangers. He told me that he felt very comfortable with me, though, and was surprised that he was so willing to share what was in his heart and his head. Partway through the conversation he asked me who I would be publishing the book under. I explained to him that I choose to keep my identity as an author separate from my identity as an everyday ordinary person. He was at first a little confused by this, but, when I explained about my desire to protect my daughter, he began to understand.

I told him I very much desired for her to grow up to be a grounded and down-to-earth young woman. I had very strong feelings about the negative affect that fame and money can have on the young. I didn't want to raise her to believe that she was better or more important than anyone else because of her mother's success. It was my intention, therefore, to keep as low a profile as possible until she was older and could separate herself from the effects that public intrusion into our lives might have. He laughed and gave me a thumbs-up when I told him that I only worked with people who could keep their mouths shut. I guess he decided he could appreciate my reasons, and he seemed very pleased with my views on the matter.

Our conversation was interrupted at this point by a rather large group of rambunctious young men exiting the casino. They, seeing a single white female sitting seemingly alone on the patio, decided to take up residence at every single table immediately surrounding mine. My new friend, however, decided to take upon himself the role of guard dog. He placed his body between me and the young men and stood there with his back slightly turned toward them, talking to me about the language and the culture while effectively keeping these drunken individuals at bay. They did, on several occasions, make the effort to get my attention, but he would very pointedly stiffen his stance and give a mild-mannered warning glance to whoever happened to be approaching the table. It was interesting to watch, as he was indeed himself a stranger to me, yet his seemingly coincidental arrival at my table ended up protecting and sheltering me from what could have quickly turned into an uncomfortable situation.

Lesson learned: I am really no safer here in the hotel than I am on the streets, and I must resolve to be more careful. He let me go to bed only after he was sure that they were long gone. Although he never openly asked me to wait, he did not stop my lessons on *Tagalog* until several minutes after their departure, at which point he asked me if I was not tired, as I had been working all day. I took his very diplomatic cue and thanked him for his conversation, agreeing that, yes, I was indeed ready for bed. I made it to my room safely, escorted by another young employee who just happened to be standing by the entrance of the restaurant at the very moment I chose to take my leave. I am very grateful for the angels I continue to encounter here and will in the future endeavor to be more cautious and aware.

Well, sweets, I really don't have much more to share. I only plan today to work on the next chapter and try yet again to get in contact with the various orphanages here, though my purpose for that is not the same as first intended. Maybe, given my change of attitude, it will become easier for me; again, we will see.

Must run; would like to check my email and look up something on the comp. I will probably get back to you later and let you know what's up...

February 25, patio of the Heritage Hotel Manila, noon

A quick note to you, hon; I was finally able to contact another home and set up a meeting for tomorrow morning. I am planning to bring along some rice for the orphanage and am thinking it is a very good thing that last night my Chinese friend and I agreed to go to Mall of Asia tonight after work. I am a very tiny girl, and I will no doubt need the assistance of a stronger man to help me cart one hundred kilos of rice back to the hotel. I hope he's willing...

February 25, patio of the Heritage Hotel Manila, 8:00 PM

Well, my darling, that was interesting—just as I was putting the pen down earlier, my rough and tough boys from the work crew happened to stop by for a lunch meeting. The twins joined me at my table afterwards and inquired what I was up to today. My hippie friend had not managed to yet make it down, but I am on pretty good terms with all the others, so it was quite comfortable to just sit with them and toss stories back and forth.

I told them my plans to go to the orphanage tomorrow and that I would be heading out later to try to get some rice from the mall to bring as gift. They asked me how much, and, when I answered one hundred kilos, their eyes popped. Pale Eyes said it best: "Bloody hell, luv, how's a tiny thing like you gonna lug one hundred kilos of anything anywhere?"

I told him I didn't know yet, but that I was sure a way would be provided. Of course they scoffed at that as well (they always do, lol), since they simply can't believe that things are given to me as I need them. If they believe that, then they will have to admit there might just be some kind of other energy at work. As they don't embrace the idea of there being anything beyond the reality of what we can see and touch, it would be expecting much too much to have them believe that my desires—or, more appropriately, my needs—are met before I am forced to take action myself.

Just as Blue Eyes was rolling those eyes at my obvious refusal to accept reality, Bear popped over to the table and took a sea; he also inquired what I was up to today. The twins explained that I needed to get some rice for a visit tomorrow, both of them bantering back and forth and joking about the very comical visual of little tiny me trying to drag a hundred kilos of rice through a store and into a cab. Of course, my big, burly, cuddly teddy came up with a solution, which shocked both of the twins into silence. He offered to give me the company truck and their driver to take me over to the mall and pick up the rice. Just as he was saying that I would need a guy to go in with me, and that he knew just who to get, Hippie showed up and asked who he was getting to do what.

Bear told Hippie he would be taking a couple hours off work to go with me to the mall and get me my rice, at which point Hippie smiled and asked if he would be paid.

To which Bear growled, "Of course you're bloody getting paid, you useless lump of sod!" then, laughing, he added, "Make sure you get a bloody receipt, gofer boy, so we can find a way to write the bloody rice off as a charitable expense."

Well, as you can imagine, the twins were... ummm... what's the word?... oh yes, stunned.

Long story short: I got my rice.

The driver dropped my hippie friend and me off at the mall and then went back to work, after we told him we would rather take the time to have dinner and were more than willing to take a cab home.

We wandered around the mall and found a beautiful little Italian restaurant that had a patio overlooking the bay. I bought Hippie a couple beers by way of thanks for the physical effort he would soon be putting in on my behalf. We were watching a really interesting spectacle across the way of a couple blow-up pools that had been inflated and laid out on the ground between the mall lot and the bay. In each pool there were two gigantic plastic balls floating in the water, and in each ball a small child was running around inside the ball, making it roll across the surface of the water. It was too comical, rather like watching a hamster in a wheel, but it did look like a lot of fun. I asked Hippie if he would seriously get paid for coming to the mall, and he explained that Bear would clock in the hours that he spent here as well as the time the driver spent in traffic getting us here. He said it was no skin off Bear's nose, so to speak. The money was there, and as it was the lead hand's decision to send him and lend me the truck and driver; he was responsible for making sure the driver and Hippie were not docked pay because they were doing something other than work directly related to the company. If they had offered themselves it would have been different, but, as it was Bear who was sending them, then it was up to him to make sure their income wasn't affected.

So we spent a couple of hours sitting in the sun, enjoying the slight breeze off the water, sipping beer, and chatting while watching the children play—not a bad way to spend the afternoon, really, and a pretty good deal for hippie: free beer, pleasant atmosphere and good conversation, and all on company time.

Hippie did ask me how the whole thing had come about, and, when I explained to him what had happened, he laughed at the twins' reaction and then asked if I always get what I want. I told him no, I very rarely get what I want, but I very often get what I need. To that, he lifted his glass and offered a toast to that amazing unseen force some of us call God…

February 26, in a cab on the way from heritage hotel to children's home, 8:00 AM

Morning, darling,

Just a quick hello; I am on my way to an orphanage here in Manila. I would like to see for myself what is being done to alleviate some of the problems caused by poverty here. I am also looking forward to meeting some of the people involved with these organizations. It would seem the more I ask around the more I discover that it is the working class here who run such organizations, not just the government and churches. I am on my way to meet the couple that runs this one, and, hopefully they can shed some light on who is behind helping the children here. I won't talk long, as I am in the car, but I will tell you I have had a few more enlightening encounters but nothing monumental. Perhaps meeting these people at the orphanage will change that.

I have to tell you, though, for all I had heard about these people before I came, when I look out the window I notice that they do not look defeated. Passively accepting, yes, but overall they seem to be content. I was talking to Blue Eyes yesterday and mentioned my observation.

He agreed that they are content to live as they do, "But then, they really don't bloody know any different, do they?" These were his words, not mine, and I have to wonder—do they want to know different? Perhaps they choose to live this way. It is still a question I do not have an answer for, but am hoping to gain some more insight into it before I have to leave. Wish me luck, luv. xo

February 26, patio of the Heritage Hotel Manila, 3:30 PM

Well, hon, I scarce know where to begin…

I just had the most incredibly uplifting visit with the people that run the Shepherd of the Hills children's home.

My first impression upon walking in was that it was just that—a home. I entered through a gate into a carport, then into a joint kitchen-living area that contained two lounge chairs and a small kitchen table. The furnishings themselves were sparse, but the room was colorful and bright. There were plants in several corners of the room and bamboo blinds covering the windows. Directly to the right were two sets of stairs, one leading up and one down. Sitting in one of the lounge chairs was a young woman holding an infant; beside her stood a playpen that was being used as a portable crib. Directly to my left was a small office that had glass windows, allowing anyone working there to have a clear view of the family area and entranceway.

And that, my friend, is all the visual description I feel I should waste my time giving. But the feeling in that house… *Contentment* comes first to mind; warmth and love were everywhere I looked.

It was a peaceful, happy atmosphere, as children moved around us going about their daily lives. Music—wow, the music saturated the home; every room held a child practicing an instrument or listening to songs; even the comfort room (bathroom), which was decorated to resemble a jungle, had music playing in it. As I said—incredible. I am finding it hard to put into words what I have seen this day. The peaceful beauty that is these children's existence cannot be described, not fairly, not accurately. I do not think it is something I can convey to you in words, it was pure feeling.

Have you ever lain down in the middle of a field of hay on a hot summer's day and just let yourself feel the simple pleasure of breathing?

Have you ever lain on a beach late at night and simply enjoyed the spectacle of millions of stars seemingly twinkling simply for the sole purpose of bringing you peace and joy?

Have you ever danced as a child in the rain, letting yourself move with complete abandon to the rhythm of the rain?

Have you lain quietly in the middle of the bush and allowed the sounds of all the surrounding nature to wash over you and wash away your fears and worries and doubts?

If you have done any of these things, then take try to remember how it made you feel, and, maybe, just maybe, you will get a glimmer of what I felt sitting in that house.

I do not think it is something I can convey to you. I simply do not know a word strong enough or pure enough, but perhaps just saying that much is enough.

I was greeted warmly and asked to sit in the dining area with the mother of these children. Understand I do not use the term lightly. Yes, she is the coordinator, but her love of these children shone in her eyes; their love of her shone in theirs. This woman, this *mother*, had a glowing warmth radiating from her, and sitting next to her was very much akin to sitting by a wood stove on a cold winter's day.

We talked about our work, my book, her shelter, and what we hoped to accomplish with both.

Her husband came to join us, and I was very much drawn to this solid, earthy father figure. He had the appearance of strength and self-assurance, but he was also blessed with gentle eyes. When he smiled at me, his wife, or his children, those eyes showed compassion and understanding. His demeanour was as causal as his wife's was welcoming, and I was drawn in by the comfort of these two magnificent souls. They live so simply; they really have very little for themselves, but they do not, I think, want for very much.

I called Revo on the way back,to the hotel and he told me to try to come back here and relax. He said I should digest it all before trying to write it out, but I felt compelled to put on paper my immediate impression. Then and only then would I be able to relax, which I am now off to do, but, before I go, I have to say that yet again I am blessed by the opportunities, and yet again I have to say thank you for this chance to be welcomed into the lives of selfless people such as these.

Their commitment to their cause and the light it brings to those they touch is something I have been very honored to witness and something I will forever cherish. I spent many hours with them, easily falling in love with the entire family and basking in the warmth of their love for each other. I am yet again uplifted by the goodness that seeps out from the core of the people I have met. I went there a stranger but left there a friend, and I am grateful. They lifted my spirit to a higher place, and it was an experience I will never forget.

Goodbye for now, my heart. I will write again soon, but for now I must make arrangements for my trip tomorrow, as they have invited me to tag along with them to Baguio to see for myself the work they do there in another one of their locations. The journey, it would appear, goes on. xoxo

February 26ᵗʰ, Patio of the Heritage Hotel Manila, 9:00 PM

Well, arrangements have been made, and my bag is packed and ready to go…

A few interesting things to note, and I will start with the effect my presence has had on some members of the work crew. They were out here around dinner time, and I took the time to sit with them and tell them I'd be out of town for a few days. When I explained where I was going, and with who, the twins were again obviously in shock. Blue Eyes just sat staring at me for a few minutes, and I had no idea until he spoke what the significance of my upcoming trip was. I'd never heard of Baguio City and had no idea what to expect…

"You mean to tell me you bloody well wander off to a bloody orphanage on a bloody whim and get invited out to stay with them in Baguio for the weekend…" He placed his hands on the table and leaned forward. "Luv, do you even have any bloody idea what weekend this is?"

"No, mate, I'm thinking our little darling hasn't a clue," laughed Pale Eyes, then added gently, "Luv, you are going to Baguio during the flower festival. You wanted culture—well, you're about to be swimming in it!"

Waving a hand at me, Blue Eyes added, "Bloody woman—off she goes to one of the biggest cultural festivals in one of the most interesting cities in this backwards country, and she hasn't a clue what it means!"

Blue Eyes grunted, "You know you need to make bloody reservations six months in advance to get a place to stay up there this weekend, and you not only have a way to get there but a place to stay—bloody freaky, if you ask me. Honestly, luv, do you always get your way?"

Of course, I again explained, after they were done with their little tirade—and, trust me, it went on for quite some time—that, no, I don't get what I want, only what I need.

Before they left, Pale Eyes confided in me that I had shown him some things his eyes had not been open to before, that his heart had not been willing to feel. He admitted he had been living here for years and was disillusioned with the thing he had seen, but that through watching my adventures he was more willing to explore the real meaning behind the why and how of the lives of these people. He ended by thanking me and admitting that perhaps there was something out there that he had not been able to grasp—but maybe now he would be more aware of his surroundings and the meanings behind what he had considered to be mere freakish coincidence.

Well, it was not my intent, but if I have opened up one heart or mind, then perhaps that heart will, in turn, open others. I am hoping I can keep in touch with these guys even after I am gone, as they have taught me much and provided me with much-needed comfort in times when I was feeling very alone. This brings me to our current phone situation.

It appears that all this time that Rev had not been responding to my messages it was not that he was avoiding me; it was that he simply wasn't getting my messages. I discovered this while sitting in the front drive of the children's home. I had just been blessed to witness the children in the home playing for me in their living room. My immediate thought was: *Wow, I wish the world could see this*—not see them playing outside the home when they did concerts, but seeing it from inside. It was an inspiring sight.

I also thought that Rev would love these kids, being a musician himself, and I wished that I could get hold of him so he could listen. I did try to call from inside the home, while they were playing, but the call wouldn't go through. After the kids were done, I took my phone outside and offered up a little prayer, asking for the phone to work for me just this once. I then dialed his number, as I had been doing for the last few days, in a futile attempt to reach him. This time, his voice washed over me from the other end—full of concern as to where I had been—with a breathless comment that he had been worried sick.

I told him not to worry about it—what I was calling about was much more important, and I explained where I was and what I was doing. I asked him to come meet the kids upon my return to Manila, and he agreed to come with me back to the home and see their talent for himself. I didn't talk long; I didn't want to take away from my time with them, but I did, as you know, call him back on my way back to the hotel.

Once back at the hotel, as you know, I made my arrangements to have my room locked until I got back, and then I spent some down time with the boys. This brings to mind another interesting thing I had previously forgotten to mention. Hippie's name is Scott—the relevance of this is not obvious now, but it will be later. We were sitting around one night talking about our tattoos, and one of the twins told a story of when he was working in Africa and had decided on a whim to go out and get a tattoo. He remembers only one thing about the whole experience: he had told the guy that was doing it to put whatever he wanted on his arm. This was years ago, and the artist in question was a tribal fellow who used the old method of body art. The process is long and painful, but the twin in question remembers none of it. He does not, in fact, even remember how he got home or the name of the fellow that did the art. When I questioned him on why he had gotten it done in the first place, he couldn't tell me the answer to that either. The whole adventure was hazy for him, but he does know one thing—he came out of his daze the next day with a simple tribal marking on his shoulder. It was a circle with a dot—the meaning of it tugs at me, and I know I should be grasping it, but for the moment it doesn't seem to be overly important, so I have neglected to research it. The boys also said that the meaning of the symbol seemed to be tucked in the back of their minds, but, try as they might, they simply couldn't seem to pull it forth at that moment. I will take that to mean that it is not yet time to know the meaning and have decided to leave it alone. Perhaps by the end of this story it will be made clear, or perhaps when I arrive home you will have the answer for me; you often do, it seems.

Well, luv, that's about it for now. I will talk to you as soon as I am able…

February 27, upper deck of SOTH, in Baguio

There's magic in this place, this city in the sky…

If you've seen the children's show *Magic School Bus*, then you will be easily able to visualize my journey to this mountainous home. We travelled in a van full of laughing, singing children, five hours through the provinces, surrounded by the beauty of nature and the poverty that comes with the desire not to destroy it.

I know I promised to get back to you sooner, my dear, but I have been rather preoccupied with the goings-on of these people and their dreams of a better world for their children. And when I say *their* children, I mean they have an undeniable love and seemingly unquenchable desire to protect all the children of this poverty-stricken nation.

I cannot say even now that I support any one religion, but I can openly admit that if this is what Christianity leads these people to then there is a definite benefit to being a member of the Christian community.

The people I have met are the real people behind an extremely strong, positive movement in this country to alleviate some of the poverty caused by oppression. They are not in power; they do not want power, and yet, they have more power to help make change than I would have previously believed.

Their hunger to help others is far beyond what we define as charity. They live each moment wrapped secure in their faith and are willing to give their lives for that faith. They eat, sleep, work, and play with one goal in mind. Their entire existence revolves around that goal, and they continue to sacrifice all they have in order to achieve that goal. It is empowering to witness how a few tiny steps begun with strength of conviction can turn into such a long and wondrous adventure.

I have witnessed those who have nothing giving of themselves, because it is all they have to offer. I have witnessed those who have only one piece of bread breaking that bread and dividing it, willingly going hungry so others can eat. I have witnessed the man who owns only the shirt on his back going bare-chested so a child would be clothed, and I have witnessed the birth of a new day, with renewed hope for a better, safer world.

One of the children just came out to sit with me, and when she saw what I was doing, she simply stated, "You need to write..."

She is only nine and her use of the English language not extensive, yet she is more able to perceive the reasons behind what I do than I myself am able to comprehend.

It is a need—one that cannot be put aside and one that will not be denied. I write to appease that need, to quench that desire, and I hope that in doing so I can share what I have seen and learned here. As I have said many times before: if you could see what I have seen, you, too, would believe.

There is magic in this place. Magic in the hearts of these people. Magic in the lives that they live. Magic in the truth of what those lives, lived as they are, mean for the future of their children, their people, and, I believe, the world.

March 4, patio of the Heritage Hotel Manila, 9:00 AM

And to think, my dear, I thought I was done. Honestly, it was my belief that in my last few days here I would not be troubling you with these letters. I wanted to take time away from this awhile and immerse myself in the endearing glow of the people I have met here, people I have grown to love.

I have to be honest: the prospect of leaving now is tearing my heart out, but from somewhere across the ocean a little girl calls. I told Rev yesterday that I would have to find some wilderness as soon as I got back. The big guy and I need to have a long chat about the price he has asked me to pay. I do not appreciate the freedom of choice he has granted me, and I very much wish to ask him why. It is difficult to explain the feelings I'm having, the conflict within. I only know that three years ago a young man wrote a song calling me home, and two days ago I realized I was.

I will come back; that has been decided by a greater mind than mine, but for how long remains to be seen. As much as I wish this one thing above all others to be granted me, I do not feel my work is yet done. I hate that Rev is right in his belief that he has to let me go. I fought the reality of it as hard as I could and denied the need with every ounce of my being. We just had two beautiful days together, and I should be grateful. I feel as if I am being selfish to ask for this—selfish to ask to be finished with this work so I can settle down and find a life for myself. The minutes tick by slowly, pulling me toward another place and another life.

You see, I can't even get it out; I can't seem to write the words I need so much to say. My soul is screaming, and as the time to leave draws closer, the agony of this is threatening to destroy what I have built here. I do not have his faith, nor do I have his strength. I never did have.

It has been a long time of shaping and molding, these years of preparation by a master craftsman. He has forged through fire and pain a weapon to use, but the blade, I fear, is flawed. I mourn the flaw and the weakness it represents. I fear the losses I have yet to endure and the sacrifices yet to be made. A life of wandering seems to be my fate. I will live out my destiny and obey the will of that higher power, but, as I said, the price will be high.

Each step taken toward a new adventure is a step away from those I love and cherish. It is a painful realization, this coming to terms with what must be. I do not enjoy the inner turmoil and am having trouble finding faith in my purpose. I will be leaving very soon, and when I go, I will leave my heart here in the Philippines, in the hands of a man whose only way to protect the heart he holds is by sending me away.

March 4, in a cab, 10:30 AM

I am on my way to meet a sister of the Catholic Church who found me while I was wandering around Baguio. She came straight to me, like a moth to a flame, and told me that when I returned to Manila I was to come see her before leaving for Canada. Of course, I never told her I was staying in Manila or that I was from Canada, but, hey, these things I am now used to. I have, at Revo's request, sacrificed my last day here with him in order to explore her world and her faith. He seems to believe there is something there that I must learn, so I will go, knowing I will not see him again for many months.

My soul still weeps at the loss of him, but, as I clung to him in our final moments of goodbye, I managed to find a way to smile. I joked with him, while we stood on the steps of the hotel, that four months was not that long. Then I watched him drive away, anguished by the price we have been asked to pay.

I have sent him a text (that I do not know if he will receive) in the hopes that somehow, someway he will find the strength to let me in. He still believes that if I am to be by his side I will suffer for it. We have spent our last two days here, in fact, arguing over it. He refuses to accept my willingness to walk into the cage that he believes his love for me would create. Yet I know that if I walked in freely, he would eventually close the door. He fears, however, his inability to reopen the door at will, knowing that eventually my work will take me away. So, I write to him one last time, trying to alleviate his fears.

Okay, so I believe if you are meant to get this, you will. If and when you decide that you are willing or want me to be yours, know that in my heart I already am. My loyalty to you will hold strong while I am gone, and if you find yourself being able to accept what I offer, all you need do is call me home.

As I said, I do not know yet if he will get it; his phone and mine have several times failed to work, and, if he does get it, I do not know how he will respond. He is stubborn in his resolve to set me free, but—as I have also said more times than I count—we will see.

March 4, sitting on the step outside St. Paul's University, Manila, 12:15 PM

I have just finished meeting with the most wonderful sister who showed me a side of the Catholic Church I very much needed to see. It is, I think, too long a story to tell to you here, but I am sure Sister Flor at St. Paul's will more than likely have her own chapter or perhaps even someday her own book. The real reason I am writing to you now is to tell you about the text message that I received during my stay here at the university.

This is what Rev wrote.

I love u just 4 that. I will.

It is the first time he has used those words (they have been implied and discussed often but never verbalized), and, though I long to hear them from his lips, it seems fitting to me that they first come to me in written form.

With that simple message I can now go back to Canada and finish what I started here, knowing that someday, when the time is right, and if the gods allow, my Rev, my conqueror, will call me home...

March 4, patio of the Heritage Hotel Manila, 1:45 PM

Well, my dear, what a strange, crazy trip it's been.

I'm writing to you while sitting outside in my favorite spot surrounded by familiar faces. It is an extremely comfortable feeling being here. Over at the next table sits one of the twins talking to his boss about their continuing struggles to get their equipment out to the job site.

You see, I was just interrupted by Blue Eyes, who stopped to tell me he will be right down for a drink. Scott dropped by quickly to tell me he'd see me tonight and we'll head over to the MOA for one last wander around. Angel has also stopped by to say hi, and it is nice to see that she both still has her job here and has apparently found happiness in it.

I honestly should not spend too much time out here; I still have to make arrangements for tomorrow, but I thought I'd take advantage of the weather to write what should be my last letter. I have no idea where to start explaining to you my last few days here. They will be in the book, of course, which you are helping to edit, so the stories themselves you can read at another time. Instead, I will try to concentrate my efforts on giving you my last thoughts and feelings about all that I have seen and done, while I try to prepare myself to leave.

Of all the things that I have been through in my short, but full, life, this has been most definitely the hardest to endure. From the moment I realized that this man I had met was to be part of my future—and all through our quest to get here, our search for purpose, right up until this very day that I sit here writing to you—this entire trip (and it has been trippy as hell) has been a crazy emotional roller coaster.

The continuing up-and-down ride, through the eyes and lives of these people as well as our own personal internal struggle between duty and desire, has been exhausting. Yet, even as tired as I am, I do not feel drained by my efforts here; rather, I am peacefully content in my exhaustion. I feel secure in the knowledge that the energy I need will be provided to me as long as I expend that energy continuing the work I have begun here.

My fears of tomorrow seem, for the moment at least, to have disappeared.

We have put into motion by our presence here a few projects that will hopefully provide these people with independent means to continue their work. We have also managed to accidentally bring together a couple of organizations that now have the opportunity to collaborate their efforts and their resources. The whole process has been quite by accident, and it is through coincidence alone that these people have found each other.

You and I, however, know that coincidence does not exist, and it will be interesting to see where this new path will lead and if and when they will choose to follow it.

As for the effects this will have on my life in Canada, I sincerely hope that I can find a way to soften the blow to those who will be affected. I have no doubt now that what we were sent here to do was important, and it is my heart's desire to allowed to come back and continue to explore the possibilities this country presents for me. I will not, of course, willingly leave behind my child. If, however, when I get back, the factors necessary for my return fall into place, I will know that my path has again been chosen. Several individual events will have to occur, but, rather than forcing the issue, I find myself more than willing to sit back and wait.

I will watch for signs, listen to my guides, and follow where they lead. I have given my life to something bigger, and, though I do not expect everybody to understand, I know that those who do are also those who are meant to share that life.

Gone are my days of trying to live up to the expectations of others. I have for far too long denied the reality of who I am in the attempt to fit in with what society deems the norm. I am mildly entertained at the thought of the shock that others will feel at the changes this trip has wrought in me. For some,

I do not think it will be easy to accept. But it was in the hopes of floating on those winds of change that we came, and it is on those winds of change that I must continue to soar.

I am again the wandering gypsy, content to explore this world and its people, content to live and learn from those who would willingly let me into their lives...

I thank our Creator for sending me an angel to wake me from my slumber and push me toward the edge.

I thank our Creator for raising me up and preparing me for flight, through loss and pain, thereby strengthening the wings I will need to fly.

I thank our Creator for giving me the courage and the will to stretch my wings.

I thank our Creator for providing me with friends and family and the safety net that they represent.

I thank our Creator for sending me angels to walk by my side as I took those first uncertain steps toward the edge and for the angels who have been sent to fly by my side to show me the way.

Lastly, I have to most humbly thank our Creator for blowing toward me those winds of change, which, I now have no doubt, will eventually allow me to fly home.

THE DREAM

To Beaner:

Start February 20, 5:50 PM

Dark imagery appears that has, as far as I can tell, no place in this tale—but I will write it to you, and, when I see you next, you can help me make sense of it.

He's screaming at me that I am his: his bride, his possession, and he will no longer share me. He came to me in my sleep and took what he thinks is his. At first it was beautiful and powerful and passionate, but when I realized that he was not who I expected, I was scared. I tried to run; it angered him, and, even after I woke, I could feel him calling me. He tells me he is coming for me, that I am his, but I do not want to give up my freedom. I do not feel, though, that I have a choice. I was his, I am his—and he will take back what belongs to him. I am wide awake, and I can still feel it. He knows where I am, and he is coming, and I cannot stop him.

But I do not know him, not in this life, and I am not sure I am ready to meet him. He will come, and even as I fear it, it excites me. Will I know him when he comes for me? I do not know...

It is hard to let go of this fear I have; I don't even know why I am afraid, but it is hard to breathe. I want to call you and talk to you, but you are far away and you cannot help me, not in this.

I am shaken and do not know what else to do but wait and see what comes of this. I want to believe that it was just a dream, but my instinct tells me it's not. Even now I feel him coming closer, and I can sense his eyes on me, his hold on me, and I have nowhere to run. He takes, in his belief that it is his right to take, that which is mine by choice to give.

What's worse is that I have been here before, and I know this feeling well, even if I can neither put a face or a name to this entity. It has from time immemorial dominated me, and it chooses yet again to impose on me its will. I do not want to face this, not now; I have too much left to do.

I am sitting out on the patio trying to calm down. Neither you nor Sophia will wake for hours yet, and by then I am afraid I will already know the answers. I wrote a text to Rev but cannot bring myself to send it.

Why? Who?

What have I to fear from him?

Why am I feeling any fear at all?

What? Who is coming? and again I ask, *Will I know it when it comes?*

They said I would be safe here; I thought I would be safe.

Why now am I in danger? I DO NOT understand…

So I wait. I ordered food but do not know if I can eat. I have to eat, need to eat, but I am not hungry.

He told me to come down here and wait, so here I am; still I am afraid and want to run. I want to stay here; I don't want to leave, not yet...

I talked to him, asking him to come and tell me what he wants. He answers that I know what he wants, and I scream NO! "I only know what you tell me," he says, "Don't argue ..."

I feel cold inside. Again I ask, "Why now?"

I am suddenly very tired, very drained and worn; I feel like we have had this argument many times before. I argue—what right does he have to tell me to whom I belong?—and he shouts back that he is the right to tell me to whom I belong.

I am trying to eat again; it tastes like ash, and between bites I am forced to write. I don't know why, just that I am being driven to document this.

I argue again that he has no right and he shouts at me again that I am HIS bride and it is his right.

What does he want?

How long do I have to wait?

I want to send that text, but something is stopping me, and again I do not understand. Every time I even look at my phone it gets harder to breathe. I can't reach over and pick it up.

Why?

Who?

I want to believe it is some kind of crazy dream and that I will wake up soon and see it as a dream—but I do not think it is a dream. Still I write...

Why?

Who?

I have to find a way to come down from this; I will not let it beat me. If he wants me, he will have to show himself to me this time and walk beside me. I will not go with him. He whispers, "You will come…"

He is purposely making me wait.

Why?

Who?

I am still trying to eat, to act as if everything is normal, as if there is nothing strange going on. You know, I half expected him to be waiting here for me. I feel as if I'm being watched. Why won't he show himself? If this is real, and I am his, why is he playing this game? What purpose is there to it? I can only sit for so long and wait, when I don't know what I am waiting for. Again I try to send the text; I can't; my hand cramps whenever I move it toward the phone.

I am calmer now; I tell him: fine if it is what he wants, I will bow to his will, but he will have to come to me—here, now, in this reality, on this plane, in human form—or I will not go. He has waited too long this time; I am stronger now; we will stand together, side by side, or not at all.

I can feel him backing off. He did not expect this, did he? No, he thought to find me weak. I am not, and, being stronger, I have nothing to fear. Oh, he's angry, so very angry. He rants and raves without words. If he wants me it will be on my terms this time. I tell him to come; I will not reject him. He tells me to go to my room; like a child I am to obey. "No," I say, "I will go when I am ready. You can come to me here; you have that power, but you fear the weakened human form."

Again I ask, *Why? Who?*

I am no threat to you; what have you to fear from this place?

I will go soon, and we will see...

I am not sure if I can stand up to him for long, but we will see. I think perhaps I am too strong this time, and I taunt him, telling him he has waited too long.

(There is a break in the writing, a point where silence and meditation was required so I could recover and regain strength...)

I am still in shock over all that I have just written, and I am gathering my strength before I go back upstairs. If I am right, and he comes to me there, it will be an epic battle of wills, but I am even now calling out to you, calling out to Sophia, Deacon, Lina, Alya, and others like you who have always come to my aid in times of weakness. You are my strength, my power, my parts that make me whole, and, with that final piece put into place, I have nothing to fear.

Who do you think he is, this entity that calls me his, this being that claims I'm his bride?

Not who is he here—who cares? It will not matter—but who is he in the bigger sense of things? From where does he come, and why does he choose to make himself known now?

If and when I see you next, I will show this to you, and we can figure it out together. If, that is, he does not show himself tonight. If he will not play the game my way, it will not be played. As I said, he is not happy about it. I'm having one last smoke and then going upstairs. I would say *wish me luck,* but I don't feel I will need it. He holds no power here; that's why he fears this place. I just felt it, and you, it seems, are waking; I felt that too.

You feel closer now, more aware of my plight, my battle. You see, I do not go unprotected or unarmed.

Alright then, let's go do battle, shall we?

End February 20, 7:27 PM

My phone beeps; it is a text, no message, only a name: Revo (7:28 PM)

THE BATTLE

To Beaner:

March 3, patio of the Heritage Hotel Manila, 9:21 AM

I don't know if either you or I will be able to read this; I very much fear the more I write, the more my hands will shake.

He is lying now asleep in my bed, and he is for the moment peaceful, but the battle that rages within will in time return.

He fights it so very hard this time, refusing to accept the price of who and what we are. As I said, he found me too late, and, even as he tries to send me away, I still maintain the power and the strength to fight.

I was lying in his arms when he asked about the dream. I couldn't deny him, even knowing he was trying to prove his point, trying to scare me off. So I told him all, and I told him I had written it down. I told him I know who and what he is and that still I am not afraid.

He argued, "Don't you see—I can't do this, not to you, not anymore..."

I told him it's my choice to make. I explained I am not weaker than him this time; my place is by his side, and that is where I choose to be. So we remain locked in a battle of wills.

He is standing over me, looking down, and my head is in my hands. I am pleading with him to see reason, but again he is stubborn and willful. He does not want to destroy anymore. He talks about Genghis Kahn and his duty to slay millions, about Mark Antony and his drive to conquer, about so many others who have come before.

I remind him that each of those men, regardless of all the pain they caused, had a woman that stood with them and loved them; I tell him again he denies me my rightful place by sending me away. He tells me he does not want to be that man again, not this time, and I remind him yet again that he has no choice.

He says that when it is time for him to fight, it will not be the man I know who does the fighting, and I answer quietly that I know, and I am okay with it. I have made my choice. I tell him how I lay in bed that night after finally coming to terms with who and what he is. I describe how I talked to him there in my sleep, telling him I was stronger this time and that it would be okay. I tell him that I argued about it for two hours lying there in the dark, and how angry he was at first that I dared to question him. I explained that after time his will had begun to bend, and he became calmer with the knowledge that he could not push me away.

He whispers, "I know, I was there…"

Then I laugh and say, "Yet, here we sit, in a stinking bathroom of a bloody hotel, having the same damned argument that we had only last week, and I tell you nothing has changed. I will not be driven away. I do NOT fear you."

He tells me he cannot put me in a cage, that I am meant to soar, and he would set me free to fly. He says, "Look how much you've done without me by your side; look how far you've come, what you've learned, what you've accomplished. I cannot—will not—take that away."

I answer softly, "But all that I've done, I've done with you in the back of my head. How can you say that you will hold me back, when it was you who lifted me up in the first place?" I look him straight in the eye and silently I plead.

He whispers to me, "But maybe that's where I belong this time, in the back of your head—then maybe I can't be taken away."

So I explain that I can live with the fact that he may eventually be taken from me. I can live with losing him through circumstance. I can live with losing him through the selfishness of others. I can live with losing him when God decides to call him home. I *cannot* live with losing him through his unwillingness to let me be hurt. I cannot bear losing him by choice.

He argues again that he will not destroy me this time, says I don't understand what I ask.

I tell him I do—I know him, and I can handle him.

He says, "But my other half is a beast, a beast that will devour you if I let it."

I answer that it was he who claimed to see me tame the lion, he who pointed out that I could...

"Not this time. You don't have to do this; you can be free of this, if you will only listen," he sounds so sad, and I have no words to comfort him.

I tell him I am stronger now, that life has molded and shaped me for this. I can handle his power; I can handle his strength. I can handle his hunger and his lust.

He bows his head, "Not my lust," and quietly again whispers to me, softly pleading with me to run while I still can.

I try to tell him yes, even that... I explain that this flesh means nothing, and as long as he holds me close inside I care not where his body goes, but he struggles visibly with the concept, telling me it would not be the same for me. I would not be allowed my freedom. I tell him I would rather live the rest of my life alone than with another man, and he whispers, "No…"

It is an old argument, we both remember; we both know we've had this conversation before, and the reality of it makes us laugh. There we stand, giggling together like schoolgirls for a moment, forgetting that we are in the process of making a monumental decision. If it affected only us, it wouldn't matter; we wouldn't care—but it doesn't, and we both feel the weight of that burden.

This time it is he who looks me in the eyes. "Maybe that is my sacrifice this time; have you considered that?"

It is a question I was expecting, but not one I am willing to answer. I do not like to think of the sacrifices he has made from the beginning, the pain he has endured; it hurts me and angers me. Though I know how necessary it had been, I cannot bring myself to justify it. He fears what he will have to become, and I cannot place blame on him for that. I cannot look him in the eye and tell him this time it will be different. I do not know that it is meant to be.

He wants to know how to control it this time; he wants to know how not to be the slayer. He wants to know how to keep form unleashing his anger on those who deserve it.

I explain that he cannot stop it, that it is what must be, but that if there comes a time when it is necessary to tame the beast, it is then my job to be there to calm the rage inside. To help direct it, to help guide it, it is my place to keep him grounded when he teeters on the brink of destruction, my role to hold him close and keep him from plunging off the edge. He disagrees that he denies me my right to live as I am meant to.

Still he argues and fights against what cannot be changed. He detests the idea of me sacrificing my freedom to fulfill the role, and I fear the consequences if I do not. I tell him not to be afraid for me. I tell him he cannot waste time protecting me. I reassure him that he cannot stop the gypsy from wandering, but that she will always come home if he will only bring himself to allow it.

It is late, or early, and we are tired, but while I am lying there in his arms, he asks me, "Do you think it was God who gave me that dark side? Please tell me it is him, that he wills this… is it for me to be his justice?"

I answer, "Not this time; not like that. It is for you to stand behind and inspire others to act. You do not have to be that kind of leader anymore; you do not have to be the slayer, but you do have to show them the way, and the price again will have to be paid. It *is* he who gives you your dark side, because he knows you will need it. It is your shield meant to protect you and shelter you from the pain you will cause. It is your weapon, to be used in this fight, a weapon you must learn to wield with strength and purpose. It is your sword and your conviction. You will do what needs to be done, and, when it is over, only he can decide who wins this battle.

He is asleep finally; his eyes are closed, and I can hear his heart as I lie with my head on his chest. I can feel his breathing; he struggles even now in his sleep, murmuring quietly, "Not this time…"

No words are needed now, but I send him a message in his dreams, "Hush, it is okay. Rest now; I am here…"

THE MESSAGE

I was not sure the dream had a place in this story. I was hoping that this time the darkness might be held at bay. I realize now that the opposite of light has its place here. It is what gives us balance. It is a struggle that has been wrestled with before. It is a battle we have already fought, a war we must continue to strive to win. It would be wrong for me to deny it its place here, so I will include it in these pages as a message to those who read them.

We are here.

We will fight.

In that fight there will be loss of life, loss of self; yet from the blood and ash comes forth hope for another chance for his people to survive.

We are here.

We will fight.

We will suffer willingly, selflessly sacrificing for a chance to make change.

We are here.

We will fight.

If we are lucky, if the Creator wills it, in the end there will be victory for the people.

We are here.

We will fight.

And if we are destined not to win this battle, we will return to fight again.

Like a phoenix born out of the ashes, we will rise to begin a new life, a new battle, and, with that battle, a new hope.

From time immemorial, we have returned.

It is an old tale; one you have heard, one you have read and one your soul knows to be true

When you read these pages, when you hear the call, will you heed it?

We are here.

We still fight.

Do we fight alone?

Will you close your eyes, your minds, and your hearts?

Or will you join us in this quest for knowledge?

Will you walk with us the path?

Will you willingly seek out the answers?

Will you open yourself to the possibility of what this world could be, or will you turn away?

Out of legend, from the beginning of time, the story unfolds to yet again reveal to the world the one thing we have been sent here to discover…

Truth

From My Heart to Yours

Well, my friends, life is full of trippy little coincidences that sometimes leave one speechless or, as my nephew just proved, sometimes leave one dancing around the living room shouting to the heavens, "No way!—that was so cool!"

Two weeks ago I picked up my nephew Derek, and when he got in the car, one of the first comments out of his mouth was, "Man, I really hate that woman!"

He was referring to the superintendent in his building, and the fact that he used the word *hate* disturbed me just a little. I asked him why he felt that way. He didn't really have an answer, except to say that she simply wasn't very nice. I explained to him that, given the work he knew I was doing with regard to my novel, he ought to know better than to use the word *hate* around me. I asked him if there was not at least one good thing that he could find about the lady. I pointed out that if he could convince himself that she was worth knowing, then perhaps his approach to her would be more positive and her response in turn would be equally positive. He, being a sixteen-year-old boy, came up with, "Well, it would be nice if she gave me twenty bucks."

So, given some of the research I have recently done, I latched onto the idea and went about cooking up a little experiment with him. I told him then that from now on when he saw her, he should smile at her and repeat in his head the phrase, "Thank you for the twenty bucks."

Then I explained the theory of unquestionable faith to him and how it's supposed to work. He asked me, "What happens if she only gives me fifteen?"

To this I responded, "Then it still proves that it works, but your faith in it working was not strong enough to actually make it work as you intended."

As we drove, he told me about a dream he had had the night before. I had come to pick him up and, instead of us using my car, he had offered to drive. In the dream, however, when we went to the garage to get his car it was a very new, very hot red Ferrari.

I told him that the dream made sense in that if the theory I was asking him to experiment with was true, then it was possible that he could use that newfound belief to start taking his own life in any direction he chose. Ultimately, it would not then be a far-fetched notion to believe that in the future he could in fact own such a car if he used the skills I taught him to create his own success.

He told me, "You're nuts, you know—but it's a kind of crazy I can appreciate; in fact, I really like your kind of crazy!"

Now for the trippy part: I was just sitting here going over the last chapter, which I had written months ago, and getting ready to write the conclusion to this wonderfully unreal adventure into self, when I received a text message from said nephew.

Guess who just gave me 15 dollars?

Of course, I simply had to call him right away and ask if it were true, and he told me that, most assuredly, it was true. It had just happened, and, oh yes, he certainly did believe now. I told him to look to the heavens and say thank you, and he told me to wait, as he walked to his window and shouted thank you to the sky.

I hung up the phone soon after and headed to my computer. I did, of course, first call Rey, as I am still trying occasionally to prove these things real to him, though he stubbornly clings to his black-and-white world.

This brings me to the point in the story that I know you are waiting for.

In fact, I would stake everything I have on the fact that you are just "dying to know."

How much of this little tale is true, and how much is not?

First, let's explore the previous statement; then we will get back to appeasing your curiosity.

"Dying to know" is an extremely common and overused expression that is uttered from the lips of thousands daily without them ever taking the time to reflect on the phrase. You are, you know, quite literally dying to know...

If you break it down and dissect it, which I must point out does not take much effort at all, really, each day you live is one step closer to death (oh yes, I did go there), and each day you live is one step close to acquiring the absolute truth.

I mean, as we grow and experience this wonderful gift called life, we learn along the way many of the truths that prophets and guides have been trying to teach us for centuries. It is a very basic principle that the teachers of today, yesterday, and tomorrow are well aware of and embrace as part of their daily routines. It is the regular Joe, the you and me of now, who seem to have problems with this concept.

What, you may ask, are these simple truths that we are meant to learn?

Well, my friends, that is the part that will no doubt shock you...

I have no idea.

No, really—I don't!

I am still learning and am not in any position at this stage of my own personal growth to tell you that even one of the truths I have written about in this book are the real truths. That is not my message to you, not my role, not my life's purpose. My message to you is that those truths that you are meant to seek are just that—YOUR TRUTHS!

You, the reader, want to know: Is it real? Do these people exist?

Yet I have to ask: What is the definition of real? Whose reality do you wish to define your truths by? Do you wish to define your life by what others tell you is true, or do you wish to seek out for yourself the truths that work for you?

I will tell you this much: the story (and it is just that, a story) is based on a true story. It is the collaboration of the thoughts and feelings of people too numerous to mention, most of whom you have already met. As to whether or not those people actually live and act and have said the things that this book claims them to have said, well, perhaps someday you will happen to run into one of them and you can ask them for yourself. I doubt very much that it will happen anytime soon, so, for the moment, perhaps it is best that you simply accept the spirit in which the tale is being told and the incredible amount of enthusiasm and creativity on the part of all of those involved that went into the telling of it.

Of course, there are a few key characters that I am sure you are curious about, and I am sure I know also who would be at the top of that list. Yes, Vincent does exist, and he is a very dear and close friend, who, through his loving and nurturing nature, has managed to bring to life in me a talent and skill that I had long ago thought to have died. I must point out that his current drive and ambition are centered on his career in the arts and his love of children. He strongly feels we must work toward a day when our children no longer need to go hungry, and it is through some of his work that others have a chance for a better tomorrow. He is not a revolutionary, not in the sense that this book portrays, but, oh my goodness, how boring would the story be if I told you he has a simple desire to provide food, shelter, and education to the countless street children who exist in his country? All of the information about the government there can be found on the Internet, and the stories of people like Jose Rizal are not in any way a secret. Yet, speaking of them can open eyes, as well as minds, to the change that has been fought for by many self-sacrificing heroes in all nations around the globe for centuries. Slowly we are advancing; with each tiny step forward, we do, as a race, come closer to a day when there will no longer be a need to save anybody, as there will be nothing to save them from. As to the story behind his name, well, I would think it much easier for you to believe that he was named after St. Vincent and that the other name is simply in honour of a random basketball team his father played on in his youth.

Oh now, don't be too disappointed. I mean, you didn't really believe that all that happened did you?

I will be honest with you and say that I did at one point take a trip to the Philippines, and I did encounter there some incredible people who were working tirelessly to help the youth of their country, and it is through that dedication to nurture and protect our young that the story of *Truth* came to life.

You see, there have always been truths and have always been guides and teachers to tell us these truths, but, as humans, we stubbornly insist on going our own way and ignoring what others out there are trying to teach us. Of course, as I said, the quest for the Grail—the quest for truth—is an extremely personal one. It is a journey, and so it is appropriate that this story be presented to you in the form of a trip to an unknown place, which happens to also be, according to the clock, in the future—yes, they are twelve hours ahead of us, so, therefore, going from the Philippines to Canada is going to the future…

I know, twisted, isn't it? We could, of course, get into the whole theory of relativity and explore the concept of time for awhile, but I am pretty sure that is meant for a later date as well, so I won't trouble you with it at the moment. What I will trouble you with is whether or not you, after reading this, are at all interested in embarking on your own personal search for answers. I cannot give them to you, but I hope that I have perhaps opened up your hearts and minds just a little—enough to at least entice you to venture out into the world with a new outlook on the possibilities that life presents. I also hope that through this adventure I have awakened in you a hunger for knowledge, a curiosity to explore the unknown and unseen. Only through fearless exploration of these things do we begin to understand the world in which we live.

A few things I should probably mention before I send you off on your adventures. The book itself was written months ago, but I was waiting patiently for the conclusion to present itself, and in the last few weeks I have been drawn to some enlightening books and drawn into some exceptionally eye-opening conversations. All seemed to point me in the same direction, and it was with these things in mind that I had encouraged my nephew to take his first leap of faith into the unknown and experience for himself what the power of believing can accomplish.

The first thing that I have to talk about is a very brief, but profound, conversation that I had with my daughter only days ago. I took a chance to ask her what she thought happened to bad people when they die. She told me they go back to God. So I asked, of course, why they didn't go to hell. She answered that hell doesn't exist. Yes, I know, it surprised me too, and it is something I fully intend to explore. I allowed myself a moment of recovery, then I asked her the one question I think we should ask all our children: "What is God?"

She said, "God is energy, I think; the closest thing to describe it would be energy, but honestly, I don't know, Mom... God just *is*..."

Well, then, okay.

Moving on, I was reading a book three days ago by Deepak Chopra, and the symbol that one of the twins had tattooed on his arm just happened to pop up in one of the chapters. Now, as often happens, I had bought the book over a year ago, randomly picking it from the shelf, not knowing at the time why I was buying it. I did not, however, start reading it until a few days ago, long after this entire novel had already been finished. The symbol leaped out at me, and so I will share its meaning with you, as it seems the appropriate thing to do. It is the symbol of all embracing reality. It is an ancient mystical belief signifying that each individual (represented by the dot) was secretly infinite (the circle), the idea being that the Creator permeated each particle of creation equally, and that the same divine spark animated life in all forms.

Why I am to bring this up now is well beyond me, but, as usual, I do not often question what I am being asked to write. I simply write, and it is only later that I am able I go back over my work to dissect and explore what I have written. I can guess, though, that to end this book with such a bold statement on the perception of reality can only mean that it will be the next step in this wondrous ongoing adventure—which also means that the story is not yet done.

But then, you and I, we already knew that, didn't we?

So, I imagine we will meet again, in another place and time, and I will have much more to share. God willing, there will be insights galore to come, and the experiencing of those insights will be as fulfilling and entertaining as this little journey has been.

In the meantime, do us all a favor, and go out exploring for yourself. I will meet you back here someday, and perhaps when we are reunited you will have learned a great many truths that you might be willing to share with me.

Don't forget, while you are out and about wandering the world, to spread a little (preferably a lot) of that love and compassion for others I talk so often about. It honestly does lighten your own burdens when you are able to selflessly give of your heart and soul to others.

And, by the way, thank you for opening your hearts to me and allowing me into your world for a short time. I so look forward to sharing with you again.

Safe journeys my friends; love, light, and laughter to you all.

God bless and Godspeed ...

Characters:

Throughout this book there are several common themes; one of those is the significance of the meanings behind the names of the people involved with this trippy little tale. Each Character in this book is a representation of some incredible individuals who I have been blessed to share my life with. Their names have been changed but the meanings behind their names were carefully researched and then those meanings used to find new names that would be a true representation of the roles each individual plays in the tale. I was very careful to keep the meaning behind the names as true to the original names as possible so when you read what each name means keep an open mind and open heart to the possibility that coincidence is merely a sign post on the road of life.

Most of the meanings were found on the 'Behind the Name' website....

Alya: Means "sky, *heaven*, loftiness" in Arabic

Given her role I would think I need not explain the connection...

Angel: Messenger of God

Bob: From the Germanic name *Hrodebert* meaning "bright fame", derived from the Germanic elements *hrod* "fame" and *beraht* "bright". The Normans introduced this name to Britain, where it replaced the Old English cognate *Hreodbeorht*. It has been a very common English name since that time.

Given that my bothers alter-ego is the outgoing side of his personality this makes sense as well...

Brigitte: Anglicized form of the Irish name *Brighid* which means "exalted one". In Irish mythology this was the name of the goddess of fire, poetry and wisdom, the daughter of the god Dagda.

Chelsea: An English name meaning messenger, pretty self explanatory...

Conrad: Meaning bold counsel, derived from the Germanic elements *kuoni* "brave" and *rad* "counsel".

Deacon: From Latin *decanus* meaning "chief of ten"

I imagine I need not explain this further....

Derek: From a Germanic name meaning "ruler of the people", derived from the elements *þeud* "people" and *ric* "power, ruler".

Who knows, if he is going to be rich enough to afford the car maybe just maybe....

Jacob: Meaning "may God protect".

Jean: Medieval English variant of *Jehanne* (see JANE). Medieval English form of *Jehanne*, an Old French feminine form of *Iohannes* (see JOHN). English form of *Iohannes*, the Latin form of the Greek name *Ιωαννης (Ioannes)*; itself derived from the Hebrew name *(Yochanan)* meaning "YAHWEH is great or gracious"

Lina: Means either "palm tree" or "tender" in Arabic or means "absorbed, united" in Sanskrit

Again most of this is pretty self explanatory; palm tree a remarkably strong and flexible tree that is able to withstand incredibly forceful winds, its ability to bend with the wind allows it to survive powerful storms. Early Christians used the palm branch to symbolize the *victory* of the faithful over enemies of the soul, as in the Palm Sunday festival celebrating the triumphal entry of Jesus into Jerusalem. Tender - she is certainly that when it's warranted and united we have stood for over 20 yrs.

Madison: Is English and means daughter of a powerful soldier; from an English surname meaning "son of MAUD". Maud - usual medieval form of MATILDA. Matilda - From the Germanic name *Mahthildis* meaning "strength in battle", from the elements *maht* "might, strength" and *hild* "battle". Saint Matilda was the wife of the 10th-century German king Henry I the Fowler. The name was brought to England by the Normans, being borne by the wife of William the Conqueror himself.

Sweet of disposition and caring of all, eyes that twinkle with mischief and mystery, her smile is given freely and lovingly and finds her a friend of everyone, full of energy and life, she knows who she is and where she's going in life, finds no challenge too great for her mind or soul, loving the feeling of accomplishment and self-satisfaction, she is loved by family and friends.

Natalie: From the Late Latin name *Natalia*, which meant "Christmas Day" from Latin *natale domini*.

Christmas can be seen as be representative of two separate things yet both of those things seem to tie into the theme of the story. First is the connection to the birth of Christ and a link to the exploration of Christianity. It could also be representative of the giving and receiving of gifts.

Norloch: Means of the lake.

I think we pretty much covered that....

Revo: The first four letters in Revolution...

Reynard: From the Germanic name Raginhard, composed of the elements ragin "advice" and hard "brave, hardy". It was brought to England by the Normans in the form of Reinard though it never became very common there. In medieval fables the names was borne of a sly hero Reynard the Fox (with the result that Renard has become a French word meaning "fox")

The fox is often described as a crafty creature and is representative of Intelligence, diplomacy, Gentleness, wildness, persistence, adaption and slyness.

Rose: Originally a Norman form of a Germanic name, which was composed of the elements *hrod* "fame" and *heid* "kind, sort, type". It was introduced to England by the Normans in the forms *Roese* or *Rohese*. From an early date it was associated with the word for the fragrant flower *rose* (derived from Latin *rosa*). When the name was revived in the 19th century, it was probably with the flower in mind.

In keeping with the theme of refusing to put only one name to the power that is our Creator, I remind you that a rose by any other name would likely smell as sweet.

The rose is believed by some to be a symbol used by the Templar Knights to Represent Mary Magdalene.

Saul: From the Hebrew name *(Sha'ul)* which meant "asked for" or "prayed for". This was the name of the first king of Israel who ruled just before King David, as told in the Old Testament. Also, Saul was the original name of Saint Paul before his conversion to Christianity.

Scott: The original meaning of the word *Scot* is debated, but it may mean "tattoo", so given because Scotsmen often had tattoos.

If you missed the connection, go back and read the conclusion...

Sophia: Means "wisdom" in Greek.

Right like that doesn't make sense....

Theo: From the Greek name *Θεοδωρος (Theodoros)*, which meant "gift of god" from Greek *θεος (theos)* "God" and *δωρον (doron)* "gift".

Oh, like that's not in keeping with the theme at all....

Victoria: Means "victory" in Latin or victory for the people. Victoria was the Roman goddess of victory.

There are several different versions of this name and it's meaning yet all go back to the same word that can be found throughout this novel "Victory"

Vincent: From the Roman name *Vincentius*, which was from Latin *vincere* "to conquer". This name was popular among early Christians, and it was borne by many saints.